HOGARTH HOUSE LIBRARY.

BOUVERIE STREET, FLEET STREET, E.C.

The following is a list of the REVISED EDITIONS of the Hogarth House Works, published in Volumes, bound in Illustrated Covers, also in Penny Weekly Numbers, all in print, and ready for immediate delivery:—

TOM WILDRAKE'S SCHOOLDAYS.

In Five Vols., price 1s. each; also complete in one Vol. as a Prize Edition, and handsomely bound in cloth and gold, price 5s. 6d.—This celebrated School Story was the first of its class ever issued in weekly numbers; and in the face of numerous imitators it still holds the foremost place. The story is a faithful narrative of the life of a high-spirited young Englishman at school—showing what he did and how he did it, and what he learnt and its influence on his after life. The story is carried on through Tom Wildrake's adventurous career, down to the time when he felt himself entitled to rest on the laurels he had so nobly won by his many brave deeds during the heartrending Indian Mutiny and in Australia and elsewhere.

YOUNG TOM'S ADVENTURES In Europe, Asia, Africa, and America.

Complete, price 1s. 6d.—This is a sequel to "Young Tom's Schooldays," and narrates his hair-breadth escapes and adventures both with wild men and animals in the four quarters of the globe.

THE BOYS OF BIRCHAM SCHOOL.

Complete, price 1s. 6d.—This story claims to be the first school story that ever appeared in a periodical solely devoted to boys. For dramatic incident and genuine fun it has never yet been equalled.

CHARLIE AND TIM AT SCARUM SCHOOL.

Complete, price 1s.—This story of the life of two boys, who are sworn chums, at school, has always been a popular one with our young friends; showing, as it does, how a sincere friendship may be formed at school which may have lasting effects on our boys' after lives. Every schoolboy should read it.

CHARITY JOE; or, from Street Boy to Lord Mayor.

Complete, price 1s.—This is the true story of an outcast, who, by his honesty and indomitable will, rose to be the Chief Magnate of the First City in the World. His adventures at school, and, accompanied by his dog Toby, with a travelling showman, should be read by every lad who wishes to know *what* an English boy can do, no matter how humble his first start in life, or how great his temptations.

OUT ON THE WORLD.

Complete, price 1s.—This history goes direct to the heart of the reader, being a story of real life, depicting the troubles and trials of two children who were stolen from their home by gipsies. Little Jack's brave defence of his fellow-prisoner, Lilly—He shoots at Tinker Tom—They escape and tramp to London—Their adventures on the way; they join a troupe of tumblers and become street-players—They are recognised by the gipsies—The fair—The booth on fire; and, after many narrow escapes, they are captured by Tinker Tom, who cruelly ill-uses them—They are traced by the players to Tinker Tom's den—They are followed and risk their lives to save the children from a horrible death—The children are restored to their parents through the skill of the detective police, and well reward those who assisted them in the days of their adversity. This work is very graphically illustrated with numerous Wood Engravings.

YOUNG TOM'S SCHOOLDAYS.

Complete, price 1s. 6d.—This is the story of the life of Tom Wildrake's son at school; and, although complete in itself, should be read by everyone who has read "Tom Wildrake," as all the readers' old friends reappear in its pages.

RAGS AND RICHES: A Story of Three Poor Boys.

Complete, price 1s.—The illustrations to this work are from the inimitable pencil of Phis (H. K. Browne), who did so much towards rendering popular many of the works of Charles Dickens. So faithfully is the story of these poor boys told, and so realistic are the scenes described, that it has been pronounced by competent critics the best story of London life published since "Oliver Twist."

FRANK FEARLESS; Or, the Cruise of the Firebrand.

Complete, price 2s. 6d.—We doubt whether for fidelity of description and stirring incidents this magnificent sea story has been equalled since the days of Captain Marryat. The story of the misjudged hero's long and troubled conflict, not only with the pirates, but with his own mistaken countrymen, should be read by every true British boy who can lay its lessons to heart and profit by them.

MIDSHIPMAN TOM; Or, the Cruise of the War Cloud.

Complete, price 2s.—This is the faithful narrative of the life of a Midshipman on board a Man-of-War, and shows the trials, temptations, and prizes incident to the career of a boy who wears the uniform of our gracious Queen at sea. Though strikingly sensational, the element of fun is not omitted.

BLACK-EYED SUSAN; or Pirates Ashore.

Complete, price 1s.—The pathetic and stirring story of William and Susan is here told in a way which is bound to enlist the sympathies of all who are possessed with a true Briton's love of adventures at sea.

THE BRIGANDS OF THE SEA; Or, the Sailor Highwayman.

Complete, price 1s. 6d.—Money Marks, the hero of this most extraordinary romance of the sea, is no imaginary character, and nearly all the soul-stirring incidents herein described are founded on fact. The career of this world-famed highwayman of the sea is one of the most sensational narratives ever offered to the reading public. It is profusely illustrated by an eminent artist.

THE WAR CRUISE OF THE MOSCA; Or, the Six Fighting Mids.

Complete, price 1s.—In this Stirring Story of the Sea, the talented author takes a wide departure from his school and military stories, and shows us that though he is familiar with the cavalry sabre, he can give us a vigorous and truthful account of the life of those whose lot it is to wield the sailor's cutlass, and fight their country's battles on the boundless deep.

FOR HONOUR; or, the Young Privateer.

Complete, price 1s. 6d.—This powerfully written story of the life of a Privateer during one of the most stirring periods of England's Naval History, is a marvellous combination of the sensational and the humorous. No British boy can read the sayings and doings of Monkey Jack and Crikey without a laugh, and no British boy can read the heroic actions of the young Privateer without feeling a thrill of exultation that he also belongs to that glorious Empire on whose domains the sun never sets.

ADRIFT ON THE SPANISH MAIN.

Complete, price 1s.—This Story of the old Buccaneers carries us back to the glorious days of good Queen Bess—the days when England settled for all time her right to the title of "Empress of the Seas."

ALL'S WELL.

Complete, price 1s.—The Story under the title of the above popular seaman's cry is full of pathos, sensation, and humour. In dramatic situations it is probably superior to any story of the sea ever written. With each copy is presented gratis a Magnificent Portrait of the greatest naval hero of modern days—Horatio, Lord Nelson.

SHEET-ANCHOR JACK.

Complete, price 1s.—A powerfully-written narrative of the life of a jolly jack tar "before the mast," and should be read by every true English boy.

THE PIRATE'S ISLE; Or, the Wonders of the Deep.

Complete, price 1s.—This is a story of adventure, both on sea and land. Full of sensation, pathos, and fun.

THE BRITISH BOY SAILOR.

Complete, price 2s.—A faithful narrative of the life of a poor boy on board a British Man-of-War, during the glorious days of Nelson, showing what a British boy's pluck can do to raise himself superior to circumstances.

WILLIE GRAY; Or, the Wreck of the Polar Star.

Complete, price 1s.—In this spirit-stirring story the entranced reader is carried into strange countries, and through strange perils by flood and field; but, from first to last, the interest is so well sustained that those who once take up the book are unable to lay it down until every line has been perused.

HOGARTH HOUSE, BOUVERIE ST., FLEET ST., LONDON, E.C.

FOLLOW MY LEADER:

OR,

LIONEL WILFUL'S SCHOOLDAYS.

WITH NUMEROUS ILLUSTRATIONS

By "PHIZ,"

(HABLOT K. BROWNE.)

VOL. I.

Publishing Office:

HOGARTH HOUSE, 32, BOUVERIE STREET,

LONDON, E.C.

ILLUSTRATIONS.

VOL. I.

VOL. II.

VOL. III.

CONTENTS.

VOL. I.

VOL. II.

VOL. III.

AS MR. GRUBBE PREPARED TO RUN HE SAW HIS ENEMIES COMING INTO VIEW BY DOZENS.

FOLLOW MY LEADER;

OR, LIONEL WILFUL'S SCHOOLDAYS.

CHAPTER I.

OUR HERO MAKES AN ENEMY.

"AND ain't they just a-goin' of it upstairs, Master Lionel?—that's all."

"Oh! they are—are they, Sam? And what are they 'a-goin' of it' about? Me of course?"

Sam, or to give him his full name, Samuel Scarecrow, was a human puzzle—a nineteenth century sphinx—in trousers much too short for him, and a green baize apron much too large.

His stature was that of a man, but his frame that of a boy—and a small boy, too; so that he presented the appearance of having been overstretched while he was very young and soft.

He possessed, besides, a shock of fiery red hair, which obstinately resisted the blandishment of the hardest brush or of any comb less persuasive in the teeth than a rake—and to these great personal advantages he added the attraction of a most diabolical squint, which rendered it impossible for the keenest observer to tell, within a few yards, the object at which Sam Scarecrow was gazing.

In point of age he might have been sixteen—or sixty—and he held the post of general factotum at Heath-end Villa, Hampstead, where the above-given scrap of conversation is taking place.

Master Lionel afforded a direct contrast to his oddly-constructed companion, with the single exception that he, too, was tall.

Dark haired, curling, crisp, and close—fair-complexioned, blue-eyed, and with an expression of the most dauntless resolution and energy in every line of his clear-cut, handsome features, he seemed the very type of what a British boy should be.

"And so they're 'a-goin' of it,' are they, Sam?" repeated Lionel

"You should have heard 'em," replied the factotum. "There's Miss Maria, your aunt, she's clicking away just like the old clock when you took the pendulum out, and there's Mr. Grubbe a strikin' in whenever he gets the chance, which ain't orfen."

"And what did my mother say?"

"Oh, nothin', Master Lionel; she never do when Miss Maria is a-goin' of it. She only looked sorrowful, like as if she wanted 'em to leave off, but didn't like to ax."

"Well, let them talk as they please," laughed Lionel. "They'll never succeed in making my mother less fond of me than she is."

"Nor no one helse, Master Lionel," said Sam, working at the crank of his knife-polishing machine with spiteful energy. "Lor', I wish I had their eds in this 'ere machine, wouldn't I turn it round that's all?"

Whirr—whirr—whirr.

"You'd find it difficult to turn them out sharper blades than they are now," said Lionel. "My aunt is bad enough, but that Mr. Grubbe, with his canting sanctimonious ways, is positively hateful."

"Which—he—are!" assented Sam, jerkily, as he bobbed up and down at the crank.

"He's a hypocrite, I know," Lionel went on; "and although he pretends to be so holy and pious that he regards the singing of a song as little short of profanity, and going to the theatre no better than going straight to the old gentleman, I feel certain that he is an artful, scheming, old rascal, and means no good to my mother. What do you think, Sam?"

"I thinks what you thinks, Master Lionel," responded Sam—as, indeed, he always did—my hero's opinion, expressed or understood, being absolute law for him.

"As for my aunt," Lionel went on, "she's about the most disagreeable thing that ever lived, I'm certain—and if it were not pretty sure to lead to the poor wretch's suicide, I could wish that some one would come and marry her straight off."

"There's a many've tried," said Sam, "on account of Miss Martinet's money, I 'spose; but, Lor' bless you, Master Lionel, nothing but a autumtytum could stand her."

"A what?"

"A autumtytum," repeated Sam—"one of them figgers as winds up like a clock, and plays at chest."

"Oh, an automaton," laughed Lionel; "well, I think you are about right, Sam; and now I'll go upstairs and hear what they have to say about me."

"That's right, Master Lionel," said Sam, encouragingly. "Don't you be afeard on 'em—I'll stand by you, as long as I've got a 'ed to slap or a ear to pull."

"No, no," said Lionel, with a smile, as he passed out of the pantry; "I'll fight my own battles, Sam; you get your ears boxed and pulled more than enough on my account now. Farewell, Sam."

"Tar-tar, Master Lionel, on we goes again."

And the whirr-whirr of the knife-cleaning machine mingled with the echo of Lionel Wilful's footsteps as he bounded lightly up the stairs.

"They are, indeed, as Sam said, 'a-goin' of it,' and with all their might too," thought Lionel as he opened the door gently, and caught Miss Maria Martinet's concluding words:

"I say again—and again—Lydia; and I will repeat it a dozen times, if necessary, that of all boys in the world I believe him to be the worst."

"Meaning me, I suppose, aunt?" said Lionel, lightly; "well, thank you for the compliment; you know I can't return it."

"Hush, Lionel dear," said his mother, a pretty, pale, delicate lady—the pallor of whose complexion was heightened by the deep mourning she had worn ever since the death of my hero's father.

Miss Maria Martinet was a tall, angular lady,

whose osseous structure had attained a remarkable development, and every line of whose sour features expressed a hatred of that sex which had neglected her in the bloom of youth; and, as Lionel entered, she shot at him a glance that would have curdled a whole dairy full of milk.

"Verily," groaned Mr. Grubbe, a big fat gentleman, with a broad white face that seemed in a perpetual state of unwholesome perspiration—"verily he scoffs: the benighted youth mocks at those who would lead him into the better path."

And drawing a handkerchief from a recess somewhere in the half-acre of broad cloth that clothed his sleek form, Mr. Grubbe sighed dolefully and mopped his flabby features.

"There is nothing the matter with you, sir, I hope?" asked Lionel polite[illegible]

"Nothing [illegible]y, Master Wilful," said the [illegible] "but my spirit—oh, that is indeed sore vexed on your account."

"Pray do not let any thought of me vex or trouble you, sir," said Lionel, with a touch of contempt—that, boy as he was, he could not help feeling for the hypocritical Mr. Grubbe.

"It is my duty," the oily gentleman replied, with an upward roll of his eyes, that left only the dirty-yellow whites visible. "It is my duty. All last night I wrestled in the spirit for your sake, and that of the *dear* lady, your mamma."

"How dare you speak of my mother in that way?" said Lionel fiercely, his face flushing scarlet. He felt such a repugnance for the sanctimonious Mr. Grubbe that it seemed like profanation to hear him even mention his loved mother's name in such a tone.

Mr. Grubbe saw the look, and though Lionel was but a boy he quailed beneath it—little knowing how near he had been to receiving a proof impression of the sharp corner of an ornamental bronze inkstand that was near Lionel's strong right hand.

"Hoighty, toighty!" said Miss Martinet, shrilly. "And how dare *you* dare to speak in that way to a gentleman who condescends to waste his time for your benefit?"

"Not *waste*, dear Miss Martinet," said Mr. Grubbe, in meek and lowly accents. "Oh, call not by such a name my poor endeavours to pluck this young brand from the fire that consumes him."

"What does all this mean, mother?" asked Lionel, in so low a tone that it failed to reach even the acute ear of Mr. Grubbe. "Did this man come here on purpose to see you about me?"

"Yes, my dear," Mrs. Wilful replied; "your aunt asked him to come, and I know you will try to like him, for my sake. He is a good man, and takes a great interest in you."

"I will try if you ask me, mother," said my hero, with an inward conviction that he would be attempting the impossible.

"What on earth is the boy whispering about now?" said Aunt Maria, sharply, for she by no means relished a conversation in which she could take no part.

"I was assuring him, Maria," said Mrs. Wilful, timidly, "that Mr. Grubbe had come here only for his good."

"Of course," snapped Miss Martinet, "and why he takes so much interest in such an obstinate, viciously-disposed boy it puzzles me to conceive."

"It *is* because he is obstinate and headstrong—we will not say viciously-disposed," said Mr. Grubbe. "There is more joy over one sinner that repenteth, you know, my dear Miss Martinet."

"If I had *my* way," Miss Maria went on, looking a whole sackful of canes and birches at Lionel, "I'd have him soundly whipped every day until he was as meek as a lamb, that I would."

"Truly, Solomon has said, 'Spare the rod and spoil the child,'" groaned Mr. Grubbe, forgetting for a time the way in which Lionel had before turned upon him, "and if Mrs. Wilful desired it, I would cheerfully inflict the necessary discipline of the rod"

"If you dare so much as to lay a finger upon me," exclaimed Lionel, his eyes flashing with anger, and his cheeks flaming scarlet, "I would knock you down with the first thing I could lay my hands on!"

This outburst of wrath was so fierce and impetuous that Mr. Grubbe recoiled as if he had actually received a blow—and backed his chair with such precipitancy against the table as to upset and shiver to atoms the china vase which decorated its centre.

And, indeed, Lionel, as he stood there—his broad chest thrown proudly out, his head back, his nostrils dilated, and his bright blue eyes flashing wrath and rebellion at Mr. Grubbe—looked manlier by far than the flabby gentleman, as he, leaning back in his chair, wiped the perspiration from his fat pale features.

"Lionel, Lionel," his mother entreated, in a frightened tone, "you must not give way to these outbursts of passion; you grieve me beyond measure, my dear."

"I am sorry mother," replied my hero, cooling in an instant; "but I could not bear the thought of that—that—Mr. Grubbe striking me."

Lionel pronounced the name as if it were spelt "Grub," as there is no reason to doubt it was originally—and Miss Martinet pounced upon this cause of offence directly.

"There again," she said sharply, "that boy takes every opportunity of insulting a gentleman, who degrades himself, in my opinion, by noticing him at all—I have told him fifty times if I have told him once that the name is pronounced "Grueby."

"It's spelt 'Grub' at all events."

"Lionel!" said his mother appealingly.

"Well, I have no objection," said Lionel, Mr. 'Grueby' then—though I think the other way just as pretty—and more appropriate," he added to himself.

"You have seen for yourself, I should think, Lydia," said Miss Martinet, "and that during the last quarter of an hour, that Lionel is utterly unmanageable. He must be sent among those who will teach him his proper level, and break his spirit. If it will not bend it must be broken; and in coming to the decision to send him away you have done one of the very few wise things you ever did in your life."

Lionel started, and looked reproachfully at his mother.

"Is this indeed true?" he asked.

Mrs. Wilful said nothing, but Lionel saw the tears gathering in her eyes.

"It is true, then," he said; "you are going to send me away from you, mother?"

"For your good, my dear," faltered his mother "you must know, Lionel, that you—you—are too headstrong, too unruly, too——"

"Too everything that is bad, in short," said the boy, bitterly—"thanks to those who have set you against me."

"No, Lionel, dear," began Mrs. Wilful, whose intention to send her boy away from her would then and there have broken down, but for the strong-minded Maria putting an end to the possibility by declaring that—

"Poor Lydia had over-excited herself,"

And straightway marching her off to her bedroom, where she administered a restorative in the shape of a good scolding.

Lionel was then left alone with Mr. Grubbe, who seemed anything but at ease as he gathered his hat and gloves, and prepared to depart.

"Er—um—good-bye, Master Wilful," he said, holding out his large flabby hand for Lionel's acceptance.

"Good-bye, Mr. *Grueby*," said my hero, disregarding altogether the flabby hand, and looking its owner full in the face; "I shall see you again before I leave Hampstead."

"I hope so," said Mr. Grubbe, "and in a spirit of brotherly love—or rather such affection as should exist between father and son, for such is the way in which the spirit moves me to regard you, Lionel. Come, you are almost a man in stature as well as in spirit, say, is it to be peace or war between us?"

Lionel's answer was prompt and decisive.

"*War!*" he said; and, moving swiftly past Mr. Grubbe, he sought the lower regions, where his fast friend and councillor, Sam Scarecrow, was still busy with his crank, but never even noticing the evil glance which the flabby gentleman threw after him.

At the very outset of his career Lionel had made an enemy.

CHAPTER II.

HOW LIONEL BAITED A TRAP FOR MR. GRUBBE.

WHEN Lionel left the presence of the oily Mr Grubbe he was calm without, but internally very warm indeed.

He knew quite well that but for the persuasion—or rather perpetual worry — to which Mrs. Wilful had been subjected, she would never have thought of parting with him—or of being separated from him, until such time as he should be of age to mount the *toga virilis* (Anglicé—tail-coat) and go forth into the world—a man.

"Ah, Master Lionel,' said Sam, with a smile that extended his mouth from ear to ear, "I told you the truth, didn't I? They was a-goin' of it, wasn't they."

"They were, Sam, and, what is more, they have done at last what they intended to do."

"And what be that, Master Lionel?"

"They have persuaded my mother to send me away."

"To send you away!" exclaimed Sam, dropping, in his excitement at the intelligence, a whole armful of knives.

"Yes."

"What, away from here—away from your ma?"

"Yes."

"And where are they a-goin' to send us to?"

"Us!" repeated Lionel, with a melancholy smile. "They're not going to send you away."

"Then I'll go athout being sent," said Sam, as with trembling fingers he began to unfasten the strings that bound him to the green baize apron.

"I ain't a-goin' to leave you no-ways—not if *I* know it."

"Then you'll have to get Mr. Grubbe's permission," said Lionel. "He seems to be master in this house now—I can't make it out at all."

"Ask *his* permisshing—*His!*" exclaimed Sam, with an ineffable sneer of contempt. "That for Mr. Grubbe! Blow Mr. Grubbe! Who's Mr. Grubbe, I should like to know? Why I'd settle him with one hand."

And, in frantic defiance of the oily Mr. Grubbe, Sam sparred, according to the strictest rule of the noble art, at the dresser, and "barked" three of his knuckles in the act.

This calmed him down a little—and closing the pantry door with a mysterious air, he approached Lionel on tip-toe and said in a whisper,

"You won't be angry if I tells you suthing, Master Lionel?"

"Angry!—of course not."

"You're quite sartin."

"I promise you."

"That's enough, Master Lionel," said Sam; "well, it's about Mr. Grubbe and—"

"And whom?"

"And your mother, Master Lionel."

"Well, fire away Sam, I'm all attention," said Lionel. "What a slow fellow you are, Sam!"

"I wishes I hadn't a begun now," said the factotum, hesitatingly. "But you'll remember your promise, Master Lionel, won't you? And. mind, I've only heard cook and the other servants talking about it, but women is generilly right in such matters—and—"

"You want me to strike it out of you, I see," laughed Lionel. "Get on a little faster, there's a good fellow."

"Well—they do say—but I only heard it, mind—that Mr. Grubbe means a-marrying of your mar."

If the conventional bomb-shell had fallen and exploded at Lionel's feet he could not have looked more startled. Such an event as Sam had just hinted at was, in his eyes, such an absurd impossibility, that instead of breaking into a violent passion, as Sam fully expected he would, he only indulged in a prolonged fit of laughter.

"Blow me if I sees anything to larf at," said that faithful henchman; "why I thought, Master Lionel, that directly I told you you'd be a-goin' of it and murdering of him right out."

"Not I," laughed Lionel, "it's too ridiculous. Why my mother, dear, gentle, timid creature as she is, would turn upon the oily sneak and startle him out of his skin if he dared to hint at such a thing."

"Neverless, Master Lionel," said Sam solemnly, "the thing's been a-talked about—and you really ought to know it; and they ses, besides, that Miss Maria's got it all up, 'cos Mr. Grubbe's such a favourite of hern."

"You're right, Sam, you're a trump," said Lionel, bestowing an encouraging pat upon Scarecrow's back, which shook all the breath he happened to have at that moment out of his body.

"Which you've got a 'eavy hand, Master Lionel," coughed Sam.

"But a light heart, Sam. This will be a capital chance to get Grubbe out of the house for good and all—and perhaps make it too warm for Aunt Maria. I'll go to mother at once."

The result of the communication to Mrs. Wilful was as Lionel anticipated it would be. She flushed crimson at the indignity that had been put upon her by such a rumour, and writing a cool but polite note to Mr. Grubbe, explaining the cause for which she so acted, gave orders that it should be given to him when next he called; but on no account was he to be admitted to the house.

Aunt Maria remonstrated, but vainly. Mrs. Wilful was firm as the Great Pyramids where her honour was concerned; and Mr. Grubbe ground his teeth with vexation, anger, and disappointment, when he received the note, and heard the message.

"This is that whelp's doings," he muttered. "Confound him, just as I had so nearly netted her, too, and persuaded her to send the youngster away. Three thousand a year, and that freehold house and grounds, all lost through that brat."

And Mr. Grubbe made use of a very unsaintly expression regarding my hero.

"But I'll be even with him yet," he went on as he made his way towards his own residence. "No one ever injured Daniel Grubbe yet, who did not sooner or later repent it."

But Lionel had not done with him yet, for even while Mr. Grubbe, bursting with malice and all uncharitableness, was walking away from Heath-end Villa, Lionel was engaged in a scheme for his further discomfiture, which seemed to necessitate the consumption of a great deal of pen, ink, and paper, and resulted in the despatch of Sam in a mysterious manner to the office of the *Hampstead Echo.*

Lionel awaited his return at the back entrance to the villa, and greeted him with an inquiry:

"Well, did you do it?"

"Which I did," gasped Sam, for he had been running all the way.

"What did they say?"

"It were four and six, Master Lionel, and the young chap in the office said he couldn't do it a penny under, as such things was low, and not considered the thing for a respectable paper. Oh, he did take a deal of persuasioning."

"Never mind, so that he did take it in," laughed Lionel; 'you can keep the change, Sam; and if that oily sanctified Mr. Grubbe bites at the bait, I'll give you half a sovereign to buy pomatum for that head of yours."

. . . .

Although Mr. Grubbe professed outwardly to be a saint, he did not carry out the idea so thoroughly as the saints of old were wont to do.

Far otherwise, indeed; he much preferred fine linen and good broadcloth to sackcloth and ashes; and liked ham, anchovy toast, poached eggs, sardines, and fragrant tea, far better than the lentils, herbs, and plain water with which the anchorites of yore satisfied the cravings of nature.

It was two days after Sam's excursion to the office of the *Hampstead Echo* that Mr. Grubbe was seated at his breakfast-table—alone—for his children (I omitted to mention that he was a widower, and had five) had their provender upstairs, under the superintendence of the housekeeper.

He had made an excellent meal, for the devilled kidneys and broiled bones were served to a nicety—the haddock a real Finnan—and his tea strong and aromatic.

Therefore Mr. Grubbe felt in an excellent condition of contentment, as such a good man should, and as he leaned back in his chair and unfolded his copy of the *Hampstead Echo*, a smile played about his placid countenance.

"'House to let,' 'Coals,' 'Dr. Birch's academy will re-open,'" he murmured, quoting the advertisements, as he glanced over the outer page. "'Hospital for Contagious Fever Petition.' Ah, Mrs. Wilful, it's just as well that I didn't marry you after all, for that pretty villa and grounds won't fetch half the original cost in a year or so. 'MATRIMONIAL.' Ah! What's this?"

An advertisement, headed with the word "Matrimonial," in capitals, had attracted Mr. Grubbe's attention, and folding the paper so as to get at it more conveniently, he read, half aloud:

"'MATRIMONIAL.—A lady, desirous of improving her soul's health, and securing for it the pious guidance of a truly good man, seeks to open a correspondence with one whose elevated moral character is above reproach. No other qualification is necessary; age, personal appearance, and worldly wealth being beneath the notice of one whose affections are fixed upon things not of this world. The lady is under thirty, is considered handsome by those competent to judge of such vanities, and is possessed of a good amount of this world's riches.—Address, in the first instance (enclosing carte), to Beta, Post-office, Hampstead.'"

Mr. Grubbe read and re-read this advertisement several times, and the more he read it the better he seemed to like it.

"Whew," he murmured; "this is something like—undoubtedly genuine, too. The repudiation of all pomp and vanity in the first place, followed by a statement of age, personal appearance, and fortune, is so thoroughly feminine. Then the request for a carte. Dear me. I've a good mind to risk it."

And Mr. Grubbe, throwing himself back in his arm chair, gave himself over to reflection.

"And yet if it should be a hoax! But no, it can't be—it is genuine on the very face of it—and even if I were to be deceived, how easy to say that seeing the advertisement I had gone to meet the young person, and warn her of the danger she was likely to encounter. Oh! yes, I'll do it. Under thirty, too—considered handsome—and possessed of the world's riches. I'll write an answer at once."

Mr. Grubbe was equal to the occasion. He sat down to his desk and spent a full hour in the composition of an epistle, which he was confident would touch the heart of the lady "under thirty, and anxious for her soul's health"—being, as it was, crammed with the most pious sentiments; and, while expressing an utter contempt for such "vanities," hinted that the writer, too, was possessed of the Mammon of unrighteousness—also five children; the delightful task of training whom in the way they should go would be the blessed office of the lady under thirty.

Mr. Grubbe despatched the missive by a trusty messenger; and, strange enough, that very day Sam happened to call at the post-office for letters.

There were several, but foremost among them was the large black-edged envelope of Mr. Grubbe, bearing a specimen of his fat, sprawling caligraphy, on the outside.

"Hurrah!" cried Lionel, "this is his writing. I know it. Pitch the others into the fire, Sam. He's bitten at the bait—and now to land him."

If Mr. Grubbe could only have seen Lionel and Sam reading the protestations of pious affection he had addressed to the lady under thirty, it is more than probable that he would have gone into a very unsaintly passion.

"Ha, ha, ha!" laughed Lionel; "if it wasn't for fear of spoiling the joke I'd show this to my mother, Sam."

"That wouldn't do no good, Master Lionel."

"Perhaps not, but it would let her see what an escape she has had from this sanctimonous old humbug, at all events."

"I think she knowed it all along. Why, the werry look of his cardewizzy's enough," said Sam, holding out the photograph of Mr. Grubbe at arm's length, and regarding it with a look of the most serene contempt.

Then the two conspirators, going to work again, produced a missive—expressive of the most holy contentment with Mr. Grubbe's sentiments, &c., and appointing an interview at the bridge on the Hendon Road, "a sweet secluded spot," where they could converse without fear of interruption. He was also particularly requested to bring his "five dear children with him."

"There's five of 'em," said Lionel, "all boys, the youngest rising ten, and the eldest about fourteen I've seen them all of a row, with their Sunday go-to-meeting tiles on; and don't they all take after their precious papa, that's all?"

The letter was despatched, and, to Lionel's infinite delight, Mr. Grubbe fell into the trap, and arranged a meeting for the following Wednesday, at the bridge—when, he promised "his dear sister in pious affection," that himself and his five boys should be forthcoming.

"Oh, dear!" gasped Lionel, as, after an extravagant fit of laughter, he was compelled to sit down and give his aching sides a little rest, "I haven't had such a bit of fun as this before. Only fancy old Grubbe's wrath when he finds out who 'the lady under thirty' is—'with considerable personal attractions and money in the funds, &c.,' eh, Sam."

"It's beautiful," replied the faithful factotum, with an admiring glance at his young master, "You can do it, Master Lionel, better than any — bar none."

"Mind, Sam, not a word to anyone, especially cook and the other girl servants, or you'll spoil all."

"Mum it is, Master Lionel."

"Mind you have all the paper bags ready with the flour and soot and ochre in them."

"It shall be did, Master Lionel—tar, tar."

"Adieu Sam."

And with a parting nod and merry smile, Lionel sped away to complete his arrangements for the discomfiture of the oily Mr. Grubbe.

CHAPTER III.

SHOWS HOW MR. GRUBBE FELL INTO THE TRAP, AND OF THE VERY UNPLEASANT RECEPTION HE MET WITH THERE.

JUST two hours before the time appointed for the meeting with the "lady under thirty," Mr. Grubbe stood before the looking-glass upon his dressing-table, putting a few finishing touches to his toilet.

His necktie was of a dazzling white—his shirt-collar and bosom were starched to a torturing stiffness—and his countenance was overspread with an interesting and intellectual pallor.

His glossy garments—sable-shining as the horny covering of the black beetle—fitted him creaselessly—he felt content with himsel, and tried in the glass the effect of a smile of pious melancholy, most touching to behold, which he thought could not fail to reach the heart of "the lady under thirty."

Then tucking a responsible-looking umbrella under his arm, and holding in his black-gloved left hand a bundle of very good tracts, with pictures of a striking character on the outer pages, he sallied forth—alone—for the five juvenile Grubbes had been sent on in advance—all black-jacketed, kid-gloved, and chimney-pot-hatted to an excruciating pitch of—ugliness.

It was a lovely spring morning—the air was balmy and delicious. The trees and hedges had put on their first garment of delicate emerald, and the birds twittered and chirruped till their little throats seemed bursting.

All this was exceedingly soothing to Mr. Grubbe, and as he ambled gently along he hummed softly the refrain of a tune—none of your low irreligious or secular melodies, be it understood, but a good solemn nasal psalm.

In this way, and distributing the tracts with an affable air—as long as there was anybody to see him do it—Mr. Grubbe passed along the Hendon Road, casting up his eyes and groaning grievously as he passed the ancient hostelry at the sign of the Bull and Bush—justly regarding such places, as all pious men should do, as sinks of iniquity, which it was a sin to tolerate in a Christian land.

"Oh!" murmured Mr. Grubbe, "alas for the corruptibility of human nature! I sigh for my fellow-creatures when I find so many amongst them willing to sell, for the filthy lucre of Mammon, pernicious poison whereby the souls and bodies of their brethren are destroyed."

Mr. Grubbe groaned deeply, and shook his head, thanking Providence that he was not as other men, even as did the Pharisee of old in the Temple. He did not think it convenient just then to take into consideration the lucre-coveting nature of his own excursion on that bright May morning.

Just where the Finchley and Hendon roads meet at right angles Mr. Grubbe came up with his five hopeful offspring—the eldest leading the way, and the four others marching two and two, like a picket of Grenadiers and their corporal.

They halted the instant that they became aware of the approach of their parent—and each young Grubbe shivered in his individual pair of shoes, for their father's rod was one of iron, and he took care that it was not spared.

They quaked visibly as his sharp eye roved over their attire to seek out the smallest blemish. A spot of mud, a necktie awry, or a glove unbuttoned, would, they knew, entail infallibly the unbuttoning of another article of clothing on their return to Hampstead.

Four passed muster—but on the left trouser of the youngest Grubbe, just three inches and a quarter from the bottom, there was a suspicious-looking spot.

With a sweet smile Mr. Grubbe pointed to it. Grubbe, junior, began a faint whimper, which was instantly checked by a prompt application of his parent's dexter hand to his sinister ear.

"If I see another spot of mud on your clothes for a month to come, sir," said Mr. Grubbe, "I'll—G-r-r-r-r-r."

And concluding his sentence with a growl that was perfectly awful from its very indistinctness, Mr. Grubbe put on his pious smile again, and taking his two eldest offspring under his own charge, bade the others walk in front.

The bridge, the place of meeting, was now in sight, and the keen eyes of Mr. Grubbe looked sharply round for some indication of the "prepossessing young lady under thirty."

At first he could see no one, and he feared that he was the victim of a hoax, but as he approached more nearly he saw leaning on the right hand balustrade of the bridge the closely-veiled figure of a female.

"There she is!" he joyfully exclaimed—inwardly.

But for once in his life the oily Mr. Grubbe was mistaken.

The figure reclined in a pensive attitude against the stone balustrade—and the bonnet appeared gazing romantically at the miniature waterfall that splashed musically beneath the shadows of the trees beyond.

Mr. Grubbe scanned critically the outlines of the figure, for he was a connoisseur of female loveliness; and he licked his thick lips with satisfaction as he saw that she was evidently young and graceful.

"Under thirty," he mentally exclaimed, as he passed his handkerchief over his face, and gave his hat a pious tilt backwards, so as to uncover the whole of his intellectual forehead, "I should say under twenty. But the bonnet is decidedly unbecoming. I must have that altered when she becomes Mrs. Grubbe."

Poor Mr. Grubbe thus speculated what the young lady under thirty would prove to be, as, motioning to his offspring to keep at a respectful distance in the rear, he advanced to the amorous attack.

"Hem!"

Mr. Grubbe sidled to within a few paces of the reclining figure, and gently coughed.

The lady moved not, neither did she betoken the slightest consciousness of her pious admirer's presence.

"Hem! a-hem!"

Mr. Grubbe coughed a little louder than before.

Still the figure showed no more sign of life than the bridge itself.

"Deaf," thought the flabby gentleman. "That is a drawback certainly; but perhaps she has gone to sleep."

To test this Mr. Grubbe advanced a little nearer, and, with elephantine playfulness, touched the figure on the shoulder and coughed again.

That cough died away in an exclamation of mingled fear and anger, for, as he touched the "lady under thirty" she reeled and slid limply to the ground, revealing to his startled gaze a blank formless face, and a bosom whereon was pinned a piece of paper bearing the words, written in large capitals—

"SOLD AGAIN!"

Mr. Grubbe continued to gaze upon the dummy in speechless dismay.

Could it be true, or was it a hideous dream?

Was it possible that any one had dared to play a practical joke upon him—the saintly Grubbe?

It was possible beyond a doubt, for there before him, leaning against the wall, in that idiotic attitude of repose which dolls assume, was the irrefragable evidence of the dummy.

"This *is* a joke!" groaned Mr. Grubbe, dismally, "but where are the jokers?"

Just then he fancied that he heard a faint chuckling sound on his right.

Mr. Grubbe turned sharply round in that direction, but there was nothing to be seen.

"I'll go!" said the flabby one, beginning to feel a little nervous.

"Come here, will you?" he added aloud to his offspring, who stood silently regarding the strange proceedings of their papa with wondering gaze.

Slowly they advanced—and received, each in succession, a sounding box on the left ear.

Then Mr. Grubbe solemnly kicked and cursed the dummy, and prepared to depart.

But he had not taken two steps when the chuckling sound that had before startled him was repeated immediately in front—then behind—then to the right and left in quick succession—and increasing in volume swelled into a perfect roar of laughter.

Mr. Grubbe turned pale and cold, and shuddered visibly. He was entrapped. He saw his enemies coming into view by the dozen—blocking up the road in front of him—in his rear, and fringing with grinning faces the parapet on either side.

If the flabby one had been a prudent man, he would have faced the situation calmly, and with such dignity as he could muster to his aid; but, confused and despairing, he attempted to do the very worst thing that he could have done under the circumstances, and clutching his eldest offspring by the hand began to run.

"Hooray!" shouted one of the crowd; "don't run away like that 'ere!"

"How's the widder?" roared a second.

"You're a pretty old rascal to bolt and leave yer young weman a-sitting on the ground," said a third.

"What'll yer take for the property?" yelled a fourth.

"I 'opes you'll stand somethin' 'andsome to drink" said another—and so on *ad infinitum*; plainly revealing, even to Mr. Grubbe's bewildered intelligence, that his persecutors were fully aware of the object of his visit to the bridge.

If they had confined their playfulness to verbal comments, Mr. Grubbe would have cared little; but scarce had he taken three strides when something white whirled through the air, struck with a thud upon his back, enveloping him in a cloud of floury dust, and causing him instantly to choke and sneeze in a manner which afforded the crowd inexpressible gratification.

"Go it, old 'un!" they roared, "we'll lend yer a pocket handkercher."

"Ax the lady for one," suggested one wit.

"She can't," said another, "don't yer see she's usen of it to wipe away the tears she's sheddin'—cos he's running away from her?"

"Oh! you wicked old sinner," yelled a third. "There's a packet of patent pearl complexing powder for you to hide your blushes with."

And with a dexterous aim the speaker hurled a half-quartern bag of flour at Mr. Grubbe, and smote him on the nose therewith.

Lamentable, indeed, was the spectacle now presented by Mr. Grubbe and his five male offspring.

From head to foot they were covered with patches of red, white, and yellow—pleasingly interspersed with the lively hue of soot, which a friendly sweep in the fulness of his heart liberally supplied from his sack.

Mr. Grubbe roared "murder!" "help!" and "police!" at the top of his by no means gentle voice, but he soon tired of that, for it invariably occurred that he no sooner opened his mouth to let out a yell than it was instantly filled with soot or ochre—both of which articles, though eminently useful in their proper places, are scarcely adapted for the food of man.

The juvenile Grubbes kept silent from the same cause, which was perhaps fortunate—for as each was furnished with a most powerful pair of lungs, the concert they could have raised might perhaps have reached the ears of the policeman on the beat, who was enjoying a pint of half-and-half a quarter of a mile away.

Foremost among the persecutors of Mr. Grubbe was a tall handsome boy, who, mounted upon one of the parapets of the bridge, directed the movements of his followers.

He, it is hardly necessary for me to state, was Lionel Wilful.

Next to him was a very tall and lanky youth, whose thatch of obstinate red hair rendered him a conspicuous object.

His mission was to serve out ammunition to the crowd from a couple of capacious sacks at his side; and from the dexterous manner in which he executed his duty—contriving, now and then, to hurl a bag of ochre himself—evidenced that he was thoroughly enjoying the joke.

"It's most all done, Master Lionel," he said, as, in spite of a fearful and wonderful squint, he managed to smite a youthful Grubbe dexterously on the nose with a bag of yellow ochre. "The flour's give out, and there ain't much of this left."

"Never mind," said Lionel; "we'll let them run for it now—tell them to open out there in front and give them a hundred yards' law."

"Hare and 'ounds!" roared the crowd.

"Hooray!"

Mr. Grubbe no sooner perceived, with the little power of vision that the ochre, soot, and flour had left him, that his enemies had cleared away in front, than he began to run at a pretty smart pace, leading the five juvenile Grubbes after him.

Throughout the whole of that terrible pelting they had steadily held fast to their hats and one another, for they knew by experience the dread penalties with which they would be visited if they returned home without those hideous emblems of respectability.

In the words of the Laureate, slightly altered—

"Flour to the left of them, soot to the right of them,
Ochre in front of them—volleyed and thundered."

But they stuck heroically to their hats and to one another, with a persistence worthy of better objects

Then how they ran! Mr. Grubbe was a sight to behold, as his plump form and short thick legs sped over the ground—and the junior Grubbes dutifully followed, or were dragged rather, till the whole train resembled nothing so much as a circus clown out for a holiday with his family.

Cheering and yelling, the crowd, led by Lionel and Sam, waited until twice a hundred yards had been covered by Mr. Grubbe and his family, and then they started in pursuit.

"This is bootiful, Master Lionel," panted Sam; "I don't think he'll come arter your mar any more."

"I don't think he will, either," said Lionel, nor after anybody else in this quarter of the world. Ha! ha! how he runs!"

"We're a gaining on him, though," said Sam, handling a bag containing about a pound of red ochre, which he had reserved for a final salute.

"Keep the other fellows back, then," Lionel said; "If we get too close to him, he'll stop and spoil the fun."

But there was little danger of that. Maddened by shame and anger, Mr. Grubbe seemed to have lost all power of reason, and ran as he probably had never done in his life before.

He had only room in his bewildered brain for one idea, and that was to reach his home, and there hide himself from the scorn of his fellow-man.

He never thought of the sensation he was likely to create when he reached the streets of that charming suburb. Safety first, and then vengeance upon his persecutors—that was enough for him just then.

Away he sped, panting, puffing, and gasping up the steep ascent that leads to the hostelry of the Bull and Bush, scarcely slackening his pace, and darted along the road that skirts Wildwood.

Past Jack Straw's Castle, past the White Stone Pond, and down Heath Mount and High-street, he ran—still followed by his tormentors, whose numbers had by this time been increased by the whole available population.

None of them knew, or cared either, what had been done by Mr. Grubbe.

There he was, running away, and that was quite enough. They ran too, and taking up the chorus, they shouted with might and main.

The chase might have been continued indefinitely but for two things. Firstly, Mr. Grubbe had run himself out, and, with a gasp and a grunt, fell opposite the Fire Engine Station, with all five of the little Grubbes on the top of him; and secondly, the police, some half dozen strong, thought it time to see what was the matter.

"It's all over," said Lionel, as he pulled Sam by the sleeve; "he ran well, didn't he?"

"That he did," returned Sam, "and if he has hisself weighted to-morrow he'll find as he's a pound or two lighter."

And as calmly as if they had been the most disinterested of the spectators, my hero and his follower strolled away towards Heath-end, leaving Mr. Grubbe to settle the matter as best he could with the helmeted guardians of the peace, who, one and all, declared that he and his five sons were drunk and incapable, and took them into custody upon that disgraceful charge.

If Lionel had known what a bitter and remorseless enemy that day's practical joke had given him in Mr. Grubbe, he would perhaps have hesitated before carrying it into execution.

But the relation of how the flabby gentleman strove to avenge himself upon my hero, and how Lionel turned the tables upon Mr. Grubbe, I must leave for a future chapter.

CHAPTER IV.

A FRESH ENEMY APPEARS ON THE SCENE.

FORTUNATELY for Lionel, Mr. Grubbe had been so bewildered by the hoax, and so blinded by the dust that had literally been thrown into his eyes, that he had not recognised any of his assailants.

If this had not been the case it is more than probable that in the first burst of his resentment he would have given anyone whom he had been able to identity into custody for an assault.

And, indeed, he had suffered enough to have made the conventional saint indulge in profanity and the sweets of vengeance. His covetousness had been disappointed—he had been covered with flour, ochre, and ignominy; and, finally, after being chased until nearly dead through exhaustion, he had been taken to the police-station and locked up on a charge of being drunk and creating a disturbance, in company with his five wretched offspring.

Of course he was released as soon as the facts were made known, but his release could not wipe out the sense of shame and disgrace; and Mr. Grubbe, burning with a desire for revenge, set his keen wits to work to trace out the author of the practical joke.

A few inquiries made at the post-office and the Hampstead *Echo*, soon put him in possession of the fact of the visits of Sam Scarecrow there—that young gentleman's personal appearance being, as my readers know, particularly distinguished.

"I might have guessed it," said Mr. Grubbe, between his set teeth. "It was that young whelp, Wilful. It's enough to drive one mad to think that I should have been made the sport of such a youngster. Well, let him laugh now: he has won this trick, but before the game is played out I'll ruin him —and his mother too, I will, by ——"

And Mr. Grubbe drowned the profane termination of his speech in a huge gulp of brandy and water.

Meanwhile Lionel felt no special apprehensions from the result of his bitter joke. He guessed, and guessed rightly, that even if the flabby gentleman discovered his share in it, he would rather grin and bear it than have the matter made public.

At present he was regarded by the pious circle of his acquaintances as a martyr—whereas, if the real object of his visit to Hendon Bridge were made known, he would certainly have his designation changed to the far from saintly one of "humbug."

He contrived, however, to let his staunch friend, Miss Martinet, know the indignity to which Lionel had subjected him; and, in due course, Mrs. Wilful was made acquainted with the circumstance.

"But, there," said Miss Maria, in plaintive conclusion, "one might as well talk to a stick or a stone, as talk to you when Lionel's faults, I will not say crimes, are in question."

"You are right, Maria," said Mrs. Wilful, "not to apply so harsh a term to my child's boyish follies."

"I don't know that it is too harsh," returned Miss Martinet spitefully. "Surely it is a crime, and one of no common magnitude, to degrade such a pious good man as Mr. Grubbe in such a way. If I had been in his place, I should not have been a sufficiently good Christian to let the rascals escape scot-free."

"Enough, Maria," said Mrs. Wilful. "I know my son's faults and I have decided on a remedy."

"Bread and water for a fortnight, and a flogging twice a day from the gardener," suggested Miss Martinet.

"I do not wish to break Lionel's high spirit by degrading him," said Mrs. Wilful. "The remedy in that case would be worse than the disease."

"Ah! I thought so," said Miss Maria. "You will let him have his own way as usual. I'm sure if it were not for the affection I feel for you, Lydia, I could not stay here for another week."

"I have written to a friend of poor Charles," said Mrs. Wilful, "asking him to recommend a fit school at which to place Lionel, and I have here a letter from him stating that his old college tutor is the very one best suited to my purpose, having a special reputation for his successful treatment of refrac—— I mean high-spirited youths."

"Aha!" said Miss Maria, a gleam of malice lighting up her little eyes—"your late husband's friend evidently understands these matters."

"Poor Charles had great confidence in him," said Mrs. Wilful, "and charged me to apply to him in any difficulties. I fervently hope that his judgment will prove good in this case."

"No doubt it will," said Miss Maria. "Who is the schoolmaster whom he recommends?"

"The Rev. Phile Styngy, of Cheetham Hall Academy," replied Mrs. Wilful, referring to the letter she held in her hand. "He will call here to-day or to-morrow, when, if everything is satisfactory, he will take Lionel with him to school."

Miss Martinet was delighted. Such good news as the departure of her nephew she had not heard for many a day, and almost atoned for her anger and disappointment at the defeat of Mr. Grubbe's designs upon Mrs. Wilful.

But there was an unsuspected listener, whose feelings were of a very different nature.

It was Sam Scarecrow, who, conceiving it a part of his duty to listen and report all that could prove of interest to his young master, had diligently applied his ear to the keyhole, where he caught some scraps of the above given conversation—and the ear-ache.

Lionel was out, and Sam anxiously awaited his return, neglecting some very important household duties that should have been performed, and getting his ears boxed by Miss Maria and the cook in consequence thereof.

"Oh, Master Lionel!" he exclaimed, running down the passage to greet his young master, "They've been a-goin' of it agin."

"What is it now? Not old Grubbe?"

"Oh, no! not him. It's a new un."

"The deuce!" said Lionel. "Why fresh enemies seem to crop up the moment that an old one is settled. Who is it Sam?"

"A chap they calls Stingy," said Sam, "and he's a schoolmaster."

"Oh, that's the game—is it?" said Lionel. "Well, it must have come some time or another, and it's just as well now."

And Lionel, with his hands thrust deep into his trousers' pockets, began to whistle.

"Well," said Sam, ruefully, "I didn't think, Master Lionel, as you'd be glad to leave 'Ampstead and your mar—to say nothin of me."

"Neither am I, old boy," replied Lionel, patting him encouragingly on the back. "I'm only resigned, that's all. Most other fellows go to school and college, and so I suppose it's necessary that I should go too."

"But I shan't be there," expostulated Sam, who seemed to regard himself as his young master's shadow, and an absolute essential to his being.

"That's a nuisance, certainly," said Lionel. "They don't allow fellows to have servants at school, or else I might take you for mine."

"P'raps they might," cried Sam eagerly, "and then you know, Master Lionel, I could do lots of little things for you. Take your whackings for you when you got into trouble, and copy out your lessons for you, eh?"

Lionel smiled at the latter proposition, for Sam's caligraphy much resembled the result that might be achieved by a tipsy spider dipped in ink, and trying to draw a map of the way home on a sheet of paper.

"If it can be done, Sam, I'll do it," said Lionel. "You may depend on that. When am I to go?"

"I didn't hear that," said Sam; "your mar only said as the reverend gent wor a comin' to-day or to-morrer to see if you was good enough for him."

"Beautiful!" said Lionel, after a moment's profound thought—"we'll do it, Sam."

"Do what, Master Lionel?"

"Why, the schoolmaster, of course," replied my hero. "He's coming to see if I am good enough, eh? Well, suppose I'm not, he'll refuse to take me, won't he?"

"But lor, Master Lionel, he won't have the cheek to say as you aint good enuf for him. You're a dashed sight too good, that's wot I sees."

"You don't understand, Sam. Suppose now that when he comes we play him a nice little series of tricks that will convince him that I'm rather too good a card for him to deal with—what then?"

Sam made no verbal reply, but slowly expanded his mouth into a perfectly miraculous grin, and squinted to such a diabolial degree that even Lionel became positively alarmed.

"You shouldn't squint like that, Sam—you really shouldn't. Suppose one of the girls was to see you now, she'd go into fits and alarm the neighbourhood; she would indeed."

"Oh, Master Lionel, its bootiful."

"Is it? You'd have a different opinion, Sam, if you'd seen yourself in a looking-glass just then."

"I didn't mean me," explained Sam. "I was a speaking of your manoverers, Master Lionel."

"My little plan about Mr. Styngy, eh, Sam?"

"That's it; what I always sees is, Master Lionel, as you can do it, bar none."

"We'll see," said Lionel; "and now, like the fox in the fable, we'll get out our whole bagful of tricks, Sam. When is he coming?"

"To-day or to-morrer"

"The deuce, then there is no time to lose. We must get ready at once. Hark! What's that?"

"A ring at the bell," said Sam. "I'll go and see, Master Lionel."

Away Sam rushed, and returned in a short time with the information that a messenger had arrived with a note from Mr. Styngy, requesting to know at what time he might have the honour of waiting upon Mrs. Wilful.

"And yer mar said," continued Sam, "that she would be happy to see him to lunch, which it only wants a hour of one o'clock."

"Then we'll be ready for him, Sam," said Lionel. "Look here, what do you think of this for the first trick?"

And bending forward, he whispered in the ear of the faithful Scarecrow for a few moments.

"Fustrate, Master Lionel; I'll do it at once."

"Mind no one sees you."

"There's no fear o' that, Master Lionel, specerly if you'll stand at the top of the stairs and just give me the horfice."

"Right you are, Sam."

And ten minutes afterwards the two conspirators were outside the drawing-room door, very busy with a ball of string and some tin tacks.

CHAPTER V.

AN AWKWARD RECEPTION AND AN AWKWARD EXIT.

THE Rev. Philo Styngy, of Cheetham Hall Academy, was built on a very large and imposing scale, as it is only fit and right that a schoolmaster should be.

He was, moreover, possessed of a deep and sonorous voice, and a manner that impressed the beholder with a profound sense of his wisdom, which was, on the whole, fortunate, as Nature had apparently exhausted the whole of her materials upon the exterior of Mr. Styngy, leaving the inner man in a decidedly incomplete condition.

He was wise enough to be in some degree aware of this, and to confine his share in the conduct of the school to overawing parents and guardians, bullying the assistant-masters, and thrashing the pupils, in each and every of which departments he was proudly pre-eminent.

Lionel and Sam were on the look-out at the hour appointed for the Rev. Philo Styngy's reception, and when they observed his tall, commanding form slowly and in the most dignified manner approaching the house they felt some slight degree of hesitation. The reverend schoolmaster did not look the sort of man to be trifled with.

"My stars," whispered Lionel, "he's a whopper, ain't he, Sam, and no mistake?"

"Him a schoolmaster!" ejaculated the disgusted factotum. "He ought to be in a carrywan—that's where he ought to be."

"I hope that string's strong enough," said Lionel, after a pause.

"Oh! it'll do, never fear," replied Sam. "*I'd* make him go if he wor twice as big."

"Cut away then; he'll be knocking at the door in another minute."

And Sam, who, on the present occasion, had donned his page's uniform, hurried away to the front door, while Lionel sauntered into the drawing-room, where his mother and Miss Martinet were already.

The latter held up her hands in dismay as my hero entered, and uttered an exclamation of mingled wonder and vexation.

"What is the matter, Maria?" asked Mrs. Wilful.

"Matter!" exclaimed that lady, "look at him, Lydia."

"He—he is looking very well, I think."

"Well! Do you call that well? Is that a fit costume to receive a gentleman in, you graceless young rascal?" said my hero's aunt, passionately. "You have not even put on a clean collar, nor brushed your hair, nor washed your hands. Just look at his hands, Lydia, my dear."

"I have," said Lionel, coolly. "The collar was clean when I put it on, and I know I washed my hands this morning—and, as for my hair, why you know, aunt, it's no use brushing that; you called it a mop yourself."

Miss Maria would in all probability have flown into a tremendous passion at this exhibition of what she termed "sauce" on Lionel's part, but for a thundering knock at the hall-door, heralding the arrival of the Rev. Philo.

Miss Maria carefully smoothed the frown out of her sharp features, and rising from the chair put on the blandest smile she was capable of producing at so short a notice.

Just then Sam threw open the drawing-room door and announced in his most impressive voice.

"The Reverend Fellow Stingy."

The gentleman thus announced advanced with his most benevolent expression and courtly bow to meet Miss Martinet—but, while his foot was yet upon the threshold, he uttered a small howl—sprang forward, stumbled and fell into the arms of Miss Maria—their heads striking together with a sound similar to that produced by the concussion of two cocoa-nuts.

The door was rapidly closed, but Lionel caught a glimpse of Sam, who had a long pin in his righ hand, and a grin of gratified malice on his features.

The Rev. Mr. Styngy arose, but he was no longer the impressive and awe-imposing gentleman of five minutes before.

The bow of his white neck-cloth was under his left ear, his collar had lost its clerical stiffness, and upon his intellectual expanse of forehead there was a large white bump.

Miss Martinet too had suffered, for Mr. Styngy's rather hard head had "collided" with her left eye, which exhibited already strong symptoms of inflammation.

"Er—er—" began Mr. Styngy, "excuse me, ma'm; I—er—really did not mean—er—it, my dear madam."

"I should hope that you did not," said Miss Martinet, stiffly.

"Quite—er—an—accident, I—er—assure you," said the Rev. Philo, tenderly feeling the bump on his forehead.

"Ahem!' coughed Miss Maria very dubiously, and then she quitted the drawing-room in search of cold water and eau-de-cologne.

It did Lionel's command of features infinite credit, for there was something, to him, exquisitely funny in the little incident just narrated, but, without a smile he proffered his services to Mr. Styngy.

"Thank you, my young friend," said that gentleman, who by degrees was recovering from the confusion the accident had caused. "It is nothing, I—er—shall be better presently. Yes, I suppose I am speaking to the young gentleman it is proposed to place under my charge."

Lionel assented with becoming gravity, and Mr. Styngy, leaning back in his chair, surveyed him as if he were some interesting little animal about to be dissected, and it was necessary to select a place to begin upon.

Then followed the usual flattering remarks upon Lionel's personal appearance and his phrenological development—a judicious application of which to parents and guardians had gained the Rev. Philo many a score of pupils; and by the time that Miss Martinet returned and lunch was announced, Mr. Styngy had succeeded in making very considerable progress in the good graces of Mrs. Wilful.

Sam waited at lunch, and his appearance seemed to cause the Rev. Philo Styngy the liveliest emotions of curiosity and surprise.

This was, no doubt, heightened by his having surprised that youth more than once in the act of pointing to the table and executing some perfectly hideous grimaces intended for the edification of Lionel alone.

"Pardon me, Mrs. Wilful," said the Rev. Philo, "but what an extraordinary lad that servant of yours seems to be!"

"His appearance is certainly peculiar," said Mrs. Wilful; "but he is very devoted and faithful; my late husband found him—a baby—exposed on the Heath yonder, one bitter Christmas-eve, fifteen years ago, and he has been in our care ever since."

"I did not need such an instance to be assured of your benevolent and Christian heart, dear Madam," said the Rev. Philo, politely; and adding in an undertone, "but he is a curious lad—ugliest I ever saw, and what hair! why, it absolutely blazes."

Sam heard these criticisms upon his personal appearance; and his heart hardened towards the Rev. Philo—he would have no mercy on him now.

The lunch was a very tasty albeit substantial one—and Mr. Stingy who was a gourmand in his way, moistened his lips with his tongue in anticipation of a treat, for the fresh air of the Heath had made him hungry.

He began with the haunch of mutton, and with glistening eyes popped a tit-bit into his mouth, and began to masticate it.

But no sooner had he tasted it than a look of vacant wonder stole over his face—followed by an expression of surprise—which was succeeded by a shuddering spasm of disgust.

"Dear me, Mr. Styngy," said Mrs. Wilful, "what is the matter?"

"Nothing, ma'am, nothing," replied Mr. Styngy, bolting the mutton and giving vent to another violent shudder, "it's—ugh—it's rather warm to-day, I think."

"Try the woodcocks or the patés, Mr. Styngy," suggested Miss Martinet. "Samuel, a clean plate for Mr. Styngy."

Sam, with a stony and immoveable expression, brought the plate and handed a dish of woodcocks to Mr. Styngy

A ray of hope dawned upon his face—he saw that both Mrs. Wilful and Lionel were partaking of the same dish. The flavour of *this* must be all right.

But no—as with the mutton so with the woodcock, the first mouthful proved sufficient, and with a still more violent shudder than before he pushed away his plate.

A decanter stood near him—the Rev. Philo snatched it, and with a trembling hand poured out a glassful and swallowed it at a gulp.

No sooner had he done so though than, with a bound, he jumped from his chair, clapped his hands over his mouth, and made for the door, while a strange gurgling sound came from his throat.

CHAPTER VI.

THE REV. PHILO STYNGY AND MR. GRUBBS MAKE A COMPACT.

THE Rev. Philo Styngy was a very polite man, especially so to the fair sex; but that was no time for ceremony.

He dashed at the door, almost twisting the handle off in his hurry, and rushed into the passage, closely followed by Lionel.

"What is the matter, sir?" asked my hero in a sympathetic tone. "Shall I send for a doctor?"

"Oh—ah—ugh!" gasped Mr. Styngy, making frantic efforts to repress his feelings by cramming his handkerchief into his mouth. "Show—bedroom—oh—ah—ugh!"

It was with the utmost difficulty that Lionel contrived to master his laughter, and conduct Mr. Styngy—not to a bedroom—there was no time for that—but to a dark cupboard of a place, the sanctum sanctorum of Sam Scarecrow—in which it was always necessary to keep the gas or a candle burning.

There was a sink in it—a huge square of yellow soap—and a jack towel—the latter being about as comfortable to use as an unplaned deal board.

Towards the sink Lionel led the unfortunate Mr. Styngy, who was extremely ill for about ten minutes, gasping and groaning as if he were in the throes of dissolution.

"Do you feel better, sir?" inquired Lionel, feelingly.

"Er—thank you, my good boy," replied Mr. Styngy, faintly, "I am a little better."

"I must apologise, sir, for bringing you to a place like this," continued Lionel, winking at Sam, who just then made his appearance in the doorway, "but I was afraid that you would be ill before I could get you upstairs."

"Quite right," said Mr. Styngy. "I should have been to a certainty. Your mama is an estimable lady, I am sure, Master Wilful, but why—oh, why—has she such a partiality for the flavour of—ugh—castor oil in her cookery?"

"*Castor oil*, sir," repeated Lionel, in a tone of horrified surprise.

"The mutton was flavoured with it—the gravy was composed of it—everything tasted of it. Ugh!" said Mr. Styngy, with a shudder, "it is a wholesome medicine, Master Wilful, but I don't like it with my meals."

"I can't think how such a thing can have happened," said Lionel, with an air of such sweet innocence that a cherub might have envied it. "It must have been an accident."

"Even when I essayed the remedial powers of wine," said Mr. Styngy, pathetically, "I found that the odious flavour of the castor oil pervaded the genial product of the Spanish grape. It was very sad!"

"Quite affecting, sir," said Lionel.

"Extremely so, I assure you," added Mr. Styngy, laying his right hand upon his waistcoat. "It will be hours before I recover. I will just bathe my features to refresh them, and then I will retire for a while if you will have the goodness to carry my apologies to your mama, and assure her that I will do myself the favour of calling on her in the evening."

Sam, at this juncture, showed remarkable alacrity in waiting upon Mr. Styngy. He wiped the basin, turned the water on, fetched a new piece of soap and a towel, and in the height of his zealous hurry accidentally turned out the gas.

"Where are the matches, Sam?" asked Lionel.

"Never mind, my young friend," said the reverend schoolmaster, "I have only to dry my face, and that I can do in the dark. Do not forget, Master Wilful, to express my regrets to your mama, and assure her that I will return when I have recovered from my indisposition."

So saying, Mr. Styngy vigorously applied the towel to his face, little suspecting that the artful Sam had, during the interval of darkness, blacked it all over with the bottom of a saucepan.

"Here's your coat, sir; shall I 'elp you hon with it?" said Sam.

"Thank you, my good boy," replied Mr. Styngy, "I—er—will reward you when—er—I get some change."

Sam duly expressed his gratitude for this generous promise, and Mr. Styngy being inducted into his outer garment made for the door, innocent of the addition that had been made to his personal attractions by the sooty towel.

WHILE MR. STYNGY'S FOOT WAS YET UPON THE THRESHOLD HE STUMBLED INTO THE ARMS OF AUNT MARIA.

Lionel, to prevent an otherwise infallible explosion of laughter, had made his way to the drawing-room to acquaint Mrs. Wilful and Miss Martinet of the reverend gentleman's indisposition.

"Dear me," said Aunt Maria; "I am so vexed. I cannot think, Lydia, what could have caused him to become so suddenly unwell."

"Nor I," added Mrs. Wilful. "I suppose that over-study and anxiety for the well-being of so many young minds must undermine the constitutions of such professional gentlemen as Mr. Styngy."

"He does not *look* delicate, either," said Miss Martinet, who, from the window, was gazing at the receding figure of Mr. Styngy. "But, dear me, Lydia, what an extraordinary coat he has on!"

It was, indeed, an extraordinary coat, for by some strange mischance the seam in the centre of the back had given way, exposing beneath it a broad expanse of the glossy black cloth of which Mr. Styngy's frock coat was composed.

As innocent of this circumstance as he was of the change in his complexion, Mr. Styngy strode along—a little unsteadily, for his sickness had made him somewhat giddy—pondering upon what he considered Mrs. Wilful's strange predilection for castor oil.

"Peculiar, very," he thought. "I must be cautious in the future how I accept invitations to lunch with ladies of whose tastes I am unaware. Good gracious! Why I might be treated one of these days to an *entrée* seasoned with assafœtida."

Absorbed in this reflection, Mr. Styngy bumped against a passing labourer, knocking him over into the roadway, while he himself sat down in a hurry.

The violence of the shock was considerable, for Mr. Styngy was a heavy man. It jerked his hat off and sent it rolling swiftly down the steep decline of the street, and it operated in the most extraordinary manner upon his overcoat, every seam of which flew apart as if, to use an ordinary comparison, they had been sewn with a hot needle and burnt thread.

"Mercy on us!" gasped Mr. Styngy.

"Dash yer," growled the labourer, as he gently administered friction to the back of his head. "What do yer go a comin' agin a man like that for? You're a dashed Christy Minstrel out o' work, I suppose, aint yer?"

"My good friend," began Mr. Styngy, as he rose cautiously from the ground—"Why, bless my soul, what is the matter with my coat?"

The reverend gentleman had indeed good cause to wonder, for as he assumed an erect position, and lowered his hands to brush the dust from his nether garments, both of the sleeves dropped to the ground, and a "solution of continuity" took place between the collar and the front parts, which fell in a heap before his astonished eyes.

A crowd had begun to collect—of course, a crowd does always collect, somehow, when anything unpleasant is occurring to anyone—and they also, as a matter of course, commented upon Mr. Styngy's personal appearance.

"Oh! 'ere's a lark, Bill!" yelled one juvenile. "'Ere's a swell hackeryback a performing!"

"Where's the cove with the drum and the mouth horgin?" asked the breathless Bill, as he joined his informant. "That ain't a hackeryback, Jim; that's a nigger—one of them as dances and sings comic songs—look at his mug."

"He's a duffer; why he ain't arf blacked hisself," said another juvenile critic. "He ain't got none on his 'ands, and where's his banjore?"

Mr. Styngy being at length brought to a sense of his undignified position by the comments of the crowd, and as he was naturally a modest man, not by any means ambitious for the applause of the vulgar, he essayed to withdraw himself from their notice.

But in this endeavour he was stayed by the labourer against whom he had "collided," and who expressed a strong objection to part so readily with Mr. Styngy.

"No, you don't!" he said, placing himself immediately in front of the reverend gentleman. "Not if I knows it, old 'un. Dy'e think yer can walk 'er Majesty's 'ighway and knock people down for nothink? I knows my rights—and I'll hev 'em; yer stand a pint, now, come!"

"My good man," said Mr. Styngy backing suddenly upon a little boy—who instantly set up a horrible yell from the gutter into which he had been knocked.

"None of yer blarney," said the labourer furiously. I knows wot Magner Carter is, I do; Dr. Kenealy's my man, he is; I reads the *Henglishman*, and down with hevery think's my motter—now where's that pint?"

"For gracious sake, my good man, go away," said Mr. Styngy. "I really fear you are intoxicated."

"I intossticated!" exclaimed the labourer with a malignant scowl, "that's a good 'un, that is, when you're as drunk as ever you knows how yerself."

"How dare you make such a vile insinuation against me?" said Mr. Styngy; "if a policeman were here I would give you into custody, you low man."

"I'm a low man—am I?" said the labourer in a furious tone, as with a dexterous twist he forced himself from his fustian jacket and planted it on top of Mr. Styngy's dismembered overcoat, "come on if you've got anythink in yer, and we'll soon see who's lowest."

The man then commenced performing a curious kind of dance around Mr. Styngy, presenting his fists at that gentleman's nose, and then withdrawing them as if they were partners in a quadrille dancing the second figure.

"Go it!" shouted some of the crowd. "Keep yerselves warm."

"Here's a lark!" bawled other excited individuals to sundry Toms, Dicks, and Billies. "Come on! two drunken men a-fighting! such a game!"

"Go away!" said the alarmed Mr. Styngy, waving his hands frantically in the air, as if he were striving to mesmerise his stalwart antagonist. "Where are the police?"

At this moment there was a commotion in one portion of the circle of spectators, and a short, stout gentleman, clad in glossy black, elbowed his way through, and addressed himself to the persecuted schoolmaster.

"Mr. Styngy," he said, in sympathetic tones, "is it possible that I behold *you* in this condition?"

"Why, bless my soul, it's Grubbe," said Mr. Styngy, in a tone of mingled astonishment and gladness.

"It is," replied the new comer, who was none other than my hero's friend—the victim of his grand practical joke.

"Then for gracious sake get me away from here if you can," said the schoolmaster. "I have been nearly murdered, or should have been, by a low fellow who had the audacity to say that I was drunk!"

But Mr. Grubbe's advent had already sufficed to send the major portion of the crowd away; for the oily one was well known, and better feared in all that neighbourhood. The juveniles dreaded his umbrella, the elders his tracts and long-winded discourses upon the virtues of water-drinking and subscribing to charities, which, in obliging deference to the old proverb, began at home—*id est*, in Mr. Grubbe's missionary-box—and ended there.

"Well," commented Mr. Grubbe, as he hastened the reverend gentleman in the direction of the Holly Tree Tavern and Hotel, "upon my word, Mr. Styngy, there was some little foundation for the belief. How did you get your face in such a state? And then again look at the coat—all in pieces!"

"Why, what is there the matter with my face?" inquired Mr. Styngy, a little indignant. "It's pale, I suppose?"

"Pale!" repeated Mr. Grubbe; "as pale as a negro's or a chimney-sweep!"

"Good gracious, you don't say so!" said Mr. Styngy, applying the tips of his fingers to his cheeks, and then regarding them with a look of dismay. "Why, so it is, I declare. How could it have happened?"

"You can tell me all about that presently," said Mr. Grubbe, as he hurried along at a frantic pace, for he feared the result to his own credit, if he were seen in company with such a disreputable object as Mr. Styngy by any of his faithful flock. "Here's the hotel."

In a few moments its sheltering portals had closed upon them, and the reverend schoolmaster was contemplating with horror and dismay the effects of Sam Scarecrow's blackened towel.

"I am the most unfortunate man in the world, I believe," he said. "The whole of this day I have been subject to a series of misadventures."

"You really shouldn't do it so early in the morning, Mr. Styngy; you really ought to be more prudent, considering your position."

"Shouldn't do *what*?" demanded the schoolmaster, exasperated almost into a condition of temporary insanity. "Surely you do not believe, Grubbe, that I—I—I have been drinking! During all the time that you were an assistant-master in my school did you ever know me to be addicted to such a vice?"

"No; but what else could anyone think who saw you in the condition you were in in Heath-street?"

"I can't understand it," said Mr. Styngy, with a bewildered air; "there was nothing the matter with me when I left home to call on the mother of a pupil I expect to get; but the instant I entered the house my misfortunes began. I stumbled over something as I entered the drawing-room, and blacked the eyes of a lady who was unluckily in the way; then the lunch made me abominably ill; and, when I leave the house to recover myself, I find my face blackened like that of an Ethiopian minstrel, and my coat—a bran new one—falls to pieces. What will Mrs. Wilful think of me?"

"Mrs. *who*?" demanded Mr. Grubbe, becoming suddenly excited.

"Mrs. Wilful," repeated the schoolmaster. "Why, what's the matter, Grubbe?"

"That's the matter," said Mr. Grubbe, emphatically. "Lionel Wilful is the matter, Mr. Styngy. It was he who tripped you up, made you ill, blacked your face, and spoiled your coat, I'm——," and Mr. Grubbe emphasised the conclusion with an emphatic bang of his fist upon the table.

Mr. Styngy looked incredulously at the oily gentleman—

"I hardly see how that can be," he said after a moment's thought. "There certainly was a boy named Lionel—"

"And another—a red-headed monster," interrupted Mr. Grubbe, "called Sam Scarecrow!"

"Yes," assented the Rev. Philo, "but Master Wilful seemed such a polite youth, of most engaging manners; and the other, Sam, was so especially civil and attentive when I became ill—that, against my usual rule, I promised him a gratuity."

"All done to blind you, to throw dust in your eyes," responded Mr. Grubbe. "This Lionel Wilful is one of the most artful and designing young villains that ever breathed. Wait till you hear the infamous trick he played upon me."

And then Mr. Grubbe told the story of his adventure on Hendon-bridge, suppressing, of course, all that portion that reflected on his own conduct, and "elevating" Lionel's practical joke almost into the region of crime.

"What a young monster!" said Mr. Styngy, aghast, when his ex-assistant had concluded. "What a narrow escape I have had, Grubbe; why if that boy were to come amongst my pupils he would utterly disorganise them."

"You will not take him, then?"

"Certainly not. I would as soon take a naked candle into a powder magazine."

"I think you will take him though," said Mr. Grubbe, with a peculiar smile.

"And I am certain that I will not," replied the schoolmaster warmly.

"I have special reasons for thinking that you will, though," said Mr. Grubbe. "It is to my interest, and it will be to yours."

Mr. Styngy shook his head doubtfully.

Then ensued a long and earnest conversation, carried on in a low and cautious tone, the result of which was, that Mr. Styngy was converted to Mr. Grubbe's way of thinking.

"I suppose I must give way, then," he said, "but it will be a dangerous thing to do."

"Not at all. Leave all that to me," replied Mr. Grubbe. "You go back now to Heath-end Villa, and at all hazards secure him for your pupil."

"You may consider it done," said the schoolmaster.

"Let that be your business; it will be mine to present myself at Cheetham Hall Academy, as your second master, and if I do not then repay Lionel Wilful for what he has done to me, and make myself master of his mother's fortune, too, may I be shut up in a lunatic asylum for the rest of my life!"

CHAPTER VII.

SAM SCARECROW IN THE HANDS OF THE PHILISTINES.

LITTLE conscious of the circumstances that had brought his future schoolmaster and his old enemy, Mr. Grubbe, into connection, Lionel revelled in the full enjoyment of the success their schemes had met with.

"He must suspect who played the tricks on him," said Lionel, "and if he does, Sam, he must be precious hard up for a pupil if he takes me."

"That be right for sartin," assented Sam. "Lor! to see him a-goin' down the road, with his face black and his coat all split up behind, it most kills me with larfin."

"Don't laugh too loud, though, Sam," said Lionel. "I don't want my mother to know it before it can be helped—it would worry her."

"'Twould worry her more to have to part with you altogether, Master Lionel. There's that to be thought on."

"It's only that which induces me to play these games at all," said Lionel. "But if they *will* interfere between my mother and me they must take the consequences."

"In course," responded Sam, "and sarve 'em right, too. D'ye think he'll come back, Master Lionel?"

"I expect so; but I shan't be sorry if he does not."

"I should think he've had enough for one while."

MUTTERED HOWLS OF AGONY AROSE FROM THE CASK, AND ALL THEIR INTEREST IN SUGAR WAS AT AN END.

"So should I; but he is almost certain to return, if only to make his apologies to mother for his abrupt departure, and——"

"And what, Master Lionel?"

"And most likely," said Lionel, emphatically, "to complain of the treatment he has received. So, if I were in your place, Sam, I should make myself scarce this afternoon."

Sam delivered himself of a slow and solemn wink, full of meaning; and began deliberately divesting himself of his green baize apron.

"I've got some horders as cook wants delivered in the town," said Sam, "and there's some books to go back to the libery; so I may as well hev the arternoon in the hopen hair."

"I would, Sam," continued Lionel; "they won't say much to me—but with you it would certainly be a case of strap and gardener."

Sam shrugged his shoulders uneasily at the mention of these suggestive words.

"He's got a 'eavy 'and," said Sam, quickening his preparations for departure, "and the way he do make that strap curl about the edges of a fellow's ribs is remarkable unpleasant."

"You remember the last time—eh, Sam?" said Lionel, "when my aunt ordered you to be strapped for sucking the new-laid eggs."

"Don't I?' said Sam, with a shudder. "That ere gardener's genurus is lost in a place like this. He ought to be appointed head garotter-whacker at Newgit or Pentonwill. My, couldn't he dror the 'owls out of 'em!"

"And a good thing, too," assented my hero; "I wouldn't mind using the cat-o'-nine tails myself upon some of those women-kickers. But cut away, Sam, or he'll be here before you've gone."

"You're sure you don't want me for anythink, Master Lionel?"

"No, Sam; I shall go and have an hour with my books. Aunt Maria is sure to, what she calls, try to expose my ignorance before the schoolmaster, and I shouldn't like to be floored. Adieu, Sam, and don't get into mischief."

"Tar, tar, Master Lionel."

And completing his out-of-door toilet, Sam Scarecrow possessed himself of the books which were to be returned to the "libery," received the list of orders from the cook, and departed rejoicing, on his way.

"All men have their failings" saith the familiar proverb, and boys, being but immature men, may be perhaps credited with the possession of a somewhat larger stock than their elders.

Sam Scarecrow had his—that fact is certain—and the greatest of them was an uncontrollable appetite.

No one with the slightest respect for the truth could have looked upon him and said that he was fat—or was reasonably plump—yet he consumed enough to fatten half-a-dozen ordinary boys, and still defied the approach of adipose deposit.

He could eat anything at any time—the tortures of indigestion were unknown to him, the horrors of biliousness a sealed book.

He had been seen to devour, without the slightest emotion, oysters, treacle, ham, jam, cheese, and pastry, concluding with a compound of the "bottoms" of beer and wine bottles mingled in one delicious draught, and it never made him ill!

It was currently believed that one small trader in cheap pastry and sweetstuffs lived entirely on Sam's custom, and the grocer regarded him with a friendly eye, for he knew how largely Sam encouraged the consumption of sugar, raisins, candied peel, and other culinary delicacies at Heath-end Villa.

Sam was always certain of a toothsome dainty whenever he took an order to Mr. Figgley, and as a natural consequence such journeys were especially captivating to the sandy youth.

There existed a rival grocer who long had paid an assiduous court to Sam, tempting him with oranges, nuts, figs, and French plums to transfer the orders from Heath-end Villa to him.

Sam took the bribes—he was not proof against temptation when it came in such form—and promised to do his best.

Time went on: three or four times a week the rival grocer presented Sam with something good, but, as he received no orders, he began to get impatient; and the sandy youth, in desperation at the idea of losing so many luscious morsels, after which his very soul hungered, made up a list of articles on his own account and delivered it to the delighted grocer, who instantly presented Sam with a whole drum of Smyrna figs.

"He wanted a horder," chuckled Sam, as he bit into a juicy fig, "and he's got one, but I don't know whether cook'll take the things in or not; I rayther think she won't.'

The cook did not. In fact she sent the things back, with an intimation to the rival grocer's young man that he had "better keep his rubbage to himself, and not bother people with things as they 'adn't hordered."

The grocer was furious, and for a whole week watched for Sam behind his door, armed with a cheese-cutter.

But the wily Sam devoured the figs, and kept out of the way of the irate donor, until he thought that the circumstance was forgotten, and even then he took the precaution to keep on the other side of the way, and turn a wary eye upon the rival grocer's doorway.

That gentleman had neither forgotten nor forgiven Sam Scarecrow, and many were the devices by which he essayed to lure the sandy youth within "spanking" distance.

On this very afternoon it so happened that Mr. Treagle, the injured grocer, had placed outside his shop an empty sugar hogshead of mighty and imposing dimensions, calculated to impress the beholder with a due sense of the enormous business transacted by the grocer who exhibited it.

Hovering round the cask were some eight or ten sugar-loving youngsters, who well knew the treasures of succulent sweets encrusted on the internal staves of the cask, but were deterred from appropriating it to themselves by reason of Mr. Treagle, who, armed with a flexible cane, stood sentry at his shop-door.

The sight of the cask at once attracted Sam's attention, and he licked his lips at the idea of the lusciously crusted interior.

He never thought of Mr. Treagle—that venomous and revengeful grocer—sugar occupied his mind, and, crossing the road, he made towards the hogshead.

The crafty Mr. Treagle retreated within his shop—even as the spider lurks in the dark recesses of his web, until his prey is well within his reach—and the unsuspecting Sam, tucking the parcel of books close beneath his left arm, looked over the edge of the cask.

He could only just do this, for his chin barely reached to the uppermost rim; but he had little need of the sense of sight, the smell was enough to assure him of the presence of the treasure.

The more timid sugar-worshippers, emboldened by Sam's example, now drew nearer, keeping a watchful eye upon the shop-door; but Sam, who had no thought of an avenging grocer in his head, was already half way in the barrel, his long thin legs dangling in the air, and his nether garments stretched temptingly tight.

No signs of Mr. Treagle being apparent, the boldest of the marauders followed Sam's example, and soon the hinder ends of half a dozen boys ornamented the upper rim of the hogshead.

It was an interesting sight, or would have been to anyone to whom the innocent enjoyment of youth is a pleasing spectacle.

From the interior came sounds of scraping and crunching, with occasional chokes occasioned by the difficulty of swallowing whilst in an inverted position; while the exterior was adorned by some dozen or so of youthful legs of all degrees of size and length, the convulsive twitching of which, as they were occasionally jerked upwards, betokened the pleasurable emotions of their owners.

The scene of bliss, like all those that visit us in this vale of tears, was not destined to last long. The flies were in the web, and now the spider stole upon his prey, or in less metaphorical language Mr. Treagle and his shopman, each armed with a long bamboo cane, sallied forth from the shop.

There was a swishing sound, a sharp crack, a muttered howl of agony from the hogshead, and all Sam's interest in sugar was at once at an end.

He struggled to withdraw himself from the trap, but Mr. Treagle had thirsted too long and too ardently for the opportunity to let it slip so easily.

With one hand he kept him fixed in the convenient position Sam had himself assumed, and the other wielding the flexible cane rose and fell with the regularity of a flail in the hands of an experienced thrasher.

"Oh! oh!! oh!!! roared Sam. "Leave orf! Murder! Oh my poor—"

The remainder of his sentence was drowned by the wails of agony from the other tormented youths, two of whom had fallen into the hogshead, and were being severely damaged by Sam, who, in his agony, whirled his long arms about as if he were competing for the champion drummership of the world, and were winning easily.

"So—you'll—swindle—a—honest—tradesman—will—you?" said Mr. Treagle, emphasizing each word by a cut with his cane. "You'll—bring—me—sham—orders—again—eh? — and—cheat—me—out—of—boxes—of—figs—eh?"

Sam kicked and plunged, and struggled, but all to no purpose; and now, the shopman finding it difficult to get at the two culprits in the interior of the hogshead, amused himself by making a few fancy cuts at Sam.

The man had been accustomed to horses, and knowing well where the most ticklish parts of the human as well as the equine animal were situated, did great execution.

This addition was too much. Sam made a tremendous effort, and launched out his long legs at random. The right struck Mr. Treagle just where he tied his apron strings, and with a sound like the bursting of an inflated paper bag he doubled up upon the pavement. The left caught the shopman on the knuckles of his dexter hand, removing an amount of skin which two-pennyworth of sticking-plaister would hardly suffice to replace.

Mr. Treagle was speechless, but the shopman used bad language enough for any two reasonable men, in spite of his having his injured knuckles in his mouth.

Sam did not stop to listen, though. He seized his parcel, scrambled out of the barrel, and removed his person out of the reach of further danger, where he soothed his smarts and bruises by levelling a series of abusive epithets and derisive gestures at Mr. Treagle.

"Blow me if ever I seed anythink like it,' snuffled Sam, as he walked stiffly and painfully along. "Who'd a thought o' my being such a fool as to run right into old Treagle's reach like that? Dash old Treagle—and bust that there cask, I ses. I shan't be able to sit down to my meals for a month. But I'll serve him out—see if I don't."

And resolving in his mind sundry dire schemes of vengeance, the very mildest of which consisted in a plan to purchase a barrel of gunpowder, light a slow match that would take a week to burn, and consign it to the unsuspecting grocer—who would be thereby blown into (according to Sam's calculation) at least a hundred thousand atoms—my hero's faithful follower proceeded on his way

CHAPTER VIII.

THE TRIUMPH OF MESSRS. GRUBBE AND STYN

LIONEL had fully made up his mind *not* to become an inmate of Mr. Styngy's establishment for sowing in the youthful mind the seeds of a select variety of knowledge and accomplishments—nearly every one of which was generally as carefully plucked out again as soon as the pupil made his entrance into the world to fight the rough battle of life.

On the other hand—as my readers know—the Rev. Mr. Styngy had made up *his* mind that Lionel should presently accompany him back to Cheetham Hall—to swell his banking account by so many pounds a year more—and to suffer all the pains and penalties of schooldom by way of solatium for the tricks that had been played upon his reverend person.

Fully anticipating that Lionel and his ally would be prepared to give him another specimen of their powers of tormenting, the Rev. Mr. Styngy acted with remarkable caution as he approached the villa—carefully looking up in the air, and down on the ground, and round about him generally, in search of snares for the unwary.

"I declare I feel quite nervous," thought the schoolmaster as he approached his hand to the knocker. "What a malicious young rascal that is! I don't think I shall ever be able to get the taste of that horrible castor oil out of my mouth again—ugh!"

And Mr. Styngy communicated such a violent shudder to the knocker that the butler was startled out of a sense of what was due to his position, and actually opened the door himself.

"Have you lost anything, sir?" asked the butler, as Mr. Styngy, instead of entering the widely-opened portals, began a close examination of the hall floor.

"No—er—that is—er—no!" replied Mr. Styngy. "Have the goodness to show me to your mistress."

The butler closed the door, and wondering greatly what could induce the reverend gentleman to follow so closely in his footsteps, led the way to the drawing-room.

"Stop a moment," said Mr. Styngy. "You have a boy here in the house, have you not?"

"Master Lionel, sir?"

"No; a page, I think. At least, he wore the ordinary habiliments of that station."

"Oh! you mean Sam Scarecrow, sir?"

"That is the boy. Is—er—is he anywhere near us?"

"No, sir. He has been out on an errand, sir, a long while."

Mr. Styngy heaved a sigh of relief, and then inquired after Lionel.

"Master Lionel's upstairs in his own room, busy with his books, I think, sir."

"Good boy," said Mr. Styngy, fervently, as he passed into the drawing-room. "I love him already; only wait till I get him to school, and I'll give him a proof of my affection!"

Mrs. Wilful and Miss Martinet were ready to receive their visitor. The latter lady, in spite of an artful adjustment of her head-dress, showed promising symptoms of a fine black eye, and Mr. Styngy, who by no means relished being in the vicinity of Lionel longer than he could help, proceeded at once to business.

It was soon settled, for there was nothing but the

terms and the manner of Lionel's departure to be arranged.

The terms were high, of course, as befitted a school of such ultra respectability as Mr. Styngy's; but as Mrs. Wilful was not addicted to bargaining, and Aunt Maria would have thought any price that rid her of her aversion moderate, no difficulty was met with on that score.

"And now, my dear madam," pursued Mr. Styngy, beaming with satisfaction, for his new pupil was to pay the highest price, and learn all the "extra's;" "now as to our dear young friend's departure. When may I expect to receive him?"

"Oh, at once, of course," said Miss Martinet, hastily. "You know he had better go at once, or you will be fretting and worrying yourself until you are ill."

"If that is the case," said Mr. Styngy, catching at the idea, "I can take my dear young friend back with me. I leave London for Cheetham Hall to-morrow afternoon, if he can be ready by that time."

"Of course he can," said Miss Martinet, immediately.

"Oh, no!" expostulated Mrs. Wilful; "not so soon, Maria. A fortnight from now will be quite soon enough."

"A fortnight!" repeated Miss Martinet. "Nonsense, Lydia. How can you think of such a thing? I should be driven crazy in half that time. Besides, you forget what an excellent opportunity it will be for ensuring Lionel's safe arrival. Under Mr. Styngy's care he will be as secure as with you."

Mrs. Wilful made a faint attempt at remonstrance, but she was far too delicate to attempt to contend against the multitude of advantages which Miss Maria urged in favour of Lionel's immediate departure, and in a very brief space the whole affair was concluded, and Mr. Styngy had risen to take his leave when Lionel strolled into the room.

"Ah, my young friend," said Mr. Styngy, with an amiable smile, "and how are you by this time, eh?"

"Quite well, thank you, sir," replied Lionel, who was under the impression that Mr. Styngy had just arrived. "I hope you are better."

"Oh, quite well now—quite well," said the schoolmaster, with a peculiar smile. "I discovered the cause of my indisposition, Master Lionel."

"That's right," thought Lionel, as he noticed Mr. Styngy's smile, and the emphasis he placed on the last sentence. "He has guessed that Sam and I played him that trick, and has come to say that he won't have me at his school. This is prime."

But Lionel, for once, had reckoned without his host. Mr. Styngy held out his hand and said with a sweet smile—

"Good-bye, my dear young friend and pupil, good-bye."

"Good-bye," repeated Lionel. "Are you going, sir? I thought you had only just arrived."

"Oh, dear no!" said Mr. Styngy, sweetly, "I have been here this long while, and your mama and I have settled everything."

"The deuce you have," thought Lionel, and it must be confessed that he looked uncommonly gloomy for a while.

"I am sure, madam," said Mr. Styngy, turning to Mrs. Wilful, "that your dear son and I will thread the pleasant paths of knowledge happily together. Do you observe that he already looks affected at the prospect of even a temporary separation?

"I shall be glad, indeed, if it is so," assented Mrs. Wilful.

"Keep up a cheerful spirit, Lionel," Mr. Styngy went on, "for we shall meet again to-morrow to part no more for many months."

"The dickens we shall!" thought Lionel, looking anything but glad or grateful. "By George, he has stolen a march upon me. But it's no use saying anything. Mother has evidently made up her mind, and I won't worry her by crossing her wishes."

With which sensible resolution, Lionel bade Mr. Styngy adieu, with as good a grace as he could muster, but inwardly resolved that before long he would make that gentleman anathematise the day that first brought him into contact with Lionel Wilful.

"I wonder how I shall like school?" mused my hero, as in the solitude of his own little study, crammed with books, cricket-bats, balls, and stumps, fishing-rods and lines, the *disjecta membra* of sundry steam-engines, electrical machines, galvanic batteries, and such other scientific toys, with which no intruding housemaid dared venture to meddle.

Miss Martinet had, indeed, once made a determined raid upon what she called a "pack of rubbish only fit for the dusthole," but Lionel forewarned, had left his largest Leyden jar fully charged in Miss Maria's way, and in handling it she received a shock that frightened her nearly out of her wits, and quite out of the room in something less than ten seconds

Lionel surveyed his treasures with a melancholy glance. Each one of them seemed to him a familiar friend from whom he was compelled to part, but whom it was doubtful if ever he would meet again.

"Aunt will play the very dickens with my things when I'm gone," he mused. "Even if I locked 'em up she'd find another key, and clear them out; and I can't take them with me, that's certain."

Just then Sam introduced the upper portion of his long body into the room, his features animated by an expression of eager curiosity.

"Master Lionel?'

"Ah! Sam, that you? Just the very fellow I want to see, come in."

Sam came in, and closed the door behind him with the greatest possible caution.

"Miss Maria—she is just a-goin' of it down stairs," said Sam in a stage whisper. "I think she must hev gone out of her mind—she looks so pleased, and she let me pass her without giving me a slap on the head."

"She is in a good temper, that's certain," said Lionel. "Do you know why, Sam?"

"I dunno, Master Lionel, unless as somebody's been and gone and offered to marry of her."

"No, not that; but Mr. Styngy's been here, Sam, and I'm going to school."

Sam's countenance fell below zero, and he looked the very picture of misery.

"You don't mean to say as the castor-oil dodge weren't enough for him?" said Sam.

"It wasn't," replied Lionel; "anyhow I'm going away to-morrow afternoon."

Sam uttered a groan of despair.

"Can't nothink be done, Master Lionel?"

"Don't think so, Sam—I must go; and, after all, there's no great hardship in it. I have heard lots of fellows say that school life is jolly enough if a fellow only sticks up for himself, and don't let the others put upon him—and I shan't do *that* you may be sure."

"I shouldn't care, either, if I was only a-goin', too," said Sam Scarecrow, dolefully. "You can do athout me, Master Lionel; but what'll I do athout you?"

"Cheer up, Sam; don't let your spirits go down," sang Lionel, as he patted the lanky one on the back. "There are the holidays, you know, Sam. I shall see you then."

"But they comes so seldom, and there ain't much on 'em at the best o' times," said Sam. "But I knows what I'll do.'

"What's that, Sam?'

"You won't let it out if I tells you?"

"Of course not. Out with it."

"Well, you knows the libery winder?"

"Yes. Cut away!"

"Well, they wants a cleanin', and I've got to do em. It ain't till to-morrer arternoon; and wher

Mr. Styngy comes to the front door, I'll fall down accerdenterly, and squash him!"

Lionel broke into a hearty fit of laughter at Sam's plan for demolishing the obnoxious schoolmaster.

"That would never do, Sam," he said, as soon as he could recover his gravity. "Besides, you would do no more harm than if a feather pillow tumbled out upon him. You're not heavy enough to squash anything except his hat."

"Never mind," said Sam, resolutely; "I'll try."

CHAPTER IX.

"DID I SPILE HIS HAT."

THE idea of such a vengeance seemed so ludicrously impossible to Lionel that he only laughed at Sam, and soon forgot the circumstance in the bustle of preparation.

Sam did not, though. The thing seemed to him perfectly justifiable and easy of execution; and the more he pondered upon his plan the more he liked it, and, never reflecting upon the danger he himself was likely to run, chuckled mightily at the mental picture he drew of the fright and discomfiture of Mr. Styngy.

"I'll let him know," mused Sam, as he plied his brush vigorously upon some of his young master's clothes. "I'll teach him to come here a-fetchin' people away agin their wills. I 'ope he'll 'ave a noo 'at on. I bets I spiles it!"

And Sam renewed his brushing with such vicious energy as to separate two or three buttons from the jacket on which he was operating, thereby incurring a severe reprimand and a smart box on the ear from Miss Martinet, who superintended the preparation of my hero's wardrobe.

"Never mind," muttered Sam, as he walked away with a blazing ear. "I can't take it out o' she, but I'll drop a little more 'eavy on the reverend gent tomorrer. Wot larks if he's laid up for a day or two!"

The morrow came, and with the sun the members of the establishment at Heath-end Villa arose, for every one had some share in the preparations for Lionel's departure.

Sam was one of the first: indeed, he had hardly slept at all for grief at the prospect of separation from his young master, and the thought of his coming vengeance upon Mr. Styngy.

He sought an opportunity of being alone with Lionel, in order to consult him as to the advisability of filling his pockets with some of the weights belonging to the kitchen scales.

But the opportunity did not occur; for Mrs. Wilful kept my hero all to herself, and so thwarted Sam's wishes.

"Never mind," mused that young gentleman; "I'll do it athout the weights. I dessay I shall be 'eavy enough; 'sides some on 'em might bump him a little too hard, and that would be orkard. I do 'ope he's got a noo tile on!"

As the time appointed for the coming of Mr. Styngy approached, Sam stole cautiously up to the library with his window-cleaning appurtenances, and set leisurely to work, keeping a keen look-out for the advance of the enemy.

"It's furder than I thought it wor," mused the faithful Scarecrow, as he cast an anxious squint beneath him; "but I don't s'pose it'll hurt much. If it do, it don't matter; it's all for Master Lionel's sake."

And Sam resumed his work—paying, however, so little attention to his mode of executing it, that, pressing too hard upon the centre of a pane of glass, it cracked, and the pieces fell, musically clashing and jingling upon the broad stone steps below.

Sam squinted at this in terrible dismay, for he knew that there was little chance of the sound escaping unheard by the sharp ears of Miss Martinet.

And he was right, for almost at the same moment he heard the shrill voice of that lady raised to an uncommonly high pitch.

Just then, too, Sam caught sight of the Rev. Mr. Styngy approaching the house with measured and stately strides, and he was in an agony of desperation lest Miss Martinet should arrive in the library before the schoolmaster was near enough to be dropped upon.

Sam was inside the library when he broke the pane of glass. He knew that Miss Martinet's action would be prompt the instant she discovered him, and she was certain to do so before Mr. Styngy's deliberate style of locomotion could bring him to the front door. There was but one resource left, and Sam adopted it.

The library windows opened vertically in the centre. Sam undid the catch, swung back the window, and stepping out upon a narrow ledge some three inches wide, passed his hand through the broken pane and refastened the catch, just as Miss Maria, crimson with anger, bounded in.

"Samuel, you good-for-nothing destructive boy, you!" shaking her hand with wrathful energy at Sam, "come away directly, you bad boy, you!"

Sam, being at the moment conveniently deaf, rubbed vigorously away at a fresh pane, casting every now and then a glance towards the slowly advancing form of Mr. Styngy.

"Oh, bust him!" muttered Sam, "Why don't he make haste? I never saw such a slow coach. I wish as how some one was ahind him with a pin. Dash it, she's a-goin' to open the winder!"

Indeed Miss Martinet, finding that Sam paid attention neither to her verbal commands nor to her tapping on the panes, laid her gentle hand upon the catch, with the intention of opening the window and dragging the refractory page in by force.

Sam held on to the window frame with one hand, while the other rubbed vigorously away at a pane of glass that interposed between his features and Miss Martinet.

"Let go this instant, you dreadful common boy!" exclaimed Miss Martinet, tugging at the catch; "oh, you will suffer for this impudence when you do come in. *I* know well enough you're not deaf."

Mr. Styngy was now slowly ascending the steps, and in another moment or two would be immediately below the window.

Sam, therefore, became suddenly conscious of the presence of Miss Martinet.

"Did you want me, mum?" he said innocently, as he ceased polishing the window, and squinted amiably upon Miss Martinet.

"You impudent, low, bad boy, to pretend not to hear me when I have actually screamed myself hoarse. Let go directly, Samuel!"

Samuel cast a glance below. The shiny top of Mr. Styngy's hat was just beneath him. He shut his eyes—and obliged Miss Maria by letting go, and in a hurry, too.

The next instant there was a loud shriek from Miss Martinet, followed by a curious "crunching" sound, part of a naughty word from Mr. Styngy, and a howl of pain from Sam, as down the steps the shiny hat, its owner and the page went, slowly turning complicated somersaults.

Miss Martinet stood at the window, gazing with horrified eyes at the scene. To her mind nothing less than instant death to both of the victims could be the result.

She waited until the acrobatic performance was terminated by the bottom of the steps being reached by the impromptu performers, and then, raising her voice in a series of peculiarly loud and piercing shrieks, Miss Martinet, with the speed and grace of a startled pussy-cat, hastened towards the front door.

By the time she reached it it had been opened, and the whole establishment, excepting Mrs. Wilful and Lionel, gathered round the victims.

The butler and the footman were busily engaged

in an endeavour to extract Mr. Styngy's head from his hat—that article having been firmly jammed over his classical features by Sam's perpendicular fall.

"Oh, is he dead?" ejaculated Miss Maria, "don't tell me he is dead!"

A muffled voice from the interior of the hat tried to articulate something. It might have been a reply to Miss Martinet's agonised query, but sounded very much like a naughty word that begins with D.

Oh, no, miss," said the butler. "he isn't dead by a long way. Hold still a bit, sir, and we'll soon get it off. Pull up on your side, John!"

A tremendous tug from the butler and the footman—a howl of agony from Mr. Styngy, and the hat came off—bringing with it, however, no small portion of the bark of his classical nose.

Up to this point no one but Miss Martinet was aware of the nature of the accident, for Sam lay quietly curled up behind one of the pilasters at the bottom of the steps—insensible.

"Where is that bad, vicious boy?" she said. "Run away, of course, after nearly killing this gentleman. I'll have him locked up for this."

"Who, miss?" asked the footman; "I'll go for a policeman, miss."

"It's that Samuel," said Miss Maria, as with her own delicate white handkerchief she endeavoured to appease the anguish of Mr. Styngy's nose. "Bring the tallest policeman you can find, John, for he is a desperate, bad boy."

"I will, miss," and John started to obey the command, when he caught sight of Sam's long form behind the pilaster, and instantly conceiving that he was endeavouring to hide himself, pounced triumphantly upon the boy.

"I've got him. Here he is, miss," shouted John, in triumph.

"Be very careful, John," said Miss Martinet, hurrying to where the elated footman was endeavouring to make Sam stand upon his legs.

But those members, never particularly steady, were now as limp as those of a puppet in Punch's show when the enlivening hand of the showman is withdrawn.

"Stand up, you young blackguard!" said the footman. "You're obstinate, are you, eh?"

"Box his ears, John," suggested Miss Martinet, "that's the only thing that does him any good."

John, with an evident relish for the task assigned him, moistened the palm of his right hand with his lips, and in another moment it would have descended with stinging force upon Sam's ear had not Lionel's clear voice rang out angrily—

"Stop that, there. What are you doing, John?"

Master Lionel, in spite of his youth, was feared as well as loved by the servants.

John put his right hand behind him, and looked sheepish, while Lioned, stooping over his faithful follower, endeavoured to restore him to consciousness

"Poor fellow," he said, indignantly. "Why, the back of his head is wet with blood. How did it happen?"

"Happen, indeed! I'd 'poor fellow' him if I had my way," said Miss Martinet. "Falling out of the library window on to Mr. Styngy. It's a mercy he did not kill that gentleman—and I verily believe he *did it on purpose!*"

This sentence brought back like a flash the thought of what Sam had threatened to do the day before.

Lionel gave a long, low whistle, and the shadow of a smile flickered on his face for a moment, but he kept the secret to himself.

Just then Sam showed signs of returning consciousness by opening one eye and launching out one of his long thin legs—the boot at the end of which struck John a painful blow on the shin.

"That's right, Sam," said Lionel, cheerfully. "Wake up. Are you better? Lift him up, John, carry him into the house."

Sam looked vacantly around him as he was raised from the ground by the crest-fallen footman—and feebly winking, as he recognised his young master, he said, in a faint voice—

"*Did I spile his hat?*"

CHAPTER X.

IN WHICH MY HERO MAKES A LITTLE MISTAKE—ACCIDENTALLY—FOR THE PURPOSE.

THE little episode detailed in the foregoing chapter did not, in spite of Sam's hopes, prevent, or even delay, Lionel's departure.

Mr. Styngy was indeed grievously bruised and disfigured—the greater portion of his intellectual countenance being covered by patches of court plaister, while other more prominent portions of his anatomy, such as his knees and elbows, were also deprived of a considerable proportion of skin.

But Sam was a still greater sufferer. His lank frame consisting principally of bony corners and projections, where, in ordinary persons flesh is to be found, had sustained great damage in the fall, being, as Mrs. Gamp puts it, "a mask of bruises" from head to foot—besides having one of his ankles sprained.

"Never mind about that, Master Lionel," he said to my hero, who was expressing his symathy for his sufferings; "I spiled his hat, didn't I?

"You certainly did, Sam," laughed Lionel, "I never saw such a hat—it had more wrinkles in it than the bellows of a concertina."

"And it was a noo 'un, too." chuckled Sam, "I see it a shinin' as he come up the drive."

The satisfaction caused by the destruction of Mr. Styngy's hat compensated Sam for all his sufferings—the pain of his ankle, the smart of his bruises were alike forgotten, and he rolled about on his little iron bedstead, chuckling with delight instead of groaning with anguish.

All this, however, did not stop Lionel's departure for even a moment.

The carriage was ordered to be at the door at three o'clock, and to the minute it arrived, crunching the gravel beneath its wheels with a sound that seemed to touch Lionel to the heart, for the time had come when he was to say good-bye to the home he loved so dearly.

Lionel bore himself bravely—and though his voice faltered a little, and his bright eyes were dimmed as he spoke the last words of farewell to his mother, he kept a smile upon his lips, and with a firm light step passed on.

The servants, one and all, with the exception of Sam, who had been deluded into the idea that his young master was not going away until the evening, were mustered in the hall, and heartily were their good-byes spoken, for they regarded with more than common affection the generous, handsome boy who had been the light and life of the house.

He had a shake of the hand and a bright smile for each, regardless of the remonstrances of Mr. Styngy who, thrusting his head out of the carriage window at intervals of two seconds, bade him make haste.

Lionel's foot was already on the step of the carriage when he heard the sound of a scuffle behind, and turning he beheld the faithful Sam, simply attired in a nightshirt, doing battle with the footman and the butler.

It was an unequal contest, for Sam's fall from the window had deprived him of the use of one leg—his left arm was in a sling, and his face so enveloped with bandages that to see was a matter of much difficulty.

"I *will* go out," Sam roared, as he fixed his only available hand in the butler's neck-cloth, causing that gentleman to become black in the face in something less than two seconds.

"Mur—der," gasped the butler, faintly, "take the willing away, John, he's a strangling of me!"

The footman, who entertained a mortal jealousy

of Sam, began a scientific twisting of the cartilage of the page's ear; but before his hold could be loosened, Lionel had arrived, and rescued him from his detainers.

"Oh! Mum—Mum—Master Lionel!" blubbered Sam; "and you was agoin' away without saying a good bye to *me*."

"There—there—Sam! its all right," said Lionel, patting the inconsolable Sam gently on the back. "Good bye, and cheer up. We shall meet again soon. Shake hands There. Mr. Styngy is calling me."

"Good bye, Master Lionel—tar, tar—likewise adoo," saluted Sam, "We'll meet agin' sooner than you thinks for. Excoos my comin' out to the carridge on account of my costoom, Master Lionel. Oh! wot a blow it are!"

And Sam, as the carriage containing his young master rolled away, turned and hid his emotion on the footman's shoulder, much to that haughty menial's disgust.

The journey to the station was performed in silence. Lionel was sad and thoughtful, and Mr. Styngy did not care to interrupt his new pupil's meditations. He reflected, and wisely, that while Lionel's mind was so occupied he would not be devising any fresh scheme for the schoolmaster's discomfiture; for, with good reason, he had learned already to dread the results of my hero's ingenuity.

It did not last long, though. The spirits of the young are too strong and elastic to be long pressed down by the superincumbent weight of care and sorrow; and when the carriage drew up before the portals of the Great Southern Railway Station, Mr. Styngy observed, with some misgiving, that the old merry, mischievous smile again lit up his pupil's features.

"Dear me," said Mr. Styngy, as he compared his watch with the station clock, "I am nearly ten minutes slow. Our train must be on the point of starting. Can I trust you to get the tickets while I see to the labelling of the luggage?"

"Certainly, sir," replied Lionel. "What shall I get?"

"Two first-class single tickets for Nobsham. Don't make a mistake—Nobsham. Have you any money?"

"Yes, sir," said Lionel, who had a five-pound note, a parting gift from his mother, enshrined in his little purse.

"Very well, get the tickets, and I will repay you by-and-bye," said Mr. Styngy, as he turned to the porter who was taking the luggage from the carriage.

"Cool," thought Lionel, who by no means relished the idea of changing his treasure for such a purpose; "but I suppose I'd better do it. Which is the booking-office, I wonder?"

Lionel plunged into the thick of the crowd that turned to and fro in search of lost luggage, wives, or children, or pressed towards the rabbit-hutch-like holes where misanthropic clerks dispensed, with haughty and aggravating indifference, sundry slips of pasteboard in exchange for good current coin.

"This way for Codsham—Codsham—Codsham!" shouted a porter, seizing a huge handbell, and performing a frantic solo upon it, with no apparent purpose but that of deafening himself and all in his vicinity.

"Codsham," thought Lionel, the spirit of mischief within him suggesting an idea; "Mr. Styngy said Nobsham, I think—but if I make a mistake it's his fault for not getting the tickets himself. I'll chance it."

And Lionel, elbowing his way to that particular rabbit-hutch having "Third-class" inscribed above it, purchased two tickets for Codsham, and returning found Mr. Styngy, with a red and anxious face, looking out for him.

The schoolmaster had a portion of his luggage with him, to wit, a handbag of plump proportions, and a travelling rug confined by straps.

Being thus encumbered, he left to Lionel the task of presenting the tickets at the barrier, following innocently enough the directions of a porter who was loudly shouting, "'Asham! 'Asham!" with all his might, apparently in the belief that he was imparting information to the bewildered passengers.

"Are you sure this is the train?" said Mr. Styngy, a little doubtfully.

"Quite, sir, I inquired of the porter," said Lionel.

Mr. Styngy was not a frequent traveller on that line; he had been to the great Southern Terminus before, but even then the worry and confusion bewildered him a little, and as there was no time for argument he followed Lionel's lead.

"Now then, sir, make haste," said the guard. "What class?"

"First, of course," said Mr. Styngy. Come, Lionel, make haste."

The carriage door was opened—the schoolmaster and Lionel entered—then it was slammed to with a crash, enclosing a portion of Mr. Styngy's skirt as in a vice—a shrill whistle from the guard, a responsive scream from the engine, and the train started.

The jerk threw Mr. Styngy forward, and about a quarter of a yard of skirt remained in the door—much to the owner's vexation, for the schoolmaster was an economical man, and the coat was a new one.

"Confound—I mean how very careless of that guard!" said Mr. Styngy. "My coat is entirely spoiled. I shall sue the company."

"It is shameful," here said a sharp-looking old gentleman, who had been seated in a corner of the carriage. "You have good grounds for an action, sir, and if you intend to bring one against the company, allow me to offer you my card. I am a solicitor, sir."

"You are very good, sir," replied Mr. Styngy. "I may be glad to avail myself of your offer. It is abominable that these careless fellows should be allowed to destroy valuable property with impunity. Are you going all the way to Nobsham, sir?"

"To Nobsham? repeated the solicitor. "*This* train goes to *Codsham*, sir—express."

Mr. Styngy gazed amazedly at his informant.

"Eh! what?" he said, in a horrified tone.

"To Codsham, sir," repeated the solicitor, in a louder tone. "We shall reach there about five o'clock if this train is punctual."

"Good gracious!" ejaculated Mr. Styngy; "we are in the wrong train!"

"The stupid company's servants again, sir," said the solicitor, soothingly. "Was your arrival at Nobsham of great importance, sir, may I ask?"

"Very," said Mr. Styngy.

"Then allow me to suggest that you make the delay the subject of an additional claim upon the company. Heavy damages, my dear sir—heavy damages!"

Mr. Styngy made no immediate reply, but stared vacantly for a moment at the solicitor. Then a sudden thought seemed to strike him, and he turned almost ferociously upon Lionel.

"Where are the tickets?"

"Here, sir," said Lionel, innocently, as he produced them.

"I thought so," exclaimed Mr. Styngy. "Third class, and to Codsham, instead of first class to Nobsham. Very good, my young friend. This is what you call a practical joke, I suppose?"

"Did you not tell me to get tickets to Codsham, sir?" Lionel asked, with a bland and childlike smile that would have done credit to Bret Harte's Heathen Chinee.

"Did I tell you to take tickets to Codsham?" repeated Mr. Styngy, wrathfully. "No, sir; I did not tell you to do anything of the sort. You know that well enough."

"There was such a noise at the station, sir," urged Lionel, "that a mistake might have been made by anybody. And I am sure that the men who called out the names might as well have spoken

FOLLOW MY LEADER.

MR. STYNGY IS REGARDED BY HIS FELLOW-PASSENGERS AS A LUNATIC, AND A SCENE OF DIRE CONFUSION ENSUES.

No. 3.

in Hindostanee. I couldn't understand them a bit."

"Quite right," interposed the sharp old gentleman. "It is perfectly scandalous. The fault clearly lies with the company's servants. I will proceed against them at once if you will favour me with instructions to do so."

Mr. Styngy muttered something relative to people letting other people's business alone, and indulged for about ten minutes in half-audible growls and mutterings that clearly indicated a most perturbed state of mind.

"My stars!" thought Lionel, "what a rage he is in! Never mind, it serves him right. He *would* have me for a pupil, and he must take the consequences as well."

Mr. Styngy opened his travelling-bag, and taking out a time-table consulted its pages with an increasing aspect of sourness.

"Just as I thought," he said, returning the guide to the depths of the bag, and closing the snap with a vicious pressure; "there is no train from Codsham to London till 7.30, and that reaches the terminus just in time to miss the last train to Nobsham!"

"Then we had better return to Hampstead, sir. I am sure my mother will be only too glad to extend her hospitality to you again."

"Hampstead be—be—bothered!" exclaimed the schoolmaster, almost choking with wrath. "Do you know that I have four other pupils awaiting my arrival at Nobsham—sons of gentlemen of the highest position—who will be kept waiting for hours in the cold, in consequence of your worse than stupidity?"

"Very sorry, I am sure, sir," returned Lionel, demurely. "I wouldn't have had it happen on any account."

"Hold your tongue, sir," thundered Mr. Styngy; "but, recollect, if through your infamous tricks I lose these pupils, I will make you pay for it, and dearly, too!"

"Pardon me, sir," said the sharp old gentleman, who did not suffer a word of the conversation to pass unheard. "As this young gentleman is apparently a minor, an action would not lie against him personally, but must be brought against his next of kin or legally-appointed guardian. If you furnish me with the——"

"I will furnish you with nothing, sir," replied Mr. Styngy, angrily, "but advise you to mind your own business."

"And I beg to say, sir," replied the lawyer, "that, in minding your business, I *am* attending to my own. But, if you feel an inclination to call me names, sir, pray do so; or, perhaps you would prefer to assault me! Pull my nose, sir; or kick me! Do! I call upon that young gentleman as a competent witness to see that I offer no resistance."

Mr. Styngy looked for a moment as if he longed with all his heart and soul to avail himself of the lawyer's invitation—but he was a prudent man, and bethought himself in time of the consequences of an action for assault and battery.

He choked back his wrath, and left the lawyer's nose unpulled, and his nether garments unsoiled by the contact of his boot.

But with Lionel it was a different matter. He could not bring an action for assault, and so Mr. Styngy, after setting aside his travelling-bag and getting into a convenient position, made a blow at Lionel's head.

But that young gentleman, anticipating such an endeavour, ducked as skilfully as that arch joker Punch, when threatened with an assault by the beadle, and Mr. Styngy's blow expended itself upon the empty air.

"What was that for, sir?" said Lionel, keeping a watchful eye upon Mr. Styngy.

"How dare you?" gasped the exasperated schoolmaster.

"What did I do?" again demanded Lionel, with the calmness of innocence.

"Keep still, sir," thundered Mr. Styngy, as he raised his hand for the second time.

"Precious likely that is," muttered Lionel.

"Let him hit you, my young friend," said the lawyer, excited at the prospect of an assault. "I am ready to bear witness that it was entirely unprovoked. Don't resist on any account. You can bring an action against him, and recover heavy damages if he is a substantial man."

"A great deal too substantial," thought Lionel; "and I'm very likely indeed to get damages if he hits me."

Mr. Styngy, however, seeing that he would in all probability gain nothing but a ruffled temper and a rumpled shirt-front, by an attempt to inflict chastisement upon Lionel, desisted, and sulked in his corner of the compartment until the decreasing speed of the train foretold its stoppage at Codsham.

Grunting, groaning, and shaking, like some mighty monster suffering from the pangs of acute rheumatism, the train entered the station accompanied with the cries of the ticket examiners on the platform—

"Tickets ready, please! All tickets ready!"

"Wilful," said Mr. Styngy, with grim politeness, as one of the officials came to the door, "hand me your purse, please."

Lionel did so, wondering what in the world the schoolmaster was going to do with it. He soon found out.

"This young gentleman and I," said Mr. Styngy, in explanation, as he handed the tickets to the examiner, "have got into the wrong train."

"Can't help that, sir," replied the official, shortly. "Full fare from London, please. Two—first class—one pound fourteen."

And, producing his excess-fare book, he rapidly scrawled out the receipts, handed them to Mr. Styngy, who paid the requisite one pound fourteen shillings out of Lionel's purse, with a grim, unholy satisfaction.

"There, Wilful," he said, as he handed back the lightened purse, "should your little practical joke entail any other expense, I may have to trouble you again: so be careful that no one picks your pocket."

"Confound it!" thought Lionel, as with a rather rueful countenance he replaced the purse in his pocket, "this is a rather awkward way of turning the tables on me. But I'll make Mr. Styngy smart for it. I haven't used up all my resources yet."

There was some two hours and a half to wait before the return train to London started, and this time Mr. Styngy proposed to utilise at Lionel's expense.

He first ascertained that there was a refreshment-room where the comestibles were not absolutely poisonous, and retailed at a little less than their weight in gold, and ordered a substantial lunch for two.

Then, his bad temper a little mollified by the march he had stolen upon Lionel, he watched that young gentleman as he paced slowly up and down the platform, little dreaming, though, of the scheme of revenge his new pupil was planning.

In the course of an nour the lunch was ready—and so was Lionel's little plot. The former circumstance Mr. Styngy announced to his pupil—the latter Lionel by no means thought it necessary to make his preceptor acquainted with.

"I hope you have a good appetite, Wilful," said Mr. Styngy. "The feast will be of your providing, you know, and you should do justice to it."

"I shall do that, sir, replied Lionel. "I have always an excellent appetite."

"Boys generally have," said the schoolmaster; "but, as you will find when we get to Cheetham Hall, it is necessary sometimes to place it under restraint. Take your seat, Lionel. That soup has really a most appetising smell."

Lionel meekly obeyed, but as he did so he contrived to slip a pencilled note into the waiter's hand, unperceived by Mr. Styngy.

The man took it, and, retiring to the counter, opened and read it.

And this is what he read—

"The gentleman with me is an escaped lunatic. He is harmless while I am with him; but be careful not to irritate him, and keep all dangerous weapons, such as cutlery, out of his way."

CHAPTER XI.

LIONEL'S LITTLE JOKE.

THE waiter was a plump man, apparently in the enjoyment of the very fullest of health; but as he read Lionel's communication the rosy hue forsook his cheeks, and his knees trembled beneath him.

"Waiter!" said Mr. Styngy, in what that poor man deemed to be a peculiarly fierce and bloodthirsty tone.

"Ye—ye—yes, sir," stammered the waiter, approaching the table by a very slow and circuitous route.

"Bring me some stale bread."

"Oh, lor!" murmured the waiter, as he hurried away to obey the order. "He must be very mad indeed if he don't think that bread stale enough for him."

With much fear and trepidation visible in his countenance and manner, he returned with some bread of a consistency that would have rendered it an admirable substitute for gun-flints.

"That will do," said Mr. Styngy, as the bread was handed to him. "Now, what are you taking my knife away for?"

"Be-be-beg—p-p-pardon, sir," gasped the waiter, as he sidled away. "Not clean, sir."

"I never saw such a fellow in my life," said Mr. Styngy, as he gazed after the rapidly retreating waiter. "He's taken both the knives and forks away, and I am quite certain that they are perfectly clean."

Mr. Styngy soon gave up wondering, though, and absorbed the soup with much evident satisfaction. It was not particularly good, but it was cheap—to him—and that atoned for a multitude of shortcomings.

The soup only whetted Mr. Styngy's appetite, and when he had swallowed the last savoury drop he rapped loudly on the table with the handle of his spoon, and called "Waiter!" with the full strength of a not very weak pair of lungs.

"Waiter!" shouted Mr. Styngy again, after an interval of a few minutes—during which Lionel regarded him with features as grave as those of the Sphinx.

"He must be a little deaf, I should think sir," said Lionel.

"Deaf!" repeated Mr. Styngy. "The man's an idiot, and I shall report him to his superiors. Remind me of that when we get to London—will you?"

"I will, sir."

"What are those noodles grinning at?" said Mr. Styngy, suddenly, as he became conscious of some half dozen pallid and anxious countenances peering down upon him from above the stained-glass partition of the door.

Lionel looked, but as if by magic every one of the heads vanished the instant Mr. Styngy turned his baleful glance upon them.

"This is the most extraordinary place," said Mr. Styngy, after another pause of ten minutes, during which he had hammered on the table and bawled for the waiter, without any result but that of denting the table and breaking a tumbler. "Here we have waited long enough for rations to be provided and cooked for a whole regiment of soldiers, and yet we cannot be served with a plain dinner."

"Shall I go and see if I can find the waiter, sir?" asked Lionel.

"Yes—no—stop a moment, Lionel," said Mr. Styngy, "I'll go myself. I'll teach those fellows that they cannot insult a gentleman with impunity. I saw that rascally waiter looking out at us over the glass door just now."

And, in a towering passion, Mr. Styngy fixed his hat on his head with an emphatic thump, and seizing his umbrella strode towards the door.

There was a sound as of footsteps in hasty retreat, but when Mr. Styngy passed through the doorway into the refreshment-room it was vacated—save by a cat, who was revelling, undisturbed, on the savoury contents of a sausage roll.

The reverend gentleman glanced around him in a very savage and unclerical manner, but there was no one upon whom to vent his wrath

The young ladies who presided over the edible and potable delicacies of the bar were absent, and the door that led into their private sanctum was fast shut.

Mr. Styngy fancied that he could hear terrified whisperings behind it, but as no one came in answer to his call he concluded that he was mistaken.

"Very odd! excessively odd," mused Mr. Styngy. "Can there be anything the matter with my personal appearance?" he added, as the thought suddenly flashed upon him that Lionel might have again decorated his features. But no, the back of the bar was radiant with mirrors, wherein he could see himself a dozen times reflected from a dozen different points of view, a little more flushed than usual with anger, but otherwise eminently grave and respectable.

Besides, there was Lionel by his side, looking innocent enough for canonization as a saint. Mr. Styngy prided himself rather upon his powers of discernment, and thought that he could have certainly detected any mischievous intention upon Lionel's part, and nipped it in the bud.

Wondering greatly to himself, Mr. Styngy strode out upon the platform, but there again the same systematic avoidance of him was manifested.

A porter who was mounting a ladder for the purpose of cleaning a signal lamp, dropped from its topmost round as if he had been shot, and crossed the line with a hop, skip, and jump.

Another, who was wheeling a truck along, stopped very suddenly when he caught sight of Mr. Styngy, and manifested a strong desire to retreat; but the reverend gentleman fixed him with his eye and beckoned to him.

"Here, my man!" said Mr. Styngy. "Come here!"

"Yes, sir," replied the porter, but he never stirred from behind the rampart of his truck.

"*Come here!*" roared Mr. Styngy. "Don't you understand English?"

"Yes, sir;" replied the porter, turning a shade paler; but he didn't attempt to move until the schoolmaster made an angry stride in his direction. Then he turned and climbed with the agility of a monkey up a perpendicular ladder into a lofty signal-box, where he barricaded himself in.

Mr. Styngy stared up at the signal-box in a vacant way, and, lifting his hat, passed his hand slowly over his head as if to reassure himself that that member was in its place.

"I believe," he said slowly to himself, "that this station is tenanted by escaped lunatics; or else I'm a lunatic myself. Lionel!"

"Yes, sir," replied our hero.

"Do you see anything strange about me?"

"No, sir."

"Have I been behaving myself in a rational manner?"

"Perfectly, sir."

"Then there is only one conclusion to be arrived at," said Mr. Styngy, calmly. "All these people must be mad. It admits of no doubt. They're lunatics, every one!"

"They can't all be mad, sir."

"They must be," said Mr. Styngy, making a wild flourish in the air with his umbrella. "It's peculiarly dangerous to the public safety to allow a parcel of lunatics the control of a railway station. We are in danger of our lives until we get away from here. Thank goodness the train is nearly due."

Indeed, just at this moment the distance signal fell, and the porter who had made his escape to the signal-box, appeared on the top step of the ladder and rang a bell.

"Look at that now!" exclaimed Mr. Styngy. "Oh, they must be all mad. Here's a waiter who will not serve us with dinner, and a porter who rings his bell on the top of a ladder forty feet high!"

CHAPTER XII.

WHO WAS THE MADMAN?

BUT a fresh surprise awaited Mr. Styngy; for, instead of the train stopping as it should have done—puffing, creaking and groaning beside the platform—it came no further than the signal-box.

"What in the name of wonder is that for?" said the schoolmaster, "I see nothing to stop the train."

Lionel guessed the cause, though. He had seen one of the porters run down the line waving a red flag, and he knew that the train had been stopped on account of the "mad man."

While Mr. Styngy was yet puzzling himself to account for the stoppage of the train, it moved on again and drew up in the usual manner alongside the platform.

But, with the exception of Lionel and Mr. Styngy, the platform remained deserted. No frantic porters rushed up and down, slamming doors, and bawling unintelligible phrases.

Lionel saw the scared faces of the passengers at the windows, and noticed that such of them as had occasion to alight at that station were getting out on to the rails, in defiance of the company's rules and regulations, but with the assistance and connivance of the porters.

"Why!" exclaimed Mr. Styngy, "the passengers are mad too! There's not a doubt of it! And all the doors are locked!"

The schoolmaster passed rapidly down the line of carriages—the train was a short one—and tugged fiercely at each successive handle, but in vain.

"Porter! por—ter!" roared Mr. Styngy at the top of his sonorous voice. "Guard! come and open this door!"

But porter and guard—for very good reasons, as they thought—were deaf to Mr. Styngy's appeals, and in another moment the signal for starting the train was given.

Just then the schoolmaster bethought himself of a knife he had, which, in addition to the usual complement of blades, possessed quite a little carpenter's chest of tools, besides a corkscrew and—a railway carriage key.

With his heart full of most unclerical anger and uncharitableness for all mankind, and railway officials in particular, Mr. Styngy produced his multifarious knife, unlocked the carriage door, and scrambled in, followed by Lionel, just as the train was getting away.

"Ha! ugh! oh! dear me!" panted Mr. Styngy, and, addressing himself generally to the occupants of the carriage. "Disgraceful! Scandalous! I shall certainly make the treatment I have received the subject of an action against the company!"

There was a stout old gentleman of bland and good-humoured aspect in the corner whom Mr. Styngy's entrance had aroused out of a nap. He took the foregoing observations as addressed to himself, and rejoined, sympathetically—

"I have been a sufferer myself, sir, frequently through the unpunctuality of trains, and the incivility of railway officials, and I can fully sympathise with you. May I ask what particular cause of complaint you now have?"

"This, sir!" returned Mr. Styngy, with much emphasis. "I have reason to believe that every one of the company's servants at the station we have just left is mad!"

"Bless my soul!" exclaimed the stout old gentleman, "you don' mean to say so?"

"I do, repeated Mr. Styngy, more emphatically than before. "They have just conducted themselves in such an extraordinary manner—as my young friend and pupil here can testify—that the only conclusion at which it is possible that a sane man can arrive is that they are all mad—stark, staring mad!"

"Dreadful!" said the stout gentleman, his rubicund face changing its hue to a pale, mottled colour. "I hope that your observation does not extend itself to the engine-driver?"

"I cannot say," said Mr. Styngy. "I had no opportunity of observing him; but I should not wonder if he were as bad as the rest. A company capable of employing mad station-masters and mad porters would not hesitate to put a lunatic engine-driver in charge of a train."

"Horrible!" gasped the stout gentleman, as he leaned back in his corner and regarded the schoolmaster with a pallid countenance.

"It is indeed," returned Mr. Styngy. "We are not safe a moment from an awful collision. What are danger signals to a mad engine-driver?"

Lionel noticed that during the period occupied by the foregoing conversation the other passengers—some half-dozen in number—were whispering earnestly together, and casting anxious and terrified glances towards Mr. Styngy and the stout gentleman, from which circumstances Lionel argued, and rightly, that they had been made acquainted with the supposed madness of the schoolmaster.

"What are they up to now, I wonder?" thought Lionel, as he saw one of them write something on a piece of paper, carefully fold it up, and turn towards the stout old gentleman, who had just accepted Mr. Styngy's proffered flask of sherry.

"Oblige me, sir," said the passenger in an impressive whisper, "by reading that—*at once!*"

"In a moment, my friend, in a moment," said the stout gentleman, who was anxious to get at the sherry by way of steadying his nerves.

"Read it directly—let me implore you!" said the passenger again. "It is of the utmost importance to yourself!"

"Surely it can wait for a moment," said the short gentleman, tilting a little of the sherry into the cup.

"Don't drink it!" whispered the passenger in a lower and a more impressive tone, as he glanced towards Mr. Styngy—who was regarding these proceedings with a wondering air—and then, sheltering his mouth with his hand, he formed the word "Mad!" with his lips.

"Bad!" repeated the stout gentleman, in a tone of angry surprise. "How the deuce can you tell whether this sherry is bad or not? I strongly suspect, my friend, that you are intoxicated."

"Do as you please, sir," returned the passenger, indignantly. "I only interfered for your own benefit. Drink it if you like: but, if you value your life, read the note first."

Thus adjured, the stout gentleman looked doubtfully, first at the sherry, then at Mr. Styngy, and then at the folded piece of paper.

He could make nothing of it. To read the note he would be obliged to relinquish the sherry. It was close beneath his nose, and the arema was very tempting. He yielded to the temptation, tossed off the sherry, handed back the flask and cup, and then, with a smile, unfolded the paper.

The smile vanished like a breath, though, and gave place to an awful look of horror and despair when he read what follows:—

Sir,—Be careful! The gentleman sitting opposite to you is a dangerous madman. We were warned by the officials at the last station whilst you were asleep."

That was all, but it was quite enough. The stout gentleman turned green with terror. He had not the least doubt in the world but that the sherry was poisoned, and felt dreadfully ill immediately.

"My dear sir," said Mr. Styngy, sympathetically, "what is the matter? are you unwell? Try a little sup more of the sherry."

"Ya—a—a—a—h," exclaimed the stout gentleman, making a frantic hit at the flask, and knocking it out of the window.

"Confound you!" said Mr. Styngy, testily, looking "daggers" at the stout gentleman, for the flask had cost him fifteen shillings—exclusive of the value of the sherry, "what do you mean by that?"

"Mur—madman!" gasped the stout gentleman.

"Bless me!" ejaculated Mr. Styngy, as he gave a dismayed glance at Lionel; "the very passengers are mad, too!"

Just then he caught sight of the note which had fallen from the stout gentleman's fingers, and as the thought flashed into his mind that it might throw some light upon the strange behaviour of the stout gentleman, he picked it up and read it.

He turned absolutely purple with indignation as he mastered the libellous contents, and shot a wrathful glance at the passenger who had written it.

"Sir!" he begun in a voice which a poet would have compared to the low muttering of distant thunder, and addressing himself to the offending passenger. "You wrote this, I believe?"

"Now—my—dear—sir," faltered the offending one, who was very pale and very polite, as frightened men usually are, "be calm."

"I will *not* be calm, sir!" thundered Mr. Styngy, upraising himself to his full height, and thereby bumping his head against the top of the carriage. "How dare you, sir—eh?"

The timid passenger, alarmed by Mr. Styngy's ferociousness, which he regarded as the preliminary to a fresh outbreak on the part of the madman—fenced himself in a corner behind a deaf old lady, who was regarding the scene with great admiration, taking it for an exhibition of private theatricals.

"No, sir!" Mr. Styngy went on, with gathering wrath and scorn, "neither subterfuge nor corners shall avail to shelter you from giving an answer to my question. Will you comply, sir? or will you render it necessary for me to inflict personal chastisement on you?"

The timid passenger faltered something indistinctly about "being calm." His companions looked wildly around for places of refuge and safety, and the stout gentleman, reclining on the seat, groaned away melodiously, in the full belief that he was poisoned, and that death was imminent.

"Lionel," said Mr. Styngy, after an awful pause, "you will bear witness that I have demanded an explanation of that—that person?"

"Yes, sir," replied our hero, gravely.

"And that he has refused to give me one?"

Lionel nodded.

"Very good," said Mr. Styngy; "then only one course remains."

And Mr. Styngy, first buttoning his coat tightly up to his chin—and tucking up his cuffs slowly, commenced to climb over the partition between the compartments.

Then ensued a scene of dire confusion—for, with an agility which one would never expect to see, except from professional acrobats, the passengers endeavoured to climb up on to the net-work provided for the reception of hats and such small articles of personal property.

The timid passenger would gladly have followed this example, but for the deaf old lady, who evidently regarded him as the cause of all the disturbance, and now prodded him viciously with the ferule of an umbrella of Kenealy-like proportions.

Mr. Styngy stared in wonder at this sudden scramble, and perhaps felt a little elated, too, that he should be capable of causing agonies of terror to agitate the frames of so many of his fellow-men. He thought it was owing to the awful majesty of his personal appearance. He forgot for the time that they deemed him a dangerous lunatic.

"Gentlemen," he said, addressing the amateur acrobats, who, in their scrambles to reach the netting, resembled nothing so much as a dish of trapped black-beetles struggling for dear life up the sides of their china prison.

"Gentlemen," repeated Mr. Styngy, in a louder tone, "you have no cause to be alarmed, I assure you. I only seek an apology from that indtvidual in the corner."

The individual thus alluded to uttered a faint howl of terror, and shrank into his corner as though he would have amalgamated himself with the horse-hair stuffing of the cushions.

Mr. Styngy's words were peaceable enough, but if they were intended to reassure the other passengers they decidedly missed their mark, for as the schoolmaster's portly form alighted on the other side of the partition, the scrambling and struggling was redoubled.

The inevitable result was that the netting, not having been constructed to bear the weight of four or five full-grown persons, gave way suddenly, and precipitated the "scramblers" on to the very person they had been most anxious to avoid.

Mr. Styngy was a strong man; but the shock was greater than he could bear. His reverend legs gave way, and his clerical nose was flattened by the bald-head of the topmost climber.

The pain, added to the consciousness of outraged dignity, was more than Mr. Styngy could bear. He forgot that he was a clergyman, a bearer of tidings of peace and good-will to men, and viciously punched the bald-head that had flattened his nose.

The owner of the bald-head retaliated, but in the confusion—that was natural under the circumstances—blackened an eye that did not belong to Mr. Styngy.

The proprietor of the injured optic, being unable to use his hands, inasmuch as some one was sitting on his back, launched out his legs, and upset the old lady who was attacking the timid passenger, and who in her turn, clutching at her opponent, brought him with a crash to the floor.

The only non-combatant was Lionel. He who had set in motion the machinery by which so many innocent persons personally damaged one another, without having the least real reason for so doing, escaped scot-free, and enjoyed himself into the bargain.

This, I know, is not practical or any other kind of justice—but it is true, and so I record, with a feeling of shame, that my hero, instead of going to the rescue of his reverend master, and doing his best to deliver him from the hands of his enemies—instead of doing this, I say, he mounted upon a seat, the better to behold the scene of battle, and, leaning against the partition, indulged in a hearty fit of laughter.

"They can't hurt one another much," was Lionel's consolatory reflection; "and Mr. Styngy will be all the better for a little exercise, for he is getting far too stout."

The confined space in which the combatants disported themselves made the struggle of much longer duration than it would otherwise have been.

For no sooner did one struggle to the top, and essay to rise, than a hand belonging to some one underneath would infallibly drag him down again, to undergo a fresh course of pummelling, kicking, and scratching.

The deaf old lady's umbrella did wonderful execution in this way. More than once Mr. Styngy, who was possessed of tolerable strength, had shaken off the grasp of his other assailants and almost succeeded in getting on his feet, when that umbrella would come soaring up, and fix its hook in his collar, or mix itself up with his legs, and fetch him back once more.

I see no reason to doubt but that the fight would have gone on until the combatants had either knocked one another into a state of insensiblity or become too exhausted to struggle any longer, but for one circumstance.

That was—the arrival of the train at its journey's end. Lionel heard the warning whistle of the locomotive, and noticing the decreasing speed, thought it high time to interfere.

"My stars!" he thought, "there'll be a pretty shine when we get to the station. I never thought of that before. Shouldn't wonder if they lock us up."

With this Lionel laid hold of that portion of Mr. Styngy that happened to be uppermost, and hauled away with all his might.

"Mr. Styngy!" he called out, at the top of his voice. "Get up, sir. The train has stopped!"

The train might stop, but Mr. Styngy wouldn't. He had just then succeeded in getting a fair hold of the timid passenger—the one who had called him mad—and was engaged in the amicable endeavour to knock a hole in the bottom of the carriage with his, the timid passenger's, head.

In the meantime the train came to a halt alongside the platform, and the stout gentleman, who had been thinking of all the things he had ever done during his half century of existence, by way of preparation for his approaching end, noticed the stoppage of the train, and, not feeling very dead, arose and lifted up his voice.

"Porter! Guard!" he shouted, in remarkably lusty tones, considering he was a dying man. "Here! Help! Let me out! There's a madman in the carriage murdering everybody!"

This startling piece of intelligence soon brought half-a-dozen officials, and half-a-hundred curious passengers, thronging to the carriage.

In a twinkling the door was unlocked, and as many of the porters as could crowd in seized upon the combatants and hauled them on to the platform.

The other passengers were only too glad to be rescued from their uncomfortable position. Mr. Styngy alone refused to be parted from the timid man. He clung fondly to the hair of his head, and when at length dragged away by main force, brought out a double handful as a token.

"Which is him, sir?" demanded the guard of the stout gentleman, who was lying in a baggage barrow, preparatory to being wheeled away to a doctor.

"That's the man," said the stout gentleman, faintly, pointing to Mr. Styngy, who was smiling complacently at the handful of hair he had secured as a trophy. "How many has he killed?"

"Their ain't none of 'em dead, sir, *yet*," replied the guard, with an emphasis which implied that although none of the injured ones had as yet "shuffled off the mortal coil," they might be expected to do so in a very short space of time.

The excitement in the station was tremendous—the terminus was thronged with passengers, who all crowded to the spot in the endeavour to get a view of the principal actor in the tragedy.

"What is the matter?" demanded one old lady.

"A madman, mum," returned one pale man, who was an authority, inasmuch as he had caught a glimpse of the back of Mr. Styngy's head.

"What has he done?"

"Broke away from his keeper, mum—killed fourteen of 'em—jumped into the express as it was goin' along at full speed—killed the driver and the stoker—cooked one in the biler, mum—and roasted the other in the furnace, mum—and *eat 'em both!*"

"Good lor' ha mercy!" ejaculated the horrified old lady, holding up her hands; and away she went to retail the story with such embellishments as her fancy suggested, while Mr. Styngy and the injured passengers were marched into a waiting-room, there to undergo an inquiry.

CHAPTER XIII.

MR. STYNGY IS CONSIDERABLY STARTLED.

AMONG the passengers on the platform who desired equally with the rest to become acquainted with the cause of the commotion, but who was far too careful to risk his person in the crush, or trust to such information as could be picked up at second-hand, was a stout gentleman in semi-clerical attire, with a pallid and rather flabby countenance, and who answered to the name of Grubbe.

"Dear me!" said that gentleman to himself, as he saw the crowd approaching the waiting-room, and two or three sturdy policemen clearing the way, "I wonder what all this is about?"

To get near enough to inquire was impossible. It was equally so to force a way through the crowd, and so Mr. Grubbe, availing himself of a pile of trunks and boxes, mounted to the top.

Mr Grubbe was not much given to expressing surprise upon any subject—he was too wary a man for that—but when his eyes encountered the spectacle of his friend and ally—ragged, hatless, bearing all the signs of recent strife, and escorted by a strong guard of railway porters and police, he nearly fell from his perch in sheer astonishment.

"Good Heavens!" he exclaimed, and for a moment his bewildered faculties refused to entertain any other sentiment than astonishment. Then his gaze encountered Lionel—and in an instant he had solved the problem.

"It's that boy!" he muttered. "Confound him—I don't know how it has been brought about, or even what it is, but if that young gentleman—or demon—Wilful, is not at the bottom of it all, call me an idiot!"

Mr. Grubbe was a stout man, but he jumped as nimbly from his perch as a lad of fifteen, and, being well acquainted with the railway station, made his way by a private passage into the waiting-room.

It was a fortunate circumstance, indeed, for the supposed lunatic that Mr. Grubbe was there to befriend him—for such a Babel of tongues, such a confusion of statements arose, when the authorities began the necessary inquiries, that would have driven crazy half-a dozen Chief Justices.

Mr. Grubbe, however, soon put matters straight, and in the course of half-an-hour, succeeded, not only in proving that Mr. Styngy was in his right mind, and had never been out of it, but so badgered and bullied the unfortunate passengers, after the approved Ballantyne fashion, that they individually apologised to Mr. Styngy for their mistake and slunk away, glad to escape from the awful threat of an indictment for conspiracy, at which Mr. Grubbe had hinted.

Lionel was, of course, an invaluable witness in all this, and he had in truth become somewhat alarmed at the serious results that at first threatened to be the consequence of his little joke. He was glad enough to bear witness to Mr. Styngy's sanity and testify that there had been a mistake somewhere.

By the time the inquiry was concluded, and all so comfortably terminated for Mr. Styngy, the last train for Codsham had departed, and the party had no other choice but to take up quarters at an hotel for the night, unless indeed, they, as Lionel proposed, returned to Hampstead.

Mr. Grubbe put a decided veto upon my hero's proposal, although Lionel was so thankful to him for his rescue of them that he would, in his excess of gratitude, have promised him a welcome at Heath End Villa.

The terminus hotel was very full that night, and

Mr. Grubbe and Mr. Styngy had to occupy a double-bedded room.

The reverend schoolmaster was very silent and thoughtful during the evening; but, when he and Mr. Grubbe were alone, he said, pensively—

"It's a most extraordinary thing, Grubbe. I have been thinking over it until my brain positively whirls, but I cannot remember anything in my conduct which led those people to treat me as a madman."

"Very likely not," returned Mr. Grubbe, "and for the simple reason that there wasn't anything particularly lunatic in your behaviour."

"Then why did they do it?"

"Do you mean to say that you don't know?" said Mr. Grubbe.

"I cannot even guess."

"It was that boy. *He* is the cause," said Mr. Grubbe.

"Impossible!" returned Mr. Styngy, "he was not out of my sight a minute."

"If Lionel Wilful was not the prime mover of the whole mischief," said Mr. Grubbe, emphatically, "I'll forfeit every penny I have in the world."

"I know that you have a clear head and a sound judgment, Grubbe," said Mr. Styngy, as he thoughtfully applied a piece of sticking plaister to the bridge of his nose, "but you must be mistaken this time."

"And I am confident that I am not," returned Mr. Grubbe, as he tucked himself snugly in between the sheets; "but we will talk of this to-morrow. Only wait till we get him safely to Cheetham Hall. His tricks will be cut pretty short there, and with a sharp knife, too."

It was a custom of Mr. Styngy's always to lock his bed-room door; and, sore and tired as he was with the events of the day, the force of habit would not allow him to forget his usual precaution.

"Why," he said as he found that the key was not in the door, "this is strange, Grubbe. Have you taken it out?"

"Taken what out?"

"The key. I feel certain I saw it in the door when we first came up."

"Perhaps it's on the other side."

Mr. Styngy opened the door and looked, but no key was there.

"It's very curious of the hotel people," grunted Mr. Styngy. "I've a good mind to ring them up. I never can sleep comfortably unless the door is locked."

"Oh, its not worth making a disturbance about," said Mr. Grubbe, who wanted to go to sleep. "Put a chair against the door, that will do as well."

This Mr. Styngy did, though with many inward misgivings—for he entertained a mortal dread of burglars."

"I'll make the hotel people allow for it in the bill," he said testily. "They will charge me for a bed-room, and a bed-room is not complete without a key in the door."

With which characteristic resolve Mr. Styngy got carefully into bed, and, shutting his eyes, endeavoured to court the favour of the "drowsy god."

There are few sensations more pleasant than that of sinking into the sweet oblivion of repose, in a comfortably-appointed bed, when both body and mind are thoroughly tired.

Mr. Styngy was thoroughly tired, his bed was a very comfortable one, furnished with a spring-mattress, downy pillows, and shaded by curtains of a most drowsy appearance. But "Nature's sweet nurse" declined to wait upon him, for the fact was, the reverend schoolmaster was so sore from the bruises he had received, that he was in a most aggravating condition of wakefulness.

It was quite otherwise with Mr. Grubbe, in less than ten minutes from the time he laid his head upon the pillow his nose sent forth strange noises, proclaiming that he was in the full enjoyment of literally "sound" repose.

Mr. Styngy tried all sorts of positions—first lying on his left side, then on his right, then on his back, but each was equally unavailing. Then he bethought himself of an excellent soporific, in the shape of a volume of sermons, written by a learned friend of his, and which he usually carried with him when travelling, for the sake of looking professional.

"If they don't send me to sleep, nothing will," thought Mr. Styngy, as he got gingerly out of bed and extracted the book from his hand-bag. "Confound that Grubbe, how he does snore."

Then the schoolmaster, turning up the lamp that stood by the bed-side, picked out the dullest and driest of the sermons, and began to read it.

He read through one, and this produced no effect; he tried another, and felt as lively as ever; then he tackled a third, so remarkably diffuse and incomprehensible that he actually began to feel a little drowsy, when, happening to glance towards the door, he beheld something which made him drop the volume, and caused his hair to slowly elevate itself with terror.

CHAPTER XIV.

FIRE!

THERE, curling through the keyhole was a dense volume of smoke, wreathing itself into fantastic shapes, as it mounted slowly towards the ceiling.

Mr. Styngy glanced at it as if doubting the reality of what he saw, but if for a moment he thought his vision had deceived him, his sense of smell came to his aid, for already his nostrils were assailed by the pungent smell of some burning substance.

He opened his mouth, and tried to call out "Fire," but he could only articulate in a hoarse whisper. Meanwhile the smoke increased in density and volume, and at length in an agony of terror he grasped the pillow and hurled it at the sleeping Mr. Grubbe.

That gentleman received the missile full in the face, one end of the pillow filling up his widely-opened mouth stopping his snoring, and awakening him at once.

"Heigh-ho-hum," yawned Mr. Grubbe, sitting slowly up.

"What's the matter! It can't be time to get up yet."

"The matter," gasped Mr. Styngy, who was frantically endeavouring to insert his legs into his coat-sleeves in the full belief that they were his trousers. "Fire's the matter! Murder's the matter! Get up if you don't want to be roasted alive!"

Just then, Mr. Grubbe, who was a heavy sleeper, became conscious of the fact that the room was half-full of smoke.

"Why, I do believe," declared the oily gentleman, as he snuffed suspiciously, "that you have been smoking in bed."

"Smoking in bed! you—you idiot!" gasped Mr. Styngy, while he tugged away desperately at his coat-sleeves. "You'll soon smoke in your bed, if you don't do something. Cannot you see that the house is on fire!"

Mr. Grubbe was a slow and heavy man, in a general way, but he no sooner comprehended the dreadful import of his employer's words than he jumped out of bed with the agility of a harlequin, alighting on Mr. Styngy's back and rolling that gentleman over and over into the middle of the room.

"Murder!" yelled the schoolmaster, who in all conscience was sore enough already, but whose agony was increased tenfold by the fall.

"Fire!" roared Mr. Grubbe, rushing to the door, through the keyhole of which the smoke was still pouring merrily in.

He grasped the handle, turned it, and pulled at it with all his force, but the door was obstinate and yielded not an inch.

"Where's the key?" he called out in terror-stricken accents. "Styngy what have you done with the key!"

"There isn't any key!" replied the schoolmaster, as with a last desperate effort he tore out the sleeve of his coat, and ruined it for ever. "Didn't I tell you last night there wasn't one in the door."

"Then who's locked it?" roared Mr. Grubbe, as with a terrific tug the handle came bodily off, and staggering back he, for the second time, upset Mr. Styngy.

This was more than mortal could bear. From Mr. Styngy's reverend lips there came the sound of a very naughty word, and, clenching his fists he actually punched Mr. Grubbe's head with considerable violence.

If they had not been so engrossed by the fancied peril of the situation the schoolmaster and his ally might have noticed that every now and then the smoke ceased to pour through the key-hole for a few seconds at a time, and that in those intervals strange sounds of chuckling and suppressed laughter came from the outer side of the door.

It was my hero, of course, who, with a huge brown paper cigar, was treating the pastor and master, whom he should have reverenced and respected, in this shameless manner. I blush to write the record of his evil doings—but is not this a faithful history, and must not the truth be spoken?

Meanwhile the two gentlemen were in close quarters on the floor, and Lionel, with his eyes at the key-hole this time, enjoyed the spectacle with silent but heartfelt manifestations of delight.

"It's beautiful," chuckled our hero. "How they are 'a-going of it,' as Sam would say. Ha, ha, there goes old Styngy's night shirt torn half-way down his back, and now he's giving Grubbe a beautiful topper on the nose. My stars, I wouldn't have missed this treat for a quarter's pocket money. I'll give 'em a little more smoke, and keep the game lively."

Lionel did give them a little more smoke—indeed, it would be more truthful to say that he gave them a great deal, enough to rouse them to the sense of their danger, and cease their combat.

"This is awful!" yelled Mr. Styngy, as he scrambled to his feet. "We shall be smothered before help comes. I can hardly draw my breath now. For Heaven's sake, Grubbe, alarm the house."

"You go to the window," said Mr. Grubbe, who was scarcely less alarmed than his friend, "and call for the police. I'll call fire at the door!"

Mr. Grubbe rushed once more to the door, and stooping, placed his mouth to the key-hole, but even as he opened it to give vent to a shout of tremendous volume, Lionel, who was quite ready for him, sent a huge puff of smoke into the unlucky Mr. Grubbe's throat.

Coughing, spluttering, gurgling, and even swearing, Mr. Grubbe started up and reeled round and round, with much of the activity and grace a tipsy man might be expected to exhibit when waltzing.

"Ugh! Oh—oh—oh! Gur—gur—get me some water! I'm cho—cho—choking!"

But Mr. Styngy, if the appeal was meant for him, was otherwise occupied. The window was wide open, and with the upper half of his manly form thrust through, was yelling "Fire!" at the topmost pitch of his musical voice.

"This is too hot to last," thought Lionel. "The people in the house will be alarmed directly, and it won't do for me to be caught here. I'll just give 'em one more dose of brown paper and cut."

My hero sent one more broadside of smoke into the room, and then quickly unlocking the door and leaving the key in, stole away just as the sounds of hasty footsteps, and loud and anxious voices were heard below.

Lionel peered cautiously over the balustrade, and saw quite a little procession coming upstairs. In front the proprietor of the hotel, looking scared and anxious, and then two policemen, and then some half-dozen servants, all in a state of the most evident terror.

"Here's a game!" thought Lionel. "My word, there'll be a row when they find out there's no fire after all! And, by George, there are the engines!"

There was a clatter of galloping horses in the street below, a cheer from the crowd that had already assembled, and the splashing of the water as it spurted from the plug-hole.

"Here!—this is the room!" said the excited proprietor, guided by the sound of Mr. Styngy's sweet voice, which was still vociferating "Fire!" with twenty costermonger power."

"Be careful how you hopen the door, sir," said one of the policemen. "Better let me do it, or the draught will work the flames up."

Cautiously he turned the handle and looked round the corner of the door into the room, expecting fully to find it a mass of flame, but there was no more evidence of a conflagration than a strong smell of burnt paper, and two elderly gentlemen in night shirts, bawling "Fire" out of the window.

"Where's the fire?" asked the proprietor, excitedly. "Is it out, policeman?"

"Is it out?" repeated the official, contemptuously, as he turned to his mate. "Here's a nice little go, Jem. Them two hold gents calls this a good joke, I s'pose?"

"Joke!" ejaculated the proprietor, whose alarm had now given place to anger. "I'll joke 'em. Here, I say, you sirs, stop that noise, and just tell me what you mean by it!"

Both Mr. Styngy and Mr. Grubbe, being half way out of the window, were unconscious of the arrival of the proprietor, and just as that gentleman was about to make them aware of his presence by the summary process of dragging them back into the room, a fire-escape was wheeled up, and the conductor, gifted with more zeal than ability, planted the machine against the window with such excellent aim as to burst it in, and dash Mr. Styngy, Mr. Grubbe, and the proprietor of the hotel in a heap to the ground.

For the next quarter-of-an-hour there was a scene of confusion—suffice it to say that when from out of the confused mass of arms, legs, and heads, each one had picked his own, and satisfied himself that these members were still attached to his body, mutual explanations began to be given and received.

"It's very mysterious; I can't make anything of it," said Mr. Styngy. "It certainly seems that it was a false alarm, but then where did all that smoke come from."

Mr. Grubbe said nothing, but borrowing one of the policemen's bull's-eye lanterns, went into the corridor.

"It must ha' been the chimney," said one of the constables.

"No, no," said the schoolmaster. "I saw the smoke, and so did my friend, pouring in dense volumes through the crevices of the door."

"It's a dashed mystery," grunted the proprietor, only he used a stronger word than "dashed;" "and if I thought anyone had been having a dashed lark with me, I'd make him blank well pay for it."

"Hush, my friend," said Mr. Styngy, whose clerical ears were shocked by such language.

"Oh, it's all very fine," grunted the proprietor. "Who's going to pay for the window that blank fireman broke in, to say nothing of a bruise on my forehead as big as an egg, and an amount of skin off my shins that a quarter of a yard of sticking-plaister won't cover."

Just then Mr. Grubbe entered with a peculiar smile on his face; but he said nothing until order was quite restored, the dispute so far settled, and himself and Mr. Styngy alone in a fresh chamber.

Then he drew from his pocket what appeared to be the stump of a very large cigar, and held it out for Mr. Styngy's inspection.

"What's that?"

"*This*," replied Mr. Grubbe, emphatically, "is the cause of all this night's disturbance; this is what has roused you and I and half the people in the hotel from their slumbers; this is the cause of our presenting the ridiculous appearance we did by appearing before all these people in our night-shirts —this is the real cause, Mr. Styngy."

"Why it looks like brown paper."

"And so it is. Brown paper when smouldering emits a large quantity of smoke, as you know. I found this just now inside the door of Lionel's bed-room, and on looking on the mat just below the key-hole, I found a quantity of ashes. Oh, there is no doubt of it, we have to thank that ingenious young rascal for all we have endured this night!"

"It seems incredible," gasped Mr. Styngy, "that he could have had the audacity!"

"He has audacity enough for anything!" said Mr. Grubbe, whose aspect was the reverse of bland and saint-like at that moment, "but only wait until I get him to Cheetham Hall, I'll break and tame his proud spirit, or I'll break—"

"What?" said Mr. Styngy.

"His neck!" retorted Mr. Grubbe, and so he gradually growled himself to sleep.

CHAPTER XV.

IN WHICH LIONEL MAKES ACQUAINTANCE WITH CHEETHAM HALL AND SOME OF ITS INMATES.

IN accordance with their preconcerted arrangement, nothing was said to Lionel connecting him with the events of the previous night. His turn was to come, as Mr. Grubbe said, when my hero was safe within the precincts of Cheetham Hall, in sight of which they safely arrived the next morning, being driven from Nobsham station in a ramshackle vehicle, curiously misnamed a fly, which the tamest of blue-bottles could have given a start of half-a-mile and have beaten easily.

With a very natural feeling of curiosity, and with a quickened pulse, Lionel leaned out of the fly as it came in sight of Cheetham Hall, anxious to see the place that was to be a substitute for home for so many months.

He could only just catch a glimpse of the upper storeys of the Hall itself, above the trees that grew within the high boundary wall; but he saw enough to show him that it was a large place, big enough for his own home at Hampstead to have been lost within the rambling precincts.

"A big place," thought Lionel. "There will have to be a good many of us to fill it—fifty or sixty I think Styngy said—it looks as if it would hold five or six hundred."

Poets have said—or if they have not I beg their collective pardon—that there is "No sweeter sound in nature than the voice of youth at play," and just as the fly halted at the gates of Cheetham Hall the voices of several youths were uplifted in play—or something else.

Mr. Styngy was not a poet, he could not have been; neither could Mr. Grubbe have belonged to that divine order, for they severally exclaimed—

"Heavens! What a hideous uproar!"

"A second Babel, I verily declare!"

It did not last long though. The gates opened into the playground, whence the sounds proceeded. As the forms of Mr. Styngy and Mr. Grubbe became visible to the youths at play, a silence as of death came upon them.

Mr. Styngy turned to Lionel with a smile of complacent condescension.

"There you see, Wilful, the effect of discipline."

"Indeed, sir," said Lionel, "I thought it was the effect of fear."

"Hem—a-hem!" coughed Mr. Styngy, who could not just at the moment find a fit answer to Lionel's comment.

"Whether it be fear or discipline," here broke in Mr. Grubbe, with a harsh manner, that startled Lionel, who had hitherto only been acquainted with one side of his disposition, "*You* will be ruled by it."

Lionel had an angry reply ready for Mr. Grubbe, for whom he felt all his old aversion, but a movement upon the part of the boys attracted his attention and directed his mind from the oily gentleman.

The pupils, as soon as they perceived the stately form of Mr. Styngy, not only ceased their sports, but hastened to range themselves in a double row, reaching across the playground from the lodge gates to the hall door, each boy, as Mr. Styngy passed him, saluting him by raising his cap.

The schoolmaster strode on with a slow and stately step, with the air of an absolute monarch receiving the homage of the humblest of his subjects, and, my hero following, looked about him with a wondering gaze.

"Well," he thought, "this is a queer sort of performance. I wonder if they kneel down and say their prayers to him. I know what I shall do if this sort of thing is expected of me. But what in the world has old Grubbe to do with it. To look at him any one would think that he was master of the school."

While Lionel yet pondered over the solution of the puzzle, the door of Cheetham Hall was reached, and standing on the steps were two gentlemen in seedy black, whom my hero at once set down, and rightly, as the assistant masters.

One was a short and very stout man, contrasting oddly enough with his companion, who was so tall and lean that scarcely any preparation would have been needed to fit him for a place in an anatomical museum.

They both agreed, however, in one thing, and that was their extreme deference, not to say servility to Mr. Styngy. Judging by their reception of him, one would have thought the head-master to be their "guide, philosopher, and friend," the benefactor of their early days, and the companion of their prime; but they did it all for twenty pounds a-year and their washing, and taught the boys beside—and very cheap it was, too, for the money.

"Mr. de Bewty and Mr. Crocklejack," said the schoolmaster, addressing the assistant masters, "this is a new young gentleman, Lionel Wilful."

Messrs. Bewty and Crocklejack, inferring at once, from Mr. Styngy being his escort, that Lionel was a pupil destined to be specially favoured, smiled upon him with a reverential tenderness, and intimated generally, in a couple of neat little speeches, that the majestic wisdom of Minerva sat enthroned upon his youthful brow.

"Bah!" said Lionel, inwardly. "The boys seem a set of sneaks, and the masters a couple of toadies. I shan't get along very well here, I'm sure."

As, in accordance with Mrs. Wilful's special request, Lionel was to occupy a separate bed-room, he was forthwith conducted to it by the stout master, Mr. Crocklejack; while the lean one, Mr. de Bewty. went with Mr. Styngy and Mr. Grubbe, to receive a lecture for allowing the young gentlemen of Cheetham Hall to indulge in low and vulgar play, and to report progress generally.

"Mr. de Bewty," began the reverend schoolmaster, in a grave tone, "I am sorry that at the very moment of my return I should witness such an exhibition of disorder."

The lean master thought that this was an allusion to his personal apparel, and nervously felt the cloudy white tie that encircled his neck.

"I—I assure you, sir," he replied, "that I brushed—"

"Brushed!" retorted Mr. Styngy, sternly; "what are you talking about, sir. What has brushing to do with the disgraceful riot in the playground?"

"I beg your pardon, sir; I thought you were alluding to—"

"It seems to me," interrupted Mr. Styngy,

warmly, "that you never *are* thinking of that which should occupy your thoughts. The interests of the school are in jeopardy whenever I leave it for a single day."

Mr. de Bewty sniffed apologetically, but answered not. He didn't dare.

"You see this gentleman," Mr. Styngy went on, indicating Mr. Grubbe with a wave of the hand.

Mr. de Bewty bowed in Mr. Grubbe's direction, as though to say he did see him and thought him a very nice gentleman indeed.

"This is Mr. Grubbe," continued the reverend schoolmaster, "a gentleman whom I *can* trust. He will in future act as my deputy, my *alter ego*, in fact, and you will have the goodness, Mr. de Bewty, to give up your desk to him."

The lean master bowed again, with a sorrowful presentiment of what was to follow.

"And, Mr. de Bewty," said the reverend gentleman, "as this addition to my establishment is, in a measure, necessitated by your neglect—yours and Mr. Crocklejack's—that is—"

Here Mr. de Bewty groaned slightly. He couldn't help it. He knew so well what Mr. Styngy was aiming at.

"What is the matter with you, Mr. de Bewty?" demanded the schoolmaster sharply. "Are you not well?"

"Quite well, sir, thank you," replied the lean usher dismally. "It is only a slight cough, sir."

"Well, as I was about to say," resumed Mr. Styngy, "your duties will be rendered lighter by the attendance of Mr. Grubbe, and, therefore, you will not, of course, object to a corresponding reduction of your salary. If you do—"

"No, no, sir!" the lean usher hastened to say, "It is only just, sir. I have no objection whatever to make."

"Very well," said Mr. Styngy, a little more graciously, "that will do for the present, Mr. de Bewty."

And away went the lean master, sighing dismally over the blighted prospect of a new suit of clothes and a week at the sea-side—both of which luxuries he had revelled in by anticipation, but which were now placed far beyond his reach by reason of the reduction in his salary.

"Why, what's the matter with you, Bewty?" said Mr. Crocklejack, who encountered the lean master at that moment.

"Matter enough," returned Mr. de Bewty, dejectedly. "I've just had notice that my salary is to be reduced—as if it wasn't small enough already."

"That is bad," said Crocklejack, in a voice of sympathy. "I wouldn't stand it if I were you, Bewty. Give him notice. A fellow with the degrees you have taken can easily get a better position."

Mr. Crocklejack's advice was not altogether unselfish. He had it in his mind that if his colleague grew desperate and resigned his situation, he (Mr. Crocklejack) might do double duty and receive a double "screw."

"It's all very well," said Mr. de Bewty; "but if I resign you'll resign too—your salary is to be reduced as well as mine."

"The devil!" said Mr. Crocklejack, and he sat down flat in the passage.

The two ushers condoled with one another, and mutually vowed that they wouldn't stand it. But they did. Ushers were plentiful, and situations were scarce, so they accepted the reduced salaries, and let off their superfluous ire upon two small boys who happened unluckily for themselves to be in the way just then.

Forms and ceremonies were in great demand at Cheetham Hall. Mr. Styngy had a very great respect for them, as they produced a deep impression upon parents and guardians, and, what was more important, cost nothing.

One of these was a formal introduction of a new pupil to the head boys of the four divisions of the school, and no new comer was allowed to mix with his future companions until this ceremony had taken place.

In due time Lionel was conducted to the library by Mr. Crocklejack, and left there while the stout usher went in search of the four head boys, intimating to my hero, by way of caution, that everything in the library was sacred, and not to be profaned by the rude hands of boys, under fear of pains and penalties a little less than death.

In a little while Mr. Crocklejack returned, accompanied by the four head boys of the forms.

Lionel's keen eyes regarded them curiously, as one by one, in order of seniority, and with much solemnity, Mr. Crocklejack introduced them.

"Frederick Flashaway," he began, "head of the fourth form—this is Lionel Wilful, a new pupil."

Flashaway nodded in a supercilious manner, as Lionel extended his hand; but this was apparently not in accordance with the rules, for the senior boy took no notice of it.

"Ah!" thought Lionel. "Very well. Master Flashaway, you're a good three years older, and nearly a head taller, besides being as strong as a bull, to judge from your build, but you've not much in you after all; your eyes are shifty, and can't look one straight in the face."

The next in order was Charles Drummond, a lad of sixteen, with delicate aristocratic features, light curly hair, and clear violet blue eyes.

They looked at one another for an instant; and then, with a simultaneous motion, shook hands heartily. That single look was sufficient; they were friends at once.

The third was a dull, heavy lad, about Lionel's age, with a downcast look, and slow in speech and manner. My hero passed him over without comment; he did not know what to make of Jabez Hunker.

The fourth was a short, sturdily-built boy of thirteen, with a broad, almost Chinese cast of feature, upon which perpetually sat a melancholy-jollity of expresssion, if such an apparent contradiction of terror can be allowed.

Lionel smiled as he shook hands with him; he could not help it, despite the solemnity with which everybody seemed to regard the ceremony of introduction; he felt for Tom Codlings, for that was his name, a pitying sympathy, in which there was something irresistibly comical.

"Mr. Wilful," said M. Crocklejack, "you are at liberty for the rest of the day. To-morrow Mr. Styngy will examine you himself, and appoint you to your form."

The stout master then walked away with as much gravity of aspect as the unclassical rotundity of his figure permitted, and the five boys were left together in the corridor.

Fred Flashaway, with his hands thrust deep into his trousers-pockets, looked superciliously at Lionel for a minute, and opened his mouth, as if he were going to speak; but, changing his mind, began to whistle, and swaggered carelessly away down the corridor.

Lionel flushed scarlet at this contemptuous treatment, and he was upon the point of following Flashaway and demanding an explanation, when a moment's reflection convinced him it would be wiser to wait. It was easy to see that the senior would soon give him a fresh opportunity for a quarrel.

And in this conjecture Lionel was right. The system of "fagging" was in full operation at Cheetham Hall, and Flashaway was then on his way to get Lionel consigned to him for his especial "fag."

CHAPTER XVI.

TOMMY CODLINGS RECOUNTS HIS WRONGS.

OF the four boys with whom Lionel had up to this time made acquaintance only two had favourably impressed him, and they were Charlie Drummond and Tommy Codlings.

For Flashaway my hero felt already as strong an aversion as if he had known him for as many years as minutes had actually elapsed since he saw him.

"He is a bully," said Lionel, "and he's got to have it taken out of him; and I'll do it, too, the first chance I get."

As I think I said before, he did not know what to make of Jabez Hunker. That young gentleman slouched heavily along the passage in the wake of Flashaway, and my hero resolved to set him aside for future consideration, with a grave suspicion in his mind that Jabez would not come very favourably out of the ordeal.

"I think," said Lionel, looking full into Charlie Drummond's clear, blue eyes, "that you and I are likely to be friends."

"I'm sure of it, for my part," Drummond responded heartily. "And Hot Codlings here, you'll like him too."

"Hot Codlings!" laughed my hero. "Why that's the name of a clown's song—isn't it?"

"Yes; and we gave it to Tommy partly because he can't sing that song or any other, but principally because of his name."

"Principally because of my luck," said Tommy Codlings, dolefully. "I'm just like that chap in the pantomime, who's always getting knocked about and upset, when he hasn't done anything. I'm a true pantaloon—I am."

"Cheer up, old chap," said Drummond, clapping him on the back.

"Oh, it's all very fine to say 'cheer up,'" Tommy Codlings went on in the same doleful tone, "*you're* not always being bullied, or caned, or dosed with impositions because somebody else laughed or did something or other."

"Are you then?" said Lionel.

"Only yesterday," replied Tommy Codlings, plaintively, "I was whacked three times on Flashaway's account. At morning prayers *he* laughed, Styngy looked at *me*—daggers were nothing to it—and, when prayers were over, he took out his cane and called me up."

"If you please, sir, what have I done?" said I.

"'Ask your conscience, Codlings,' says he, sternly, and then he laid into me hot and strong."

"That was a shame," said Lionel, sympathetically.

"Then in the class-room," Codlings went on, with a growing sense of injury, "Flashaway shied a book at one of the young 'uns. 'Who did that?' says Styngy, directly. 'Come here, Codlings, I know it was you.' Though I was ever so far away. And of course I had to go; and of course I got it hotter and stronger than ever, being the second time."

"What!" said Lionel, indignantly, "hadn't Flashaway honour enough to come forward and say that he threw the book?"

"Honour!" said Charlie Drummond. "He has no more of that article than an Old Bailey barrister, who'll do all but swear that his client's innocent when he knows quite well that he's guilty."

"Well," pursued Tommy Codlings, the doleful look upon his face intensifying as he recounted his wrongs; "in the afternoon Flashaway chalked up a countenance of old Styngy on the big black board, and threatened to smash anyone who rubbed it out. So, when old Styngy came into the class-room, the first thing he saw was the drawing, but he never said a word till he got to his desk. Then he stood and looked all round till he came to me. I turned red, I know. I couldn't help it. But he thought it was me again.

"'Codlings, come here,' he said.

"I went up, of course, I was obliged to; and I could feel myself turning hot and cold by turns.

"'I see, Codlings,' says he, 'that you are developing into an artist; but,' he says, 'the proper place for the exercise of your talent is not this school, Codlings, but *Punch*. Do you hear—*Punch!*'

"And then he gave me one on the side of the head. Such a staggerer.

"I couldn't say anything, of course. If I had denied it he wouldn't have believed me, and, of course, I couldn't play the sneak and say who had really done it."

"I don't think I should have been so particular," Lionel put in indignantly; "Flashaway's a cowardly bully, and deserves no consideration."

"Hush!" said Drummond and Codlings together, for they had now entered the playground, and were within hearing of some of the boys. "Hush! or some of the fellows will hear you, and there are plenty ready to carry a tale to Flashaway to get in favour with him."

"Let 'em," retorted Lionel, in a still louder tone. "Let 'em carry as many tales as they like, but it won't alter the fact that the fellow who lets another suffer for his fault is a coward and a sneak."

"Hush, for goodness sake," said Tommy Codlings, whose doleful look had given place to one of alarm and wonder at Lionel's bold defiance of the bully of Cheetham Hall. "Sombody will be sure to hear and tell him, and if he gets you for his 'fag'—he always gets the new boys—you'll suffer for this; he'll torture your life out."

"Fag," repeated Lionel. "If he gets me for his 'fag?' What's that?"

"Why, you'll have to run on errands for him," explained Charlie Drnmmond, "get him hot water in the morning—he's beginning to shave, though he's got no more moustache than an egg—and wait on him generally whenever he wants you."

"The dickens I shall!" exclaimed Lionel, in a tone half wondering, half angry. "Is it one of the rules of this precious school to make the new boys servants to the old ones?"

Charlie Drummond, and Codlings uttered an emphatic confirmation.

"Have you been 'fags'?'

Drummond assented again. Tommy Codlings groaned, and showed the whites of his eyes in a very expressive manner. It was evident to Lionel that he was a very much "fagged" boy.

"It doesn't seem the thing quite—does it?" said Charlie Drummond, in an apologetic tone. "*I* didn't think so at first; but it's the rule, and there's an end of it."

"It's done at lots of places," said Tommy Codlings; "tip-top schools, too. I had a cousin at Rugby, and he had his leg broke fagging—made him get out of a high window at night to smuggle some prog in, and he slipped and fell, and he's a cripple now."

"If it's the rule, and you fellows do it," said Lionel, reluctantly yielding, for he had a great respect for rule and order, "of course I can't object. I wouldn't mind fagging for you, for instance, or Codlings here."

The unfortunate Tommy looked at my hero in unutterable wonder. The bare idea of anybody being *his* fag was so utterly preposterous.

Charlie Drummond shook his head.

"That's against the rule, too. It's only the big fellows in the upper form who are allowed to have fags. Flashaway or one of his set will get you."

"Will he! not so; don't think it," replied Lionel resolutely. "I'd sooner leave the school to-night than be his fag."

"By jingo!" exclaimed Drummond at this moment; "you'll have to make your mind up pretty quickly, for there he is."

Just then the tall powerful form of Flashaway elbowed its way despotically through a knot of the younger boys, scorning to go a yard out of its direct course.

FOLLOW MY LEADER.

MR. STYNGY AND THE USHERS, ATTENDED BY THE PUPILS, WELCOME HIS IMPERIAL HIGHNESS, THE JAPANESE PRINCE.

No. 4.

He looked about him for a moment or two, as if in search of some one; and, then, perceiving Lionel and his two new friends, called to him.

"Hallo, there! you new fellow."

"Don't you hear him?" whispered Tommy Codlings, who was already pale; "he's calling you."

"He knows my name," retorted Lionel coolly; "if he calls me by it, well and good; if he doesn't choose to, I'll pay no attention."

Flashaway hailed the new fellow in a louder tone, and in the same terms as at first; but Lionel took no notice, and coolly strolled on.

The bully, puzzled at what was quite a novelty to him, hesitated for a moment, and then strode forward, and placed himself directly in front of my hero.

"Hallo, you new fellow!" he said, wrathfully; "didn't you hear me call you?"

Lionel stopped and looked at him with an expression of such calm innocence that Flashaway became more enraged still.

"No," replied my hero; "I didn't hear anyone call me."

"That's a lie!" said Flashaway, angrily. "And if you lie to me I'll wring your ear off!"

"I never tell lies or bully boys younger than myself," retorted Lionel, with the same refreshing coolness. "That seems to be more in your way."

Flashaway gazed in mute astonishment at the boy who thus dared to openly affront him. Quite a crowd of other boys had gathered round, too, by this time, and they looked on with awe and bated breath.

"I see what it is," said Flashaway, after a pause of a few minutes, during which Lionel sturdily regarded him; "you're cheeky, and the cheek will have to be taken out of you. Do you know what fagging is."

Lionel professed to be ignorant, in order to hear what Flashaway might have to say upon the subject.

"Well," the bully went on, "I'll tell you. Out of school hours, whenever I want my fag—day or night—he belongs to me, to do what I tell him, to go where I want him, and when I want him. Do you hear that?"

"Oh, yes; I hear that," said Lionel, pleasantly.

"It's lucky for you that you do, for you're *my* fag, and you'll find me a tough customer if you don't obey sharply and to the letter."

"Shall I, indeed?" said Lionel, in the same pleasant voice.

"I'll look over your cheek just now, because you're a new fellow."

"That's very kind of you, indeed," said Lionel, with affected gratitude.

"But," Flashaway went on, quite taken in by my hero's affected humility, "if it happens again look out for squalls."

"I will, indeed," said Lionel, in the same tone of affected innocence; "I can't bear windy weather."

"Now," Flashaway resumed, "come up to my room, and I'll set you to work. I want my books dusted and put in order."

Never doubting but that Lionel would follow, Flashaway turned, and walked towards the house. He had nearly reached the hall door before he discovered that Lionel, instead of following at his heels, was sauntering calmly in the opposite direction, with his hands in his pockets, and his lips whistling a lively tune.

Flashaway halted, and stared after Lionel's receding figure with a gaze of blank astonishment. Then, at a rapid pace—almost a run—he returned, and, as he came up behind Lionel, aimed a heavy blow at his head.

The blow took effect, but not where intended—Lionel had timed his movements nicely, and sprung forward just as Flashaway's hand descended—it smote the unlucky Tommy Codlings on the ear, and laid him prone in the dust of the playground.

"—— you," said Flashaway, white with anger. "I'll knock your young head off for that."

"What," said Lionel, scornfully, "you are a blackguard as well as a bully, eh, and add swearing to your other accomplishments?"

Flashaway had his hand raised to strike again, but he kept it suspended, principally in consequence of a dawning fear of the boy who looked at him so defiantly and treated him so contemptuously. He allowed the hand to fall harmlessly to his side, and tried remonstrance.

"Look here, young Wilful," he said, "you'd better give in, and do as you're told. You'll have to, you know; and, the sooner you do it, the better. Don't make me force you."

"I don't know any thing of the sort," retorted Lionel; and, as to forcing me to do anything against my will, that is what neither you nor any one else can do."

In his eager defiance of Flashaway's authority Lionel took a step forward and raised his hand to emphasize his words. As he did so the bully involuntarily raised his arm, as if to ward off a blow.

That motion was enough—it showed Lionel that he had a coward as well as a bully to deal with.

The same sentiment seemed to be getting ground amongst the boys who were looking on. A murmur of applause broke out amongst them, and one or two said audibly—Tommy Codlings, holding his hand to his injured ear, as if it would drop off, was very audible indeed—

"Well done, Wilful!"

The unfortunate Tommy's reward—he being at a convenient distance—was a blow on his left ear, which compelled him to close that with his disengaged hand, and so shut himself out from the hearing of the further proceedings.

Flashaway was white hot with wrath, but he was cowed. He was big enough to have crushed his opponent by sheer weight, but in that respect he was like some dull, heavy piece of ordnance—fully charged, but impotent without the tiny spark of fire. What Flashaway wanted was a spark of courage, and he hadn't got it.

Lionel had won, for the time, and turning, with a last contemptuous look at his adversary, walked calmly away.

Flashaway hesitated for a moment, and then followed his example, his little soul, full of hatred, malice, and all uncharitableness, as your bully always is when he finds himself defeated.

He had scarcely gone twenty yards when a shout of ringing, derisive laughter, made his blood tingle with shame and anger, and he paused as he muttered an oath.

"I'll have it out of the young whelp for this. It will be all over the school by to-night that I have been braved by him. Lucky for him that he was so young or I'd have thrashed him within an inch of his life."

And so deceiving even himself as to the real cause of his defeat, Mr. Fred Flashaway skulked into the hall for his hat, and skulked out again in search of some of the upper form boys—his special associates, who were of his way of thinking, and with whom he designed to concoct a plan for the deception and disgrace of Lionel Wilful.

What he did and how it was done I must defer for a chapter or so, for the current of my story bears now upon its bosom a remarkable and important personage.

CHAPTER XVII.

LIONEL AND MR. STYNGY RECEIVE SOME STARTLING INTELLIGENCE.

THAT evening Lionel underwent an examination for the purpose of ascertaining in what class his mental attainments entitled him to be placed.

The duty fell to Mr. Crocklejack, and that gentleman being in an exasperated condition of mind, consequent upon the reduction of his salary, found Lionel very bad, and decided that he was only fit for the lowest form, of which Tommy Codlings was the head.

It was undeniable that Lionel felt some degree of shame at thus being in a way degraded, but he consoled himself with the consciousness that it was not deserved, and that he would soon elevate himself in the school by the exertion of a little industry.

It was at this time, too, that the mystery of Mr. Grubbe's power at Cheetham Hall, was solved—that is, solved as far as his actual presence was concerned. As to the wherefore of his reduction from the station of a semi-clerical gentleman of independent means to that of a tutor, with no means at all, it was still a mystery to Lionel.

But a greater wonder than all this soon started my hero's mind from Mr. Grubbe. He had scarcely settled down to the work he had to do, when one morning the post brought several letters, amongst which was one for Lionel and one for Mr. Styngy.

Lionel's was from his mother, which, after the usual maternal and endearing protestations of affectation for her darling boy, and entreaties to him to do his duty, and subdue, as far as possible, his h gh spirts to the dictates of reason, went on to give the following startling piece of intelligence.

"My dear Lionel, I have to tell you something which distresses and grieves me sorely. Samuel, in whom we all placed so much trust and confidence, *has run away*. I can imagine well how sorry you will look when you read this; you can hardly be more sorry than I am. Bills have been printed offering a reward to anyone who will be the means of restoring him to me, and I have advertised as well, but without effect as yet. I did not know how much I missed him, ungainly and uncouth as he was, until now; but he had been so faithful and devoted to you, dear Lionel, that it almost seems to me as if I had lost you twice over. Your Aunt Maria insisted, at first, that he had run away with something valuable; but after counting the plate over herself three times, and comparing the furniture with the inventory, even to the mahogany bedsteads and dining tables, which could by no possibility have been stolen by him, she was reluctantly compelled to admit that the boy was honest. I think, my dear boy, that Samuel may possibly come to you—if he had any object in running away from here, it must have been that—should he do so, ask Mr. Styngy to treat him kindly and considerately, and send him back."

"Well," thought Lionel, as he looked with widely opened eyes at the letter. "Here's a pretty go! Poor Sam! What the dickens made him run away, and where can he have gone to?"

The contemplation of this piece of news caused Lionel almost totally to ignore the five pound note enclosed in the letter until it fell to the ground, whence he mechanically picked it up, and, restoring it and the letter to the envelope, went to consult his chum, Charles Drummond.

In the meantime Mr. Styngy had been equally astonished—though the astonishment was of a pleasurable nature—by *his* letter.

This is what the letter said—

"TO THE REV. PHILO STYNGY, CHEETHAM HALL,
DUNBROWNSHIRE.

"My dear sir,—Though years have passed away since we climbed the giddy heights of Mount Parnassus, I yet retain a lively sense of our old friendship, and with it a desire to render you such service as I can. A young Japanese Prince has been confided to the care of the Government by the Mikado, for the purpose of imparting to him a sound English education. The trust I confide to you, my dear sir, confident that you will do him and me justice. The Prince is a most unpretending young man, and purposes coming alone, unattended by any of his suite or the insignia of his Royal birth. I cannot possibly inform you when he will arrive, but it may be at any moment after you receive this letter.—I am, my dear sir, with professions of the profoundest respect and esteem, "MEDDLE-DE-MUDDLE,

"*Secretary of State for Foreign Affairs.*"

When Mr. Styngy read the letter he felt a conscious glow of pride pervade his whole frame, from his toes to the roots of his hair, and break out in little warm shoots all over him.

"This is very gratifying," he mused, holding the letter at arm's length, and surveying it with that species of admiration with which he might have regarded some priceless work of art. "I cannot call Lord Meddle-de-Muddle exactly to mind, though, just now. It must have been at Harrow, I suppose, but my memory is not so good as it used to be."

Mr. Styngy raked in the ashes of his memory, and stirred up the shadows of many long-forgotten forms and figures, but in all, that goodly company there was no trace of his gracious lordship.

"Never mind," thought the schoolmaster, "he remembers me, and that is quite sufficient. A Prince, too, for a scholar! Very gratifying, really. I wonder if he speaks any English? It will be rather awkward if he does not.

Of course such a visit was not to be kept from being communicated to the assistant masters of Cheetham Hall. Mr. Styngy instantly summoned all the ushers and professors to the library, and there imparted the contents of Lord Meddle-de-Muddle's letter.

Messrs. Bewty and Crocklejack, Signor Tomkini—the eminent linguist—and Herr Krakjauer—the professor of gymnastics, &c.—expressed themselves in ecstasies at the prospect of receiving the Prince amongst them, and exalted to the skies the wonderful discernment of Lord Meddle-de-Muddle, who had made choice of so super-excellent a tutor as Mr. Styngy.

Mr. Grubbe alone was very moderate in his reception of the letter. If any one had been looking at him just then they might have perceived a smile of incredulity upon his face.

"Now gentlemen," said Mr. Styngy, who, as the prospective preceptor of a Prince, became more stiff and dignified at each moment, "the question is how are we to receive his Imperial Highness. Lord Muddle's letter says that he may be expected at any minute."

Mr. Crocklejack had some grand ideas about a triumphal arch and fireworks, as being necessary to a Royal visit. Mr. Styngy received the suggestion with scorn.

"Absurd," said the head master. "Pray are you aware of the time required to erect a triumphal arch, even if we had the means at our disposal, and are you acquainted with the charming effect of fireworks in the middle of the day."

Mr. Crocklejack cowered beneath the withering rejoinder; and Mr. Bewty, encouraged in his turn by his fellow tutor's defeat, suggested a procession to meet the Prince, and a brass band.

"Good Heavens!" exclaimed Mr. Styngy making a frantic clutch at his hair. "If you can do no better than offer me such maniacal suggestions, you had better go. For goodness sake, Grubbe, give me a piece of reasonable advice!"

"Well, since you ask it," replied that gentleman; "my advice is, do nothing at all."

"Why, that's worse than the triumphal arch and fireworks, or the procession and brass band."

"Not at all, if this is really a Prince."

"Really a Prince!" repeated Mr. Styngy. "Why, what do you mean, Grubbe? Here's Lord Meddle-de-Muddle's own letter."

"You're well acquainted with his lordship, of course?"

"Does he not say himself," returned Mr. Styngy reflectively, "that we were boys together?"

"And you know his handwriting?"

"Of course I do," said Mr. Styngy, testily. He could not bear to have a doubt cast upon the matte

"Then, of course, in that case it's all right," said Mr. Grubbe. "What I should do would be this: place somebody on the road between here and the station to give us notice of the Prince's approach; at the signal, you and the rest of us can receive him at the gate, make a neat little speech welcoming him to Cheetham Hall, and so conduct him in."

"Very good. Thank you, Grubbe," said Mr. Styngy, radiant with satisfaction. "Very good, indeed. Mr. Crocklejack, will you send one of the boys to the station with orders to run back here and give us notice the instant he sees the Prince."

"But, now," said Mr. Bewty, a shade of anxiety covering his features like a cloud, "who is to make that little speech, sir? It will have to be made in Japanese if his Imperial Highness doesn't understand English."

Mr. Styngy looked blank for a moment, but suddenly he turned to Professor Tomkini, the linguist of the establishment.

"Signor," said Mr. Styngy, blandly, "have the goodness to write out for me a neat little speech in Japanese, will you?"

"Really sir," stammered Tomkini, who knew as much of Japanese as he did of that mysterious language known as Double-Dutch, "I—"

"No excuse, sir," said the head-master, sternly. "You were engaged here as professor of modern languages, and Japanese is a modern language, I believe?"

"Oh, certainly, of course it is," said the other assistant master, in a confirmatory tone.

Signor Tomkini made a desperate resolve, he had an old book upstairs, printed in curious spidery characters, which might be Japanese or anything else. He would copy some of that out; Mr. Styngy would be none the wiser, but his reputation would be saved.

The Signor retired, and in a quarter of an hour returned with a large sheet of paper on which he had traced some most extraordinary hieroglyphics.

Mr. Styngy received it, looked at it with a puzzled air, turned it upside down, but finding it quite as incomprehensible in that position, said sternly—

"What's this, Signor Tomkini?"

"The Japanese speech, sir."

"Oh! the Japanese speech, is it? Perhaps you will oblige me by reading it."

This put the professor of modern languages into a fresh fix, for he knew less, if possible, of the pronounciation than of the caligraphy of that tongue. But it had to be done, or ruin stared him in the face, so taking the document in his hand and clearing his throat with a prefatory "hum," he began—

"How, chow nobble hi ching chang, how chi ho woo chew ho fi hang chang whang."

"Is that Japanese?" asked Mr. Styngy, doubtfully.

"Pure Japanese, sir," replied Signor Tomkini, confidently.

"It sounds more like Gibberish," said Mr. Styngy. "What does it mean?"

"It means, sir," said Tomkini, who was now getting desperate, and didn't care what he said; "hail, illustrious and mighty Prince from the far-off land of the Eastern Sun, thy slaves of the West humbly bow the neck and prostrate themselves in the dust before thee."

"I say *that* won't do!" said Mr. Styngy, indignantly.

"It's the Eastern style, sir, flowery and poetical. Quite correct, I assure you, Mr. Styngy."

"Flowery fiddlesticks!" exclaimed the head-master. "Why, if I said such a thing as that to him, he'd expect me to do it. Besides, I could never learn to pronounce all that 'Hang wang chow' rubbish at five minutes' notice."

"Then I can tell you what to do," said Mr. Bewty. 'Address him in English, sir, and Signor Tomkini here, who speaks Japanese so fluently, can act as interpreter."

The unhappy Signor turned upon Mr. de Bewty a look of mortal hatred. He was his foe for life from that moment.

"Capital!" said Mr Styngy, delighted at the suggestion. "That's the very thing. Don't be too flowery in your interpretation, Signor."

The poor Tomkini, who expected that he really would have a live Japanese to deal with, thought madly of running away, but was too late, for at th moment Mr. Crocklejack entered the room in a sta of great excitement.

"He's coming, sir."

"*Who* is coming, sir?" said Mr. Styngy.

"The Japanese Prince, sir."

"Then let me tell you, Mr. Crocklejack, that you should have announced the arrival of his Imperial Highness in a more becoming manner. Gentlemen, follow me; Signor Tomkini, keep close to my right hand, if you please."

And in a solemn and dignified way the procession filed out to meet his Imperial Highness the Prince of Japan.

CHAPTER XVIII.

IN WHICH PROFESSOR TOMKINI REALISES PRACTICALLY THE TRUTH OF THE OLD ADAGE, "OUT OF THE FRYING-PAN INTO THE FIRE."

THE intelligence that a real live Prince was coming to Cheetham Hall soon spread in that wonderful way which news has of apparently communicating itself, and the pupils were, as a matter of course, on the tiptoe of expectation.

"Some hungry German duffer, I expect," grunted Tommy Codlings. "Styngy will get precious little besides the honour out of him."

"Perhaps it's the Prince of Wales," suggested another.

"The Prince of Wales' grandmother," ejaculated Lionel. "That's just about as likely; the Prince finished his education long ago, and his head is so full of learning, that there isn't room enough in it for the roots of his hair."

"Is that why he's bald?" said Tommy Codlings, innocently.

"Of course it is, and if it isn't, it's quite as good a reason as anyone else can give you."

This, and other similar scraps of conversation, passed in the class-room, where the boys were assembled for the pursuance of their daily duties, when the tutors were summoned by Mr. Styngy.

As the school was left in charge of the monitors, for whom the pupils of Cheetham Hall had no fear, and consequently no respect, the discussion of the arrival of the expected Prince was carried on in a very animated way, even resulting, in one instance, in a pitched battle between two youths, who differed as to whether the new-comer would make his appearance crowned and robed in princely fashion, or habited as an ordinary mortal.

The fight, and indeed all other discussions were put a stop to by the entry of Mr. de Bewty, who rushed in hatless and breathless, to summon the pupils to the playground.

"Fall into rank!" panted de Bewty as he made hasty endeavours to wipe the heat from his features, with his pocket-handkerchief. "Flashaway, and Drummond, and Codlings head your classes, and follow me. His Imperial Highness the Prince is close at hand."

"Blow his Imperial Highness" muttered Codlings. "What's he, that all this fuss should be made about him. I'll punch his Imperial head, if I get a chance."

"What's that you are saying, Codlings?" asked Mr. de Bewty, angrily.

"Nothing sir," replied Tommy, a little confused, lest his revolutionary threat should have been overheard by the usher.

"If I catch you speaking again without permission, Codlings," said Mr. de Bewty, in an awful voice, "you—you shall be deprived of the honour of assisting at the reception of the Prince."

"I shan't die of grief if I don't," thought Codlings, but he affected to be very much depressed at the dreadful threat, and headed his class meekly out of the schoolroom.

In the playground they found Mr. Styngy, Mr. Crocklejack, and the professors, looking very excited and nervous as the time approached for the arrival of the distinguished visitor.

Professor Tomkini was excessively pale, and looked as if he would gladly have inhabited his boots in preference to any more conspicuous position.

His agony of mind was something terrible to witness. Having no doubt whatever but that the expected Prince was a genuine Japanese, he was, of course, equally assured that the nature of his Japanese address would be discovered.

"If he does not speak English himself," thought the unhappy Tomkini, "he is sure to have an interpreter with him, and I shall be found out that way. I don't bear any malice against his Imperial Highness, but if he would only fall down in the road and break his neck I should be a happy man, and save my situation."

While yet the agonies of doubt and suspense racked poor Tomkini's mind, the disturber of his happiness himself appeared before the gates.

Such a Prince! Imagine a tall boy of fifteen with closely shaven head, on which was perched a saucer-shaped cap; features so ugly as to be irresistibly comical, eyes which squinted in a fearful and wonderful manner, and habited much as one might suppose a Chinese scarecrow, of extra magnificence, to be.

But it was the Prince. Mr. Styngy and his ushers (Mr. Grubbe had disappeared) expected him, had no doubt of him, and bowed to the ground before the representative of Japanese Royalty, while the pupils of Cheetham Hall sent up a hearty welcoming cheer. With one exception—and that was my hero. His cap was raised, his mouth opened, to shout with the rest; but, as he gazed upon the "Prince," his eyes dilated with wonder, and, instead of a cheer, his lips gave utterance to the remarkable words—

"*It's Sam Scarecrow!*"

Fortunately a second burst of cheering broke out at this moment, or Lionel's words must have been heard—as it was he had time to reflect that there might yet be an opportunity of extracting Sam from the scrape into which he would certainly get when the imposition was detected.

"It *is* Sam," muttered Lionel, as he took another amazed stare at his faithful retainer, returning in the most affable manner the bows of Mr. Styngy and the masters. "And yet it seems like a bad dream, to see him there; and, what is *more* extraordinary still, is that Styngy and the rest of 'em take it all in. I can't believe it's real."

Lionel rubbed his eyes and stared again, but he knew Sam too well to be mistaken. The red hair was gone, but the squint was unmistakable, and he could only wonder and wait, until a chance occurred of hearing the solution of the mystery from the lips of Sam himself.

Meanwhile, that young gentleman seemed thoroughly to identify himself with the part he had undertaken to play, and was prepared to listen to the address which the unlucky Tomkini held in his trembling hands.

"Go on, sir," said Mr. Styngy in his sternest whisper. "Don't you see that you are keeping his Imperial Highness out here in a climate which is not suited to his delicate constitution."

"I—I—really—er. Don't you think, sir?" faltered Tomkini.

"I really think, sir!" said Mr. Styngy, fiercely, "that you're a fool, sir! And if you don't go on with that address I shall request his Imperial Highness's permission to kick you out of the gates."

Thus adjured the professor began—

"Chingaree—hi—chang—chow—colley-wobbles—Ho—fi—"

"Louder, sir," whispered Mr. Styngy. "His Imperial Highness cannot hear you!"

"Certainly, sir," returned the professor, fervently hoping that his Imperial Highness was extremely deaf.

And then in a slightly louder voice he went on.

"Hi—ching—chowly—wol—rum-ti-teddity—"

"That isn't what you said before," said Mr. Styngy, fiercely. "If you attempt to impose upon me, sir, I'll—I'll kick you into splinters!'

It is difficult to say into what peculiar Japanese dialect Professor Tomkini, now almost insane with fright, would have wandered had not his Imperial Highness Sam Scarecrow come himself to the rescue.

That illustrious young gentleman, perceiving that an address in some foreign tongue to which he was expected to reply had been made, stretched forth his right arm, and squinting amiably upon the assembled group, addressed them in the following remarkable language—

"Rumbustifugus — also chickaleary — likewise wimble-wumble."

Professor Tomkini was staggered. Evidently the Prince had understood his speech, and was replying to it. Could it be that without his own knowledge he had actually framed a speech in good Japanese."

Bewildered by this thought, the professor stared in a most uncourtier-like manner at the Prince, until admonished of his rudeness by a painful poke in the ribs from Mr. Styngy.

"Tomkini!" said the schoolmaster, severely, "recollect yourself, sir. Listen to what I am about to say, and translate it into Japanese for the benefit of the Prince. Ahem—"

Mr. Styngy cleared his throat with a respectful cough, and putting himself in a good parliamentary attitude, addressed the Prince—

"May it please your Imperial Highness—translate that, Tomkini."

"Oh, why won't he let me alone!" thought the unhappy professor of languages. "I got over the address, but I shall certainly be floored if I attempt to talk to him."

But Mr. Styngy's warning elbow nudged Tomkini again, and the professor translated—

"Ching a ring how chi—"

His Imperial Highness nodded his princely head in an affable manner, as if he perfectly comprehended what was said.

The professor was more astonished than ever, and began to think what a clever fellow he must be to be able to speak Japanese without having ever learnt a word of that language. Mr. Styngy's confidence in Tomkini was being rapidly restored, and he went on—

"I welcome your Imperial Highness to my humble dwelling, which though lowly to one accustomed, like those of your Imperial Highness's station, to the gay and festive splendours of a court, is yet the abode of Minerva. Translate that, Tomkini."

"I say, he's coming it strong," thought Lionel. "My stars, what will he say when he finds out what sort of Prince this is."

In the meantime, Tomkini, running short of gibberish—I beg pardon—Japanese, translated Mr. Styngy's flowery speech in two syllables—

"Tum tum."

"I say," whispered Mr. Styngy, "is that all? It's rather short, isn't it?"

"Very expressive language, the Japanese, sir," said Tomkini.

"Humph," said Mr. Styngy, and then resuming his parliamentary attitude, he went on—

"To form the minds of the young, is always a high and pleasant privilege, your Imperial Highness, but to be entrusted with the task of instructing and

"THE IDEA OF BRINGING DEAD RATS AND SUCH VERMIN INTO MY KITCHING," SAID THE COOK TO PROFESSOR TOMKINI.

guiding along the pleasant paths of knowledge one who is in the not far distant future to be the ruler and arbiter of the destinies of millions of mankind, is indeed a proud position, and one that should be filled more worthily than I can ever hope to do. Translate that Tomkini."

"This is awful," thought Lionel. "He'll kill Sam when he finds him out."

Professor Tomkini had by this time became so bewildered that he knew as little of gibberish as of Japanese.

"I—I beg pardon, sir, but would you mind repeating—"

Mr. Styngy darted a withering glance at the professor. He was particularly proud of the little speech he had just made, and hoped to impress his Imperial Highness with it. He would have repeated it, but he fancied he saw symptoms of impatience developing themselves in the royal listener—and to weary royalty, he deemed little short of high treason.

"You are an incompetent idiot, sir," he said. in a wrathful whisper, to the professor. "Tell his Imperial Highness that the doors of my humble house are open to him, if he will honour it by walking in and taking some refreshment.

It was noticeable that the eyes of the Prince squinted brilliantly at the mention of refreshment—just as if he understood the English language as well as Japanese—and before the bewildered Tomkini could attempt to translate it the Prince moved for the house.

Mr. Styngy, with a low bow, preceded him to the library, where his Imperial Highness was left, with Messrs. de Bewty and Crocklejack waiting on him, with the air of mutes at a funeral, while Mr. Styngy consulted Professor Tomkini upon an important point.

"Look here, Tomkini," he said, taking that gentleman by the top-button of his coat, "his Imperial Highness is sure to stand in need of some refreshment. What shall we give him?"

"A glass of wine and—er—and a biscuit," suggested Tomkini.

"Pooh, nonsense," said Mr. Styngy, impatiently. "I want to give him a real Japanese dinner. Now, you know all about that sort of thing—or ought to—and I want to know what to do?"

The professor was in despair again. He knew no more about the manners and customs of the Japanese than he did about their language. But to confess his ignorance would be to expose himself to his employer's wrath, and so he went on, in a confident tone—

"I only suggested the wine and cake, sir, as probably acceptable to his Imperial Highness until a dinner *secundum artem Japonica* could be prepared."

"Well, well," said Mr. Styngy: "but as to the dinner. What dishes shall there be?"

"There's rice, sir," Tomkini went on. "That's a staple food of the Japanese."

"Good," said Mr. Styngy. "That is not expensive. What else?"

"Then there's birds'-nest soup."

"Birds'-nest soup?" repeated Mr. Styngy; "that's a curious thing."

"Very much appreciated in that country, sir," said the professor.

"Any particular kind of birds'-nests?"

"No, sir," said the professor; "any kind will do, though I believe they have a preference for peacocks."

"There are some very fine old crows' nests in the elm trees at the back, but I don't know how they are to be got at."

"Some of the boys will climb up and get them, sir."

"We'll see about that directly. What other dishes do you propose?"

"Puppy-dogs are great favourites with the Japanese nobility," the professor went on; "also cats and rats."

"Ugh!" said Mr. Styngy, with a shudder and a lengthening face. "I hope he wont expect us to dine with him."

"Not at the same table, sir," responded the professor. "That would not be etiquette."

"I'm glad it isn't," said Mr. Styngy. "Puppy-dogs, cats, and rats. Ugh! I shall never be able to get the cook to prepare them."

"She might object, certainly," asserted Professor Tomkini.

"Besides," Mr. Styngy went on, "she doesn't know the correct way. I tell you what, Tomkini You know how, don't you?"

"Oh yes, sir."

"Then you shall cook the dinner."

The professor opened his eyes and his mouth, and stared at his employer in unutterable dismay.

"I know," Mr. Styngy went on, "that it is not quite the thing for a professor of languages to turn professor of cooking. But consider the position, Tomkini, consider the circumstances, and do this for me. I shall be eternally grateful to you. Will you?"

Of course Professor Tomkini would—he could do nothing else, without offending his employer, and that was not to be thought of.

"Thank you—thank you, Tomkini," said Mr. Styngy, warmly. "Will you set about it at once?"

"I will, sir."

"You'll find plenty of materials, you know. The gardener's bitch, old Rose, has a litter of puppies three weeks old. There are lots of cats about the place; and the keeper will catch some rats for you in the stables."

And away went Mr. Styngy, delighted, to pay his court to the Prince—by looks and signs—while the professor—transformed into a cook—stalked moodily in the direction of the kitchen, to prepare the grand Japanese banquet.

CHAPTER XIX.

MY HERO PLAYS A GAME AT "HIDE AND SEEK," AND FINDS SOMETHING THAT HE NEVER LOOKED FOR.

To say that Lionel was puzzled by the appearance of Sam Scarecrow at Cheetham Hall in this remarkable manner would be to say very little.

He was fairly bewildered, and quite at a loss how to act; and, as all work for the day had been suspended in consequence of the Prince's arrival, he separated himself from his companions, and went up into the dormitory to think it out.

"Here's a pretty kettle of fish," he thought, as he sat on the bed and stared alternately at his boots and then at the ceiling, as if in search of the solution of the difficulty. "How, in the name of wonder, can I get poor Sam out of this mess? and what the dickens did he come here for? and how has he managed to impose upon Styngy and the others? Any one would think that such a flaming piece of imposition would be seen through directly. The idea of Sam pretending to be a Prince!"

The bare idea seemed so outrageously comical to him that he was obliged to indulge in a long fit of laughter, but the reflection that there was a serious side to it soon subdued him.

"I can't think of anything," said my hero to himself again, after mature reflection. "I must wait till I get a chance to speak to him, and, in the meantime, I'd better go down and see what the other fellows say about him."

Lionel soon found that the "other fellows" were much divided in opinion as to the merits of the Prince. Many thought that being a Prince necessitated being perfection, and that all detraction from such exalted personages could only be prompted by jealously.

The minority were jealous, and openly said so. Who was this "chap" (the young Red Republicans actually dared to insult the Prince by calling him a "chap," and speaking loudly too), that all this fuss was made about him. If he had come covered with gold, and bristling with diamonds, it would have been different; but he was shabby, and squinted fearfully. Some even took the liberty of doubting whether he was a Prince at all, and declared their belief that "old Styngy" had been "sold."

Among these latter doubters was Tommy Codlings, and as he appeared to be the head of this particular party, Lionel took him confidentially aside.

"Look here, old fellow," said my hero, "will you do one thing to oblige me?"

"Of course I will," replied Codlings. "We're chums, you know."

"Well, will you oblige me by going in for the Prince?"

"Going in for him?" repeated Tommy, putting up his hands and sparring scientifically. "Like that? Well I don't mind, for your sake, but a squinting chap's precious awkward to tackle. You can't tell when they're going to hit."

"No, I don't mean that—I mean backing him up. You don't believe in him, do you?"

"I don't!" said Tommy, emphatically.

"Well, I want you to—"

"But I *can't*. What! tell me that a chap that squints like that is a Prince! Princes never squint; look at our Royal family, you can't find one of 'em even with a cast in his eye. It wouldn't be allowed."

"Well, at any rate, I want to appear to believe in this one, Codlings, and to make the other fellows do the same."

Tommy scratched his head gently with one forefinger, and looked puzzled.

"Well, it's a queer thing to do," he said. "I've been running him down for the last half-hour, and now I've got to run him up again."

But Codlings was a boy of his word; and he set about the "running up" task without a moment's delay, and with a zeal which totally outdid his previous detracting performance.

That little piece of diplomacy effected—Lionel went in search of Charles Drummond, whom he found surrounded by a circle of sympathisers, loudly grumbling because, in consequence of the advent of the Prince, they were not permitted to go in the playground.

"For fear lest our noise should awake his Highness when he has his Royal nap after his Royal dinner. I wonder if he snores with his Royal nose?"

"Who'd have thought of Tomkini speaking Japanese like that?" said another. "In my opinion he spoke it better than the Prince."

"Why, what do you know about it? How can you tell who speaks it the best when you don't know a word of it yourself," commented Lionel.

Hullo, it's the new boy," said the youthful critic. "Don't you be so sharp—you're not cock of the walk, yet."

"I can crow over *you*, my bantam," said Lionel, coolly, "so shut up."

The speaker—one of the elder boys—looked monstrous fierce, and seemed inclined to dispute the point, but he didn't, and retired from the circle, growling something about "cheek," and expressing an intention of "punching" somebody's head.

"Now," said Charlie, "we can't stay moping here all day. Let's have a game of some sort."

"Touch," suggested one.

"Too noisy. His Imperial Highness would hear us, and we should be stopped."

"Hide and seek."

"That'll do—we can't make much noise at that," said Drummond. "Here, Hot Codlings, we want you."

That young-gentleman approached slowly, with an open clasp-knife held to a large blue bump on his forehead.

"Hallo, been having a turn up?"

"Yes, with Twister."

"Did you lick him?"

"Lick him! No, do I ever lick anybody? I never knew a chap with such luck as I've got.

"Never mind, Codlings," said Lionel, consolingly. "You've got pluck, and that's everything; what was it about?"

"Oh, that dashed Prince. I was sticking up for him, and young Twister said I was a turn-coat, because I'd been running him down five minutes before, just as if a fellow couldn't change his mind if he wanted to."

"You're a brick, Codlings," said my hero, patting him on the back.

"I wish I was," grumbled Tommy; I shouldn't get bumps and bruises then. I never saw such a thing, every time I was going to hit young Twister his fist came out somehow and hit me instead!"

"Cheer up, Tommy, better luck next time," said Drummond. "Come and have a game at hide and seek."

"All right," replied Tommy, shutting up his knife, and restoring it to his pocket. "Who's going to hide?"

"I will," said Lionel.

"But you don't know the house."

"All the more fun. I shall get into some place where you fellows wouldn't think of going."

"Take care you don't take your nose where it'll get stung."

"Trust me," said Lionel, with a laugh. "How much law?"

"Two minutes," replied Charlie, taking out an old-fashioned silver watch.

"All right, off it is."

And away Lionel sped—light and noiseless, down the corridor to the left of the class-room, up one flight of stairs and down another, then along another passage, and down a third flight of steps, where he was met by a strong smell of cooking, and an echoing sound of angry voices.

"This is the very thing," thought Lionel. "The kitchen must be close at hand. They won't think of coming after me there."

And without hesitating he descended the stairs—cautiously, though, for fear of being heard—and so came upon the source of the smell and of the sounds.

The kitchen door was ajar, and through the opening Lionel could see a very stout woman, with a very red face and a very voluble tongue, heaping injurious epithets upon a mild-looking little man, who had a large white apron tied round his neck, while in one hand he held a brace of dead cats by the tails.

In this mild little man Lionel recognised, to his astonishment, Signor Tomkini, the interpreter of that morning, the stout lady with the voluble tongue was, beyond doubt, the cook, and the former was speaking.

"But I assure you, my good woman," the professor began to say, as Lionel came up.

"Don't 'good woman' me," fiercely interrupted the cook, "you low whiffing-sniffing, parley-vooing professor—you. I won't have it. The idea of bringing dead rats and such wermin into *my* kitching."

"But my dear madam—" began the professor again.

"I won't have none o' your 'dear madams.' My name's Mary Hann," said the cook, putting in a most prodigious aspirate.

"Well, Mary Ann, then," said Tomkini, in an agony at the delay, lest Mr. Styngy should visit the kitchen with a view to inspecting the progress of the Japanese cookery, "I tell you again that the Prince—"

"Don't talk to me about the Prince," exclaimed the indignant cook. "I saw him—a dried-up scarecrow of a thing; and no wonder if he lives on dead rats and cats. I shouldn't wonder if he's a cannon-ball—(she probably meant cannibal)—and wants one o' the boys for dinner."

"I can't bear this," said the professor, in desperation. "It's positively treasonable. Once for all, Mary Ann, will you—"

"I'll have nothing to do with the beastly things," interrupted Mary Ann, flinging down the gridiron she held so close to Tomkini's toes that he jumped a foot high in alarm. "Cook 'em yourself."

The professor looked ruefully at the cats in his hand and the rats and litter of puppies on the floor. He had reckoned upon securing the cook's aid by means of a bribe, but that irate lady had strongly resented the intrusion into her kitchen, and still more strongly objected to the introduction of "warmints," as she phrased it.

"What on earth shall I do," murmured the unfortunate Tomkini. "The Prince might have pretended to understand what I said to him out of politeness, but, if it comes to giving him something to eat which he doesn't like and refuses, I shall be exposed, and lose my situation."

But, for all that the dinner had to be cooked, and, as the kitchen maids had followed the example of their chieftainess, and quitted the kitchen, he had no chance of getting help.

Around him all things necessary to the culinary art were grouped; pots, pans, kettles, gridirons, frying-pans, rolling pins, moulds, *et hoc genus omne*, and a huge fire burnt redly in the grate; but Tomkini didn't know in the least what to do with them.

There was a huge carving-knife on the dresser, which at last the professor clutched, with a desperate hand, and impaled one of the rats upon the point.

"I'm not a bloodthirsty man," Lionel heard him mutter, as he glared at the rat, "but I wish you were a Japanese Prince just now."

"If this isn't a game," thought Lionel, nearly black in the face from his efforts to restrain his laughter, "I never saw one. Ha, ha, ha! only fancy, they're treating Sam Scarecrow to a Japanese dinner—rats, cats, and puppies. My stars! I can fancy Sam walking into it and finding out afterwards what he's eaten!"

Lionel was not selfish; he scorned to keep such a good joke to himself, and running lightly up the stairs again, he whistled softly, by way of signal to those who were seeking for him.

The signal soon collected them from the different quarters of Cheetham Hall; where they had been seeking for my hero—and to them he imparted what he had seen.

"Easy does it," said Lionel, restraining the impetuosity of one hasty youth. Keep quiet, or he will hear and we shall be caught out."

The kitchen door was safely reached, without attracting any notice, the offended cook and her satellites having retreated to an inner sanctum, where they vilified the professor, the Prince, and Mr. Styngy, to their full content.

"Now you can't all look at once," said Lionel; "each of you fellows must take a turn at peeping. Drummond and I will stand in front to keep you from crowding."

"Here, that's good, that is, for you two, you'll be looking in all the time, and we shall only get a peep."

"Grumblers shan't peep at all," said Lionel, imperatively—and that dictum settled the complainant.

Just as Lionel and the others arrived, the professor, overcoming his repugnance, addressed himself fairly to the task before him.

He had set aside a huge saucepan in which to stew the puppies, the cats were to be baked, and the rats roasted—thus affording what he considered an excellent variety of dishes, which could not fail to please his Imperial Highness.

"I don't mind the cooking so much, but the dissecting work is very unpleasant," murmured Tomkini, as with the carving-knife he prepared to cut open poor pussy. "Anyhow, here goes."

He made an incision with his weapon, and the next moment recoiled to the opposite extremity of the kitchen, with an expression of disgust upon his features, and his nose held tightly by the fingers of his left hand.

"Ugh!" he exclaimed, with a shudder. "The confounded cat is 'high,' and that can hardly be, either, for I saw the gardener kill it."

He gazed upon it for a moment with a woeful countenance, which was not made more lively by the sound of a heavy footstep descending the kitchen stairs.

The boys had heard it before, and took refuge at the end of the passage. For the unhappy Tomkini there was no refuge, and he looked very downcast indeed when the schoolmaster stalked in.

"Well," Mr. Styngy began; but scarcely had he entered a yard into the kitchen than he recoiled and clasped his nose in his fingers.

"Poof! Whatever is this dreadful smell, Tomkini?"

"It's—it's all right, sir," replied the professor, deciding not to incur the blame of Mr. Styngy by an admission that anything was wrong.

"It don't *smell* right, Tomkini."

"Perfectly right, sir. The Japanese always like their meals a little gamey, sir."

"Well, you kdow best, Tobkidi," said Mr. Styngy, speaking as if he had a very bad cold in his head, in consequence of the tightness with which he held his nose; "but is the didder dode?"

"Sir?"

"Is the didder ready or *dot?*" repeated Mr. Styngy. "His Imperial Highdess is very hudgry."

"It is not ready yet, sir," said Tomkini, apologetically. "I have been delayed, sir."

"Add who has dared to delay the preparatiods for the Pridce's didder?"

"The—the cook, sir."

"The cook, Tobkidi?" said Mr. Styngy, with much severity. "Thed she shall have a modth's warding this instadt. Where is the wobad?"

Tomkini indicated the locality where she might be found; and Mr. Styngy, glad to escape from the atmosphere of the dissected cat, went thither, and left the professor to his cooking.

It was then that Tomkini became reckless. He knew nothing before—he cared less now—and, slicing and hacking away at the animals before him, had the puppies in the stewpan, the cat in the oven, and the rats suspended from the roasting jack before Mr. Styngy's return.

He had had quite enough of "dissection," in the little operation on the cat; the puppies went into the stewpan with their "in'ards" complete, and the professor was once more able to breath freely through his nose.

Mr. Styngy returned from his errand of conciliation, looking very red and wrathful. It was plain that he had not succeeded.

"All right, sir?" queried Professor Tomkini.

"No, sir," replied Mr. Styngy, stiffly; "it's not *all* right. Mary Ann is the most rebellious and obstinate woman on the face of the earth."

"So she is, sir," said the compliant Tomkini.

"But what a cook she was. Her entrées were perfect," Mr. Styngy went on, regretfully. "I shall never get such another."

"Oh, yes you will, sir," said the professor, in a consolatory tone. "Cheer up, sir."

"I say, sir," Mr. Styngy continued, emphatically. "I shall *never* get such another. She could make up a dinner for the boys out of anything, and flavour it so that it was impossible to tell what it was. Her hashes were marvels of cheapness and flavour.

"Peace be to her hashes," murmured Professor Tomkini.

"Tomkini, you forget yourself," said the schoolmaster, sternly. "No low jokes here, if you please; and if the dinner is not ready for the Prince in ten minutes, you and I will part."

"It's ready now, sir," said Tomkini, who began to feel very unwell from the combined aroma of baked cat, roast rat, and stowed puppy.

"Are you sure?"

"The Japanese nobility always take their meals underdone, sir."

"Very good," said Mr. Styngy; "but be careful, Tomkini. If any of it disagrees with his Imperial Highness, we part that instant."

There was an imposing array of plated covers and dishes on the kitchen dresser, which articles had just undergone the process of cleaning.

These Tomkini appropriated, and carefully arranging the puppies on one, the cat on another, and the rats on a third, announced that all was ready.

"But, good gracious me!" said Mr. Styrgy, who had been eying these strange products of the culinary art through his gold-rimmed eyeglass, "haven't you made a mistake?"

"How sir?"

"Why, these—these animals are not skinned."

"They never are, sir, in Japan. The nobility peel their game themselves."

"Very strange custom," said Mr. Styngy, doubtfully. "Very strange, indeed."

"No doubt about that, sir," said the professor, as he eyed the awful-looking viands. "But I beg your pardon, Mr. Styngy, how is the dinner to be taken up?"

"By you," replied the schoolmaster, after a moment's pause. "There is no degradation of dignity in waiting on royalty, you know, Tomkini."

"But I can't carry all at once, sir."

"You have two hands, Tomkini."

"I can only carry two dishes with those, sir."

"Then put the other on your head."

"That's quite against Japanese etiquette, sir," said Tomkini, struck with a brilliant thought. "There must be a separate bearer for every dish."

"Humph," muttered Mr. Styngy, floored by this argument. "There's no time to lose. I'll carry the biggest, and go in front, you follow close behind me and you won't be noticed."

There were unseen listeners to this conversation, in the persons of Lionel and Charlie Drummond, and if Mr. Styngy had been a little quicker, he might have seen their youthful forms scudding on before him.

Lionel had a long piece of cord in his hand and some pins. The old mischievous look was in his face, but Drummond seemed grave and a little anxious.

"I don't half like it," he whispered, as they reached the upper corridor and made swiftly but lightly for the apartment in which his Imperial Highness was waiting for his dinner.

"Don't funk," said Lionel, in the same low tone.

"I won't; but you don't know what a Tartar old Styngy is, and what he will do if we're caught."

"Bosh! I don't care for forty old Styngys. If you won't come with me I'll do it myself."

"Oh, I'll come. I never back out of a thing when I'm once in."

"That's right. Here we are now. Make haste. Drive the pins well in. Don't strain the cord. Now off we go; I can hear 'em coming."

And in the same noiseless way the two conspirators dodged round the corner, Lionel still holding in his hand one end of the cord, and watching for the approach of the amateur footmen.

On they came. The door was reached, and Mr. Styngy, bearing the great covered dish, kicked gently at the door. It was opened by Mr. Crocklejack, and the schoolmaster passed in, announcing, in a loud voice, the Japanese for "his Imperial Highness's dinner is served!" which, according to Professor Tomkini, was "Crockery dickory boo."

Tomkini followed; but just as he stepped upon the threshhold, Lionel gently pulled the cord he held in his hand. The professor tripped, tried vainly to recover his balance, and then fell headlong with a crash against the reverend back of Mr. Styngy, and into the august presence of the Prince.

Neither Lionel or Charlie waited to see the result of their little joke. They heard the sound of the collision, the howl of the injured Mr. Styngy, and then fled down the corridor, not pausing until they were compelled to, by tumbling themselves over Tommy Codlings, who, as usual, happened to be in the way.

"I never see such a thing," said the unlucky Tommy. "When I was a baby I was always falling down on somebody, and now somebody's always falling down on me. I lost a fortune that way once."

"What—through somebody falling over you?"

"No. Through my falling down on somebody.

"How was that, Tommy? Tell us," said Drummond.

"Well, you see, it was my uncle I fell on, a cantankerous old bacheler, who'd never been married himself, and would, I believe, have poisoned any one who did marry him. I don't recollect the thing myself, for I was only a baby at the time—in fact it was at my christening it happened—but I've been told of it over and over again since, and blamed for it, too, as if a baby six months old could help where he fell."

"Never mind, Tommy. Cut away. Tell us about your uncle."

"Well, he'd been invited to the christening of all my brothers and sisters—I'm the youngest of fourteen you know—and he'd always refused. When it came to my unlucky turn to be born the invitatation was sent as usual, and to my father and mother's surprise he accepted it."

"Why?" asked Lionel."

"*I* don't know," replied Tommy, gloomily. "Because I was born to be unlucky, I reckon. Anyway, he said he'd come; and there was such a fuss made to give him a swell reception, for he was regularly rich you know, and my parents thought he'd leave me some money."

"That was rather mean, wasn't it?" said Charlie Drummond."'

"I don't know. How could I? A baby six months old can't be expected to know what's going on. Anyhow, the house was turned upside down, all the swell things got out, a dinner ordered, with all the old chap's pet dishes, and I was rigged out in a new christening robe, that cost I don't know how many guineas, and tied up with ribbons, till, as my old nurse often told me, I looked like a little angel."

"You've changed since then, Tommy."

"P'raps I have; anyway, I don't think I could have had such fat cheek as they give the angels on the tombstenes, if they're like the real article."

"I'm not a judge," said Charlie.

"Well, at any rate, there we were togged up to the nines, and waiting for my old uncle. At last he came—two hours behind time. My father and mother rushed down to the door to welcome him, while the nurse had me at the top of the stairs, for I was delicate and had to be kept out of the draught.

"They don't take so much care of you now, Tommy."

Codlings grunted an expressive approval and went on—

"The old chap came upstairs ahead of all the rest—grunting away, as nurse told me, like an old bear. He'd got half way up, when the girl who was holding me leaned over the bannisters to have a look, and dropped me plump on to the top of my uncle's head."

"Ha, ha!" laughed Lionel. "That was an early fall in life, Tommy."

"And that wasn't the worst of it, for, you see, the

"COME ON!" YELLED SAM, AS HE DEALT A BLOW AT MR. STYNCY. "WHY DON'T YOU STAND STILL AND FIGHT FAIR."

No. 5.

fall shook me up, and, being delicate, I was dreadfully ill, all over my uncle. He swore in an awful way—they say that he even kicked me—and then rushed away out of the house, and was never seen any more."

"And you didn't get his money?"

"Not a copper. He left it all to found an institution for old maids who'd never had an offer of marriage in their lives—but that didn't flourish, for none of the applicants could be got to say that they couldn't have been married if they'd wanted to."

"Poor old Tommy," said Lionel. "Come along with us, and we'll see how old Styngy is getting along with the Prince by this time."

CHAPTER XX.

IN WHICH THE JAPANESE PRINCE, INSTEAD OF PUTTING A DINNER INSIDE HIM, IS PUT INSIDE A BED HIMSELF.

THERE was an awful crash, followed by a dread silence for a few moments, and then, Messrs. de Bewty and Crocklejack's gravity being as completely upset as the gravy, they ignored the presence of Royalty, and burst into a roar of laughter.

The countenance of his Imperial Highness, too, was radiant with mirth for a moment, but only for a moment, as it suddenly occurred to him that he was extremely hungry and that his dinner was spoiled.

The reverend schoolmaster was in a towering rage at this untoward occurence. He had fallen in a most undignified position, with his coat-tails over his head, and his nose lovingly nestling on the interior of the principal dish.

He scrambled up, frantic with wrath, and, grabbing the metal dish-cover, brought it down upon the unfortunate Tomkini's head.

There was a sound as of the beating of a gong, a smothered howl of agony from the professor of languages, and a rush of de Bewty and Crocklejack to the spot.

"Be calm, sir," said Mr. de Bewty.

"Restrain yourself, sir," said Mr. Crocklejack.

"I will *not*," said Mr. Styngy, bursting with passion, as he flourished the dish-cover in the air. "Let me go."

"We will not," panted Mr. de Bewty. "Crocklejack, hold him tight on your side."

"I'll annihilate the villain!" roared Mr. Styngy, making a frantic endeavour to free his right arm.

"Think better of it, sir," said Mr. de Bewty, soothingly.

"Think of his Imperial Highness, sir," said Mr. Crocklejack.

These words had the desired effect. Mr. Styngy ceased to struggle and dropped the dish-cover on Mr. Crocklejack's most tender corn.

"Thank you for reminding me, Mr. Crocklejack," he said; "I will be calm; but bear me witness that the presence of his Highness alone restrains me from inflicting summary and serious chastisement upon the wretch."

"I couldn't help it," murmured Tomkini. "I tumbled over something."

"Don't make foolish excuses, sir," said Mr. Styngy, in a ferocious whisper. "You're *always* tumbling over something. Apologise in my name to his Highness for the accident at once, sir."

"I can't."

"What's that you say, sir?"

"You gave me such a blow on the head, sir," replied the injured Tomkini, "that it has quite confused my faculties, and I can hardly speak English, far less such a difficult language as Japanese."

At this point Mr. de Bewty nudged his superior gently in the side, and whispered—

"Look at his Imperial Highness, sir. He is ill I think."

Mr. Styngy glanced in that direction, and saw the Prince going through a series of evolutions of the most complicated nature.

"First he pointed slowly to the ground, where the ruins of the feast lay strewn, then he pointed to his mouth—opened to the widest of its wide extent—and then, with the palm of his right hand, slowly, and with a circular motion, rubbed the lower part of his tunic, just where the bottom waistcoat button would have been had he worn one.

"Good Heavens!" exclaimed Mr. Styngy; "the sight of Tomkini's unseemly conduct has been too much for him. Run for the doctor, somebody! Mr. Grubbe! Where is Mr. Grubbe?"

The schoolmaster missed his deputy for the first time, and accustomed to rely upon his astuteness in matters of difficulty, called for him now in a frenzied manner.

But Mr. Grubbe answered not; and Mr. Styngy, bidding one of his assistants run for medical assistance, advanced to the Prince and motioned to him to sit down.

The Prince shook his head with emphasis, and again repeated the mysterious signs that had alarmed the schoolmaster.

"Dear me, this is dreadful!" said Mr. Styngy. "His Highness is certainly out of his senses. I would not have had such a thing happen for a thousand pounds. Where is that idiot, Tomkini?"

"Here I am, sir," said the professor, in a faint voice.

"Then come here and ask his Highness what is the matter with his Imperial stomach."

"I can't."

"You *must*, sir. Get up directly. How dare you have the audacity to sit down in the presence of the Prince?"

"I can't stand—I'm too giddy, sir. That blow on the head you gave me—"

"Pooh, nonsense," exclaimed Mr. Styngy, unpolitely. "A little thing like that wouldn't hurt *your* head."

"Excuse me, sir, but it was a very knobby dish-cover."

"Knobby fiddlesticks," said Mr. Styngy, sternly. "Get up at once, sir, or—"

Tomkini knew that instant dismissal was impending, and staggered to his feet, almost instantly tumbling down again though—clutching at Mr. Styngy and taking away a portion of his shirt front and the whole of his cravat.

Again did Mr. Styngy capital D the professor of languages, and, once more forgetting that he stood in the presence of Royalty, did the knobby part of the dish-cover descend upon Tomkini's head.

There is a point of outrage to go beyond which is said to cause even the worm to turn, and that point Mr. Styngy passed when he struck the professor in the same tender place with the same offensive weapon.

"I won't stand it," yelled Tomkini, dancing frantically about with pain. "Take that. I'll teach you to cut down a man's salary and then assault him with dish covers."

"That" was the cat, which the now reckless Tomkini seized by the tail and, swinging it round his head, brought it with full force against Mr. Styngy's reverend nose.

The result was dreadful—far too much so to be more than hinted at in these pages. Suffice it to say that Mr. Styngy became intimately acquainted with the internal development of the feline species.

With a gasp and a groan he fell upon his back, and lay there shuddering, while with both hands he endeavoured to remove from his classical features the obnoxious traces of the cat.

"Oh! you shall suffer for this," he panted. "You villain, I'll have you locked up. Po-lice!"

Just then the door was opened, and Mr. de Bewty, followed by a doctor, came in hurriedly.

"Good heavens!" ejaculated the assistant master, hurrying to Mr. Styngy and raising him into a sitting position. "What is this? My respected principal is murdered."

"Very nearly," gasped the schoolmaster, "and by that beast, Tomkini. Don't let him go, de Bewty. Send for the police."

"But here is the doctor, sir, for his Imperial Highness. There will be nobody to translate to the Prince."

"True," said Mr. Styngy, gasping worse than ever. "Oh, that confounded cat!"

The professor of languages, who already repented of the violence into which he had been led, was ready enough to do anything which would reinstate him in the good graces of his employer, and advanced boldly to interpret a language of which he did not understand one word.

Poor Sam—we beg pardon, his Imperial Highness—watched the preparations of the doctor with a dismayed countenance. He was not ill—only hungry—but he dared not express his feelings in the only language which he could speak, for fear of detection, so he suffered the doctor to feel his pulse and look at his tongue, while, from the bottom of his heart, he wished that he had never come there.

"Hum," said the doctor. "His Imperial Highness is in a very bad state. Symptoms of fever already apparent."

"Dear me, how unfortunate," said Mr. Styngy, dismayed.

"The worst may yet be averted," the doctor went on. He never had the chance before of getting a Prince for a patient, and was determined to make the most of this one.

"I hope so," said Mr. Styngy presently. "What do you advise, doctor?"

"His Imperial Highness," said the doctor, who was thinking already how well "Physician in Ordinary to his Imperial Highness the Prince of Japan, etc.," would look on his cards, "must be put to bed at once."

His Imperial Highness looked very miserable.

"And," the doctor went on, "kept upon a low diet, say toast and water."

His Imperial Highness groaned audibly.

"He is worse," said Mr. Styngy, hurriedly. "Tell his Highness, Tomkini, what the doctor advises."

His Highness did not want telling, he knew too well already, and he groaned again.

"I will see the Prince put to bed," the doctor went on, "and then return to my surgery and compound the necessary medicine."

"His Highness had better be carried, he's too weak to walk."

The Prince groaned again, and oh, how fervently he wished that he had never come to Cheetham Hall.

Still, to protest would involve the worse fate of detection, and, with a groan that put the former ones in the shade, so doleful was it, he suffered de Bewty and Crocklejack to lift him up and bear him from the room.

My hero was not far off, and as he saw the procession, he thought at first that the impostor had been discovered, and that Mr. Styngy, in the first burst of his wrath, had killed Sam.

"No, that's not likely," said Charlie Drummond, to whom Lionel confided his suspicions. "He has very likely given him something warm for himself, but he hasn't killed him. He wouldn't dare to kill a Prince, you know."

For a moment Lionel thought of confiding fully in his new chum, but thinking it advisable to keep his secret for a while longer—he kept silent on that point.

"Let's go and see what they are going to do, at all events, Charlie."

"What's the use. There is no fun in that, and we should certainly get caught."

"Well, I shall go, so you stay here then, Charlie, one is more likely to get clean off, than two."

On tiptoe and with the utmost caution, Lionel followed the procession, and as they were proceeding at a very gentle rate, arrived just in time to see them enter the best bedroom, which had been specially prepared for the reception of his Highness.

The door was shut upon Lionel, but by way of the keyhole he soon saw and heard enough to convince him that Sam was far from dead, inasmuch as he made such a frantic resistance to all attempts to undress him; that it was finally decided to put him to bed as he was: it being probably against Court etiquette for a prince to be undressed in company.

Then they left him to repose, it being absolutely necessary, said the doctor, that he should not be disturbed; and Lionel had barely time to hide, in a dark corner of the corridor, when the party came out again, and filed slowly away.

"Now's my time," thought Lionel, as he heard the footsteps dying away in the distance. "I'll go in and see Sam, and contrive some way for him to get out of this mess."

And crossing the corridor on tiptoe, Lionel gently opened the door, and entered the august presence of his Imperial Highness, Sam Scarecrow.

CHAPTER XXI.

MY HERO HEARS SAM'S EXPLANATION—THE DISCOVERY OF THE IMPOSTURE AND HOW MR. STYNGY REWARDED IT.

HIS IMPERIAL HIGHNESS was sitting up in the bed when Lionel entered, looking as much unlike a Prince as it was possible for a mortal to do; and so absorbed in his melancholy thoughts was he that he did not notice my hero's presence until a light touch on his arm aroused him from his reverie.

In an instant his expression changed from one of the profoundest melancholy to the most extravagant joy—he squinted worse than ever, and his mouth expanded in such a way as to alarm Lionel for the possible consequences.

He leaped out of the bed, and performed a dance round his young master which seemed to be a compound of Indian war-dance and Highland fling.

"Oh, Master Lionel, I am so glad. I thought I should never be able to get to speak to you."

"Don't make so much noise, Sam; but sit down on the bed, and tell me whatever induced you to come here in such a way? and how in the name of wonder did you make old Styngy believe that you were a Japenese prince. *I* should have known you if you had come disguised as a whale."

"Oh, that's the hi of affection, Master Lionel. Sim'ly likewise I should know you if you was disguised as a hangel with a 'arp and a pair o' wings—though why they prefer 'arps, which must be orkard to 'andle while flyin', I don't know."

"Never mind about that Sam; but tell me how you did it. They'll be back directly."

Sam's features became overcast with melancholy again.

"Oh, Lor'! that beastly toast-and-water, and the physic!" he said, with a shudder. "All I wants is a good cut o' beef and some taters, and I daresn't say so."

"Serve you right, for being such a stupid as to come," said Lionel.

"Oh, don't say that," murmured Sam plaintively. "I couldn't bear to be away from you no longer."

"Then why didn't you come in a proper way?"

"'Cause he wouldn't have let me come amongst you if he knowed who I was," said Sam, in a slightly injured tone. "He would have remembered the tricks we played upon him at Hampstead—wouldn't he?"

"Perhaps he would, Sam."

"Well, so I insulted with a chap."

"Consulted, Sam."

"Consulted with a chap as used to come about sometimes with partitions."

"With what, Sam."

"Partitions, yer know, is for a widder as have lost her cow, and is left a dissolute orphan, with sixteen small children; or when a poor man has had three of his arms blown orf by a omblebus runnin' over him. That's the sort of thing, Master Lionel."

"Oh, petitions, I see; he was a begging letter impostor. You fell into good hands, Sam. Go on."

"Well, I insulted him, and he bein' a very clever chap told me that he'd do what I wanted all right and proper for arf a sovereign; so he writ a letter as if it come from a lord, you understand, which did the business bootiful."

"Yes; and it'll do *your* 'business bootiful,' as you call it," said Lionel. "Do you know that you can be sent to prison for ten years, or, perhaps, twenty."

Sam's countenance lengthened in a manner truly alarming.

"You don't mean to say that, Master Lionel? It were only a lark."

"It will be a serious lark for you if you're caught," said my hero.

"Pe—pe—penal servitude?" gasped Sam.

"That's it, Sam, with a whacking once a week to make you lively," said Lionel. "I wouldn't stand in your shoes for a trifle."

"No more will I," said Sam, darting from the bed, with a pale and alarmed countenance. "I'm orf, Master Lionel."

"Where are you going," said my hero, clutching Sam Scarecrow by the arm.

"Anywheres but penal servitude. I can't stand that. Let me get out o' the winder."

"You'll break your neck. You haven't got Mr. Grubbe to fall on this time, remember. Do as I tell you—stay here quietly till night comes, make 'em understand that you want to be left alone, and when all's quiet I'll slip down and let you out."

"Can't it be done afore?" said Sam, dolefully. "Think of the toast and water and the medicing, Master Lionel, and I'm so hungry."

"You'd better take that than what they were getting ready for your dinner," said my hero, smiling, "unless you are fond of rats, cats, and puppies."

"I think I could a'most eat them now," said Sam, musingly, "I'm that dreadful hungry."

"Go to sleep and forget all about it, Sam. The time will soon slip away. I must go now or we shall be caught. Cheer up, Sam, and don't let your spirits go down."

"I won't let the medicing go down if I can help it, but I shuddn't mind a drop o' sperrits."

"You shall have something by-and-bye, Sam," said Lionel. "Good-bye.

"Adoo, Master Lionel," said Sam, in a doleful tone, as he drew the counterpane up to his chin.

And then, with a word of encouragement, Lionel left the room, and cautiously closed the door behind him.

As he stepped into the corridor he thought he saw a figure disappear behind an angle some distance ahead. He hurried forward at the risk of being heard, but the figure, if there had been one, was out of sight.

Lionel felt relieved—but had he known that the figure he had seen was that of Mr. Grubbe, and that nearly every word of his conversation with Sam had been overheard, he would have felt just a little anxious.

* * * * * *

With the feelings of a criminal awaiting the arrival of Calcraft to pinion him, Sam lay quaking in bed, dreading the coming of Mr. Styngy and the physic.

"I wonder wot they'll give me?" he thought. "Salts and senny, or caster ile. Ugh! I can't abear it."

And already in anticipation Sam's stomach turned at the thought, and he bitterly regretted the unlucky thought that had led him to visit Cheetham Hall in disguise.

In a little while after Lionel's departure, though it seemed an age to Sam, he heard the footsteps of his executioners approaching, and a moment after they entered the room, looking preternaturally solemn, and Sam noted, too, with wonder, that Mr. Styngy, as well as his assistants, carried canes, which they exhibited in a ferocious and alarming manner.

Sam looked at them, and they looked at him, and as they did so, shook their heads and groaned, in a way that was certainly not calculated to raise his spirits.

"Wot the deuce is the matter?" thought Sam, breaking out into a cold perspiration. "Wot are they lookin' at me like that for?"

Sam was not left long in suspense, for the schoolmaster, the doctor, with the assistants, having ranged themselves round the bed, and Mr. Styngy addressing Professor Tomkini, who had his head tied up, as if he was suffering from a very bad toothache, said—

"Now, professor, oblige me by looking at that—that person."

The professor looked, and did it in such a vindictive manner, that Sam shuddered.

"Well, sir," Mr. Styngy went on, in an awful voice, "now that you have looked, are you convinced that he is not a Japanese?"

"I am, sir," said the professor, with great alacrity. "I was, from the very first, sir, but it was not for me to question the actions of my respected principal."

"Never mind that, sir," said Mr. Styngy, frowning. "And are you also convinced that he does not speak or understand the Japanese language?"

"Quite convinced, sir," returned the professor, positively.

"Then in pretending to understand him, and inventing fictitious replies, you were as great an impostor as he is, sir," thundered Mr. Styngy. "But I will talk to you on that point presently."

The unlucky professor slunk into the background, invoking blessings manifold upon the head of the impostor Sam.

"Now, doctor," said Mr. Styngy, turning to that gentleman; "what is your opinion of this case?"

The doctor looked at Sam, in a knowingly severe manner, with his head on one side. Then he ordered Sam to put out his tongue, and shook his head at that; then he felt his pulse, and shook his head at that; and finally gave a series of grave nods, as one who had quite made up his mind upon the subject, and was not to be shaken by any earthly consideration

"Well, doctor?"

"I should say, mad. Decidedly mad," said the doctor. "Not violently mad, but insane and subject to delusions."

"I ain't mad," here broke in Sam.

"What did you do it for then, you—you scoundrel?" said Mr. Styngy, wrathfully.

"Only—for a lark," faltered Sam.

"Only—for—a—lark," replied the doctor in slow and contemptuous syllables. "He is mad, without a doubt, Mr. Styngy; and it is your duty, sir, to have him placed under restraint."

"I ain't mad, indeed, sir," said Sam, again; he felt very much inclined to cry, but bore up bravely in the presence of his persecutors.

"You are. Don't contradict *me*," said the doctor, who was nearly wild with suppressed wrath, at having been disappointed in his expectations of having a Prince for a patient.

"It will not avail you to attempt to carry on this deception any longer," said Mr. Styngy. "The conversation with Lionel Wilful was overheard and repeated to me by a gentleman whose word I cannot doubt. You have committed forgery, in affixing the signature of my old friend, Lord Meddle-de-Muddle to a letter, and I could prosecute you for the same, but as in the opinion of the doctor you are insane, and the victim of a delusion, I pity you, and will do my best to restore you to your senses. Doctor I leave the patient in your hands."

The doctor, with great readiness, placed a case he had with him on a chair, and drew therefrom a bottle containing a villainous-looking green mixture and a sort of funnel.

Sam eyed these preparations with great dismay, but when the doctor approached him he shrunk back in the bed, and took refuge beneath the counterpane, from whence he was heard to declare, "That he couldn't and wouldn't take any medicine."

"Gentlemen," said Mr. Styngy, addressing De Bewty and Crocklejack, "you will be so good as to assist the doctor."

They were only too ready. Mr. de Bewty seized one arm, Mr. Crocklejack another, and Professor Tomkini, anxious to revenge his injuries upon somebody, sat upon Sam's legs.

Thus deprived of all power of resistance, Sam was an easy prey for the doctor, who, putting the nozzle of the funnel between Sam's teeth, and pinching his nose firmly with his fingers, poured about a pint of the nastiest stuff he had ever tasted into him.

Sam gurgled and spluttered, and writhed, but all in vain. The doctor was an old hand at curing refractory patients, and not until every drop had been swallowed, and Sam was nearly black in the face, did he remove his fingers from the sufferer's nose, and allow him to breathe again.

The first use he made of his recovered breath was to lift up his voice and howl with rage and anguish. Then seizing the pillow, he hurled it at the doctor, with so good an aim, that that genleman, who was returning the funnel to its case, was knocked to the ground in company with his instruments, and bled himself involuntarily with a lancet.

"Stop him!" said Mr. Styngy, as Sam made frantic efforts to dig up the bolster. "De Bewty, Crocklejack, stop him or he'll do some mischief;"

"I don't care!" yelled Sam, defiantly. "I'll murder the lot, I will! I ain't goin' to be poisoned for nothink!"

And wildly flourishing the bolster round him Sam leaped from the bed, and charged full upon his pale and frightened enemies.

CHAPTER XXII.

IN WHICH HIS IMPERIAL HIGHNESS PRINCE SAM SCARECROW MAKES AN IGNOMINIOUS EXIT FROM CHEETHAM HALL.

THERE is little doubt but that the assailed would have beaten a precipitate and ignominious retreat from the room, had not Sam been between them and the door.

As it was, their escape was cut off. Their only chance of evading the fury of the maniac lay in successful dodging, and really it was wonderful, considering the sedentary nature of their pursuits, what extraordinary activity they displayed.

It must have been many years since Mr. Styngy played at leap-frog, and yet to have seen the way in which he took De Bewty and Crocklejack flying, and landed on his head in an arm-chair beyond, you would have fancied that he was quite fresh from a game of fly-the-garter.

His assistants were not far behind him in point of agility, and if they had been boys of fourteen just let out of school, and playing a game of touch, they could hardly have dodged with more consummate ability.

And certainly their activity was needed, for Sam was furious. His long legs seemed to bear him into all parts of the room at once, the while he whirled the bolster round his head, aiming it at nothing in particular, but bringing some article of furniture to the ground with a crash at every blow.

"Come on!" yelled Sam, as he dealt a mighty blow at Mr. Styngy, and smashed the wash-hand basin instead. "Yah, you cowards! Why don't you stand still and fight fair?"

This was exceedingly good advice, no doubt, from a boy's standard, but the gentlemen advised didn't seem to see it. They would have called for help but they had not breath enough to spare, and as long as the stimulus of fear lasted they ran.

Had it not been for a device of the doctor's, they most probably would have gone on running until exhausted nature could no longer hold out, but that gentleman, with the agility of an elderly monkey, clambered up one of the posts of the solid mahogany bedstead, at the hazard of his neck, and seizing the bell-rope tugged at it with all his might.

Ring-ring — ding-ting — jingle-tingle, went the resounding alarum, startling the servants in the lower regions of Cheetham Hall.

"It's that furrin Prince, a nasty feller, drat him; I wouldn't go, Mary, if I was you. 'Tain't safe for a unprotected female to trust herself with one of 'em."

"I don't mean to, cook," said Mary. "They're all Turks or Mormons, or worse."

"Then I dont go anigh him," said Susan, the second housemaid.

Ring-ting—jingle-jingle—ding-ding!

With increased violence the bell gave out its summons. Cook folded her arms and sat with a grim and resolute expression of countenance, that seemed to defy anything short of an earthquake to move her; while the housemaids tossed their heads and looked scornfully at the swinging clapper of the bell.

Suddenly there was a loud "snap," and the bell ceased to agitate its noisy tongue.

"He's broke the wire!" said the cook.

"We shall have master down here directly," said Mary, who began to feel a little nervous for the consequences of her disobedience.

"Here he is!" exclaimed Susan, starting up affrighted, as the door opened slowly, and gave entrance to the figure of a stout, broad-shouldered, ruddy-faced man, upon whose features there dwelt a smile of the most aggravating simplicity.

"Lawk, it's only Noodles," said Susan, hastily. "I never saw such a man. What do *you* want here, frightenin' people out o' their wits.

"Yes," added the cook. "Drat your imperence. Arter the beer agin, I suppose."

"Ax your pardon, ladies," said the man. "But I thought I'd come in to see if you heard the bell."

"Drat the man," said the cook, tartly. "Do he think we're deaf!"

"How was I to know, ladies? I heard the bell a ringing away like anythink, and I thinks to myself, thinks I—"

"Never mind what you thought," said the cook, cutting him short. "If you're so very anxious to know what the bell's ringing for, you'd better go and see, *we* ain't."

"'Tis ever a dooty and a pleasure to me to obey the gentler sect," replied the man, grinning more than ever. "And if ever I can persuade any nice young female to change her name to Noodles, I'll hev that took out of the married service where she'll promise and wow to obey—I'll do that part myself."

And, with an ineffable grin, Mr. Noodles betook himself slowly upstairs, towards the apartment reserved for his Imperial Highness, the Prince of Japan.

"They be having a bit of a lark," mused Mr. Noodles, as the sound of the stamping of feet, the breaking of crockery, and the frenzied shouts of Sam, fell upon his ears. "A war-dance, most like; or perhaps he's a cannon-ball, and hev took a fancy to master for his supper. Darn all manner of furriners, say I."

With which thoroughly English and patriotic sentiment, Mr. Noodles turned the handle of the

BEFORE TOMMY CODLINGS TOUCHED THE TOWEL THE CANE SWISHED, AND HE LEAPT UP WITH A DOLEFUL HOWL.

door and entered the apartment at a critical moment.

Exhausted nature had given way. Mr. Styngy and his two assistants were lying on the floor in the helpless attitude assumed by Punch's victims when that murderer has slain some half-dozen, and arranged them in a row, while Sam, acting the part of Punch himself, was pounding what little breath their exertions had left them, out of their bodies.

Mr. Noodles paused on the threshhold, and stared at the scene in amazement—at the three gentlemen lying helpless on the ground, and Sam wielding the bolster with all the energy of a thresher handling the flail, and then at the doctor still perched on the top of the bedpost, jerking away at the wire with the desperation of fear.

"Its a game, I do s'pose," thought Mr. Noodles, scratching his head in a meditative manner. "I've seen the young gents in the playground playin' at summut as they called 'baitin' the bear,' and this be main like it. I s'pose I'd better wait a bit till they be done."

And so, leaning complacently against the door-post, with the same broad grin upon his face, Mr. Noodles watched for the 'game' to conclude—and most probably would have waited (as he never was in a hurry) for an hour or two had not the doctor spied him.

"Hi! you sir; hulloa!" yelled the doctor, frantically. "Why don't you go and help your master? Don't you see he's being murdered?"

"Be he? He didn't say so," said Mr. Noodles. "I thowt 'twere a game."

"Go and help him, I tell you. Knock him down, or there'll be murder done."

"But he be knocked down a' ready," said the odd man, thinking that the schoolmaster was alluded to.

"The boy, the boy!" exclaimed the doctor, frantically. "Knock him down I tell you!"

"Why that be t' prince," muttered Mr. Noodles, as he slowly advanced. "If I knock him down I shall ha' my 'ed cut off, and if I don't knock him down master 'll be murdered. What'll I do? I'll hit un as soft as I can, and then p'raps he won't say nowt."

Sam was still pounding away with undiminished energy at the three prostrate bodies of his enemies; but the bolsters, unaccustomed to such rough usage, had split a little at the ends, and at every blow a shower of feathers flew out, covering Mr. Styngy and the assistants, until they looked like some strange species of monstrous birds.

Mr. Noodles, with a considerable amount of misgiving, approached from behind, dexterously caught the bolster as it was raised to deal a blow, snatched it from Sam's grasp, and felled him to the ground.

"Werry sorry, your Royal Highness," said the odd man, as he laid the bolster on Sam and then sat upon it, "werry sorry, I'm sure, if I inconweniences you at all, but dooty's duty."

The odd man was heavy, and all attempts at resistance were fairly crushed out of Sam. He could only kick feebly with one leg, as a sign that the treatment didn't agree with him.

"Have you got him safe, Noodles?" said the doctor.

"Werry safe, sir," replied Noodles. "There ain't more nor a kick and a 'arf in him."

"You're quite sure?"

"Sartin, sir; come and see for yourself."

Reassured by this, though with no small degree of trepidation, the doctor dismounted from his perch, and hastened to raise the fallen schoolmaster.

He was so covered with feathers that the doctor at first addressed several pathetic observations to Mr. Styngy's boots, mistaking them for his head, but he found out the right end at last.

"My dear sir,' said the doctor, "how do you find yourself after the brutal attack?"

"First class in arithmetic," murmured Mr. Styngy, looking wildly around him. "If one bolster makes a bump, how many bruises make an acher?"

"Bless me!" exclaimed the doctor. "His mind is wandering."

"May it please your Imperial Highness," murmured Mr. Styngy again. "Unaccustomed as I am to play with bolsters, nevertheless, it affords me great pleasure to receive your Imperial Highness into my humble dwelling. The best of cats—I've had it from a kitten—let the Prince have the cat-o'-nine-tails."

"His mind is gone," said the doctor, affected in turn. "This is dreadful—and the others seem to be dead. Holloa, there, Mr. de Bewty, Mr. Crocklejack!"

"'Tain't time to get up yet," murmured Crocklejack, faintly, as he rolled over and struggled up into a sitting position. "What a hard bed this is—it hasn't been properly made. I'll—why where am I?"

"Now another one's gone out of his mind," said the doctor in alarm. "Good gracious!—can it be that madness is, as some have said, contagious? Heavens! I—I really begin to feel a little mad myself. Noodles, do you feel at all insane?"

"Not pertikler so, not more 'n usual. I had a pint o' beer for my dinner, sir."

"Here's another," gasped the doctor. "He answers me at random—I'll go for help."

In his agitation he released Mr. Styngy's head, which fell with a sounding bump upon the floor; but, as he reached the door, he was confronted by Mr. Grubbe, behind whom stood two calm matter-of fact-looking policemen.

"My dear sir," said the doctor, nervously, "I am delighted to see you. You could not have arrived more *à propos*."

"Why, what in the name of wonder does this mean?" said Mr. Grubbe, staring aghast at the prostrate forms of Mr. Styngy and his assistant. "Where is the rascally impostor?"

"Do you mean the Prince?"

"Prince!" said Mr. Styngy, scornfully; "I mean the Scarecrow rascal—that companion of young Wilful's—who I believe is at the bottom of all this mischief."

"There he is," said the doctor, pointing to two long thin legs, protruding beyond the bolster, and which were from time to time agitated by a faint convulsive movement.

"Why he'll be smothered!" said Mr. Grubbe. "Come off Noodles."

"Which I will, sir, with pleasure," returned the odd man, rising, "for he's bony even through the bolster."

"Take care," exclaimed the doctor, retreating towards the door, "he's mad."

"Mad?"

"As a March hare," said the doctor. "One of the worst cases I ever encountered. You see the condition to which he has reduced Mr. Styngy and those other gentlemen. I only escaped by a miracle, and Noodles just managed to overpower him after a terrific struggle."

"Which it were frightful," asserted Noodles, who saw a prospect of beer, "and makes a man werry dry."

"Indeed," said Mr. Grubbe, with a peculiar smile, "that alters the case. You are ready to give a certificate to that effect, of course?"

"Quite ready."

"Very good; then we shall have no occasion for you, policemen," Mr. Grubbe went on. "You can't take an insane person into custody on a charge of false pretences."

Mr. Grubbe slipped something that chinked like money into the palm of one of the officers, and they withdrew, having first promised to send a straight-waistcoat for poor Sam's especial benefit.

He was not in much need of it just then. All the fight had been knocked out of him by the pressure of some sixteen stone of odd man, and so possibly thought Mr Grubbe as he looked at him.

"Mad is he?" muttered that gentleman to himself. "No more mad than I am. But if the doctor will only sign a certificate that will shut him up for a year or so in a lunatic asylum, it will punish him sufficiently for the tricks he and that young whelp Wilful dared to play upon me. Mad, eh? Yes, it is a capital idea, and could not have fallen out better."

* * * * * * *

Mr. Grubbe lost no time in effecting his purpose—in less than half an hour the certificate was signed, the beadle sent for, and the unlucky Sam on his way to become an inmate for an indefinite period of a pauper lunatic asylum.

CHAPTER XXIII.

THE BULLY AND HIS VICTIM—LIONEL ONCE MORE TO THE RESCUE.

IT must not be supposed that "Fast Fred," or "Frederick Flashaway, Esq."—as he preferred to be addressed in all written communications, as an acknowledgment of his claims to manhood—had either forgotten or forgiven how Lionel had checked his bullying and exposed his cowardice.

For the bully is always a coward, and seldom dares to act directly or alone, preferring to get his dirty work done by means of his satellites and toadies, with which creatures bullies are generally well infested.

Flashaway had his; for though he was overbearing and violent—all bullies are—he was the son of a wealthy baronet, a member of Parliament for Nobsham, to whom Mr. Styngy was distantly related.

Thus "Fast Fred" was a personage of no small importance. The heir to a baronetcy, and a kind of relation of the head-master's, he was allowed more licence than fell to the lot of the other pupils.

He had plenty of money, too; and now and then, with an ostentatious liberality, he would treat his own especial toadies to an excursion, from which, it must be said, they generally returned with pallid faces, aching heads, and persons smelling strongly of cigar smoke, from which it may be inferred that they had taken something besides fresh air into their systems.

Be that as it may, these jaunts and the heroes of them were regarded with a kind of fearful awe by the less favoured youngsters, by whom Flashaway and his chums were looked upon with reverence, as mortals to whom the mysterious pleasure of smoking was revealed, and who knew what gin-and-water and champagne tasted like.

Sometimes, too, Flashaway had been known to extend his invitation to one of the juniors, but the result in these instances did not seem to be so satisfactory.

Tommy Codlings had been one of those so highly favoured by the upper form boys. He started off pursued by the envy of his companions, he returned about tea-time, red hot, dusty, and so tired that he could hardly drag one leg before the other.

"Hullo, here's Codlings come back," shouted one. "Now we shall know all about it. What did they treat you to, Tommy?"

"Did you have any champagne?" demanded another queriest.

"Did you smoke, Codlings?"

"Don't you see him smoking now," put in a third youthful joker.

"Some water," was all the unfortunate Tommy could feebly gasp, and as he began to turn round in an alarming manner and clutch at the boys nearest him, some water was fetched, and Tommy supported to a seat, where he told his doleful story—

"They're the meanest set of beggars out; I only wish I was big enough to pitch into that Flashaway. I'd show him something."

"What did he do then, Tommy. Didn't he stand treat. Didn't you have a ride?"

"Yes, and a walk too," growled Tommy. "They drove out about eight or nine miles in their dashed trap, when Flashaway dropped the whip accidentally—I thought he did—and asked me to get out and go back for it. I did, and handed it up; but just as I was going to get in again, he drove on, and left me lying on my back in the road."

"What a shame; but perhaps it was an accident, Tommy?"

"Was it," grumbled the unlucky Codlings. "Why didn't they wait for me then?"

"Didn't they?"

"No they didn't," returned Tommy, with a sour and discontented expression of feature. "I ran after 'em till I was tired out, asking 'em to stop, but all that brute Flashaway said was that I was too heavy for the trap, and wished me a pleasant walk back."

"And did you have a nice walk, Tommy?"

"Did I!" said Tommy, indignantly. "You try it, and see how you like it. Ten miles along a hot dusty road, after I'd been fagging all the morning at cricket. Try it."

"Poor old Tommy. It's a confounded shame!" murmured the sympathisers; but his fate did not prevent others from hankering after "the flesh pots of Egypt," and being treated as badly, or even worse, than Tommy Codlings.

One unlucky youth was brought back from one of these excursions hopelessly inebriated, in consequence of having imbibed an unknown quantity of warm porter and gin, and having attempted to smoke a long clay pipe. He was ill for a week, and received at the expiration of that time a handsome flogging from Mr. Styngy for going out of bounds without permission.

My readers will see that Lionel had made himself an enemy, who had both the power and the will to annoy him.

Mr. Styngy, to do him justice, always discouraged any attempt on the part of the older boys to oppress the younger; but it was impossible to detect every case of the kind, and, until the coming of my hero, "grin and bear it" had been the rule.

The arrival of his Imperial Highness, the Japanese Prince, alias Sam Scarecrow, and the subsequent discovery of his identity, diverted Flashaway's attention from his youthful foe for the time; but as soon as the unfortunate Sam had departed in safe custody for the pauper lunatic asylum, and the school was restored to its usual condition the bully began to lay his plans.

Regarding Sam, Lionel's mind was quite at ease. Mr. Styngy had told him that the unlucky personator of Royalty would not be punished for what he had done, but placed in safe hands, whereby Lionel understood that he would be sent back to Hampstead.

Of how my hero was mistaken, and the further scrapes and misadventures into which Sam managed to get, I shall have more to tell in the future chapters of this true history.

For the present, I must confine myself to Lionel, from whom I have already wandered too much.

Two or three mornings after Sam's ignominious departure from Cheetham Hall, in the custody of the beadle, the sonorous clang of the getting up bell awoke the echoes in the long corridor and the boys in the dormitories.

"Ugh!" grunted Tommy Codlings, as the noisy summons aroused him from a dream of a paradise in which all the fountains were ginger beer, all the streams iced lemonade, and the fruits of the earth, almond-rock, three-cornered puffs, and Bath buns. "Ugh! Blow that bell! I believe they ring it earlier every morning on purpose."

"At that rate we shall have to get up the day before yesterday to be in time for this morning's lessons," said Charlie. "Hallo! there's the big fellows calling for fags. Whose turn is it?"

"I'm one, I suppose," grumbled Codlings. "I'm always in it, I am. I never get a rest."

"Hurry up, then, Tommy, or you'll get something that will wake you up effectually. Flashaway's wild this morning, I can tell, by the sound of his voice. Now then, Smalls junior, you're the other fag, make haste and turn out."

"Oh no I ain't, come now," retorted Smalls junior, who was an undersized, dough-coloured boy, with an expression of countenance that seemed to indicate that the wearer was suffering from a perpetual stomach ache.

"Well, who is then?" shouted Charlie Drummond.

"The new fellow, of course. I heard Flashaway tell him the other day that he was to be his fag."

"Did you?" said Lionel, coolly. "Then perhaps you heard me tell him that I shouldn't be anything of the sort?"

"Oh, that's nothing. That was only cheek. He said you were to be his fag, and you've got to do it."

For all answer Lionel gave a short, contemptuous laugh, and began to whistle.

"I say, you'd better go," said Smalls, who trembled for his own safety, as he heard the harsh voice of Flashaway shouting down the corridor.

"Go yourself," said Lionel. "I told him I shouldn't fag for him or any one else—and I mean it."

Tommy Codlings had, by this time, scrambled through his dressing, and bolted into the corridor, where he was met by the great Flashaway himself, habited in a gorgeous crimson dressing-gown.

"Take that, you lazy young hound," said the bully, bestowing a slap of the first magnitude upon the unlucky Codlings's head. "Keeping me standing here all the morning for my hot water. Where's the other fag?"

"Smalls won't come," replied Tommy, who had a mortal hatred of that young gentleman, which sentiment was fully reciprocated.

"Oh, Smalls won't come—won't he?" replied Flashaway, and, disappearing into his own apartment, he returned with a pliant gutta-percha riding whip, a taste of which he gave first to Tommy Codlings, bidding him make haste with the hot water, and then went in search of the refractory Smalls.

The appearance of the bully in the dormitory of the youngsters made just such a consternation as that of a kite in a poultry yard will do, and Smalls, who was in the middle of the room, with one leg in his trowsers, uttered a preliminary howl of dismay, well knowing what was coming.

Flashaway wanted no words—his victim was in a favourable position—he could not run away, for he had one leg in his trowsers and his shirt was short.

There was a swishing sound, a smart crack, and then a yell of pain from Smalls, who tried to run, tripped himself up with his braces, and fell, face downwards, on the floor.

The position was more favourable than ever. Flashaway, who was never happier than when torturing some one who could not retaliate, plied the whip with calculating cruelty; but he had not given half-a-dozen strokes, when the weapon was wrenched out of his hand, and Lionel stepped in between him and his writhing victim.

CHAPTER XXIV.

LIONEL TRIUMPHS OVER THE BULLY—TOMMY CODLINGS GETS INTO TROUBLE AGAIN, AND THEREBY OVERHEARS A VERY INTERESTING CONVERSATION.

"OH! it's you again, is it?" said Fast Fred, between his set teeth, while his face flushed into a colour that rivalled the crimson hue of his dressing-gown.

"Yes, it's me again, Mr. Bully Flashaway," retorted Lionel, politely, "at your service."

He kept a wary eye though upon his foe, for he knew what an advantage Flashaway had in weight and strength, and was fully aware that if he only screwed his courage up to the striking point, and took Lionel unawares, a chance blow might give the victory to the bully.

Fast Fred was, however, by no means inclined to come to blows.

Lionel had cowed him.

But, on the other hand, he saw that the other boys, gathered round at a respectful distance, were whispering and chuckling in high glee at this, his second discomfiture by the new fellow.

If he put up with this, good-bye to his supremacy in the school.

"Look here, young Wilful," he said, trying to control his voice, though he was trembling with passion, "you're a jolly sight too cheeky. I put up with it once before because you're a new fellow; but I shan't stand any more of it. Give me that whip."

"And look *you* here, Flashaway," returned Lionel, "as I've told you before, you're a great deal too much of a bully. You drink, and smoke, and swear, and think yourself a man because you've got a moustache coming; but it don't make you a man to ape a man's vices, and, I tell you straight, you're only a hobbledehoy, and a poor one at that."

A very audible laugh passed round as Lionel delivered himself of this emphatic opinion.

Flashaway turned from red to white, and white to red, in a breath, clenched his fists, and scowled; but made no movement to strike.

Lionel was ready for him if he had.

Just then plump Tommy Codlings looked into the dormitory, holding a jug of warm water in his hand.

"I say, Flashaway, here's your water, and a precious hard job I had to get it. Cook says she won't let us have any more."

"You needn't trouble yourself about it, Tommy," said Lionel, cheerfully; "Flashaway's getting his hot water here."

It does not take much to make a schoolboy laugh under such circumstances, and a perfect roar went up at the mild little joke of my hero.

Flashaway ground his teeth audibly, and almost made up his mind to hit Lionel. He was big enough and strong enough to have ensured the victory, but his heart was too small; if he could have shot down Lionel where he stood, or have stabbed him safely, he would have done it at that moment.

Lionel stood quietly tapping the floor with the whip, but keeping a steady watch upon the shifty eyes of his adversary.

He hoped that the bully would bring matters to an issue, for his fingers tingled with the desire to thrash him soundly; but as he hoped to find a better time and place wherein to perform that operation, Lionel confined himself to words.

"Now, Flashaway," he said again, with no attempt to conceal the scorn he felt for the hulking bully; "you had better go. This room is not big enough for you and me, and besides, your shaving water is getting cold."

Here Tommy Coldings, who still stood at the door, burst into a delighted chuckle, and even Smalls junior varied the howling, which he had continued since he received his thrashing, with a spasmodic smile.

That was a little too much to bear. With a profane oath Flashaway rolled Smalls junior over by a kick, and striding to the door, bestowed a box upon the unlucky Tommy Codlings right ear, which upset him in company with the hot water, and left my hero master of the situation.

He shut the door with a bang, that resounded along the corridors, but not in time to shut out the derisive cheer which followed his ignominious exit.

"My stars, Lionel," said Charlie Drummond, admiringly; "you're a plucky fellow and no mistake!"

"Nonsense! I tell you, Charlie, the fellow's a cur. He'd turn tail and bolt from you or any one else who showed fight to him."

"But look at his age! Why, I thought once or twice that he was going to hit you, and I got the water jug ready to shy at him."

"There wouldn't have been any need of that, my boy, as you'll see before long. I've made up my mind to give him a thrashing in a fair stand up fight, and I'll do it, lad!"

"You'll never do that, Lionel. Don't you remember—oh, you weren't here though—but Jabez Hunker told us how one day when Flashaway was out he thrashed three labourers! Men, you know."

"Then Jabez Hunker told a lie, that's all," was Lionel's answer; "and now you fellows cut away and dress, for there goes second bell."

In the excitement of the scene between Lionel and the bully, the boys of No. 3 Dormitory had forgotten the stringent regulations that existed regarding punctuality, and were remorselessly booked for punishment by Mr. Crocklejack as they limped in to prayers.

The unfortunate Tommy Codlings was rejected altogether, as presenting a totally unfit appearance for that pious exercise.

"What do you mean by it, sir?" demanded Mr. Crocklejack, sternly.

"Mean by what, sir?" said Tommy, who was quite unconscious that his toilette—though perhaps a little negligé, was not good enough for a promenade in the fashionable parks.

"You haven't even washed yourself," Mr. Crocklejack said, regarding the defaulting Tommy with a look of horror. "Your hair is positively disgraceful, your braces are hanging down, and you've only got one boot on."

And catching Tommy by one ear, the tutor led him into the corridor, and dismissed him with a sound box upon his already red-hot ear, and a faithful promise of a sound thrashing to follow.

With a sensation in his head as of several thousand bells jangling themselves cracked therein, poor Tommy slowly bent his way towards the dormitory, there to rectify the omissions of his toilet.

"Blow old Crocklejack! and everlastingly blow that bully Flashaway!" muttered Tommy Codlings, savagely. "What did they want to go and both pick out the same ear for? It feels as if it had been flayed, and then boiled, and afterwards fried a little."

And the injured Tommy tenderly handled the smarting organ with the tips of his fingers, as if he feared that it would come off if touched too roughly.

His sense of hearing, though, was in no way impaired, for as he was about to enter the dormitory he distinctly heard the sound of Flashaway's unpleasant voice proceeding from that gentleman's own apartment.

Hullo!" thought Tommy, "there's bully Fred turned back as well as me, or has he got excused from prayers. Styngy is too strict for that, though. I'll listen a bit."

Listening is scarcely defensible upon any grounds, but Tommy Codling's morality, like his toilet, was not strictly irreproachable, and without the least compunction he crept on tiptoe along the corridor, and applied his eye to the keyhole of Flashaway's room.

"I never saw such a mean chap," thought Tommy, "he's left the key in, and I can't see a bit. Never mind, I can hear though. Hullo, what's that!"

Flashaway was speaking, and Tommy just caught the concluding part of the sentence, which was—

"I tell you, Hunker, if I could, I'd kill him!"

"It's nonsense to talk like that," said the slow quiet voice of Jabez Hunker. "You can serve him out well enough without going as far as that."

"I wonder if he means me," thought Tommy, as a cold perspiration broke out all over him. "Because I didn't get his water in time this morning."

"Tell me how," Tommy heard the bully say, eagerly; "and you shall have that ring of mine—that one you were admiring yesterday."

"It's a bargain," said Hunker. "And I'll help you all the more readily, because I hate the youngster myself. But first, how do you want him served out?"

"I should like to have him cut in pieces, or flayed alive!" exclaimed Flashaway, fiercely.

"Yes, yes. I daresay, but you can't have that, you know," said Jabez, in the same slow deliberate tone. "But as far as a good thrashing goes, one that will keep every bone in his skin sore and aching for a week, how will that do?"

"That will do to begin with," responded Flashaway, "but who's to do it? I would myself, but you know, Hunker, it would be called cowardly if a sixth form fellow pitched into a chap of his size to that extent."

"Of course it would," replied Jabez, turning round to conceal the contempt which even he could not help feeling for Flashaway. "But if there is no one in the school, there are plenty outside."

"Whom do you mean?"

"Why some of those overgrown louts, who are always hanging about the farms, fellows with fists like legs of mutton, and hides as thick as an ox's. Three or four of them, for a shilling a piece, would give Master Lionel a thrashing that he wouldn't get over in a fortnight."

"But can it be managed so that there would be no fear of discovery?" said the bully, eagerly. "Suppose one of the louts should split."

"No fear of that," said Hunker. "Leave all that to me. Is it a bargain?"

"Done," said Flashaway. "Only let me see the young cub brought home here, black and blue, and aching in every limb, and the ring's yours, Jabez. When can you manage it?"

"Next half-holiday—that's the day after to-morrow. What's that at the door?"

A sound as if something heavy had fallen against it startled the two conspirators. They turned pale, as their guilty faces looked at each other, and then they made a simultaneous rush for the door.

CHAPTER XXV.

TOMMY CODLINGS FINDS HIMSELF IN HOT WATER AGAIN.

IT was the ever-unfortunate Tommy, who, in the endeavour to get his ear in a more convenient position with regard to the keyhole, had brought the back of his head into violent contact with the handle of the door.

His first thought was to run for it; but Tommy's thoughts were like his movements, slow, and before the idea of flight had fairly entered his mind, the door flew open and the Philistines were upon him.

As a matter of course his tortured ear was the part picked out for punishment.

First Flashaway boxed it, Hunker followed suit, and then the former gentleman led him, still keeping a hold upon the tender organ, into the room.

"Oh, lor!" howled poor Tommy. "Don't. It'll come off."

"All the better, you spying young rascal. What do you mean by coming listening at my door, eh?"

"I wasn't," said Tommy. "Mr. Crocklejack wouldn't let me into prayers, because, he said, I wasn't tidy enough, and so I came to see if you wanted anything. You told me to always when I wasn't at lessons."

This was true.

Tommy's wits were sharpened by desperation, or he never would have been able to make such an excuse.

Flashaway seemed relieved, and relaxed his hold of his captive's ear, which Codlings immediately felt himself to make sure that it was still in its place.

WHEN FRED. FLASHAWAY AND JABEZ HUNKER CRAWLED OUT OF THE POND THEY PRESENTED AN ABJECT SPECTACLE.

No. 6.

"You're sure you weren't listening, then?" said Flashaway.

"Of course I wasn't," returned Tommy, with an injured air.

"What was that noise at the door, then?" demanded Jabez Hunker, whose suspicious nature was not yet fully satisfied.

"I knocked," said Tommy.

"People don't generally knock at the handle of a door," Jabez went on, but Flashaway interrupted.

"Oh, it's all right, Hunker. What should he be listening for? Besides, he'd be afraid, he knows I'd flay him alive if I caught him at anything of the kind."

"I know you'd like to," thought Tommy; but he made no audible comment beyond a sniff.

"Then let the cub go," said Hunker.

"Don't you want me to do anything, sir?" said Tommy.

"No—yet stay a minute," said Flashaway, and then he whispered something to Hunker which Tommy could not catch.

Jabez shook his head, and replied in the same low voice to Flashaway.

This time, however, Tommy caught the words "wouldn't be safe."

"Oh, it wouldn't be safe, wouldn't it?" thought Tommy, with a chuckle, as he received his dismissal and left the presence of the bully and his toady. "Perhaps it won't be safe for you, my jokers, when I tell Wilful what I know."

And then and there in the corridor Master Codlings executed a slow and solemn dance of defiance opposite Flashaway's door, and then re-entering the dormitory proceeded to make up the deficiencies of his toilet.

"Let me see," thought Tommy, after he had washed his face and hands and proceeded to dress himself. "Shall I get a birching or only be caned over my clothes. Caned I fancy, for I haven't been up for punishment lately. I'll chance it."

So saying, Master Codlings selected a couple of the driest towels, and carefully folding them, placed them over those portions of his anatomy most likely to be visited by the stinging cane, and then with considerable difficulty managed to button his waistcoat and jacket.

"What a nuisance it is that the tailor always makes my clothes so tight," thought Tommy, as an uncomfortable sensation of suffocation stole over him in consequence of being over-buttoned; "I fancy they must know that a whacking hurts more when a chap's clothes fit him too much, and so they do it on purpose. I hope the towels don't show through."

And Tommy nearly gave himself a fit of apoplexy in the endeavour to get a peep over his shoulders. Failing in the attempt, he went down to breakfast, presenting as nearly the appearance of a well-stuffed sofa-cushion as it is possible for a human being to do.

Master Codlings' appetite was always a good one. This morning it happened to be especially sharp, and he sniffed the fragrance of the aromatic coffee, and bestowed a hungry—not to say wolf-like—glare upon the tall piles of bread and butter.

Mr. Crocklejack growled at him, and Mr. Styngy gave him a glance which meant two dozen at the least; but Tommy heeded them not; he had no eyes for anything but breakfast.

He took his accustomed seat next to Lionel, bestowed upon him a wink full of meaning, and took a huge bite of bread and butter.

Tommy swallowed it and felt uncomfortable; then he took another bite, swallowed that, and felt worse. His third mouthful refused to go down at all, and the awful conviction burst upon Tommy that he was buttoned up too tightly.

"Here's a go," he thought, as he glanced ruefully at the tempting meal before him; "If I try to eat I shall choke, and if I unbutton, the towels will drop down. What on earth shall I do?"

The stacks of bread and butter were disappearing with magical celerity. Another five minutes and there would be none left. Tommy made a desperate effort and gulped down the obdurate mouthful; as he did so a button flew off.

"Oh, dear!" thought the unfortunate Tommy; "there goes the bottom one! By the time I get through the slice they'd all be off, and I should be found out."

With a groan he resigned the idea, and, leaning back in the chair, gazed despairingly at the unfinished slices.

"What's the matter, old fellow?" whispered Lionel. "Ain't you well?"

"Never felt better in my life," moaned Tommy.

"Why don't you eat your breakfast, then? Time's almost up. Have you lost your appetite?"

"I feel like a cannibal," responded Tommy.

"Then pitch in, or you won't have time to get any more."

"I can't," whispered Tommy, ruefully. "*It's the buttons!*"

Before Lionel had time to ask what buttons could have to do with his friend's loss of appetite, Mr. Crocklejack gave the signal for departure for the class-room. Tommy thought for a moment of taking his bread-and-butter with him, but the impossibility of getting it into any of his pockets stayed him.

Mr. Crocklejack stood at the door, and, as the offenders of the morning passed him, he read out their names and allotted the punishments.

All escaped with a slight infliction, only Tommy Codlings was condemned to pay a visit in private to Mr. Styngy's study.

"I hear a very bad account of you, Codlings," said that gentleman, as he opened a drawer and felt in it, the guilty Tommy knew too well for what.

"I—I'll never do it any more, sir," faltered the culprit. "It—it was quite an accident."

"It always is an accident in these cases," said Mr. Styngy, in a sweet voice. "Consider, if you please, that it is quite by accident that I give you this dozen. Hold out your hand, Codlings."

Horror and dismay filled unlucky Tommy's mind. He was to be caned on the hands, then, and not on the back. All his precautions were useless, and he had lost his breakfast for nothing.

There was only one course to pursue though, and that was to obey. He held out his hands, one after the other, and took his dozen in anything but a martyr-like manner, for Tommy's hands were plump and tender.

He turned to go, and was groping his way, with tear-blinded eyes, towards the door, when Mr. Styngy's soft persuasive voice called him back.

"Ye—ye—yes, sir?" sobbed Tommy.

"Come here, Codlings."

Codlings obeyed, wondering what it was for.

"Turn round, my boy."

Tommy turned slowly round, and a cold chill crept down his back, just as if the towels he bore had been dipped in iced water.

Then Mr. Styngy prodded him gently from the nape of his neck to the base of his spine, and at the conclusion of the examination said, in the same mild voice—

"Take off your jacket, Codlings."

"Oh, lor," thought Tommy, "it's all over. He's found me out."

Slowly and reluctantly Tommy "peeled," and disclosed the armour that had been intended to protect him from the head-master's vengeance.

"I thought so," said the schoolmaster. "For the attempt to evade just punishment, Codlings, I am reluctantly compelled to flog you again. Turn your back to me and pick up those towels."

Tommy turned and stooped, but before his fingers touched the towel the cane swished through the air, and the culprit leapt up with a doleful howl.

"Try again, Codlings," said Mr. Styngy, sweetly.

Codlings did try again with the same result, for exactly four-and-twenty times, then, and not till then, did the head-master suffer him to resume his jacket and waistcoat, and leave the study, sore and furious.

"Blow him! Blow everybody! Blow anybody!" sobbed Tommy. "It's all that beggar Flashaway's fault, but Lionel will pay him out for it, I know, when I tell him."

And, indeed, my hero did.

CHAPTER XXVI.

OWING TO A SLIGHT DIFFERENCE OF OPINION ON A MATTER OF ENGLISH HISTORY, HIS IMPERIAL HIGHNESS SAM SCARECROW MAKES HIS ESCAPE.

THE beadle of Nobsham was a man proud of his office, of the importance of which he held an exaggerated idea—not clearly defined it is true, yet ranking himself somehow with the Chief Commissioner of Police, the Lord Mayor, and the Archbishop of Canterbury.

The race of the Dogberries and Verges is not yet extinct in the fair realms of England.

Sam Scarecrow was for him a prize, and his arrest an event of importance in his official career.

It was nothing new to him to have a boy in custody; in fact, he generally apprehended one or two every week to keep his official dignity up and his official hand in.

He had, indeed, once tried to "comprehend an vagrom man," a sturdy Irish agriculturist, but as the result was that he had been confined to his bed-room for three weeks afterwards, he wisely limited his exertions to the rising generation.

Boys were safe prey.

But Sam was an exception.

The beadle had heard that he claimed to be a prince, and that very claim raised the prisoner in his estimation.

"There must be summat in it," thought the beadle, as he eyed poor Sam, "or they wouldn't have made such a fuss. There's more in this than meets the heye. I'll just step over to Mr. Swiller's and have a pint over it afore I take him to the Board."

Mr. Swiller was the landlord of the "Nobsham Arms Hotel," and to that hostelry Mr. Bumpshus proceeded straightway.

"Mornin', Mr. Bumpshus; mornin', sir," saluted the landlord. "Another o' the young wagabones, eh? I wonder you stands it; if you wasn't a strong man, Mr. Bumpshus, your 'ealth would break down under the continual strain. I knows it would."

"Hush!" said the beadle, with an air of mystery. "This aint no or'nary offence, Mr. Swiller. A prisoner of State, Mr. Swiller."

The landlord opened his eyes and stared at Sam.

He did not exactly understand what a prisoner of State was; but that was of no consequence.

"You don't mean to say so? Come in, Mr. Bumpshus: come in, sir. There's a nice little party in the parlour."

The beadle shook his head, and grew more mysterious than ever.

"I dursn't, Mr. Swiller; I dursn't. State secrets ain't to be talked of, nor looked upon by common he..es. This is a Tower affair."

"Ah!" said Mr. Swiller, nodding his head gravely, though he understood still less what was meant by a "Tower affair" than what was the dread importance of a "State prisoner."

"A Tower of London affair," the beadle went on, "and let me tell you, Mr. Swiller, that if this had 'appened a few years ago, that there prisoner would have 'ad his 'ed cut off, as sure as I'm goin' to have a pint of your old stingo."

Mr. Swiller took the hint, and fetched the "old stingo," leading the way then, in a fit of abstraction no doubt, into the parlour, whither the beadle and Sam followed him.

Mr. Bumpshus returned with a grave and preoccupied air the salutation of the company in the parlour, and fencing his prisoner into a corner with his chair, laid upon the table the order signed by the doctors, and his staff of office, as if they were cabalistic spells capable of preventing any attempt at an escape.

"Your 'elth Mr. Swiller, and gen'lemen," said the beadle, taking his first sip. "Ah, it's a strange world."

The company had already been informed by sundry mysterious nods, winks, and whispers that the beadle had in custody a prisoner of no ordinary importance, and suspending their own conversation, which concerned the crops, they listened with breathless interest to the oracular utterances of Mr. Bumpshus.

"Ah," the beadle went on, after a pause, during which he finished the "stingo." "It's a strange world, as I were a sayin', and if every one had their rights, some one in this room wouldn't be sittin' where he is."

"That's true enough, Mr. Bumpshus," said the landlord. "If your merits had their doo, you'd be up in London, at this blessed minnit. I won't say percisely wheer, but put it some'ere up Guildhall way."

"No, no, Mr. Swiller, you're too partial, you air indeed; but I worn't alludin' to myself, but to—"

Here the beadle paused significantly, and pointed with his thumb over his left shoulder, to Sam.

The eyes of the company were turned upon Sam, as if they had been set going simultaneously by machinery.

"Ah! Him!" said the beadle. "I could tell you somethin' as would make you stare, only as Mr. Swiller knows, it's a State secret, and musn't be told, no not for untold gold."

Here Mr. Bumpshus thoughtfully looked into the empty measure. The landlord took the hint and the pot, returning with it in something less than ten seconds for fear of losing a scrap of the conversation.

"You remember, Mr. Swiller," said the beadle, after he had again refreshed himself; "when George the Three had his 'ed took off by Cornwall becos he wouldn't sign Magna Charta."

Mr. Swiller nodded to comply that he had a perfect recollection of the historical fact.

"That were in fourteen ninety three, worn't it?"

"Fourteen ninety four, I think," said Mr. Swiller.

"Oh, perhaps it were. Say fourteen ninety four. Well, arter George's 'ed were off, Cornwall—"

"It was Cromwell," here interrupted a solemn-faced little man, who occupied the important post of parish clerk. "And it wasn't in fourteen ninety four at all, and—"

"Or—der," roared Mr. Swiller, bringing his fist down upon the table with an emphatic bang. "I'm ashamed of you, Parsons, interrupting a man like Mr. Bumpshus."

"Oh, never mind him," said the beadle, bestowing a contemptuous glance upon the parish clerk.

"But—" began Mr. Parsons.

"Or—der," roared Mr. Swiller, with a more emphatic thump than before, and the clerk subsided into an inarticulate murmur of protest against the beadle's history.

"Well," as I was sayin', afore that person interrupted me, the beadle went on, "arter George's 'ed were cut off, Cromwell he made a law forbiddin any of the said George's ancestors comin into Hingland, or if they did *their* 'eds was to be took off immediate. Well, gen'lemen, from fourteen-ninety-five till the day afore yesterday, none on 'em did come back."

"For a very good reason" said the parish clerk, with a short laugh.

"And what was that, Mr. Parsons?" demanded the beadle, sternly.

"Because there wasn't any of 'em," retorted the

parish clerk. "George never had his 'ed cut off, it was Charles; and that wasn't because he wouldn't sign Magna Charta—that wasn't invented then—but because he hacked up Fair Rosamond, who was Wat Tyler's darter, the Mayor of Bethnal Green. There now!"

"There's history for you!" sneered the beadle, contemptuously.

"Ah! There's history; you find better if you can," said the excited Mr. Parsons; "you and your George's, indeed!"

"Parsons," said the beadle, "you is a hignorant bass!"

"Bumpshus," retorted the parish clerk, "you're another!"

"Parsons," said the beadle, "if it weren't that I respect the lor, and therefore am forbid any hacts of wiolence, I'd pull your hugly nose."

"You daren't do it!" exclaimed the excited little man. "You're afraid! Who hid himself behind the haystack when he was wanted to go arter the baker who stole Farmer Green's chickens?"

"Swiller," said the beadle, turning very pale; "hold me back, or I shall do that man a mischief! I don't want to sile my 'ands——"

"I don't mind silin' mine a bit!" said the angry Mr. Parsons, and, before any one could interfere, he rushed forward, and bestowed a blow upon the extremity of Mr. Bumpshus's nose that seemed to spread it all over his face.

The beadle uttered a howl of anguish, and clutching his assailant by the ear with his left hand, hammered wildly at him with his right; while the little clerk, nothing daunted, made good play upon what the "Fancy" term the "conk" of his opponent.

The company stood aghast for a moment, and then with one accord rushed upon the combatants and dragged them asunder—Mr. Bumpshus retaining in his grasp a goodly portion of the parish clerk's hair.

"I'll—I'll murder him!" gasped the beadle. "Let me go, Swiller."

"No, no, Mr. Bumpshus! for 'evin's sake be calm, sir; think of your posishun, Mr. Bumpshus!"

"Yes, that's jest what I do think on," said the beadle, wrathfully. "Look at my nose. How on earth shall I be able to go afore the Board with the—— Why, *where's the pris'ner?*"

The chair that Sam had occupied was vacant. That young gentleman had seized his opportunity; and the "State prisoner" had, in vulgar parlance, bolted!

CHAPTER XXVII.

IN WHICH TOMMY CODLINGS HAS ANOTHER SLICE OF HIS OWN SPECIAL LUCK—STRONGLY FLAVOURED.

THE dastardly plot which Flashaway had conceived, and intended to carry out upon Lionel, caused that young gentleman far less alarm than it did to Tommy Codlings as the time drew near.

Poor Tommy had been so long under the influence of the merciless bully that it was not easy for him to get rid of his dread at so short a notice.

At every available opportunity Tommy would, at the imminent risk of drawing some punishment upon him, whisper some caution or counsel to Lionel, which pieces of sage advice my hero received with a careless nod.

He had already decided in his own mind how to act.

For about the twentieth time Tommy slipped from his seat, and dodging under the desk, reached Lionel, who was calmly solving a problem in Algebra after the approved method—

"If $xy + 22 =$ Oh! what the dickens is that? and my hero drew his right leg sharply up, and for a good reason. Tommy Codlings had run a pin into it for the purpose of attracting his attention.

"Wilful!" Mr. Crocklejack called out, severely; "talking again in class. The next time you shall have a heavy imposition."

"Something, sir," began Lionel—

"Nothing, sir," interrupted Mr. Crocklejack, severely. "If I hear another word from you until you are requested to speak, I shall report you for punishment to Mr. Styngy."

"It's all very fine," muttered Lonel; "but I should like to know what that was pricking my leg?"

He would have stooped, but he saw that the tutor was keeping a vicious eye upon him, for Mr. Crocklejack had borne him a grudge ever since the discovery of the counterfeit Japanese Prince.

Just then though the mystery was solved by a husky whisper that came from underneath the desk in the well-known accents of Tommy Codlings.

"I say, Wil—ful."

"Oh, it's you, is it?" replied Lionel, in the same low voice. "Confound you, Tommy. Did you run that pin into my leg."

"Only just to let you know I was here. Did it hurt?"

"Did it hurt?" repeated my hero. "I should think it did, and if anyone else but you had done it, I'd warm him after school. What's the matter?"

"Oh, about that affair. You know."

"What, Flashaway?"

"S-s-sh, not so loud," whispered Tommy, alarmed at the very mention of the name. "Some one'll hear you."

"Well, why the dickens don't you wait till class is over?"

"But I say, is it all right?"

"All right—of course it is," replied Lionel. "Cut away and get back to your seat, or we shall both be caught, and the game spoilt."

This was so true that it quite overcame even Tommy's insatiable appetite for knowing whether the affair was "all right," and he turned to crawl back to his own seat, which he would have probably reached unperceived, but for the greediness of Smalls junior.

That covetuous young man had witnessed the loss of a peculiarly valuable species of marble by a boy seated a couple of yards away. The said marble had passed through a hole in the pocket that confined it, meandered gracefully down the trousers-leg, and rolled slowly down an incline in the boards till it found a resting place near the seat of Smalls junior.

It was then that that the evil genius of covetousness seized upon him. He had a fine collection of marbles, but not one of this particular kind, and he resolved to have that marble or be caned in the attempt. Smalls stooped down beneath the desk, crawled along the floor, and had just reached the coveted prize, when the head of Tommy Codlings came into violent contact with his own little pug nose.

He uttered a howl—he couldn't have helped it if death had been the penalty—and dropped the marble to lay hold of the injured organ of smell. The combined noises attracted Mr. Crocklejack's attention. He took two strides to the spot, stooped, and then much as a periwinkle is extracted from its shelly lair, drew forth from underneath the desk the wriggling form of Smalls junior and the ever unfortunate Tommy Codlings.

"This is pretty conduct in class," began Mr. Crocklejack, keeping a tight hold with either hand upon an ear of each of the culprits. "What were you doing on the floor then, Codlings and Smalls?"

Smalls junior opened the ball with a whine, of course. He never did anything else when punishment threatened him.

"Oh, if you please, sir, it was the other boy, it was, indeed, sir."

Mr. Crocklejack looked at Tommy, who, with his hands deep in his trousers pocket, was calmly awaiting the punishment which he knew would follow

He was so used to it, indeed, that a day without a caning or a heavy imposition would have been a startling novelty.

"Codlings," said the tutor, "you hear Smalls junior? He says that you put him under the desk?"

"It's a lie. Oh!"

"How dare you use such language?" said the tutor, giving Tommy's ear a pinch, that seemed to turn it red-hot on the instant. "A simple denial would have been quite sufficient."

"That was the simplest I could think of, sir."

"A—hem," coughed Mr. Crocklejack, and then he twisted the flabby ear of Smalls junior by way of variety. "I mean, Codlings, that you need not have been so concisely abrupt in your denial. Now, once more, will you tell me why you were under the desk instead of in your proper place?"

"I—I—I was only looking for something I dropped, sir," stammered Smalls junior.

"If you please, sir," here interposed the original loser of the marble, "he was looking for something I dropped. Here it is, sir. He was going to keep it, sir. He always does."

"Very well, Johnson, playing at marbles in school-hours. I shall report you. Now, Codlings, what have you to say? Why were you on the floor?"

"I—er—only for a little change of air, sir," replied Tommy, who was too bewildered to think of a decent excuse.

This reply instantly produced a titter from the boys, and a stinging box on the ear from Mr. Crocklejack.

"There, sir, go to your seat," said the tutor, angrily, "and take that for your insolence. After lessons you will go to Mr. Styngy's room."

Tommy Codlings wandered in a decidedly staggery way to his seat, and as he went cast a glance of despair at Lionel.

"Oh, Lor'," he thought, dismally; "it's all over: old Styngy is never satisfied with caning a chap—he's sure to keep me in, and I shall miss the fun this afternoon. It's just my luck."

CHAPTER XXVIII.

IN WHICH MY HERO BELIES HIS CHARACTER BY RUNNING AWAY FROM AN ENEMY.

TOMMY CODLINGS was perfectly correct in his anticipations. Mr. Styngy not only gave him a very handsome flogging, but added to the physical torture the mental one of construing four pages of his "Delectus," and being, of course, "kept in" until his task was completed.

"Here's a miserable go," he grumbled; "and I shan't be able even to speak to Lionel before he starts. Such a pity, too. There's a piece of advice I could give him which would carry the thing out splendid."

But he was compelled to keep his advice to himself, for when the bell rang, announcing that the morning classes were over, and the other boys, noisily putting away their books, trooped out of the schoolroom, the unhappy Tommy was sternly bidden to remain behind, and threatened with further severe punishment if he dared to move or speak.

"Just like that Codlings," thought Lionel, as he ran lightly up the stairs to the dormitory. "He's sure to get into trouble just as I want him. He could have watched Jabez Hunker nicely while I got ready, and—by Jupiter, here he comes out of Flashaway's room with his hat on."

Lionel began to whistle a lively tune, and his clear fearless blue eyes looked straight into the dark lowering features of Hunker, as the boys passed one another.

"Ah," was the thought that passed through Jabez Hunker's mind, "you'll whistle another tune by and by, my boy."

"There goes one of the conspirators," thought Lionel, in his turn. "He little thinks how nicely his precious plot will be turned against himself."

My hero only waited until the echo of the toady's heavy footfall had died away, and then, concealing his cap beneath his jacket, he strolled along the passage.

"I wonder where that Flashaway is. Can he be waiting about any where to see if I follow his toady, Hunker. Ah! here's Charlie Drummond—perhaps he's seen him."

"Just the very fellow I was coming after," said Drummond, as he ran up. "Come into the playground, Wilful."

"Why? Is Flashaway there?"

"Come, and you'll see," Drummond said, pulling his chum by the arm.

"No—but tell me first is Flashaway there? I've a particular reason for wanting to know."

"Well—yes, he is, and the best of the joke is he wants to see you."

"I don't want to see him, then," said Lionel, releasing himself from Drummond's hold.

"You're not afraid of him?"

"Afraid!" repeated Lionel, contemptuously. "I've shown that pretty plainly, I think."

"That's true—I beg your pardon, old chap—but Flashaway was in the playground and some of the bigger chaps were chaffing him about you, when, all at once, he turned round and said—'Look here, you fellows, I'm not afraid of young Wilful or anyone else, only I didn't want to thrash him because he's a new chap and not up to my weight and size, but he's gone too far, and I'm waiting now to make an appointment to give the whelp the hiding he deserves.'"

"Did he say that?" exclaimed Lionel, the hot blood flushing into his cheeks.

"He just did, and so I ran off to fetch you at once."

"Con-found it," muttered Lionel, giving an angry stamp with his foot, "and I can't come."

"Can't come!" repeated Charlie Drummond.

"No—and what's more I must get out of the house without Flashaway seeing me. Did you happen to see Jabez Hunker pass out."

"Yes, he went through the playground and out of the gates just as I came after you."

"Then, I'm off. You know the crib better than I do. Charlie, can I get out without being seen by the fellows in the playground. I can't tell you why now—there isn't time—for I must catch up with Hunker; but you know I'm no cur, Charlie, and that it isn't because I'm afraid of Flashaway."

"I deserve to be kicked for thinking such a thing for a moment, Li," replied Drummond, hurrying along the passage. "I'll show you a way, through the head master's private garden. Hunker's gone towards old Grumpy's farm, and you'll just be able to take the short cut across the five-acre field and catch up to him."

And so, hurrying up the corridor, down one flight of stairs, up another, turning to the right, then to the left, then to the right again, with bewildering rapidity, they reached the basement, traversed a stone passage, unbolted a door, and emerged into a partially covered yard, where the out-houses were situated.

"It's lucky none of the slaveys were about," said Drummond, "or they might have reported us. That's your way, Li—over this wall—straight across the garden—never mind the flowers. There's a gap in the hedge low down by the side of the old plane tree; get through that, turn to the left across the five-acre field, and you'll catch up with Hunker before he makes old Grumpy's—unless he's been running, and that's out of his line."

Before Drummond had concluded his instructions, Lionel, with the activity of a cat, had scaled the wall, nodded an adieu to his chum, and dropped on the other side.

Charlie listened for a minute, heard the creaking

of the twigs, and the soft footfall of his chum as he made his way across the flower beds, and then chuckling as he pictured to himself the wrath of Mr. Styngy at the damage, he retraced his own steps to the playground.

With the rapidity of a coursed hare Lionel followed his friend's instructions, and in a few minutes found himself close to the hedge which separated the five-acre field from the road down which Jabez Hunker had to pass.

"I wonder whether he's gone past?" thought Lionel. "Confound the hedge! it's so thick I can't see through it. Oh, here's a chance!"

There were a few scrubby pollard oaks overlooking the road. It did not take Lionel long to climb one, separate the foliage with one hand, and glance swiftly up and down the road.

"Just in time, by Jupiter!" said our hero, as he just caught sight of Jabez Hunker's round shoulders and slinking figure, shuffling along at a rapid rate, some twenty yards down the lane. "I must be careful, though, for he has the sure eye and cunning of a fox."

Lionel watched until the ungainly form of Jabez had disappeared round a bend in the road, and then swung himself lightly from a branch to the ground.

Then hurrying forward a few paces until he was again in sight of his enemy, Lionel, keeping close to the hedge, followed on, never losing sight of him until Hunker turned aside and entered a low, dirty-looking ale-house, dignified by the title of the "Pig's Whisper."

Lionel came to a halt, and looked unutterably dejected. He had expected that Hunker would confer with the roughs in some place where he could overhear the particulars of their plan; but this hope was frustrated.

"There's nothing for it but to wait," thought Lionel. "When Hunker's gone I shall be able to drop in upon these fellows and settle matters. I can pretty well guess what will pass between 'em."

A dirty little lane—serving as an entrance to the garden at the rear of the Pig's Whisper—skirted that hostelry, and down that Lionel cautiously turned, stooping so that his head did not rise above the level of the hedge. He guessed that Hunker would go directly back to inform Flashaway of the success of his shameful errand.

Lionel was right; in less than a quarter of an hour he saw Jabez slink by, with something like a smile upon his usually surly features.

"You spider," muttered Lionel, as he looked after his retreating foe; "you've spun your little web very nicely, I dare say; but here goes to spoil it."

CHAPTER XXIX.

IN WHICH HUNKER PLOTS AND LIONEL COUNTERPLOTS.

MY hero, once assured that Jabez had passed the bend in the road, emerged from his concealment, and entered the low portal of the "Pig's Whisper," whence he was almost driven back though by the combined fumes of stale beer and bad tobacco smoke.

"Ugh!" and Lionel gave an involuntary heave. "If it smells like this in the passage, I wonder what sort of a flavour the tap-room has?"

He turned the handle of the door, and entered as coolly as if he were an old customer, accustomed to fuddle his brain and debilitate his digestion in the parlour of the "Pig's Whisper" every day.

There were only three occupants of the room, and Lionel knew at once they were the men he wanted.

They were talking noisily, so noisily that his light footfall was not heard.

"Th' young gent he promise fair enow," said one; "but waat I loikes be money down."

"Well, he's gi' us soom, aint he?" said the second.

"Waat I say be," added the third, "that it bain't enow for t' job. Waat be foive shillun 'mongst three."

"Loight work, loight money," said the one who had first spoken. "It be on'y to gi' youngster a hidin', and I'd a done that for a quaart o' yale."

This conversation was just reaching an interesting point for Lionel, when it was interrupted by one of the yokels making a discovery that there was an addition to their number.

"Hullo! who be there?"

"Don't let me disturb you, gentlemen," said Lionel. "I've only come on a little matter of business."

"Moor bwoys to drash mebbe," muttered one.

"That's just it," said Lionel, who caught the words; "you hit it exactly."

"This waun't do," said the biggest of the thre who looked half-lout, half-poacher, and all blac - guard. "I say, youngster, didn't 'ee hear waat we wur sayin'?"

"Some of it," replied Lionel; "and it happe ed to be the very thing I had come to you about."

"Drashin' th' youngster, eh?"

"That's it," said my hero, drawing a chair to th table.

"I zee," and the lout grinned a grin of satisfaction. "T'oother chap sent 'ee back wi' th' mon y?"

"No he didn't," replied Lionel; "I came vit! some of my own."

"I wor right," murmured a lout; "More boy to drash it be."

"Haud thee tongue," growled the biggest. "Now, young measter, waat be 'ee coom for? Ye bain't goin' to gi' mooney for nowthin'?"

"Your intelligence is really remarkable," said Lionel. "I am not."

"Waat be't foor, then?"

"That young—er—gentleman, who just left you," said my hero, with great deliberation, "gave you five shillings?"

"Naw a didn't," interrupted the lout. "We got tew shillun, and th' yung gent promised to gi th' t'other three when th' job weer doon."

"I'm sorry for that," said Lionel, "for he didn't intend to keep his word. The two shillings you have is all you'll get for thrashing me."

"Drashing thee!" exclaimed the lout. "Be 'ee th' lad we was to wollop?"

"That's me," said Lionel, calmly. "That boy who was here and another, are at the same school as I am, and because I thrashed one of 'em, and they're too cowardly to take their own parts, they've hired you to give me a hiding. Now do you see this?"

The rustics did see it, if opening their eyes to the very widest extent and staring at the sovereign Lionel held up, would enable them to accomplish the object.

"'Ees!" they exclaimed in one voice.

"When was the thrashing to come off?" asked Lionel.

"Morrer arternoon," replied the big lout, licking his lips in anticipation of receiving the soverign.

"Where?"

"In t'field yonder, back o' th' pond; yong chap as comed here was goin' t' bring 'ee oop t' foight wi' his mate. Then we were to drop on 'ee, drash 'ee we'in a hinch of's life, while t'other two runned off t' bring th' constable."

"By George," thought Lionel. "A well-laid trap, and I certainly should have fallen into it but for poor Tommy Codlings. I'll stand him a blow out of whatever he likes for this."

Then he went on aloud—

"Now, this sovereign is yours on this condition. We will all be in the field yonder to-morrow afternoon, but, instead of pitching into me, you must tackle the boy who came here and his mate, and if you duck them in the pond as well, I'll stand another five shillings. Is it a bargain?"

"Gi' us holt!" said the big lout, clutching at the tempting peice of yellow gold.

"Promise first," said my hero, drawing his hand away.

"It be a bargain, I tell 'ee young gen'leman," said the lout; "we'll drash 'um till 'em can't see, then we'll dook 'em to bring 'em round agin."

"And earn another five shillings," said Lionel, "or perhaps ten, if you roll 'em where all that green slime is."

"Sartin sure we'll do it, young measter," replied the rustic, "we'll 'arn t'other ten shillun. Won't we mates?"

"Sartin," grunted the others, in chorus. "Good day, measter."

And Lionel, with a quiet smile of satisfaction, left the "Pig's Whisper." Thirty shillings was a good deal of money, but the satisfaction of seeing his cowardly enemies fall into their own trap, was cheap at the price.

CHAPTER XXX.

THE TABLES TURNED COMPLETELY UPSIDE DOWN.

ON his return, that amiable young man, Jabez Hunker reported to Flashaway the full success of his scheme. "You're sure it's all right?" said the bully anxiously. "I would not have the scheme fail for fifty pounds."

"It can't fail," replied Hunker; "the louts would engage to thrash half-a-dozen fellows like Wilful for a quart of ale apiece. I only regret having offered them so much."

"If I'd had to pay them five pounds apiece for doing it," said Flashaway, savagely, "they should have had it. Why, Hunker, it will be worth any money to see the young whelp howling for mercy, kicking and struggling in the grasp of those louts. I hope they're strong?"

"Oh, they're strong enough to throw a bull between 'em," replied Jabez. "But where is young Wilful. Have you challenged him yet?"

"Not yet, I've been waiting for him. He's in the house somewhere. Young Drummond has just told me so."

"Ah, and there he is, just coming out of the door," said Hunker, in a low tone. "Now's your time, Flashaway. Keep up a bold front, and speak out so that all the other fellows can hear you."

In spite of the advice, and the knowledge that he was tolerably safe in what he was about to do, it was with a very ill-assumed appearance of cool indifference that Flashaway stalked towards my hero, and Drummond, to deliver his defiance.

Lionel had just returned from the "Pig's Whisper," by the back way, and after giving himself a few minutes to cool after his run, strolled into the playground, with as innocent an air as if he had been perfectly unaware of the plot.

He was close to a knot of the fourth form boys—most of them Flashaway's toadies and companions—when the bully walked up and called his name.

"Wilful, I say, Wilful!"

"Did you call?" said my hero, turning and coolly confronting the bully.

"Yes, I did," said Flashaway, with a poor attempt to look as if he were perfectly calm and self-possessed. "I want a few words with you, Wilful."

"Make haste and get it over, then," said Lionel; "for as you very well know, Flashaway, your company isn't agreeable to me."

"I'll make it a little less agreeable before I've done with you," said the bully, giving his hat a ferocious cock and nodding it menacingly towards Lionel. "I've put up with too much of your cheek, young fellow, and we've got to have it out."

"You don't mean to say that you're going to fight?" exclaimed Lionel, in affected surprise.

"That's just what I mean," retorted Flashaway, "as you'll find out to your cost."

"Why, where have you been laying in a stock of pluck?" said my hero. "You hadn't got an ounce the other day, and now you seem to have at least a hundredweight. I hope it's some of the right sort, and will keep a while."

"It'll keep long enough for *you*," retorted Flashaway; "and it's no use your trying to sneak out of it, you provoked it, and fight you shall."

"Oh, *I* don't want to get out of it. I'm only too happy to oblige you, Flashaway. Clear a ring, you fellows. Drummond, take my jacket."

"Not now, not here," said Flashaway, recoiling two or three paces and turning several shades paler. "I'm not going to fight here."

"Why not?" said my hero, calmly tucking up his wristbands. "Better have it out now, while that stock of pluck lasts."

"Fight him, Flashaway. Off with your jacket. Put up your hands, man," observed those of the bully's party who were not in the plot.

"No; I tell you, no," said Flashaway, retreating sullenly as Lionel advanced. "I'm not going to fight here, where we're liable to be stopped any minute by Styngy or one of the ushers."

Where will you have it, then?" asked Lionel, with a polite smile. "I'm quite willing to oblige, only let it be soon, for there's only half an hour before the bell rings; but I think I can manage to polish you off in that time."

"Don't be so sure of that," said Flashaway, sullenly. "I'm going to take my time over it, and I'll fight you to-morrow afternoon in old Grumpy's two-acre field.

"Where the duck-pond is?" said Lionel, with a slight emphasis on the word "duck."

Flashaway started, and Jabez Hunker's sallow face turned a shade paler, as the thought came simultaneously to each that Lionel suspected something, but my hero's face bore so innocent an expression that they dismissed the doubt, and the final arrangements were made as to the time and place of the encounter.

"I shall bring up Jabez as my second, and a couple of others to see fair," said Flashaway, "and I propose that the witnesses on each side do not exceed four.

"Why?" asked Lionel.

"Because the more there are that know about the fight, the greater the chance that Styngy hears of it, and I wouldn't have it stopped for a hundred pounds."

"Neither would I," said Lionel, with a meaning smile. "Good afternoon, Flashaway. Keep your spirits up."

The bully nodded sullenly, Jabez Hunker bent his heavy brows, and laughed a short, harsh laugh, as arm in arm the two worthy companions walked away, little thinking how completely my hero had outwitted them.

My readers may imagine the state of Tommy Codlings, whose misfortune in the morning had condemned him to be "kept in" during the play hour.

In spite of the "warming" he had already received Tommy could not help quitting his seat and crossing stealthily over to Lionel, when he and Drummond entered from the playground.

"Is it all right, Li?" Tommy whispered, eagerly.

"What a chap you are," said Lionel. "You'll get yourself into trouble again, and miss the fun tomorrow."

At that moment the stern voice of Mr. Crocklejack was heard.

"Codlings, come here with your imposition."

The unfortunate Tommy hurriedly approached from a quarter in which he had no business to be, and the usher fixed an ominous glare upon him.

"Absent from your place again without leave," said Mr. Crocklejack. "Your imposition is doubled, Codlings, and if you offend again to-day I shall give you a task that will keep you in all tomorrow afternoon."

"Oh Lor'," said Tommy; "what a donkey I am! I shan't see the fun to-morrow, after all. I never saw such luck."

"No muttering, Codlings," said Mr. Crocklejack. Stand upon that form, sir, and turn your face to the wall."

And in that undignified position Tommy had to remain until tea time, with the pleasant prospect of having to pass the evening until bed time in the class-room over his untouched composition.

Tommy communicated his sorrows to Lionel by means of a few words scrawled on a piece of paper, and my hero soothed him with the assurance that he and Drummond would between them write out his imposition, so as to make matters safe for the morrow.

This they did; and when the important moment arrived Tommy passed his examination creditably, and was pronounced free to spend his half-holiday with his companions.

Tommy received the intelligence with a demure and sober expression of countenance, as if he were rather sorry than glad to have his liberty; but no sooner did he reach the playground than he walked to a corner and stood on his head in the fulness of his joy.

But Codlings-the-unlucky was unused to this species of gymnastic performance, and being once wrong end upwards found the utmost difficulty in geting right end up again.

In fact, it is more than probable that a fit of apoplexy would have terminated his sufferings, had not the friendly hand of Lionel restored him to his normal position, and stood him up against the wall where he leant—purple and gasping.

"There never was such a fellow as you, Tommy," said my hero. "What on earth did a fat chap like you want to stand on his head for, you're nearly black in the face, now."

"I—know—I—am," gasped Tommy. "Oh—dear, I—thought—I—should—bust."

"It's a wonder you didn't," said Lionel. "But come along if you're going with me. I want to be on the ground as soon as Flashaway and his party."

"Is it all right?" gasped Codlings, whose feelings may be compared to those of a man who had been hanged for a quarter of an hour, and cut down before the breath had quite left his body.

"Yes," replied Lionel. "Drummond's coming on behind with all the fellows he can muster."

"But won't that make Flashaway suspicious?"

"He won't see them till it's too late, Drummond's going to keep 'em behind the hedge until the ducking begins."

"I see," said Tommy. "Then we've all to rush out and chevy 'em back to the school."

"That's it," said Lionel, with a nod of approval. "But don't talk too loud, Tommy, or we may be overheard and the game spoiled."

Codlings was mute as a fish after that hint, and, beyond an occasional chuckle of joy at the prospect of the discomfiture of Flashaway and the toady Hunker, gave utterance to no other sounds.

As Lionel hoped, he was first on the ground, and as he passed the gate he caught sight of the louts, who were skulking along the road at a short distance.

Lionel beckoned the leader, and drawing the half-sovereign from his pocket, held it up.

"Don't forget," he said. "Duck them in the slimiest part of the pond—but wait till the ring is made and the fight is begun before you interfere—and this is yours."

The lout grinned, nodded, and slouched away again, while Lionel and Codlings chose a nice piece of turf near the pond and waited the arrival of the foe.

In a few minutes the long form of Flashaway was seen hurrying along accompanied by Jabez Hunker and three of his particular friends.

"That's all right," thought Lionel. "I'm glad he hasn't brought more, for if any of them had pluck enough to pitch into the louts it might have spoiled the fun."

My hero noticed, too, that both Flashaway and Hunker looked anxiously about them as they neared the gate; but the louts had disappeared.

"Do you think they'll come?" said Flashaway, nervously. "They won't back out of it at the last moment—will they?"

"Who? Wilful do you mean?" said Hunker.

"No, confound him!—the louts, will they be here?"

"Certain. A few shillings are a little fortune to such chaps. Confound it, Flashaway, you're trembling like a leaf. 'Pon my word I'm almost ashamed of you myself."

And, indeed, the bully, big and strong as he was, looked such a pale and frightened coward at the bare thought of being obliged to fight that even the toady Hunker could not repress a feeling of contempt.

Biting his white lips until the blood flowed, Flashaway tried to control the nervous twitching of his features and strolled towards my hero with as much of his old swagger as he could assume.

"Aha," said Lionel, greeting his adversary with a pleasant smile. "Here you are at last, Flashaway. Cold, ain't it?"

It was in reality rather warm for the time of the year, but to judge by the trembling form of Flashaway it might have been mid-winter.

"Never mind," said Lionel, airily, as he divested himself of his jacket, and rolled up his shirt-sleeves, "I'll soon warm you, you know. Come, Hunker, peel your man and put him up."

"Don't be in such a hurry," growled Hunker, while his shifty eyes wandered about in search of the louts. "Your time will come soon enough."

"Well, you'd better make haste, for I'm not fond of waiting. Besides, I've got an appointment in half-an-hour. Now, Flashaway, off with your jacket or I'll pitch into you as you stand.

The bully was paler than ever, as with trembling, reluctant fingers, he began to pull off his jacket, aided by the three fourth-form boys he had brought with him, but who were quite ignorant of Flashaway's plot.

"Off with it," said one, as he tugged away at the sleeve of the bully's jacket. "Now your waistcoat and—"

But Flashaway repulsed him with something very like an oath. He was resolved not to fight, he dare not. But Lionel was getting impatient, and still the louts did not arrive.

"Now, Flashaway!" exclaimed my hero, to whom the fear and anxiety of the bully afforded the utmost delight, "are you going to be all day? I tell you now that I'm going to count twenty, and if you're not ready then I'll slip into you, jacket and all?"

"Lor! isn't it beautiful?" chuckled Tommy Codlings, in an ecstacy of rapture. "My, what a fright he is in to be sure."

"One—two—three—four—five," counted Lionel, in slow, measured tones.

"Ain't they coming yet?" whispered Flashaway,

"No," replied Hunker, who was looking anxiously round him.

"Six—seven—eight—nine—ten," counted Lionel, stepping out into the ring, and placing himself in a most scientific posture of self-defence.

Just then Jabez caught sight of the louts, skulking leisurely along the hedge towards the gate, and his heavy features lightened up with a smile.

"Here they come," he said, in hurried whisper to the bully. "Now for it, Flashaway. Pretend to show fight at least."

Flashaway first assured himself that the louts were really approaching, and then resumed the confidence which had so completely forsaken him while he doubted their arrival.

"So young Wilful," he said, "you really are rash enough to mean to fight me."

"Eleven—twelve—thirteen — fourteen — fifteen," added Lionel. "Look out Flashaway, I'm only going to count five more."

"I'll give you just as many minutes to beg my pardon, young Wilful," said Flashaway, as with his long arms folded, he stood smiling mockingly at my hero, carefully watching, though, the approach of the louts, who were now within a few yards of the ring.

"Look out," said Lionel, determined to have one good "prop" at the bully before the arrival of the louts. "Sixteen—seventeen—eighteen—nineteen—*twenty*."

And as the last word left his lips, he sprang forward and delivered a telling blow full upon the nose of the bully, who had never expected such a present.

Almost at the same moment the broad shoulders of the louts scattered Flashaway's supporters right and left. Two of them seized upon the bully, and two laid hold of Jabez, with a horny-handed grip.

"What be all this?" said the biggest lout, giving the paralyzed Flashaway a shake, that made his teeth rattle. "We don't 'low no foighting 'ere. What d'ye mean by't, eh?"

"You're making a mistake, my men," whispered Jabez, hurriedly. That's the boy you're to thrash, that one with his jacket off."

"Noa it beant," said the lout, with a broad grin, and a wink at Lionel. "We be roight, beant we mates?"

Jabez Hunker shot one single glance from the grinning faces of the louts to where Lionel stood, calmly replacing his jacket, and that one look told him that his scheme had been discovered and frustrated.

"We're sold," he said to Flashaway, in a whisper. "If you've got a spark of courage in you hit out, and run for it."

But that was just the quality which the bully had *not* got. He was pallid as death, trembling in every limb, and as helpless as an infant in the grasp of the louts.

Just then Charlie Drummond and his little army broke through the hedge and swarmed up to the scene. Jabez Hunker thought he saw a chance of rescue, and raised his voice in a shout.

"Help, here. Help. Res—"

That was as far as Jabez got, for a particularly dirty fist filled up his widely opened mouth and choked back the final syllable.

Jabez had just enough courage to turn to bay like the worm, when it is trodden upon, and with a vicious "take that," he let one of the louts have a heavy kick on the shin.

It was an unlucky kick for Jabez. Instead of loosening his hold the countryman tightened it, and returned the kick with such good interest that the toady howled aloud for mercy.

"Dang it," growled the lout. "I'll let un ha' it. Dom thee, coom awa' to t' pond."

"Let me go," yelled Flashaway, frantic with fear. "Help! Murder!"

"I'll murder 'ee," said the big lout who held the bully by the collar. "I'll teach 'ee to coom foightin' in my father's field. Coom awa' and be dooked."

"Wilful," gasped Jabez Hunker, struggling desperately every part of the way, "help us! Don't let us be murdered."

"Oh, yes," replied our hero, coolly. "I'll help you—to what you intended for me, you cowardly sneak. You've fallen into the trap you laid for me, my boy, just see how you like it."

"Hooray!" shouted Codlings, who in the wild exuberance of his joy was performing a series of extraordinary capers on the grass. "Hooray!—let 'em have it. Duck 'em."

"Close up," old fellow," said Lionel to his chum Charlie. "We mustn't let those friends of Flashaway's interfere.

But the bully's friends had evidently no intention of doing anything of the sort. The sight of the square shoulders and huge muscles of the louts was quite enough for them, and one by one they slunk off to a distance and watched the fate of Flashaway and Jabez Hunker.

The distance from the ring to the pond was only a few yards, but Flashaway and his toady suffered a whole eternity of torment during that short passage.

The louts were honest men in this one instance at least. They earned their money fairly. The unlucky conspirators were hauled, pushed, pulled, punched, choked, kicked, and shaken to within, as the louts had promised, an inch of their lives.

"Hang it," thought Lionel, as he watched their white, despairing faces, "I hope those chaps won't go too far. They'd better not be ducked, they won't have strength to get out again."

But it was useless to interfere now. The louts were fully enjoying the fun of "dooking schule-boys," and remorselessly the two were dragged to the very edge of the deepest side of the pond.

"Now mates, in wi' 'em," shouted one big lout, as he grasped Flashaway by the ankles, and his mate did the same office for the bully's shoulders. "One—too—dree and awa."

Like a stone from a catapult Flashaway was whirled into the air, looking like a confused mixture of arms and legs, then with a loud splash he descended into the very midst of the pond, scattering the green slime and duckweed in every direction.

Jabez Hunker fought hard and desperately, kicking, biting and scratching, but all in vain. The water had scarcely closed over the head of Flashaway, than the toady followed him, taking his involuntary dive in the very same spot.

The pond was not more than three feet deep in the middle, and in a moment the heads of the two defeated bullies rose up, gasping and spluttering, while their arms clung fondly round each other.

"Lor', ain't they affectionate?" exclaimed Tommy. "Look at 'em, Lionel."

"True friends in adversity," laughed Lionel; "they cling to each other."

"How much for your new suits?" roared another. "What a beautiful green!"

It was an inexpressibly comic spectacle to behold the baffled and defeated bullies slowly crawling through the mud and slime to the shore.

At nearly every step Flashaway or Jabez Hunker would slip in the greasy mud, and clinging to his comrade with a tight embrace, drag him once again beneath the water, and at every such occurrence a roar of laughter went up from Lionel and his companions.

When at length they did crawl out of the pond—soaked from head to foot and literally smothered in duck weed, mud, and slime—they presented as abject a spectacle as it is possible to conceive.

Indeed, so miserable did they look that Lionel almost pitied them, and for his part would have let them go without further molestation.

But Tommy Codlings was unmerciful. He had numberless injuries to avenge, and he determined to have payment in full for all the fagging and bullying he had undergone.

Lionel caught him in the act of preparing a pile of clay balls, of the softest and slimiest nature, while he eyed with a vicious glare the shivering figures of the defeated bullies.

"What are you going to do, Tommy?"

"What am I going to do?" repeated Codlings. "Why, I should have thought you could see that—I'm going to pelt 'em home."

"Don't do that—they've had enough already. Let 'em go, Tommy."

"Yes, I'll let 'em go," replied the vindictive Codlings, as he launched a huge clay ball at Flashaway and smote him heavily on the ear. "There goes one. Hooray!"

The example was infectious. In an instant twenty pairs of hands were busily engaged in pelting Flashaway and Hunker, with clay, mud, tufts of grass, or anything that came first.

"Help!" yelled Flashaway, who was fairly cowed, and as terrified as a hunted hare. "Murder!"

Jabez Hunker would have added the sounds of his sweet voice, but unluckily for him, the instant he opened his mouth, it was filled by a well-aimed dab of mud from Tommy Codlings, who had been watching for the opportunity.

"Hooray, give it 'em," shouted Tommy. "Let 'em have a start, and make them run for it."

"Chevy chase; Chevy 'em," shouted the others, and a fresh shower of mud and clay whizzed about the heads of the unlucky bullies.

Tommy was particularly precise. He never threw away a shot, he knew better. His plan was to advance within a couple of yards of Flashaway, and Hunker, and then wait until he saw an opening, when his clay ball would fly with unerring aim into the ears, eyes, or mouths of one or the other.

"Run," gasped Flashaway. "I can't stand any more of this, both my eyes are full of mud, my ears are stopped up, and I've got pounds of the beastly clay down my neck."

Hunker could not reply, his mouth was too full of clay, the consequence of Tommy Codlings's first shot, but he understood the meaning of Flashaway's words, and clearing just enough mud out of the corner of his right eye to enable him to choose his direction—he began to run, with all his might, for the gate.

"Hooray!" shouted the crowd. "Gi' it to 'em!"

And a fresh volley of clay, mud, and turf flew after the fugitives—who ran like deers—now that they were fairly started.

Some of the more eager of the crowd continued the pursuit; Tommy Codlings followed to the very gates of the school; but Lionel and his chum Charlie stayed behind, as did the louts anxious to receive the promised reward.

"There's the extra half-sovereign," said Lionel, "and very well you deserve it. Now, if you'll take my advice you'll make yourselves scarce for a little while."

The louts grinned, winked significantly, and slouched away.

Before night fell they had placed twenty miles between themselves and the probability of pursuit.

"I say," said Drummond, "there'll be a row about this."

"Not a bit of it. They daren't say a word, Charlie. If they did they know quite well that I should expose them, and even old Styngy dare not defend them, when he found out what a cowardly trap they had laid for me."

"They'll try, at all events, to take it out of you, Lionel."

"Let them try," replied my hero, with a laugh. "I'm on my guard, now, and twenty Flashaways, with as many Jabez Hunkers to back them, wouldn't frighten me."

"Well, I should think he'd had nearly enough of you by this time," laughed Charlie.

"Not quite," said Lionel. "I haven't done with him yet."

"Why, what on earth are you going to do now?"

"As soon as he's got over the bruises he had to-day," replied my hero, "I mean to make him fight. He challenged me you know, everybody heard him, and he shall either fight or be jeered at for a cur and a coward by the smallest boys in the school."

CHAPTER XXXI.

SAM SCARECROW'S WANDERINGS—A FIGHT FOR A DINNER—A FRIEND IN NEED.

I MUST now turn aside from Cheetham Hall for a brief space and introduce my readers once more to Sam Scarecrow, whose condition was almost as unenviable as that of Messieurs Flashaway and Hunker, as detailed in the last chapter.

When that unlucky youth made his escape from the custody of the beadle he took the first direction that presented itself—for all were alike to him—turned down a narrow lane, scrambled through a gap in the hedge, crossed a couple of fields, waded through a ditch, and finally sank down, gasping and exhausted, beneath the friendly shelter of a hay-rick.

"Oh, Lor'! Oh dear me!" panted Sam. "What an unlucky chap I am to be sure. And I do feel so bad. I wish I was dead, I do."

In truth, poor Sam had good cause for feeling unwell—he was faint with hunger, he had been very roughly handled, to say nothing of being set upon by Noodles, and, above all, the powerful medicine with which the doctor had dosed him was beginning to work its sweet will upon his frame.

"Ugh!" groaned Sam, with a shuddering heave. "I think I can taste it now. Castor ile was in it, I know, and jollop; also salts and senny. Oh! how it is a-hurtin' of me."

Sam crossed his hands over the lower part of his tunic, and worked himself backwards and forwards in agony, giving utterance to a suppressed howl every now and then when a pang of extra violence griped him.

At length over-burdened Nature could endure no more—Sam turned his face to the rick, opened his mouth to its widest extent, and gave vent to his emotions for fully ten minutes.

He was dreadfully ill. He had never been so ill in his life; and when it was all over Sam cautiously felt round the place where anatomists say the digestive organs are situated to ascertain if he had any left.

"Oh, Lor'," he moaned. "How empty I am! I feel like one large hole."

And in time that hole would want to be filled. This was the worst of the matter. Sam knew that in a little while he would be desperately hungry, but where was he to get anything to eat?

It was a particularly unpleasant position, and one to which Sam was quite unaccustomed. Until now he had always been well clothed, inside and out, and to be hungry, without any prospect of satisfying that hunger, was a most unwelcome idea.

"There was a chap called Nebuchadnezzar," mused Sam, as he glared hungrily round him, "as lived on grass, once upon a time. Blowed if I don't think I shall have to be Mr. N. number two."

Poor Sam was dreadfully weak, too, and only the fear of being pursued and taken to the lunatic asylum could have induced him to journey onwards—whither, he knew not.

"I'll have to take my chance," thought Sam. "I've got a good nose; and if there's anything to eat cooking within 'arf a mile, I'm bound to smell it."

And onwards the unlucky Samuel trudged, with only chance to guide him to a destination.

It was a beautiful country from a picturesque point of view, but a very unpleasant one to trudge on foot, as Sam soon found out.

He chose, for safety's sake, to cross the fields, and as most of them were ploughed, and heavy with the recent rains, and as the ditches were all full from the same cause, and the hedges were particularly stiff and thorny, poor Sam found his path anything but one of roses.

"I must give it up," he thought. "I can't stand no more of this. There's a road of some sort. I'll go down it. I've heard of chaps as sold themselves for gold. "I'd sell myself just now for a good tuck-out of Irish stew, or a steak and inguns."

And Sam sniffed, as if the flavour of the savoury viands his imagination conjured up already tickled his palate.

It was just at that moment that Sam caught sight of a boy, dressed in smock frock and gaiters, seated on the top of a stile, whereon also reposed a tin can, while in his hand he held a huge slice of bread and fully three-quarters of a pound of plump and juicy pork.

It was in taking a sharp corner that Sam alighted on the youthful chawbacon, and the sight of the eatables roused Sam's hunger to a pitch of madness.

Involuntarily he stretched out his hand and made a grab at the pork, but the rustic youth was too quick, and drew his dinner out of danger. Sam only grazed the pork with the tips of his fingers, but he licked those, and resolved to have that pork or perish.

"Oi say, wnat be 'ee arter?" said the lout, keeping the savoury morsel behind his back.

"I want that there pork," said Sam, in a determined tone, as he dodged first to one side and then to another, in order to get a second grab at it.

"Not loikely," replied the lout, who was as tall as Sam, and nearly twice as heavy. "Eat thee own pork. Thee shant ha none o' mine."

"I will," said Sam, savagely. "I'm starving, I tell you. I'm as empty as a drum, and I ain't got no money, and I'm going to have that pork."

"Will 'ee?" retorted the lout, gaining courage, as he compared his own size and weight with that of Sam. "Noa 'ee won't nayther."

And keeping a watchful eye upon Sam, the lout deposited his bread and pork by the side of the can, spit on his hands, rubbed them together, and clenching his fists, revolved them with a slow and circular motion.

"He's twice my weight, and I feel as weak as a kitten," thought Sam, "but I mean havin' of that pork."

Sam had one advantage though; like most boys who have been brought up in London, he knew how to box, while the lout was as ignorant of the use of his fists as a windmill.

"I've got plenty of wind," thought Sam; "there isn't nothink else inside of me, and if my strength only lasts, I'll have that pork."

The lout's tactics were very simple—in fact a good deal too much so. He just flourished his arms about in a few wild contortions, and then rushed at his foe.

But Sam nimbly slipped aside, and as the rustic rushed by, dealt him a blow on the right ear, which made all his teeth rattle again.

Sam would have closed with him then, but he knew he was too weak, but he eyed the pork with a hungry glance, and waited for the enemy to come on again.

"Dom thee," said the lout, tenderly feeling his injured ear. "I'll gi' it to 'ee, when I ketches thee."

Sam waited for him with a grim and resolute expression, and as the lout came lumbering up, a little more cautiously this time, dodged under his guard, and landed a "hot-un" on the rustic's nose.

This time the blow was more effectual, the lout sat down in the road, and clasped his nose in his right hand, while the "crimson stream" meandered slowly through his fingers.

Now Sam thought he saw his opportunity, and he made a rush at the stile whereon reposed the coveted pork, but the lout was hungry too, and before Sam could touch the dainty morsel he had scrambled up, and placed himself in front of his dinner.

"Noa 'ee don't," said the lout, fiercely. "I beant agoing to ha' my he'd pooncbed and lose my dinner too—not loikely."

"Get away," roared Sam. "I tell you I'm going to have the pork—give it up."

"'Taint loikely," retorted the rustic, who still held his injured nose with the fingers of his right hand, as if fearing that it would drop off. "I'll call my feyther."

Sam's hunger would no longer allow him to be prudent. He made a feint at the lout, dodged the blow that was aimed at him, returned one straight from the shoulder, loosening two of the bumpkin's front teeth, and snatching the bread and pork from the top of the stile, ran as he had never run before in his life.

Before the unlucky lout had recovered from the shock of the blow Sam was a quarter of a mile away, tearing along like an express engine, and with the stolen dinner safely in his clutches.

The slice of bread was nearly equal to an ordinary half-quartern loaf, and the pork was proportionate, but in six bites Sam disposed of the lot, and glanced hungrily around for any crusts he might have dropped.

"It were lovely," mused Sam, licking the tops of his fingers. "I don't think I ever eat anythink so delicious. I wonder how that poor chap feels? It were raytber too bad, certingly, but I couldn't help it. Lor', how hungry I was to be sure! I think I'll have a nap now; he won't follow me as far as this."

There was a nice dry piece of turf by the roadside, and there Sam, tired out by his exertions, coiled himself up, and slept that sound sleep which only youth and a good digestion can bestow.

It was pitch dark when Sam awoke shivering, and sitting up wondered drowsily where he was.

There was not a star to be seen in the sky—the wind had risen, driving before it a chilling misty rain, and Sam could hardly discern the dark outlines of the opposite trees. It was a wretched night, and promised to be worse.

"Here's a go," thought Sam, getting stiffly on to his feet. I wonder where I am. Oh, I remember now. That poor chap's dinner. He's luckier than me though, for he's got some place to sleep in, and I haven't. I shall catch my death o' cold out in this rain."

Sam looked up the road and down the road, and over the hedges as far as he could, but no friendly gleam of light told of shelter near, and still the wind rose, and the pitiless rain came down faster and faster.

There was nothing for it but to go on and trust in Providence to bring him to a shelter. Sam drew his thin clothes closer around him, and turning his back to the wind and rain, tramped wearily on.

He had gone on in this way for nearly a mile, when he fancied he heard just in front of him the sound of voices.

Sam paused to listen for a moment, and peering eagerly ahead, thought he saw something like a large waggon looming up in the centre of the road. His voice was just raised to hail it, when there seemed to shoot up from the ground before him a blinding blaze of light, then followed a deafening crash, and Sam was hurled—as by some giant hand—stunned and insensible into the ditch.

CHAPTER XXXII.

IN WHICH SAM SCARECROW, AFTER GETTING A "BLOW UP," GETS A "BLOW OUT."

SAM'S first conjecture, when he recovered his senses, was that he was the victim of some stray earthquake, which had wandered from the more genial climate of Peru, and burst with disappointment at finding itself in a country where its species is artificially manufactured by means of gunpowder, boiler and colliery explosions, railway collisions, and such other highly satisfactory substitutes.

It was dark enough before, but it seemed darker still to Sam now, as he slowly and painfully crawled out of the ditch, wet through and shivering.

"Where the doose am I now?" thought Sam. "Blow me if I can see anythink! If it wasn't that I can feel the ground under my feet, I might be in the clouds this blessed minnit, for all my eye tells me to the contrary."

Sam groped his way a few steps with the slow uncertain footing of one who is blind, then slipped, uttered a yell, and found himself up to his neck in water.

AS HE TURNED THE CRANK, THE AUTOMATON SWUNG ITS ARMS ABOUT AND QUICKLY DISPERSED THE SPECTATORS.

No. 7.

With his usual good luck he had crossed the road, and tested practically the quality of the other ditch.

"Bust it!" growled Sam, as he groped his way once again on to dry land, "this ain't exackerly the night for a cold bath, and here I've had two of 'em in ten minnits."

Once again Sam started, very slowly though, carefully feeling the ground before him with one foot, ere he ventured to trust the rest of his body to the treacherous soil.

But it was dreadfully slow work, it took him five minutes to go as many yards, and he was so chilled by his recent immersion that only the most violent exercise would have sufficed to restore the warmth to his numbed limbs.

He had just made a desperate resolve to dart onwards, and run the risk of falling into another ditch, when he fancied he saw a faint glimmer of light dancing about in an erratic way, a few yards ahead of him.

"Oh lor!" groaned Sam, dropping down in the road, "there's another o' them airthquacks!"

He shut his eyes, and cowered close to the ground, in the full expectation that he was once more going to be blown up; but as no explosion followed, he ventured to open his eyes, and saw the light still moving in the same irregular manner about the road.

"It's a Jack o' Lanting," thought Sam, "but no; that can't be, for I've heard thy're blew, and this is yaller—and—why yes, it's a real 'un, I can see the man's hand a holdin of it."

The prospect of human companionship, was quite enough for Sam. He would have fraternised with a set of murderers almost if they had offered him a prospect of warmth and food; and hobbling forward, he was soon up to the bearer of the lantern.

"Hullo!" said Sam.

The man did not appear to hear him, and still holding the lantern close to the ground, appeared to be in search of something.

"Hullo!" said Sam again—this time enforcing the remark by touching the man on the arm.

The man started, and raised the lantern so suddenly, that it grazed the tip of Sam's nose.

"Why, Jem, I thought you were—Hullo! It isn't Jem Who may you be?"

"Blowed if I hardly know," replied Sam. "But I knows *wot* I am, and that's precious cold and hungry; and if you could tell me where I can get a shelter—"

"Shelter!" exclaimed the man, with a growl. "Precious likely that, when my carawan's just been blowed to bits. Where do you come from?"

"Out of the ditch," said Sam; "out of two ditches I might say."

"You choose a lively place to sleep on a night like this."

"*I* didn't choose 'em," retorted Sam. "I was a comin' quiet enough along the road, when there was a blaze and a bang, and when I woke up I found myself in the ditch."

"It's lucky for you you didn't find yourself made a hangel of by this time," said the man. "So you were blowed up too, was you?"

"I *was*," replied Sam, emphatically. "Did you let it orf?"

"Let it orf!" growled the man. "No, I didn't; it let itself orf. But if you was blowed up by it you've got a kind o' claim on me, and as soon as we've found my partner, I'll do wot I can for you."

"Was he blowed up, too?" asked Sam.

"Ah! he just was. I want to find a bit of him to take to his missus; she'll never believe it without."

"A bit of him! Is he dead, then?" said Sam, horrified.

"I reckon he is, unless there's a doctor handy who can put about four thousand bits of a man together, and shake life into 'em arterwards. Poor Jem! he was a cross-grained sort of mate; but there's wuss than him—out o' the world and in it."

"Don't you be too sure of that," said a faint voice, in a gasping whisper, so close to the showman, that he jumped back and dropped the lantern. "That point's open to argyment."

"*It's Jem's voice!*" whispered the showman. "He's dead, and that's his ghost a' speakin'."

"Don't you be too sure of that," said the whispering voice again. "It's open to argyment. Come and help me out of this, Bellers."

Sam's only idea of a ghost was a tall figure in a white sheet, and with flaming eyes. He had no particular dread of a voice, and the instant he heard it he caught up the lantern and went to the spot from whence the sound came.

Its dim light fell upon a sight, though, which might have startled him a little, for from out the muddy waters of the ditch their protuded a pair of long pair of thin legs, terminating in two huge splay feet, from which the voice seemed to be proceeding, as there was nothing else visible.

"Make haste, will you?" said the boots again.

Sam set the lantern on the ground, and grasping the feet, pulled at them with all his might.

The first effort was unsuccessful, for the boots came off, and Sam sat down with considerable emphasis in the road, while a spluttering cough from the ditch told that the owner of the boots was in worse difficulties.

Fully satisfied by the tangible proof of the boots that he had a man, and not a ghost to deal with, Sam returned to the charge, grasped the feet, which were vibrating convulsively, and with a few hearty tugs, landed—not a bit of a man, but the whole of a very long thin one.

The showman had been watching Sam's operations with a dreadful interest, but, when he saw the long form slowly upraise itself, he dashed forward, and shook it energetically by the hand.

"Bless my soul, Jem!" exclaimed the showman; "it really *is* you, then—*all* of you?"

"Well, I *think* so," replied the long man slowly; "but I'm not quite certain. It's open to argyment."

"Blow argyment!" said the showman heartily; "there's enough ot you to last for another forty year, if you don't go into the firework line again."

"Ah!" replied the long man in a sorrowful tone, "wot a waste it wos, Bellers—ten pounds' worth, and nobody to see 'em go orf."

"It's lucky there's anybody left to see you come back again," growled the showman. "Why that there young chap, a quarter of a mile orf, was blowed up as high as the Monyment, and only escaped by fallin' on his 'ed, which ain't delikit. But come on, Jem, now you're found; we'll go and look arter the cairywan."

"Wot, is there any of that left?"

"A goodish bit, I should say. Any way, the old mare she bolted with the balance when she heard the blow-up, and I know she won't go far. Come on, young 'un."

"It's a dreadful pity about them fireworks, though," said the long man, who seemed to regard his own sufferings with remarkable indifference. "Wot a orjeance we should have had, Bellers, if we announced the drammer of 'Guy Fox' with a real exploshing!"

"Like them wot wos bought?" said the showman. "No, thankee, Jem—not for me; I ain't so fond of the dashed public to let myself be blowed up sky high, with the chance of coming down in more bits than would take a week to count."

"But think how it would dror!" said Long Jem. "There's the young chap, now—he's been blowed up, perhaps he wouldn't mind doin' of it again?"

"No, thankee," replied Sam, in a very decisive tone. "I'm nervous, and going up in a 'urry like that wants practice."

"That's open to argyment," said Long Jem. "I say that a ammyture can be blowed up as well as a perffessional the first time."

"Wery likely," responded Sam, gruffly; "but I knows more about it than I want to already."

Long Jem, who thought himself strong in argument, would have replied, but he was cut short by the showman, who suddenly gave a shout, and ran forward.

"Come on," he said; "here's the cairywan, as I said it would be, and the old mare still atween the sharves."

The caravan was indeed there, but wofully damaged, as they could see, even by the dim light of the lantern. The back part was entirely gone, as was also the greater portion of the roof.

Mr. Bellers was so rejoiced, though, to find anything at all left, that an ordinary spectator would have thought that he had found a small fortune, instead of having the whole of his stock-in-trade and his life imperilled.

"Jump in, Jem. In with you, my lad," he said gleefully. "The old mare's all right, and we'll be in Bungleford in less than an hour."

"But I say, Bellers, stop—but——"

"Wot for?" demanded the showman.

"There may be some of the fireworks left. Perhaps they didn't all go orf."

"Dash the fireworks!" growled Mr. Bellers. "I wish I'd never listened to you when you proposed to buy 'em. Jump in."

And jump in Long Jem and Sam did. Mr. Bellers touched up the old mare, and away the caravan rattled towards the thriving little market town of Bungleford.

CHAPTER XXXIII.

SAM'S NEW FRIENDS, BELLERS-TO-MEND AND LONG JEM—SAM'S COOKERY, AND ITS RESULTS—MR. BELLERS RESOLVES TO CONVERT SAM INTO AN AUTOMATON, AND THE IMMENSE SUCCESS OF THE PLAN.

THE old mare seemed to have been less frightened, as she was less injured, by the explosion, than either Mr. Bellers, Long Jem, or Sam Scarecrow; and, trotting along the road at a good pace, rattled the caravan into Bungleford in little more than half an hour.

They reached a particular hostelry, designated by the particularly incomprehensible title of the "Sun and Bagpipes," which had been honoured by the patronage of the strolling fraternity from time immemorial, and opposite its door Mr. Bellers reined in the old mare.

"I'm afraid to look at it," said the showman, as he descended from his perch in front. "How's the figgers, Jem?"

"How can I see," growled Jem, in an unamiable tone, "the lantern's out. Here, youngster, get down, and holler at the door. Wot do they mean by going to bed afore other people?"

"That's open to argyment," said Sam, repeating Long Jem's familiar phrase.

Long Jem's only reply was an application of his long foot to the small of Sam's back, thereby ejecting the young gentleman from the caravan in an unpleasant hurry.

Sam put up with the indignity, though. He was too cold and hungry to quarrel with the prospect of a warm shelter and a good supper for such a trifling cause as a kick, so he contented himself with retaliating upon the door in a way which soon brought down the landlord.

Sam prudently dodged to one side, as he heard the door unlocked and flung violently open.

It was fortunate that he did so, for the landlord appeared at the door armed with a stout stick, with which he aimed a mighty blow into the darkness, on the bare chance of hitting something.

He did hit something—the head of Long Jem—but that gentleman, being an accomplished acrobat, instantly closed with the landlord, and favoured him with a cross-buttock, which stretched him on the floor in an attitude of elegant repose.

"Why wot's come to you, guv'nor," remonstrated Long Jem, "is this wot you calls the right way to treat old customers; *you* may say so if you like, but I ses as it's open to argyment."

"Why, it's Spider Jem!" said the landlord, getting slowly up.

"It just is, and Bellers-to-mend is outside with the cairywan, but if you ain't got anything better to give us than that stick we'll go on farther."

And Jem turned away sulkily, but a reconciliation was soon effected, for the showman and the landlord of the "Sun and Bagpipes" were old friends, and in a very little while Sam, to his inexpressible delight, was warming his shivering limbs before a blazing fire, and sniffing the savoury odour of sundry huge slices of ham, which were broiling for supper.

"You and the boy had best have a rig out," said the host, speaking to what appeared to be two pyramids of steam, but which in reality were Long Jem and Sam Scarecrow, drying themselves before the fire.

"Well, I don't mind if I do," replied the man, "and I don't 'spose the kid will either, though that's open to argyment."

Sam didn't think it necessary to argue. He accepted a pair of trousers from the landlord, one leg of which would have made Sam a suit, Spider Jem accepting a similar accommodation. They soon began to feel a little less like animated snowballs in a rapid thaw.

Just then Mr. Bellers stalked in with a remarkably woful expression of countenance, returning the salutations of the landlord as if they had been prophecying his approaching end.

"Why, what's the matter with you, old chap," said the host; "anything gone wrong?"

"Gone wrong?" repeated the showman, in an exasperated tone. "Just go into your shed, and look at my cairywan. The roof's orf, the back's bust in, and my wonderful collection of waxwork is blowed to bits; it would take a week to sort 'em!"

"That's bad, certainly, Bellers," said the landlord, when he had been told the story of the explosion. "But it might have been wuss. Sit down and comfort yourself with a bit of supper, a glass of summat hot and a pipe, and we'll see what can be done in the mornin."

But in spite of this consolatory advice, Mr. Bellers remained in a very gloomy condition all the evening, and took leave of his friends at bedtime with the cheerful air of a man who has made up his mind that suicide is the only thing he has left to live for.

Sam Scarecrow, on the contrary, was in a very cheerful mood. He was very comfortable, and had appeased the pangs of hunger with a mighty rasher of bacon, and the half of a huge loaf, washed down with a foaming jug of home-brewed.

He had eaten enough to give two ordinary men the nightmare; but it never affected Sam, and that night he snored the peaceful sleep of youth and innocence.

By daybreak Mr. Bellers and Long Jem were up examining into the condition of the caravan, and the wax figures, and debating the best means of repairing the damage.

"Tain't so bad arter all," said Mr. Bellers. "If there's a handy carpenter in the village, he'll do up the cairywan. A few pots of paint will make it look smarter nor ever, and you and me get the figgers to rights."

"And the boy?"

"Oh, he'll make himself handy; I've been having a little patter with him, and he ses he's been doing the Japanese bus'ness."

"He ain't one of us, though?" said Long Jem.

"Not reg'lar; he's took to strollin' in a hammytoor way. Did you twig his rig out?"

"Not me, I had too much to do with thinkin' of own," growled Jem.

"Rummy looking things, they are," said Mr. Bellers; "with a few spangles and a bit of lace here and there, they'll do for a Chinee costoom, and the boy's hugly enough for any kind of foreigner."

"That's troo," said Jim. "Lor, how he do squint!"

"He'll earn his livin' never fear," said the showman. "And I've got a capital plan in my 'ed, too, that'll make him pay better than fireworks."

"That's open to argyment, though," retorted Long Jem. "If we could only get him to let himself be blowed up, same as he was last night, how it would draw?"

"Don't be a fool, Jem. How often do you think a chap could stand that? Why, he'd be shattered to hatoms the first time, and we should be collared for murder! Set to work on the figgers, Jem; you've got fireworks on the brain, I think."

"That's likewise open to argyment," replied Long Jem, and then he turned to his work of repairing the damaged figures, and for the time dismissed from his mind the grand idea of blowing up Sam Scarcecrow.

Working with a will, Mr. Bellers, Long Jem, and Sam, aided by a carpenter, had all the necessary repairs concluded by nightfall, in plenty of time—as the showman said—to make their pitch in Swiggletown by the following morning.

It was Sam's first taste of strolling life, and it agreed with him admirably. The men were rough, but they were good-hearted and true to each other, and, if the fare was as coarse as their manner, it was as good as their natures, and plentiful.

Sam fell in with their ways as if he had been born in a caravan. Long Jem, who thought his profession of acrobat as dignified as any, put Sam through his paces, and our eccentric friend gained his good will by the proficiency he exhibited.

"There's a want of helegance about him," said Long Jem, confidently to Mr. Bellers, "but he's as nimble as a monkey, and with a little of my tooition he'll come at it as well as the 'Japanese Jumper of the Jumbo Jungle.'"

"That's a good title," said Mr. Bellers, reflectively; "but it'll come heavy on the printer who has to find all them 'J's' for the posters. I've got a notion, too, and, if it don't draw, I'll try yours."

"What is it?"

"You rek'lect old Bobson's automyton, don't you?"

"What! the figger as used to play chest, and all manner o' games at cards, and lick anybody at it?"

"That's it. Well, old Bobson, he told me the dodge afore he died, and I means reviving it."

"How?"

"With this here boy, the Japanese."

"But he's alive, and Bobson's was an automyton, as went by clockwork."

"No it was'nt. That was Bobson's dodge. It was a live chap, wot he trained and made up to look like a wax figger. This chap 'll just do; he looks as if he was made out o' wood."

"That's a first rate idea," said Long Jem, "though whether it's better than the firework dodge is open to argyment."

"Blow your argyments," said the showman, "they're no good. The boy's got to be a automyton; and if that don't draw, then we'll see what you've got to say about the fireworks."

Sam had been busily engaged in a corner of the caravan, glueing down some portion of the garments of Oliver Cromwell, which had come unfixed, but his ears were sharp, and he had heard quite enough of the foregoing conversation to make him curious.

"Goin' to make an autommyton of me are they," said Sam, "we'll see about that, 'cos if there's any more blowing up goin' on, I decline the contrack, as the man said when they were goin' to feed him on train-ile, 'stead of roast beef, 'cos it were more fattenin'."

By the time the sun was fairly up, the caravan was half-way to Swiggletown; and then Mr. Bellers called a halt for breakfast.

"You must learn to make yourself handy now," said the showman to Sam, "and you begin by gettin' the grub ready, while me and Jem has a stroll to stretch our legs. You can cook, I 'spose?"

"Oh, yes, I can cook," replied Sam, who never doubted his ability to do anything until stern experience convinced him that he had failed.

"All right, then, light the fire stove; there's the wood and matches over there; you'll find the corfee and bacon in that locker, broil three rashers and cook some heggs, don't bile the heggs, but break the shells and fry 'em in the fat; and look sharp, for we shall be back in arf-an-hour."

Now, the fact was that Sam had never cooked anything in his life—devouring it after it had undergone the culinary process being considerably more in his line—but he went about the work with the calm confidence of a Soyer or a Francatelli, and cramming the stove full of wood and paper, Sam sent a blaze roaming up the pipe, which made it red hot in something less than ten minutes.

"Now for the corfee," thought Sam, "and the bacon. He said they was in the locker; but what's a locker? something that locks up—than he means a cubbard."

There was a curious little recess in the front portion of the caravan which might have passed for a cupboard when there was not a real one to compare it with.

Sam opened the door, and after a good deal of rummaging found a jar containing some dark brown lumpy powder, and a block of something which looked like a mass of petrefied bacon a few thousand years old.

Sam looked at it doubtfully, and tested it with his finger nail and his nose.

"It doesn't smell right," mused Sam, "and it don't feel right. Been smoked too much, may be. Prap's it 'll come soft in the cookin'."

The time was fast slipping by, and, anxious to show his zeal, Sam fetched an old coffee-pot and a frying-pan that were in a corner, filled the first half full of the dark brown powder, added some water, and placed it on the fire to boil, while he attempted to cut some rashers from the bacon.

But at the first attempt the blade glided off and chipped a knuckle away, a stronger effort only ended in his breaking the knife short off at the handle.

"It'll have to go in as it is," mumbled Sam, despairingly, licking his wounded finger, "though if it don't come a bit tender in the cooking, I wonder how they'll get their teeth into it."

There was plenty of fat left in the frying-pan, and as that began to frizzle, and fill the caravan with a savoury smell, Sam's hopes rose.

The coffee, too, began to simmer, but as Sam sniffed it there was something suspicious mingled with the aroma not altogether suggestive of the aromatic Arabian berry.

But time was too short to allow Sam a critical examination. There was one department in which the lanky youth was tolerably proficient. He could lay the table neatly, and he got the cups, saucers, plates, knives and forks, and other breakfast paraphernalia in order just as Mr. Bellers and Long Jem came back from their walk.

"Whew!" whistled the showman, halting on the top step of the caravan, and sniffing suspiciously.

"What on airth have you been cooking? You've let those rashers burn, my lad."

"No, I ain't; your comin' out o' the fresh hair makes it smell a bit strong."

"Well, let's have it, for me and Jem's precious sharp set."

And Mr. Bellers, drawing a stool up to the table, clutched his knife and fork, and licked his lips in anticipation.

"There's the corfee," said Sam, pouring out into the cups some muddy brown fluid from the coffee-pot, "and the bacon's 'most ready."

Sam had it on the plate in a twinkling, and presently it reposed beneath the nose of Mr. Bellers.

"Why wot on airth made you cook it whole?" said Mr. Bellers. "Didn't I tell you to cut it into rashers?"

"Well, you did," replied Sam; "but I couldn't find a hatchet or a saw handy, and the knife wasn't no good. I broke that."

Mr. Bellers was about to make some critical remark upon this, when his attention was attracted by the curious conduct of Long Jem.

That gentleman had just swallowed at a gulp three parts of the contents of his cup, and for a moment sat looking at the balance with a curious expression of discontent upon his features.

Then he took up the cup, and shook the sediment slowly round and smelt it; then he went to the little window, put his head out, and for five minutes there was a sound as of a half-choked pump in full work.

When he brought his features in again they were very pale, but solemn and determined, and without a word he stalked up to Sam, tucked the lanky one's head under his left arm, and unbuckling the strap which confined his waist, commenced flaying the unlucky Samuel.

"Why, Jem, what's the matter?" demanded Mr. Bellers, half afraid that his companion had gone mad.

"*Taste the corfee,*" said long Jem, in a sepulchral voice, but never ceasing to apply the strap with unfailing aim and merciless vigour.

Mr. Bellers *did* taste the coffee, and then he undid his own waist belt and went to help Jem for a quarter of an hour, at the expiration of which time they had all had enough exercise, especially Sam.

That tortured individual's first thought was to go for a jug or two and throw them at his tormentors, but all the hands he had were wanted just then to rub himself with, so he hurled a quantity of personal abuse instead.

"Yah, you cowards!" sobbed Sam, "to hit a poor boy—two of you—you call yourselves men, I 'spose? Put down them straps, and come on one at a time. I'd like to pison you, I would."

"It's my belief, my lad," said Mr. Bellers, with the calm air of conviction, "that it's wot you've been tryin' to do."

"That's open to argyment," commented Jem; "but still he might tell us why he biled up a bit o' brown paint, and gave it to us for corfee."

"And why," added Mr. Bellers, "did he fry this dashed old chump of painted wood, and call it bacon."

"I didn't," said Sam; "you told me where the corfee and the bacon was, and I got 'em ready."

"Then p'raps you'll have a little tuck-in all to yourself," replied Mr. Bellers. "There's plenty on it; we don't want any more."

"I shan't be able to touch a mouthful all day," said Long Jem, with an involuntary heave, as the taste of the burnt umber and water surged upward into his mouth again.

Disappointed of his breakfast, the showman again urged on the old mare, for there was no time to lose, and at the end of a couple of hours reached Swiggletown.

After hastily refreshing the inner man, Mr. Bellers-to-mend secured his "pitch" in the centre of the market-place, and then, after a long conference with his mate, visited a ricketty printing-office, and after a quarter of an hour emerged therefrom radiant with satisfaction.

"I've done it, Jem," he said, giving the long acrobat a slap on the back, which nearly dislocated his lumbar vertebra.

"Precious nigh," coughed Jem; "but don't do it again, Bellers. A whack like that'll last me a month."

"I've been round," continued the showman, aiming a second friendly blow at his mate, which that gentleman adroitly dodged; "and we'll have a good day afore any of the others pitch here. And the bills, Jem—you should see them!"

"Well, where are they, and wot are they about? My fireworks?"

"Dash your fireworks," growled Mr. Bellers; "you're always at that, you are. No; the bills is about the Ortommyton."

"But how about the boy? He'll turn up nasty arter the weltin' we give him."

"Not he. Boys like a whackin' now and then; it keeps 'em lively. Where is he now?"

"Down in the tap-room, peggin' away like one o'clock at the cold beef. I never see such a chap, since Tadman's donkey ate the load of hay, and swelled his skin so that all the hair come off."

Mr. Bellers went below, and found Sam pegging away at the beef and pickles as if he had spent the fortnight previous at sea in an open boat on a diet of old boots.

"Now, my boy," said Mr. Bellers, "you cum along wi' me. If you eat another hounce o' the beef, there'll be an inquest. I've got something to show you."

Very reluctantly Sam quitted the table, and accompanied Mr. Bellers and Long Jem into the High-street, which they traversed until a dead wall was reached, on which a man was busy in posting an enormous poster.

"Stop a bit, till he's done," said Mr. Bellers, coming over to the opposite side of the street. "Now come here, Sam, and read that."

Sam was not a very proficient scholar, but the type of the poster was so large, not to say startling, that a board-school scholar might almost have managed to read it.

And this is what Sam read:—

"A Miracle! A Miracle!!

To-night. To-night.

The Great Japanese Automaton, exhibited before all the Crowned Heads of Europe, Asia, Africa, and the rest of the uninhabited globe.

Professor Billoso begs to inform the Royalty, Nobility, Gentry, and Inhabitants of Swiggletown generally, that he has purchased from the

TYCOON OF JAPAN,

at an enormous expense, the sole right of exhibiting the

MARVELLOUS AUTOMATON JUMBARELLO,

which, on being wound up, will talk, sing, play cards, chess, or any other game, at the wish of the company; and the wonderful performance will terminate with a

SPARRING EXHIBITION,

when Jumbarello will box with any person present for

FIFTY POUNDS ASIDE.

Be in time! Be in time! Admission Sixpence! Remember, these wonders can be seen for a few days only. Be in time!!"

Long Jem and Sam stared for a few moments in wondering admiration of the placard. Then Sam said—

"Who's Jumbarello?"

"You," replied the showman.

Sam staggered back in astonishment, but recovered his balance by falling against Long Jem and upsetting him.

"But come along," continued Mr. Bellers, catching Sam by the arm. "We've got to show to-night, and there's everything to be got ready, happyratus and all. I'll tell you all about it as we go along."

And Sam, in an utter state of bewilderment at the new and strange character he so suddenly found himself transformed into, allowed himself to be dragged away, muttering in a vague tone the one word—

"Jumbarello!"

CHAPTER XXXIV.

THE AUTOMATON STRIKES A "HATTITOOD."

FEELING very like a criminal about to be led to execution, Sam suffered himself to be dragged away by Mr. Bellers towards the place where he was to be transformed into Jumbarello.

"Wot are you goin' to do with me?" said Sam "If it's any more fireworks, I'm not awailable. When I *do* go to heaven, I don't want to start in such a hurry—'Slow and sure's' a motter good enough for me."

"'Slow and sure,' be dashed," said Mr. Bellers; "I'm in a hurry now, and you've got to be so, too."

"It's all werry fine," grumbled Sam, "but I'm not goin' to be blowed up any more for you nor nobody helse. You jist let me go, will yer?"

But the showman resolutely declined. He kept a tight hold of Sam, and that young gentleman followed involuntarily and with nearly as much noise as the tin-kettle accompanies the dog's tail to which it is attached.

Mr. Bellers never halted until he had reached the market-place, where a crowd was already assembled, and through which he forced his way with very little ceremony.

Then up the few steps he strode, and so into the caravan, where he forced Sam into a corner, and regarded him with a glare which had to the lanky youth something positively ferocious in it.

"Now, you stop there," said Mr. Bellers, shaking his fist in an admonitory way at Sam, "and don't you move till we're ready. Now, Jem?"

"But ——" began Sam.

"Don't you say a word," said the excited Mr. Bellers; "that there bill's bound to draw!—like a mustard-plaster. We've got to get you ready to show to-night, so none of your larks, if *you* please."

"But ——" said Sam, again.

"Look here," retorted the showman, catching up a terrible-looking property sword, with a wooden blade, covered with tinfoil. "You're fond of your wittles, I know. Well, if you're quiet, and does wot you're told, there's as much grub as ever you can peck at; but if you goes agin' me, you has a taste o' this here weppin' and a free perpetooal pass to the outside of my cairywan."

The threat to deprive him of his food was quite enough for Sam. He remembered only too vividly the pangs of hunger which he had so lately endured, and stood mute in the corner, watching Mr. Bellers and Long Jem engaged in some mysterious preparations.

The waxwork figures had already been arrayed in order round the caravan, and from amongst them Mr. Bellers, after much deliberation, selected Guido Fawkes, and with very little ceremony hauled that illustrious conspirator off his perch.

"Now," said Mr. Bellers to Sam, "you get in that."

"Wot for?" asked Sam, regarding the stand lately occupied by the effigy of Guido Fawkes as if he thought it concealed a hundredweight or so of fireworks, designed to send him once again into the upper regions of the air

"Never you mind wot for," growled Mr. Bellers; "do as you're told."

"But," remonstrated Sam.

"If you gives me any more of your 'buts,'" said the showman, viciously, "I'll give you a taste of my strap, my lad. Sit up, will you?"

Sam had a particularly keen recollection of that strap, the buckle-end of it too, and he got upon the pedestal without a murmur, while Mr. Bellers, falling back a little way, regarded him with half-closed eyes, much as a connoisseur might survey the Apollo Belvedere.

"He'll do beautiful," said the showman. "Now, my lad, strike a hattitood."

"Come a bit nearer," said Sam.

Mr. Bellers unsuspiciously advanced, and Sam, shooting out his right fist, smote the showman in the mouth, and marred the symmetry of his two front teeth.

"Dash you!" mumbled Mr. Bellers, as he felt about his mouth for the damaged teeth. "Wot did you do that for?"

"You told me to."

"I told you to strike a hattitood."

"How did I know wot names you wos goin' to call yourself?" retorted Sam. "You calls me 'Jumbarello' in that there bill, and 'Hattitood's' quite as pretty."

There was no time to argue the point then, for the first exhibition of the wonderful automaton was to take place within half-an-hour, but Mr. Bellers bestowed upon Sam a look which meant "strap" unlimited at the very first available opportunity.

"Your eddecation's been neglected, my lad," said Mr. Bellers. "I'll have to teach you wot a hattitood means by-and-by. You see that there figger of Oliver Cromwell?"

"That fat chap with the big boots and the red nose?"

"That's him," said Mr. Bellers. "The public *will* have him with a jolly large weskit and a nose like a public-house sign; but that's because they don't know any better. If there was a few more like Mrs. Abel Heywood, of Manchester, things would be different."

"Who's she?" asked Sam.

"A true Englishwoman, my lad," replied Mr. Bellers, "who has been the first to erect a monument to one of the truest and greatest Englishmen that ever lived—and she deserves a statue herself for doing it. But time is short, my lad. Strike—I mean, put yourself in position."

Sam looked towards the effigy of the Great Protector, and arranged his own angular limbs as nearly as he could in imitation of Cromwell.

"That'll do," said Mr. Bellers, delighted. "You look as if you was made out o' wood, and jinted with wire. It only wants a little paint to finish you orf with."

"Wot are they goin' to do to me next?" thought Sam, as Mr. Bellers proceeded to daub his face with a thick layer of white paint, touching up the cheeks with rouge, till Sam looked like an interesting case of consumption in its last stage.

"Now," said Mr. Bellers, producing an instrument resembling a highly magnified clock winder, "you see this?"

Sam nodded in reply. He dared not speak, for the paint on his face was drying, and he was afraid that some of it would crack if he opened his mouth.

"Well," continued Mr. Bellers, "you stand in your present hattitood till I winds you up with this crank; arter that, at the word of command, you will do wotever you're told. D'ye see?"

"I don't mind," said Sam, in a voice which proceeded apparently from the pit of his stomach. "I'll do anythink so long as there's no more fireworks."

"Don't you be afeard o' that, my lad said," Mr. Bellers; "you won't be blowed up so long as you does wot I tell you. If you don't, a ton of gunpowder couldn't blow you up more than I will. Now, Jem, it's time we went on parade."

By "parade," in stroller language, is meant the preliminary discourse and flourish of trumpets *outside* the show, intended to lure the paying public *inside*.

When they had departed, Sam glanced around him

in despair. He was still in a vague and uncertain state as to the intentions of Mr. Bellers towards him, and had some dim idea that a second edition of the blowing up was to be the end of all this preparation.

"I won't stand it," thought Sam. "I can't. If I could only hide anywheres."

Again he cast his despairing glances around the caravan. But there seemed nothing in which a body of his length could be hidden, until he suddenly caught sight of the big drum, which instrument, in company with the Pandean pipes, it was Long Jem's especial province to play.

"I'll hide in that," thought Sam, "if I can get the top orf. They'll never think of lookin' for me there."

It was a desperate resolve, and one which only Sam Scarecrow, perhaps, would have thought of making; but he was in such a condition of fear, that any means of escape would have seemed possible.

To get the top of a drum off, though, is no very easy matter, and so Sam found it, even when at last he had to cut the cords at one side, and prize the top open sufficiently to admit his long thin figure.

Then, holding the severed ends of the cords, he drew the top down again, and waited.

He was only just in time, for almost at the same moment the outer door of the caravan opened, and a heavy footstep shook the whole structure with its tread.

Sam's heart sank within him as he heard the owner of the feet approaching the drum; and it only occurred to him just then that the drum might be wanted to play on.

It was too late to retract, though; for almost before the horrible thought had time to pass through Sam's brain, he felt the leather strap attached to the drum lifted up, and an instant afterwards the instrument itself was suspended from somebody's shoulders.

"Dash my wig!" muttered the voice of Long Jem, as he staggered beneath the unexpected weight. "What on airth makes this dashed drum so dooced heavy to-night?"

"Now, then, Jem," said Mr. Bellers, putting his head in at the door at this juncture, "are you going to be all night."

"I should like to know what's the matter with this 'ere drum," growled Long Jem, as he laboured heavily towards the door. "Blowed if any one wouldn't think as I wos tight."

And indeed, if anyone had taken Long Jem's uncertain method of progression as a test, that gentleman would infallibly have been pronounced to be under the influence of alcohol.

But Sam was more uncomfortable still than even Long Jem, for he was in mortal dread of being found out. He had never calculated upon the possibility of the drum being wanted to play upon, or he would never have got into it.

"Now, then," growled Mr. Bellers again; "are you comin'?"

Just as Mr. Bellers thrust his head into the caravan to hurry up Long Jem, that individual lurched round the corner, and brought the drum into violent contact with the showman's head.

"Bust you!" growled Mr. Bellers. "Wot did you do that for?"

"You was in a hurry, wasn't you?" retorted Jem.

"Hooray!" roared the crowd, who took the little accident to be a part of the performance. "'It un another."

"If he does, I'll smash him," thought Mr. Bellers, casting a vicious glance at Jem. Then he added, aloud—

"Play up there, Bag-o'-Bones!"

Now, if there was one thing more than another calculated to curdle the milk of human kindness within the bosom of Long Jem, it was an illusion to his want of plumpness. It was, of course, impossible to retaliate upon Mr. Bellers before the audience, but Long Jem thought he would let the drum have it, and, lifting the right-hand drumstick high in the air, he brought it down upon the parchment with a mighty blow.

But instead of the usual sonorous "boom" there came from the drum a yell of mortal agony.

"Wot's that?" gasped Long Jem, turning pallid.

"Play up!" roared Mr. Bellers. "Do you call that a drum?"

"Play up yourself," retorted Long Jem; "I'm not a goin' to play on a drum wot makes a noise like that."

"Give us hold," said Mr. Bellers, viciously; and in a minute he had lifted the drum from Long Jem's shoulders and snatched the drumstick from his grasp.

"Now, ladies and gen'lemen," he roared at the topmost pitch of his voice, "you are about to behold the most wonderful sight that ever was seen. The rep-presentations outside of the cairywan are nothin' to the marvellious realities inside of it. Walk hup! walk hup! Oh, my good gracious! wot's that?"

At the conclusion of his address, Mr. Bellers had given a tremendous bang on the drum by way of emphasis; and the blow, as in Jem's case, had been followed by a melancholy howl as of some one in mortal anguish.

Of course it was the unlucky Sam, upon whose head each time the drumstick had descended. The space being limited, the ex-Japanese Prince was unable to dodge, his knee being already in contact with his chin.

The showman with remarkable rapidity had unfastened the strap from his shoulders, and, setting the drum upright on the platform, stared at it with an expression of wondering dismay.

"Hi!" roared the crowd; "there be a ghost in t' droom."

Just then Sam gave some confirmation to the idea. Mr. Bellers had set the drum down with the wrong end uppermost, and the lanky youth, finding his position remarkably uncomfortable, made an effort, and shot his thin legs through the upper parchment, whence they emerged quivering, to the intense delight of the crowd, who looked upon the incident as specially provided for their entertainment.

The showman was fairly shaking with wrath when he saw what was really the matter. In an instant he had dragged Sam out and hauled him into the caravan with one hand, while with the other he unbuckled his waist-strap.

"I'll teach you," growled the showman, "to well nigh frighten me into a fit, and spile my drum besides. Take that."

The strap was flourished in the air, and in another moment would have been curling around Sam's lean body, but for the interposition of Long Jem.

"Stop a bit, Bellers," whispered the acrobat. "Think of the ordience. It's time to open now, and, if you larrups the boy, wot's to become of the ortommyton?"

Mr. Bellers unwillingly relinquished Sam, and a hollow truce was patched up. Even personal animosity must give way to considerations of business.

"Now," said Mr. Bellers, sternly, "don't let's have no more o' this. You get up on that there stand, and do your dooty by me and I'll do mine by you."

Sam dolefully obeyed, received Mr. Bellers' parting instructions, and stood upon his feet in a stiff and constrained attitude, looking a very monument of human misery.

The flaming placards had produced an immense effect at Swiggletown. The wonderful automaton, that had been viewed with such favour by royalty, excited the public curiosity to a tremendous pitch; and when Mr. Bellers, after cooling his heated brows with some of the contents of a gallon can of beer, went on to the platform, he found spectators enough to fill his caravan a dozen times over, ready with their sixpences.

"Walk hup! walk hup!" roared Mr. Bellers. "Only forty at a time can be admitted, ladies and gentleman, to see the wonderful Jumbarello. Stand back, you boys, and let the ladies pass."

The forty, and one or two more, perhaps, had deposited their sixpences in Long Jem's hands and passed into the caravan in about as many seconds, and now stood staring at the dingy curtain which screened the wonderful automaton from their gaze.

There was a breathless interval of suspense while Mr. Bellers passed behind it, and, bestowing a warning look upon Sam, pulled at the rope and swung the screen aside.

A murmur of admiration greeted this, Sam's first appearance on any stage, and he certainly felt a little uneasy at being the focus for so may pairs of widely-opened eyes; but he played his part very creditably, and the fixed and glassy nature of his squint could not have been surpassed by the most hideous piece of waxwork that ever caricatured nature.

"Now, ladies and gen'lemen," said Mr. Bellers, "I'm goin' to wind up the wonderful Jumbarello, when, at the rekwest of the company, he will play cards or chest, or sing a song, or arnser any question that may be put to him. With one turn of this here crank he plays cards; with two he is ekal to a game of chest; with the third he arnsers any questions you like to put; at the fourth he sings a song in his native language, and another turn will enable him to knock Tom Sayers into a cocked hat."

At this moment two stout, broad-shouldered countrymen, with broad, red faces, wearing a most ferocious expression, forced themselves to the front.

"Dang it, showman, we'll ha' a go at th' chap. Gi' un t' five turns. We'll box un for t' brass. Here't be."

And much to Mr. Bellers' alarm, one of the countrymen produced two greasy five-pound notes, and placed them on the pedestal.

"My turn fust, Jacob," he said to his friend. "When I ha' polished un off, thou can slip into un. Wind un up, showman."

Mr. Bellers was in a dreadful fix. He had never intended the challenge to be accepted—had never thought that any one would have had the courage to stand up before the mysterious automaton, and now here was two intoxicated countrymen bent upon the ruin of the wonderful Jumbarello.

"Be careful, gen'lemen," said Mr. Bellers; "you ain't got no idea of the strength of the springs. It were only last week as he knocked a Hirish labourer's 'ed clean off."

"I don't care—I ain't afeard o' un," retorted the countryman, sparring up to Sam, and putting his right fist immediately under the young man's nose, as if he were required to pronounce an opinion on its odour. "Wind un up and set un goin', I tell 'ee. Oh!"

Sam had, up to that moment, preserved his statue-like immobility, but as the two countrymen came within reach he shot out a long and bony arm on either side, and floored his two antagonists as easily as if they had been nine-pins!

CHAPTER XXXV.

THE NEW PUPIL—THIS SIDE UP, WITH CARE.

LIONEL'S judgment was not at fault when he predicted that the bully and Jabez Hunker would keep silence regarding the "ducking" they had received.

They accounted to Mr. Styngy for the condition in which they arrived at the school, by saying that they had fallen into a ditch in taking a short cut across a field. Mr. Styngy was perfectly satisfied, and the bullies went to bed, and stayed there for a week, writhing with pain, and swearing fresh schemes of vengeance against our hero.

Even when they did once more take their places in the school, Jabez Hunker's scowling eyes and heavy brows were concealed by a deep green shade, while Flashaway, owing to the loss of four front teeth, could only speak in a mumbling whisper, and limped in his walk in consequence of the kick he had received from the heavy boots of the louts.

Every eye was turned upon them as they entered, and a murmur of curiosity buzzed around the schoolroom.

There was no pity for them—neither of the two had a true friend in the school. Flashaway's money purchased him companionship, but nothing beyond.

"Young gentlemen," said Mr. Styngy, rising from his stool, and waving his hand benignantly towards Flashaway and Hunker. Your companions are doubtless as glad as I to welcome you back amongst them after your recovery from the lamentable accident which befel you a week ago. I do not approve of noisy demonstrations as a rule, but if they like to give you a cheer, I shall not forbid it."

There was a dead silence for a moment or two, then the voice of Small Junior piped out a feeble "Horray," a few of Flashaway's favourite toadies followed suit in a shame-faced way, but the majority sat silently looking on or whispering to one another. Lionel laughed audibly.

"A-hem," said Mr. Styngy, in a short, dissatisfied cough. "Go on with your studies, young gentlemen. Flashaway, I have a letter from your father, Sir Frederick, in which he states that, in consequence of typhoid fever having broken out on his estate, he intends sending your brother to me at once, and requests that you will meet him at the station this afternoon."

"I can't go in this state, sir," mumbled Flashaway, sullenly.

"I thought that perhaps you would be too unwell to undertake the journey," said Mr. Styngy blandly; "but it was only right to mention Sir Frederick's wishes. I will see to the matter, Flashaway."

Lionel's place was close to the head master's desk, and he had heard every word that passed between Mr. Styngy and the bully.

"H'm!" thought our hero. "So Flashaway's brother is coming here, is he? I wonder if he's anything like his precious relative yonder; if he is, the school will be rather too rich for me. I've felt bilious as it is, ever since I came."

"I say, Charlie," he whispered to his chum, "did you hear what old Styngy was saying just now."

"What! about the cheering?"

"No; about Flashaway's brother coming."

"The dickens he is," said Charlie. "When?"

"This afternoon. Old Styngy wanted Flashaway to go and meet his brother, but bully Fred don't care about encountering the public gaze just at present."

"I should think not," laughed Charlie, silently. "He never was good looking, but he just *is* a guy now. I wonder what his brother's like?"

"So do I."

"He won't turn out a sell, will he, like your Japanese Prince, Li?"

"Never fear; Styngy isn't to be caught twice that way. But I should like to see this new scion of the house of Flashaway. Suppose we trot off after class and take stock of him; we shall be able to tell then whether he's one of the right sort, or whether he takes after his precious brother."

"I'm on," said Charlie; and then, the class being called by Mr. Cracklejack, their conversation had to terminate.

As a matter of course, some latent idea of mischief was in Lionel's mind. He was never without a handsome stock of that commodity, but his plans were not yet matured; he wanted to get a peep at Master Flashaway the Second before he could tell what to do to him."

Tommy Codlings was of course invited to join the party, and that young gentleman scenting some fun, at once consented.

"We shall have a clear field," said Tommy, "for I heard Mr. Styngy saying to Crocklejack what a nuisance it was that young Flashaway was coming to-night, for he's invited to dine at the rector's."

"Who's going to meet him, then, at the station?"

"Noodles is going with the trap," replied Tommy. "Styngy sent for him only a quarter of an hour ago, and told him he was to be at the station in time to meet the half-past seven train."

"Did Styngy tell him about Flashaway?"

"No; the 'head' knows what a stupid Noodles is, and he never puzzles him with long directions. He was told to go to the station and wait till he was asked for."

"That'll do," said Lionel, as the light of mischief sparkled in his eyes; "I've got it!"

"What'll do, and what have you got?" demanded Tommy Codlings.

"Never mind, Tommy; you come to the station with us, and you'll see. We can slip out after ten, and be there long before old Noodles. Styngy will be gone out to dinner, and nobody cares for the ushers."

Tommy Codlings was forced to be satisfied with what Lionel told him—not that he was discontented; on the contrary, he was never happier than when playing at "Follow-my-Leader," with our hero for his chief.

Tea-time passed. Mr. Styngy, arrayed in his glossy black, departed for the rectory to dine, and our hero, with his two chums, slipped out of the school-gate, and trotted lightly away towards the railway.

Lionel did not halt until one-half of the distance between the school and the railway was covered. Then he pulled up, and looked anxiously about him.

"What are you looking for now, Li?"

"You don't see anybody about, do you, Charlie?"

"I don't see a living creature in sight, except the cows yonder, and that young donkey in the paddock."

"Ah, that's it!" said Lionel. "I didn't see it at first, I thought they'd taken it away."

"What in the name of wonder do you want with it, Li?" said Charlie.

"Can't you guess?"

"No, that I can't; unless you mean having a ride with it to the station."

"I mean that, old fellow, and something else, too," replied Lionel. "Just keep watch here, Charlie, while I go and fetch our young friend."

Lightly and gracefully Lionel vaulted over the paddock gate, and, first picking a tempting bunch of thistles, advanced cautiously towards the donkey.

It seemed a very amiable, unsuspecting young animal, for it allowed Lionel to walk close up to it, nibbled at the thistles with an appetite, and apparently had no earthly objection to our hero mounting on its back and riding it out of the paddock.

"That was neatly done, Li," said Charlie. "The last time I tried to get a ride out of the little beggar he ran me into a corner, and let out with his heels as if he wanted to make putty of me."

"Now," said Lionel, dismounting, and taking from beneath his waistcoat a large placard; "do you see this?"

On one side of it was written, in large Roman capitals—

MASTER FLASHAWAY, JUN., CARE OF
THE REV. PHILO STYNGY,
CHEETHAM HALL.

And on the other, in the same bold text—

THE NEW PUPIL.
THIS SIDE UP—WITH CARE.

"Well, I never!" gasped Tommy Codlings.

"You don't mean to say——" began Charlie Drummond.

"But I do," said Lionel, with a clear ringing laugh. "You see something may prevent the real Master Flashaway from turning up this evening, and it will be only good-natured to provide a substitute."

"But Noodles will never take that to the school."

"Why not? How does he know? He only had orders to go to the station and wait till he was asked for. You heard what Styngy said, Tommy?"

"Yes; that was it," replied Tommy.

"Then come on, my noble companions, and you shall see what you shall see."

"All right; I'm willing," said Charlie. "But there's a mile and a half to go yet, Li; let's all have a turn at the donkey."

So by easy stages the three chums reached the station, and hailed the porter, who, having to work, on an average, for a salary of eighteen shillings a week, was wondering how on earth he managed to solve the weekly riddle of clothing, feeding, and keeping a roof over the heads of himself, his wife, and six children.

"Porter!" said Lionel.

"Hallo!" returned the porter, surlily, for the continued attempt to solve the weekly riddle had ended in souring his temper.

"Do you want to earn half-a-crown?"

"I jist *do*," was the porter's emphatic reply.

"Then just look after this young donkey for half-an-hour. There'll be a man here for it from Mr. Styngy by that time."

The porter looked a little suspiciously at the donkey; he thought he had seen it before. But there was half-a-crown to be earned, and he was blind at that price.

"All right, sir," he said, taking the half-crown, and tethering the donkey to the palings.

Lionel walked calmly away, but as soon as he reached the rear of the goods shed, where he was free from observation, he indulged in a pas seul of triumph.

"What's that for?" said Tommy Codlings.

"You'll see, my boy; the trick's as good as done. Hark! don't you hear the sound of wheels?"

In fact, a minute later the noise of some vehicle crunching the gravel was heard, and, peeping round the corner of the shed, they saw the startled Noodles drive up and look around him with a vacant air.

"Hallo," said the porter, "you're Mr. Styngy's man, ain't you?"

"I am," replied Noodles, after a moment's hesitation, as if he were afraid of committing himself.

"Called for something, ain't you?"

"Yes," said Noodles; "there's a new pupil. Ha, you got him?"

"There you are," returned the porter, unfastening the donkey and pushing it towards the odd man; "that's the sort of pupil you keeps at your school—carridge paid."

Mr. Noodles looked at it in a doubtful way, as if he, in his turn, had a riddle to guess; but, not finding an answer, he slowly tied the donkey to the tail-board of the trap.

"There's the address on the card round its neck," said the porter; "you can read, I s'pose, as you're odd man at a school?"

"Oh, yes, I can read," said Mr. Noodles, verifying his statement by slowly spelling through the address which Lionel had written.

That seemed to settle the matter. The odd man

had no further doubts, and, wishing the porter "good arternoon," climbed into the trap, and drove away, the donkey following patiently behind.

"Beautiful!" laughed Lionel, executing a second dance of triumph as soon as Noodles was fairly out of sight. "My stars! if he don't startle old Styngy to-morrow, call me names."

"If *who* don't startle old Styngy?" asked Tommy Codlings.

"The new pupil, to be sure. But quiet, boys; it's nearly half-past seven, and the genuine Flashaway Junior has to be settled yet."

"Lor, I never thought of that!" said Charlie. "Why, old fellow, when he gets to Cheetham Hall he'll spoil all the fun?"

"Yes; *when* he does," said Lionel quietly; "but he isn't there yet, Charlie. Hallo! there goes the distance-signal—the train's due."

A distant whistle from the approaching engine—a sound like that of a distant storm—a groaning and shrieking as of some giant in mortal agony—and the 7.30 train rolled slowly into the station.

Only five or six passengers alighted, whom Lionel watched keenly one by one as they passed along the platform, and it did not take him many seconds to pick out his customer—a pale, sickly-looking boy, with a Jewish, ill-natured face, yet bearing so strong a likeness to Flashaway that no one could have mistaken the relationship.

Motioning to Charlie and Codlings to keep back, Lionel advanced, and greeted Flashaway Junior with a ceremonious mock politeness.

"What do *you* want?" said the new pupil in a particularly disagreeable tone.

"Have I the pleasure of addressing Master Flashaway?" said Lionel in his sweetest voice, while he politely raised his cap.

"That's my name," replied Flashaway Junior, with a shade more civility in his tone. "Do you come from the school—Mr. Styngy's?"

"I do, and with bad news," said Lionel gravely. "Mr. Styngy has sent me to say, with his compliments, that in consequence of geological peritonitas of the cerebellum having suddenly made its appearance in the school, he doesn't think it quite safe for you to come there at once."

"Good gracious!" exclaimed Flashaway Junior, dreadfully alarmed at the bare mention of this disease with the long name. "But what shall I do—there is no train back to my father's place to-night?"

"There's a capital hotel close by, where you can stop for the night," said Lionel. "I'd show you the way, but I'm not quite sure that I haven't got the geological peritonitas of the cerebellum myself. The porter yonder will show you the way."

Flashaway Junior did not wait to hear any more. He had a mortal dread of any infectious disease, and recoiled from Lionel as if our hero had been red hot.

Lionel raised his cap gravely, but when he once more joined his chums, a third fantastic dance of triumph was performed.

"Did you settle him?"

"Beautifully," said Lionel. "There he goes with the porter and all his luggage to the hotel. Only fancy what old Styngy will say when he asks for the new pupil in the morning, and Noodles brings out the one I gave him."

CHAPTER XXXVI.

IN WHICH THE ODD MAN COMMUNICATES THE ARRIVAL OF THE NEW PUPIL TO MR. STYNGY, AND IS REWARDED WITH THE ORDER OF THE BOOT (WELLINGTON)—CHURCH PARADE AT CHEETHAM HALL—TOMMY CODLINGS AGAIN IN TROUBLE—A SNEEZE AND ITS CONSEQUENCES.

THE Rev. Mr. Styngy was a gentleman who had a thorough appreciation of the good things of this life, especially regarding those grosser indulgences of the carnal appetites—such as eating and drinking—with a veneration that seemed strange, to say the least, in one of his reverend profession.

He never missed an invitation to dine at the rectory on any account, for the rector kept a cook who was facile princeps in his craft, and, moreover, had a cellar wherein were stored such magnums of claret and '47 port as had not their equal in the United Kingdom.

There was only one drawback to these little indulgences. Mr. Styngy had a delicate digestion, and, whenever he dined sumptuously, there was sure to be a skeleton at the feast, in the shape of an attack of indigestion, which cost a week and a small fortune in medicine to be rid of.

So it happened that on the morning after his visit to the rector, Mr. Styngy had a violent headache, and, moreover, a severe pain in the abdominal regions, known to the vulgar as a stomach ache. He loathed the very sight of his breakfast, and evinced an extraordinary thirst for cold water, emptying in succession his water-bottle and ewer, and even then casting a longing eye at the contents of his bath.

In fact, Mr. Styngy was so unwell, that he decided to remain in bed all day, and as it was Sunday, use it literally as a day of rest. His headache was so severe that he had forgotten all about the arrival of the new pupil.

Mr. Noodles, in the pursuance of his duty, had indeed got the donkey into the stable, littered it down, and duly provided it with fodder, and, on Sunday morning, after visiting his young charge, to see that it was all right, proceeded to Mr. Styngy's room to make his report.

"Who's there?" demanded the schoolmaster, sharply, as Noodles' knuckles tapped upon the panel of the door.

"It's me, sir."

"Go away," said Mr. Styngy, in a very acid voice. "I gave orders that I was not to be disturbed."

This was true, and Mr. Crocklejack had made public announcement of that fact; but as Mr. Noodles had a great contempt for the under masters, and looked upon himself as responsible only to Mr. Styngy, he had treated the order with contempt.

"But I say, sir," persisted the odd man, despite the schoolmaster's angry tone——

"*Will* you go away?" roared Mr. Styngy, who was racked just then by a most agonising twinge.

"But if 'ee please, sir," said the obstinate Noodles.

Mr. Styngy was silent for a moment; but there was a sound as of some one groping on the floor in search of some article, and then Mr. Styngy's voice said—

"Come in."

Noodles turned the handle, but scarcely had his head got fairly round the corner than a boot—a Wellington boot—was discharged at it with such force and accuracy that the odd man staggered back, and sank down upon the oil-cloth in the passage with a shock that shook the house to its foundations.

"Take that!" roared Mr. Styngy, "you impertinent, meddling fellow; and learn to obey orders next time, will you?"

The three inseparables were passing the end of the corridor just then, on their way to adorn themselves for church. The vicinity of the head master's room was forbidden ground, but curiosity overruled prudence, and our hero, Charlie Drummond, and Codlings ran towards the fallen Noodles.

"Hallo," whispered Lionel; "what's the matter, old chap?"

Noodles pointed first to his forehead, whereon the heel of the boot had inflicted a huge blue bump, then to the Wellington, and finally to the door of Mr. Styngy's room.

Lionel nodded significantly, and helped Noodles to regain an erect posture, which, however, he seemed to have some little difficulty in maintaining, for his locomotion was of a decidedly "staggery" character.

"What did he do it for?" asked Lionel, as soon as they were out of contact of the wrathful head master.

"*I* don't know," replied Noodles, sulkily; "I wur only goin' to tell him I'd got the new pupil safe in th' stable, when he ups with a boot and downs me like a skittle-pin."

"And serve you right, too," retorted Lionel; "you ought to know better than to worry the 'head' about new pupils on Sunday."

"I should think so," added Charlie Drummond, with affected indignation. "If I'd been Styngy, you should have had the water-jug instead of a boot."

"All you've got to do," Lionel went on, "is to look well after the poor little chap; give him plenty of prog, groom him well, and wait till Mr. Styngy asks you for him. Ta-ta, Noodles."

And speeding away towards their dormitory, Lionel and his friends were soon busy arraying themselves in all the glory of their Sunday clothes.

It was a scramble to get dressed in time, for the church bells had already been clanging out their solemn assembly for some time. Lionel and Charlie just managed to get through as the voice of Mr. Crocklejack was heard along the corridor, but the unfortunate Tommy was in trouble, as usual.

"Dash the tailor!" growled Tommy; "he must do it on purpose, I know he must. He never makes any allowance for a chap growing. Just look at my waistcoat; I can't button *that!*"

"You'll have to wear stays, and take to tight lacing, Tommy," said Lionel; "anyhow, make haste, for here comes Crocklejack."

Tommy made a desperate effort, and, by dint of holding his breath, succeeding in buttoning his waistcoat; but it was extremely painful, and he was compelled to walk along the passage in a doubled-up condition."

"It's awful," whispered Codlings, as he took his place next to our hero; "I can't breathe. Oh! blow that tailor."

Mr. de Bewty was inspector-general of costume in the absence of Mr. Styngy, and, being a very precise man in his own person, he was extremely severe with regard to any deficiency of neatness on the part of the pupils.

Unbuttoned gloves, an unbrushed jacket, and dusty boots, were crimes little short of high treason in his eyes. Poor Tommy was generally deficient in one of these respects, and Mr. de Bewty eyed him with unusual severity.

"Codlings?"

"Yes, sir," said Tommy, in a faint voice.

"Are you hump-backed, Codlings?"

"Not that I'm aware of, sir," replied Tommy, in a husky whisper, occasioned by his being unable to breathe freely.

"Then straighten yourself, sir," said Mr. de Bewty, in an awful voice; "at present you have more of the appearance of a dromedary than a boy."

A cold perspiration bedewed Tommy's forehead as he slowly drew himself up. He could feel the waistcoat-buttons creak and strain, but the tailor's work was good, and, as yet, they held firm.

"If I see you with such a pair of round-shoulders again, Codlings," said Mr. de Bewty, "you shall have something which will straighten them for you very effectually."

And he shook his substantial umbrella menacingly at the unhappy Tommy; who felt himself rapidly growing giddy, and weak from partial suffocation.

"I shall bust," he said, in a gasping whisper, to Lionel. "There never was such an unlucky chap as I am."

"Never mind," replied Lionel; "I'll lend you my knife when we get to church, and you can let out a few stitches."

"Silence!" exclaimed Mr. de Bewty. "Fall into rank, young gentlemen."

And two and two the pupils of Cheetham Hall marched soberly and demurely towards the church.

The place assigned for Mr. Styngy's young gentlemen was just in the rear of the pulpit, facing the pews occupied by the Misses Trotems' young ladies, and, indeed, in full view of the whole congregation.

It was on this account that the head master of Cheetham Hall was so precise regarding the costume of his young gentlemen, and so severe upon any little peccadilloes that they were only too apt to indulge in, even beneath that sacred roof.

Tommy Codlings, who had felt his waistcoat buttons growing weaker and weaker all the way to church, would gladly have taken a back seat; but for his sins—it is to be supposed—he was placed in the front row, and directly facing the centre aisle, with every eye, as it seemed to the unhappy Tommy, fixed upon his waistcoat.

The organist had not yet finished playing the congregation in, and, under cover of the melodious drone, Tommy whispered to Lionel the one word—

"Knife!"

But just then Mr. de Bewty's eye rested upon our hero, and he dared not move.

"Lionel," whispered Tommy again, "your knife; my buttons are going!"

Our hero, under cover of his church-service, sought his right-hand trouser's pocket where the penknife reposed; but just then, Mr. Crocklejack passed along the line to take his place, and Lionel was obliged to become intensely devout once more.

Just then, Tommy felt a slight tickling sensation at the tip of his nose. A stray hair wafted by the breeze had alighted on the tip. Tommy hastily brushed it away, but the mischief was done; he knew that he was going to sneeze.

The sonorous strains of the organ ceased, the rustling of dresses and the fluttering of the leaves of prayer books were stilled, and the clergyman mounted into the lectern.

Tommy grew worse, he was nearly black in the face by reason of his efforts to restrain the explosion, but he held on a little longer, though his eyes were streaming with water, and, with his mouth wide open, was gasping like a freshly-landed fish, greatly to the amusement of the Misses Trotems' young ladies.

Meanwhile, the clergyman proceeded—

"Dearly beloved brethren, the scripture moveth us in sundry places"——

Just then, Tommy Codlings' powers of restraint were exhausted, and he let off a sneeze of such prodigious power that it startled the congregation like the report of a pistol; at the same moment his much-tried waistcoat buttons gave way, and there was the unhappy youth lying back gasping in his seat, with the whole of a wide expanse of shirt front exposed to the horrified gaze of the modest Misses Trotem and their fair pupils.

The clergyman paused, and fixed a glance of mild rebuke upon Tommy. Not so Mr. de Bewty, for, darting like a tiger from its lair, he pounced upon the culprit, and, catching him by the arm, hurried him along the aisle.

But Tommy hadn't done yet, and, in the transit to the door, exploded no less than seven times, each sneeze seeming to be louder than its predecessor.

Arrived outside, Mr. de Bewty propped Tommy up in a convenient corner, and bestowed a stinging slap upon his right ear, following it up by a second on the left, to enable him to keep his balance.

"Oh, you abandoned little vagabond!" said Mr. de Bewty, wrathfully.

"How could I help it?" sobbed Tommy.

FOLLOW MY LEADER.

AS THE HAMPER OF "GAME" WAS OPENED, A GIGANTIC FIGURE QUICKLY ROSE FROM ITS DEPTHS.

No. 8.

"Don't tell me, sir," retorted the usher, in a towering passion, for he was enamoured of the youngest of the three Misses Trotem, and the disgrace of Tommy fell in some measure upon his shoulders. "Why didn't you say you had a cold before you came out?"

"I *haven't* got a cold."

"Then you must have done it on purpose," said Mr. de Bewty; "and, not content with sneezing once, you must repeat your filthy behaviour all down the aisle. Just look at the sleeve of my coat, you—you hardened young reprobate."

And, for the second time, Mr. de Bewty gave the unlucky Tommy a couple of staggerers.

"And your waistcoat, too!" continued the usher, for the first time noticing the total absence of buttons upon that portion of Tommy's attire. "It's positively indecent. I blush for you, sir!"

Tommy was blushing for himself just then, for the open-handed smacks Mr. de Bewty had inflicted upon his cheeks made them red-hot in feeling as well as in colour.

"It was too tight," retorted Tommy, becoming rebellious under a sense of unmerited injury. "How can I help that? Pitch into the tailor, if you must pitch into somebody."

"Don't be insolent, sir!" thundered the usher; "go back to the school, and get off by heart the collect and epistle for the day. I shall expect you to be perfect by the time I return."

And Mr. de Bewty, having first removed the effects of Tommy's sneezing from the cuff of his coat, re-entered the church on tip-toe, leaving the unlucky Codlings to his reflections, which were not of the most cheerful character.

"I'm the most miserable chap in the world, I believe," he murmured. "I've no more memory than a cat at the best of times, and what little I had old Bewty has spanked out of me. Then he'll report me to Styngy, and I shall get it hot from him, for he's in a lovely temper. Two dozen I shall get at the least, and an imposition that'll keep me without holidays for a fortnight. Blest if I won't drown myself."

There was a nice little pond, overhung by a large willow, in a meadow nearly opposite, which Tommy thought would just suit him, so he went and had a look at it.

But, as usual, "distance lent enchantment to the view." It didn't seem nearly such a nice pond when he got close to it, and there was a lot of dark mud and slime, which would have spoilt his clothes. Besides, Tommy felt sure that the bottom was muddy, and then what a lot of trouble he would be giving people in fishing him out and holding an inquest! No; Tommy thought it would not be the genteel thing to do, so he did the most sensible thing that he could have done—walked back to Cheetham Hall and resolved to take his punishment manfully, but equally resolved to "take it out of" Mr. de Bewty the very first chance he got.

And the chance came to Tommy Codlings a great deal sooner than he hoped for.

CHAPTER XXXVII.

MONDAY MORNING AT CHEETHAM HALL—THE BLACK LIST—NOODLES ANNOUNCES THE ARRIVAL OF THE NEW PUPIL—THE NEW PUPIL ARRIVES—HIS RECEPTION "BY" MR. STYNGY, AND HIS RECEPTION "OF" MR. STYNGY.

MONDAY morning dawned, and with it the clang of the "getting up" bell—the scrambling out of bed of the awakened pupils—the fight for the clean towels—the hasty dressing by the dim, cold light—the encounter between so many keen young appetites and sundry piles of bread-and-butter, in which the latter were literally and figuratively "licked"—and then the school-room, with Mr. Styngy, perfectly green with bile, an hour earlier than usual at his desk.

"My stars!" whispered Lionel to Charlie; "some of you will catch it hot, to-day. Don't old Styngy look fierce?"

"I wouldn't be the *new pupil*, for something," returned Drummond. And at the very thought of the little joke he had perpetrated, Lionel was obliged to dodge behind a desk, and choke back a fit of laughter.

As the pupils entered, and took their places, in a much more quiet and orderly manner than usual—for Mr. Styngy's look was ominous—the head master took up a slip of paper from his desk, and consulted it.

Those who had been guilty of misdemeanour on the previous day shuddered, and poor Tommy Codlings turned livid. The slip of paper over which the spectacles of Mr. Styngy wandered was the Black List.

Mr. Styngy laid down the paper, and, beginning at the pupil nearest his left-hand, passed a cold and stony glare slowly along the form, until his eyes encountered those of Tommy Codlings, and then he stopped.

"I knew it," thought Tommy, as a cold chill crept down his spine; "I shall be flayed alive!"

Mr. Styngy's lips were slowly parted to pronounce the name of the unlucky one, when the sagacious Noodles entered the school-room, and saved Tommy for the time.

"Now, Noodles," said Mr. Styngy, sharply; "what is the matter?"

"Nothink, sir, as I'm aweer on," replied Mr. Noodles, civilly.

"What do you *want?*" demanded the head master, with a tremendous emphasis on the last word.

"*I* don't want nothink, sir," replied the stolid Noodles, upon whom Mr. Styngy's angry glance was entirely thrown away.

"Will—you—tell—me—what—you—want—man!" thundered the schoolmaster, putting a pause between each word in order to make the speech more impressive.

"It's about the new pupil," said Mr. Noodles, not in the least ruffled by Mr. Styngy's ferocious demeanour. "I thought you might want to know how he was a gittin' along."

"The new pupil," gasped Mr. Styngy, as the thought of his neglect burst upon his mind. "You mean, young Master Flashaway, Noodles?"

"That's him, sir," returned Noodles, cheerfully, for he had spelt out the placard by the light of his lantern.

"How is it that I was not informed of his arrival before?" demanded Mr. Styngy, majestically.

"Well, I wanted to yes'day mornin'," replied Noodles, in an injured tone. "But 'stead o' listenen', you shies a boot——"

"There, that will do, Noodles—that will do!" said the schoolmaster, hastily. "Where is Master Flashaway?

"In the stable, sir."

"In the stable?" repeated Mr. Styngy, horrified.

"Yes, sir, and very comf't'ble he's a makin' of hisself. A rare good happetite he's got, sir—put away best part of 'arf a 'undred weight of 'A, 'sides a lot of beans, and now he's amoosin' of his little self with chewin' up the manger."

"Hay?—beans?—chewing up the manger?" repeated Mr. Styngy, with a distracted air. "Are you a maniac, Noodles?"

"Not as I'm aweer on, sir, but I've had the measles," replied the odd man, with a stolid imbecility that would have done credit to a brazen monkey, or a modern First Lord of the Admiralty inditing a Slave Circular.

"This is a pretty state of things," said Mr. Styngy, glaring at his assistant masters in a manner that made them tremble in their shoes. "While I am indisposed, a new pupil, the son of my right honourable friend Sir Frederick Flashaway, is confided to the care of an Idiot and allowed to grovel in a Stable!"

"We knew nothing of it, I assure you, sir," said Mr. Crocklejack, almost weeping.

"Knew nothing of it!" repeated Mr. Styngy, with withering scorn. "It seems, sir, that it is your especial province to know nothing of anything. Noodles, bring Master Flashaway here at once. Flashaway Senior, I trust that you will excuse me to the right honourable baronet, your papa, for this unfortunate occurrence."

"Oh, lor," murmured Lionel; "I shall certainly burst—I can't hold out much longer!"

As for Charlie Drummond, he had lifted up the lid of his desk, and buried his head amongst his books, stuffing the better half of a handkerchief into his mouth by way of further precaution.

As for Tommy Codlings, he preserved his gravity tolerably well, by thinking of the thrashing he was certain to get directly.

Noodles had been gone five minutes, and all those not in the secret were eager to get a peep at the strange pupil who preferred sleeping in a stable, and dined upon hay and beans.

Their curiosity was soon gratified. At the expiration of the five minutes, the heavy tread of Noodles was heard, accompanied by a strange "Click-click, clack-clack," then the voice of the odd man was heard saying, "There he be, sir," and then trotted into the schoolroom, not a boy, but a benevolent-looking young donkey.

Mr. Styngy had a little speech all ready, and, as was his usual manner, delivered it with his head erect, and his eyes half shut.

"Master Flashaway," he said, "I beg you to excuse——"

He stopped then, for an irresistible roar of laughter drowned all other sounds—a roar that was taken up again and again, before the bewildered schoolmaster had comprehended its meaning.

But when he *did* open his bewildered eyes to the fact, and saw the placid young donkey standing there—when he did read the words upon the placard, and comprehended at length the nature of the joke that had been played upon him, his wrath was terrible to behold.

The assistant masters cowered behind their desks, the pupils seemed to become part and parcel of theirs, and even the usually unimpressionable Noodles closed the door of the schoolroom, and made his way towards his own particular sanctum.

Only the donkey remained unmoved, as, with a ferocious glare, Mr. Styngy rushed to his desk, and, seizing his cane, strode down the centre of the room, determined to have revenge on someone or something.

That donkey was not such a fool as he looked. He waited until Mr. Styngy, with uplifted cane, was well within range, and then, wheeling round on his fore-legs, as on a pivot, and letting go his hind-hoofs, kicked the schoolmaster just in the spot where his gold repeater was reposing.

My readers may remember that Mr. Styngy was exceedingly bilious that morning. I may therefore safely leave to their imaginations the sequel to the kick inflicted by that calm young donkey.

To say that Mr. Styngy was in a furious passion, would very justly describe the state of the gentleman after he had sufficiently recovered from the effects of the kick to be able to speak.

In the intervals, when he was not occupied in confidential communication with the basin which it had been necessary to fetch, Mr. Styngy gasped out an order that the donkey and Mr. Noodles should be shot.

"I'm dying!" said the schoolmaster. "I know I am; but before I go I'll be revenged! Crocklejack, you have a double-barrelled gun in your room, I know; oblige me by shooting Noodles and the donkey at once!"

"But—but—" returned the usher, turning very pale, "that would be—be—murder, sir!"

"Murder? Nonsense! It's justice!" said Mr. Styngy. "Haven't they killed me? I'll give fifty pounds to anyone who will shoot them! Ugh! Oh, dear me!"

And again the schoolmaster turned his attention to the basin, while the usher looked at him with pallid and alarmed features.

"The shock has been too much for him," said Mr. de Bewty. "His mighty intellect is unsettled!"

It is almost needless to say that the boys were highly delighted with the fun of the scene. Of course, this was very wrong; they should, properly, have been filled with grief at the misfortunes of their revered preceptor. But the fact was that they were all thoroughly enjoying themselves, especially Tommy Codlings, who had retired to a convenient corner, where, leaning his head against the wall, he indulged in suppressed laughter, till he was on the very verge of apoplexy.

There was only one exception to the general merriment, and that was Flashaway. He had not the least doubt in his mind but that Lionel was the author of this fresh insult to him; and, if possible, the hatred he felt for our hero was redoubled.

Only too gladly would he have carried out Mr. Styngy's frantic sentence upon Lionel himself, but, as that was out of the question, and as his mean soul burned with a desire to revenge himself upon something or somebody, he offered to be the executioner of the poor little donkey.

"If you'll lend me your gun, Mr. Crocklejack," he said, "I'll do it."

"Great heavens, Flashaway!" exclaimed the usher. "What are you talking about? It would be murder! Mr. Styngy is not in his right senses!"

"What!" added Lionel; "offer to kill your own brother, Flashaway? This is a modern edition of Cain and Abel with a vengeance!"

"You hold *your* tongue," said the bully, savagely. "Nobody asked for your advice. If Mr. Styngy wants the donkey shot, I'll do it!"

"And I say that if you attempt to injure the poor brute," retorted Lionel, "I'll give you such a thrashing as you never had in your life; so, now."

The bully thought that he was safe from Lionel while the master was present, and stepping forward he made an attempt to grasp the donkey; but that sagacious animal, recognising an enemy, reared up on his hind-legs, and shooting out its fore-feet with the skill and force of an accomplished boxer, struck Flashaway full in the chest, and sent him reeling over the recumbent form of the head master.

"Take the donkey away," whispered Lionel to Charlie, "or the poor beast will suffer for this. Lead him out into the road, take the placard off his neck first, and he'll find his way home; make haste!"

Charlie obeyed, and giving Lionel a wink full of meaning, led the little animal out of the schoolroom. Neddy, as if quite capable of distinguishing his friends from his enemies, made not the slightest resistance, while the confusion caused by the fall of the bully allowed the manœuvre to be executed unnoticed.

It was a long time before anything like order could be established in the schoolroom, Mr. Styngy was so dreadfully ill that he had to be carried to his bedroom, and Flashaway was much in the same condition.

"Never mind, old chap," said Tommy Codlings to the bully, as he was being led away by Jabez Hunker; "it was very unbrotherly of him to kick wasn't it? If I were you I'd ask my father to cut him off with a shilling, and stop his weekly allowance of thistles!"

Flashaway was too weak and ill just then to retort as he would like to do, but he treasured up the recollection of Tommy's taunt, and resolved to repay that usually unfortunate young gentleman at the earliest possible opportunity.

CHAPTER XXXVIII.

MR. STYNGY'S PLAN FOR THE DISCOVERY OF THE "PRACTICAL JOKE," AND HOW IT SUCCEEDED—TOMMY CODLINGS GETS "IN FOR IT" AGAIN, AS USUAL—HIS REVENGE, AND THE CONSEQUENCES THEREOF.

When Mr. Styngy had a little recovered from the effects of Lionel's practical joke, his first step was to institute a strict inquiry into the cause of the advent of the donkey to Cheetham Hall.

That inquiry resulted in the discovery of the real Master Flashaway at the hotel, and the certainty that some one had been audacious enough to trifle with one of the members of the illustrious house of Flashaway.

Then came the question—"Who did it?" An easy one to ask, but a difficult one to answer, when Mr. Styngy knew himself surrounded by some sixty odd youths all "boiling over" with animal spirits.

"If I find out who has done this," said Mr. Styngy, giving his pillow an emphatic thump, and addressing himself to Mr. Crocklejack, "I'll prosecute him!"

"And very rightly too, sir," replied the usher. "It's scandalous!"

"Shameful!"

"Disgraceful!"

"Ought to be whipped at a cart's tail!"

"He shall be whipped at his own tail when I find him," said Mr. Styngy. "The idea of telling Master Flashaway that there was some dreadful infectious disease here at Cheetham Hall. That's libel, I think, Crocklejack?"

"Undoubtedly, sir—very much so," was the obedient reply of the under master.

"Now, Crocklejack, there is one way of getting at the culprit. Master Flashaway Junior saw and spoke to the author of this abominable practical joke at the station, did he not?"

"He did, sir."

"Very good, then, Master Flashaway will be able to recognise the culprit—either by sight or sound. He shall have the whole school paraded before him, Crocklejack, and when he *does* pick out the culprit, I'll——"

Mr. Styngy did not finish his sentence, but the awful pause which followed his concluding words sufficiently indicated the fate in store for the victim *when he was caught.*

This little conversation took place in Mr. Styngy's bed-room, two days after the events recorded in our last chapter. From which circumstance my readers will naturally infer that the unfortunate school-master had not recovered fully from the combined attacks of biliousness and donkey-kicks.

He kept his word with regard to parading the school, though, to do him justice, he was not of a particularly malicious or revengeful nature; but the joke had been carried a little too far this time, and he meant "having it out of" somebody.

"My eye!" said Drummond, when on the third morning Mr. Styngy, supported by Mr. de Bewty on one side and Mr. Crocklejack on the other, entered the room, "doesn't he look shaky, Li?"

"He just does!" replied our hero, emphatically; "and it's my belief, Charlie, that he'll make some of us look shaky before the day's out."

"Do you think he's found out anything?" asked Drummond, looking suddenly pale.

"No, but he's going to try; and if anyone chanced to see us about the station that afternoon we shall be in for it."

"Then I'm afraid *you're* done for, old fellow. Young Flashaway is sure to pick you out."

"I don't think so. He's one of those down-looking chaps who can never look you straight in the eyes; besides, he dodged away from me as if I'd been red hot, when I said I had the geological thingummy."

"I don't feel quite comfortable, though," whispered Charlie, with an ominous shake of his head.

"You're safe enough, and so is Codlings," said Lionel. "Hush! there's old Styngy going to speak."

"Is every boy present, and in his place?" demanded the schoolmaster, speaking with slow and measured accents.

The assistant masters reported every boy present, and the more timid, though innocent ones, began already to feel as if their spines had been iced.

"Flashaway Junior," Mr. Styngy observed, "be kind enough to stand here by me, and, as the pupils pass you in order, look at them attentively, and pick out the boy who spoke to you at the station."

Class after class filed slowly by. Lionel and Drummond had both safely passed the ordeal, and only Tommy Codling's class remained.

Now Flashaway Junior was fully determined that someone should suffer; and as he had not the faintest possible recollection of Lionel, it became necessary to pitch upon the one least capable of retaliation.

There was something very tempting about Tommy's appearance that morning. He was so plump and rosy and happy looking—for he felt confident that *he* had not been seen—that Flashaway Junior, who was invariably miserable, felt aggravated, and, looking straight at Tommy, said—

"That's the one, sir."

"I thought so," said Mr. Styngy, glaring in such a ferocious way at Tommy that the blood of that unhappy boy seemed to freeze in his veins. "Codlings, come here!"

But Tommy was petrified by the unexpected accusation. He could neither speak nor move until a smartish cut from Mr. Styngy's cane awoke him to the reality of his position.

"You hear what the young gentleman says, you abandoned young profligate?" said Mr. Styngy—touching Tommy up again—"you hear, sir?"

"Oh, if you please, sir!" said Tommy, pathetically; "it isn't true. I never spoke to him in my life, sir."

"You are quite sure this is the boy?" said Mr. Styngy, addressing himself to Flashaway Junior.

"Quite certain, sir; I recognise the sound of his voice now, perfectly."

"Oh, what a lie!" exclaimed Tommy, forgetting for a moment the august presence in which he stood. "I'll warm you for that. Oh!"

Tommy's threat was interrupted by Mr. Styngy's cane, which descended with a vicious "swish," and nearly cut him in half.

"You audacious vagabond!" thundered Mr. Styngy. "You dare to threaten the young gentleman before my very face."

"What did he want to tell lies about me for, then? Oh!"

Mr. Styngy had got off his stool, and, taking good aim, caught Tommy for the second time just below the tail of his jacket. The yell and the frantic leap which the unlucky one immediately executed would have done no discredit to a first-class Shaker in good practice.

"Now hold out your hand," said Mr. Styngy.

"I won't," replied Tommy, smarting with pain and a strong sense of injustice. "I'm not going to be whacked for nothing."

Flashaway Junior was thoroughly enjoying Tommy's torments; he had no small share of his elder brother's mean and cruel disposition, a nature which absolutely revelled in the infliction of pain—the sort of nature, in short, with which Nero is usually credited.

Tommy, in the midst of his suffering, caught sight of the smile upon Flashaway's pale face. It was that last straw which broke the back of Tommy's patience. Regardless of the consequences, he dodged by Mr. Styngy, and bestowed upon his enemy a kick on the right shin, which was distinctly heard throughout the schoolroom.

It was Flashaway's turn to howl now, and howl he did with such vehemence, that a pig in danger of his life from the butcher would have been musical in comparison.

As for Tommy, he was instantly pounced upon by the three masters, each one grabbing some portion of him, and so was hauled away to the torture chamber, alias the library.

"Poor Tommy!" said Lionel. "My eye, won't he catch it this time! What did you hold me for when I wanted to go up and tell the truth?"

"Because it wouldn't have done any good," replied Charlie. "You would have had a thrashing, but it wouldn't have saved Tommy."

"Perhaps not. Only I shouldn't like Tommy to think I'm a sneak, who let another fellow suffer for what I did."

"No fear of that, old chap. I say, what a hot 'un he let young Flashaway have on the shin!"

"Yes; look at him over there. He's pulling up his trousers to look at the place. See, there's a good six inches of the bark taken off. Ha! ha! ha!"

"That will comfort Tommy in the midst of his sufferings. If he could only see how he has barked that little sneak's shin, he wouldn't mind his own back being flayed."

* * * *

It was a whole week before Tommy re-entered the schoolroom and took his usual place.

It was easy to see that he had suffered during that period, for he was very pale, and almost thin, and there was a savage glare in his eyes which betokened the thirst for vengeance that was strong within him.

Immediately after class was over, Tommy was surrounded by a crowd of sympathisers, all eager to hear the account of his sufferings. Foremost amongst them were, of course, Lionel and Charlie.

"Poor old chap," said our hero. "Why, they've been starving you, Tommy; you couldn't burst your waistcoat buttons now."

"Bread and water for a week would pull anybody down; and I didn't get too much of that, either. But where's that Flashaway?"

"What for, Tommy? I should think you've had enough of meddling with him."

"If I was to be beheaded for doing it the next minute, I'd punch his ugly head," said Tommy, viciously. "Ah! there he is."

Codlings was after him like a flash, and had him penned into a corner of the playground in less than no time.

"Now, you just let me alone, will you?" said Flashaway Junior, nervously.

"Oh, yes; I'll let you alone, when I've done with you. Just take off your jacket, unless you prefer being thrashed while you're in it?"

"I'll tell Mr. Styngy, if you don't let me alone."

"I know you will, so I'm going to give you a hiding while I've got the chance. Will you fight?"

"No I won't; and I'll go away, I will. I won't stop in a school where there are low vulgar boys, always wanting to fight."

"Make haste and get it over," whispered Lionel; "there's old Crocklejack looking this way."

"Now, I'm going to give you one on the nose," said Tommy, squaring scientifically up to the frightened Flashaway Junior. "Don't say I didn't give you warning. One——"

Tommy hit straight and true from the shoulder, Flashaway's nose was flattened out, and two thin crimson streams trickled into his mouth.

The sight aroused Tommy's appetite for blood, and he punched away merrily at his antagonist, who yelled, and kicked, and scratched, and finally lay down on the ground.

But Tommy had not had enough yet. He lay down on the ground, too, and, encircling Flashaway's head with his left arm, pegged away with his right in splendid style until, flushed and triumphant, he was dragged up by a strong hand, and found himself face to face with Mr. Crocklejack.

"What is the meaning of this, sir?"

"Only a little turn-up, sir," replied Tommy, cheerfully. He had had his revenge, and was quite prepared to take the consequences.

"Only a little turn-up!" repeated Mr. Crocklejack; "you shall have a turn-up of a very different nature directly. Come with me, and you, too, Master Flashaway."

Tommy went like a lamb to the slaughter, and his fate may be imagined. Mr. Styngy spoilt four canes, and tired his arm so that he was unable to write for the rest of the day. Poor Tommy writhed in anguish on the mattress in the solitary room where he was locked up, but he thought of Flashaway Junior's flattened nose and blackened eyes, and felt comforted.

There was another reflection that comforted him, too, and that was a certain plan he had formed for Mr. Styngy's especial benefit.

"I'll teach him," murmured Tommy, "to flay a chap alive. Only wait till he lets me out of this, and I'll pay him out beautifully."

CHAPTER XXXIX.

TOMMY CODLINGS IN SOLITARY CONFINEMENT—HIS SUFFERINGS THEREIN—HIS VOW OF VENGEANCE—MR. DE BEWTY MAKES A PRESENT OF A "LITTLE GAME" TO MR. STYNGY.

It is an old proverb that "Revenge is sweet," and one which is generally accepted as truthful. Tommy Codlings found his revenge, while he was taking it out of Flashaway Junior, very pleasant indeed, but the punishment was proportionately unpleasant.

For a fortnight after he had enjoyed the delicious joy of flattening his enemy's nose, the unfortunate Tommy languished on bread and water in solitary confinement, which was only enlivened by the daily appearance of Mr. de Bewty, who, to keep the culprit from catching cold—for there was no fire in the room—gently stimulated the circulation of the vital fluid in Tommy's veins by the free application of a long and limber cane.

Mr. Styngy would have expelled him, but it happened that Tommy's friends were abroad, which was a fortunate thing for the plump youth, inasmuch as his guardian was a stricter disciplinarian than even the schoolmaster, and Tommy's fate would indeed have been a dreadful one.

On the last morning of his confinement, Mr. de Bewty, who quite enjoyed this department of his profession, unlocked the door, and, as usual, greeted Tommy with a pleasant nod and smile, as if he were about to confer some great favour instead of a couple of dozen stripes from the cane he flourished so gracefully in his right hand.

"Good morning, Codlings," said Mr. de Bewty. "Cold—is it not?"

Tommy gave a sulky nod—eyed the usher malignantly. He did not appreciate politeness under the circumstances.

"This is the last morning I shall have the pleasure of visiting you—at least for the present," Mr. de Bewty continued; "and, therefore, I am willing to grant you a little favour, Codlings."

FOLLOW MY LEADER.

MR. STYNGY ASSUMED AN ATTITUDE OF DIGNIFIED INDIGNATION AS THE NEW PUPIL WAS INTRODUCED.

Tommy brightened up. The usher was going to let him off this time.

"Thank you, sir," he said, gratefully. "I am getting very sore indeed, sir."

"All for your good, Codlings—all for your good," said Mr. de Bewty, amiably; "but, as I was saying, this is your last flogging, and so I will allow you to choose whether you will be caned over the hands or on the back; or, if you like, you can have a dozen each way."

"I don't call that a favour," grumbled Tommy, disconcertedly. "Flay me where you like, I don't care."

"That is ungrateful, Codlings; but never mind—I am used to ingratitude from boys. Are you ready?"

"It would be all the same if I wasn't," grumbled Codlings. "Make haste, please, and get it over, sir."

Mr. de Bewty rather delighted in the refinement of torture, and he aggravated poor Tommy's pain by sundry ingenious devices. He would make a point to cut him in one place, and then, as Tommy involuntarily raised his arm to ward the blow, deliver a stinger on some unprotected portion of his frame. Then he would make a great show of accurately counting the strokes, and pretending to forget, pause, and ask Tommy's opinion as to whether he had had seven or eight stripes, while the tears were yet coursing down the sufferer's cheek and he was writhing with agony.

It is certain that Tommy was one of the best and gentlest boys that any one could have encountered in a long day's march, and it is equally certain that the severe and even cruel punishment inflicted on him was sowing the deadly seeds of hatred, malice, and all uncharitableness within him. Had he possessed such a nature as the bully Flashaway, Mr. de Bewty's life would hardly have been safe.

"Oh, lor, how I do smart!" groaned Tommy. "What a beast that Bewty is. Don't I wish I was a man, that's all. Let me see: in six years I shall be over twenty. I know I shall be strong, and big enough to pitch into him then. I'll take lessons from a prize-fighter, and then won't I let him and old Styngy have it."

The contemplation of his coming vengeance obliterated for a time the pain of his bruises, and Tommy, propping the bolster up in the corner to represent his tormentor De Bewty, rehearsed the scene of his revenge, and punched the bolster with hearty good will until the arrival of Noodles with the prison diet—a large slice of dry bread and a tumbler of cold water.

"I should think, Master Codlings," said the odd man, with a grin, as he watched Tommy pegging away at the dry bread, "that you feels a bit bilious arter a fortnight o' that rich kind o' grub."

"Never you mind whether I'm bilious or not," replied Tommy, shortly. "If you're anxious to know you can try for yourself. What are you waiting for. Why don't you go?"

"I'm waitin' till you're done," replied the odd man. "You're to come alonger me to the school-room when you've polished orf that there plate o' roast weal and that there glass o' wine."

"There's the bone for you to pick," said Tommy, dexterously throwing a hard piece of crust, which fitted with painful accuracy into the orbit of Mr. Noodles' right eye.

"Your temper ain't improved, Master Codlings," said Noodles, as he removed the crust. "Likewise, no more have Mr. Styngy's."

"If you think that a fortnight on bread and water and two dozen stingers every morning is the way to turn a boy into a first-class angel, you're mistaken, Noodles—that's all. But there, cut away, I'm glad to get out of this hole at any price."

Arrived at the schoolroom, Tommy was formally handed over to the custody of Mr. de Bewty, who solemnly marched him up the centre towards the desk of the head master.

It was evident that Mr. Styngy had not yet recovered from his illness, for he was very pale, and the stern glance which he bent upon Tommy showed that his wrath was unappeased.

"Codlings," the head master began, after silencing with a tremendous frown some faint symptoms of applause which had accompanied Tommy's entrance, "you have now suffered the just punishment of your shameful behaviour. It is painful indeed to see one so young give evidence of such a malicious and revengeful disposition as prompted you to attack Flashaway Junior in so savage a manner."

"What did he want to say it was me for, then?" said Tommy, in a decidedly rebellious voice.

"Silence, sir!" thundered Mr. Styngy. "If you speak another word in that tone I order you back to solitary confinement."

That was the only threat which had any force to quell Tommy. He would not have minded a fresh "round" of caning, but he could not endure a second course of bread and water diet.

"As you have now completed the allotted term of your punishment, Codlings," Mr. Styngy went on, "I will permit you once again to resume your place amongst your schoolfellows; but, before doing so, I hope you are sufficiently penitent to confess your sorrow for what has taken place?"

"I am—very sorry indeed, sir," said Tommy, in an unmistakable tone of sincerity.

"And you will say as much to Flashaway Junior?" demanded Mr. Styngy.

"I'd say so to anybody, sir," replied Tommy. "I'm very sorry indeed that I've been caned and kept on bread and water for a fortnight."

This was such a doubtful kind of repentance that the head master frowned sternly at him, and seemed half inclined to exact the apology he required; but reflecting probably that the culprit had had enough punishment for the present, he dismissed him to his seat, and the usual duties of the school were resumed.

But what a crowd of sympathising questioners surrounded the unfortunate Tommy when the classes were dismissed at twelve o'clock! He would have needed forty tongues to have replied to a tithe of the questions that were showered down upon him.

Tommy solved the problem by replying to none, and sought refuge with Lionel and Drummond in a secluded corner of the playground, where, as the sentimental novelists say, "he poured forth his sorrows into the sympathising bosoms of his friends."

"It's a confounded shame!" said Lionel, when Tommy had concluded his tale of woe. "That makes just three weeks of bread and water, not counting the whackings; and my stars, ain't you thin!"

"I don't mind that so much," replied the sufferer. "I always had a fancy for a genteel figure; but the way that brute De Bewty used to cane me! oh my!"

And Tommy writhed, as if he were once again under the torturing influence of the usher's cane.

"He never spared me a single cut," Tommy went on, "and often he used to pretend that he'd lost count, and give me one or two extra to make sure, though he knew I was so sore that I could hardly bear to have my shirt on."

"Tommy, said Lionel, resolutely, "we must pay De Bewty out for this."

"I've been thinking of it ever since I was locked up; but I couldn't think of any plan, Li. I've no more invention than a peg-top."

"We'll think of something for you," replied our hero. "Don't be afraid, Tommy; he shan't get off scot-free."

"If," said Codlings, with a vengeful gleam in his eye, "we could only poison him a little—not much you know, but just enough to make him feel uncomfortable."

"Nonsense, Tommy," laughed Lionel. "We

mustn't meddle with such things as that. Why, you'll be challenging him to fight a duel next."

"I should jolly well like to," replied Codlings, viciously. "I wish I was big enough, I'd do it."

"I say," said Drummond, who had been deep in thought for some minutes, "do you know that De Bewty has a hamper of game coming up from the country?"

"No; has he?"

"Yes, and he means making a present of it to the 'head.' I heard him telling Noodles that if a hamper came while he was out, to pay the carriage, and take it up to De Bewty's room."

Lionel reflected for a moment, and then gave Tommy a slap on the shoulder, which made that young gentleman roar with anguish.

"I beg your pardon, old fellow, I forgot that you were so sore; but I've hit upon a plan to serve De Bewty out."

"Have you, though," said Tommy, forgetting his sufferings on the instant. "Hooray! what is it, Li?"

For a few moments the heads of the three friends were so close to each other that they might have been growing on one pair of shoulders, while our hero whispered his confidential communication.

The result was peculiar. Charlie Drummond went to the wall, and, leaning up against it, went through a series of convulsions which might have induced anyone out in the street to think that he was suffering dreadful internal agony, but he was only laughing; while Tommy Codlings, in spite of his aching back and limbs, indulged in a frantic pas seul, composed of an Irish jig and an Indian war dance, with a few fancy steps of his own invention thrown in.

This little incident occurred during the ten minutes' interval between the dismissal of the morning classes and the ringing of the dinner bell. It was scarcely over, and Tommy was yet merrily "jigging" away, when the bell rang, and almost at the same moment the carrier entered the school gate, bearing a hamper on his shoulder.

Noodles was not at his post, of course—he never was, when wanted. Lionel's quick eye sighted the man at once, and he seized the opportunity and the hamper.

"Come, now; you ain't De Bewty, Heskwire?" said the carrier. "If yer air, there's two and thruppence to pay."

"All right," said Lionel, whose only object was to ascertain that the hamper was really the one destined for the usher; "it's for our second master. I'll send him to you."

And away he ran towards the school, whispering to Charlie as he reached him—

"It's all right—the hamper's come. Shall we do it?"

"Rather!" replied Charlie.

"Suppose we're missed out of our classes?"

"No fear of that, for half-an-hour. Crocklejack always goes to sleep on his desk, after dinner."

"All serene, then. I'll send Noodles out to the carrier; and, while you go in to dinner, I'll take notice of where De Bewty tells him to put it. He won't give it to Styngy till the evening."

All went well with the conspirators. Noodles strolled out to the carrier in a leisurely way, which greatly aggravated that personage, paid the carriage, and hauled it up to Mr. de Bewty's room, in all of which operations he was carefully watched by Lionel.

The mid-day meal over, the boys of Cheetham Hall dispersed for the usual quarter-of-an-hour, which they industriously employed in playing such games as "leap-frog" and "touch," for the purpose, no doubt, of shaking their food well down, and getting it as far away from their brains as possible.

Lionel and his chums were generally foremost in the fun, but on this occasion they might have been seen stealthily creeping up the staircase, in the direction of the usher's bed-room.

"Don't you think you'd better stop behind?" said Drummond, to Tommy Codlings. "It don't matter so much if we're caught, but if you're dropped on to-day, you'll be murdered."

"Stop behind?" said Tommy. "Not if I know it! I wouldn't miss the chance of serving old Bewty out for six months' pocket-money."

The usher's bedroom was close to the dormitories—an artful arrangement of Mr. Styngy's, in case of any surreptitious "larking" on the part of the pupils, which the proximity of the usher would compel him to hear, and arise shivering and grumbling in his night-shirt and trousers to put a stop to.

The door was unlocked, and, with the noiselessness popularly attributed to ghosts, they entered, and reclosed the door behind them.

"There's the hamper," said Lionel. "You untie the strings, Charlie; don't cut them, whatever you do. You, Tommy, listen at the keyhole, and give us the tip if you hear anyone in the corridor. I'll go to work on the sofa. Make haste, everybody; there's no time to be lost.

* * * *

A quarter of an hour afterwards the three conspirators might have been seen descending the staircase as cautiously as they had mounted, just in time to mingle with the last of the stragglers from the playground, and enter the schoolroom unsuspected.

During the whole of that afternoon Mr. de Bewty's features wore an expression of such perfect content that he looked positively happy. Mr. Crocklejack noted the change, and wondered at it, but the second master knew what he was about; the present of game to Mr. Styngy would soften that stern individual and avert a further reduction of salary, which Mr. de Bewty, as one contemplating matrimony, could not bear to think of.

The moment the afternoon classes were over and the boys dismissed to tea, Mr. de Bewty ran up stairs to his chamber, panting with eagerness to bestow his present upon Mr. Styngy.

"It's almost a pity to give away so much," thought the usher, as he took a letter out of his pocket and glanced through it. "Let me see. Here's the list. Two brace of pheasants, two hares, and four rabbits—a nice little hamper that. I don't think he'll offer to cut down my salary this quarter."

Mr. de Bewty retired to the little sofa, and "plumped" down upon it with the intention of regarding his pet hamper from a new point of view; but, to his horror, he felt the seat give way beneath him, just as if he had sat upon an inflated paper-bag.

"Well, that's curious," mused the usher, when he had extricated himself from the sofa and patted the horse-hair seat. "I'm certain that there were some springs in it when I sat down yesterday—and—bless my soul! what has become of my new hat?"

That article of personal attire—Mr. de Bewty's best Sunday one—was missing from its accustomed peg. He hunted in all the drawers, looked under the sofa, under the bed, and searched the most impossible corners, but the hat was gone.

"Perhaps Noodles has taken it away to brush," thought Mr. de Bewty; "but there's no time to inquire now. I must get this hamper down before Mr. Styngy goes out."

The usher grasped the handles, but it was as much as he could do to stagger to the door with it.

"Whew!" he panted; "I didn't think game was so heavy as this. I must get someone to help me. Hi! who's there?"

Just then, by a remarkable coincidence, Lionel, Charlie Drummond, and Tommy Codlings happened to be passing along the corridor. It is just possible that they had been waiting there on purpose; but Mr. de Bewty never thought so.

"Oh, it's you, is it?" said the usher. "Do you think you are strong enough to help me downstairs with this hamper. It's a little game, which I am going to make a present of to Mr. Styngy."

"With pleasure, sir," replied Lionel and Charlie together, as they took hold of one side of the hamper, while Mr. de Bewty supported the other, and so staggered down the stairs.

"Rather heavy, isn't it?" panted the usher, as they reached the bottom of the first flight of stairs.

"Very, sir," said Lionel, gravely; "but I hear that the game is extremely fine this year."

"So it need be," replied the usher. "Whew! It weighs half-a-ton, I believe."

"Oh, it's nothing, sir," said Lionel, with a wink to Charlie. "Trifles light as hare."

It was perhaps fortunate for our hero that Mr. de Bewty was too much occupied with his hamper to notice this little joke. To keep the wicker-work away from his shins was quite as much as he could conveniently manage, and when they arrived at the library door he heaved a sigh of relief.

"Don't go yet, Lionel," he said. "I shall want you to help me in with it."

And just pausing while he hurriedly arranged his necktie and brushed the dust from his trousers, Mr. de Bewty put on his most captivating smile, and tapped at the door.

"Come in," said the voice of Mr. Styngy.

"Oh, I beg your pardon, sir; I didn't know you were engaged," said Mr. de Bewty, pretending to draw back as he saw Crocklejack and Professor Tomkini in conference with the head master.

"Come in, come in, Mr. de Bewty," said Mr. Styngy, amiably.

"It's only a little hamper of game, sir," continued the usher, "which has just been sent to me from the country, and which I have the pleasure of offering for your acceptance."

"Oh, indeed; you are too kind. Couldn't think of depriving you," murmured Mr. Styngy, as the usher, Lionel, and Charlie staggered in beneath the weight of the hamper, Tommy Codlings following close behind with a bit of straw, being determined to see the fun.

"A mere trifle, sir—a mere trifle," said Mr. de Bewty, in an off-hand way. "Just a few pheasants, a couple of hares, and some rabbits."

Mr. Styngy involuntarily licked his lips. He was particularly fond of pheasants, and quite doted upon jugged hare, though the latter delicacy invariably made him bilious for a week.

Mr. Crocklejack and the professor looked daggers at De Bewty. What a mean sneak he must be, they thought, to curry favour with his employer by bribing him with game. They couldn't have done such a thing for worlds, not they.

"Hum," murmured Mr. Styngy, as a pleased gastronomical smile lit up his features. "Pheasants, hares, rabbits. Ha! Really very kind of you, Mr. de Bewty. Suppose we look at them?"

Mr. de Bewty was burning with the desire to exhibit his present, and annihilate his rivals' chances for the favour of the head master. His pocket-knife was out in an instant—the straps were cut—when, with a crash, the lid flew open, and then sprang upwards with alarming suddenness a hideous, unearthly figure!

CHAPTER XL.

MR. DE BEWTY'S "LITTLE PRESENT OF GAME," TURNS OUT TO BE ANYTHING BUT A "LARK"—TOMMY CODLINGS HAS A VERY NARROW ESCAPE.

MR. STYNGY'S reverend nose was immediately over the hamper when the startling event with which we concluded our last chapter occurred; and, as a natural consequence, the tall hat which the unearthly figure wore smote him with considerable violence as it sprang upwards.

The schoolmaster was still nervous by reason of his recent illness, and, giving utterance to a yell of terror, he leaped backwards into a corner, where, for a few moments, he stood gazing with dilated eyes at the weird shape, which was nodding to and fro with the regular frequency of a Chinese mandarin paying a visit of ceremony.

Poor Mr. de Bewty was even more startled than the principal; he had shot backwards as the figure shot upwards, stumbled over a chair, and sat down in Mr. Styngy's model aquarium, much to the alarm of the gold fish therein contained.

Mr. Crocklejack and the professor had been also startled, but only for a very short time. They recovered their presence of mind almost instantly, and demonstrated the harmlessness of the figure, by hauling it out of the hamper, and pulling it to pieces, when it proved to be composed of nothing more unearthly than some sofa springs, an old coat, a fifth-of-November mask, and Mr. de Bewty's missing hat by way of summit to the edifice.

Mr. Styngy had been angry—very angry indeed, when the young donkey was introduced into the schoolroom, but then he was violently passionate. Now, he was very calm, and very pale, as he silently eyed Mr. de Bewty and the hamper. The usher felt that he would much rather have had the schoolmaster rave, stamp, or even swear.

"I see, sir," began Mr. Styngy, in a tone of dreadful calmness. "I fully appreciate your delicate attentions—a present indeed worthy of my acceptance. Believe me, Mr. de Bewty, I shall not forget this little "GAME."

The poor usher was still lodged in the aquarium, apparently quite indifferent to the fact that he was getting extremely wet behind, and that the gold fish were much annoyed at his intrusion. He was trying to collect his scattered senses, and understand what was the matter.

"Mr. de Bewty meant no harm, sir," said the rival usher, affecting to conciliate the wrathful "head." "It was only a little joke, no doubt."

"I am astonished at you, Crocklejack," said Mr. Styngy, sternly. "Do you think that I am the proper subject for a joke—the principal of this establishment, and his employer?"

"Don't be too severe with him, sir," said Crocklejack again, knowing quite well that the more he pleaded on De Bewty's behalf the more angry the schoolmaster would become. "It was intended as a pleasant surprise."

"A pleasant surprise!" ejaculated Mr. Styngy, wrathfully. "A very pleasant one indeed, to promise a gentleman a hamper of game, and then nearly startle him out of his senses by a tomfool's trick. I'll 'pleasant surprise' him!"

And Mr. Styngy, red-hot with wrath, strode forward, and before any one could prevent him—if any one, indeed, had felt inclined—bestowed upon Mr. de Bewty a vigorous "punch" on the head.

The blow was what is usually described in pugilistic language as a "hot 'un," and it aroused Mr. de Bewty to a sense of his position. He saw Mr. Styngy getting ready to let him have another, and, in making one mighty struggle to force himself from the aquarium in which he had become embedded, the fragile glass gave way with a crash, and the unlucky De Bewty sat down in the midst of the fragments.

A more uncomfortable seat than a floor carpeted with broken glass it would be difficult to find, and so the usher thought, as he uttered a doleful howl, and scrambled up only to be instantly knocked down again by his principal.

"Ow—ow—ow!" yelled Mr. de Bewty. "Murdah!"

"Calm yourself, sir!" said Crocklejack, catching Mr. Styngy by one arm.

"Think of your position, sir!" added Tomkini.

"Let me go!" thundered the schoolmaster, whose anger, which had been simmering for many days, now fairly boiled over. "I will *not* be restrained."

Until now Tommy Codlings had confined the expression of his joy at the sufferings of De Bewty to pantomime, but at this point his exultation at the downfall of the tyrannical usher overcame his prudence, and he said aloud—

"Brayvo! Go it! Let him have another!"

Up to this time Mr. Styngy had forgotten the presence of Lionel and his friends, he had been so engrossed by his passion. The sound of Tommy's voice, though, reminded him that he was compromising his dignity by fighting in the presence of his pupils.

"H'm—ha," muttered the schoolmaster, letting fall the hand with which he was about to smite De Bewty for the third time. "I—er—had forgotten—that is—I—was unaware that you were present, young gentlemen. As it is, you will oblige me, out of consideration for—for Mr. de Bewty, not to mention to your schoolfellows the ridiculous scene which has just occurred. I address myself particularly to *you*, Codlings."

Tommy, who was perspiring at every pore with fear lest Mr. Booty should have heard his unlucky words, stammered out—

"Of course, sir—certainly, sir; I shouldn't think of mentioning it, sir."

"Take care that you do not," said Mr. Styngy, with such a fierce look and emphasis, that Tommy literally shuddered himself a couple of yards towards the door. "Now, young gentlemen, you may go," he added, to Lionel and Charlie; "and send Noodles to me to clear away this rubbish."

By the way in which the schoolmaster looked at Mr. de Bewty, as he spoke these last words, it might easily have been imagined that he included his assistant in the contemptuous epithet. But the usher did not hear him—he was too much occupied just then in the slow and painful process of picking out the pieces of broken glass.

"What a fellow you are, Tommy," said Charlie, as soon as the three chums were safe in the passage. "If it hadn't been that the 'head' wanted the affair kept quiet you would have had another fortnight of solitary confinement for saying what you did."

"I couldn't help it," replied Tommy. "Lor, what fun it was to see him punching De Bewty's head! I do wish he'd given him another topper; I'd have taken a licking for it, and felt happy!"

"It's more than I should," said Drummond, "if I had been dosed with cane like you for the last three weeks. Why you look as if you'd been made out of bits of a broken rainbow, now, when you're stripped."

"It's my natural condition," said Tommy, cheerfully. "The nurse used to spank me black-and-blue when I was a baby, and somebody or other has kept the game alive ever since."

"Talk about something else," said Lionel, in a lower voice; "here comes some of the other fellows, and we must keep our promise to Styngy."

CHAPTER XLI.

A NEW PUPIL ARRIVES (A REAL ONE THIS TIME)—WHAT HE HAD TO SAY TO LIONEL—AND WHAT LIONEL HAD TO SAY TO HIM—FRENCH AGAINST ENGLISH—THE QUARREL—THE CHALLENGE—THE DUEL.

BOYS are proverbially careless as to what they say or do, and, in a general way, a promise is almost as soon forgotten as made; but Lionel's sense of honour was very strong, and he managed somehow to communicate it to all with whom he was intimate. So it happened that not a word was whispered in the school affecting Mr. de Bewty's little hamper of game, and the promise was religiously kept.

The only thing regarding his little practical joke that made Lionel uneasy, was the fear that the usher might lose his situation. Boy as our hero then was, he knew to some degree how poorly paid were the men who devoted their lives to the teaching of the young.*

It was a great relief to him when he saw Mr. de Bewty take his accustomed place in the school on the following day; though Lionel was hardly able to refrain from breaking out into a laugh, when he noticed that the unlucky usher carefully avoided sitting down, and seemed to walk with exceeding difficulty, as if the joints in his legs had become suddenly stiffened.

Utterly indifferent to the fact that he had not prepared a line of his lessons, Tommy watched the usher with a grim, unholy satisfaction, and every time that Mr. de Bewty's features contracted with pain, as some unremoved pieces of glass gave him an extra pang, Tommy dived behind his desk and indulged in a perfect volley of chuckles.

At any other time Tommy would have been severely punished for his ignorance that day, but Mr. de Bewty was utterly incapable of using the cane. Any violent exertion would have caused him the most exquisite torture, and as for stooping to take hold of his victim, the very thought would have made him shudder.

On that very day a fresh surprise occurred to Mr. Styngy. At one o'clock, just as the afternoon classes had taken their places in the schoolroom, Noodles showed himself at the door, and stood there as was his custom, till he was questioned.

"What is it now?" demanded Mr. Styngy.

"There's a boy come," said the odd man, "with a bellycram."

"A what?"

"A bellycram," repeated the imperturbable Noodles. "And in my 'pinion he'd best kep it for himself, for he be mortal skinny surely."

"Go with that idiot," said Mr. Styngy, to one of the ushers, "and see what it is. If I get near him I shall knock his ridiculous head off."

It proved to be a telegram, which Noodle's ingenious idea of euphony had altered to bellycram. Mr. Styngy took it from the usher, tore open the envelope, and as he perused the contents he frowned heavily.

The telegram ran as follows:—

"From Josiah Sweetman, London, to Rev. Styngy, Cheetham Hall, Dumbartonshire.—Shall arrive by 3.38 train with new pupil. Be at station to meet me."

Mr. Styngy had been rendered so suspicious by recent events, that he decided at once that the telegram was another hoax. Josiah Sweetman was the name of his London agent, and at any other time he would have accepted the telegram as genuine; but he had not yet forgotten the advent of the Japanese Prince, and the substitution of the donkey for Master Flashaway Junior, and the sham hamper of game, were yet fresh in his mind.

"If this is an attempt to impose upon me again," thought Mr. Styngy, "I will show no mercy to the perpetrator."

Then, he added aloud to the odd man, who was still at the door.

"Noodles, go down to the police-station, and ask

* As bearing upon the fact above mentioned by the author, we refer those of our readers who may be interested in the subject, to the "Evening Echo," of Friday, January 14th, 1876, from a letter in which, signed "A Hated One," we quote the following paragraph:—

"The masters in these (large non-public schools) receive salaries varying from £30 to £80 and residence, or from £80 to £160 non-resident; and this in many cases after years of study at public schools and universities. I know at the present moment honours men, and wranglers, who do not receive as much as ordinary mechanics. I have been seventeen years a tutor, and do not now get the wages of a journeyman tailor; and the pay of lady teachers is even worse."

AS THE PARTY REACHED THE LAST OF THE LONG LINE OF PORTRAITS, MR. STYNGY'S ANCESTOR GAVE A DECIDED WINK.

No. 9.

the inspector to be kind enough to place three or four of his best men at my disposal for an hour or so."

Tommy Codlings turned pallid, and Charlie Drummond felt a little uncomfortable at the order. What could it mean? had Mr. Styngy found out the real authors of the "hamper joke," and were they to be locked up for it?

Lionel was of course appealed too, but as he was ignorant of the contents of the telegram he could not solve the mystery, until about an hour afterwards, when an adroit spy returned with the intelligence that Mr. Styngy had gone out, and, accompanied by two constables, was marching in the direction of the station.

"It is no use worrying," said Lionel, when he was again appealed to for his opinion. "If we wait, we shall know all about it."

Lionel was right in some degree. After an interval of some two hours Mr. Styngy returned, ushering into the room with great ceremony, a sallow faced boy, with closely cropped black hair, and small round restless black eyes. He was dressed in black clothes, of a somewhat foreign appearance, but of extreme and almost painful neatness, and he wore a supercilious, haughty expression on his features, which made our hero dislike him at once.

"Young gentlemen, stand up," said Mr. Styngy, pompously. Flashaway Senior, oblige me by coming forward."

The senior pupil, in his labouring, sulky way, obliged, and the keen black eyes of the new comer flashed all over him at once.

"Mr. Flashaway, and young gentlemen," said Mr. Styngy, "I have pleasure in introducing to you a new comrade, who will, I trust, accompany us for a lengthened period along the pleasant paths of knowledge. Monsieur le Vicomte de Chateaux-en-Espagne, this is Mr. Frederick Flashaway, eldest son of my friend the Right Honourable Baronet, Sir Frederick Flashaway."

Mr. Styngy had a great respect for the aristocracy, and the titles rolled off his tongue with the smoothness of oil. The telegram had been a genuine one after all. His agent Mr. Sweetman had really arrived at the appointed time, and with a real pupil.

The French boy who owned such a sounding name and title, bowed gracefully on the introduction; and Flashaway, who could never do anything with ease, nodded in a clumsy half-sulky way.

"As it wants but a quarter of an hour to tea-time," Mr. Styngy went on, in an amiable tone, "the classes may break up now, and you, Flashaway, can introduce our young friend from La Belle France to the senior pupils."

"I shan't like that fellow," said Lionel to Charlie, as he placed his books in his desk. "Did you see the contemptuous way in which he looked round at the fellows?"

"A mangy French beggar!" said the voice of Tommy Codlings at this juncture. "I mean to have a go at him, Li."

"Nonsense, Tommy," replied our hero; "that fellow is as active as a cat, and strong too, although he is so slender."

"But you know, Li, an Englishman is a match for three Frenchman; so why shouldn't an English boy be able to double up one French boy. I wish he was twins, I'd have a go at the two, I should like to lick somebody."

"I don't think he'll be long here before he does quarrel with somebody," said Lionel. "He's a proud fellow evidently, and pride don't go down in a school. Then, Flashaway's got him in hand—some mischief is sure to come of that."

"Do you think he'll try to fix a quarrel on you?" asked Charlie.

"Very likely he will, if he thinks the Frenchy's game," replied our hero. "I shan't seek a quarrel, but I shan't avoid one."

"Come on, any how, and let's have a look at him," said Charlie; "all the other fellows are gone already."

Most of the boys, though possessing a full share of that lasting British contempt for foreigners, also had in their bosoms that equally British sentiment of respect for a title; and so although they crowded about the new comer, they refrained as yet from putting the peculiar questions usually asked of a fresh pupil.

The young vicomte took it as a matter of course. He was fresh from Normandy, where the Legitimist peasantry still look upon their feudal seigneurs as infinitely superior to the common mass of humanity. His step-father, being a man of advanced views, had seen that the boy was being ruined by much flattery and worship. He was, as many high-class Frenchmen are, a great admirer of England and English institutions. Without warning he had taken the boy from his mother, and launched him at once into the miniature republic called a school.

Tommy Codlings looked upon the advent of the young French aristocrat as a golden opportunity to retrieve his laurels. Although he had never succeeded in thrashing either an English, Scotch, or Irish boy, he felt certain that he could give a foreigner a hiding, and he burned with desire to begin.

"If that chap Flashaway would only go," muttered Tommy, "I'd get a chance. I'll say something, any how."

And making a speaking trumpet of his hands, Tommy roared out, "I say, Frenchy—Waterloo!"

It happened that Lionel and Charlie were passing close to the group, when Tommy levelled his sarcasm at the French boy, who, turning sharply round as he heard the voice, came face to face with our hero.

"Canaille!" he hissed, as his sallow face turned livid with passion. "It is you who have say that!"

CHAPTER XLII.

SHOWING HOW THE DUEL WAS FOUGHT—AND HOW THE REV. MR. STYNGY ARRIVED AT A MOST INOPPORTUNE MOMENT.

"YES, see," whispered Lionel to Charlie, "it is as I told you. Flashaway is egging Frenchy on to quarrel with me, but I'll disappoint him if I can."

Then turning calmly to the excited little foreigner, he said aloud—

"You are mistaken. Until this moment I have not spoken to you."

"Don't believe him," whispered the bully to the French boy; "he's afraid."

He took the hint, and frowned until his keen deep-set black eyes were almost hidden beneath his eyebrows.

"Vous mentir—vous été un lâche" (you lie, you are a coward).

And, stepping forward, he struck at Lionel with his open hand.

Our hero's reply was prompt and to the point. His right fist shot out straight from the shoulder, and laid his opponent sprawling in the dusty ground.

He was up in an instant, his face a deathly yellow-green with rage, save where a thin stream of blood trickled from his mouth.

"Sacré canaille d'Anglais!" he spluttered; "you have knock me down. I demand dat you fight me sur le champ."

"With all the pleasure in life," returned Lionel, coolly. "I'll knock you down as many times as you like."

"Non, non, non. I fight vit no more like zat. I am noble. I know not ze box; zat is for ze canaille. You fight me wiz ze sword, and zen I wash out dis insult in your blood."

"It's precious little of my blood that you'll see," said Lionel; "unless I cut my knuckles open against your teeth."

"Den you refuse to fight. Hein?" hissed the French boy, whose anger and excitement seemed to increase with every moment. "Forçat canaille d'Anglais! Je crashe à la figure!"*

And before Lionel, who little expected such a salute, had time to dodge, the French boy spat full in his face.

We take it for granted that no greater insult could be offered to anyone than this. It was tolerably certain that Lionel thought so. His face flushed scarlet, then paled to a marble whiteness, and he would have sprang upon the French boy and have punched him into a jelly but for Charlie Drummond and Codlings, who, alarmed at the expression of his face, seized him and held him back.

"Let me go, I tell you," panted Lionel, as he strove to break away from his chums. "Take your hands off, Charlie?"

"Aha, you fight me now, hein?" said the young vicomte, with a sneer in his voice which made Lionel's blood boil. "You English are cold. It take a great deal to make you show your courage."

"You will find me warm enough presently, I promise you," said Lionel. "I will fight you anywhere and anyhow you please. You and that fellow Flashaway have forced this quarrel on me, and you must take the consequences."

"Allons donc," said the French boy, his black eyes sparkling with a savage, satisfied gleam. "I have a pair of fleurets (foils) in ze portmanteau; de ends can be made sharp wiz a file, and den, nous verrons" (we shall see).

"We shall," said Lionel, gravely. "Come, where shall we fight; I am as impatient as you are?"

"It had better come off in the box-room," said Flashaway, who could hardly refrain from openly showing his delight at the prospect of witnessing the defeat of our hero. "The vicomte's portmanteau is there, and we shall have more room?"

Lionel nodded, and, turning, walked with a hasty step towards the school, accompanied by his two chums, who, as yet, hardly realised the serious nature of the affair.

Flashaway was the only one of the party thoroughly contented. He thought Frenchy was certain to be the best fencer, as the use of the sword formed a part of every well-born French boy's education, while scarcely one in a hundred of our English youths know how to handle a foil. Then, too, he reflected that the young vicomte was fiercely angry, and the sharpened point of his foil would effect as dangerous a wound as a sword.

"Even if the worst happens, and that young cub Wilful is killed," thought Flashaway, "I can swear that I tried to prevent the fight. Jabez will back me up in that. At any rate he is sure to get a nasty wound. I saw the Frenchman's eyes shine like a snake's when Wilful said he would fight."

Charlie Drummond and Codlings, on the other hand, felt exceedingly uncomfortable—a feeling which was only slightly relieved by the spice of romance surrounding the circumstance of its being a real duel.

"It's all my fault," said Tommy. "It was me who called out 'Waterloo,' and I'd have told him so, but you were at it hammer-and-tongs before I could get near. Let me fight him instead."

"You, Tommy?" laughed our hero. "He'd run you through like a cockchafer at the first pass. No, old fellow, I must fight him now."

"But can you fence?" said Drummond, anxiously. "Those French chaps are always well up in that sort of thing."

"Fortunately I am too," said Lionel. "Flashaway hopes that I cannot handle a foil; but I had a lot of lessons from a French exile, who had been a friend of my father's. I wasn't as tall as the foil I used, when I began to learn."

"Then," said Tommy Codlings, "I suppose you understand the language too, don't you? What did he keep on calling you a 'canal' for?"

"Oh, 'canaille,' you mean. That's about equivalent to an English expression, 'the scum of the earth.'"

"Complimentary, that," growled Tommy. "If he calls me that I'll pitch into him English fashion, and chance it."

By this time the box-room had been safely reached. Lionel, Charlie Drummond, and Codlings entered, closely followed by Flashaway and the French boy, Alphonse de Chateaux-en-Espagne, to give him his full name.

Jabez Hunker had been sent to the gardener's out-house, where the tools were kept, for the purpose of getting a couple of files, and also to keep back any of the more inquisitive of the boys, who from the scene in the playground might have scented the coming fight.

He soon returned, and reporting in his usual quiet, subdued voice that the course was clear, the door of the room was locked and the preparations for the duel commenced.

A strange quiet seemed to have fallen upon them all, now that the dangerous nature of the scene in which they were about to engage was impressed upon them.

Tommy Codlings' face changed gradually to a livid white colour as Jabez and Flashaway seized each a file and one of the foils, and commenced filing the buttons away. Charlie Drummond, too, who, as Lionel's second, watched the operation to see that it was fairly conducted, was paler and quieter than usual.

Lionel was at one of the windows, looking out upon the bright landscape, lit up by the rays of the afternoon sun, and thinking—he could not help it—of the pleasant hills and vale of Hampstead, and of the mother there who loved him so fondly. There was no trace of fear in what he felt. He could not have drawn out of the fight for any earthly consideration, for the memory of the insult was too fresh in his mind.

Alphonse, the French boy, was watching the preparations with a half-concealed sneer upon his sullen features; and then he began leisurely to divest himself of his jacket and waistcoat, as if a duel was a matter of every day occurrence, the while he sang in a low mocking voice the refrain of some Parisian street song:—

> "Mon père c'est à Paris,
> Ma mère c'est à Versailles,
> Et moi je suis ici
> Par moi tout ce canaille."

"There he is, with his 'canals,'" growled Tommy Codlings, viciously; "I'd like to knock him down with the old stool, I would. Dash him! How cool he seems to take it, and I'm shaking like a leaf."

Poor Tommy was indeed in a dreadfully nervous condition. The sharpening of the foils was nearly completed now, and as he saw Hunker and Flashaway testing the points with their fingers, he felt an insane desire to rush to the door and summon some of the masters to interfere.

But it was too late—almost as the thought flashed into his mind, the work was complete; and Charlie Drummond, taking one of the foils, approached Lionel.

"All's ready, old fellow," he said, in a low voice; "the beggars have made them as sharp as needles. This is a dreadful affair. Is it too late to stop it?"

"I wouldn't have it stopped for a hundred pounds," said Lionel, as he took the foil, and tested

* I spit in your face.

its flexibility by pressing the point against the ground.

The young vicomte had already taken up his position, and the very attitude he assumed convinced Lionel at a glance that he was an accomplished fencer.

"But," urged Charlie, "if anything serious should happen, Li."

"Let me go for old Styngy, or call for the police," said Tommy, who was almost blubbering.

The French boy gave a little impatient stamp with his foot, and Lionel, who would rather have died ten times over than have shown any reluctance, pushed his chums aside, and placed himself in position.

"Oh, lor, they're at it," muttered Tommy, as the foils crossed with an ominous clash, and then involuntarily he closed his eyes, and retired into a corner.

The French boy saw at once that he had no mean adversary to deal with, as Lionel's early training had not been lost upon him, and he felt his antagonist's blade with his own, following its every movement, and anticipating every feint, as if there existed some subtle electric communication between them.

For some moments both fought on the defensive—Lionel, because he did not intend to injure his opponent, and the young vicomte, for the purpose of ascertaining our hero's weak points, but, to his vexation, he could discover none.

But this blade of steel was a whole suit of armour to Lionel. Quick of hand, eye, and foot, he thwarted every movement of the French boy, and baffled every attempt to find an opening.

The sinister smile that had played about Flashaway's pale lips was gone now. He had thought to see Lionel gasping, wounded, on the ground at the first pass; but now even he could see that the French boy had at least met his equal, if not more than his match, and he trembled for the success of his foul design.

The young vicomte was getting excited now, and, abandoning his caution, though none of his skill, attacked Lionel fiercely, lunging almost every time he disengaged, but with no better success than at first.

Lionel had made up his mind to act wholly on the defensive. He knew that he was much stronger than the French boy, and his longer reach gave him an advantage, too.

But it is a great deal easier to make a resolution of this kind than to keep it when made. So Lionel found. The clash of steel—the evident determination of the French boy to wound him—the sight of the sallow face, the thin, firmly-compressed lips, and the black, snake-like glitter of the eyes into which he was gazing, fired Lionel's blood, and in a little while his resolution was forgotten, and he lunged fiercely at the French boy in return.

For full five minutes they fought without further result on either side than Alphonse's shirt-sleeve being ripped up from the elbow to the shoulder.

Even this point, unimportant as it was, sufficed to increase the anger of the French boy to a pitch of madness. He had anticipated an easy victory, but, instead of stretching Lionel at his feet in the first half-dozen passes as he meant to do, he had not only been foiled at every point, but very nearly wounded.

He lost his self-possession, the most invaluable quality in a fencer, and made lunge after lunge without coming to his guard again. Lionel saw that the French boy's intention was to wound him at any cost, and he determined to disappoint him in his effort.

The opportunity came: Alphonse made a desperate attempt to beat down Lionel's guard, and then sent in a thrust over the point. Lionel parried it with a half-parade, lunged straight out, and sent the keen point of his foil through and through the French boy's shoulder.

He uttered a sharp, shrill cry of pain, dropped his foil, and staggered back into the arms of Flashaway, just as the heavy tread of Mr. Styngy sounded in the passage, and his hand was laid upon the handle of the door.

CHAPTER XLIII.

THE FURTHER ADVENTURES OF SAM SCARECROW—THE MILD CURATE ENGAGES THE WONDERFUL JUMBARELLO IN A TOURNEY AT CHESS—CHECKMATE.

IT is high time now that we returned to the adventures of Sam Scarecrow, whom, for the past few chapters, we have neglected without apology.

That young man, our readers may remember, had, while personating the famed automaton Jumbarello, "floored" the two antagonists who had dared to face him, not only to their astonishment but also to that of the showman, Mr. Bellers-tomend.

"Brayvo!" shouted the male spectators, especially the juvenile portion, while such of the ladies who had eligible male friends near them fainted away, or pretended to do so, which latter method was quite as effectual.

"You will observe that there is no deception," said Mr. Bellers, recovering at once his professional composure. "Who'll have another try? Only five pound a time."

The two fallen rustics slowly rose to their feet, amidst the ironical cheers of the audience. One had a beautiful, beautiful nose, which before the wonderful Jumbarello operated upon it had been in colour and shape like unto a turnip radish, but which now rivalled the beetroot in elegance of contour and brilliancy of bloom.

The other, as he got up, might have been observed closely scanning the floor in his immediate neighbourhood in search of a couple of front teeth which Jumbarello had dislodged from their natural resting place.

"Never mind them, sir," said the showman, cheerfully. "It's only your wisdom teeth gone. It's plain you ain't got any wisdom, or you wouldn't have tackled Jumbarello. Better let 'em both go together."

And amidst the ironical laughter and cheers of the audience the two young farmers slunk out minus two five pound notes and plus sundry aches and pains, which they would not get rid of in a week.

The fame of the marvellous Jumbarello "spread like wildfire" through Swiggletown, and the caravan was regularly besieged by the crowd of applicants for admission.

The receipts far exceeded Mr. Bellers' expectations, and Sam was regaled when the last performance was over with a liberality perfectly astounding to that young gentleman.

"Horder wot you like," said the showman. "Sassidges and champagne, with turtle soup to follow, if you've got a fancy for that kind of thing. You've done well, my lad, and I'll do the 'ansom' thing by you."

"If we'd only had the fireworks!" said Long Jem, regretfully.

"Dash your fireworks, and you, too!" exclaimed the exasperated showman. "Do you think they'd hev drored like this ere ortommyton dodge?"

"Wot I ses is, as it's open to argyment," replied Long Jem, obstinately.

"Jem," said Mr. Bellers, solemnly, "if this warn't a night of rejicin', I'd send you to bed with a skinful of sore bones. Bust me if I wouldn't. You're enough to aggerawate a saint, *you* are."

"It's all werry well to talk," growled Jem; "but if you'd only put in the bills about the wonderful ascent of Jumbarello in the midst of fifty pound worth of squibs and Roman candles, you'd have drored twice as much."

"We couldn't have drored another penny," said Mr. Bellers, "unless we'd had the Agricultooral 'All to show in. Ain't we been obliged to turn away money to-night, you awaricious old sinner. Just go on with your beer, and don't talk nonsense."

Just then the landlord came in with a note, pink-coloured and perfumed, and addressed to "The Proprietor of the Automaton."

"Hullo!" said Bellers, turning the note over and over, and upside down; "what's this 'ere?"

"It looks like a billy-doo," said Long Jem. "It's from some gal, Bellers, as fell in love with you in the cairywan; I noticed one, with a pink bonnet and a yaller shawl, as looked uncommon sweet at you."

"You dry up," growled the showman, as he opened the envelope and slowly spelled over the contents, during which operation his face lengthened out into a very doleful expression.

"Here's a go!" he said, when he had reached the bottom of the letter.

"Wot's a go?"

"This 'ere letter. Listen!"

And Mr. Bellers-to-mend slowly read aloud, as follows:—

"The curate of Milkington-cum-Chalkery presents his compliments to Professor Billoso, and wishes, in company with a few friends, to have a private view of his automaton. The curate takes a great interest in chess, and the object of his visit will be to engage in a contest with the automaton; the hour of 10 a.m. to-morrow will be the most convenient to the curate, who will feel obliged if the professor returns an answer by the bearer of this."

Mr. Bellers refolded the note, and glanced dolefully round at his companions.

"I wish I hadn't been in such a hurry with that 'ere poster," he said. "You got oncommon well out o' the boxin' difficulty; but how about the chess? You don't know no more on it than the big drum, I'll be bound."

"I knows, yer plays it on a board, and shoves little things about," replied Sam; "for I've seen Miss Mariar, at Hampstead, play the game!"

"Anybody knows that," said the showman, impatiently; "but it's shoving 'em about the right way, that's what we want to know. We can't miss the bespeak, for it'll be a clean fiver in my pocket; but, on t' other hand, if the parson finds out the sell, we shall be bust up."

"I've got it then," said Long Jem; "look here, Bellers, you work it this way—when the parson comes in, have everything all ready, chess, board, and all, and just as he's goin' to sit down, you let's orf some fireworks, and——"

The exasperated showman rose to his feet, and aimed a blow at Long Jem's head, which would certainly have made him see some phantom fireworks, had it taken effect.

"Dash and jigger you and your fireworks!" he roared. "I tell you wot, Jem, if you mentions the subjeck of fireworks to me agin, we parts company!"

Just then the landlord entered, and intimated that the curate's messenger would be glad of an answer as quickly as suited Mr. Bellers' convenience.

"Pass me a sheet o' paper and a henvelope, and pen and ink," said the showman, desperately. "I'll chance it!"

And in a few minutes he had written a reply, which was more remarkable for being brief and to the point, than for any great beauties of grammar and diction.

"There," he said, when the note had been despatched. "Now I've done it; but how we're to get out of the mess to-morrow, beats me."

"Leave it to me," said Sam, who since he had floored the two countrymen had a considerable belief in his own ingenuity. "I'll manage it."

"I hope you will, my lad. You've done fust rate, so far; but it won't do to go floorin' the parson, mind that; 'cos there's sure to be a lot o' ladies with him. They always hang round arter those pet curates."

Mr. Bellers was remarkably silent that evening, for he was trying to think of some way out of the difficulty. Long Jem was silent, too, because he was sulky; and Sam was fully occupied with his supper, of which he ate so much, that he fell asleep, like a gorged boa-constrictor, and snored peacefully with his nose reposing in the pie-dish.

The party were up light and early, though, the next morning, getting the caravan in readiness for the reception of the bespoke party. The figures were rearranged and dusted. Sam received a fresh coat of paint, while his Japanese costume was adorned with a few extra spangles.

"You do look the real article uncommon!" said Mr. Bellers, admiringly. "Blow me, if ever I see a boy so much like a Dutch doll, afore!"

Long Jem had been sent into the town to purchase a cheap chessboard and a set of men. A little table had been placed in front of Jumbarello, and a couple of chairs—one for the automaton and one for the curate.

Punctually to the appointed time arrived the curate, attended by some dozen ladies. Mr. Bellers was glad to see that he was a very mild-looking young man, with scanty, fair hair parted in the middle, a pair of spectacles, and a figure with about as much symmetry as a pump.

Mr. Bellers bowed politely, and bestowed on the ladies one of his most fascinating professional smiles as he stowed them away on the forms.

"Mornin', ladies—mornin', sir," he said. "You're here to a minnit, sir. Well, you knows, no doubt, as I do, that punctuality is the thief of time."

With which slightly mixed aphorism Mr. Bellers gave the signal to Long Jem to draw the curtain.

"There he is, sir," said the showman, waving his hand towards Sam, who looked hideously unlike a human being. "There's the wonderful Jumbarello, ladies and reverend sir. The admiration of the universe and the envy of all the profession. I'm obligated to have him watched by two men night and day or he'd be stole from me in no time."

The mild curate and the ladies crowded so eagerly round the automaton that, had not the showman taken the precaution to rope off a space, it is more than probable that Sam, chair and all, would have been upset.

"You'll find him uncommon lively this mornin', sir," continued the showman. "He had a very hearty breakfast, and——"

"You don't mean to say that you feed your automatons," exclaimed the surprised curate.

Mr. Bellers saw that he had made a slight mistake, but he soon rectified it, by adding—

"Only a professional joke, sir; by givin' him his breakfast, I mean ilin of his inside."

"It must have a curious and complicated piece of machinery within him," said the curate. "Where is it situated? There, I suppose?"

And the curate actually prodded Sam in the lower portion of his tunic, nearly causing him to utter a yell, for he was ticklish.

"The machinery's all over him," said Mr. Bellers. "Harms, legs, head, body, and all, and very powerful it is. You didn't hear, may be, of wot happened yes'day, sir."

"I heard of no special accident," said the curate.

"You see that line in the bill, sir?" the showman continued, "where it says as Jumbarello will box anyone for fifty pounds a side."

"Yes," said the curate, turning a shade paler.

"Well, two young chaps comes in, and would have a go at my ortommyton, being—beggin' the ladies' parding for mentionin' such a thing—raything drunk at the time. I begs of 'em not to; I tells 'em

A SHARP CRY OF PAIN FROM THE FRENCH BOY TOLD THAT HE WAS HIT.

how Jumbarello had knocked a Hirish labourer's 'ed clean orf, only a day or two afore——"

"Good gracious!" exclaimed the curate, while his very spectacles trembled with agitation; "you don't mean to say that is true?"

"I do indeed, sir," replied Mr. Bellers, with much gravity and solemnity. "We got up a very fair subscription for the widder though, arterwards. But, as I was saying, these young chaps *would* tackle Jumbarello; spite of all I could say, they squared up to it, and the consekence was that a minnit arterwards they lay welterin' in their gore—just where you're a standin' now!"

The curate gave a nervous little jump, and felt round for his hat. He had a very nervous system, and the vision of the headless Irish labourer and the two countrymen weltering in their blood, had shaken that system to its centre.

"But—but—my good man," he said. "This—this—is dreadful; it ought not to be allowed; it's—it's positively dangerous!"

"Lor bless you, sir, not a bit," said Mr. Bellers, cheerfully. "He's quiet as a lamb when he ain't wound up to the full pitch. Are you ready for that there little game of chess, sir?"

The curate was *not* ready for that little game of chess. His own "little game" was getting away from the bloodthirsty automaton as quickly as possible, and he would have done so, too, but for the ladies in his company.

There was something delightfully wicked about this automaton, who had knocked one man's head off and demolished two others; and they longed to see it exhibit its powers in a game with the curate.

"Oh, *do* play, *dear* Mr. Mildew," said one fascinating maiden of forty-seven. "The automaton is *so* deliciously ugly, and we should *so* like to see you beat it. There *can* be no danger, you know, if the showman says there is not."

"That's it, sir. Go to work," said Mr. Bellers, leading the reluctant curate to his chair. "Perhaps you wouldn't mind settin' the chessmen, sir, while I winds up Jumbarello?"

"M—m—mind you do not overwind him, my good man," said the curate, as he nervously placed the men in position—keeping one eye, though, fixed upon the dreadful automaton.

The showman balanced the crank, and with much solemnity gave the required number of turns, and then pronounced the automaton to be ready.

"There's only one thing I forgot to tell you, sir," said Mr Bellers. "You is a good player, I suppose?"

"I—er—am generally considered so."

"That's all right, then," said Mr. Bellers, with a satisfied air. "I'm glad o' that, for you see, sir, Jumbarello can't abear anyone to make a mistake. So sure as he does, he ups with the chessboard and gives 'em one on the head. That were the only reason why the hemperor of Japan got rid of him. The hemperor, you see, were a very bad player, and the top of his head got so sore with the continual whacks Jumbarello gave him that he couldn't stand it no longer."

Just then there marched into the caravan with very little ceremony a short stout man, with a stern, business-like expression of countenance, who, walking straight up to Sam, laid his hand upon his collar and said—

"Now, young feller, you come along with me. I'm a detective, and I hold a warrant to apprehend you for absconding from Heath-end-villa, Hampstead!"

CHAPTER XLIV.

"BIRDS IN THEIR LITTLE NESTS AGREE," BUT THE INSIDE OF A NEST OF BOXES DOES NOT AGREE WITH TOMMY CODLINGS—THE FENCING MATCH, AND HOW IT CAME TO A SUDDEN TERMINATION—AN EXPLANATION—THE BULLY EXPOSED.

LIONEL and Charlie alone of all their companions preserved their presence of mind. Flashaway and Hunker turned green with fright, while Tommy Codlings, in an ecstasy of terror, opened a large empty box and got into it, shutting the lid down, and lay curled up, shivering and perspiring at once with terror.

"Quick!" said Lionel to Charlie, as Mr. Styngy had impatiently rattled the handle of the door. "Put on Flashaway's jacket, and shake him up. We must pretend that we were only fencing in play, and that he feels a little faint through over exertion. Make haste."

Charlie executed Lionel's instructions with more rapidity than gentleness, for there was no time for ceremony, while Lionel went to the door and said sharply—

"Now, you be off, you boys. You can't come in here."

"Let me in instantly," said Mr. Styngy, severely.

Lionel looked round. The French boy had recovered his senses, and was standing by the window, with Charlie whispering to him. It was all right then. He knew that Flashaway and Hunker would not betray themselves.

"I'm sure I beg your pardon, sir," said Lionel, politely, as he unlocked the door and threw it wide open. "I did not know it was you."

"Whether or no," replied Mr. Styngy, sharply, "you have no right to be here at all. Ah," he continued, as he caught sight of the others, "Monsieur le Vicomte and Flashaway. What is all this?"

"We have been practising a little with the foils, sir," said Lionel. "Monsieur is very fond of the exercise, and, as I knew something of fencing, he challenged me."

"Oh, indeed," said Mr. Styngy, graciously, for he was quite satisfied with the explanation. "A very graceful and charming exercise; but you should not fence without masks. You might chance to lose your eyesight, monsieur."

The French boy fortunately had some spice of chivalry in his nature. He was not a sneak, and he fell in readily with Lionel.

"Dere is no danger," he said. "Monsieur Weelful is so adroit as myself. It ees only wiz de maladroit fencer zat de danger come."

"Possibly," said Mr. Styngy; "but still it is iser to be cautious. Have you a pair of masks?"

"Oh, yais—jacket and glove—toute la boutique, monsieur."

"Then," said Mr. Styngy, seating himself on the box in which Tommy had hidden, "if you and Wilful please, I should like to see a specimen of your skill. It is always my wish to encourage healthful sport and recreation."

"Confound him," thought Lionel. "Here's a fix! Frenchy can't fence with that hole in his arm, and if he does, and we fence with these sharpened foils, ten to one but we shall get angry again, and thrust in real earnest."

The French boy got Lionel out of the difficulty in a way that made our hero begin to have a real respect for him.

It was his left arm that was hurt, and though it was evident that the wound, though slight, must have pained him considerably, he extended that hand, and, with a smile, took the foil which Lionel still held.

"Pardon," he said. "I hafe a better pair in my portmanteau, if you will be so kind to help me get zem."

"With pleasure," said Lionel, and, picking up the other sharpened foil, they were speedily exchanged for a pair of blunt ones. The masks and leather jackets were donned, and, placing themselves opposite Mr. Styngy, they saluted according to form, and began.

By the set teeth and contracted brows of the French boy Lionel knew that he was suffering no slight pain from his wound, but he bore it with a fortitude that won the admiration of our hero, and he resolved to make a friend of him, and expose the malicious meanness of the bully, Flashaway.

They had not exchanged more than half a dozen passes, when Mr. Styngy, who at first showed the greatest interest in the exhibition, began to look uneasily about him, and at length held up his hand.

"Stop a moment, young gentlemen," he said. "I fancied I heard a cry as of some creature in distress."

Lionel and the French boy paused, and all listened intently, but they could hear nothing.

"There," said Mr. Styngy. "I fancied I heard it again. It was a sound like——Oh!"

The schoolmaster gave a convulsive bound, and leaped some three feet into the air as he uttered this ejaculation, and, turning, he regarded the box with a fierce and bewildered expression.

But what were his feelings when the lid was slowly lifted up, and Tommy Codlings appeared—his mouth wide open—his features purple—his eyes nearly starting out of his head—while in his right hand he still clutched an open penknife!

Lionel, Charlie, and Alphonse burst out into a hearty laugh. They could not have helped doing so if extermination had been the penalty; and even Flashaway and Hunker contorted their features into the semblance of a smile.

"I—I—hope—I—didn't hurt you much, sir," gasped Tommy; "but—but I was nearly dead—indeed I was, sir."

Mr. Styngy was speechless with wrath and indignation—perhaps with pain, too, for he kept one hand behind him, and was tenderly passing it over the wounded part. Had it not been for the presence of the young vicomte, Mr. Styngy would have "had it out of" the luckless Tommy there and then.

"What business had you in that box at all, sir?" thundered the schoolmaster in his severest tones. "I have a great mind to punish you severely for this."

Tommy sniffed meekly; he had no excuse to offer.

"If you please, sir, I hollered till I hadn't got any breath left, and then I put the blade of my knife through a crack in the lid, and you——"

"There, there, that will do," said Mr. Styngy, hastily; "and if I have any more of your nonsense for a month to come, I will write to your friends to say you are expelled, and keep you on bread and water till they come to fetch you."

The threat of this punishment, as my readers know, had always more effect upon Tommy than any other. He shuddered, and endeavoured to hide himself from Mr. Styngy's baneful glare, behind his protector Lionel.

"As for you, Alphonse and Wilful," he continued, "I shall have great pleasure in witnessing an exhibition of your skill at another time, when we are not liable to be interrupted by clumsy and mischievous tricks."

These latter words were emphasised by a second malignant glare at Tommy, which curdled his blood, and he seemed to be quite two sizes smaller until Mr. Styngy had departed, to court-plaister the wound inflicted by Tommy's penknife.

No sooner was he fairly out of sight than Alphonse turned to Lionel with the quickness and vivacity of his nation, and held out his hand.

"Monsieur Weelful," he said, "dey tell me that you was coward, and mean, and base; but dat cannot be, for you fight me like a gentilhomme de bonne race. Voilà ma main."

Lionel took the French boy's hand and shook it cordially, while Flashaway and Hunker stood looking on with sullen, lowering looks.

Our hero thought it was his turn to offer an explanation, but Alphonse was too quick for him, and, facing round, regarded the bully with his keen black eyes flashing with angry scorn.

"It is you," he said, "who have tell me dis. It is you who take me by ze arm, and make me to see Weelful, while you say, 'Prenez garde à lui—he is méchant, he is liar, he is coward.' And what do I find? Dat it *you* who are ze liar and ze coward. Canaille!"

"There he goes with his 'canails' again," thought Tommy; "but I'm glad Flashaway's getting it 'stead of Li."

The French boy had delivered the speech with such volubility, and with such abundance of gesture, that it was impossible for any one to get a word in. Flashaway, pale as death, was retreating towards the window as Alphonse in his excitement approached nearer to him.

"I don't know," said Lionel, at this juncture, "how you found out the true character of that fellow, but you are quite right. He is all that you have said, and more too."

"Do I not know it," said Alphonse, throwing his hands above his head, apparently forgetting his wound in his excitement. "I begin to see it when I insult you in ze cour, I see it more as we come to dis chambre, and I see it more still when you fight so brave, and he look on so pâle and tremblant."

The bully was white hot with wrath; while shame, hatred, thirst for vengeance, and a dozen other violent passions were struggling within him.

"Brayvo Frenchy," said the exultant Tommy, delighted at seeing Flashaway cowed and defeated—it did not matter in the least by whom. "Give him a topper—he won't hit you back."

If Lionel had not been there, the chronicler of this faithful history verily believes that Flashaway would have struck the French boy—he had not forgotten that one arm was nearly useless; but one look at the calm, contemptuous face of our hero daunted him, and, sick with shame and fear, he turned, and skulked away.

The French boy looked after him for a moment, and then faced suddenly round upon Lionel, with a peculiar smile upon his face.

"Somebody he say to me, little while ago, 'Waterloo.' How many like zat when you fight us at Waterloo. Hein!"

"None, I hope," said Lionel, flashing red himself. "Else we should have had little chance of winning the battle."

"If I had one tought in my mind," said Alphonse, "dat zere was in de world a Français so coward as dat, I go myself a tousand mile and kill him."

"There are cowards of all colours and of all nations," said Lionel, who by no means liked the subject of the conversation; "and if you and I were to devote ourselves to the slaughter of all the cowards in the world, we should have enough to keep us busy if we lived as long as Methusaleh. But what a thoughtless fellow I am," he added, suddenly. "I had forgotten all about your arm. It must be seen to at once."

"It make me pain a good deal," replied the French boy, with a faint smile; "but it is nossing."

"You bore it like a hero," said Lionel. "Here Charlie, lend a hand, and we'll carry him up to our dormitory. You, Tommy, run on a-head, and let me know if anyone's there."

Before Alphonse had time to protest, their strong young arms had lifted him from the ground, and were bearing him along with the utmost tenderness. A brief half hour ago each was doing his best to spill each others blood, and now they were firm friends. The bond of mutual courage and sympathy had united them.

CHAPTER XLV.

TOMMY CODLINGS' JEALOUSY—THE RECONCILIATION—TOMMY OFFERS TO GIVE THE FRENCH BOY A LESSON IN BOXING, AND GETS ONE HIMSELF INSTEAD—A LITTLE GAME AT "FOLLOW-MY-LEADER," AND WHAT IT LED TO.

THE wound was not a dangerous, nor even a severe one, but it had bled a good deal, and seemed inflamed. Lionel would have sent for a doctor, but Alphonse would not hear of such a thing, lest it should cause an inquiry into the case, and get his new friend into trouble. So it was bathed and bandaged as well as their very slight surgical knowledge permitted, and, under pretence of having bruised his arm, Alphonse carried it in a sling.

The friendship between Lionel and the young vicomte grew daily in strength; each recognised intuitively the good qualities of each other, and made willing allowance for the defects they encountered.

This was not at all to the taste of Tommy Codlings. He had an intense admiration for our hero, and looked upon Alphonse as an intruder, a sort of poacher upon the preserves of his friendship, whom he would willingly have fallen upon and "punched."

"Whatever can Lionel see in that chap?" he muttered, sulkily. "He never goes in for a lark now, and he's always parleyvooing with that dashed Frenchy, so that a fellow can't understand 'em. Why if I was Li, I should be ashamed to be seen with a chap who has hair like a worn-out blacking-brush, and a face that's more the colour of a bad penny than anything else. Blowed if I'll put up with it!"

And Tommy became so furiously jealous and offended by Lionel's partiality for the "Frenchman" that he actually became cool to our hero, took no notice of him, pretended to be looking another way when they passed, and altogether behaved in so strange a manner that our hero was at loss to account for it.

"I say, Tommy," he said, meeting that young gentleman one afternoon in the playground, "what's up, old fellow?"

Thereupon Tommy affected to be very deaf, and continued his walk, bursting into melody, and singing the chorus of "The Miller of the Dee":—

"I care for nobody—no, not I;
And nobody cares for me-e-e-e!"

But Lionel was not to be shaken off in that way. He ran after Tommy and slapped him on the shoulder, whereat Tommy turned round and pretended to be profoundly astonished at seeing him.

"Oh, is that you, Master Wilful?" he said.

"What do you mean, you stupid old Tommy, you?" said Lionel, with a half serious, half amused look, as he caught Codlings by the shoulders and turned him round.

"I will thank you, Master Wilful," said Tommy, haughtily, "not to take any liberties with me. Go to Frenchy if you want to do that."

Lionel stared at Tommy for a moment, and then burst into a fit of laughter.

"Oh, that's the way the wind lies, is it, Tommy," he said. "Why, you donkey, you don't mean to say you're jealous."

"Jealous!" repeated Codlings. "Oh dear no. What should I be jealous of?"

"Hein!" said the voice of Alphonse, who came up at that moment. "M'sieu Tommee est jaloux! He is in loafe, eh?"

Tommy turned crimson with rage and spite. To be laughed at by Lionel was bad enough, but to be taunted by his rival was unbearable.

"No," he said, wrathfully, curling up as much of his little snub nose into a sneer as he could, "at least not of *you*, Monsieur Cock-a-doodle-do. Waterloo! There, Frogs! How do you like that?"

"Have you gone out of your senses, Tommy," said Lionel, shaking Codlings sharply by the shoulders. "Come away with me, old fellow, and let's have this out."

Lionel led him away into a corner of the playground, and, with a few gentle words, coaxed out of him the real reason of his strange conduct. Poor Tommy was almost blubbering with the soreness of his wounded feelings; but our hero had him all right again in no time, and, what was more, reconciled him to Alphonse.

"I tell you what," said Lionel, "it's a beastly afternoon, and is likely to get worse. We three and Charlie will have an hour or two in the box-room, and amuse ourselves with a little fencing and sparring. Charlie's got a set of gloves."

Tommy's good humour was quite returned now, and, he readily assenting, Drummond was found, and the quartette of friends ran off to the scene of their afternoon's amusement.

There they passed away an hour pleasantly enough. Lionel and Alphonse paired off with the foils, while Tommy amused himself by receiving Charlie's boxing-gloves in regular succession upon all the tenderest parts of his face and body.

Then they changed, Lionel and Charlie taking the foils, and Tommy promising to give Alphonse a lesson in the noble science.

He thought that his time had come now. It was impossible for anyone but a native of the British Isles to know anything about the pugilistic art, and Tommy promised himself to land the "Frenchy" one or two.

But here again his usual luck attended him. Alphonse indeed knew nothing of the "art," but he was quick of eye, and he knew where Tommy's nose was.

"Now," said Codlings, squaring scientifically up to his opponent, "posture's everything in boxing. Just put your left arm—so, and your right arm—so, and then you wriggle 'em a little, and you——Oh!"

Tommy had intended to land his right fist on the intellectual forehead of his antagonist, but the quick eye of the French boy had seen the blow coming, and parried it by smiting Tommy on the nose, and flooring him.

Alphonse made him a polite little bow, and smiled.

"I hope I note hurt you too moche?"

"I never saw such a thing," said the bewildered Tommy. "An English chap actually knocked down by a Frenchy, who knows nothing of boxing. I don't believe I *am* English? I *can't* be."

"Hallo, Tommy," said Lionel. "Come to grief, eh?"

"Never mind," retorted Tommy, sulkily. "I see how it is; you've been giving him lessons on the quiet, and he practices on me."

"Why, Tommy, you surely don't mind a tap on the nose."

"Not from an English chap," said Tommy, gloomily; "but think what a disgrace it is to be floored by a foreigner."

"Why what an old donkey you are, Tommy!" laughed Lionel. "You're a thorough going patriot, if ever there was one; but we've had enough of this for the present. What shall we do now?"

"Let's go on an exploration," said Charlie.

"Where? Not out of doors—the weather's too bad."

"No, I mean about the house! You've no idea what a queer old crib it is, Li. There's a lot of it shut up and never used—gloomy old passages, big rooms full of spiders, and mice, and beetles, and that sort of thing."

"It is tempting, certainly," said Lionel; "but how about Styngy?"

"Oh, he's safe enough. He's got some friends to lunch, and De Bewty, Cracklejack, and the rest, see too much of us at lessons to worry about us now."

"I'm on!" said Lionel. "Come on, Alphonse; come on, Tommy. "Which is the way, Charlie?"

"We'll take the way that comes first," replied Charlie. "All beyond this part of the house is deserted. Suppose we have a game of Follow-my-Leader?"

"Follow-my-Leader," replied Alphonse; "qu'est que c'est?"

The rules of the game, which we are quite sure it is unnecessary to repeat to our readers, were explained to Alphonse, Lionel was chosen as Leader, and they started.

Lionel chose the corridor opposite the box-room, as having the gloomiest appearance, and went down it at a run, until his progress was checked by a door, black with age, and thickly covered with dust and cobwebs, but still evidently of great strength.

"We must go back, and try the other way," said Charlie.

"Wait a bit," said Lionel.

There was a grating, some eighteen or twenty inches square, in the centre of the door. By standing on tip-toe Lionel could peer through the dusty bars.

"There's another passage, beyond," he said, "and a dim sort of light at the end, that looks promising."

"What's the use, if you can't open the door?"

"There are more ways than one of getting through a door," said Lionel, and, covering his right hand with his handkerchief, he struck the grating a heavy blow.

The fastenings were nearly rusted through, the woodwork rotted away, and the grating fell in with a dull sound.

"You're not going through there?" said Charlie.

"I am, though," replied Lionel, coolly; "and you'll have to come too—it's Follow-my-Leader, remember!"

And the next moment, with the agility of a harlequin, he sprang up and squeezed himself through the opening, falling lightly on his hands and knees inside.

Alphonse followed with the ease of a cat. Then came Charlie's turn, and he got through safely, only bruising one knee a little in the fall; and next the plump features of Tommy Codlings appeared in the opening, puffing and gasping in the apparently vain endeavour to get the remainder of his portly person through.

"Come along, Tommy," said Lionel; "there's a draught through that grating, and you'll catch cold if you stop too long."

"Oh, I dessay," puffed Tommy; "I ain't a skeleton, like you fellows! Oh, don't! Let me alone, Charlie!"

Drummond, with a view of aiding Tommy in his gymnastic feat, had laid hold of the plump one's ears, and hauled away vigorously at them.

"Never mind if it hurts a bit, Tommy; it's the only way to get you through. Come and lend a hand, Li."

Panting, puffing, and gasping out protests, poor Tommy Codlings was hauled up, and a vigorous pull brought him through with such suddenness that all three rolled over on the dusty floor of the passage.

"Are you hurt, Charlie?"

"No; are you, Li?"

"Not a bit; only a mouthful of dust. How are you, Tommy?"

"Oh, there's nothing the matter with me, of course," replied the unlucky Codlings; "there never is. I've only got two front teeth loose, and all the skin off my elbows and knees, and my nose is bleeding!"

But a little thing like that could not ruffle Tommy's good nature for long, and he trotted contentedly on after Lionel, with his handkerchief held to his injured nose.

At the end of that passage was a window, so obscured by the dirt and dust of years, that it was almost as difficult to open a view through it as to open an oyster.

It was managed with the aid of a little patience and a pocket-knife, and then the boys saw that it opened out upon a beautifully kept garden.

"I've been in there once," said Charlie, "and Styngy has no end of lovely grapes, melons, and things growing in the hot-houses."

"Has he though?" said Lionel.

"Yes, and they're in season pretty nearly all the year round. I heard my father say when he saw the garden, that it must cost no end of money to keep it up."

"The greedy old beggar never gives us a taste," growled Tommy, as he licked his lips at the thought of the tempting delicacies. "Didn't you say those were pine-apples, Charlie?"

"Yes; whoppers. My father said that they were worth a couple of guineas apiece."

"And I say," whispered Lionel, who was at the window, "here's old Styngy and some ladies and gentlemen just come out of one of the hot-houses, and there's old Noodles behind 'em, bringing some fruit in a basket. Now they're going indoors."

"Was there a pine-apple?" asked Tommy.

"I believe you—a beauty; such a rich yellow, it looked as if it was modelled in gold. We must have a peep at those hot-houses, Charlie."

"What now?"

"No; not in such a hurry as that. But some evening, you know, Charlie," said Lionel, with a wink, "when we're not likely to interrupt anybody."

"To be interrupted by anybody, you mean," laughed Charlie. "But push on, Li. Let's finish our exploration. Time's getting on."

Another passage branched sharply off to the left, but it was unlighted, and before they had gone half a dozen yards they were in complete darkness.

"Be careful, Li," said Charlie; "there may be a trap-door or something in the way."

Just as he spoke his own foot caught in some obstruction, and, putting out his hand to save himself from falling, his arm went through the wall, a shower of pieces of mortar and rubbish clattered to the ground, and a flood of daylight and cold air rushed in through the aperture.

"What's up," said Lionel, coming back as he heard the noise. "What have you done, Charlie?"

"Bother me if I know," laughed Drummond; "except that I've let a little light in where it was wanted. Here, you Tommy, get out of the way, and let me look."

"That's always the way," growled Tommy. "You always want the first of everything."

"I made the hole, didn't I?" said Drummond, as he elbowed Tommy away and looked through the aperture. "Why, Li, this looks into a picture gallery—such a jolly crib. Old armour and things of that sort all about the place."

"Make haste, and let us see," said Lionel. "This is a discovery that may lead to something."

"It's my turn next," said Tommy. "Here, Drummond, you've been looking long enough."

"I'm ashamed of you, Codlings," said our hero. "Where's your politeness? Here's Alphonse, a new boy, and you want to push yourself in before him."

"Oh, ah," grumbled Tommy. "You didn't want to look yourself, I suppose. Oh, yes."

Alphonse had a good stare, and expressed himself delighted with the view of the picture gallery. Then Lionel's turn came.

FOLLOW MY LEADER.

AS HE ENTERED MR. STYNGY'S BEDROOM, EVERY PORTABLE ARTICLE IT CONTAINED WAS PUT IN MOTION.

No. 10.

"I say, Charlie," he said, "old Styngy goes in for this sort of thing pretty heavily, doesn't he?"

"It seems like it," replied Drummond. "I suppose they're the portraits of his ancestors. There's an old cure in a bag-wig opposite with a nose exactly like his."

"Hush!" said Lionel, at this juncture. "I can hear footsteps and somebody talking."

"Who is it?"

"Don't know yet, but it sounds like Styngy's voice. Ah! now I can see something. Yes, by George, here they come—the same party we saw in the garden. Old Styngy's showing 'em the pictures."

"Here, I say," whispered Tommy, pulling Lionel by the jacket, "it's my turn now."

"Don't be in a hurry, Tommy. What a fellow you are. I want to hear what they're saying."

And, kicking out behind with his right foot, Lionel gave Tommy a gentle reminder in the waistcoat not to be so impatient.

The hole which Charlie's arm had made was a large one, and afforded a clear view of the long room or gallery below from end to end.

Mr. Styngy was at the head of his guests, moving slowly up the centre of the gallery, describing with much pomposity and satisfaction the various portraits of his ancestors.

He was yet some distance from Lionel, so that our hero could look and listen with perfect safety.

"There," said the schoolmaster, indicating with a wave of his right hand the portrait of a most villanous-looking elderly gentleman, dressed in a suit of key-rings, "is the 'counterfeit presentment' of William, Baron de Styngy, who accompanied Richard Cœur de Lion to the Holy Land. He was a model of piety and benevolence. He slew no less than fourteen hundred Saracens with his own hand at Ascalon, and it is chronicled that the royal Richard himself was jealous of his prowess, and accused my ancestor of having cheated in counting up the corpses."

"What a de—ar man!" said an elderly lady, surveying the features of the lamented baron through her double eyeglass. "How his family must have adored him! Oh, those lovely crusaders!"

"You are very complimentary, ma'am," said Mr. Styngy to the elderly lady, who was the rector's wife. "Here is the suit of armour which he wore while in Palestine, and the very sword he used at Ascalon."

Ten minutes of rapturous exclamations of delight and admiration at these relics of the deceased Baron de Styngy, and the party moved on to the next ancestor, which was exactly opposite the hole through which Lionel was gazing.

"This is getting a little too close," thought Lionel. "I'll let Codlings have a peep now."

"Now then, Tommy," he said aloud, "it's your turn. Mind how you go—it's rather high up for you. Charlie, help me give him a leg up."

It so happened that the hole which Charlie's arm had made happened to be through one of Mr. Styngy's most cherished family pictures, and in the very spot where the features of that ancestor were delineated.

The boys were, of course, quite unaware of this circumstance, and when Tommy was hoisted into position he ruthlessly enlarged the hole, not finding it quite large enough for his purpose.

"Take care what you are doing, Tommy," whispered Drummond.

"All right," returned Codlings; "they won't look up this way—the pictures are on the other side."

Just then, to Tommy's horror, he heard Mr. Styngy say—

"I am fortunate, ma'am, in the possession of two portraits of this distinguished ancestor, who fought so gallantly for Charles the First against the usurper Cromwell, and forfeited his estates in consequence. The one you were looking at was painted at the age of fourteen, but the other was taken when he was a war-worn bearded veteran, eighty-seven years old."

And Mr. Styngy, wheeling suddenly round, waved his hand directly towards the spot where Tommy Codlings' round head and plump cheeks were in full view.

Tommy was petrified with terror. He dared not call out to his companions to release him, lest he should be heard. Neither could he signify his wish to be let down by a kick, for both his legs were tightly held.

"Dear me!" said the old lady, gazing up at Tommy through her glasses. "What age did you say, Mr. Styngy?"

"Eighty-seven, madam," replied the schoolmaster. "Observe the sorrowful expression upon the bronzed, worn features of the old warrior. You can trace in his very look the fact that he has staked and lost all in the service of his royal master. Connoisseurs have declared that the texture of the long grey beard is one of Lely's happiest efforts."

"Beard?" almost shrieked the old lady. "Why, my dear Mr. Styngy, he hasn't got any!"

Up to this time the schoolmaster had been watching the effect of his oratory upon his audience, and not looking at the picture at all. His feelings may be imagined when, looking up, he beheld—instead of the grim, gaunt visage of his ancestor—the plump, round features of the unlucky Tommy Codlings!

CHAPTER XLVI.

TOMMY CODLINGS IN A WORSE DILEMMA THAN EVER—THE MYSTERIOUS PORTRAIT CAUSES A DIFFERENCE OF OPINION—MR. STYNGY DISCOVERS THE SECRET.

THE position was indeed a dreadful one for Tommy. There was he, looking down at the schoolmaster, and there was the schoolmaster looking up at him, petrifying him with a basilisk-like glance.

Big beads of perspiration stood out on Tommy's brow, and an ice-cold chill crept slowly down his back. If Mr. Styngy's incensed countenance had been the head of the fabled Medusa, which turned everyone who looked upon it into stone, the effect upon poor little Tommy could hardly have been greater.

Lionel and the others were quite unconscious of what was going on in the gallery. They could only hear Mr. Styngy's voice sounding in an inarticulate growl, and believed that Tommy was thoroughly enjoying himself; in fact, enjoying himself a little too much, for he was heavy, and they were tired of holding him up.

"Now then, old chap, haven't you had enough?" whispered Lionel.

"Wake up, Tommy," added Charlie Drummond; "we're tired."

But Codlings heard them not. He was fascinated by Mr. Styngy's glare much as a young bird is held in thrall by the glitter of a serpent's eyes.

"If you don't come down, we'll let you drop," said Lionel. "So look out, Tommy."

Still Tommy made no reply, and together our hero and Drummond let go his legs.

But Codlings did not fall—he was not lucky enough. Some of the lathes had caught in his jacket-collar, and held him there suspended as firmly as if Mr. Marwood had been operating on him with a half-inch rope.

With Tommy's head stopping out the light, the corridor was so dark that neither our hero nor his companions could see the real reason why he remained so silent and so fixed.

"We're going now, Tommy," said Lionel. "You'd better come too, or you'll never been able to get through the grating in the door by yourself."

"He's sulky," said Drummond, when they had

waited in vain for an answer. "Don't wait for him, Li. Let's see if the weather has cleared up as we may have a chance of half an hour's run before tea time."

"All right," said Lionel; "you will come too, Alphonse?"

"Oh, yais," replied the French boy. "I come avec plaisir."

And, quite unconscious of the predicament in which the unlucky Tommy was left, our hero and his two chums retraced their steps, and, scrambling through the grating in the old door, reached the dormitory without having been observed.

Meanwhile, poor Codlings' position was becoming extremely critical. Mr. Styngy glared up at him for a few moments in silence, unable quite to decide whether or not he was the victim of an optical illusion.

"It's—it's—very extraordinary," he said at last, "My sight is not quite so good as it was—but would you do me the favour, Mr. Bilbury, to give me your opinion on the subject."

Mr. Bilbury's sight was considerably more imperfect than Mr. Styngy's, but he set his double eyeglass astride his nose, and took a good long stare.

"I certainly do *not* perceive any symptoms of a beard," replied Mr. Bilbury; "but the painting is certainly a wonderful piece of art; the eyes seem actually to follow one."

Mr. Bilbury was quite right. Tommy's eyes were indeed following his every movement, with an appealing look in them, which, if a painter could have transferred faithfully to canvas, would certainly have made the fortune of the artist.

"I must see into this," said Mr. Styngy. "I have had that portrait in my possession for years. I have seen it every day, and am as familiar with it as with myself; but never before did I observe any change in it. What miracle, I ask, can have transferred the wrinkled, bearded features of an old warrior, into those of a boy, and a fat boy too, apparently."

"Very fat," said Mr. Bilbury, emphatically; "but perhaps it's the weather. I have heard that the weather has an extraordinary effect upon old paintings."

"If it has had such an effect as *that*," said Mr. Styngy, "it is little short of a miracle. Master Bilbury, will you oblige me by bringing here a pair of steps? You will find them at the end of the gallery."

Master Bilbury, a good-looking lad of sixteen, who had been watching the portrait of Mr. Styngy's ancestor with a look of amused satisfaction, hastened away, and the schoolmaster returned to the contemplation of the picture.

But now he found that a fresh change had come over the features of his ancestor. They had been very pale but a moment ago—now they were of a deep red. The eyes were rolling in their sockets with a wild expression, and the mouth was slowly opening and shutting like that of a newly-caught codfish, who finds that fresh air does not agree with him.

"Lord bless me!" exclaimed Mr. Styngy. "What's that? Why, it's making faces at us."

Mr. Bilbury gazed too in wonderment, and his mind reverted to certain miraculous pictures of which he had read, which could weep and wink and do other strange actions not usually associated with the work of the painter.

"Wonderful!" was all that he could say, opening his mouth as widely as Tommy's. "Won—der—ful!"

The rector's wife, who was rather given to superstition as being rather fashionable (spiritualism was in great vogue just then), retreated to the opposite side of the gallery, where there was a convenient lounge, and got ready to faint.

Up to this time none of the spectators had had any idea but that what they saw was really a picture, the face of which, by some strange chance, had become altered. The schoolmaster himself had not the least suspicion of the existence of the corridor into which our hero had penetrated, otherwise it is likely that he would sooner have solved the mystery.

At that moment young Bilbury returned with the steps, and Mr. Styngy, full of wonder and curiosity, slowly mounted.

But as he got nearer to Tommy his expression changed from wonder to wrath. He was within a yard of the unlucky one, when the truth flashed upon him, and, reaching out his hand, he grabbed Tommy by the ear.

"Oh! don't, sir," howled Tommy. "I couldn't help it, sir; it was quite an accident."

"Come out, you—you—ineffable young villain," roared Mr. Styngy. "What sins have I committed in my life that I should be plagued with such a daring young scamp as you? Come out?"

"Whatever is the matter!" said Mr. Bilbury.

"It is the spirits," screamed the old lady. "Take care, dear Mr. Styngy, not to offend them, or they may do you a mischief."

"I'll 'spirit' him," said Mr. Styngy, viciously. "Come out, I say, you scoundrel."

The schoolmaster took a firm hold of Tommy's other ear, and hauled away at him with such success, that he not only brought Tommy bodily through the canvas, but overbalanced himself, and and, falling backwards, floored Mr. Bilbury and a stout, mild looking old gentleman, who had been too bewildered to say anything.

Tommy was shot over Mr. Styngy's head like a rocket, and, turning a couple of somersaults, finally deposited his plump person in the lap of the old lady, who instantly assaulted the unlucky youth for taking a liberty.

Mr. Styngy was up again in a moment though, and had Tommy by the ear again in "less than no time," as the popular saying has it.

"Oh! don't," exclaimed the agonized youth. "You're always catching hold of my ear, and it's so tender."

"I'll catch hold of you somewhere else before I've done with you, sir," said Mr. Styngy, grimly. "Now, tell me at once how you came up there, behind that picture."

It flashed at once upon Tommy's mind that to reveal the secret of the passage would be to implicate Lionel and the others—and that he would have died rather than do—so he replied, with a vacant air—

"I don't know, sir."

Mr. Stygny instantly gave Tommy's right ear an excruciating twist, and then bestowed a similar complaint upon the left, lest he should be accused of partiality.

"Now, will you answer, you hardened young wretch?" thundered Mr. Styngy, in his most awful tones.

"I can't," sobbed Tommy. "I don't know. I was walking in my sleep, and fell through, I believe."

This was such an audacious and preposterous fib, that Mr. Styngy turned crimson, and gasped with anger. Of course Tommy's ears suffered again. Then the schoolmaster held him out at arm's length, and surveyed him with a look of despair upon his classical features.

"What am I to do with such a boy as this?" he said, appealing to Mr. Bilbury and the short stout gentleman, the former of whom had received Mr. Styngy's head in his waistcoat, while his spectacle-glass fell from the eye into which some one's elbow had rammed it.

"I should recommend a sound thrashing," said Mr. Bilbury.

"Oh! he has one nearly every day," said Mr. Styngy; "and it doesn't seem to do him any good!"

"Try bread and water for a week, and solitary confinement," suggested the stout gentleman.

"He is used to that, too! In fact, I believe he rather likes it."

"Try them in conjunction then, my dear Mr. Styngy," added the old lady; "but be sure and give him a *good sound* flogging. You know what the wise Solomon has said regarding the spoiling of children by sparing the rod. I am afraid that you treat your boys too kindly."

"Oh, lor!" muttered Tommy. "Does he?" Much *you* know about it. I wish you were here for a week, and you'd think different, I'll wager."

"I must think over it," said Mr Styngy, at length, "and devise some fitting punishment for his audacity; but I will at once place him in solitary confinement, if you, madam, will have the kindness to excuse me for a few moments."

So Tommy, still held by his smarting and suffering ear, was led from the room, and conducted to the cell, where he was left smarting and tingling to an almost unbearable extent, and with the pleasing prospect of worse punishment in store.

"Here I am in for it again," muttered Tommy, as he soothed his burning ears with his pocket-handkerchief. "More bread and water, and more whackings, I s'pose. Blest if I don't think that I was made on purpose for old Styngy to cane. I wonder if he got it as hot as me when he was a boy. I hope he did; it would be some consolation if a fellow only knew that."

Meanwhile, Lionel, Charlie, and the French boy, finding that the weather had considerably improved, slipped out of the school gates for a run, returning breathless, with muddy boots, and cheeks glowing healthily, in time for tea.

As they trooped into the tea-room, after changing their muddy and disordered clothes, Lionel's thoughts naturally reverted to Tommy Codlings; but that unhappy youth, as my readers know, was pining in the "cell," and only Mr. Styngy was aware of his imprisonment.

Lionel passed the word round in a whisper, but none of the boys had seen Tommy since dinner.

"My stars!" thought our hero. "I hope Tommy hasn't stuck fast in the grating of the door. It was thoughtless of me to leave him. I'll run up directly after tea, and see."

He was really anxious about him; but Charlie Drummond only laughed.

"It'll do him good, Li."

"How?"

"Improve his figure, of course. If I were Tommy I'd practice getting through that grating every day. He'd be as slim as you or I in a week, and a couple of inches taller."

"That's a novel way of doing Banting," laughed Lionel. "But, I say Charlie—seriously—if poor old Tommy has got stuck in that hole, he'll hurt himself."

"Nonsense—we didn't."

"No—but Tommy will. You know how unlucky he is; he can never get out of a lark like anybody else."

"Suppose old Styngy caught him looking through the hole?" said Charlie.

"I hope it isn't as bad as that, Li. Depend on it we shall find him stuck fast in that door. We ought to have waited for him."

Tea over, Lionel and Charlie made their way cautiously towards the deserted portion of the house, but to their consternation, when they arrived in the corridor, they saw a workman—a carpenter—busily engaged in barricading the entrance.

"My stars! Here's a go!" said my hero. "He's blocking up the place, and p'r'aps poor Tommy is in there."

"There's Noodles," replied Charlie. Let's ask him if he's seen Tommy."

"No," replied that stolid gentleman. "I ain't seen him."

"Not in there?" said Lionel, indicating the deserted corridor.

"No—I ain't seen him nowhere."

"Then let one of us go and look," said Lionel. "I tell you, I think Codlings is up there, and if you bar the place up, so that he can't get out, he'll starve, or be smothered to death."

"Codlins'," repeated Noodles, thoughtfully. "Be that the fat boy that's always getting wolloped?"

"That's him."

"Then he's all right. Mr. Styngy 've found he."

A cold perspiration broke out on Lionel's forehead.

"Mr. Styngy's found him? Are you sure, Noodles?"

"Sartain sure. I took un up some bread and water 'arf a hour ago. Oh, he's all right, *he* is."

Lionel very much doubted this when he heard the news, and he would gladly have heard how and where Mr. Styngy had effected the capture of the unlucky Tommy; but of that Noodles knew nothing.

"Poor old chap!" murmured our hero. "I say, Charlie, what can we do?"

"I don't see that we can do anything," replied Charlie. "I never saw such a fellow—he's always in some mess or another."

"And never gets out of one without tumbling into something worse. I say, Noodles?"

"Well, Master Wilful?"

"When you go again to take Codlings any grub, will you give him a note from me?"

"Clean agin the rools," said Mr. Noodles.

"Oh, bother the rules. Half-a-crown will break all the rules *you* have to keep."

"Well, it'll break that there one," replied the odd man, as he pocketed the coin with a grin of satisfaction. "Where be the letter?"

Lionel, with a pencil and a scrap of exercise paper, scribbled a few words of comfort to the imprisoned Tommy, as follows:—

"Cheer up, old fellow. Charlie and I beg your pardon for leaving you in the hole, but we thought you were following. We mean to come and see you if it can be done, and bring something good with us. Give Noodles a note in answer to this. You can trust him."

"There," said Lionel, folding up the missive and handing it to the old man; "give that to Codlings, and if you bring back an answer you shall have another half-crown."

Mr. Noodles winked a slow and heavy wink full of meaning; and so Lionel and his chums departed, wondering how on earth Tommy had managed to be unlucky enough to fall into the clutches of the schoolmaster.

"He'll get it uncommonly warm this time, Li," said Charlie, as they made their way back to the class-room, to prepare evening lessons.

"Yes. I wonder what Styngy will do to him? I've a good mind, to take all the blame on my shoulders."

"That wouldn't be of any use," said Drummond. "You'd only get into hot water yourself, and do poor Tommy no good."

"That's true," replied our hero, gloomily. "Old Styngy's a regular brute, for pitching into Tommy as he does."

"We all get a taste, for the matter of that; but I must own, that Tommy generally gets a double dose."

"Then I tell you what, Charlie," said Lionel; "old Styngy shan't have it all his own way. He's sure to give it very hot and strong to Tommy, this time; so suppose we be his champions, and give the 'head' a dose?"

"A dose of what, Li? Not poison."

"Not exactly," laughed Lionel. "Serve him out, I mean. Give him a regular startler. I've got a plan in my head."

"What is it, Li?"

"Hush! I'll tell you at bed-time. Here's old Crocklejack."

CHAPTER XLVII.

TOMMY CODLINGS IN A NEW CHARACTER—THE SENTENCE—THE CONSPIRATORS' PLOT—MIDNIGHT—THE EXECUTION OF THE PLOT, AND WHAT CAME OF IT IN THE MORNING.

MR. STYNGY was a long while before he could make up his mind what kind of punishment to inflict upon the unfortunate Tommy.

To do him justice, he was not apt to be needlessly cruel, though he certainly spared no one who came in his reach when he was angry.

"It will be of little use to flog him," he mused. "I have tried solitary confinement and prison diet before, and they have been of no benefit. Ah, I have it. I will try the effect of degrading him. Most boys have a keen sense of the ridiculous, and I will shame him into better behaviour."

It was late in the evening when Mr. Styngy arrived at this decision; but he acted on it at once, and rang the bell for Noodles.

That solemn-faced gentleman produced himself to order.

"Noodles."

"Yes, sir."

"Is Master Codlings still safe in the cell?"

"He be, sir."

"Asleep, I suppose."

"He be, sir. Which he said as it were the best thing but wittals for a hempty belly."

"Then wake him up," said Mr. Styngy, "and bring him here. Be careful, Noodles, that he doesn't play you any tricks on the way."

"I'll take care o' that, sir."

And Noodles, departing, returned in a very brief space of time with Tommy tucked comfortably beneath his arm, but habited only in his night-gown.

"There he be, sir," said Noodles, as he set Tommy down upon his feet.

"What do you mean by bringing him here in that state? you—you—idiot," said the schoolmaster, sternly. "Why is he not dressed?"

"You didn't say nowt about that. You only said as I was to bring un here, and see as he warn't to play no larks."

"Take him back and dress him instantly," said Mr. Styngy; "and then bring him to me in a decent state."

This little error was rectified, and Tommy produced with his usual proportion of every-day clothes on him.

"Now, Codlings," said Mr. Styngy, sternly, "as I find that, in spite of repeated warnings and punishments, you will *not* behave yourself like any of the other young gentlemen in this school, I intend to keep you constantly near me—under my own eyes, in fact; but as you cannot reasonably expect to lead an idle life, and you *will* not apply yourself to your lessons, I shall employ you in such domestic services as I think fit."

Tommy stared at Mr. Styngy in a bewildered way. "Domestic services! Was Mr. Styngy going to make a 'buttons' of him?"

"Do you hear me, Codlings?"

"Oh yes; I hear you, sir."

"Do you understand me, Codlings?"

"No, sir, I don't," replied Tommy, which was quite true.

"I will explain myself," said Mr. Styngy, pleasantly. "This evening, for instance, you will go to the kitchen and bring me the basin of arrowroot which the cook will have prepared. Then you will read me a few pages of Blair's Sermons until I feel drowsy, when Noodles will lock you up again in your room. In the morning Noodles will arouse you at six o'clock, when you will employ yourself in cleaning my boots and brushing my clothes, and at half-past seven precisely you must bring me a pan of hot water. Do you understand that, Codlings?"

"Why," said Tommy, aghast, "you're making a servant of me, sir."

"Ex—actly," replied Mr. Styngy, blandly, "and that is all you are fit for at present, Codlings. When I see an improvement in your conduct you shall resume your place among your companions."

With a curious sensation as if the room were going round and round, and he was spinning with it, Tommy suffered himself to be led from the room by Noodles, and marched to the kitchen, where he received the arrowroot, and, escorted by Noodles, marched back again.

"Just to see as you don't play no larks, you know," said the odd man. "In you go."

"Put it on that table," said Mr. Styngy, who was undressed and in bed, "and stand there till I call you."

"Well, I'm dashed," moaned Tommy, "if this ain't a pretty go—making a slavey of me! I wonder what my father would say to it."

But as Codlings senior was many miles away, his opinion could not be asked, and Codlings junior had nothing to do but obey.

Mr. Styngy tasted the gruel, and poured in a little of something out of a bottle, which he said contained medicine, but which smelt suspiciously like rum.

"Codlings," he said, wrapping himself comfortably in bed.

"Yes, sir," replied Tommy, dolefully.

"Bring me that large book lying on the table yonder."

Tommy brought it with, I am afraid, a vicious desire in his mind to drop it on some tender portion of Mr. Styngy's frame.

The schoolmaster took the volume, rapped Tommy on the head with it, "to keep him from going to sleep," as he said, and then picking out the very driest and dullest of the sermons, bade Tommy read it aloud.

It was a dreadfully tiresome task for the unlucky youth. He hated reading generally, but a dose of Blair's Sermons was not calculated to increase his taste for literature. Then the volume was so dreadfully heavy—in more senses than one—that he was obliged to hold it up with both hands.

Then the way in which Tommy stumbled over the long Scriptural names, and the manner in which he dashed at the Latin and Greek quotations—much as a clumsy foxhunter scrambles over a five barred-gate—would have made any disinterested listener split his sides with laughter.

But it was no joke to Tommy. He was dreadfully sleepy. His arms ached with the burden of that ponderous volume.

He tried once to skip a page, but Mr. Styngy found him out in a minute (for he knew that particular sermon by heart), and gave Tommy such a "twister," that he dared not try it again.

But everything must have an end—so Codlings came at last to the final paragraph, and pronounced the "Amen" with a fuller appreciation of the beauty of that word than he had ever had before.

"If he wants me to read another," said Tommy to himself, "I'll shy the book at him and bolt. He can't like it himself—nobody could."

Fortunately for Tommy, Mr. Styngy did not want him to read any more, and, after keeping him waiting in the agonies of suspense for about two minutes, he said, sleepily—

"That will do, Codlings. Put the book down on the table, and ring the bell."

Tommy gladly obeyed, and, in answer, Mr. Noodles appeared to conduct Tommy back to his prison.

"Good night, Codlings," said Mr. Styngy. "I hope that the pious and learned words you have read to-night will make a deep impression on your mind."

"They have, indeed, sir," said Tommy, fervently. But he didn't mean what Mr. Styngy meant.

"I am glad to hear it," replied the schoolmaster. "You shall read one to me every night, in the same manner. There are only ten volumes, but when we have got through them, we can begin all over again. Take him away, Noodles, and mind that he is here at the right time with my boots and hot water."

Tommy turned faint and giddy, and clung to the odd man for support. Ten volumes! It would kill him—or worse, drive him crazy.

Arrived at the cell, Noodles set down his candle, and produced, with an air of mystery, the note which Lionel had scrawled.

Tommy read it, and the tears came into his eyes.

"He's a real good chap to think of me," he said. "But tell him, Noodles, not to get into any scrape on my account. It would only make me feel worse if he did."

"Is that the messidge?"

"Yes," said Tommy. "That's all."

"Then p'r'aps you'll ha' the kindness to write it down," continued the odd man. "Which my mem'ry ain't fust-rate, and I might make a horror."

He produced a stumpy pencil and a piece of paper, and Tommy wrote a few words in his peculiar spidery caligraphy.

Noodles took it, nodded, and then took himself off in company with the candle; leaving Tommy to get into his narrow bed in the dark.

Either rum in arrowroot, or Blair's Sermons, or perhaps both, had made Mr. Styngy particularly sleepy that night. Almost before Tommy and Noodles had quitted his room he began to snore, and in two minutes after, his nose was emiting sounds which a dying pig might have failed to emulate.

Midnight! The great clock in the hall below chimes forth the hour, and as the sound of the last stroke dies away, two ghostly forms steal noiselessly along the corridor and halt opposite the door of the head master's room.

They cannot be ghosts, although they look so spectral in the gloom; for, instead of going through the key-hole as is the well-known custom of such ethereal beings, one of them, after listening intently, softly turns the handle, and, listening once more cautiously enters.

Then, looking towards the bed where Mr. Styngy is snoring away with undiminished vigour, they laugh softly and in a very unghostly fashion; and one of them, who bears remarkable resemblance to our hero, produces a huge ball of twine.

Then the two spectral figures flit noiselessly about the room, visiting for some strange and occult reason, every article of furniture in the room and performing some mysterious manœuvres with the ball of string.

This lasts for about half-an-hour, when the two ghostly figures approach one another, and again laugh softly.

"My stars!" whispered one, in a voice which sounded very like Charlie Drummond's. "What a lark it will be in the morning."

"Yes; and won't old Noodles get it hot in the morning," replied the second ghostly figure, who looked like Lionel. "But come on, he *might* wake up."

"Let's have a peep at him first. I should like to know what he looks like when he's asleep."

And, gently drawing aside the curtain, the ghost, who looked like Charlie Drummond, peeped in upon the sleeping schoolmaster, and gazed with awe (and reverence, we hope) upon his classical features.

A sleeping infant is regarded by the poets as the type of innocence and beauty. Mr. Styngy had long ceased to be an infant, and truth compels us to say that he was anything but beautiful in repose. This was chiefly due, perhaps, to the fact that he slept with his mouth very wide open, and twitched his features into horrible grimaces, as if his dreams disagreed with him.

"My!" whispered one spectre; "don't he look an old guy?"

"He just does. If he only knew that we had been here, wouldn't he be wild?"

Then, softly replacing the curtain, the ghostly figures glided away through the door, closed it noiselessly, and left Mr. Styngy to solitude and sleep.

* * * *

Punctually at six Tommy was aroused, shivering, by the stern Noodles, and conducted to the boot-cleaning department, where he wasted the blacking and knocked the skin off his knuckles in the attempt to clean seven pairs of boots and shoes.

"Now," said Noodles, when the last boot was beautified; "it's time for the governor's hot water. Come along, and look sharp; he don't like to be kep' waitin'?"

Tommy followed the odd man gloomily to the kitchen. He was thinking about the coming night and the sermons, and whether it would not be advisable to fall down stairs and break an arm or a few ribs, as an excuse to avoid the reading.

The hot water was ready in a large foot-pan, nearly as much as Tommy could lift. He managed to stagger upstairs though without spilling more than a quarter of it, and reached Mr. Styngy's door in safety.

But as he crossed the threshold his foot caught in some obstruction, and he shot forward in a flying attitude, while, by some mysterious and alarming means, every portable article in the room was set in motion!

CHAPTER XLVIII.

THE CATASTROPHE—LIONEL AND CHARLIE FIND OUT THAT THEY HAVE MADE A LITTLE MISTAKE —TOMMY IN THE "BLACK HOLE" OF CHEETHAM HALL.

IT was a dreadful catastrophe for poor Tommy. With his usual luck, he had managed to fall into the trap his friends had made ready for Noodles.

Of course Lionel and Charlie, when they paid that ghostly visit to Mr. Styngy's bedroom, had not the least idea that Tommy Codlings would be the first to enter, but, as says the proverb, "Luck is everything," and it was Tommy's fortune always to get into a scrape when anyone else would easily have avoided it.

The foot-pan had been shattered to pieces in the fall, and Tommy had tumbled in their midst, where, scalded by the boiling water and lacerated by the broken crockery, he set up a doleful howl.

He couldn't get up either—that was the worst of it; he was held down by a perfect network of string, and the more he kicked the tighter he was held, while every plunge brought down with a crash some article of furniture.

The little table by Mr. Styngy's bedside—the basin—the lamp—the bottles, spoons, and glasses —the clock and ornaments on the chimney-piece— the pictures on the walls—the very chairs—all seemed endowed with life and a reckless desire to smash themselves, which latter object they were achieving with immense success.

Mr. Styngy, thus suddenly aroused, passed his classical head between the curtains and gazed with dismay and horror upon the scene of destruction.

He gazed for a moment, and then, jumping out of bed, made a grab at his favourite reading lamp, as it danced merrily about the floor.

But he only succeeded in cutting his fingers with the broken glass, and then he too became entangled in the twine, and sixteen stone weight of him came "crash" down upon poor Tommy.

He had often come down heavily upon Tommy

before, but never so much as now; besides, there was no satisfaction in it, for he hurt himself.

It may have been only fancy, or owing to the position in which he found himself, but Tommy thought he heard, and afterwards declared solemnly that Mr. Styngy gave vent to several very naughty words, which, in a general way, are only supposed to issue from the lips of bricklayers overcome with beer.

Lionel and his chum Charlie were, as may be supposed, on the look-out for the result of their little joke. They dared not venture within peeping distance, but the instant they heard the crash of the falling Tommy they ran like hares to the spot.

The door was still widely open, and they arrived just in time to see Mr. Styngy prostrate himself in all humility, but with unpleasant suddenness.

Neither of the boys had as yet the least idea that Tommy was the sufferer. They were in the full belief that Mr. Noodles was the victim, and their enjoyment, we are sorry to record, was doubled when Mr. Styngy fell into the trap.

"Oh, look at him! Isn't it beautiful?" whispered Lionel, as he peeped round the corner of the doorway. "I wonder how Noodles likes it?"

"Hasn't he just got long legs?" chuckled Charlie, in the same tone; "and ain't he kicking?"

"But ain't Noodles quiet over it," added our hero. "He's strong enough to pitch old Styngy out of the window, and yet he doesn't seem to move."

"Yes, he does. I saw him wriggle then. There's his head now. Why, I say, it isn't Noodles after all."

Lionel looked, and then he too dodged round the corner, aghast. There was no possibility of mistaking that plump form, and those rounded features owned by Tommy Codlings.

"Did you ever know such a thing?" said Charlie.

"Was there ever such an unlucky chap in the world?" added Lionel. "The idea of his getting in there."

"And, hark, now how he's howling! Old Styngy is pitching into him red hot."

"We'd better go in."

"Yes, and get welted ourselves," said Drummond. "No, thank you."

"He won't touch us. We can say we heard the row, and thought the place was on fire."

"Somebody else has heard it, too," added Charlie. "Hark, there's Noodles coming. Hide up, Li."

But our hero had resolved not to leave his comrade in distress, so he darted into the room, panting, and with an air of having just arrived from a great distance.

"Did you call, sir? Is anything the matter?"

Mr. Styngy had just got Tommy into a convenient position, and holding him by one ear, was preparing to pepper him with his right hand, when Lionel entered, and he became aware of the extreme indecorousness of his attire, considerably more of his legs being visible than is usually deemed decent to expose to the public gaze unclothed.

He gave Tommy a parting twist, and scrambled back into his bed before he replied—

"What do you want here, Wilful?"

"I'm sorry if I disturbed you, sir," said our hero, sweetly; "but there was such a noise, sir, that I thought something was the matter."

"You have no business to think," retorted the schoolmaster, sharply, for he was considerably ashamed of being found in such a position, "and you have no business to come here at all, unless you are sent for. Tell Noodles to come here instantly."

But that stolid gentleman himself putting in an appearance, rendered the message unnecessary.

He stood there in the doorway, gazing at the disarranged furniture and broken glass and crockery with a bewildered look, then finally his glance rested upon Tommy Codlings, sitting up in the midst of the wreck, feeling his ear with an air of deep interest.

"Bin havin' a bit of a game, eh?" was the odd man's sage remark; "who be goin' to pay for t' crockery?"

"Noodles," said Mr. Styngy, in a very sharp and vinegary voice.

"Here I be, sir."

"Come here. But first turn Wilful, and any other boys that may be lurking in the passage, away, and take down their names. Do you hear, Noodles?"

"All right, sir," replied the odd man, lumbering heavily towards the door, but of course before he reached it Charlie and Lionel had vanished.

"Poor old Tommy," said our hero, "he's in for it again."

"Yes, I'm afraid so."

"We must own to old Styngy that we did it, Charlie."

"It wouldn't do a bit of good, Li; Codlings would get it just as hot as ever."

"I don't care. It makes me feel mean to think that poor Tommy is getting welted for what I did, or helped to do; and he had no hand in it at all, this time, you know."

"That's true enough. Well?"

"Well, I vote you and I go back, and I shan't feel comfortable unless—or, if you like, I'll take all the blame."

"Not exactly, Li. If you think it's right, and will help poor Tommy out of the scrape, I, too, go with you."

"That's the way, Charlie. I didn't think you were the chap to leave a friend in a mess. Here we are. Hallo! they're at it already."

Just as they reached the door they heard Tommy's sweet voice uplifted in a tearful wail, and accompanied by a peculiar "swishing" sound, which they knew only too well.

Lionel rapped loudly at the door, and, as he did so, it must be confessed that he felt a little nervous at the thought of the ordeal he was about to undergo.

There was a pause, and then the voice of Mr. Styngy said sharply—

"Who's there!"

"It is I, sir—Wilful and Drummond. We want to speak to you, if you please, sir."

"Go away instantly," said Mr. Styngy, angrily. "If you dare to stay another instant you shall be severely caned."

"Neck or nothing," whispered Lionel. "Come on, Charlie."

And turning the handle of the door, he boldly entered, and beheld a rather curious spectacle.

Noodles was standing by the bed holding the unlucky Tommy tucked beneath his left arm, the lower half of the young gentleman hung thus presented to Mr. Styngy as if the schoolmaster had desired to hold an inspection as to the soundness of the seat of Tommy's trousers.

Mr. Styngy himself was setting up in bed, looking wonderfully fierce and vicious, and wielding in his right hand a long and limber cane.

He had never caned a boy in such an attitude before. There was something luxurious about it, and he felt proportionately annoyed at being interrupted.

"Stop, if you please, sir," said Lionel, hurriedly. "Don't flog Codlings any more. It was I who tied the string to all the things in the room."

"And I helped, if you please, sir," added Charlie.

"Oh," said Mr. Styngy, with sarcastic politeness. "You were the author of this mischief, were you, Wilful? and you aided him, eh, Drummond?"

"Yes, sir," replied Lionel; "and we hope that you will let Codlings off, for he had nothing at all to do with it, sir."

Now, there is no reason to doubt but that Mr. Styngy would have let Tommy go free; and, in reward for our hero's pluck in taking the blame to himself, would have allowed both Lionel and Charlie to escape with slight punishment, but Codlings, with his usual luck, spoiled everything.

They had shown a desire to sacrifice themselves upon the altar of friendship, but Tommy was too proud to allow them to do it.

"Don't believe 'em, sir," he roared, trying to wriggle himself round the odd man's elbow, so as to get a view of Mr. Styngy. "They had nothing to do with it, sir."

"Indeed we did, sir," said Lionel, earnestly. "Drummond and I did it last night, sir, after you were asleep."

Mr. Styngy looked at the boys in angry perplexity.

"This is a strange thing," he said at last. "You boys generally strive to fix the blame of misconduct on another's shoulders, yet now you absolutely wish to be thought guilty of a shameful practical joke."

"We have told you the truth indeed, sir," said Lionel.

"And I always tell the truth, sir," said Tommy, in a choked voice, for he found it rather difficult to carry on a conversation upside down.

"Then," said Mr. Styngy, decisively, "I shall not believe either of you; you must be trying to impose upon me, and I shall therefore punish you all. Noodles, turn Codlings a little more this way."

"There's a chap!" thought Lionel, fairly exasperated. "After trying such a risky dodge to get him out of the mess, he runs himself, and us too, into it."

Charlie Drummond's thoughts were of the same description; but Tommy didn't see things from that point of view—he was confident that he had done something brave and heroic, and took the rest of his caning without a wriggle or a cry.

Fortunately for Lionel and Charlie, Mr. Styngy had had enough of it by the time he had polished Tommy off, and so they escaped the stinging visitation of the cane.

But I very much doubt if they would not far rather have been flogged, and handsomely too, than have been condemned to a week's imprisonment on bread and water, which was the sentence passed upon them. Their only consolation was that they were not to be separated.

"I shall have an opportunity," said Mr. Styngy, when he had done raising blisters all over poor Codlings, "of finding out now, who are the real authors of the audacious tricks which have been played of late in the school. If they cease while you are in confinement, I can come to no other conclusion than that you are the culprits; but on the other hand, if they continue to be perpetrated, I will not relax my efforts until I discover the practical joker. Take them away, Noodles. Lock them up, and bring the key to me."

Whether or not the audacious larks the schoolmaster complained of, ceased, and whether he succeeded in bringing the real culprit to justice, our readers will discover if they trace the progress of this truthful history.

CHAPTER XLIX.

IN PRISON—A DISCOVERY AND AN ADVENTURE—THE MAGIC DINNER.

THE stern mandate of the head master was carried out to the letter. Noodles had a strong sense of duty, especially of his duty to himself.

"I say, Noodles," said our hero, as he, Charlie, and Tommy, were marched into the prison chamber, "look sharp, and let's have some breakfast. I'm peckish."

"I ain't got no horders 'bout that yet, Master Wilful. I mun wait till th' guvnor tells me afore I brings ye owt."

"Look here," Lionel went on, persuasively, jingling some loose money in his trousers pocket, "I've got another half-crown or two somewhere."

"You owe me one now, Master Wilful," said Noodles, taking the scrap of paper Tommy had given him on the previous evening and passing it to Lionel; "there's the harnser to your messidge."

Lionel took it, looked at it, laughed, and slipped two half-crowns into Noodles' horny fist.

"There's one for the footman," he said, "and one for the waiter. Bring us something good, and we won't forget you."

"Which them is capital ticklers for a bad mem'ry, Master Wilful," said Noodles, regarding the half-crowns with a heavy grin of satisfaction; and, so departing, he left our hero and his chums alone.

"Well," said Lionel, after a pause, which he employed in looking steadfastly at Tommy, "you're a nice chap, ain't you?"

"Well," replied Tommy, taking the praise in perfect sincerity, "it's very kind of you to say so, Li; but I really think that I did it pretty well, considering."

"I should think so," Charlie struck in sarcastically. "Here we are, locked up for a week on bread and water, and you with a precious good tanning. I rather think that you have done it pretty well, considering."

"I couldn't do anything less, you know," Tommy went on, not in the least perceiving that his friends were speaking sarcastically. "It was only right to speak up and try and save you fellows. I couldn't let you get into a mess on my account, you know."

There was something so truthful and honest about poor Tommy's way of putting the matter that neither Charlie nor our hero had the heart to be angry with him any longer.

"But don't you see, Tommy," said Lionel, "that if you hadn't cut in at the wrong time and contradicted me, old Styngy would have let you off altogether, and us, too, for speaking the truth."

Tommy did see it then; but the idea had never occurred to him before. Ideas seldom did, in fact, until they were useless.

"Dash it!" he said, desperately, pulling a lock of hair. "What a fool I am!"

"Don't call yourself such bad names," laughed Charlie, "and I wouldn't pull my hair out, if I were you—you haven't got too much."

"The idea," Tommy went on mournfully, "of having got you two fellows locked up here—and all through my dashed thick head."

And Tommy, as if to test its solidity, battered it at the wall, where it sounded like a cocoa-nut.

"Try again, old chap," laughed Lionel; "a few 'props' like that, and you'll make a hole into the passage. Hallo! that sounds like Noodle's elephantine tread."

It was Noodles, bearing a long and doleful countenance, and a tray, whereon were ranged a jug, three tumblers, and three thick slices of dry bread.

"Hallo, Noodles, *that* won't do," said Lionel, as he regarded the contents of the tray with a very unamiable countenance. "Haven't you got anything better than that?"

"Which Measter Styngy hev been to the cook hisself, and giv pertickler horders as nothink helse but this should go out of the kitching."

"Mean beggar!" grumbled Lionel.

"And there's the 'arf a crownd," continued Noodles, placing that coin on the tray; "and werry sorry am I as I couldn't 'arn it by bringing of you somethink better."

"Never mind, keep it all the same, and see what you can do for us at dinner time."

"Which the horders is too strick, I'm afeard,

Master Wilful; but I'll try. Though if I shuld get holt of anything, be keerful, for Measter Styngy he said as he were comin' to see you frequent hisself."

"Much obliged," growled Tommy; "but he can keep himself to himself it it's all the same to him, especially if he brings that dashed cane with him."

"Which I've got to wax-end a dozen new 'uns this werry mornin', Master Codlins."

"That looks cheerful, don't it?" laughed Lionel. "They're being got ready for your benefit, old chap."

"I wouldn't care," grumbled Tommy, "if he would only give a fellow decent grub; but it's too bad to keep one's inside empty, and whack the outside as well."

"So it is, Tommy," said Charlie, in a tone of sympathy.

"Just as I was filling out, too, and getting my figure back again. My father wouldn't know me now."

"I don't see much alteration, Tommy," said Drummond, as he glanced at the well-filled suit of clothes, which had the unlucky Tommy inside them; "you'd keep fat on anything."

Codlings grunted an inarticulate reply, and attacked his slice of bre: d as if it had been a mortal foe whom he was bot nd to annihilate in a given time.

Breakfast over, Mr. Styngy appeared, armed with a cane, and followed by Mr. Crocklejack, bearing an armful of books.

The schoolmaster gave Tommy a passing cut or two, just to keep his hand in, apparently, for the unlucky one hadn't committed any fresh crime just then, and ordered Mr. Crocklejack to distribute the books.

"And mind," said Mr. Styngy, "that they are properly learned. Fasting is said to clear and stimulate the mind; when I come this afternoon, to hear you repeat your lessons, I hope to find that the diet has had a beneficial effect upon your brains."

Then, touching up Tommy again once more, just to see him skip, Mr. Styngy left them once more to the solitude of their prison chamber.

"A double dose, and all to be got by heart, too," commented our hero. "Well, my memory's pretty good, and there's nothing else to do, so here goes. How are you off, Charlie?"

"First rate," was the reply. "He's marked me off a lot of lessons that I know by heart already."

"And you, Tommy?"

"Don't ask me," groaned that miserable object of persecution; "I haven't got a bit of memory. When one thing's hammered into my head, number two drives it out again directly, like an old nail. I shan't try—it's no use."

"Don't give in, Tommy; we'll help you," said Lionel.

"It's not a bit of use," said Codlings, dismally. "If it were sums or written exercises, I'd ask you; but I can't get more than half-a-dozen lines by heart at once."

So the time passed away. Lionel and Charlie applied themselves to their books, while Tommy piled his books carefully in a corner and went to sleep, until the arrival of Mr. Styngy and Noodles—the former bearing his cane, the latter the dinner allowance of bread and water.

Our hero and Charlie acquitted themselves creditably. Tommy, of course, did not know a word, and said so.

"And *why* not, Codlings?" asked Mr. Styngy.

"Because—because I haven't learnt them," said Tommy.

"And *why* have you not learned them, Codlings?" asked Mr. Styngy again, the while he tucked up the wrist of his right coat-sleeve, in a careful and scientific manner.

"Because I couldn't, sir—there's too many of them; and besides, if you please, sir, I can't learn on bread and water."

"Now, Codlings," Mr. Styngy resumed, in the same soft bland voice, "don't tell me such nonsense. Philosophers, men far wiser than you in all probability will ever be, hold that a light spare diet leaves the brain more free—separates it, in fact, from the grosser bodily elements. Do you understand me, Codlings?"

"No, I don't, sir," replied Tommy, whom deprivation of his dinner had reduced to a state of obstinacy.

"I see what it is, Codlings," said Mr. Styngy, playing suggestively with his cane. "You require stimulating. Your system is sluggish. Turn round, if you please?"

Tommy turned round, and Mr. Styngy stimulated him for ten minutes, at the expiration of which time the unlucky one was much redder in the face, and much sorer somewhere else, but he looked not a bit the wiser for the stimulant.

When the schoolmaster was gone, Tommy lay down upon the bed and cried a little—he couldn't help it, poor fellow, for he was very sore, while Lionel and Charlie did all they could to soothe him.

"Never mind, old fellow," said Lionel; "a week soon passes, and then think how we shall enjoy our liberty again, and pitch into the regular dinners."

"There's a little consolation in that," sniffed Tommy. "But I declare if I have much more of this I'll jump out of window—I will."

"You couldn't, Tommy," said Lionel. "They're all fastened down, I expect."

Our hero tried one, and found that, though the sash stuck a good deal from long disuse, it opened with a little trouble, and a rush of keen, cool air swept in.

It was welcome, for the room smelt close and musty. Lionel propped it open with a piece of wood, and then naturally put his head out to survey the scene below.

The window was not more than thirty feet from the ground, and looked upon some out-buildings, beyond which lay the kitchen garden, which supplied the school with vegetables.

"Too far to drop it, Li," said Charlie, who had joined our hero.

"Yes—unless Tommy will go first, and let us fall on him."

"I should go off with a bang like a bladder, if you did—I'm so empty," rejoined Tommy.

"What's that queer little crib with a skylight—looking as if it grew out of the wall?" asked Lionel.

"That's Noodles' country house; he sleeps there in the summer, and takes his meals there generally. The cook won't have him in the kitchen, because she says he's so vulgar, and eats too much."

"That's likely; Noodles looks like a good feeder."

He doesn't keep a waistcoat of that size on dry bread," grumbled Codlings. "I wonder what he has got for dinner to-day."

"I don't know; but if you're curious, Tommy, you had better watch at the window. It's near his dinner time, and you'll see him bring it from the kitchen."

"Do you think he'll bring us up a bit? Lor, if it's only roast pork!" Tommy went on with a meditative and rapturous look. "I've got a fancy for roast leg of pork to-day, with plenty of stuffing and apple sauce."

"Don't, Tommy—you're making my mouth water," said Lionel.

"The last time I tasted roast pork," Tommy continued with the same rapt air of abstraction, "the crackling was done to a turn, and the gravy——"

"Dry up, will you," said Charlie Drummond, in an exasperated tone. "Don't you know better than to talk about such things when we've got a week of dry bread before us."

"We'll have something better than that," said Lionel, in a mysterious manner.

"What do you mean, Li?"

"You don't mind running the risk of breaking your neck for the chance of a good feed."

"Not if I had twenty necks. But what's the dodge?"

"You see that ledge just below?"

"Yes; well?"

"It won't be very difficult to drop down on that, nor dangerous, if we hold tight to the window-sill."

"No," said Charlie, peering down at the ledge, which was about a foot wide; "I think we can do that."

"Then we can work ourselves along the ledge, until we are close to the wall, and then, dropping down on the top, we can run along, and so get to Noodles' cabin."

"Ah, I see!" cried Charlie. "You're going to ask him to give us some of his dinner!"

"No, that I'm not. Do you think that Noodles, with his appetite, would share his prog with three hungry chaps like us?"

"Then what are you going to do? Fight him for it?"

"Not exactly—I'm going to borrow it."

"Without his leave, of course?" said Charlie, with a delighted wink.

"You've hit it; and now, are you on? Don't come unless you're a good climber, for it would be an ugly fall to the ground below."

"I'm a cat at climbing; but how about Tommy —he won't be able to come?"

"Oh, won't he," said that young gentleman, opening his little round eyes, indignantly. "Don't you think that I'm going to be left out of it, Master Charlie."

"But you'll never be able to get along that ledge; it's only a few inches wide—and we shall have to stick as close to the wall as flies."

"Oh," added Lionel, "Tommy's too fat!"

"I'm not," retorted Codlings, in an obstinate way. "I'm coming, I tell you."

"Now, Tommy, old chap, don't be a fool," said Lionel, with more friendliness than politeness in his manner. "If we get the prog we'll bring it back, and you shall have a fair share."

"Honour?"

"Of course," said our hero, indignantly. "Did you ever know me cheat?"

So it was settled, and Tommy, in a rather sulky and discontented way, consented to remain behind, while Lionel and Charlie started on their rather perilous journey.

But what boy thinks of peril when fun or sport is in question? We have seen boys many a time run risks at which men, and brave men too, would hesitate.

Once on the ledge, it was only a question of time and care to make the journey in safety—barring the accident of a loose brick, which would have put a sudden and dangerous termination to the expedition.

They found the ledge so narrow that they were compelled to shuffle along it, their faces pressed closely to the wall, and their arms extended in a cramped position—sticking as closely to it in fact as flies, to use Charlie Drummond's expression.

The distance was trifling—not more than twenty yards; but so slow was their progress, that it took a quarter of an hour before they were able, much to their relief, to quit the ledge and drop down upon the wall.

They were a little damaged. Charlie had scraped all the buttons off his waistcoat, and some of the skin from the tip of his nose; while the epidermis of Lionel's fingers had suffered, and he had worn a hole in the knee of his trousers.

But such trifles as these were only made to be laughed at, and now the two chums prepared for the more difficult portion of their enterprise.

"First," whispered Lionel, "is there any chance of being seen?"

"Not much. All the windows that look out upon this part belong to the deserted part of the house, and only Noodles and the gardener come out here."

"Then on we go."

And Lionel, crouching down, crept along the top of the wall, which was on a level with the skylight of Noodles' "country house," until he could peep through the glass into the room below.

"No one there," said Lionel; "but there's a dirty cloth laid on the table, and a knife and fork, and a cruet-stand. Wonder if the old beggar's had his dinner?"

"Not he. I know his time well enough. But you haven't told me what your little game it yet?"

"I'll show you presently," replied our hero, opening the strongest and keenest blade of his pocket-knife. "Don't talk more than you can help; a whisper goes a long way sometimes."

Charlie was silent, and watched his chum with deep interest as he carefully loosened the putty which held one of the panes of glass in its place; and, when he had completed that operation, he removed the glass itself.

Then he replaced the knife in his pocket, and produced two long fishing lines of fine gut, each weighted at the end and provided with three sharp, strong pike-hooks.

"I see now," said Charlie, admiringly. "That's a capital dodge, Li. You mean fishing up the dinner?"

"That's it exactly."

"But," said Charlie, "how about getting away with it? Old Noodles is sure to spot us before we can get back to our room."

"Not he. It'll be a quarter of an hour before he understands that he's lost his dinner; and when he *does* come out to see what has become of it he'll stare about in every direction but the right one."

"Well, we must chance it. Hush! I hear him."

The door opening from the kitchen was close by where the two chums were stationed, and they could plainly hear the heavy footfall of Noodles and the "bang" of the closing door.

Then, peeping cautiously out, they saw him coming in with a covered dish, from which a savoury steam was exhaling, and a quart pot, creaming with the foam of freshly-drawn porter.

Tommy had seen him, too, for he was still at the window watching the progress of his chums with great anxiety, and at the appearance of Noodles he manifested by signs his exuberant delight.

The movements of the odd man were unusually quick on this occasion—he was in his little cabin in less than no time, and, depositing the dish on the table, removed the cover.

Tommy's vision was realised. It was a small leg of pork, the crackling roasted to a delicious brown, and bathing in a perfect pond of gravy.

Noodles looked at it for a moment, with a fond, contented expression, and then took a draught of beer to whet his appetite.

Lionel was watching for his opportunity, and like a flash he dropped one of the almost invisible gut lines, and hooked the leg of pork by the knuckle.

Noodles put down the beer, and turned to take hold of a chair. In the instant Charlie had dropped the line, and hooked the pot by the handle.

"It's done to a turn," murmured the odd man, as he grasped his knife and fork, and licked his lips anticipatorily. "For what we're going to receive, and settera—— Oh, lor!"

Just as Noodles completed this very short grace before meat, Lionel and Charlie, with a swift strong pull, hauled up the lines, and, as if by magic art, the dinner vanished through the skylight!

CHAPTER L.

OUR HERO'S LITTLE PLAN TO GET A DINNER MEETS WITH SUCCESS—TOMMY CODLINGS NEARLY MANAGES TO GET LIONEL AND CHARLIE INTO A WORSE SCRAPE THAN EVER—THE DINNER IN THE PRISON—MR. STYNGY'S VISIT—SAGE AND ONIONS.

"DONE!" whispered Lionel, as he hastily detached the joint from the hook, and wrapped it in his pocket handkerchief. "Come on, Charlie."

"But how on earth are you going to manage, Li?" said Drummond. "It was hard enough to get along that ledge with our hands empty—we can never do it with this grub to hold."

"We must," replied Lionel. "I wouldn't lose that pork for any money. It'll last all the week if we don't let Tommy get at it."

It strikes me that Tommy won't have the chance," said Drummond. "We shall never get back to the window with these things."

"Yes, we shall," rejoined Lionel. "Do as I'm doing, Charlie. Tie your handkerchief to the handle of the pot and sling it round your neck."

This little operation was soon effected, and then the two chums were ready to start on the return journey.

"There's Noodles," said Lionel, taking a final peep through the skylight, "still sitting at the table, staring up like one o'clock. He can't make it out yet. My, won't he spin a yarn when he gets back to the kitchen! But come along, Charlie. Hurry up."

As noiselessly as cats the two boys crept along the top of the wall until they reached the ledge, and, scrambling up to it, began to edge themselves along in the same slow, undignified way they had traversed it before.

"How do you feel, Charlie?"

"Precious bad," replied Drummond, in a husky, gasping voice. "That handkerchief has slipped round my windpipe, and the weight of the dashed pot is throttling me."

"Never mind, old chap, we are half way there now, I should think—only I can't turn my head to look. Blow it! There's a sharp piece of brick just taken a corner off my nose."

"Hush! I think I can hear Noodles," said Drummond. "Isn't that his footstep on the gravel?"

"Sounds like it," replied our hero. "But a fellow can't see anything with his face jammed up against the wall in this fashion. How far are we from the window?"

Charlie, who was in front, turned his head with considerable difficulty, so as to get a peep in the direction of the window; but what was his astonishment, when he found his nose almost touching the little snub nasal organ of Tommy Codlings.

There he was, no doubt of that, and in a terrible fright, too. His arms were stretched, and to their fullest extent; and his plump little body was pressed as closely to the wall as it would go.

"Move on, Charlie," said our hero, impatiently. "If old Noodles casts his eye up here, we shall be nabbed, to a certainty, and lose the pork!"

"I can't!" replied Charlie, savagely. "Here's that ass, Codlings, stuck in the way."

"Blow it! what did he want to come out here for. Shove him along, Charlie, there ain't a minute to lose."

"Move up, Tommy—do you hear?" whispered Drummond. "What a chap you are! Make haste!"

"I can't!" replied Tommy, in a shivering voice. "A hook or something has caught in my breeches, and I can't move either one way or the other."

"Here's a pretty go, Li; now we're in for it." growled Charlie, as he imparted this piece of information to his chum.

"You're the unluckiest chap I ever had anything to do with," said Lionel, fairly exasperated by the fix into which Tommy had succeeded in getting himself and his friends. "Bother me, if I sha'n't have to give up your company; it's a dashed sight too expensive."

"Don't say that, Li," pleaded Tommy, sorrowfully. "I was so hungry, and you seemed gone such a long time, that I couldn't wait."

"You'll have to wait long enough now," retorted our hero. "Hark, Charlie! who's that talking?"

Drummond listened for a moment, and then said in a thrilling whisper—

"It's all up, old chap. That's old Styngy's voice."

"He may not see us, though," added Lionel. "We must get along somehow. Can't you unhook Tommy?"

"I can't get my hand down low enough without overbalancing myself."

"Well, then, shove him along. If the hook tears his breeches it can't be helped."

To this process Tommy had a strong objection, for he was in mortal fear of falling; but it was out of his power to help himself beyond letting off a little groan of terror, as he felt Charlie's shoulders slowly but surely pressing him onwards.

"You make that noise again, and I'll shove you clean over!" whispered Charlie, ferociously. "On you go."

"Is the hook giving way?" asked Lionel.

"No; but Tommy's breeches are. Push a little harder, Li."

The push was given, and, with a sharp, tearing sound, the hook was out, leaving a rent some four inches long in Tommy's pantaloons.

Just then they heard the voice of Mr. Styngy raised in tones of anger.

"Nonsense, Noodles!—utter nonsense! How can you expect a human being to believe such a story. The idea of your dinner flying away through the skylight. Preposterous!"

"I tell 'ee it's troo, sur," said Noodles, obstinately. "I see it wi' my own heyes, and I'll take a haffydaved on it. There."

"If you have really lost your dinner it must have been a trick of some of the boys, and that is not possible, for they are all at class except Wilful, Drummond, and Codlings, and *they* are safely locked up."

"P'r'aps they got hout, sur," suggested Noodles. "Them boys is the werry dickens for larks, 'specially Master Codlins'."

"It may be so; but we can soon ascertain," said Mr. Styngy. "Come with me, Noodles, we will go to the room at once."

A cold perspiration had broken out over the three chums, and, crouched close against the wall, they waited; dreading every moment, that Mr. Styngy would look up and see them.

But fortunately the schoolmaster never thought of the window. It is doubtful, whether he even remembered that it looked out upon the kitchen garden, and in another minute the boys had the satisfaction of hearing the footsteps of Mr. Styngy and the odd man, receding rapidly in the direction of the back door.

"Now's our time. Cut along," said Lionel. "Wake that slow chap, Tommy, up, Charlie. We sha'n't have time to get through the window before Styngy unlocks the door."

Tommy was hustled along with very scant ceremony. The window was reached, and one by one they scrambled in, Charlie upsetting more than a pint of the beer down his own neck in his haste.

"Now, then, under the bed with these things," said Lionel, hurriedly. "Out with your books, and begin gabbling away as if you'd been at it ever since he left. Hush, here he comes! Sit over in that dark corner, Tommy—your nose is bleeding."

FOLLOW MY LEADER.

"THAT'S THE WAY I SPELLS IT," SAID NOODLES, AS HE BROUGHT THE DICTIONARY DOWN WITH A CRASH.

No. 11.

Tramp, tramp came the heavy feet of Mr. Styngy and the odd man along the corridor. The door was unlocked and flung open, and there, sure enough, were the three boys—quiet, studious, and respectful.

"You see, Noodles," cried Mr. Styngy, "you are mistaken. These boys are safely under lock and key, and all the others are in the schoolroom. Be careful, Noodles; you seem subject to delusions, and I fear that you drink more than is good for you."

"Dang it," growled Noodles, "that be too bad, that be—to lose my dinner, and then to be told as I be subjeck to collusions, and that I drinks too much. Dashed if I put up wi' that."

"No muttering, Noodles," said Mr. Styngy, sternly. "Get back to your work, and you boys mind that those lessons are properly prepared by tea-time. I address myself particularly to you, Codlings."

Codlings looked up at him and smiled. He was blissful in the thought of the coming feast, and he actually dribbled at the corners of the mouth with excess of appetite.

He could hardly wait until the door was locked and the schoolmaster gone, and for a minute he even felt jealous of Lionel and Charlie for being there to deprive him of a part of the delicacy.

"Now, Tommy, keep your fingers off till you're helped," said Lionel, administering an admonitory rap on the knuckles to him, as he grabbed a loose piece of crackling. Where are your manners?"

"Oh! blow manners. Make haste, Li; there's a good chap. Lor, if you only knew how hungry I am!"

"So are we," returned our hero, coolly; "but we're not going to feed like pigs, for all that. Make yourself useful, Codlings—tear some leaves out of the exercise-book, for plates."

"Where shall we have the peck, Li?"

"On the bed—that's the most comfortable place. Take care Tommy doesn't get all the pillows to himself."

"Why, anyone would think that I was greedy to hear you talk," said Tommy, in a tone of indignation.

"So you are, old chap; only you don't know it," said Lionel. "You don't mean to be, I know; but you're too fond of the good things of the world to let any of 'em pass you without making a grab."

"If I thought you were in earnest, Li," said Tommy, "I should feel quite hurt; but you don't mean it. Lor! how delicious that pork does look—be sure and give me plenty of crackling—and I'm fond of stuffing—and I'll take a little fat, please—and if there's any gravy, I should like a drop."

"Now, what do you call that but being greedy?" said Lionel, "and it's an insult to me besides, Tommy, for you doubt my dividing the prog fairly. Now to teach you better, and all for your own good, you shall be helped last."

Tommy sniffed indignantly, and retired sulkily to a corner of the room—but the sight and smell of the roast pork was too much for him; he came forth again, and took his place on the bed, licking his lips contemplatively till his turn came to be served.

But when it did!—that was a sight to have cured an alderman of a fit of indigestion. Lionel had calculated that the pork would have lasted throughout the term of their captivity, but their appetites were too keen; indeed, I rather think that Tommy himself could have eaten the leg—it was only a small one—and have left very little on the bone for a dog of average voracity.

"Just a little bit more, Li, please—off the knuckle, if there is any," Charlie would say.

"And I'll have a little fat and some crackling," Tommy would add; "and if there's any stuffing, I should like some."

Lionel was not much behind his companions; for, to tell truth, he had a very unheroic appetite, heroes of the romantic type being popularly supposed to exist upon love and blood, and to disdain the coarser food of ordinary mortals.

But our hero pegged away merrily at the savoury pork, enjoying it as he thought he never had enjoyed a meal before. This was, of course, principally owing to the fact that it did not belong to him, and that he had no possible right to be eating it. It was only another proof of the old adage which tells of the sweetness of stolen fruit.

Tommy was the last to give in; and, with a sigh of satisfaction, he sank back on the bed, greasy from head to foot, and smelling like a cook-shop.

"Oh, it was beautiful," muttered Tommy. "What a pity there isn't any more of it."

"It's precious lucky there wasn't any more of it," said Lionel, "or bother me if I don't think you would burst, Tommy. I never knew such a chap for a tuck-out."

"Come now," retorted Tommy, "you've done pretty well, Li. But lor, who's to blame; that stuffing was perfectly lovely."

"Yes, and that reminds me of something," said Lionel, getting hurriedly off the bed. "Old Styngy will be here presently, and he'll smell us, as sure as my name's Wilful; and what's to become of the bone, and the pot."

"Pitch 'em out of window," suggested Charlie.

"That wouldn't do," said Lionel; "somebody would find 'em, and we should be suspected."

"Then let them stay where they are."

"Worse and worse. There's nowhere to put them, except under the bed, and they would be seen directly when the room is cleaned."

"Well, what can you do, then, but swallow them?"

"Not exactly, unless Tommy feels equal to the task. No, Charlie, we must put them back where they came from."

"That's the idea," exclaimed Tommy; "and then we can get something more to eat—eh, Li? I know I shall feel hungry again before supper."

"Shut up, you boa-constrictor," said our hero. "You've had enough to eat to last you the week; why, a moderately hungry man might dine off the smell of you."

"Take my advice, Tommy," said Drummond. "Go to the basin there, have a good wash, and rinse your mouth out, while Li and I go and put these things back."

The window was again cautiously opened, and once more Lionel and Charlie, after satisfying themselves that the coast was clear, started for Noodles' "country house."

They reached it safely, and, dropping lightly from the wall, entered it by the door this time, and deposited the bare bone and the empty pot upon the table, leaving a note in a very much disguised hand, thanking Mr. Noodles for his kindness, and promising to renew the visit on an early occasion.

Then Lionel made a hurried inspection of the cupboard, but nothing eatable rewarded his trouble, as, in consequence of predatory cats, the odd man preferred keeping his food in a safer place. There was only a half-emptied bottle of gin, which Lionel humorously filled up from the paraffin can.

"That'll cure the old vagabond of drinking," said Lionel. "He won't make much of a beast of himself with that bottle."

"Time we were back, Li," said Charlie. "It must be getting near old Styngy's time. It's jolly fun this, ain't it?"

"Yes; and if we're careful, there's no chance of getting caught either. I hope old Noodles won't take the alarm, and dine in the house for the future."

"No fear; they won't let him in the kitchen. But come along, Li; I'm afraid of old Styngy getting into the room while we're away."

The return journey was made with much more rapidity than the first. Practice was perfecting them, and they shuffled along the ledge at a fair pace.

Lionel was the first to reach the window; but, as he grasped the sill and raised himself up a little way, he suddenly let go his hold and nearly fell off the ledge.

"What's up?"

"It's all up," whispered Lionel, with an alarmed look. "The window's shut down, and I can hear old Styngy turning the key!"

CHAPTER LI.

MR. STYNGY IS PUZZLED, AND TOMMY CODLINGS SUFFERS—THE DISCOVERY AND THE RELEASE—THE VISIT TO THE SPELLING BEE, AND HOW NOODLES GAINED A PRIZE AND LOST HIS TEMPER.

IT was too—too true. The window was shut down, but through the lower panes Lionel had caught a glimpse of Mr. Styngy, glaring about him in a puzzled and ferocious manner.

That unlucky Tommy was the cause, as usual. He had felt sleepy after that surfeit of roast pork, and shut the window down to keep away the draught while he had a nap, forgetting, for the moment—for he was not thoughtful—that he was cutting off the only chance his chums had of entering the room.

There he was, lying on his back, his little snub nose sending forth such sounds that an imaginative listener might have fancied that the pig Tommy had eaten had come to life again, and was giving utterance to its complaints at the way it had been treated.

Mr. Styngy had his cane with him—he was never without it when he visited the prisoners—and, advancing softly to the bed, he rolled Tommy gently over, until the convenient part of him was uppermost, and then brought the cane down with a vicious "swish."

It was a cut that would have awakened any one of the Seven Sleepers. Poor Tommy started up with a howl—broad awake in an instant. He had been aroused from such a delicious dream, in which he fancied himself king of a land where the most tempting luxuries—eatable and drinkable—grew ready for consumption on the trees, with nothing to pay for them.

"What's that for?" said Tommy, in a defiant tone, as he rubbed his eyes with one hand, and the injured place with the other.

"What's that for, sir?" thundered Mr. Styngy. "What do you mean, Codlings, by going to sleep in the middle of the day, when you should be hard at work—and where are Wilful and Drummond?"

This question, and perhaps a second cut from 'stinger," aroused Tommy to a sense of his position, and he began to realise the danger in which he and his chums were placed.

He glanced towards the window, but it was still shut down, and there were no signs of his chums to be seen, so he answered, innocently—

"I'm sure I don't know, sir."

This reply resulted in his reception of a third application of the cane—a cut that seemed to sting him all over at once.

"Ow!—ow!" yelled Tommy. "Oh, don't."

"I'll don't you," said the angry schoolmaster. "Answer me at once. Where are your companions, or shall I flay you alive?"

"Up—up the chimney," gasped Tommy, resolved to perish, rather than betray his chums.

But this was, of course, about the worst and most unlucky answer he could have made, for it so happened that there was no fireplace, and consequently no chimney in the room.

This time Mr. Styngy wasted no words; but, gripping Tommy by the nape of the neck with his left hand, he plied the cane so vigorously with his right, that the sound resembled that made by a steam thrashing machine in full operation.

Lionel and Charlie, stationed outside on the ledge, heard the sound, mingled with Tommy's yells and shrieks; and they would have gladly given themselves up, if only for the sake of effecting a diversion in the unlucky Tommy's favour; but they could not by any possibility open the window from the outside.

"Poor old Tommy," whispered Lionel, "how he is getting it."

"Serve him right," growled Charlie. "What did he shut the window for?. We might have had a chance to get in before old Styngy if he hadn't done that."

"Our turn will come presently," said Lionel. "We shall catch it quite as hot as Tommy."

"Suppose we go back along the ledge, and hide up for a while," suggested Charlie. "I don't much fancy a welting from old Styngy when he's in such a temper."

"But what about Tommy?"

"Oh! we can't do him any good. He's had his licking, and it's all over. Peep in, Li, and see what the head is up to now."

Our hero did, and a most unlucky peep it was, for just as he cautiously raised his head above the level of the window sill, Mr. Styngy glanced in that direction; their eyes met, and Lionel knew that he was discovered.

The schoolmaster was at the window in two strides, the next moment the sash was flung up with a crash, and his head was out; but he had not reckoned upon the sash-lines being rotted away, and, with a crash, the lower half of the window came down, after the manner of a guillotine, upon his neck.

"Oh! dear me!—oh! murder!" gasped Mr. Styngy, who, for the moment, fully believed that the assault was the work of the revengeful Codlings.

With no little difficulty he raised the sash again, and released his neck from its painful situation.

Then, as he held the window wide open, our hero and Charlie climbed in, and looking, if the truth must be told, rather sheepish and confused—anything, in fact, but heroic.

Mr. Styngy let the window down again, and facing round, regarded the culprits silently, with a meditative and thoughtful, but not an angry expression, as, in obedience to his stern question, Lionel made a clean breast of the whole affair.

"What the dickens is he going to do?" thought Charlie.

"A storm brewing, and a hot one too," was Lionel's inward conviction.

But they were both wrong, for after having contemplated them in this silent and unexpected way for a few moments, Mr. Styngy said—

"Really, Wilful and Drummond, I am at a loss what to do with you. I have had mischievous boys, and unruly boys, in my school before now; but I generally managed to cure, or, at least, curb them. It seems to me, though, that there are some faults which are incurable, either by the suaviter in modo or the fortiter in re. You seem to be afflicted in this respect, and I am as reluctant to punish you for it as to flog a boy because he was hump-backed or lame, or afflicted with any physical infirmity. You understand what I am saying, I hope?"

They understood that Mr. Styngy was not going to punish them, and for that they were supremely grateful.

"But," continued the schoolmaster, "you will understand this—Wilful, Drummond, and Codlings—I cannot submit to have my peace of mind utterly ruined by your misconduct. I have had absolutely no rest or comfort since your arrival.

You will take your places, as usual, amongst your schoolfellows for another week, but if, during that time, these tricks are continued, I shall expel you —one and all."

"We are very much obliged to you, sir," said Charlie, a little confusedly. He meant, of course, that he was grateful for being unpunished, whereas his reply seemed to intimate that he was thanking the schoolmaster for the threat of expulsion.

But Mr. Styngy took no notice of the remark, and, turning from the boys, strode away in his most majestic manner.

"Well," said Lionel, wonderingly, "that's the queerest start I ever heard of. What does it mean?"

"It means that we're let off when I thought we were in for a precious good hiding," said Charlie; "and that's quite enough for me."

"How about *me?*" sobbed Tommy, joining his sweet voice to the debate. "I've had my whacking. There never was a chap with such luck as mine."

"You ought to be grateful for your celebrity then, Tommy," laughed Drummond. "To be the unluckiest boy in creation is something to be proud of."

"It's all Tommy's fault," said Lionel. "We should never get into mischief if it wasn't for him."

"Come now, I like that," said the ill-starred Tommy. "Who is it that always gets in for the whackings and the impositions. *You* get off sometimes, but I *never* do."

"Cheer up, Tommy; you're right for a week to come, anyway. We shall all have to be good and virtuous now."

"It don't matter to me," said Tommy, gloomily. "If I was an angel, I believe I should drop in for my whackings just the same. I was born to be unlucky."

"Well, console yourself for the present with some tea. There's the bell going. Come on to the dormitory, and have a wash first. We must change our clothes, too, for we're all over brick-dust, and there isn't a button left on my waistcoat."

* * * *

Noodles had to go without his dinner that day—for the cook, with whom he was at mortal variance, refused for any earthly consideration to let him have any more in place of that which he had lost.

"You're a nasty guzzlin', gormandizin', low beast, Noodles, that's wot you are," she had said in answer to the odd man's pathetic appeal; "and you has no more wittles out o' this kitching, I can tell you."

"But," pleaded Mr. Noodles, in desperation, "think o' wot it is, Marey Hann, for a man like me to be deprived of his dinner! How do you s'pose that I can get through my day's work, and come in contack with them himps of boys onless I'm kep' up with a reg'lar supply of grub."

"I don't know, and I don't care," retorted the cook, with much asperity; "but I do know this, if you don't take your hugly 'ed out o' that there doorway, I'll throw this pail o' water over it!"

Mary Ann was a determined character, and a woman of her word, as Mr. Noodles had often learned by experience. He, therefore, removed his "hugly 'ed" from the dangerous vicinity of Mary Ann, and went to pour his tale of woe into Mr. Styngy's ears.

But, as our readers have seen, he was unsuccessful in that quarter, for his master refused to give any credence whatever to the story.

"I'll strike!" said Noodles. "That's wot I'll do. I aren't goin' to be deprived of my wittles, and work too. I'm blest if I don't run over to the pub., and have a pipe and a pint."

This, in truth, was a rather favourite amusement of Mr. Noodles, and the very slightest excuse would suffice to make him go in search of the refreshing "pint" and the soothing "pipe."

His hat was in his "country house"—a place of bitter memories now to the odd man—and, as he entered it, he cast a mournful glance around, when almost the first objects that met his gaze were the pot and the well-picked bone.

"Well, I'm dashed," muttered the odd man, as he slowly spelled through the note Lionel had left on the table. "They're polite, anyway, them sperrits; but they might hev' left a morsel on the bone."

Thinking of spirits put the odd man in mind of a certain bottle in the cupboard, and he poured himself out a liberal glassful.

"It's rayther 'eatin' in the middle o' the day," thought the odd man; "but I've been upset, and my nerves rekwires stimulatin'."

He raised the glass to his lips, and threw his head back with the jerk of a practised tippler; but it had scarcely gone down his throat than it came back again, and Noodles rushed wildly out of the cabin—his mouth widely opened—his arms waving frantically in the air the while he spluttered, gasped, and choked in a violently alarming manner.

The odd man's agitation is not to be wondered at, when our readers recollect that Lionel had mingled about half-a-pint of paraffin with the "Old Tom," and if they are at all acquainted with the flavour of that un useful, but drinkable liquid, Mr. Noodles' condition will not seem extraordinary.

He sank down in the midst of a bed of early cabbages, and, after giving vent to his emotion for about ten minutes, he was able to return to his cabin, when he instantly sacrificed the bottle to his wrath by smashing it, and, putting on his hat, departed in search of comfort.

"Why, Mr. Noodles, sir, this is a pleasure," said the landlord. "We don't orfen see you so airly in the day as this."

"Well, I've bin upset," replied Noodles, dropping into a chair.

"You don't mean to say so," Mr. Noodles, said the landlord, soothingly. "Have a little drop o' something to cheer you up, sir?"

Mr. Noodles did have a little drop of something, and then he thought that he could "peck a bit" as well; and then, having disposed of a pound or two of cold bacon, with a corresponding allowance of bread and beer, he felt better, and unburthened his mind to the landlord.

"And so you think it was sperrits, Mr. Noodles?"

"Or boys," replied the odd man.

"Might be both"—with some vague idea of a joke—"you know what sperrits boys has."

"I wishes I had the sperritin' of em," said the the odd man, viciously; "they worries the life out o' me."

"You don't take no change, you see, Mr. Noodles; you ought to go about a bit more, and see things, and then you'd be hable to put up with them warmints o' boys with deparative compunity. Why, now, don't you go to the spellin' bee to-night?"

"The wot?" said the odd man. "I've seed many shows in my life, but there warn't ne'er a bee among 'em all as could spell."

"You will have your little joke, sir. 'Taint *that* kind of a bee I means. This 'un is up at the Lectoor Hall, and you goes up on a platform, and there's a couple of chaps with big dictionaries, and they axes long words out o' the book, and them as spells 'em right gets a prize."

This rather incoherent definition of a spelling bee was pondered deeply upon by the odd man, and when at last he had got its meaning fairly into him, he said—

"Prizes, did 'ee say, Muster Bungler? Wot kind o' prizes?"

"All kind, and main good some on 'em be, tew Silver watches, and chains, and new hats, and weskuts, and deskes, and halbums, and sitch."

"Then blame me if I don't hev a go," said the odd man, "You're sure about the giving away?"

"Sartin."

"And all as you've got to do is to spell wot you're axed?"

"Jest so. Will you come? I m a goin' myself."

"I will," said Noodles, emphatically.

"But you're not a goin' in for the spellin', are you?"

"Why not, Mr. Bungler?" demanded the odd man, in a slightly offended tone.

"Nothin', sir—nothin'. Only some o' the words they axes is enough to give a ordinary chap the lock-jaw to hear, let alone tryin' to spell 'em."

"There ain't a word in the Henglish languidge," said Mr. Noodles, with reckless confidence, "as I don't know how to spell. Why, up at our place they calls me the 'walkin' dickenary.'"

"Do they indeed, sir?"

"They does, and well I desarves the name," Mr. Noodles continued, growing more daring in his assertions as he went on. "Spell! Why, how many chaps is there, I wonder, as can spell any word of twenty sillybulls backwards if they were axed?"

"Not many, I dessay," replied the landlord, deferentially.

"Not many? There ain't only one, and that's me. You'll see how I'll polish 'em up to-night, Mr. Bungler. I'll have every blessed one o' those prizes—every blessed one—see if I don't."

And in the full confidence that he would that night return laden with prizes from the competition, Mr. Noodles became extravagant, and ordered a pint of old stingo for luck, and then another pint to keep the first company; then a little drop of rum, to prevent the beer from turning acid; then a second "go," because the first was so good, concluding with a half-quartern hot Irish—at the landlord's suggestion—just to keep his tongue oiled.

The consequence of these frequent and mingled potations may be imagined. When the time arrived to go to the Lecture Hall, Mr. Noodles' gait was unsteady, and his speech slightly thick and incoherent, while Mr. Bungler, the landlord, was very little better.

"How d' yer feel, Misser Noodles?" said Mr. Bungler. "We'll get here lee'le early, 'cos I've got to 'range sheats."

"All ri'," replied the odd man, lurching out of the doorway—"never berrer."

The fresh air steadied them a little, and in a tolerably respectable fashion they reached the scene of the spelling bee.

The hall was empty, for it wanted quite an hour of the time appointed for the "bee" to commence, so Mr. Bungler, conducting his friend by a side entrance, led him on to the platform, where Noodles instantly reeled into a chair, and went to sleep in a corner."

"They won't notice him," thought the landlord; "and if they does, it won't matter. There's always a lot of 'em goes to sleep at these here lectures."

And so the odd man was left in peaceful possession of his corner. Indeed, the landlord could hardly have done anything else, for Mr. Noodles was apt to be obstinate when in liquor, and he was far too heavy to be carried out.

At length the hour came, the doors were opened, the questioner, the referees, the committee, and the competitors crowded on to the platform, while an eager and expectant audience crowded the seats in front.

No time was lost, the questioner produced his dictionary—a huge volume, enough in itself to make any but the stoutest-hearted spellers tremble—and then the competition proceeded.

All went merrily for half an hour—the audience laughed, applauded, or hissed the competitors according to their success or failure, and the questioner had just let out a particularly long and difficult word, when the voice of Noodles was heard, and the ponderous frame of that gentleman came lurching heavily to the front of the platform!

"Where's them there prizes?"

Such was the husky demand growled forth by the intoxicated Noodles—startling the questioner, who was a nervous little gentleman, so that he nearly fell off his chair.

"Wh—who—are you, sir?"

"I'll soon let you know who I am," replied Noodles, fiercely, as he swayed about in the vain endeavour to maintain an erect and dignified position. "I'm champion shpeller of 'e world."

"Indeed!" said the questioner, not knowing what else to say, and backing himself a little farther away.

"Yes, tha's wa' I am," said Noodles; "and I want them there prizes."

"Oh—indeed," faltered the questioner, giving an appealing glance around him for help; but no one volunteered to touch Noodles—he was a big man, and there was a ferocious gleam in his eyes.

"Where are them there prizes? I wan't' see 'em," demanded the odd man again, as he pitched heavily forwards, and brought himself up with a lurch that upset an old gentleman who was standing just behind him.

"You will excuse me, sir," said the questioner, frightened into politeness; "but—er—is it—your intention to take part in the contest?"

"I sh'think 't was," replied Mr. Noodles, doubling his fists and revolving them slowly around one another. "I'll fi' anybody!"

"Excuse me," said the questioner hastily, as he edged still further away; "but you are under a slight misapprehension—this is not an assault-of-arms, but a spelling bee."

"I'm aweer on it," replied the odd man, in an injured voice; "don't I come to spell?"

"Oh, that's a different thing, my dear sir," said the questioner, hoping that if he got Noodles quietly into a seat, he would fall off to sleep. "Take a chair, sir—take a chair."

This Noodles had no objection to do, for he was particularly unsteady on his legs; and he dropped into a chair with a crash that spoke well for the good workmanship of the upholsterer who had supplied it.

The questioner went on with his task; but both he and the referees were so nervous, that many an error by which competitors should have been ruled "out," were passed unnoticed.

Noodles looked on with a fixed and glassy stare.

"He's going to sleep, I think," whispered one of the referees. "I've sent for the constables, and when they come we'll have him put out quietly."

"Where are those police? Confound them, they're never at hand when wanted," said another.

"I'll lodge a complaint with the inspector," said a third. "It's shameful. Who *is* this man?"

"Never saw him before. How he got in I don't know," replied the questioner, as he turned over the pages of his dictionary in quest of a fresh word. "Hallo! Confound him, he's woke up again."

At that moment the odd man, who had been apparently composing himself for a nap, straightened himself with a jerk, and said in an unnecessarily violent manner—

"Now, where's them there prizes?"

"My dear sir," replied the questioner, in his most polite terms, "according to the rules you must spell correctly the words that are asked you before a prize can be awarded."

"Fire away," said the odd man, huskily. "There ain't a wor' as I ain't ekal to."

"Then suppose you begin with an easy one," said the questioner. "Will you spell parallelogram?"

"Tha' ain't a word," replied Mr. Noodles, with much disgust.

"It is, I assure you," said the gentleman. "But

FOLLOW MY LEADER.

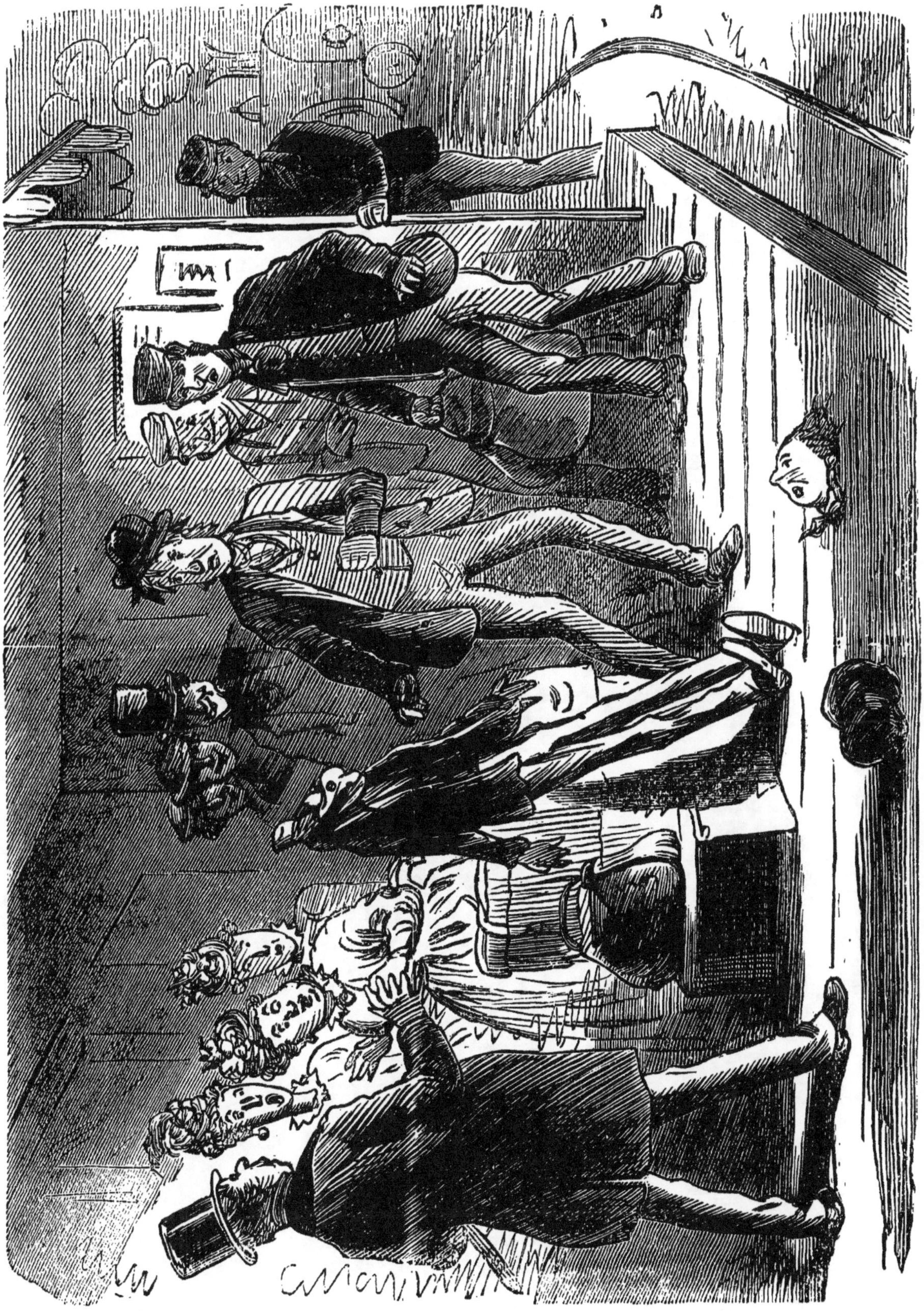

AS THE DETECTIVE DELIVERED THE BLOW HE SAW SAM SCARECROW'S HEAD FALL OFF.

perhaps you did not hear distinctly. Allow me to repeat it," which he did with much distinctness and with a strong emphasis on every syllable.

"I tell 'ee 't ain't a word," said the odd man, with ferocious obstinacy.

"You may think it is not," rejoined the questioner; "but the opinions of such eminent men as Johnson, Walker, and Webster are against you. Take the dictionary, sir, and look for yourself. *They* call it a word, I can assure you."

"Oh! they calls it a word, do they," said Mr. Noodles, taking the dictionary, and rising unsteadily from his seat. "Well, then, that's the way I spells it."

And he brought the heavy volume with a crash upon the head of the unlucky questioner, felling him to the floor as if he had been shot.

In an instant the lecture-hall was in a state of utter confusion. Noodles' appetite for blood was aroused, and, lurching hither and thither, he attacked, indiscriminately, everyone who came within his reach.

In five minutes he had flattened as many noses, made free gifts of four black eyes to respectable old gentlemen who didn't want them, and sent several false teeth down the throat of their unlucky owners.

Some few of the bravest, rendered desperate by danger, endeavoured to capture and bind the odd man, but he was strong and heavy, and floored them like skittle-pins.

The younger portion of the audience enjoyed the scene amazingly, and amongst them, we very much regret to state, were some young gentlemen who ought to have known better.

The sight of a number of elderly, respectable gentlemen being "punched" with much severity by a tipsy man, ought to have inspired in their bosoms feelings of sympathy and compassion; instead of which we grieve to record that these young reprobates mounted the chairs and tables, and applauded as if they had been spectators at a pantomime, and really, if our hero and his chums had been there we think they would have done the same.

"Police!" roared those who were dodging to get out of Noodles' way.

"Murder!" yelled those who had already suffered.

"Turn him out!" shrieked the audience, who, not being on the platform, were comparatively safe.

But the police didn't come, and nobody seemed able or willing to tackle the odd man single-handed, when the landlord, Mr. Bungler, who had been having a comfortable little nap in a back room, appeared.

"Hallo! here's a go!" he thought. "There'll be a row, and I shall get into it, if he don't go afore the police comes."

His course of action was soon decided on. Moving cautiously behind the unsuspecting Noodles, who was engaged in a playful attempt to twist a very snuffy nose off an old gentleman's face, Mr. Bungler suddenly grabbed him by the collar of his coat, and what sailors call the "slack" of his breeches, and "ran" him skilfully across the platform, shot him down the stairs like a sack of coals, picked him up at the bottom, ran him out into the street—which was, fortunately, nearly empty—and never relaxed his exertions until he reached his own house, where he tumbled Noodles into a corner, and sank into a chair, exhausted.

There for a time they must be left to recover their breath while we return to follow the fortunes of Sam Scarecrow.

CHAPTER LII.

THE WONDERFUL JUMBARELLO UNMASKED—MR. BELLERS-TO-MEND INVOKES THE AID OF A POWERFUL SPIRIT, COMMONLY KNOWN AS IRISH WHISKY—HOW THE DETECTIVE WAS CHARMED THEREBY, AND THE MARVELLOUS OCCURRENCE ON THE PLATFORM OF PENDLETOP STATION.

THE announcement made by the detective was a startling one for all.

The curate and the ladies with him saw that they had been imposed upon. Mr. Bellers-to-Mend and Long Jem were much afraid—not because of the deception they had practised, but because it had been found out; while Sam himself turned pale and faint at the idea of being taken into custody.

"Oh you low man!" said one of the indignant curate worshippers. Take them all into custody, policeman."

"It is shameful," added the curate, burning with a mild species of wrath, and holding his umbrella as if he meant to hit the sham automaton. "I'll bring an action against you for obtaining money under false pretences."

"Don't you be in a 'urry, old feller," retorted the showman. "We ain't seen the colour of your coin yet, so you ain't got no call to holler."

The fascinating maiden of forty-seven before mentioned gave a little scream of horror.

"Oh, the impudence of the wretch," she said. "He actually called dear Mr. Mildew 'old fellow!' Why, he would have the audacity to call me old next."

"No I shan't, mum," growled the showman. "There ain't no 'casion for that. Anyone can see it without bein' told."

If a look could kill, Mr. Bellers would have fallen lifeless on the instant, so scathing was the glance the enraged spinster shot at him.

Then, with an indignant sniff, she turned and stalked haughtily from the caravan, followed by Mr. Mildew and the others.

"Now," said Mr. Bellers, when he had carefully fastened the door of the caravan, to prevent intrusion. "Wot's all this?"

"Just as I ses," retorted the detective, shortly. "I wants this chap, Samuel Scarecrow, alias Jumbarello, on a charge of abscondin' from Heath-end-villa, Hampstead. It's a fifty pound job, and worth it too, considerin' the trouble I've had."

"And now, young feller," said Mr. Bellers, "wot ha' *you* got to say?"

"You're a nice treat, ain't you?" added Long Jem, indignantly, "to come and parse yourself orf as a honest cove, when you've been boltin' from willas and collarin' no end of plate, I dessay."

"I ain't!" said Sam. "I never stole a thing in my life."

"Oh—ah—yes—no doubt," said Mr. Bellers, sarcastically. "Innocent as a unborn babe, ain't you? Wot do you say, policeman?"

"Well, there ain't no charge agin' him for stealin'," replied the detective; "in fact, one of the ladies said so, and told me special not to be rough. Seems he's a kind of orfen which they adopted."

"P'r'aps he weren't well treated," suggested Mr. Bellers. "Got more clouts on the head than bread an' butter inside of him. Some o' those old ladies do come the Brownrigg game, and no error."

"No," said Sam, tearfully. "I were well treated—fust rate, I may say. The only one agin' me was Miss Mariar, and I always give her back as good as she sent."

"Then wot the blue blazes did you bolt for?" asked Long Jem.

It did not take Sam long to tell his little history, to which they all listened with interest, particularly to that portion referring to the visit to Cheetham Hall, disguised as a Japanese prince.

"Blow me, but that was a rum start," said Mr.

Bellers, with a hearty laugh. "You seem to be a fust-rate hand at getting yourself into messes, though. But there's no bad in you, and I'm sorry I said wot I did a while ago. You're glad to go back, in course?"

"No I ain't," replied Sam, tearfully. "Miss Mariar 'll worrit the life out o' me now; and Master Lionel ain't there, and likely as not they'll keep me away from him altogether."

"Well, you've got to go, young feller," said the detective, whether you likes it or no. So pack up your traps, if you've got any, and we'll be orf."

"Which way are you going?" asked Mr. Bellers, who had just exchanged a wink of peculiar and profound meaning with Long Jem.

"Well, I hardly know; this part o' the country is strange to me. I came over here in a fly, from Cragymoor. I s'pose I'd better go back that way, and take the train from there to London."

"That's miles out o' your way, and dear too: considering you'd have to change at Crushington Junction, and p'r'aps not get the up-train for four or five hours."

"Wot's the best thing to do, then."

"Go on to Pendletop, there you'll be able to catch the arternoon up-express; that'll land you at Euston in a hour and a arf."

"Thanky," said the detective; "that'll do fust-rate. How far is it to Pendletop?"

"'Bout five or six miles. We're going there soon, for the pitch is bust up, now; and if you like, you can stop in the caravan, and save the walk."

"Thanky," said the detective, again; "you're wery kind."

"Not at all," replied Mr. Bellers. "I'm rather glad, in fact, that you've got the boy, for we didn't hardly know wot to do with him. The werry fust job we puts him to, he gets us into a mess, and spiles the best pitch in the circuit."

"How could I help it?"

"I didn't say you could help it, my lad," returned Mr. Bellers; "but you've *done* it, for all that. What's your faverite tap, perliceman?"

"Well, I gen'rally take a drop of Irish, if you've got any handy," replied the detective; "but fust, if you don't mind, I'll slip the bracelets on this covey, for I've heard as how he's a slippery one."

Accordingly the unlucky Sam's hands were handcuffed behind him, and a cord attached, which the detective fastened to his belt.

The whisky was produced—a bottle of Kinahan's LL., and the detective smacked his lips over the first glass, and looked at the bottle as if he would like to try another.

Mr. Bellers was very liberal with the liquor; and the detective, now that he had accomplished his object, and thought himself secure of the fifty pounds reward, was inclined to make merry.

Both of the showmen were practised "soakers," and could drink with impunity a quantity of liquor which would have given an ordinary man a fit of delirium tremens; and between their united efforts, and those of the detective, the contents of the first bottle soon vanished.

"Let's have 'nother borrle," said the detective, whose speech was already becoming a little thick.

"Certainly," said Mr. Bellers. "I've got two left, and we can get through that little lot before we get to Pendletop."

"I sh'—hic—think so," said the detective. "Fifty pounds ain't picked up every day in our lives."

"In course not," said Mr. Bellers, with a wink. "Here's luck."

"Same t' you, old f'ler."

"Jem," said Mr. Bellers, "put the old mare to, and we'll start, else this gent won't catch the train in time."

"Wot's the odds, s' long's you're 'appy,' said the detective. "Let's 'ave another drop."

He had another drop, and then broke out into a popular melody, the burden of which was anything but complimentary to himself, inasmuch as he there exalted himself above all the wicked ones of the earth, and affirmed that neither Cain nor "Sir Roger," nor Brigham nor Odger, were fit to hold a candle to him in point of iniquity.

Long Jem seemed an equally long time in putting the old mare between the shafts, and when he did re-enter the caravan, he had a bundle with him, and was very much out of breath.

"Have you done it?" asked Mr. Bellers, in a low tone.

"Yes."

"And got the clothes?"

"Yes; there they are in the bundle."

"All right. You go to work behind the screen. I'll keep this chap up here all night. He's as drunk as a lord already."

Just then the song ceased, and the voice of the detective was heard apostrophising the empty bottle.

"It'll cost 'arf a quid for whisky," muttered Mr. Bellers; "but it's wuth the money. Hark at him a cussin' the bottle 'cos it's empty. Fire away, Jem."

Long Jem gave a nod of assent, and, retiring behind the screen with his mysterious bundle, disappeared from view.

"How are you a gettin' along, old chap?" said Mr. Bellers, slapping the detective on the back with a force that made him cough.

"Fust rate—only the whisky's all gone. Let's have 'nother borrle."

"There you are," said Mr. Bellers, producing the third bottle of the amber fluid. "And now you'll excuse me, mate, for I must go outside and drive. Make yourself at home, and give us another song. I can hear you outside."

Again the detective burst forth into melody, but this time his song was of a sentimental, not to say lachrymose character, concerning a certain ill-regulated young person of the female sex, who trifled with the affections of her sweetheart until the wretched youth was driven to bury his sorrows in a neighbouring pond, much to the gratification of the eels who lived there.

It was so affecting that he cried over it before he had got half-way through, and, like Mr. Richard Swiveller, bewailed his hard fate at being left a "dissolute orphan," finally laying his head upon the table and going to sleep.

No sooner had he arrived at this stage of intoxication than Long Jem slipped out from behind the screen, bearing in his arms a figure that bore a striking resemblance to Sam Scarecrow in general appearance, though it was dressed in modern costume.

The original Sam, who had been sitting silent and sorrowful in a corner, looked up as Long Jem softly whispered his name.

"Hallo!" he said, dolefully.

"Hush—don't make a row. It's all right. Do you see this?"

"Yes—wot is it? Another ortommyton?"

"Not azackly. It's you."

Sam looked down at himself and then up at the dummy, as if to make sure of his own identity.

"It's this way," said Long Jem. "You see when we gets to Pendletop, it'll be gettin' darkish, and this chap will be so muddled that he won't be able to see over and above well. D'ye understand?"

Sam nodded.

"Well—we'll wake him up, and tell him your clothes must be changed; you goes behind that screen, but you don't come out again—only this here figure does, and you're so unwell that you has to be carried. D'ye see?"

Sam did so, and grinned a grateful grin.

"Wery good then. Now keep dark, and mind wot yer does when the time comes."

The time was not long in coming. In less than an hour they had reached Pendletop, and Mr. Bellers, re-entering the caravan, gave the detective a vigorous shake.

The only answer to this was an equally vigorous snore.

Then Mr. Bellers adopted a harsher method, and seizing him by the hair, bumped his head against the table half-a-dozen times.

This had the desired effect, and the detective looked sleepily up.

"Now then, mate—here we are," said Mr. Bellers.

"From inf'mation I received, your washup," the detective feebly muttered, evidently under the belief that he was giving evidence in a police-court.

"From inf'mation I've received," shouted Mr. Bellers, "you'll miss you train if you don't look sharp. Hold up, will you."

"All right," answered the detective, sleepily. "Where's pris'ner?"

"There he is, where you put him," rejoined the showman. "Come young feller, and change your togs. Time's short."

"Never mind 'bout changing clothes," said the detective. "He'll do for me."

"But it won't do for me," said Mr. Bellers. "That soot o' clothes is worth ten pound if it's worth a 'apenny. Let him put his own on."

"Well, loo' sharp," the detective added, sourly. "I ain't going to waste my time about here all day. Got drop more whisky?"

"Take them things off the boy, fust," said Mr. Bellers.

"What things?"

"The handcuffs, in course; you don't 'specks he's a Davingpot brother, do you, to undress hisself with his hands tied."

With a good deal of grumbling, and a proportionate amount of fumbling, the handcuffs were removed, and Sam retired behind the screen in an apparently limp and exhausted condition.

"Poor chap," said Mr. Bellers, in a tone of sympathy. "He's done up—that's wot he is."

"Then he's a' ungrateful young ruffian," growled the detective, who seemed to have awakened in an unpleasantly vindictive humour. "Wot—arter all this trouble's been took over him? A man of my standing in the force—paid fifty pound and expenses to collar him, and he pretends he ain't satisfied. I'll satisfy him."

"You'd best be careful," said Mr. Bellers, in a warning voice.

"Why?"

"How much was the reward?"

"Fifty pound."

"Fifty pound, eh?"

"Yes—and a good price, too, for such a cove as that. I wouldn't have offered fifty pence if he'd belonged to me," growled the detective.

"Wot's the terms?"

"I told you, didn't I?"

"Yes; but you didn't say *how* he wos to be took back."

"Wot in blazes do you mean?"

"Is he to be took back dead or alive?"

"Alive, of course."

"Then you be careful. He's got a remarkable delikit constitution, and if you frightens him with them Bow-street hairs o' yourn he'll kick the bucket, and you won't get no reward."

This was enough to alarm the detective, who, in his muddled condition, had no suspicion that the showmen were attempting to impose upon him.

"All right, ole cock," he said; "I'll treat him like his own father. I mean—hic—you no wa' I mean."

"Just so," said Mr. Bellers, cheerfully. "Here he comes. How is he, Jem?"

"Werry queer," replied Long Jem, with a grave shake of the head.

"Poor chap," added Mr. Bellers. "He's overcome at the idea of parting with us. Jem's obligated to carry him in his arms like a baby."

"G' 'im little drop whissey," suggested the detective, alarmed lest his prisoner should shuffle off this mortal coil, and so deprive him of the chance of the reward.

"No, no," said Mr. Bellers, hurriedly, "he can't abear it. The smell on it would make him wuss."

"Let's have medikle man."

"There ain't no occasion for that," replied the showman. "He'll be all right as soon as he gets into the fresh hair."

"He's better now," said Long Jem, who was holding the sham Sam in his arms, after the fashion of a nurse dangling a baby."

"How's his pulse?"

"Werry low," said Jem. "It's gone down to a pound and a arf, but it's gitten' better now."

"Bring him along—gently down the steps," said Mr. Bellers. "Will you go fust, policeman?"

The policeman did go first, and rather in a hurry too, inasmuch as he went down all at once, head first, and was picked up out of the mud by the showman, in a state of confusion.

The railway station was not far off, and thither the party proceeded—Mr. Bellers and the detective arm in arm—and Long Jem going on ahead, with his inanimate burden.

"How is he now, Jem?"

"Better—better. He's breathin' more reglar."

"That's the style," said Mr. Bellers. "He'll be all right, mate, by the time you get him to Euston."

"He'd better be all right," growled the detective, thickly. "Wot right sich young varmints got to be ill t' all?"

"That's troo. Here's the bookin' orfice—wot class are you going to travel?"

"Fust, my boy," replied the detective, with a wink, "all 'xpenses paid, y' know."

"Shell out, then!" said Mr. Bellers, cheerfully.

After a good deal of fumbling and feeling in the wrong pockets, then producing a brass button and insisting on having change for it, then dropping a handful of copper and silver and accusing the porters and passengers of having picked up and appropriated a portion of it, the tickets were procured and paid for by the detective; and, supported by Mr. Bellers, he reeled on to the platform.

There were a few passengers waiting for the up-express, amongst them a stout starchy old gentleman, with an equally stout and starchy wife, and two lean prim daughters.

These regarded the advent of the tipsy detective with disgust, and elevated their noses in the air with a simultaneous motion, as if they had been marionettes animated by the same string.

"Scandalous!" said the old gentleman.

"Disgusting!" added the wife.

"Low fellows!" commented the prim daughters, in a very audible voice.

"So they are, ladies," said the detective, affably, thinking that Mr. Bellers-to-Mend and Long Jem were alluded to.

"Don't speak to us—you low man, you," squeaked the two young ladies, indignantly.

"They sha'n't, mum," said the detective, with a confidential and reassuring wink. Then, assuming as much of his stern professional voice and dignity as he could under the circumstances, he seized a mild inoffensive young gentleman by the arm, and giving him a violent "shove," uttered the characteristic cry—

"Move on, there!"

The mild young gentleman spun round like a teetotum in the last stage of exhaustion, and brought himself up with a crash against a pillar—ruining his hat, and breaking his spectacles.

"My good man," he gasped, as soon as he had extracted the bridge of his nose from the brim of his hat, "what's that for? What have I done?"

"I'll soon show you wot you've done," said the detective, with a show of ferocity quite out of keeping with the occasion. "I'll run you in."

And he lurched towards the timid young gentleman in such a hostile manner, that in defiance of the company's regulations, he jumped from the platform, and ran across the line to the other side.

Long Jem and Mr. Bellers had deposited the sham Sam against a pile of luggage, propping it as nearly upright as they could, and then returned to the darkest corner of the platform, whence they could in safety watch the progress of events.

The detective watched the flight of this mild young gentleman with a sleepy, but satisfied air, and then the thought of his prisoner flashed across his mind, and he glanced wildly around him in the sudden fear that he might have escaped.

But no—there he was, leaning against the pile of luggage, in a listless and apparently inanimate condition, with his head bent forward, and a shabby tall hat was shadowing his features.

"Oh! there you are, young f'ler."

Sam made no answer to this polite remark, but remained standing in the same listless attitude.

"None o' your sulks with me. Up you comes," the detective continued, punctuating his remark with a punch in Sam's ribs.

The figure doubled up a little more, but made no verbal reply.

Just then the home signal fell with a "clack," and a porter, seizing a bell by the handle, began agitating it in an unnecessarily violent manner.

"Now then," said the detective, viciously, "*are* you comin', young feller. Here's the train."

But Sam never moved an inch.

"I see wot it is," growled the detective. "You're sulky, and this is the way I cures such chaps as you."

And, using his right hand, he took careful aim, and let the reeling figure have "one" on the ear; but, to his horror, as he delivered the blow, he saw Sam Scarecrow's head fall off, and roll upon the platform!

CHAPTER LIII.

SHOWING HOW LIONEL AND HIS CHUMS DETERMINED TO BECOME VIRTUOUS, AND FORSWEAR PRACTICAL JOKING, AND HOW THEY KEPT THEIR WORDS—FLASHAWAY AND JABEZ BUNKER AT WORK AGAIN—RUNNING THE GAUNTLET.

THE evening after their unexpected and welcome release from captivity, our hero, together with Charlie Drummond, and of course Tommy Codlings, held a solemn and serious conclave, the object of which was to decide upon pursuing a more orderly course of life.

"I say, old fellow," Lionel began, with a very demure countenance.

"Well?"

"This sort of thing won't do, you know."

"That's true."

"We must give up sky-larking."

"I've said so before, lots of times," sighed Charlie; "but it's no use."

"We shall have to, though, that's flat," continued Lionel, decisively. "We narrowly escaped being expelled this time, and old Styngy will certainly keep his word if we get into trouble again."

"Then *I'm* done for," said Tommy, with an air of desperation; "with *my* luck I'd get into trouble anywhere—if you were to lock me up in a cell at Newgate, or leave me alone in the middle of a desert!"

"Well, we must try," continued Lionel, "and perhaps the head will take the will for the deed."

"But Crocklejack and de Bewty wont," said Charlie. "We've got a bad name; and they'll be down on us, cause or no cause."

"We don't bear the best of characters, and that's a fact," Lionel resumed. "There's Frenchy, for instance—just as we'd got to like him, and be sociable and chummy, Styngy declares that we are corrupting his morals, and forbids him our company."

"A jolly good job, too," growled Tommy, who had never got rid of his feeling of jealousy. "Whatever you could see in that chap, I don't know."

"He was a good little fellow at bottom," said Lionel. "It was only the way in which he had been brought up that spoilt him. We should have cured him of all those nonsensical notions about his rank and birth; but now, I expect, Flashaway's got hold of him again."

"A good job, too," Tommy was heard to growl again, in an indistinct voice.

The result of the conference was, that for exactly three days, Lionel, Charlie, and Tommy were the most circumspect of school boys. Their lessons were always carefully prepared (poor Tommy had indeed, a mild attack of brain fever, in consequence of his superhuman efforts), they were invariably regular in their attendance in the class-room, and never detected talking in school hours; and only in the play-ground relaxed from the severity of their self-imposed discipline.

Mr. Styngy was as much astonished as delighted. The assistant masters were equally astonished, but extremely incredulous as to the durability of the conversion.

"You see," said the head master, in the course of a conversation he was holding with his assistants, "the consequences of well-timed leniency. If I had kept these boys closely confined, the probabilities are that they would have persisted in playing these scandalous practical jokes, instead of which—as you yourselves know—they have been, for the past three days, the best behaved boys in the school."

Mr. Crocklejack lifted up his eyes, and groaned slightly.

"What is the matter with you?" demanded Mr. Styngy, sharply.

"Nothing, sir—I was only thinking."

"Thinking what, sir?"

"How long this will last, sir. You will excuse my respectfully calling to your recollection an old proverb, which says that a calm always precedes a storm."

"The old proverb does nothing of the kind," retorted Mr. Styngy, with much asperity. "The proverb says that 'after a storm comes a calm.'"

"We shall see," thought Mr. Crocklejack, but he did not hazard the quotation of any more old proverbs just then, for he saw that Mr Styngy was getting out of temper, and so the conversation terminated.

This took place on the evening of the third day. It was on the morning of the fourth that our hero and his chums became engaged in a "lark" of such magnitude and importance that its recital imperatively demands a fresh chapter all to itself.

Their self-imposed task of being good and virtuous had grown unutterably wearisome to our hero and his chums, for only one little incident had relieved the monotony of those three days.

"Heigh-ho, hum!" sighed Lionel, stretching out his arms, and indulging in a tremendous yawn. "How do you feel, Charlie?"

"Too good to live," replied that young gentleman; "I shall break out before long, I know I shall."

"Let's make up the week, as we said we would," Lionel went on; "it's only four more days, and one of those is Sunday, when we're not so likely to get into a scrape."

FOLLOW MY LEADER.

EACH STROKE OF THE KNOTTED HANDKERCHIEFS BROUGHT FORTH A HOWL OF ANGUISH FROM THE BULLIES.

No. 12.

"We *may* do it," said Charlie, doubtfully; "but then, you see, there's Tommy Codlings—he'll never be able to keep good for the rest of the week. How he's managed to do it so long is a mystery to me."

"Oh—ah—now! I daresay!" growled Tommy, looking up from the "delectus" he had bought, in an excess of zeal, to coach up for afternoon class. "You're a pretty grateful beggar, ain't you? After nearly driving myself mad with 'cramming' for three mortal days!"

"Never mind him, Tommy, you've been a brick," said our hero. "Only keep it up till the end of the week, and we'll go in for a spree."

"I say, Li," said Charlie, suddenly, "isn't that Flashaway and Hunker over in yonder corner? And look, there's a little chap between 'em!—young Twister."

"We must see into this," added Lionel. "Come on, Charlie, creep close along this side of the wall; their backs are turned, and they won't hear us till we get close."

Following out this manœuvre, the three chums arrived within a few paces of the bully and Hunker, who were fencing into the corner a youngster about twelve years of age, whose name was Twister, and who was objecting strongly to the position in which he was placed.

"Now you just let me go; I haven't done anything to you!"

"Not before you lend me that sovereign, you young beggar," said Flashaway, giving Twister a playful rap on the ear.

"I can't! I've got to pay my score at the tack-shop out of it; and I want a cricket bat, and lots of other things."

"Now, look here, young Twister, it's no use being obstinate; you are going to lend me that sovereign, you know you are."

"You're going to steal it, you mean!" retorted young Twister, raised to an unwonted pitch of courage at the prospect of the loss of the whole of his pocket-money.

"What!" ejaculated Flashway, with feigned indignation. "You call me a thief, you young vagabond, do you? Hold his arms, Jabez!"

The toady pounced upon Twister like a spider on a fly, and held his arms behind his back, while the bully felt in the youngster's pockets, and, after a little search drew out a small leather purse, which he held up triumphantly.

But at that very moment he felt it snatched from his grasp, and turning, saw our hero confronting him with a look of scorn.

"Upon my word, Mr. Flashaway," said Lionel, with mock courtesy, "you improve wonderfully! Not content with being a bully, a liar, and a sneak, you add to your accomplishments that of a highway robber."

"It's a lie!" said Flashaway, turning alternately green and white with shame and fear. "I was only having a game with him—wasn't I, young Twister?" he added, frowning furiously at that young gentleman, as an intimation of what he might expect if he did not answer as the bully required him to.

But Twister felt safe under our hero's protection, and he said, boldly—

"No; I wouldn't lend you the sovereign, and you were going to thieve it."

During this little colloquy, and while Lionel kept Flashaway and Hunker safely fenced up in the corner, Tommy Codlings had trotted off to bring a few select friends to see the fun.

They came, to the number of twelve or fourteen, all boys who disliked the bully and his follower—for Tommy had been very judicious in his selection.

"Hullo, Wilful, what's the row?"

"Just caught a couple of pickpockets, that's all," returned Lionel. "There's enough of us to form a court. Suppose we try 'em for felony!"

"School rules?"

"Of course, a fair field and no favour; but first secure the prisoners. Constables Drummond and Codlings, do your duty.

The two officials named, aided by half-a-dozen amateur policemen, soon had the prisoners' hands firmly secured behind them; then they were ranged in the corner which represented the dock.

Lionel was unanimously elected lord chief justice; Twister acted as clerk. Charlie and Codlings acted as warders, standing guard over the prisoners, and the rest formed the jury.

"Now, then, Twister," said the lord chief justice, in a magisterial voice—"I should say, clerk of this honourable court—what is the charge against the prisoners at the bar?"

"That they did skilfully, and with delicious aforethought," began Twister, with some hazy recollection of an indictment he had seen in a newspaper, "kill, slay, and otherwise feloniously steal from me the sum of one sovereign, all the blessed money I had in my pocket, and I hope, my lord, you'll give it 'em hot."

"Have you any witnesses to call?"

"Why, you saw 'em do it yourself!"

"You mustn't address the bench that way," said the lord chief justice, severely. "What do you say, gentlemen of the jury; are you satisfied with the evidence?"

"We are," cried the jury unanimously.

"And do you find the prisoners at the bar guilty or not guilty?"

"Very guilty indeed!" was the verdict roared in chorus as before.

"It only remains, then," said the lord chief justice, putting on his cap hind-side before, "to pass sentence upon you, prisoners at the bar; and the sentence is, that you be taken hence to the place of execution, there to run the gauntlet as long as we jolly well please."

"The court is dissolved," shouted Twister. "Get toko ready!"

"Toko" was a weapon much in vogue in Cheetham Hall, being used chiefly for such games as bait-the-bear, and even for personal conflict of a mild description. Its formation was very simple, consisting only of a piece of knotted rope, a foot long, or a pocket handkerchief with a chestnut tied up at one end.

"Now, you be careful, young Wilful," said Flashaway, between his set teeth, and drawing back as our hero advanced to take him by the collar. "I'm not going to put up with this, you know."

"What's the good of saying that, when you know you can't help yourself," retorted Lionel, coolly. "There, your hands are untied, and if you like you can have a turn-up with me instead."

But that would have been to jump out of the frying-pan into the fire, as the bully well knew, and, with a scowl of hate and impotent rage upon his dough-white features, he was shoved along to the head of the double file of executioners.

Jabez was there already, waited upon by Drummond, Tommy, and Twister—our plump friend indulging in the luxury of a preliminary cut or two.

"One, two, three. Start 'em!" cried Lionel.

The two culprits began to run, but such a storm of "toko" hailed down upon them from the front and rear, from left and right, that they got bewildered, turned round and round, fell over one another—did anything, in fact, but run straight forward.

"Oh, this is prime!" murmured Tommy Codlings, who had got into a good place, and had marked out for his own a particularly plump and tender portion of Flashaway's frame—"let 'em have it."

And "have it" they did, for fully a quarter of an hour, when, bruised, sore, and blinded with tears, they were allowed to limp away, with such a dose of "toko" as ought to have satisfied the most unreasonable boy.

"Do you think they'll split to Styngy?" said Charlie.

"Not they—I wish they would," replied Lionel. "We could prove that he tried to prig young Twister's coin, and, severe as he is with us, he wouldn't doubt our words, and I'm certain that he wouldn't keep a thief in the school, though Flashaway's a relation."

My readers will see by this how severe Master Wilful was with regard to dishonesty, and this is a feeling which no doubt all the subscribers to THE BOY'S STANDARD share with him.

But there is a species of dishonesty which all boys—and especially boarding-school boys—look upon as not only venial, but praiseworthy; and that species may be represented, say, by the robbery of an orchard.

To pluck an apple from a tree against the wish of the owner, is just as much an act of larceny as to appropriate the first gold watch we happen to meet in company with a waistcoat; but your true schoolboy never did, and never will, see the matter in that light. He has a lex non scripta—an unwritten law—to the effect that fruit is his property, whenever he can get at it.

Our hero, we are sorry to say, was no exception to this rule. He had been haunted for a long time by a vision of the delicious pine-apples, grapes, melons, and other luscious fruits, of which he had caught a glimpse in the schoolmaster's hot-houses.

He "coveted his neighbour's goods," and, worse than that, he resolved to st—— no, that is an ugly word—suppose I say, annex—them; and, with this view, called a council of his chums, Charlie Drummond and Codlings. The French boy—for what reason Mr. Styngy best knew—was never allowed now to mix with the rest of the scholars.

"It's awful risky, though," said Tommy, dubiously.

"Of course it's risky. You don't expect the pine-apples and things to drop into your mouth, do you?"

"Who said I did?" demanded Codlings, in an injured tone.

"Nobody; but it looks like it, when you begin to talk about 'risk;' but then we'll get the fruit and share it with you, while you stop here—same as we did with the pork, Tommy."

"Now that's an unkind thing for you to say," said Codlings, almost blubbering. "That's as good as saying I'm a coward, and afraid to go."

"There, there, Tommy, cheer up. I didn't mean to hurt your feelings."

"He hasn't got any feelings, bless you," laughed Charlie Drummond—"that is, not feelings of that sort. It's only a cane that can tickle him up."

This conversation was taking place in the class-room, which was deserted by all but the three friends; for it was Wednesday, and a half-holiday. Tommy pulled out two of the forms, and placed them at right angles to the two lines of desks which traversed the class room longitudinally, and at a distance of about eight feet from each other, so as to form an enclosed square place.

Then Tommy deliberately divested himself of his jacket and waistcoat, unnoticed by our hero and Drummond, who were again deep in conversation; until Tommy, with his shirt-sleeves rolled tightly up, approached, and delivered unto Charlie a severe "punch" in the ribs.

"Oh!" exclaimed the punched one. "Here, I say, what are you up to, young Codlings?"

"Come on," said Tommy, revolving his fists in a sprightly but very unscientific manner. "I'll teach you to say I ain't got any feelings. I'll find out where some of yours are before I've done. Come on!"

And his plump little fists revolved more swiftly, and he danced to and fro like an enraged Cupid dressed in nineteenth-century costume.

Lionel and Charlie looked at him for a moment, and then burst into a roar of laughter.

Tommy burst into a roar too, and rushed valiantly upon his tormentors. Lionel put out his fist as he passed, and the unlucky Codlings pitched head first over a form, bringing that useful article of school furniture with a crash to the ground.

At that moment the tall figure of Mr. Styngy strode into the schoolroom, and his stern voice was heard.

"What is this?" he said. "Wilful, Drummond, and Codlings at your old tricks again! I thought your promises of reformation would soon be broken."

"We were staying here quietly in the class-room, so as not to get into mischief," answered Lionel.

(Oh, Lionel, Lionel, what a fib!)

"Ah, I dare say," the schoolmaster went on. "And Codlings, there; does he think that he will the more easily keep out of mischief by taking off his jacket and waistcoat, and upsetting the forms, eh?"

"He was only taking a little exercise, sir—as he preferred to stay with us, instead of going into the playground."

"Hum," muttered Mr. Styngy; "as your conduct has been so exemplary, I will say no more. But do not attempt again to convert the schoolroom into a gymnasium."

And the schoolmaster departed, perfectly satisfied with our hero's explanation.

"There, now, Tommy, see what you've done again."

"Yes," said the luckless one, feeling the bridge of his nose and the extremities of his elbows, "I don't want to see what I've done—I can *feel* it. There's all the skin off my nose, and off my elbows too."

"Well, never mind, Tommy," said Drummond, soothingly. "It saved me the trouble, you know."

"Let him alone, Charlie. Don't tease him any more. We haven't had our consultation out yet. Come along, Tommy."

But that young gentleman had put on his outer garments, and, without replying, was stalking away with an air of insulted dignity till Lionel went after him and coaxed him back.

"You are the stupidest old donkey of a chap I ever knew," said our hero, by way of paying a compliment. "What's altered you so lately? You're as touchy and short-tempered as my aunt Maria when her parrot's got the pip."

"You began it," growled Codlings. "You told me I was funky, and then Drummond said I hadn't got any feelings."

"There, there; it's all over now. Think of the whoppers I had to tell old Styngy to get you out of the scrape. But come, how about this foray into the enemy's camp."

"We shall have to try it by the back way," said Charlie.

Lionel shook his head.

"No use, old fellow."

"Why not?"

"There's old Grumpy's field to cross, and you know what he does if any of us are caught tres-passing. There's always some labourers at work."

"We could dodge 'em easy enough."

"Well, if we did, there's the quick-set hedge enclosing the rector's rosary, to get over, for nothing but a cannon-ball could ever get through it."

"That's a tight 'un."

"And then there's always some of the family in the gardens looking after the flowers, whether they're in bloom or not; and then there's the dog."

"That'll do, Li," said Charlie. "You've shut me up. Now about your plan?"

"You remember that little window down the passage where Tommy got stuck in the wall?"

"I should think I did," laughed Drummond; "and so does Tommy, I'll lay a wager."

Tommy Codlings wriggled as the recollection of that day came back to him, but he only sniffed sorrowfully.

"Well, if you recollect, that window looked out upon this very conservatory."

"What's the use of that? The passage is blocked up."

"But it may be undone again, dear boy. It's only a deal partition—not over strong, I dare say; for these carpenters don't put themselves out when they're at work, if they can help it."

"We shall want some tools, though, and they make no end of a row."

"Only a strong screw-driver," said Lionel, "and that we can borrow from Noodles' tool-house. As for the noise, there'll be nobody to hear us; the slaveys have made the beds and all that sort of thing long ago, and nobody else ever comes up that way on a half-holiday."

"I'm on then. Who's to get the screw-driver?"

"Tommy will. No, stay; you'd better go, Charlie, for you can run faster than Codlings. Look out for Styngy."

Drummond gave a knowing wink, and trotted off, while Lionel and Tommy, putting on their most innocent and demure expression, sauntered slowly in the direction of the blocked passage.

They reached it fortunately without encountering anyone likely to put troublesome questions, and Lionel examined the species of hoarding the carpenter had constructed, with the eye of a judge of such matters.

To all appearance it was strong, and it looked neat; but, with a very slight effort, Lionel found that he could bend the centre plank so far inwards as to obtain a peep through the interstice.

"Why, a moderate draught would blow this down," said Lionel. "We shall have an easy job. Don't sneeze, Tommy."

"I'm not going to."

"That's right; for if you did you'd make the whole partition fall, and we only want one plank out. Ah! here comes Charlie. All right?"

"I believe you," replied Drummond, producing a powerful screw-driver, eighteen inches long, from his jacket collar, like a long iron pigtail.

"Didn't see anybody?"

"Only old Noodles."

"Where was he?"

"In the tool-house."

"How did you manage to get this, then?"

"Oh! he was asleep."

"Just like him; that's why he gets so fat."

"He's been doing a little carpentering, for there was a glue-pot on the fire, and there were some boots to clean; so I poured the glue into the boots, just to warn Noodles not to go to sleep over his work any more."

"Ha—ha—ha!" laughed our hero. "Good for you, Charlie. I hope the glue won't dry before Styngy puts the boots on. But hand over the screw-driver. Here goes."

Using the tool as a lever, Lionel gently prized at the centre plank from the bottom, until it was only held in its place by the topmost nails, and with a little squeezing, especially on Tommy's part, who held his breath until he was black in the face, they got through the aperture, and stood in the dusty disused corridor.

The old door, which had formerly barred their passage, had been broken open when Mr. Styngy made his exploration in search of Tommy, so that there was no obstacle between them and the window.

Our hero, by right of leadership, was the first to look through the peep-hole he had before scraped in the begrimed window-pane, and certainly it was a tempting sight that now met his view.

A brilliant sun was shining, lighting up the glass of the conservatories and hothouses, till they looked like fairy palaces in miniature; while here and there, gleaming through the glass, he could catch purple and golden glimpses of the fruity treasures within.

He enjoyed his look so much, and seemed so little inclined to give his chums a turn, that they each scraped a look-out for themselves, and immediately fell into an ecstacy of admiration.

"Oh, don't it look beautiful!" said Tommy, while the water of covetousness trickled from the corners of his mouth.

"It just does," murmured Charlie; "but how the dickens are we going to get down there?"

"We'll find a way somehow," said Lionel. "We must. Why, look at Tommy—he's dribbling like a baby, and, 'pon my word, my own mouth feels watery."

"It's a good twenty feet from the ground," added Drummond; "and I don't see any ledge below that we can crawl along."

"Let's open the window, and make sure. Hand over the screw-driver."

It was one of the old-fashioned casements, not lifting up like a modern sash, but opening outwards on a swivel.

It had been nailed down, but the nails were rusty and broke away easily. Lionel pushed it gently open, and a current of cool fresh air rushed in.

"Keep a little back, you fellows," said our hero, "in case there's any one about. Three heads are more likely to be seen than one."

With the utmost caution Lionel put out his head a little way, and surveyed the scene of their proposed predatory excursion.

On his left, so close that he could almost have touched it by stretching out his arm, was the wall of that part of Cheetham Hall where Mr. Styngy's state apartments were situate; but to Lionel's great relief, he saw no window openings in the wall from which his guilty deed might be espied.

There was the door, though; but Lionel had a plan in his head concerning that. The survey, on the whole, was satisfactory, and now it only remained to decide upon the means of getting down.

"There's a ladder propped against the garden wall opposite," said Lionel; "but it might as well be at Jericho."

"Let's get some blankets and sheets, and tear 'em up for rope."

"No; that won't do. It would take too much time, besides the chance of being caught, and then the blankets would have to be accounted for. I know what to do."

"What's that, Li?"

"You'll see. Hold the window back for me."

Charlie pushed the window back to its fullest extent. Lionel got upon the window-sill, and, taking a firm hold of the ledge with both his hands, began to let his body slide gently over.

"Here, Li, stop a minute!" said Charlie, in a tone of alarm. "You're never going to drop all that way; you'll break your neck!"

But Lionel was already suspended from the edge, and, swinging himself a little, so as to clear the wall, he dropped upon the bed of newly-turned earth beneath.

It "jarred him some," as our American cousins say, but Lionel righted himself in a moment, and stepped out upon the gravel path, treading as lightly as if he were walking on eggs for a wager.

"He's going to fetch the ladder," said Charlie, who, with Tommy, was anxiously watching our hero's moments.

"He is a plucky chap, ain't he!" responded Tommy, admiringly. "Hullo! look, Charlie, he's going to the door!"

Our hero, in fact, had crept on tiptoe to that sacred portal whence Mr. Styngy was wont to emerge when he desired to indulge in the society of those lovely goddesses, Flora and Pomona—or, in more ordinary language, when he wanted to pick his flowers and eat his fruit.

Lionel, after listening (most improperly) at the

keyhole for a few moments, opened the door gently, and, with the dexterity of a conjuror, transferred the key from the inside to the out, turned it twice, and put it in his pocket.

Then, running lightly across the path, he took the ladder, which was not a very heavy one, in spite of its length, and placed it beneath the window.

Charlie came down with the agility of a cat. Tommy, in trying to imitate him, slipped along a dozen rounds before he could stop himself, and once again his knees and elbows suffered.

"What were you doing to the door, Li?"

"Only locked it on the outside, and put the key in my pocket; so we can't be disturbed."

"That's prime!"

"Is it, though," moaned Tommy. "Oh, my poor knees!"

"Well, you have done it this time, old chap," laughed Lionel, as he glanced at Tommy's pantaloons, which were awfully damaged about the knees, to say nothing of the skin beyond. "But come on, Charlie; think of the —— Oh, my goodness! We're done for!"

There, just turning the corner of a winding path, was Mr. Styngy himself, with a select party of ladies and gentlemen. He had been in another portion of the grounds, and Lionel had not locked him *out*, but *in!*

CHAPTER LIV.

A SHORT CHAPTER, BUT ONE WHICH IS FULL OF FRUIT, FOR REFLECTION—A FALL IN CODLINGS!—GRAPES DOWN AGAIN!—AND MR. STYNGY MORE "DOWN UPON" TOMMY THAN EVER.

FORTUNATELY Mr. Styngy was coming along at a very slow pace, halting at almost every step to explain, or call attention to the beauty and rarity of some horticultural treasure.

The two gentlemen who were of the party were also amateurs, and made the air hideous with verbal cork-screws, eighteen and twenty syllables long, which they pretended were the correct names in gardener's Latin of the various plants and flowers. They would have scorned to call a rose, a tulip, or a pansy by its simple English name. Unless it bore some such title as Pollywobblesophia Snooksiensis, it couldn't be worth looking at.

Our hero made the most of this opportunity by clambering up the wall which ran along one side of the hothouse.

Charlie followed in that short space of time popularly supposed to be taken up by the "twinkling of a bed-post," and then Tommy essayed to mount.

"Come on," said Drummond. "Make haste, or you'll be caught!"

The wall was not a high one, but poor Tommy was shorter still. He jumped, and tried to catch the top, but he only bumped his forehead. Then he tried frantically to dig his little fat fingers into the mortar between the bricks, and broke his nails off to the quick, and Mr. Styngy could be heard coming nearer and nearer.

"Catch hold of him," whispered Lionel, in an agony lest the schoolmaster should detect them. "Confound it! he'll spoil us all if he stays down there."

Thus adjured, Drummond leaned over the edge, and grabbed one of Tommy's hands; Lionel did the same kind of office for the other, and, after a good deal of wriggling and subdued groaning on Codlings' part, he was hauled up.

"Now then, follow me," whispered our hero. "The sloping roof of the hothouse will hide us from the path."

It was a very uneasy wall to crawl along, for it was little more than six inches wide, and the top at one time or another had been ornamented with broken glass; the mortar had long since rotted away, and had been washed down by the rain, but here and there a spiky piece of bottle remained, rendering a sharp look out very necessary.

Lionel was soon in a place of safety, and so was Drummond, for in the position they had taken up behind the sloping roof of the hothouse they could not be seen from the path.

Poor Tommy, though, was in dreadful trouble. Tears of agony were in his eyes, and great beads of perspiration dropped from his forehead and the tip of his nose, while muffled wails of woe, resembling the distant tuning of a violin, escaped him.

And no wonder that these evidences of the torture he was enduring made themselves seen and heard. Tommy's knees were already raw; and it seemed to him that every piece of glass left in the wall got in his way on purpose, to say nothing of the gravel and the mortar.

He was still well in sight when Mr. Styngy and his friends reached the entrance to the hothouse, but the party were so busy discussing the merits of some ugly little vegetable with a particularly long name, that Tommy escaped notice.

The door of the hothouse was secured by a huge padlock, and, producing a key of corresponding size, Mr. Styngy opened the door, and threw it open with a flourish.

"There, ladies and gentlemen," he said; "I think I am showing you as perfect a specimen of a vine as you have ever met with. And as for the pines, the great magnate of this county, the Duke of Dunbrownshire, acknowledged to me that they were finer than any he had on his estate."

The fruit certainly well merited the eulogium Mr. Styngy passed upon it. The tapering bunches of grapes, with the delicate purple bloom—the rich yellow of the pines, with their dark green "bunch of daggers"-like coronet, formed a picture that the late William Hunt would have longed to group and paint.

"Perfectly lovely!" exclaimed one young lady.

"Divine!" said a second.

"Quite; too charming!" added a third.

But the comment of the fourth lady, who was stout and of a resolute appearance, was practical.

"Do me the favour to cut me a few bunches, my dear Mr. Styngy," she said, sweetly, but in a tone that plainly meant—"It's no use saying 'No,' for I mean having 'em."

"I shall be delighted," replied Mr. Styngy, wondering at the rudeness of the old lady, who was the widow of a prosperous grocer, who had been uncomfortably converted into a baronet, for the very good and sufficient reason that he happened to be Lord Mayor of London when a Royal babe—we forget which, there are so many—came into the world.

"And while you're about it," continued Lady Lollopper, "you may as well put in some o' them pine-apples. I'll take this one—and this—and this, I think."

"Is that *all*, Lady Lollopper?" said Mr. Styngy, in his most sarcastic manner.

"Since you are so pressin', Mr. Styngy," replied Lady Lollopper, taking Mr. Styngy's words in earnest—for she was as impervious as an elephant to sarcasm—"p'r'aps my girls would like a few."

Two of the young ladies, who happened to be Lady Lollopper's daughters, blushed crimson, and hastily declined.

"Now don't be foolish, gals," said Lady Lollopper, in a loud whisper. "Take all you can get—that was always your pa's motter."

The poor girls, who were really well-bred and modest, in spite of their mamma, turned redder and redder, and were almost ready to faint with shame, when a little incident occurred, which we must go outside again to account for.

Lionel and Charlie were still upon the wall, but

THERE WAS A YELL, AND THE PLUMP FORM OF TOMMY CRASHED THROUGH THE ROOF.

they had assumed a sitting position, as being more comfortable, while Mr. Styngy was in the hothouse.

Tommy had not moved a "peg;" he was still in full view of anyone coming out of the conservatory; and our hero and Drummond were passing the time in making signs to the unhappy one to come further up the wall.

"If you don't come," Lionel telegraphed, in unmistakeable pantomimic language, "I'll come and drag you."

This threat induced Tommy to try again. He got over the first yard in about five minutes, and was "well into" the second, when suddenly he uttered a yell, sprang up, and fell with a crash through the glass, clinging frantically to the sacred vine in his fall, demolishing whole bushels of grapes, and kicking over the choicest of pines, in his desperate efforts to save himself.

The young ladies screamed with affright as the grapes fell in showers upon them. One of the scientific gentlemen had his left whisker neatly shaved off by a piece of the broken glass, and, when he turned round to see what had done it, Tommy gave him a black eye with his boot; so by the time that unlucky youth had gyrated to the ground, and found a resting-place on two of the finest pine-apples, things looked pretty comfortable.

We ought in this place to describe Mr. Styngy's anger, fury, wrath—what shall we call it?—but we find myself really unequal to the task. The pen of Homer, or Shakespeare, or Dante alone could do the scene justice. We must content ourselves with remarking that but for the united efforts of the two scientific gentlemen, we firmly believe that Mr. Styngy would have had Tommy's blood with a pair of garden shears.

The ladies had run ont into the garden, screaming, of course, as 'tis their nature to—but not fainting, because there was nobody to hold them up; for no well-bred young lady would think of fainting unless there happened to be an eligible young gentleman within fair catching distance.

One of the most disturbed was Lady Lollopper. The very bunches of grapes she had selected, the very pine-apples she had set her heart upon, this young ruffian had demolished; and it was in the hope of seeing him suffer exemplary chastisement, that that estimable lady kept peeping round the corner of the doorway.

When the two gentlemen considered that it was safe to release their hold of Mr. Styngy, they did so, exhorting him to be calm, and send for a policeman.

"I can't do that," replied Mr. Styngy, gloomily.

"Why?"

"Because he's a pupil of mine."

"Then you have a right to take the law into your own hands," said one of the scientific gentlemen, cheerfully. "I'm sure if you feel disposed to chastise him now, I shall be happy to assist as far as holding him goes."

"And I shall be delighted," said the other gentleman, who had the black eye.

Poor Tommy had been so shaken by his fall, that he still sat where he had alighted, flattening out the pine-apples and staring before him in a vague and wondering manner.

The scientific gentleman with the black eye hauled Tommy out of that reverie by his right ear, and then gave him a slap on the side of the head that sent him spinning gracefully towards the other scientific gentleman, who gave Tommy another that rolled him into Mr. Styngy's arms, where he lay affectionately and warmly embraced for full a quarter of an hour.

At the end of that time Tommy was released—probably on account of the schoolmaster having been so affectionate to him before company, while Mr. Styngy, looking at a pile of splinters by his side, said—

"Really, now, the stem of the grape vine is a capital substitute for the ordinary cane!"

"But expensive," said the scientific gentleman with the black eye.

"We are keeping the ladies waiting," suggested the other.

"True," said Mr. Styngy, with a doleful glance at the wreck around him; and, taking the sore and sorry Tommy by the ear, he apologised for the delay, and moved towards the door.

But here a fresh complication of affairs conspired to trouble him, for, as our readers know, the door was locked, and the key—a patent Chubb's—safe in our hero's pocket.

CHAPTER LV.

LOCKED OUT—MR. STYNGY SENDS FOR THE BLACKSMITH—THE STORM—STRUCK BY LIGHTNING—THE FIRE.

MR. STYNGY pulled at the handle of the door, pushed it vigorously, turned it to the right, then to the left, and finally came to the conclusion that it was locked.

Then arose the question, who had locked it? Mr. Styngy felt perfectly certain that he hadn't, and he remembered quite well leaving the key in the lock inside.

Of course his suspicions turned upon Tommy at once, and regarding that unhappy young gentleman with a look worthy of a Lord Chief Justice about to pass sentence, he said—

"By which way did you gain access to this place, Codlings?"

Tommy, true to his resolve not to say a word likely to betray his companions, turned round, and, including a whole parallel of latitude in a wave of his hand, replied—

"Over there, sir."

"Did you not come through this door?"

"No, sir," said Tommy, very emphatically.

"I regret to say that I cannot believe you, Codlings. I must search you to ascertain if you have the missing key in your possession."

Tommy's pockets were accordingly turned out, and the treasures of odd marbles, bits of string, buttons, "nickers," a top without a peg, and some pebbles, which our young friend cherished in the belief that they would some day turn out to be precious stones of marvellous value, were ruthlessly scattered on the ground by Mr. Styngy; but of course he didn't find the key.

"This is extremely awkward," said Mr. Styngy. "I really do not know how we are to open the door."

"Let us go round the other way," said one of the scientific gentlemen, offering a brilliant suggestion.

"But there happens to be *no* other way," replied Mr. Styngy.

"Then," said the other scientific gentleman (the one with the black-eye), "let us call through the key-hole till somebody comes."

"An excellent idea. This boy can do that," said Mr. Styngy. "Codlings, shout for Noodles through the key-hole, till he answers you.'

Tommy set to work, and as it somewhat relieved the smart of his injuries to use his voice freely, he yelled with such good will, that in about five minutes the heavy step of Noodles sounded in the passage.

"Here he is, sir," reported Tommy.

"Ah!" said Mr. Styngy, much relieved. "Have the goodness to unlock the door, Noodles."

"Where be t' key, sur?" demanded the odd man.

"In the lock, isn't it?"

"Noa, there baint nary key here, sur."

"It must have dropped out. Look on the floor."

A pause, and a sound of groping and scraping, and then the voice of Noodles again—

"Noa, 'taint on t'floor."

"Tut, tut, tut. Dear me, dear me," said Mr. Styngy. "I don't know what to do. That is one of Chubb's best locks, and can't be picked."

"Send for the blacksmith, to break it open," suggested one gentleman.

"Look at the expense of a new lock, besides the damage there would be done to the door."

"But, my dear Mr. Styngy, you can't keep these ladies here all night, and it's coming on to rain."

Mr. Styngy glanced up, and a heavy drop immediately fell in his eye. There was a low growl, as of distant thunder, and the clouds were getting black and heavy overhead.

"Go for the blacksmith, Noodles," said the schoolmaster, reluctantly.

Meanwhile, our hero and Drummond had not been slow to note the coming change in the weather. The clouds, drifting together from all quarters of the sky at once—angry looking clouds, with rugged edges, that were constantly changing their shapes, as is the way with clouds heavily charged with electricity—told them what they might expect within a very short time.

"I say, Charlie, " whispered our hero, "we must mizzle."

"But how? Where? We can't drop back into the garden, till old Styngy and his friends are gone, and it'll be half an hour before Noodles gets back with the blacksmith."

"We must drop over on this side, that's all."

"How about the dog? You know what a beast he is, Li."

"We must chance that. I don't see him about anywhere, and I haven't heard him bark. Come on, Charlie; drop over."

And Lionel, setting the example, swung himself neatly off the wall, into the midst of a newly-planted flower bed, just as the first vivid flash of lightning shot athwart the sky, followed by screams from all the ladies in Mr. Styngy's company, and a rattling peal of thunder.

"Come on," said Lionel, pulling up the collar of his jacket, and preparing for a run, "that clap will bring down the rain in a minute."

They started, but they had not gone a couple of yards, when there was a hoarse growl some distance ahead, and looking, they saw a huge brown mastiff coming up the path, his white fangs showing, and his back bristling like a boar's.

"Oh lor! here's a go," faltered Charlie, as he turned and bolted towards the rectory. "There's the man-eater, Li!"

Lionel needed no telling. In half a dozen bounds he had reached the French windows of the rectory, which were luckily unfastened, pushed them open, dragged Charlie in, and closed them again, just as the black muzzle of the fierce brute touched the glass.

It was a fortunate escape for the boys. The mastiff had earned his nickname of man-eater by having in one night dragged down and throttled two burglars, who had made an attempt to break into the rectory.

The storm seemed to have enraged it, for as the second flash of lightning and peal of thunder came out of the sky, the huge brute lifted up its massive head, and barked hoarsely—defiantly, as it seemed to the boys.

"We'd better hide up somewhere," suggested Charlie. "That blessed dog's barking will bring some of the slaveys here."

"Not a bit of it—girls are too funky of the lightning," replied Lionel. "I say, look at the table! here's a jolly lunch laid out for somebody."

It was indeed a "jolly" lunch, as Lionel called it. Cold ham and chicken, game pie, Perigord pie, pâtés de foies gras, delicate preserves and jellies, and, in short, a hundred and one delicacies to set a schoolboy longing, and to make his mouth water.

"I say, don't it look nice?" said Lionel, after an interval of silent admiration. "If the old boy was here, he'd be sure to ask us to lunch. Charlie, suppose we help ourselves?"

"Wha—at? In—this storm?" said Drummond, who was beginning to turn rather white, and showed a desire to get into the darkest corner of the room.

"Why not. You're not afraid of a thunderstorm, surely, Charlie?"

"I never was before—much. But this is such a dreadful one. Oh, there was a flash!"

A steel-blue flame filled the room at that instant, so bright and vivid, that the boys were fairly blinded for a moment or two. When Lionel was able to look about him again, Charlie had vanished, with the exception of the soles of his boots, which might have been seen sticking out from underneath a sofa.

The only effect the storm produced upon Lionel seemed to be to sharpen his appetite. He coolly drew a chair to the table, and helped himself to a taste of everything he fancied, altogether heedless of the storm, which seemed to increase in violence.

Suddenly Lionel became aware of a peculiar sensation upon his face, as if he were being tickled with cobwebs, while a peculiar smell, like that which may be observed near an electrical machine at work, took the place of the savoury odour of the lunch.

Our hero had scarcely time to notice these peculiar phenomena, when a violent shock dashed him from his chair. He saw a thin, serpentine line of dazzling fire run along the table, scattering everything upon it. Then it seemed to dart at the French window, shatter it into splinters, and, with a crash, was gone.

Lionel knew that the house had been struck by the lightning, and he scrambled hastily to his feet, a little confused, and trembling too. There was a curious numbed feeling in his left arm, and, on easing it with his right, he saw that his jacket sleeve and shirt were ripped up from the elbow to the wrist, and just at his feet there lay the plated dessert knife he had had in his hand—the blade completely melted away by the awful power of the mysterious electric fluid.

Our hero shuddered as he thought of his narrow escape, and he was just looking around for Charlie, when he distinctly heard some voice crying out, in alarm, "Fire!"

It was in the house, and not far off, as Lionel made out. He stayed a moment to haul Charlie out from under the sofa, extremely dusty and fluffy, but looking pale even through that complexion powder.

"Is it all over?"

"Yes—come on; the lightning's set the house on fire, I think! Make haste—we may be of use."

The cries were still heard, but more faintly, as if the persons uttering them were exhausted. Following the direction, Lionel sped on like a hare, until in a passage he discovered two large cans of water, apparently left there by the housemaids in their fright at the outbreak of the storm.

Lionel seized one, Charlie the other, and, turning the corner, they came upon the room from whence the cries—very faint now—were issuing.

The door was dashed open, but both Lionel and Charlie recoiled.

"We can't go in there," gasped Charlie.

"We must. Get on your hands and knees. Crawl in—it's easy that way. Shove the can along before you. That's it."

The room was so full of the smoke from burning sheets, blankets, and feathers—for it was a bed that the lightning had fired—that it was impossible to see a foot ahead.

Lionel knew the danger; the door was open now, and a draught might at any moment fan the smouldering fire into a blaze. At last he caught sight of the red sparks dropping through the smoke upon the floor, and cried out—

"This way with the water, Charlie."

Then holding his own breath, he stood upright, seized his can, and, staggering forwards, poured a deluge of water on the bed."

Charlie was not slow to follow suit, and the effect was instantly to check the on-rolling volumes of smoke. Fortunately they had poured the water on that very portion of the bed which was smouldering, and at once extinguished it.

"Now for the gals," said Lionel. "I wonder where they are; they've left off squeaking. Go to the door and call for help, Charlie, while I feel about for 'em."

The smoke had now cleared off sufficiently to allow Lionel to see in which direction lay the window.

He crawled as rapidly as he could towards it, with the intention of opening it, when his progress was checked by something—the body of a woman lying on the floor.

Lionel hurriedly crawled over it, but, to his horror, there were two more immediately beyond.

He hesitated no longer, but, rising to his feet, staggered blindly through the smoke till he reached the window, which he had just strength enough to throw wide open.

A torrent of rain and cold air rushed in, and whirled the smoke away as the rising sun dispels a mist.

The storm was still raging, though the lightning was less frequent and vivid. The rain was dashed in at the window in sheets of water, but Lionel was glad of it, for it cleared and purified the air.

As well as his strength would let him, Lionel raised the bodies, which he recognised now as the daughters of the rector, with two other ladies whom he did not know, into a setting posture, propping them up with anything that came to hand, so that the fresh air and the rain could play upon them.

"I hope they're not dead," thought Lionel, beginning to feel very uncomfortable. "Poor things! don't they look pale! Hallo! that one moved a bit, I think. Why don't somebody come? Charlie isn't hallooing half loud enough."

It seemed that he had, though, for at that moment some half dozen pale and anxious gentlemen, headed by the rector himself and a doctor, rushed tumultuously into the room.

CHAPTER LVI.

IN WHICH OUR HERO AND CHARLIE DRUMMOND DISCOVER SOME OF THE SPECIAL ADVANTAGES ATTENDING HERO-WORSHIP — THE RECTOR'S GRATITUDE—THE PRESENTS—ANOTHER FIRE, BUT OF A VERY DIFFERENT NATURE.

IF we were to attempt to give in detail a tithe of the compliments, congratulations, and laudatory epithets that were showered down upon our hero and his chum, we should exhaust the dictionary, and certainly our readers' patience.

Lionel, as is the custom with brave boys—or men—thought very little of what he had done, and would gladly have let the matter drop altogether, quite content that his conscience told him he had done his duty.

But that was not to be. He found himself elevated all at once into the rank of the heroes of the first water, with Charlie a star of little less magnitude by his side.

Mr. Styngy almost shook their hands off, and gave them a week's holiday to "recover from their fatigue," as he said—a boon which they appreciated very much.

The head master, too, in the first warmth of his admiration, had promised them any favour they chose to ask. Need we say that a free pardon for Tommy was requested, and granted.

The story got wind in the villages about, of course, and as Lionel and Charlie were pretty well known, they were followed and cheered by crowds of admiring yokels—old and young—until, as our hero said, "It was getting a little too hot to be pleasant."

But there was one result of this adventure which rather touched Lionel and Charlie—light-hearted, thoughtless boys though they were—and fixed the memory of that time deeply in their minds.

It was a few days—some four or five—after the storm, when a message came from the rector, asking that Masters Wilful and Drummond might be allowed to step round.

Of course the permission was instantly given, and our hero and his chum, faultlessly attired (Lionel, by the way, was obliged to carry his left arm in a sling, for the electric flash had injured the nerves), presented themselves at the rectory gate.

There the butler, who was a very stiff and formal gentleman, utterly ignoring the existence of boys in general, except when he condescended to kick one, actually received our heroes with a respectful bow, and conducted them to the breakfast room as if they had been young dukes.

The rector had it in his mind to improve the occasion, and had prepared a neat little speech containing allusions to various historical acts of bravery, and concluding with an exordium concerning the beauty of modesty when united with courage—and so on.

But, when the two boys entered, all the speech-making went out of the poor old gentleman's head, and he could only say, brokenly, as he passed their hands into his—

"My dear boys—God bless you!—you have spared me the unutterable sorrow of a childless old age."

Then Mrs. Rector—fairly crying, she was—hugged them each in turns, and then both together in a loving matronly manner that was very pleasant; and, finally, the young ladies they had rescued—who looked very pretty in their pallor—kissed them (which they seemed to like), and things generally got very comfortable.

Of course they had a glorious tuck-out—a better one even than that to which Lionel had helped himself on the day of the storm, thought of course he said nothing about that.

When they left, they received an invitation to come again and have a similar feast whenever the rules of the school permitted. The kisses were gone through again. (I am sadly afraid that young rascal, Lionel, enjoyed that part more than was correct and decorous.) The young ladies gave each of them a keepsake. The rector, remembering his own school-days, slipped a five pound note into each of their hands.

But that was not all. A week after, there arrived at the school two neat little packages about four inches square, one for Lionel and one for Charlie.

On being opened, they proved to be morocco cases, each containing a small, beautifully finished gold medal, bearing on one side an emblematical figure of Courage, and on the other an appropriate inscription.

"I say, this is handsome on the old boy's part, ain't it?" said Lionel, as he tried the effect of the medal in the button-hole of his jacket.

"First rate," replied Charlie. "But I say, Li, I don't half like taking this, for it was all your doing, you know. Those poor girls would have been smothered and burnt a dozen times over, before I should have heard 'em under that sofa."

"Nonsense! you worked away like a brick when you did come out."

"Ah, but that's not all," said Charlie, in a dissatisfied tone. "I feel like an impostor, Li."

"Why, you're getting as big a donkey as Tommy Codlings, Charlie. Didn't you bring up a can of water and pitch it on the bed, and didn't you yell out at the top of the stairs like half a dozen town criers?"

"Laugh away, old fellow," said Charlie. "But, never mind, if all these good things are pitched at me, I'm not going to throw 'em back."

"Right you are," replied our hero. "I'm very glad my mother's abroad, though, and that old Styngy hasn't got her address, or he'd write such a letter as would bring her here post-haste if she were five hundred miles away, and the dear old mater would make such a fuss."

"My governor would work it all by the rule-of-three," laughed Charlie. "He'd say—'How much did you get by it—five-pound note, gold medal worth so much, and so many feeds at so much apiece. What did you risk?' Then I'd say—'Nothing; because I stayed outside and let my chum in for all the danger.' Then he'd say—'You're a sensible chap, and know how to make a good bargain.'"

"You've got a practical kind of governor, Charlie."

"Rather. You don't get much in the way of a joke out of him."

"I say, Charlie, suppose we go into class and astonish the fellows with these medals. Besides, I'm getting rather tired of this holiday."

"I am with thee," replied Charlie, dramatically. "Onward."

And into the class-room they went side by side, amidst a murmur of admiration from the boys, hardly one of whom, we are glad to chronicle, were mean enough to envy them the honour they had so well deserved.

As for the medals, our hero and his chum little dreamed of the good service these two pieces of gold would do them in the years to come, when the hand that gave them had long since mouldered in the dust.

CHAPTER LVII.

SHOWING HOW THE DETECTIVE FAILED IN HIS LITTLE PLOT TO CAPTURE SAM—THE TABLES TURNED—AN IMPORTANT DISCUSSION AS TO SAM'S FUTURE IS DECIDED BY A MASTER-THOUGHT OF GENIUS OF THE LANDLORD—AND SAM APPEARS IN AN ENTIRELY NEW CHARACTER.

WE ought here to apologise most humbly and sincerely to Master Samuel Scarecrow for having left him so long in such a painful position, as our readers will remember that at the conclusion of Chapter LII. no satisfactory explanation of the consequences of that painful operation was given.

Truth to tell, it did not hurt Sam at all, for, as our readers have no doubt surmised, the tipsy detective had only decapitated the "dummy" which Long Jem had so cleverly made up and passed off upon him.

But the detective, fully believing that he knocked the head off a real boy, stood for a moment aghast and trembling.

"Oh, the wretch!" screamed the horrified old lady.

"He's killed the boy!" cried the old gentleman. "Po-lice!"

Some of the railway officials, who were near enough to see that the figure was only a dummy, looked upon the whole affair as a good joke, and helped to carry it on.

"You've done it now, old chap," said one, gravely.

"Fourteen years' penal servitood, at least," added a second.

"The jury'll bring it in 'wilful murder,'" said a third. "I heard him myself say he'd do for the boy."

"I never sa' so—hic," faltered the detective, not a little sobered by the occurrence, but still exceedingly drunk. "I on'y mean give 'im a li'le 'olesome c'rrection."

"Precious 'olesome, to begin by knocking the poor kid's 'ed orf," said a porter. "Now, Bill, is that stretcher ready, and is the perlice come yet?"

"Here in a minnit," replied the other; "but here's the up express a comin' in. Shove 'em into the lamp-room till we've got her orf."

"The corpse, too?"

"Yes, both together; bless you, t'other chap won't object, and I don't s'pose the body say'll anything."

"And here is my card, my good man," added the old gentleman, as he produced a slip of pasteboard. "I will gladly be a witness at the trial of that cold-blooded villain."

"Certingly, sir," replied the porter with a grin, as, aided by a mate, he bundled the detective unceremoniously into the lamp-room, and laying the figure of the dummy on the floor, with its head under its arm like St. Denis, covered it with a spare tarpaulin, and locked in the murderer and his supposed victim.

"Le' me out," yelled the terrified detective, as he scrambled amongst the old lamps, empty oil cans, and other odds and ends that were lying profusely about. "I ain't goin' to be shut in here with dash corpsh."

But all his remonstrances were drowned by the groaning and shrieking of the in-coming train, and the bustle of the passengers and the porters on the platform.

Now, it so happened that the guard of this particular train brought news of a break-down on the down line, at a small station some eight miles away. Immediate help was needed, as some heavy mineral trucks had been upset, and the station master decided to send all the available porters, besides the plate-layers, to act as a "break-down gang."

They were sent off on a light engine, a few minutes after the up express had gone, flying on her road to Euston; and so it happened that there was no one left at the station who was aware of the imprisonment of the unlucky detective. No more trains stopped at that platform until early the next morning, and our readers may imagine the extremely happy and comfortable position of Sam Scarecrow's murderer.

Meanwhile, the genuine Sam had been rejoined in the caravan by Mr. Bellers-to-Mend and Long Jem. The old mare had been urged to her smartest pace—which was neither a trot nor a walk, but a compound of the side-wise, and up and down movement, very suggestive of the motion of a steamer crossing the channel in a chopping sea.

The jolting thus produced precluded all attempt at conversation, and it was not until Mr. Bellers drew rein in front of a quiet little hostelry, situated just at the top of a gentle slope, leading to a small, but pretty town, that conversation was able to find a vent.

"Ha, ha, ha, ha!" roared Mr. Bellers, giving way to a long-continued expression of laughter, as he dropped the reins on the old mare's back and stepped from his perch into the caravan; "of all the games as ever I—— Ha, ha, ha, ha! Oh, dear me!"

And the jovial showman, quite overcome by the recollection of the scene on the platform of the railway station, dropped into a corner, and laughed until strong apoplectic symptoms developed themselves.

Long Jem, being of a more grave and taciturn disposition, was content to express his appreciation of the joke by an occasional broad grin, or well-developed chuckle; while Sam, who had seen nothing of the fun, and had not yet heard the history, stood in wonder at his employer's uproarious mirth.

HERE, THERE, AND EVERYWHERE, EXCEPT BEHIND HIS BACK, MR. STYNGY SOUGHT FOR TRACKS OF THE FIRE.

No. 13.

"Is he often took like that?" asked Sam, of Long Jem.

"Not quite so bad, in a gin'ral way."

"How long is it a goin' to last?"

"Wot do you want to know that for?"

"Wot for!" replied Sam, in an injured tone; "becos I'm hungry—that's why. Larfin's all very well in its way, but I'm dashed if I can larf on a empty stummick."

"Wot a chap you are for your innards!" growled Long Jem. "I've knowed some fairish peckers in my time, but, for size and weight, you lick 'em all!"

By the time this little piece of dialogue was terminated Mr. Bellers had sufficiently recovered to be able to get up, though he was still very weak through excess of laughter; and even as he descended the steps of the caravan with Long Jem and Sam, he let off little cachinnatory explosions, as often as the recollection of the detective came back to him.

Here, as indeed at all the places where the showman put up, Mr. Bellers and Long Jem were recognised, and welcomed as old friends. A substantial supper—to Sam's special gratification—was got ready; and afterwards, to a select little party in the landlord's private parlour, the story of the detective and the dummy was told.

It was received with laughter hardly less hearty than Mr. Bellers himself had exhibited; and when he was sufficiently recovered to speak, the landlord asked—

"And wot become o' the chap arter all, Mr. Bellers?"

"Blowed if I know," returned the showman; "we left him a reelin' backards, and starin' at the 'ed on the platform, as if he really thought he had killed the boy; while some of the porters, goin' in for the joke like, threatened to send for the perlice."

"And did they?"

"In course not. They must ha' found out in a minnit or two as it were only a dummy. But there, to see the look on that chap's face when the 'ed came orf——"

And again Mr. Bellers burst forth into a prolonged roar, which seemed to indicate that, in spite of his nick-name, his "bellows" were in very good order indeed.

"And wot are you goin' to do with the boy?" was the landlord's next question. "You ses there's a reward offered, and this chap I'll be arter him again—sharp and savage—the minnit he gets sober."

"Well that's been puzzlin' me a bit, I must confess," said Mr. Bellers. "You see the boy and us have got accustomed like, and I didn't mean to part with him, unless he's willin' to go."

"Which I ain't," said Sam, promptly. "Leastways, not back to Amstid."

"You'll have to tog him up afresh," suggested the landlord; "another soot o' clothes, and a touch o' paint, and his own father wouldn't know him."

"P'r'aps not—but these blessed detectives would," said Mr. Bellers. "I'd got him made up beautiful as a ortommyton, when that werry detective, as had never clapped heyes on him afore, spotted him d'reckly."

Sam was becoming interested in the conversation, for he had finished his supper, and had time to listen.

All sorts of disguises were proposed and rejected, nearly every character in history and out of it being suggested, when, suddenly, the landlord gave his thigh a tremendous slap.

"I've got it, Bellers!"

"Got wot?"

"The idea you want."

"Out with it, Peter."

"Why, you remember poor old Jones, who bought Wilkins' menagery, and had such bad luck."

"Ah! I remember. All the beasts died off one by one with the rot or consumption, or somethin'. Some said they were pisoned, but I don't believe that."

"Well, he stopped here the night his werry last animal died—it was the big blue-nosed baboon, the finest specimen as had ever been seen in England. He skinned it himself, and buried the body in my garden. Three days arter he went away, sayin' he'd come back for the hide, which he'd dressed most careful; but, poor chap, no one ever see him alive agin, and a week arter his body were found in the canal."

"But wot air you adrivin' at?" said Mr. Bellers, still puzzled.

"Why can't you see?" answered the landlord. "Stop a bit, I'll get the skin."

And he returned in a few minutes with what appeared to be a door mat of irregular construction.

"Well?" said Mr. Bellers, staring at the door mat, and scratching his head in a state of woful perplexity.

"Don't you see, Bellers, that it's the werry thing for your boy. It'll just fit him. I knowed the size o' that baboon to a hinch. Your chap may be a trifle too long, but you can easily piece it out with some oakum at the ankles and wrists."

"Well, I'm dashed!" gasped Mr. Bellers. "That *is* a idea. Turn me inside out if ever I should ha' thought o' makin' a monkey o' the lad. It's splendid!"

"It's open to argyment, though," said Long Jem, thoughtfully.

"Blow your argyments!" retorted Mr. Bellers, contemptuously. "What do you say, Sam? Ah! that boy's asleep. Never mind, *he* won't have no injections."

"He've got a bootiful mug for the part," said the landlord, contemplating Sam as he lay back in his chair asleep, with his mouth wide open. "He's as like that there baboon as a twin brother. You won't want no mask for him."

"I don't know whether that's a compliment to Sam or the monkey," laughed the showman; "but it's just as well the lad ain't awake to hear it."

But Sam was too fast asleep, and over another generous jorum of grog and a pipe, the plan for transforming our eccentric friend into a baboon was completed.

How Sam took to his new station in life, and how he astonished the public by his wonderful performance as the Blue-nosed Baboon of Barbary, we have to tell in a future chapter.

CHAPTER LVIII.

LIONEL AND HIS CHUM DESCEND FROM THEIR HEROIC PEDESTALS AND BECOME ORDINARY BOYS AGAIN—MR. STYNGY'S LITTLE SPEECH UPON THE NECESSITY OF KEEPING CALM AND COOL IN CASE OF FIRE, AND HOW OUR HERO TESTED THE TRUTH OF THE SCHOOLMASTER'S WORDS—FIRE! BUT WHERE?—THE DISCOVERY, AND AN UNCOMFORTABLE CLIMAX.

"WELCOME, young gentlemen," said Mr. Styngy, affably, as Lionel and Charlie passed up the centre of the school. "Welcome back to the pleasant paths of Parnassus."

"The leave you so kindly gave us, sir," replied Lionel, "is not up yet; but, in fact, we had got tired of a solitary holiday; and so, with your permission, we will take our places in class."

They were now just under Mr. Styngy's eye, and that gentleman caught the glitter of the medals.

"Aha!" he said, putting up his double eye-glasses. "What is that you have on your jackets?"

"A—a—momento—a present, which the rector kindly sent us this morning, sir," replied Lionel.

Mr. Styngy examined the medals with great attention and satisfaction, and then as he returned them to our hero, he said—

"You have well earned those tokens of my reverend friend's gratitude, Wilful and Drummond. In after life may the sight of them inspire you with the resolve always to do your duty as calmy and courageously as you did on this occasion. Coolness is especially necessary in case of fire—always remember that. I have been in a house on fire myself, and I know the importance of keeping perfectly calm and cool. You can go to your seats, young gentlemen."

Lionel nearly exploded with laughter when Mr. Styngy made that illusion to his having been in a house on fire; for he remembered well that scene at the hotel, where he had puffed the smoke through the key-hole.

"He's a nice chap to talk about being cool at a fire," said our hero, when he had recounted that little incident to Charlie. "You should just have seen him and old Grubbe scampering about the bed-room, and holloaing, "Fire!" out of the window.

"No—did he though?"

"Rather; till he alarmed the whole hotel, and brought half a dozen fire-engines round the place. I should just like to try him again."

"How?"

"Why, by just setting something on fire, to make a bit of a smoke. You see what a stew he'll be in when he smells it."

"Let's burn some brown paper in our desks."

"No; he'd find that out directly."

"Somebody else's desk, then."

"Worse. Styngy would discover it just as soon, and we should get an innocent chap into a row."

"Well, you'll have to get up a dodge yourself, Li. I can't think of anything."

"I tell you what, Charlie; we'll set him on fire himself."

"What!" ejaculated Charlie, aghast.

He spoke so loudly in his astonishment, that Mr. Styngy was obliged to take notice, in spite of his desire to indulge the "heroes."

"Drummond," he said, "your holiday has apparently caused you to forget the necessity of discipline in the school-room. I must request silence."

"How different from a week ago," whispered Drummond, with a grin. "Then, if I had roared out in that style, I should have got half a dozen 'handers' or a heavy imposition."

"Very likely," returned Lionel, with affected dignity; "but it would never do to cane a hero, Charlie. Fancy Julius Cæsar curling up under a birching, or the Duke of Wellington holding out his hand for a dozen."

"Come, now, Li, draw it mild. We are not quite up to any of those big swells."

"Who said we were? You might know I was only chaffing. But about this little spree?"

"Well, I suppose you were chaffing me about that," said Charlie Drummond.

"Not a bit of it. Have you got any touch paper?"

"Not a scrap."

"Nor any powder?"

"No. Stop a minute, though; I've got two or three squibs that got spoilt last November by getting wet."

"They'll do prime; get 'em for me when class breaks up."

"What are you going to do with 'em, Li?"

"You'll see, presently. Hullo! here's our class called for Virgil. I hope it's an old bit, that I know."

Thanks to the many "impositions" our heroes had undergone, Virgil was tolerably familiar to them, and they passed muster creditably.

"I am glad to find, Wilful," said Mr. Styngy, as he dismissed the class, "that your holiday has not dulled your scholarship. You may take for your motto, 'Tam, Marti quam Mercuris.'"

Lionel bowed, and blushed a little, too, at this handsome compliment. Charlie, who did not quite understand it, promised himself that he would look it out in his lexicon and grammar, after class.

But there were the damaged squibs to be got from amidst a very nest of odds and ends, the accumulation of nearly eighteen months—for this particular box Charlie kept at school, carefully locked, of course.

The squibs were found, or, rather, the empty, crushed cases, for the powder had mixed itself up with the flue and dust at the bottom of the box; Lionel contrived to gather up enough for his but purpose.

A strip of brown paper half a yard in length, and a tin worm-box, perforated in the lid, was all that Lionel required to construct his infernal machine, and by the time the bell rang for dinner it was ready.

* * * *

Dinner was over, the young gentlemen of Cheetham Hall had re-assembled in the class-room. Mr. Styngy, the autocrat, had taken his seat at his high desk, and his satellites—De Bewty, Cracklejack, and the professor—were bullying the less important of their pupils, and dealing out boxes on the ears and cuts with the cane with the very greatest partiality.

Mr. Styngy generally "took it easy" in the afternoon, contenting himself with sitting at his high desk, and taking a short nap or two if he felt sleepy, or with caning the bigger boys who were beyond the under masters' control, if he felt wakeful, and, consequently, ill-tempered.

On this occasion he was sleepy, and his reverend head gradually sank below the level of the high rail in front of his desk, and, by-and-by, a slight choking sound proclaimed that he was taking the usual forty winks.

Suddenly, however, he started up, and, seated on his high stool, looked about him in a scared fashion, and sniffed suspiciously.

Lionel nudged Charlie in the ribs, and pointed to the head master.

"The fun's beginning," he whispered. "Old Styngy's got the first whiff."

"Has he? Oh, oh! look at his old nose, routing about the desk like a porker among the turnips," returned Charlie.

Mr. Styngy was indeed sniffing about, in the most suspicious manner. He opened his desk, and smelt that; then he got off his stool, and peered under the desk, and beneath the stool, sniffing all the while. Finally, with a look of vague alarm upon his reverend features, he called Mr. Crocklejack.

"Sir?" said that gentleman, hurrying up at the call of his employer.

"Do you — sniff — smell fire anywhere, Mr. Crocklejack?"

Mr. Crocklejack began sniffing on the instant, as if he were taking a dose of the most delicious snuff.

"Well—yes—I—I certainly do smell something, sir."

"I didn't ask you whether you smelt something, Mr. Crocklejack," said the head master, sharply; "I asked you if you smelt fire."

"Yes I do, sir," replied the usher, humbly.

"Where is it, then?"

"It—it seems to be somewhere about here, sir."

"Can you see any smoke?"

"No, sir," replied Mr. Crocklejack, after looking up at the ceiling, and all round the schoolroom.

"We must have this seen to," said Mr. Styngy. "It is evident, by the absence of smoke, that the fire has gained no ground as yet. Send for Noodles."

That stolid gentleman arrived in due course, and the question was put to him.

"Noa, sir, I ain't seen ne'er a fire, 'cept the one in the kitching. There ain't no other, as I knows on."

"Idiot!" growled Mr. Styngy. "Don't you smell fire here, Noodles?"

"Well," replied the odd man, after taking a prolonged taste of the atmosphere with his nose, "I don't smell no fire, but I smells smo—ake!"

"Get down stairs, you—you egregious ass," said Mr. Styngy, wrathfully. "Search the cellars and basement thoroughly, and, if you see fire anywhere, put it out at once."

Noodles ambled off on his errand, and then, as the smell of burning became stronger, the schoolmaster, now thoroughly alarmed, despatched De Bewty and his professor of languages to search the rest of the house, while he and Crocklejack remained in the schoolroom.

"Here's a game," said Lionel. "He's afraid to go himself, don't you see, old boy, so he's sent the ushers. My stars, when he does find out where the fire is, won't he be wild!"

"Rather. Halloo! he's beckoning to us—come on, Li."

In effect, Mr. Styngy, suddenly recollecting the amateur firemen, called our heroes to him, and put the inevitable question.

"I certainly do, sir," replied Lionel, affecting great alarm. "It is just such a smell as there was at the rectory fire, sir."

"Good gracious!" ejaculated Mr. Styngy; "this is dreadful. But there is no smoke."

"All the more dangerous, sir," said Lionel. "It is a sign that the fire is smouldering somewhere, and, when it does break out, it will be ten times worse!"

"Good heavens!" gasped the schoolmaster; "what can be done? The smell of burning gets stronger."

And, frantically rushing from side to side of the schoolroom, Mr. Styngy peered into every possible and impossible place where an incipient fire could conceal itself, Mr. Crocklejack and our heroes aiding him energetically.

"The fun will soon be up," said Lionel, in a whisper, to Charlie. "Only the smell has come out of his coat tails as yet, but now the smoke begins to show."

In fact, the rapid movements of Mr. Styngy had considerably hastened the combustion of the "infernal machine" which somebody had placed in his coat-tails, and now, not only the smell, but the smoke began to pour forth in volumes.

The pupils, who had been regarding the proceedings of the schoolmaster and his assistants with wonder—not unmixed with alarm—now began to smile, then to titter, and, finally, one rash youth laughed out loud.

"Who was that?" demanded Mr. Styngy, sharply. "Who dared to laugh?"

"It was Codlings, sir," said Smalls Junior, rising in his place to denounce the culprit, "and, if you please, sir, there's a lot of smoke coming out of your coat-tail."

Mr. Styngy, on getting into an upright position (he had been peering up the chimney), became aware that there was a halo of smoke around his reverend head.

"My coat!" he said alarmed. "Mr. Crocklejack, is there anything the matter with my coat?"

Mr. Crocklejack withdrew his head from a desk which he had been examining, but, no sooner did he look at his respected principal, than he rushed at him, and began to violently divest him of his outer garment.

"What are you doing, Crocklejack—are you mad?" cried Mr. Styngy as he struggled with the usher.

"Take your coat off, sir," gasped the usher, as he tore that garment half way down the back, "you're on fire!"

The coat came off in an instant, and then the mystery was solved. The right hand tail pocket was nearly burned through, and Mr. Crocklejack, after scorching his fingers, drew therefrom, an oblong tin box, from the sundry holes in the lid of which there curled upwards a quantity of evil-smelling smoke.

"Your matches have caught fire, sir," said Mr. Crocklejack, waving his scorched digits in the air. "Most dangerous thing to carry matches in the pocket, sir."

"Confound you, sir," said Mr. Styngy, trembling with passion. "I *never* carry matches in my pocket. This is some infamous trick. Give me that box, if it is cold enough."

But it had to be cooled, by carefully pouring water over it, before it was fit to handle, and then Mr. Styngy—who looked awful in his shirt-sleeves—took the box to his desk and examined it carefully.

In the interior he found nothing but the ash of the burnt touch-paper, but the exterior of the box gave him what he thought would prove to be a sure clue to the perpetrator of the little joke.

"I say," whispered Lionel to his chum, "I don't like the look of old Stygny. He's found out something."

"D'you think so? Well, he does look rather like an Indian chief who's just got a new scalp."

"He's going to have somebody's scalp over this. I say, Charlie, was there any name or anything of that sort on the box when you gave it me."

"'Pon my word I don't know," replied Charlie. "I borrowed the box from some fellow, I think, last half; or else I picked it up."

"Hush! he's going to speak."

Mr. Styngy had tapped with his ruler on the desk to attract attention, and, in an instant, the buzz of whispered conversation ceased, and some three-score pale and anxious faces were turned towards him.

"All the pupils," he said—in that low musical voice of his which always betokened mischief to come for somebody—"will assemble here, in the class-room, immediately after tea. Mr. Crocklejack, you will take especial care that every boy is present."

"I will, sir."

"Tell De Bewty and Tomkini that they need search no further, as the cause of the fire has been discovered, and let the duties of the school proceed as usual."

So saying, Mr. Styngy took his damaged coat over his arm, and with the little tin box under his arm, stalked forth, leaving some of the boys with an uncomfortable feeling in the region of the spine.

CHAPTER LIX.

MR. STYNGY IS RESOLVED TO FIND OUT THE CULPRIT—A CLOSE EXAMINATION—CIRCUMSTANTIAL EVIDENCE—SMALLS JUNIOR IN A FIX—CONVICTION—NO PITY FOR A SNEAK—VERDICT, "SERVED HIM RIGHT."

WITH a very uneasy feeling that all was not quite as right and safe as it should be, Lionel and Charlie marched after tea back again to the class-room, in company with all the other pupils, the solitary exception being the French boy.

"He's spotted somebody, that's certain," whispered Lionel to Charlie; "but who, I wonder?"

"It can't be you, for if he'd felt you slip the box into his pocket he would have been down upon you then."

"No—that's right enough. It's something about the box itself that he twigs; but we shall soon know. Here he comes."

Mr. Styngy entered at that moment, looking

about two sizes larger than usual, and holding in his right hand the mysterious tin box.

The roll was called. Every boy was reported in his place, and then Mr. Styngy, beginning with the upper form, called each boy in turn, and, holding up the tin box, asked him—firstly, if it belonged to him; and, secondly, if he had ever seen it before.

All the upper form boys replied in the negative to the first question, and to the second, two or three replied that they had seen such a box before, but could not say in whose possession.

When it came to Lionel's turn, he examined the box rather narrowly, and there on one side he discovered the initials, "S. S. Jr.," neatly scratched with the point of a knife.

He replied, of course, as the others had done, taking as his maxim the great principle of English law—that no one is bound to criminate himself.

Charlie Drummond did the same, and all went on smoothly till the last of the younger boys came, when one promptly identified the box as belonging to no less a personage than Smalls Junior.

Two or three others followed suit, and then it came to the turn of Smalls Junior himself, who, with pallid countenance and shaking limbs, strongly denied ever having set eyes on the box before.

Mr. Styngy let him pass on, and so boy after boy was questioned until all were done. Then the schoolmaster, in a terrible voice, bade all those who had spoken to any previous knowledge of the box stand forward.

About half a dozen obeyed the mandate, and then Mr. Styngy spoke again.

"Smalls Junior, come here!"

That little sneak, in as mortal a state of terror as could well be imagined, tottered forward, whining as he came—

"Oh! I don't know anything about it, if you please, sir. Indeed I don't, sir. I never saw the box before in my life, sir. Indeed I didn't."

"Hold your tongue, and wait till you are accused before you begin to defend yourself," said Mr. Styngy, sternly.

Smalls Junior was silent, but his teeth chattered like castanets.

"Six of your companions," the schoolmaster continued, "speak positively to having seen this box in your possession. Now I find scratched on one side the initials, "S. S. Jr.," which apply to the name of no other boy in the school but you."

"I remember him doing that with his knife, sir," said one of the witnesses. It was young Twister, who many a time and oft had suffered from the tale-bearing of the sneak Smalls, and thought this a good opportunity for vengeance.

"Oh! you saw Smalls mark his initials on the box, did you?" said Mr. Styngy. "You are generally a truthful boy, Twister. What have you to say to this evidence, Smalls?"

"It's all lies, sir," said the sneak, in an agony of terror; "it is indeed, sir. "They're only saying this to get me into trouble."

"How dare you make such a lame and paltry excuse, sir?" thundered Mr. Styngy. "How dare you expect me to believe that six of your schoolfellows would combine for the purpose of getting you unfairly punished."

The sneak, of course, in his desire to get out of the scrape, had gone too far, and had told a lie which was instantly detected. If he had simply confined himself to the truth, and owned that the box had once belonged to him, but that he had lost it, he would have stood a good chance of escape; but Mr. Styngy saw in his equivocation a sure sign of guilt, and condemned him without mercy.

"This is poetical justice, Charlie," said Lionel. "It's capital fun to see that little sneak fall into a trap that was never intended for him."

"He'll get it uncommonly warm," said Charlie, who looked rather solemn.

"Serve him right; he's such an artful little beggar in a general way, that it's almost impossible to bowl him out in any of his own tricks. This is poetical justice, I tell you, Charlie."

"Well, of course, as he's a sneak it don't matter much what happens to him. But I say, what a wonder that Tommy Codlings didn't get in for it."

"He would if the 'head' hadn't dropped on Smalls. I saw him looking precious hard at Tommy before young Twister spoke."

"Hush!" said Charlie. "Styngy's looking out for his longest cane—and now he's calling Smalls up. Put your fingers in your ears, Li, for his howls are dreadful."

In fact, at the sight of the cane, Smalls Junior began to yell; at the first cut he roared, and then set up such a succession of hideous screams, that the remonstrances of a full-grown pig, holding a last interview with a butcher, would have sounded operatic by comparison.

Mr. Styngy gave him about a quarter of an hour of it, and then, standing him on a solitary stool at the upper end of the school, Mr. Styngy passed sentence on the limp and tearful sneak.

His lessons were doubled for a month. He was to be deprived of all holidays whatsoever during that half, and every other day, for a fortnight, he was to receive a tickling, similar to that which the head master had bestowed upon him.

"I punish you so severely, Smalls," said Mr. Styngy, "not because of the gravity of your offence, but because it is *you* who have committed it. You are ever the foremost to detect and expose the shortcomings of your schoolfellows, and now I find that you are as bad yourself—worse, indeed, for you have shown yourself a hypocrite. I fully believe, now, that many of the misdeeds, for which I have punished other boys, were committed by you, and that, by your cunning, you contrived to fasten the guilt upon the innocent."

This little speech was just calculated to rouse the boys into a state of enthusiasm; and rising, headed by Lionel and Charlie, they gave Mr. Styngy three hearty cheers.

"Beautiful!" said our hero, rubbing his hands in high glee. "I think, Charlie, that the sneak of the school is settled for good and all."

CHAPTER LX.

A LITTLE DIGRESSION CONCERNING SNEAKS IN GENERAL, AND MASTER SMALLS JUNIOR IN PARTICULAR—MR. STYNGY HEARS AN ALARMING REPORT, AND HOLDS A CONSULTATION WITH HIS ASSISTANTS—THE RESULT THEREOF.

THAT which our hero curiously described as the "warming up" of the sneak, was a source of the utmost satisfaction to nine-tenths of the pupils of Cheetham Hall. The exceptions to the rule were, of course, our old acquaintances, Flashaway and Hunker, and their associates, who had found the craft and cunning of Smalls Junior too useful on many occasions, for them not to regret sincerely the temporary loss of his valuable services.

The doubling of the lessons Smalls Junior would have cared little for, as, to do the little sneak justice, he was intelligent enough, but the deprivation of all holidays, and especially the canings, were to him fearful.

These latter were performed publicly every other day, according to order, before first lessons, and directly the boys came in from the breakfast-room.

Exactly the same formula was gone through each time. Smalls Junior, although he knew quite well that no prayers of his could stop the course of his punishment, sobbed and screamed, and wailed and howled in the most abject manner, until the caning was over, when he was led back,

FOLLOW MY LEADER.

AS NOODLES ENTERED THE ROOM EVERY CHAIR COLLAPSED AS IF BY MAGIC, AND——

sobbing, to his solitary corner, vowing incoherently that he would "write to his pa, he would."

This little episode was regarded by the pupils in the light of a performance got up for their benefit—an oasis in the Desert of Learning—a gay little prelude, to fit them for the more serious portion of the day's work.

"Do you think it will cure him?" said Charlie Drummond, to our hero, one morning, as the classes settled into their places, after the usual performance.

"It'll never cure him of being a sneak," replied Lionel, decisively.

"You don't think so?"

"I'm certain of it. There's only one thing that could do that."

"What is it?"

"Cutting his head off."

"A sharp remedy that, Li," said Charlie, with a smile.

"A fellow who's a born sneak, like that Smalls, is sure to be one all his life. He'll be as bad a man as he is a boy."

"That's a comforting look out for somebody," said Charlie. "If he does as much mischief in the world as he does at school, those who deal with him will suffer."

"Yes, and so will he in the long run," replied Lionel, with a more acute perception of character than he dreamt of having. "It's such chaps as Smalls that you read of in the papers—fellows who get up those dummy companies and sham banks. They thrive for awhile, but some one is sure to put salt on their tails at last."

"Which is a comforting thing to know," said Charlie, arranging his books. "Well, here goes for Euclid; though why on earth any sane man could be found to pass his life in writing such a book as this, I don't know."

"Don't you?" said Lionel.

"No—do you?"

"Yes. He was a boy-hater, and he resolved to invent something which should prove a curse and a torture to boys for all generations to come. That's why he made up all these beastly propositions."

"Gammon," was Charles's reply, and the next minute the two chums were deep in the mysteries of the great mathematician.

A whole week passed away quietly enough as far as our hero and his friends were concerned. They were virtuous and well-behaved—not, we are sorry to record, because these young gentlemen had resolved to quit the thorny paths of practical joking and tread evermore the smooth high road of duty—but simply because they had had no opportunity of indulging in their favourite pastime.

But they managed to make themselves pretty comfortable with the legitimate games of the playground. Football was in full season, and many a goal did the light foot and quick eye of Lionel Wilful score for his side.

There were rumours, too—vague and uncertain as yet—regarding the probable establishment of a rival school near Cheetham Hall. The very mention of such a possibility was enough to set the boys, our heroes especially, on the very tip-toe of expectation.

Mr. Styngy had heard of the proposed establishment of the rival school, too, and had at first laughed the idea to scorn; but when the fact was known beyond dispute, that the Manor House, so long deserted, had been taken on lease by a person who called himself Mr. Trixham Trot, Ph.D., M.R.C.S., F.S.A., with several other honorary initials which we forget just now, and that circulars of a particularly sugary character had been largely circulated in the neighbourhood, the proprietor of Cheetham Hall thought it time to bestir himself.

"The bare idea," said Mr. Styngy, in consultation with his assistants—"the bare idea of a fellow like that having the impudence to send out circulars like this."

"It's abominable," said Mr. Crocklejack.

"Perfectly sickening," added M. de Bewty.

"He ought to be prosecuted," said Professor Tomkini.

"If you have no better suggestion to offer than that, Tomkini," said Mr. Styngy, sharply, "you can retire. The man is an—an ass; no doubt a presumptuous donkey; but we can't prosecute him for that."

"Certainly not," murmured De Bewty and Crocklejack, in chorus.

"Then, the question arises, what shall we do to prevent this person from undermining our influence and position in the county."

Mr. de Bewty ventured to suggest that Mr. Styngy's reputation was far too well established for such a nameless adventurer to weaken it.

"Very well said, De Bewty," replied the schoolmaster; "but people like novelty, and if this fellow gets the thin end of the wedge in, there is no telling what may happen."

Again the unfortunate professor hazarded an imprudent suggestion.

"Why not," he said, "issue some circulars, too, sir, and denounce him as an impostor."

Mr. Styngy glanced wrathfully upon him. He would very much like to have done what the professor suggested, but the impossibility of doing it only rendered the idea more aggravating.

"Tomkini," he said, "do me the favour to retire, and at once; your idiotic suggestions are—are—only worthy of the brain from which they emanate."

And with this withering sarcasm clinging to him, Professor Tomkini meekly departed from the room.

"Now," said Mr. Styngy, "that we have got rid of that insane person, I will tell you, gentlemen, what I think best to be done."

The two assistants inclined their heads gravely.

"There is nothing," Mr. Styngy began, with the air of a man who is about to make a speech, and a long one, too, "which so welds together the framework of society as social intercourse."

"Hear, hear," said Mr. de Bewty.

"Certainly. Very good," added Mr. Crocklejack.

"Therefore," continued the schoolmaster, bringing his speech to an abrupt conclusion, "I have decided that the best course to pursue to maintain and preserve those friendly relations which have hitherto existed between my neighbours and myself, will be to give a series of dinner parties, inviting all, without exception, and thereby, I trust, opening the eyes of my friends to the ridiculous pretensions of this adventurer—what's his name?—Trixham Trot."

Again the assistant masters expressed their admiration of the wisdom and liberality displayed by their employer, and this time there was something genuine in their congratulations, for whenever there was a dinner party they invariably came in for some small share of the feast.

So this matter was settled, and the head master, with many anathemas against Mr. Trixham Trot, who had forced him into this enormous outlay, began to calculate the number of the guests whom he must invite, and the probable cost of the series of entertainments.

He found that there were at least eighty people whom he would have to invite, and as his dining-room would not accommodate more than ten or a dozen at once, six or seven dinner parties would be an inevitable necessity.

"What must be, must be," said Mr. Styngy. "I will not be undermined by this seedy swindler—I'm sure he's a swindler, and seedy, too—without an effort. I'll crush him. I'll drive him out of the county the instant he sets foot in it."

This was hardly the sort of declaration to be

made by a master of christianity; but then Mr. Styngy had to look at matters from a worldly point of view. There was the reputation of the school to be maintained as well as his own, and, perhaps, he had hit upon the very best means possible.

How he fared in his endeavours, and what evil machinations were set on foot to destroy his hopes of success, we proceed to narrate in the following chapter.

CHAPTER LXI.

THE PREPARATIONS FOR THE DINNER PARTY—TWO SIDES TO A QUESTION—THE RESULT OF NOT RECEIVING AN INVITATION—AMATEUR UPHOLSTERERS—THE PARTY, AND WHAT HAPPENED THEREAT.

IN a very little while the report that Mr. Styngy was going to give a series of splendid entertainments in order to "cut out" his coming rival, found its way into the school, and to the ears of none more quickly than to Lionel and his chums, Charlie Drummond and Codlings.

"Dinner parties, eh!" said Tommy, musingly, as he gave a prophetic sniff. "Oh! when I grow up to be a man, Li, won't I just give some dinner parties!"

"Why, what would you have for dinner, Tommy?"

"Oh, everything," said Tommy, wrapped in an ecstatic dream. "Roast fowls, and ginger-beer, and raspberry jam, and nuts, and oranges. No, I don't think I'd have them, because they're common. I'd have pineapples and peaches, like those we saw in the hot-house, and——"

"And a pretty idea you've got of a dinner," laughed Lionel. "You wouldn't get many to dine with you a second time, unless you asked the ostriches from the Zoological Gardens."

"Well, it would do for me," said Tommy, perfectly satisfied that his bill of fare was one that would have satisfied the most exacting gourmand.

"Old Noodles tells me," said Lionel, "that Styngy's going to give five or six of 'em."

"What, altogether?"

"No, stupid; in succession of course. I wonder if he'll ask any of us."

"Not he; you be sure of that. He's got us, and we can't do any good or harm to this new fellow—Trixham Trot, ain't it?"

"Yes, that's the name," said Lionel. "Well, if Styngy doesn't ask us, Charlie, there'll by something wrong with the dinner. That bully, Flashaway, is invited."

"The dickens he is!"

"Yes; old Styngy says it's because Flashaway is a relative; but I know it's because he's the heir to a baronetcy, and the head likes to say as often as he can, when he's introducing him—'Permit me, my young friend Frederick Flashaway, Esq., eldest son of the Right Honourable Sir Frederick Flashaway, Member for this county.'"

"I say, it sounds well."

"That's it; nothing like having a title or two in a school, it 'draws' better than any advertisement."

"Confound that hulking brute," grumbled Charlie. "You're sure he's invited, Li?"

"Certain; he was showing the card round this morning, and I know he meant me to see it; though of course he didn't dare to speak."

"It's a beastly shame if that chap's invited, and we're not."

"Never mind, Charlie," said our hero, with his peculiar quiet mischievous smile; "we'll be there in the spirit, if we're not in the body."

"What do you mean, Li? You're not going to 'ghost' the old boy."

"No, no; only to give him something to remember us by. A word in thine ear, Charlie. The dining-room chairs are going to the upholsterers' to be re-covered; they will come back looking bright and new, but good luck to anybody who tries to sit down upon them."

"And even now I don't understand," said Charlie; "you're talking riddles, Li."

"Am I? well, here's the answer."

And stooping down, our hero whispered a few words in his ear, the effect of which seemed to be to fill Charlie with wonder, and a dash of alarm.

"You can't mean *that*, Li."

"But I do, though. Will you be in it?"

"Of course. Don't I always follow your lead."

"What's it all about?" asked Tommy, suddenly awaking from his reverie; "the dinner party?"

"Yes, Tommy; we're not invited to it. I said it's a shame, and so we're just going to help to make the guests comfortable, to show that we bear no malice."

Lionel and Charlie happened to be present in the hall—quite by accident, of course—when the upholsterer came to fetch the chairs away in his caravan, and four days afterwards they happened to be present at the re-delivery of those articles of furniture, brilliant and glossy as when they first, in all their pristine beauty, blinked upon the world in Piccadilly.

The dinner was not to be for two days yet to come. The chairs were carefully stowed away in the box-room, while the dining-room was put through a course of soap and water, and thither on the evening before the festive day, three youthful forms might have been observed cautiously stealing in the twilight.

There were twelve chairs, and there were three conspirators. Each of the latter noiselessly appropriated four of the former, and for the ensuing three-quarters of an hour a peculiar rasping sound, such as that produced when a fine saw is in contact with wood.

Need we further detail the shameful deed that was being perpetrated. The three youthful forms were owned by Lionel, Charlie, and Codlings, and armed each with a fine saw, dipped in oil, they were cutting the chair legs three parts through.

As a matter of course, Lionel and Charlie had completed their nefarious work long before Tommy, who ran the saw into his fingers more often than into the chair legs, which, perhaps, served him right.

"Done, Charlie?" whispered Lionel, as he rose from his last chair.

"Just upon—only this leg. There, that's it. How's Tommy getting on?"

"First rate," responded Tommy, cheerfully. "I've got through two of my fingers already."

"Bother your fingers!" said Lionel, taking up the candle end by which they had been working, and going over to Tommy; "why, confound you for a noodle, what are you sawing through the middle of the leg for, just where it can be seen? Up here's the place, where the legs are carved."

And Tommy was unceremoniously thrust aside, and left to suck his wounded fingers, while Lionel and Charlie completed his share of the work, and replaced the chairs in order.

"There now, that's beautiful," said Lionel, stepping back to admire the effect. "The cuts don't show a bit, only I hope nobody'll take a fancy to sit down in 'em before the dinner party."

"Never fear; old Styngy will take good care of that. I say, Li, won't he be wild—just a little, that's all."

"We shall see what we shall see," replied our hero, gravely, and then, as the candle went out, they went out too, carefully locking the door upon the chairs, which were the pride of Mr. Styngy's heart.

* * * * *

At length the day arrived—the day of the first of Mr. Styngy's formal dinner parties. Seven o'clock was the hour announced in the invitations, and with very commendable punctuality the guests arrived.

Mr. Styngy felt almost reconciled to the expenses as carriage after carriage, and fly after fly rolled up and deposited sundry hungry dames on the steps of Cheetham Hall.

The schoolmaster, in a resplendant tail coat, with bright buttons, was ready to receive his guests in the drawing-room, flanked on either side by the two scions of the house of Flashaway.

Everything was lovely and serene—the guests had all arrived. Mr. Styngy looked at his watch; it was twenty minutes past seven, and he had given Noodles strict orders to announce that dinner was served at the quarter after.

Now Mr. Styngy, having got Noodles up in an expensive livery, naturally desired that the odd man should do credit to his costume; and had taken pains to instruct him personally in the way in which he should fling open the door and announce, as if it were a piece of intelligence upon which the fate of Europe trembled—

"The dinner is served!"

It was rather disappointing then to the schoolmaster, when Noodles opened the door of the drawing-room but a few inches, and just putting his head in, said in a confidential growl—

"The grub's ready!"

The company tittered—of course they couldn't possibly have helped it under the circumstances. Mr. Styngy darted a look at him that would have killed a dozen basilisks, but it had no effect upon the odd man; and then, offering his arm to the oldest and ugliest (and richest) lady in the room, Mr. Styngy led the way to dinner.

The famous chairs were there, radiant in the splendour of their crimson satin. The gentlemen handed their partners to their seats. There was a flutter of silk and muslin as the fair ones settled down; then the gentlemen took their places; and finally Mr. Styngy himself plumped into his chair.

There was an ominous "cra—a—ck" as he did so; but Mr. Styngy, unsuspicious of the coming catastrophe, heeded it not, and smiled blandly round upon his guests.

Just then there was another "crack," sharper than the first, on the right of the table; followed almost immediately by another on the left. The guests looked at one another in alarm, and shifted their chairs as if the cracking was the prelude to some terrible explosion.

That shifting of the chairs was fatal; without a second of warning, every chair collapsed as if by magic, just as Noodles appeared in the doorway with the soup.

It was really a touching and pathetic sight to behold those ladies and gentlemen, but a few brief moments ago seated calm and orderly, waiting for their dinner, and to see, as if by the enchantment of some wicked fairy, the whole scene changed into one of disorder and confusion.

Not one had escaped. Even the sylph-like forms of the ladies had come into violent contact with the ground. Some had fainted—the rest were screaming, and such of the gentlemen as were not upside down endeavoured to restore them.

Mr. Styngy himself was the greatest sufferer; he had fallen with the back of his head against the fender, and, after seeing several thousand more stars than astronomers account for, and a stray comet or two, he came to the conclusion that he was stunned, and had better stay where he was.

One very stout old gentlemen, who had brought a still stouter wife and daughter with him, was dreadfully indignant at the treatment they had received. He professed to believe that the break down of the chairs was a little joke arranged on purpose by Mr. Styngy.

"But I'll joke you! See if I don't!" growled the irate old gentleman, as he shook his fist close to Mr. Styngy's unconscious nose. "Ask ladies and gentlemen here to dinner, and then play fools' tricks on them! It's no use you're pretending to be asleep, or in a faint. I know better. Let us see if you will treat with a little more respect the friend I shall send to you in the morning, sir!"

Having uttered which speech, with a tremendous emphasis on the last dozen words, the stout gentleman stalked off with his wife and daughter, an example that was speedily followed by the other guests.

Mr. Noodles, after seeing all the company depart in much wonder, bethought himself of his master, and, when he had looked at him a quarter of an hour or so, to decide upon the best way of catching hold of him, lifted him out of the fire-grate, and, propping him up in an arm-chair, took the vinegar cruet, and poured the contents down his throat.

It brought Mr. Styngy to his senses almost instantly. His first action was to rub the back of his head, his first words to inquire whether the dinner was ready.

"Ah!" said Noodles, "t'dinner be ready, but there be nobody to eat 'un."

By degrees, Mr. Styngy's eyes opened upon the wreck about him, and he began to comprehend the full extent of his disaster.

The floor was covered with broken pieces of crockery and glass, knives, forks, and spoons; and, above all, the fragments of the shattered chairs, the cause of the fell disaster.

"Go, Noodles," he said, mournfully. "Leave me to myself, and, if anyone comes, I'm not at home."

And then Mr. Styngy, from the shelter of the arm-chair, gazed at the wreck and ruin around him, even as Marius did, and, like that hero, too, he did not disdain to drop a silent tear over his lost hopes.

CHAPTER LXII.

MR. STYNGY RUMINATES ON HIS BLIGHTED HOPES —WAS IT AN EARTHQUAKE?—"IT'S AN ILL WIND THAT BLOWS NOBODY GOOD."

IT was a terrible blow to Mr. Styngy—disastrous in more senses than one—for our readers will remember that he was a heavy man, and that he had fallen with the back of his head against the fender.

He sat there in the easy-chair, the bump outside his head growing rapidly larger, and the sense of his misfortunes increasing at a tremendous rate inside his reverend cranium.

"This is a truly dreadful thing," he murmured; "but half an hour ago, all was an atmosphere of peace and soup; and now regard the fearful wreck of my happiness and my furniture."

Mr. Styngy, being by this time a little less confused, arose from his arm-chair, and, helping himself to a glass or two of wine, began to reason upon the nature and cause of the strange accident.

"It was like an earthquake," mused Mr. Styngy; "a sudden shock, and we were all precipitated to the ground. I recollect seeing eight or ten legs above the tables when they ought to have been underneath. Then I fell myself, and all was a blank."

At this moment a knock sounded at the door, and the head of the odd man appeared calm and solemn as the Sphinx.

"Now, man, what do you want?" said Mr. Styngy, angrily. "Did I not desire to be left alone?"

"You did, sir, there's no denyin'; but cook wants to know whether the dinner's to be left alone too, 'cos it's a spilin', she ses."

"Bother the dinner. What concern have I with dinners now? Tell cook to do what she likes—or stay—let it be served up to the young gentlemen for their supper."

Noodles stared; but he was not fond of argument, and so contented himself with conveying the message to the cook.

"That at least will not be wasted," thought the schoolmaster, mournfully. Then stooping down, he picked up one of the broken chair legs, and for the first time noted that they strewed the ground in every direction.

A horrible suspicion crossed Mr. Styngy's mind. He picked up three or four more legs and examined them closely. Then giving utterance to a very naughty word, he rang the bell furiously.

"Send Mr. Crocklejack, De Bewty, and the professor here at once," he said to Noodles, who answered the bell with wonderful rapidity, he having, in fact, been outside the door all the time, waiting for a chance to get at the wine.

"Gentlemen," said the head master, as soon as the assistants entered, "an atrocious crime has been perpetrated."

The trio looked round with eager curiosity. They had heard of the sudden departure of the guests, but knew nothing of the cause. Flashaway Senior was sulky, because he had received a black eye from a flying decanter, and would answer no questions, while a very stout lady had sat upon Flashaway Junior and squeezed all the conversation out of *him*.

"There is indeed evidence of a terrible struggle, sir," said Professor Tomkini, looking at a place on the carpet where a bottle of claret had been spilled. "I see the gore. Have the villains escaped?"

Mr. Styngy turned upon him in desperation and anger.

"What an extraordinary thing it is, Tomkini, that I never summon you to ask your advice but you outrage all sense and probability with your ridiculous suggestions."

"Ha, ha. The idea—gore!" sneered Mr. Crocklejack.

"'Have the villains escaped too,' he said; that's very good," added Mr. de Bewty, who knew nothing at all about the matter, but pitched into the professor on principle.

"I'm very sorry, sir. I really——"

"'Really' you had better hold your tongue," said the head master. "Now, gentlemen, do me the favour to examine these chairs."

The evidence of the fractures and of the manner in which they had been accomplished was too plain to be mistaken, and the trio said together—

"Why, these legs have been sawn through, sir."

"Not a doubt of it," said Mr. Styngy, with an air of mystery. "Now comes the question—who has done it?"

"Some of the boys," hazarded Mr. de Bewty.

"'The boys,'" repeated the head master, contemptuously. "Think you that any boy would have the audacity to plan and carry out such a deep-laid scheme as this? No, gentlemen," he added, lowering his voice to a whisper, "the arch villain is Trixham Trot."

"The man who is going to set up a school at the Manor House? said Mr. de Bewty, aghast.

"Exactly;" and his confederate is the upholsterer."

"I see!" said Mr. de Bewty, speaking very rapidly, so as to get ahead of Crocklejack. "Trot heard of your dinner-party, and bribed the upholsterers to saw the chair legs, so as to spoil the party, and cover you with shame and confusion."

"That's it, exactly," replied the head master, in appreciation of his assistant's acuteness of perception.

"What will you do with the miscreant, sir?" asked Mr. de Bewty. "Drag him before the outraged tribunals of his country?"

"Certainly not," said Mr. Styngy. "That would only be heaping ridicule upon my own head—the very thing this fellow Trot desires. Besides, I can prove nothing, unless we make the upholsterers confess."

"They might be bribed," suggested Mr. de Bewty.

"This unfortunate affair has already cost me far more money than I can afford," said the Reverend Mr. Styngy. "Ah! gentlemen, I know it is wrong to harbour the desire, but how I wish that my clerical character could be put off for awhile, and I enabled to meet that miscreant in the field!"

The assistants sighed, and shook their heads as if they thought it a great pity that Mr. Styngy was not able to offer himself as a mark for Mr Trixham Trot's pistol bullet, at twelve paces."

"Had I a friend now, who—but no, I will not think of it. Leave me, gentlemen—leave me, I beg of you."

And Mr. Styngy, as if too overcome by his emotions to bear the sight of his fellow-man, dismissed them from the room with a wave of his hand, and sank into his arm-chair, the picture of woe.

The assistant masters had, of course, smelt out the fact that the dinner was to be given to the young gentlemen for supper, and, as a matter of course, took their places at the table.

It was excellent, though there was not too much of it; for a dinner, provided for a dozen people, becomes rather meagre when there are forty to partake of it.

The elder boys, of course, came in for the lion's share, and amongst these lucky ones our heroes were, of course, numbered. Tommy's appetite was "fearfully and wonderfully" made, as usual, and he tasted everything on the table, from the mustard to the mutton, and from the vinegar to the vol-au-vaut.

By-and-by Lionel's attention was attracted by a word or two that fell from Mr. de Bewty's lips—a word which at once enlisted his sympathies and aroused his curiosity at once, for it was the word "duel."

To say he listened would be an impolite word to use; we will say, therefore, that he did not close his ears, which were very keen, and by the time the dinner was over he had picked up and pieced together enough of the conversation to disclose to him the secret conversation in the dining-room, and the comments of the assistant masters made the whole affair still clearer.

Immediately the dinner—or, rather, supper—was over, Lionel sought out Charlie, with a face full of lurking fun and mischief.

"Here's a game, Charlie," he said, hardly able to contain himself till they were safe out of hearing. "Such a game as we shall never have again in all our lives."

"What's that?"

"You know what we did to the chairs, and how the affair went off?"

"Rather," said Charlie, with a wink.

"Well, Styngy thinks that the new chap that's going to set up school bribed the upholsterer to saw the chairs, and, by George, he's asked De Bewty and the others to call him out and fight him, as he can't do it himself because he's a clergymen."

"Come, Li; no larks," said Charlie, as he dropped himself into a seat with excess of astonishment.

"Fact, though—I heard it."

"And will any of 'em fight?"

"Not they. They is too fond of their precious carcasses! but I tell you what, Charlie; we'll make one of 'em fight whether he likes it or no."

"You can't do that, you know."

"It's as easy as A B C. Look here!"

And Lionel run off and returned in a moment with his desk.

"Now, which one shall we make fight? they've none of 'em got any pluck; but which do you think is the funkiest?

"De Bewty, I fancy," said Charlie, "because he

VOL. II.—ONE SHILLING.

MR. STINGY ASSUMED AN ATTITUDE OF DIGNIFIED INDIGNATION AS THE NEW PUPIL WAS INTRODUCED.

Or, Young Wilful's Schooldays.

LONDON:—HOGARTH HOUSE, BOUVERIE STREET, FLEET STREET E.C.

HOGARTH HOUSE LIBRARY.

BOUVERIE STREET, FLEET STREET, E.C.

The following is a list of the REVISED EDITIONS of the Hogarth House Works, published in Volumes, bound in Illustrated Covers, also in Penny Weekly Numbers, all in print, and ready for immediate delivery:—

TOM WILDRAKE'S SCHOOLDAYS.

In Five Vols., price 1s. each; also complete in one Vol. as a Prize Edition, and handsomely bound in cloth and gold, price 5s. 6d.—This celebrated School Story was the first of its class ever issued in weekly numbers; and in the face of numerous imitators it still holds the foremost place. The story is a faithful narrative of the life of a high-spirited young Englishman at school—showing what he did and how he did it, and what he learnt and its influence on his after life. The story is carried on through Tom Wildrake's adventurous career, down to the time when he felt himself entitled to rest on the laurels he had so nobly won by his many brave deeds during the heartrending Indian Mutiny and in Australia and elsewhere.

YOUNG TOM'S ADVENTURES In Europe, Asia, Africa, and America.

Complete, price 1s. 6d.—This is a sequel to "Young Tom's Schooldays," and narrates his hair-breadth escapes and adventures both with wild men and animals in the four quarters of the globe.

THE BOYS OF BIRCHAM SCHOOL.

Complete, price 1s. 6d.—This story claims to be the first school story that ever appeared in a periodical solely devoted to boys. For dramatic incident and genuine fun it has never yet been equalled.

CHARLIE AND TIM AT SCARUM SCHOOL.

Complete, price 1s.—This story of the life of two boys, who are sworn chums, at school, has always been a popular one with our young friends; showing, as it does, how a sincere friendship may be formed at school which may have lasting effects on our boys' after lives. Every schoolboy should read it.

CHARITY JOE; or, from Street Boy to Lord Mayor.

Complete, price 1s.—This is the true story of an outcast, who, by his honesty and indomitable will, rose to be the Chief Magnate of the First City in the World. His adventures at school, and, accompanied by his dog Toby, with a travelling showman, should be read by every lad who wishes to know *what* an English boy can do, no matter how humble his first start in life, or how great his temptations.

OUT ON THE WORLD.

Complete, price 1s.—This history goes direct to the heart of the reader, being a story of real life, depicting the troubles and trials of two children who were stolen from their home by gipsies. Little Jack's brave defence of his fellow-prisoner, Lilly—He shoots at Tinker Tom—They escape and tramp to London—Their adventures on the way; they join a troupe of tumblers and become street-players—They are recog nised by the gipsies—The fair—The booth on fire; and, after many narrow escapes, they are captured by Tinker Tom, who cruelly ill-uses them—They are traced by the players to Tinker Tom's den—They are followed and risk their lives to save the children from a horrible de ath—The children are restored to their parents through the skill of the detective police, and well reward those who assisted them in the days of their adversity. This work is very graphically illustrated with numerous Wood Engravings.

YOUNG TOM'S SCHOOLDAYS.

Complete, price 1s. 6d.—This is the story of the life of Tom Wildrake's son at school; and, although complete in itself, should be read by everyone who has read "Tom Wildrake," as all the readers' old friends reappear in its pages.

RAGS AND RICHES: A Story of Three Poor Boys.

Complete, price 1s.—The illustrations to this work are from the inimitable pencil of Phiz (H. K. Browne), who did so much towards rendering popular many of the works of Charles Dickens. So faithfully is the story of these poor boys told, and so realistic are the scenes described, that it has been pronounced by competent critics the best story of London life published since "Oliver Twist."

FRANK FEARLESS; Or, the Cruise of the Firebrand.

Complete, price 2s. 6d.—We doubt whether for fidelity of description and stirring incidents this magnificent sea story has been equalled since the days of Captain Marryat. The story of the misjudged hero's long and troubled conflict, not only with the pirates, but with his own mistaken countrymen, should be read by every true British boy who can lay its lessons to heart and profit by them.

MIDSHIPMAN TOM; Or, the Cruise of the War Cloud.

Complete, price 2s.—This is the faithful narrative of the life of a Midshipman on board a Man-of-War, and shows the trials, temptations, and prizes incident to the career of a boy who wears the uniform of our gracious Queen at sea. Though strikingly sensational, the element of fun is not omitted.

BLACK-EYED SUSAN; or Pirates Ashore.

Complete, price 1s.—The pathetic and stirring story of William and Susan is here told in a way which is bound to enlist the sympathies of all who are possessed with a true Briton's love of adventures at sea.

THE BRIGANDS OF THE SEA; Or, the Sailor Highwayman.

Complete, price 1s. 6d.—Money Marks, the hero of this most extraordinary romance of the sea, is no imaginary character, and nearly all the soul-stirring incidents herein described are founded on fact. The career of this world-famed highwayman of the sea is one of the most sensational narratives ever offered to the reading public. It is profusely illustrated by an eminent artist.

THE WAR CRUISE OF THE MOSCA; Or, the Six Fighting Mids.

Complete, price 1s.—In this Stirring Story of the Sea, the talented author takes a wide departure from his school and military stories, and shows us that though he is familiar with the cavalry sabre, he can give us a vigorous and truthful account of the life of those whose lot it is to wield the sailor's cutlass, and fight their country's battles on the boundless deep.

FOR HONOUR; or, the Young Privateer.

Complete, price 1s. 6d.—This powerfully written story of the life of a Privateer during one of the most stirring periods of England's Naval History, is a marvellous combination of the sensational and the humorous. No British boy can read the sayings and doings of Monkey Jack and Crikey without a laugh, and no British boy can read the heroic actions of the young Privateer without feeling a thrill of exultation that he also belongs to that glorious Empire on whose domains the sun never sets.

ADRIFT ON THE SPANISH MAIN.

Complete, price 1s.—This Story of the old Buccaneers carries us back to the glorious days of good Queen Bess—the days when England settled for all time her right to the title of "Empress of the Seas."

ALL'S WELL.

Complete, price 1s.—The Story under the title of the above popular seaman's cry is full of pathos, sensation, and humour. In dramatic situations it is probably superior to any story of the sea ever written. With each copy is presented gratis a Magnificent Portrait of the greatest naval hero of modern days—Horatio, Lord Nelson.

SHEET-ANCHOR JACK.

Complete, price 1s.—A powerfully-written narrative of the life of a jolly jack tar "before the mast," and should be read by every true English boy.

THE PIRATE'S ISLE; Or, the Wonders of the Deep.

Complete, price 1s.—This is a story of adventure, both on sea and land. Full of sensation, pathos, and fun.

THE BRITISH BOY SAILOR.

Complete, price 2s.—A faithful narrative of the life of a poor boy on board a British Man-of-War, during the glorious days of Nelson, showing what a British boy's pluck can do to raise himself superior to circumstances.

WILLIE GRAY; Or, the Wreck of the Polar Star.

Complete, price 1s.—In this spirit-stirring story the entranced reader is carried into trange countries, and through strange perils by flood and field; but, from first to last, the interest is so well sustained that those who once take up the book are unable to lay it down until every line has been perused.

HOGARTH HOUSE, BOUVERIE ST., FLEET ST., LONDON, E.C.

AS THE MYSTERIOUS MONKEY SPRANG FORWARD TO EMBRACE THE STOUT GENTLEMAN, THE KEEPER LAID HOLD OF HIS TAIL.

No. 14.

always pitches into the smallest boys in his class, and lets the big ones off."

"A good reason. We'll have De Bewty. Now, keep quiet a minute."

Lionel scribbled away with his pen, and in a quarter of an hour had produced the following elegant epistle, which he handed to Charlie Drummond, and which we will take the liberty of reading at the same time:—

"TO THE IMPUDENT BLACKGUARD AND SWINDLER, KNOWN AS TRIXHAM TROT.

"Your rascally machinations, whereby a certain dinner party was broken up, are discovered. You can no longer crawl like a toad in its slime, and hide in your native mud; for this is to give you notice—you low thief—that I shall pull your nose, and otherwise assault you as I think fit, upon the first opportunity; and, after that—if you have sufficient courage to enable your spindle-shanks to bear you upright before the face of a man—I will give you satisfaction.

(Signed) "ERNEST DE BEWTY,
Cheetham Hall."

"I say, that's uncommon strong," said Charlie, looking in some dismay at the letter.

"I wish I knew how to make it stronger," said Lionel. "Anyhow, here goes."

And in a very short space of time the letter was placed in an envelope, sealed, directed, and posted to its destination by the ever convenient Noodles.

What dreadful complications and dire mishaps came of the posting of that little scrap of paper, future chapters will show.

CHAPTER LXIII.

MR. TRIXHAM TROT ARRIVES AT THE MANOR HOUSE—AN EASY METHOD OF MEETING ACCOUNTS HALFWAY—LIONEL'S LETTER ARRIVES—THE EFFECT THEREOF—GOOD-NATURED JOHN SENT TO SPY OUT THE NAKEDNESS OF THE LAND.

NOW Mr. Trixham Trot, to whom our hero had addressed that very blood-thirsty letter, was one of the most fiery and quarrelsome little men it was possible to meet, whenever he considered himself insulted or his rights infringed.

Therefore our hero's little scheme promised to "come off" with "flying colours," presuming the colour to be red or ruby, and that it was to fly from Mr. de Bewty's nose.

"How long do you think it'll be before old Tricks (the young rascals had already nicknamed him) sends you an answer?"

"Sends me an answer? He won't send *me* one," said Lionel, with a mischievous smile. "Why should he? You know it was old De Bewty who wrote to him."

"Oh, ah, of course it was," replied Charlie, with a responsive wink. "Well, how long will it be before Bewty gets one?"

"All depends, my boy, whether Tricks is at the Manor House, and whether he's a peppery customer. If he's both, we may expect him down to-morrow morning."

"Early, eh?"

"Just so."

Now our readers are already informed that Mr. Trixham Trot *was* of a peppery character, and he arrived at the Manor House on the very evening that Lionel despatched the letter.

He was in a furious temper because the bills for the alterations and repairs which it had been found necessary to make in the Manor House had been sent in, and, as a matter of course, he disagreed with the amounts charged.

"It's monstrous—it's infamous," he gasped, working himself up into a perfect whirlwind of rage in something less than two minutes. "*John!*"

This name was bellowed forth in a prolonged roar, and accompanied by a tremendous tug at the bell-pull; and almost immediately a short stout man with a round red face, which wore an expression of imperturbable good humour, appeared. He was dressed very neatly in the conventional dress of a butler, and bowed politely as he entered, and gently closed the door after him.

"John."

"Yes, sir."

"Look at these rascally bills! You know what work has been done—or ought to—for I told you to look after the scoundrels of workmen, and keep 'em up to it."

"And so I did, sir; though they used to leave pails on the stairs for me to tumble over, and they'd drop their tools on me from the scaffoldin', and upset their paint on my clothes, and all manner of games, sir."

"You should have picked out some of the rascals, John, and prosecuted 'em," said Mr. Trot; "but never mind that now. I want you to take these bills, and knock off—say about half."

"Fifty per cent., sir," said John, looking doubtfully at his master. "I don't think they'll stand that."

"D—— what they'll stand," roared the peppery Mr. Trot, using, we am sorry to record, a very naughty word. "D'ye think I'm going to stand being robbed?"

"Certainly not, sir. Couldn't be thought on, sir," was John's conciliatory reply.

"Well, then, do as you're told; and if it ain't properly done, I'll take fifty per cent. off your wages."

"Very good, sir," said John, gathering up the bills, and speaking as politely as if his employer had agreed to add fifty per cent. to his salary.

John departed, and Mr. Trot proceeded to open the remainder of his correspondence, which seemed to be rather large.

He was not, apparently, what is called a "good scholar," for he haggled a great deal over the letters, and occasionally had to spell through a word longer than usual.

They seemed to afford him no more satisfaction than the bills, for he certainly used bad words, and tore up and trampled on the letters as he read them, in a way that was terrifying to behold.

"Here's a pretty go!" he said, giving a bewildered look around him. "Here's the school ready, and no dashed scholars to put in it."

Here we may as well explain in a few words who and what was Mr. Trixham Trot, and his object in coming to set up a school at the old Manor House.

Mr. Trot was a vulgar, uneducated man, but a cunning one. He had made a little money at betting, but, having married about that time, he resolved to achieve respectability, and invested part of his capital in the purchase of a small middle-class school.

By judicious puffing and toadying of parents, and screwing the expenses down to the very lowest point, Mr. Trot managed first to quadruple the number of pupils, and then to sell the goodwill for a handsome sum, besides having already made a considerable profit.

With the money thus obtained he determined to launch out into a wider field, and, after long deliberation, he pitched upon the old Manor House (which had been deserted for years, and was consequently to be had cheap) as the spot for his operations.

As for pupils, Mr. Trot had devised a cunning plan, which he thought could not fail.

He sent artfully-worded circulars to all the parents and guardians and so forth, whose children were still at the school he had sold, and, after intimating the innumerable superior advantages his new establishment had over the old, offered to take pupils for about a third less than the sum they were then paying.

"It's sure to draw," said Mr. Trixham Trot to

his better half. "Put it to yourself, my dear. If you can get a thing cheaper and—ahem—better at one shop than another, you transfer your custom to the cheapest shop, don't you?"

"In course," said Mrs. Trot, who in point of vulgarity far surpassed her husband; "it's natur'."

But the letters which the new schoolmaster received in the evening when we personally introduce him to the reader, convinced him that there was an alarming lack of "natur'" in some people.

The majority treated his circulars with contemptuous silence. Several, as we have seen, sent short and indignant comments on his dishonesty and presumption, and two only consented to transfer their children, and these two Mr. Trot knew never paid.

It was lucky for Mrs. Trot that she had not yet arrived from London, or she would have had to bear the brunt of a terrible storm, as Mr. Trot regarded her as the legitimate target for all the arrows of his displeasure.

When he couldn't get at Mrs. Trot, John was the sufferer, though he never cared, and through it all "smiled away like clockwork," as Sam Weller says.

When he went to bed he was still furious. He kicked a stray cat from the top to the bottom of the kitchen stairs with a fiendish satisfaction. He ground his teeth as he went to his bedroom till he made them ache; he banged down the candlestick with such force that the candle jumped out, and, falling on its head, extinguished itself.

Then he cursed the candle, and roared out at the top of the stairs for matches, though he knew there were half a dozen boxes in the room, and after bestowing a final anathema of prodigious power upon John, he undressed and got into bed, clutching his pillow with both hands, as if it had been an enemy whose life he wanted to choke out.

In the morning he was worse, for he had had nobody to bully and keep awake during the night, and he went down to breakfast with a face that would have put Medusa's to the blush.

There was only one letter lying on his plate, and Mr. Trot pounced upon it as does a cat upon a mouse. He wanted something to vent his anger upon.

The address was in a handwriting unfamiliar to him, but Mr. Trot did not stay to scrutinize that. He tore open the envelope, opened the letter, and then ——

We utterly fail in the attempt to describe the wrath of Mr. Trixham Trot when he read Lionel's letter. It can't be done.

When we record that he kicked the breakfast table over, that he smashed the new pier glass (value thirty pounds), and that he sent his new boots flying through the plate glass of the dining-room window, it gives not the least idea of his fury, and so we abandon the attempt.

"John!" he roared, as soon as the first paroxysms was over.

But even that usually immoveable personage had taken fright, and hidden himself in the coal cellar; while the two maid servants had locked themselves, with the cook, in the pantry.

"John!" roared Mr. Trot again, with a bell obligato.

"I think I'll go," thought John, as he unfastened the cellar door. "His fit's over, I think. I don't hear no more smashin'."

"Why didn't you come before, you dashed scoundrel?" was Mr. Trot's very natural question.

"I thought you were busy, sir," replied John, still smiling calmly on, aud glancing at the damaged furniture.

"Busy? Yes—I was busy calling you, Thick-head," growled Mr. Trot, "and I had to break all these things to wake you up, Sleepyhead; but you shall pay for 'em out of your wages. Dash me, if you shan't. Now look at this—this scrawl."

John did look at it, round it, turned it over and over, and said as he handed it back—

"It's very unpolite, sir."

"Dash the unpoliteness! D'ye know the handwriting?"

"I do not, sir."

"Then find out. There's the address—Cheetham Hall; it's a school close by. I've heard of it. Get hold of one of the boys; get what you can out of him, and don't come away till you've got a sight of this—this ass, De Bewty. I'll Beauty him. And bring me back a particular description of him, d'you hear? And have it ready by the time I come back from London. I start to-night."

"Certainly, sir. I'll go at once, sir," and the good-humoured John backed out of the room as reverentially as if he had been quitting the presence of royalty.

Leaving Mr. Trixham Trot to fume and fret, we will turn to a chapter on matters intimately affecting the comfort of Mr. Styngy.

CHAPTER LXIV.

MR. STYNGY'S SECOND DINNER PARTY—A DINNER, AND NO ONE TO DINE—TOMMY CODLINGS SHOWS A STRONG DISPOSITION TO SLEEP, AND MR. STYNGY EVINCES A PREFERENCE FOR SCALDING SOUP OUT OF A TUREEN.

MR. STYNGY did not suffer the failure of the first party to depress him long.

On the second day he had quite recovered, and set his assistants to work so vigorously upon elaborate notes of apology to the late sufferers, besides fresh letters of invitation, that little or no work was done in the school for at least one day.

"What the dickens are they all up to?" said Charlie. "Styngy seems to have gone quite off his head this last day or two."

"Enough to make him," replied our hero. "That last joke of ours was really too bad."

"It's led up to some first-rate fun though."

"It will, you mean," replied Lionel. "I say, we'll just let this dinner party go off all right, won't we? No tricks this time; we're getting really too bad."

"How about that letter to Tricks and De Bewty, then?" said Charlie; "that don't look much like reform."

"I only want to leave Styngy alone awhile. I don't care what happens to De Bewty. I shall never forgive him for the way he paid into poor Tommy when he was black-holed. Never let him off a single cut."

The dinner was given upon rather short notice, only three days being allowed for the diners to decide whether they would accept or refuse.

Mr. Styngy was rejoiced when the day came at last, and not a single refusal had reached him, but he was rather surprised, too, that he had not had any of the usual formal acceptances.

"Too short notice, I suppose," mused Mr. Styngy as he turned the matter over in his mind; "wouldn't take the trouble of writing; they'll come sure enough."

Mr. Styngy had spared no expense over this banquet, for he knew that he owed a recompense to those who had suffered before.

This time, however, he had tested the furniture in person, going over every article, and even making Noodles—who weighed about twenty stone—sit down on the chairs.

"Serve the dinner punctually at half-past seven, Noodles; and see that the waiter who helps you does not get drunk," were Mr. Styngy's last orders to Noodles.

"I'll try, sir; but he've got a fearful love of licker. He'd smell it out if you was to bury it twenty foot under ground."

As the assistants were to be of the party—under

strict orders to amuse the company and enliven it whenever it showed signs of getting dull—the boys were left to do as they liked until bed-time.

Lionel and Charlie were naturally anxious to hear if Mr. Trixham Trot had made any reply to the note, and, with this object, dogged De Bewty and Crocklejack with the pertinacity fo Indian warriors on the war-trail.

"They're in the dining-room now," said Lionel; "who'll listen at the key-hole a bit; old Styngy isn't there."

"I will," said Tommy; "my ears are first rate."

"All right; you'll do. You're short, and won't make your back ache stooping so much as we should. We'll stop at the end of the passage, old chap, and give you the whistle when anyone's coming"

"Right you are," said Tommy, and at once placed his ear to the key-hole.

But after about a quarter of an hour he found the position fatiguing. Besides, there was a draught, and he was afraid of the ear-ache.

"I'll lie down on the mat," thought Tommy. "I can hear better underneath the door, and it's more comfortable."

It proved, in fact, so comfortable, that Tommy went to sleep in something less than five minutes. He snored, too, but the sound was muffled by the woollen tufts of the mat.

A quarter past seven, and no arrivals!

Mr. Styngy was in the dining-room, in an agony of doubt and fear.

Half-past, and still no welcome rattle of carriage wheels on the gravel-drive brought relief to him.

"I must go and tell them to put back the dinner," said Mr. Styngy, desperately. "They must come soon."

Noodles punctually obeyed his orders. Exactly as the hall clock chimed the half-hour, did that gentleman make his appearance in the passage, bearing a huge tureen of smoking soup.

Lionel and Charlie saw him, and the warning whistle was given; but in vain, for Tommy was fast asleep as a top.

Tommy was quite invisible to Noodles, for that gentleman had his eyes carefully fixed on the tureen, which was quite full, lest he should spill any, and he was debating whether he should kick at the door for somebody to open it, or set the tureen down, and open it himself.

Before he could decide this knotty question, the door was suddenly opened by Mr. Styngy. He took one step forward, kicked against Tommy, stumbled, and fell face forward in the scalding soup!

The tureen fell from Noodles' hands, and he clasped his falling master in his arms, writhing and roaring with agony.

Need we say that Tommy Codlings was aroused, when we record that two quarts, at least, of the boiling soup fell just below the tail of his jacket?

He bounced up like an india-rubber ball, his mouth wide open, his eyes starting almost out of their sockets, and with both his hands pressed tightly behind him. He uttered an awful yell, and tore down the passage like a maniac, and without the least notion of what had happened to him, except, perhaps, a general idea that he was on fire.

The assistants were out of the drawing-room in a twinkling, and the reason of the disorder was laconically explained by Noodles.

"He chucked hisself into the soup tooreen!"

"Impossible!" exclaimed the assistant-masters in chorus.

"Get me some water!—some oil!—I'm scalded to death! Oh!" groaned Mr. Styngy.

The situation admitted of no delay. Mr. de Bewty hurried to his bedroom for his water jug. Crocklejack raced to the kitchen to get a flask of oil from the cook; while Professor Tomkini did the wisest thing of all, and went for a doctor.

The oil, the water, and the doctor, arrived about the same moment. The assistant-masters were hustled into the background; Noodles was ordered to carry his master to his bedroom; and then, with the dexterity of a conjurer, the doctor oiled his smarting visage, and covered it with a thick layer of cotton wool, keeping up the while a running fire of questions as to how the accident happened.

"Very unfortunate, very!" said the doctor. "Dinner party, too, I hear, isn't there?"

"There be a dinner," said Noodles; "but there baint no paarty!"

"Eh?" said the doctor, not understanding the odd man.

"Quite true, sir," added Mr. Crocklejack. "Mr. Styngy had issued invitations for a dinner party this evening, but no one has come!"

Mr. Styngy was unable to speak on account of the cotton wool; but he gave a confirmatory groan and wriggle.

The doctor shook his head dubiously.

"Very strange," he said aside to Crocklejack and De Bewty; "it really seems as if some malignant fate had taken a spite against our friend, in heaping all these misfortunes upon him in succession."

"It does indeed, sir," sighed Crocklejack, who had a presentiment of coming misfortune. He knew that the head master would propose to cut down his and De Bewty's salary, to make up, in some degree, for the loss he had sustained.

"And I hear, too, that a Mr. Trixham Trot is about to set up a school in rivalry to this?"

"Quite true, sir."

"Ah! I hear he's a very smart fellow. Tell our friend, Styngy, to keep his eyes open."

A cool recommendation, rather, coming from the doctor, who had just carefully plastered them up with oil and cotton wool; but Mr. Styngy had not heard the words, and so it was of little consequence.

"The mystery to me is, how it happened," continued the doctor. "Mr. Styngy usually walks so stately and slowly, that it is difficult to conceive him slipping or stumbling."

"There wos a boy in it," said Noodles, at this juncture.

"A boy! what boy?" exclaimed De Bewty, Crocklejack, and Tomkini, altogether.

"I can't say, sir, 'cos I didn't see him; but I heard him squeal when the soup went over him."

That was enough for the assistant-masters, and, with one impulse, they hurried out to search for any boy who was scalded, and denounce him as the miscreant who had endangered Mr. Styngy's life.

Poor Tommy's chance of escape was small indeed!

CHAPTER LXV.

IN WHICH THE GREAT JUMBARELLO DISAPPEARS, AND THE BOUNDING BLUE-NOSED BABOON OF THE BANKS OF THE BOMBENDAH MAKES ITS FIRST APPEARANCE BEFORE AN ENGLISH AUDIENCE—MR. BELLERS' OPENING SPEECH—THE VINEGARY OLD GENTLEMAN OBJECTS TO ILLUSTRATE DARWIN'S ORIGIN OF SPECIES—A LONG-LOST FATHER.

IT would have been as easy to wake one of the Seven Sleepers as Sam Scarecrow after he had had what *he* called a good supper, with a proportionate allowance of beer, and so Mr. Bellers and Long Jem, after two or three attempts, gave it up for a bad job, and carried him up to the room which they were all three to share.

With the dawn, though, they were up again, and found the old place—half hostelry, half farm—all alive with the dairy maids and farm labourers come in from the fields to breakfast.

Sam would have dearly liked an hour longer between the coarse, but clean sheets of the inn; but the certainty of getting no breakfast if he delayed, made him hurry, and he was down in the long low kitchen as soon as the showmen.

There was milk and huge loaves of bread, which seemed only fit for a giant to handle. Such fat pork, that a microscope would have been required to detect the faintest streak of lean; smoking dishes of fried ham and eggs, and a huge pot of what passed for coffee, but was more probably a decoction of ground beans and chicory.

It was after the breakfast—to which, we need not say, Sam did ample justice, despite his heavy supper—that the new plan was unfolded to that lanky youth, very much to his astonishment.

"Why, wot the doose are you a goin' to make on me next?" said Sam, with an air of deep injury upon him. "That there Jumbarello were bad enough; but I'm dashed if I likes bein' turned into a monkey."

"Don't you see it's all for your own good, Sam?"

"No, I don't," replied Sam, very shortly.

"Well, it is then. D'ye s'pose that detective chap 'll let you alone when he's to get fifty pound by it, to say nothing of revenge for the trick we played on him."

Sam's long features grew a little longer at this. He had almost forgotten that little circumstance till it was brought to his mind.

"And the skin's werry light, and the work's werry easy," continued Mr. Bellers. "All you'll have to do 'll be to sit in the cage when we shows, and jump about a bit when I stirs you up with the pole."

"And you knows," added Long Jem, as a clencher, "that you always gets your grub reg'lar, and plenty on it."

"I knows I do," said Sam, touched by this last appeal to his feelings. "All right, I'll do it."

Then came the settling of the score, the hearty good-bye, and then the jolting of the old caravan; which Sam, however, had grown to like heartily, and regard as a second home.

The alteration of the monkey's skin—so that Sam's angular limbs might go safely into it—was Long Jem's task, as he was the official property-man of the caravan; and many a curse—not loud, but deep—did he utter over the difficulty of his task.

And when that was done, there was Sam to be trained. Monkeys—although some philosophers claim for them relationship to the human race—do not exactly walk, sit, and eat after the manner of mankind.

So the long youth had to be taught how to squat on his haunches, and spring from thence to a parallel bar or trapeze; how to scratch himself, and how to grin and chatter in a properly ferocious way.

To the great delight of the showmen, Sam took to it wonderfully. He was as active as a cat in spite of his awkward shape; and he had no more fear of falling from a height than the animal he represented.

"Lor, if it ain't as nat'ral as life. The real monkey hisself couldn't do it better," said Mr. Bellers.

"That's open to argyment," said Long Jem; "but cander compels me to admit that he ain't bad."

"Not bad! He'll make our fortunes."

"Look here," said Long Jem, struck with an idea—a very rare occurrence; "why shouldn't he tell fortunes?"

"Tell fortunes!" said Mr. Bellers a little taken aback.

"Ah! there's learned pigs; why shouldn't there be learned monkeys?"

Mr. Bellers looked for a moment at his friend and partner, lost in admiration; and then he gave him a slap on the back, that set him coughing for five minutes.

"That's an egstraonary idee," he said—"that's a magnifishent idee; and if I don't stand the best supper old Nopples at the Three Lobster Pots can give us, may I never make a pitch again."

* * * *

Again was Sam made famous on mighty posters, printed in all the colours that the local printing office could furnish; but not as the Great Jumbarello. No. Sam was now glorified as "The Bounding Blue-nosed Baboon of the Banks of Bombendah!"

Then followed, in smaller type, a list of his marvellous achievements; including, of course, the fortune telling, and the *singing of a song* in the African dialect, spoken by his captors, one of whom would accompany him on the tom-tom.

"It's a bootiful bill," said Long Jem; "but how about the tom-tom; we ain't got ne'er a thing as will do, onless it's the big drum."

"That's easy enough," returned Mr. Bellers. "Get a empty butter tub at the grocer's, stretch a bladder over the end, make it dirty, and there you are."

These and all other preliminaries had been concluded, when the time came to raise the barrier at the entrance to the huge canvas tent, which Mr. Bellers, anticipating "large and crowded audiences," had purchased of a brother showman retiring from business.

There was a rush when the "doors" were opened, and both Mr. Bellers and Jem had as much as they could do for twenty minutes to take the money, and then Mr. Bellers returned to introduce the monkey and give the preliminary lecture.

Mr. Bellers was rather proud of this piece of patter, as he had happened to pick up a second-hand copy of "Darwin on the Origin of Species," and introduced some of the arguments from that famous book, altered and flavoured to suit his own taste.

This introductory address was an immense success, for Mr. Bellers, with a showman's ready wit, printed his remarks relative to the connection between the Simian and the Human species by pretending to find marked resemblances between the ugliest and most ill-tempered of the audience and the blue-nosed baboon.

These sallies were received with uproarious applause by all except of course the unlucky individuals alluded to.

Of these, the most annoyed was a very vinegary-looking old gentleman, who satisfied himself with audibly growling his displeasure the first two or three times; but his hot temper got the better of him, and, rising, he shook his stick violently at Mr. Bellers.

"You darned impudent scoundrel!" he roared. "How dare 'ee do't."

"There, ladies and gentlemen," continued the unmoved Mr. Bellers; "the resemblance is now more plainer than ever. In fact, it seems to me that there may be a closer relationship atween the parties than we knows on. Were you ever in Africky, sir?"

The little joke was fully appreciated, and the audience burst into a tremendous roar of laughter. The old gentleman shouted and flourished his stick till he was breathless with rage.

Just then Sam thought that it was high time for him to take an active part in the joke, and, making a tremendous spring, he bounded through the air and clasped the sour old gentleman in his arms, uttering, as he sprang, in a sharp, shrill squeak—"*Me long los' fader!*"

FOLLOW MY LEADER.

AS MR. STYNGY ENTERED THE ROOM, HE LURCHED FORWARD, AND TOOK AN INVOLUNTARY DRAUGHT OF SOUP.

CHAPTER LXVI.

THE LONG LOST FATHER STRONGLY OBJECTS TO THE CLAIMS OF HIS RELATIVE—SO DOES THE LONG LOST MOTHER, WITH AN UMBRELLA—MR. BELLERS THREATENED WITH SOMETHING "HOT" FOR HIMSELF—HE REPLIES WITH AN OFFER OF A LITTLE "COLD WITHOUT"—A GOOD DAY'S WORK—PEACE AND PLENTY, ESPECIALLY OF THE ROSY WINE—THE EVENING'S ENJOYMENT, AND THE MORNING'S REFLECTION.

MR. BELLERS had seen Sam's movement, but not quickly enough to prevent it. He made a desperate grab at his tail, but that frail member parted close to the root, and the desperate leap was done.

The audience were for a few moments dumb with astonishment at hearing a monkey (for they never doubted but that it was a real one) speak intelligible English; but their surprise soon merged into laughter, and peal after peal of boisterous merriment shook the frail supports of the tent.

"Murder!" gasped the old gentleman, half frantic with terror. "Git un off. Do'er year. Oh, lor! It's t' ould un! Murder! Help!"

Here an elderly lady, the very counterpart in petticoats of the old gentleman, elbowed her way through the crowd, and gave Sam such a punch in the ribs, that with a gasp, he unwound his arms from his "long los' fader's" neck, and taking a couple of somersaults backwards, was promptly grabbed by Mr. Bellers, and secured by a piece of rope thick enough for a ship's cable.

"Ladies and genelmen," roared Mr. Bellers, at the topmost pitch of his voice. "The hanimal is now under the control of a two-inch rope, which will affectooilly restrain his family infections. You can sit down, sir," he added to the irate old gentleman. "If you don't want to claim your young relation, there ain't no call on you to do it. *I* don't want to part with him."

Another roar of laughter from the audience, who began to settle into their places once more.

"What," ejaculated the old lady, in a scream of forty locomotive power—"what does the imperent willin' say, Gearge? I'll '*relation*' him and his monkey."

And flourishing her umbrella in a manner worthy of some doughty champion of the chivalric age, she charged over the rails towards Mr. Bellers.

That gentleman was always ready for any little emergency of this sort, and, without moving an inch, he called out—

"Jem, pass the hose o' the fire-engine, and turn the water on."

Long Jem appeared in an instant with the tube of an old garden-engine, which Mr. Bellers had bought with the tent.

"Now, mum," said Mr. Bellers, holding the nose in a direct line with the old lady, "I ain't considered disrespeckful in a gin'ral way to the fair secks, but this here stage is privit, and if you comes on it, it will be my onpleasant dooty to spile that werry putty bonnet as you've got on."

Here Mr. Bellers showed his diplomacy in dealing with an angry woman. If he had threatened her with personal violence, she would have charged him like a bull—all the more enraged because of the red-rag of defiance—but to spoil her new bonnet, the pride of her heart! The idea was too dreadful. She was vanquished, and retreated at once.

"That's right, mum," said Mr. Bellers encouragingly; "you're a sensible woman, and there's only one fault in you, my good mum—you won't own your poor relation."

Another tremendous roar, under cover of which the old gentlemen and his missus sailed out, trembling with wrath, and declaring, in very unsaintly language, "that they would have the lor on that impident wagabone."

"That's gratitood," said Mr. Bellers, addressing the audience. "I become the humble means of bringing relations together from the furderest corners of the airth, and all I gits for it is a threat to hev the lor on me."

"Shame!" howled the audience.

Just then, Sam managed to pick Mr. Bellers' coat pocket of his handkerchief, and was wiping his eyes in the most pathetic manner, in token of his grief at the abrupt departure of his supposed father.

This burst of pathos, of course, sent the spectators into another fit of laughter, and, in a word, Sam's performance was a complete success.

The tent was filled again and again with spectators, eager to see the wonderful monkey who could do everything but talk, and could even manage a little of that, and the private money-box of the showman was filled to overflowing.

The proprietors of the opposition shows were mad with jealousy. In vain did they bang their big drums, and almost crack their cheeks upon already cracked trombones and cornets-à-pistons, while their mates dilated upon the wonders and beauties to be seen inside.

Giants, dwarfs, bearded ladies, spotted boys, calves with half a dozen legs, fat women, all paled their ineffectual fires before the marvellous monkey.

At length the day was over. Mr. Bellers dismissed his last audience with an announcement that the wonderful Blue-nosed Baboon would be on view every day till further notice—the health of the illustrious baboon, which was delicate, permitting.

"We'll hev a buster over this," said Mr. Bellers, when the three—red-hot, but triumphant with success—had closed the tent, and were in the seclusion of the caravan; "you remembers old Nopples, Jem?"

Long Jem replied with a wink. He had used up too much wind that day, to have any left for unnecessary speech.

"Well, he'll reklect us when we used to work this circuit ten year ago, and, if he ain't changed, he's the chap to turn us out a supper that'll make Sam, there, grin agin. Ah! and he's got a bottle of good wine in his cellar, too, and dash me, but we'll hev a few."

"That's open to argyment," gaped Long Jem, slowly; "leastways, so far as the boy's consarned. If he's seen out o' the carawan, he'll bust the 'ole affair."

"Dash it, I never thought o' that," said Mr. Bellers—"I never thought o' that."

"And you jist mind this," said Sam, getting greatly excited at the bare prospect of missing the luscious treat the showman had sketched out. "I ain't goin' to be done out o' that supper now, you mind that, or I never puts this blessed dress on agin."

And the long youth, who had not yet divested himself of his hairy attire, began tugging vengefully at the head-piece, as if he meant to bring it up by the roots.

"Stop Sam, stop!" exclaimed the showman; "you shall go. It's all right, Jem; we can rig him out with a piller under his weskut, and nobody 'ud know him agin."

"That won't do," said Sam, decisively; "no pillers for me."

"Wot for, you aggrawatin' chap?"

"Where's the wittles to go?" demanded Sam, sullenly. "If I has my weskit buttoned over a piller, I shan't be able to get a tater down."

"That's heasy got over," said the showman. "We'll hev a privit room, and when the wittles is on, you can drop the piller."

With this arrangement all had to be satisfied, for time was passing with relentless speed, and they were all tremendously hungry.

Fortunately Mr. Nopples, the landlord of the "Three Lobster Pots" was unchanged by the lapse of ten years.

Everything that could contribute to Mr. Bellers' notions of a good supper was ordered, and checked off by the landlord, until the list was of such a length, that Mr. Nopples demanded how many were going to partake of the supper.

"Three," said Mr. Bellers. "Here we are; it'll make four if you'll jine."

"Gracious me!—and you've got enough here for thirty. Wot's the little game? Are you goin' to eat for a wager?"

"Not we, Jo Nopples; but I've hed a fust-rate day, and I means to hev a fust-rate supper, and a bottle or two o' wine arter."

"Well, and ye can hev a good supper, Bellers, without orderin' enow for a ridg'ment o' sodgers! Why, you'd hev to eat your supper in two rooms, if I cooked all you've got down here, and it 'd take a couple o' days to get it ready. You leave it to me, and I'll send ye up a rare supper in an hour."

Their confidence in Mr. Nopples was rewarded. In less than the promised hour there appeared, in quick succession, a leg of mutton boiled to a turn, with appropriate accompaniments, two boiled fowls, two roast ditto, plenty of vegetables and home-made bread; and finally, a cold apple pie of prodigious size, and a piece of cheese, so strong that the very smell was strong enough to knock a man down.

Sam's pillow was under the table the instant the boiled mutton was under his nose, and such a a knife and fork did he play, that the landlord, who joined them at supper, could not refrain from expressing his admiration.

"Is he allers like that?" he inquired.

"Pretty nigh; he don't care wot he pecks—bread and cheese or boiled mutton's all the same to him."

"It must come pretty hevey on the hexchequer, Bellers. You need hev a good day, and a good many on 'em, if you has him to keep."

"Oh, he's a good lad, and arns his grub. But where's the wine, Nopples? I swore I'd hev a bottle or two, and it's well knowed as I never breaks my word."

"Wot shall it be—port or sherry?"

"Let's see; there's four un us. Bring up arf-a-dozen, Jo, three of each sort—that won't hurt us."

"Well, it's rare good stuff, or I wouldn't anser for that. You ain't used to tackin' a couple o' bottles o' wine under your belts; but there's nothing like 'spear'nce."

Their experience the next morning was that commonly felt by gentleman who have indulged too freely in alcoholic fluids. Their throats felt as if lined with scorched parchment, and each one's head was one tremendous conglomeration of aches, of all sizes and patterns; while the rest of their bodies burned with a consuming fever, and their hands shook as if with the palsy.

"Jem," said Mr. Bellers, in the feeblest and huskiest of whispers.

"Hullo!" came the reply, fainter and huskier still.

"Water," was Mr. Beller's laconic demand.

"Git 't yerself," was Long Jem's ill-tempered reply.

"I can't move; I'm too ill."

"I'm wuss."

"You're a liar; you can't be wuss—no man could."

"That's open to argyment; an' if I could get hout o' bed, Bellers, I'd drop you a prop on the nose for that."

"It wouldn't be no good; I'm that dry, there ain't a drop o' blood in my weins."

Just then a groan, long and dismal, came from Sam's bed, and that young gentleman feebly pushed back the coverlet from his head, and tried to raise himself.

Sam was never, at the best of times—as our readers have seen by the life-like portraits of "Phiz"—what is usually termed handsome; on this fatal morning he was absolutely hideous—about as good-looking, say, as a dead gentleman, who has been forgotten by his despairing relatives, and left out in the sun for a week.

"There's the boy at it now."

"Well, he's got as much right as you, ain't he?" said the surly Jem.

"No, he ain't. He's a boy; wot bisness had he to get tight?"

"Wot bisness had you to show him the way?" was Jem's scathing reply.

This was too much. Mr. Bellers made an effort, leaned out of bed, grabbed a boot, and flung it at Long Jem.

He was too exhausted to look for himself and see if his aim had been true, but he heard a faint husky howl, and that was quite as satisfactory.

Whether or no Long Jem would have retaliated will never be known, for at that moment the jolly voice of Mr. Nopples was heard at the door, and then that gentleman himself appeared, bearing three pint glasses, with a dose of brandy in each, and a corresponding number of bottles of soda-water, at the very sight of which the thirsty ones gasped with rapture.

What a draught that was! what nectar! So thought Mr. Bellers, Long Jem, and Sam, as, with the gas in their throats and noses, they held out their glasses and demanded more.

They had a second bottle apiece, and still thirsted for a third; but Mr. Nopples resolutely refused.

"Not me," he said; "why, you'd blow up and bust, or else float out o' the winder like berloons. You just give yourselves a good freshener with cold water, and come down to breakfast. Yer ain't got much time to lose if you're going to show this mornin'."

"I don't think I'm ekal to it," said Mr. Bellers.

"I don't blow no thundering old trumpets, nor beat no dashed old drums to-day," growled Long Jem.

Sam was about to assert his incapability of performing as well, when a look from Mr. Bellers stopped him.

"I tell you wot it is, Nopples," he said; "none on us ain't fit to show to-day. I ain't had such a tyin'-up since my weddin' day, so I'll just get up and go down to the tent and stick up a notice that in consekens o' the illness of the great baboon, the performances is suspended till to-morrow."

"I likes the idea," growled Long Jem. "I agrees to that."

"It'll only stimulate their appetites," Mr. Bellers continued, as he got painfully out of bed, "and we shall do all the better to-morrow."

But if Mr. Bellers had only known what mischief his enemies would do while he was making holiday, no headaches or feverish throats would have kept him from his tent that day.

CHAPTER LXVII.

MR. JOHN JUBILEE PLAYS THE SPY, AND FALLS IN WITH LIONEL AND CHARLIE, WHO GIVE HIM A QUANTITY OF VALUABLE INFORMATION, WHICH IS HARDLY APPRECIATED—NOODLES UNDER THE PUMP—MR. TRIXHAM TROT RETURNS TO THE OLD MANOR HOUSE—THE MESSAGE TO DE BEWTY—THE MEETING—"BLOOD, IAGO! BLOOD!"

MR. JOHN JUBILEE, the factotum of Trixham Trot, Esquire, did not find his task quite so easy or pleasant as he had imagined.

He waited about the school gates for some likely boys to "pump," but unluckily for himself he pitched upon Lionel and Charlie Drummond.

Our hero and his chum had already noticed Mr. Jubilee loitering in the road, peeping in at the school gates when he thought he was unobserved, and otherwise acting very much after the fashion of a spy, and with utmost artlessness they put themselves purposely in his way, to ascertain, as they very strongly suspected, whether or no he was an emissary of Mr. Trot.

"Good afternoon, young gentlemen," said John, politely, as he passed them by the purest accident in the world, of course. "Nice day."

"Beautiful," replied Lionel and Charlie, together.

"Going for a walk, I suppose?" said Mr. Jubilee, blandly.

"Yes—we thought of doing so," replied Lionel, as mildly as if he had never done anything worse than sing Dr. Watts' hymns all his life. "The country is so pretty and beautiful, with the birds singing and the trees waving, and the brooks flowing on so calmly. Don't you think so, sir?"

"Hallo!" thought Mr. Jubilee, to himself. "There's a couple of soft uns here. I shall get all I want out of these chaps easy."

Then he said aloud—

"Yes, my dear young gentlemen—you are perfectly right. There is indeed something very different in the lovely serenity of the country from the folly and dissipation of the town. You must indeed have excellent moral teachers at your school. That was your school I saw you come out of, I believe?"

"Oh, yes!" chorussed the two young hypocrites, lifting up their eyes as if the school was only just a shade below paradise.

"It's indeed delightful to see the young so excellently trained," continued Mr. Jubilee. "I have boys of my own, and when they are old enough, I shall certainly send them here. May I inquire the names of the masters?"

Lionel gave them with becoming gravity, and the factotum made a note of each in his pocket-book.

"Charming names," he said, "the very sound is enough to fascinate a parent's ear. This Mr. de Bewty, here. There's a name for a schoolmaster!"

"Not half good enough," said Lionel.

"You don't say so! Is he indeed so good a man? I should like to know him. He don't happen to be anywhere about—in sight I mean?"

"Oh, no, he never goes out of doors," said Lionel.

"Never! That's a curious fancy."

"It is rather. When he wants a little fresh air, he gets a ladder and climbs on to the roof and sits on the kitchen chimney-pot till the servants light the fire and it gets too warm for him."

"Is this chap a chaffin' of me?" thought Mr. Jubilee. But, as Lionel's face was calm and serene as that of a sleeping infant, Mr. de Bewty was eccentric, that was all.

So he said aloud—

"Rum taste, rather."

"Yes," said Lionel, "but you see his temper is very hasty, and several times when he has been out walking, he has nearly killed people who have been rude to him, so now he stops indoors."

"Dashed queer story, this," mused Mr. Jubilee, getting a little puzzled. "Blow me if I can make out whether they're a chaffin of me or not."

"But he is such a good man," Lionel resumed, suddenly, as if he had been meditating on the excellence of Mr. de Bewty and couldn't hold his praises in any longer. "He thinks of going out as missionary next year, to Africa."

"I'll bet he don't, if my guv'ner gets hold of him," thought Mr. Jubilee, but he only said aloud—

"A good man indeed, young gentlemen."

"You see," continued Lionel, "the savages over there are in a dreadful state of ignorance. They don't even know the use of pocket-handkerchiefs; but I hardly like to say it, it's so vulgar."

"Oh, never mind me."

"Well, they actually blow their noses with their fingers," said Lionel, in a tone of awe, "and missionaries are to be sent out with a ship load of pocket handkerchiefs, to teach them this great step in civilization."

"Dash it, they must be a sellin' of me," thought Mr. Jubilee. "No one would be such a dashed fool as to send out handkerchers to flat-nosed niggers."

"Won't you contribute a mite towards the mission, sir," said Lionel, holding out his hand. "We don't take less than half-a-crown as a rule, but as your moral character is so high, we'll let you off with a bob."

"Very sorry," mumbled the spy; "no small change. I'll send a post office order to-morrer. By-the-by, I might meet Mr. de Bewty, and then I could give it to him. What sort of a man is he?"

"Didn't I say he never went out of doors?" replied our hero, "but if you see him sitting on the top of the chimney, and hold out half-a-crown, he'll come down to you. He's a very tall, big man, seven feet high, with a wooden leg and red hair, and he always has a telescope and a blunderbuss with him, on account of the cats."

"Now," said Mr. Jubilee, waxing suddenly wrathful, "do you expect me to believe all this?"

"I don't expect anything," replied Lionel, carelessly; "but you can, if you like, you know."

"Dash you, you've bin a chaffin' me all through," roared Mr. John Jubilee, losing his temper, and making a futile rush at Lionel and Charlie. "I've been took in by a couple of dashed schoolboys. Only let me get hold of you, that's all!"

"Good-bye, John," said Lionel, cheerfully, sending a good shot at the spy's name. "Whenever you want a little more information, don't forget us."

"And remember to look up at the chimney-pot, if you want to see Mr. de Bewty," added Charlie. "About four o'clock's the best time."

Mr. Jubilee made another rush at Lionel and Charlie, but he might as well have chased a couple of wild goats amongst the Welsh hills.

"Them boys is the wery dooce. To think of *me* being took in like that. I only wish we had 'em at our school, I'd give 'em a turn. If all the other boys is like them two, I shan't get to know what I wants in a month. Hallo! who's this a coming?"

This happened to be Mr. Noodles, who sauntered out of the gates in his usual leisurely way, but with an expression of extra solemnity upon his manly features.

"He'll do," thought Mr. Jubilee, after a moment's scrutiny. "There ain't no games about *him*."

"Mornin'," he said aloud, as Noodles approached.

"Mornin'," growled the odd man, in reply.

"I'm a stranger 'bout here," continued the spy, and as my walking made me thirsty, I thought you might be able to tell me where they sell the best in the village yonder."

Noodles looked up hopefully. He had quarrelled with the cook that morning, and she had cut off his allowance of beer. He had no money, and less credit at the inn; but here was a chance of slaking his thirsty throttle.

"You've hit on the right man, mate," he said. "I'll show 'ee—I wur goin' there myself."

"You looks like a man as knows a good drop o' stuff when he sees it," said Mr. Jubilee.

"Reyther!" replied Noodles, with the nearest approach to a wink his heavy eyelids could manage. "But tastin' of it's the way to tell."

"Right you are," said Mr. Jubilee, approvingly; "You're the chap for my money. Is this the crib?"

Mr. Noodles signified that that was the inn honoured by his patronage, and they entered, the landlord eyeing Noodles with a strong glare, intended to remind him of a long and unpaid score.

But he speedily became civil when Mr. Jubilee ordered two pints of the best old Stingo, two screws of tobacco, and a couple of pipes.

Here's luck!" was Jubilee's laconic toast, as he raised his mug to his lips.

Then Noodles echoed the sentiment, and when he put his mug down there was just enough ale left to drown a melancholy blue-bottle, who had, apparently, been crossed in love.

"Have another!" suggested Mr. Jubilee.

"You're werry kind; don't mind if I do," rejoined Noodles, who had no scruples whatever about drinking at a stranger's expense.

"Rare good stuff," continued the spy; "don't keep such up at your place, do they?"

"Wot our guv'nor? Not he; Styngy by name, and stingy by nature—that's wot he is."

"Ah! like all the rest on 'em. There's only one advantige in livin' at school, and that's the opportunity a man has of improvin' his mind; now, anyone can see, with half a hye, that you're a superior bloke."

"Hem!" coughed Mr. Noodles, who always bolted his flattery whole. "I ain't far behind some on 'em."

"I should think not. I took you for one o' the masters."

"No, I ain't exactly one o' the masters; not in the schoolroom, you know. I could be, if I liked, but the boys werrit a man so. As for larnin', I won't say anythin' 'bout that; but you should ha' seen me at the Spellin' Bee, a while ago."

"Ah!" said Mr. Jubilee, "you floored some on 'em, eh?"

"I just did," replied Noodles, emphatically.

And this time he told the truth, as our readers will remember.

"There was a chap I knowed once," said Mr. Jubilee, leading up to the point he wanted to reach, "as was a rare good speller—he was a schoolmaster, too, and his name was De Bewty."

"De Bewty!" exclaimed Noodles. "Why we've got a' chap o' that name at our place, as pertends he can teach. Why, though he's only a poor man, I've forgot more than he ever knowed."

"P'r'aps it's the same chap," said Mr. Jubilee "What is he like?"

"A young-looking cove, thin as a herrin', werry flash in his dress, wears about two pound of copper watch chains, and pins, and rings, and he fancy we thinks 'em gold—ha, ha!"

"That's the werry chap," said Mr. Jubilee. "I'm glad I've found him, for there's a little account atween us, which he never settled, but I means to make him. Would you mind givin' of him this note from me? I shouldn't be able to get nigh him for a week myself, he's such a shuffler."

"In course I will," said Noodles, readily. "Give us hold."

"Don't forget it. You can say it was left at the gate."

"Let's have another pint," said Noodles.

They had another pint, and then they parted, mutually satisfied. Noodles returned to the school quite oblivious of the errand on which he had been sent by Mr. Styngy.

At the gate stood the very gentleman he sought. Mr. de Bewty was looking mournfully up at the sky, and seeking there a solution of this problem—Given, a salary of twenty pounds per annum, paid quarterly; required, to maintain an irreproachable position, and to keep out of debt upon that sum.

In the very midst of this Noodles pounced down upon him with the note, and smiled sardonically as the tutor turned it over and over, and then slowly opened it.

He had not read half a dozen lines, when he staggered back against the gate, and, with a wild look in his eyes, asked Noodles who had left the note.

"A big chap," replied Noodles—"gen'leman, I should say, 'bout six foot and a 'arf 'igh, and strong as a bull. He giv' me five shillins, and said you was to attend to the letter immediate."

"Shut the gates, Noodles," exclaimed Mr. de Bewty, in an agony of terror; "and if that person comes again, don't let him in. He's a madman."

"I can't shut the gates without horders from the guv'nor," replied the odd man; "and as for the gen'leman, he ain't no more mad than you be."

Mr. de Bewty waited for no more, but, casting a fearful glance up and down the road, he turned and ran into the school as fast as his long legs could carry him, never stopping till he reached the bedroom occupied in common by himself and Crocklejack.

Mr. Crocklejack was there, examining some shirts, and mourning over their dilapidated condition, when his fellow-usher rushed in, locked the door, and sank down, pale and exhausted, upon one of the beds.

"What on earth's the matter?" demanded Mr Crocklejack, turning pale himself. "Is it fire?"

"No," moaned De Bewty. "Worse than that."

"What is it, then?"

"This letter," he panted, holding out the missive. "I'm a dead man, Crocklejack."

"Nonsense; you're not dead yet, anyhow, and how can a letter kill you?"

"Read it. It's awful. It's from that fiend, Trixham Trot."

"You don't say so? Give it to me."

Mr. Crocklejack eagerly snatched the letter from his friend's hand, and read as follows—

"Mr. Trixham Trot respects himself, and the noble profession to which he has the honour to belong, to retort upon you in the filthy and disgusting language you have not scrupled to use; but he begs to inform you that the instant he returns from London, he will do himself the pleasure of pulling your nose, punching your head, and kicking you until you or his boots are wore out. And as soon after as may be possible, he will send a friend to meet any friend of yours (if a man stooped so low in blackguardism is possessed of one), and arrange for a meeting. Pistols!"

"There—what do you think of that?" panted Mr. de Bewty.

"Think of it," repeated Crocklejack, rising and shaking him warmly by the hand. "Why, that you are a hero, De Bewty. Our respected principal placed his honour in your hands, and you will not disgrace him."

"Eh!" said Mr. de Bewty, with a vague stare of wonder.

"When did you send the challenge to this villain, Trot? You might have told me, De Bewty."

"I—I never sent him a challenge," De Bewty almost shrieked.

"Come, come now, that won't do. None of this among friends, De Bewty. It's very well done, but you shouldn't try it on me. It's really noble of you, old fellow, to stand up for the governor like this."

"That I didn't. I won't—I'll have the police in. I'm not going to be murdered in cold blood!" exclaimed the unhappy victim of Lionel's practical joke, as he rose from the bed, and performed a frantic dance about the room.

"Of course not. You'll have as good a chance as he will. You're a capital shot, for I've heard you say so. Now first, about the assault. You'll pull his nose, I suppose, and kick him a little, just to give him good grounds for fighting."

"Me? Why, he's a fellow seven feet high, and as strong as an elephant. Noodles told me so."

"All the more credit to you, De Bewty. You'll do it easily. These big fellows are always clumsy."

"But I tell you I won't have it. I'm not going to pull anybody's nose. I'm not going to fight. It's all a mistake. It—it—must have been you they meant."

"Oh, no," said Mr. Crocklejack, with great promptitude; "there's the name too plain for that.

MR. STYNGY DROPPED HIS INSTRUMENT OF TORTURE AS THE CLOUD OF SNUFF AROSE AND SET EVERYONE SNEEZING.

No. 15.

But you leave it all to me, old fellow. I'll see you safe through it."

"Will you—will you, though?" gasped De Bewty, clutching his friend firmly by the hand.

"Yes; trust to me. I'll see this Trixham Trot—or whoever he sends—and arrange it all. I don't care if he's ten feet high."

"You're a true friend," exclaimed De Bewty, fervently. "I don't know how to thank you, Crocklejack."

"Thank me when it's all over," he replied, putting the letter in his pocket, and leaving the room. "By-by, old fellow; keep your spirits up."

When Mr. Crocklejack was fairly outside the door, he indulged in a chuckle indicative of much silent merriment; and meanwhile his thoughts ran thus—

"What a precious ass that De Bewty is! He thinks I'm going to play the peacemaker, and prevent the duel. Ha—ha—ha! Let's see, how can I manage it? I had better go and see this Trixham Trot, work him up into a tremendous passion—he seems to be a regular fire-eater—make an appointment for the fight in some quiet place, take De Bewty there under the belief that it is for a reconciliation. That'll do. I'll be off at once."

CHAPTER LXVIII.

THE PLOT CONCERNING THE DUEL IS A LITTLE FURTHER DEVELOPED—LIONEL AND HIS CHUMS VISIT THE OLD MANOR HOUSE—MR. JOHN JUBILEE AGAIN—A CIVIL QUESTION AND A WELCOME OFFER—THE GROUNDS OF THE OLD MANOR HOUSE, AND WHAT OUR HERO SAW THERE.

THE anger which Mr. Styngy, in so unchristian a manner, had cherished in his breast against that unscrupulous wronger of his peace—Mr. Trixham Trot—had been considerably added to by the melancholy failure of the second dinner party.

It could not be laid directly to his charge, but that was nothing; Trixham Trot had been the spoiler of the first party, and to that and to nothing else was to be attributed the wreck of number two.

"If I only had him here, within reach of me," thought the schoolmaster, wrathfully, "I fear that I should forget my peaceful profession and strike him. Yes, verily," he added, putting himself in a very scientific posture of self-defence, "I—I think I could punch his head with pleasure."

Poor Mr. de Bewty was hardly less agitated than his respected principal—but by fear, not anger. He experienced a little relief when Crocklejack offered to take the matter out of his hands; but that soon vanished, and he became as anxious as at first.

Mr. Crocklejack, indeed, was the only one of the three who derived any satisfaction out of the matter. He had arranged a little plot in his own head which promised to bring some very sweet little fish to his net, and he was jubilant.

Lionel and his chums were also in a state of glee. They had heard nearly every word that had passed between the two under-masters, and as our hero was pretty well acquainted with Crocklejack's disposition, he understood perfectly what that gentleman meant when he told De Bewty to "leave it all to him."

"It couldn't be in better hands," said Lionel, when they had reached a secluded corner of the playground. "Crocklejack will arrange the rest of the business better than we could do it, and there'll be no chance of our getting into a mess, which is something gained, especially when Tommy Codlings is in the spree."

"Thankee," said Tommy; "at me again."

"No; only a drive at your bad luck, Tommy."

"Same thing; but never mind me. I want to know, Li, if Crocklejack's going to manage all this, how shall we get any fun out of it?"

"Easily enough. We've only got to keep a sharp look out, and we shall find out when the fight comes off, never fear."

"Precious sharp, I expect," said Charlie. "They'll keep it as dark as they can, Li?"

"Of course they will; but Crocklejack won't be on his guard against us. He believes that De Bewty wrote the letter, and is frightened now and wants to get out of it."

"Well, we shall see what we shall see," said Charlie; "for it would be a shame to have the game spoiled. Fancy old De Bewty fighting a duel. He, he! Why he'd faint with fear if any one only pointed a pistol at him."

"Suppose we stroll up by the old Manor House," suggested Lionel.

"How about the practice at cricket," said Charlie. "You know you promised to go, and I want to see how you can bowl."

"Oh! that can wait. Let's have this fun out first."

"Anything you like, Li—only remember old Crocklejack's gone up there, and he may smell a rat."

"Not he. He'll only think we've come up to have a peep at the new school. Come along."

Noodles was at the gate, an unusual place for him, as he much preferred sitting to standing in general, and sleeping when there was no eating or drinking going on. Now, however, he was wide awake, and looking alternately up and down the road with great show of interest.

"Hallo!" said Lionel. "The end of the world's coming. Here's Noodles actually awake in the afternoon!"

"What's happened, Noodles?" added Charlie. "Has that wife you left in the workhouse in London come to look after you?"

"With the ten small children?" said Lionel.

"That's the beadle's cocked hat coming round the bend in the road," said Charlie. "Look out, Noodles; you'd better bolt."

"I ain't afraid o' no beadles," rejoined the odd man, with a look of contempt, "and as for wives, why I can prove I've been a single man ever since I war born."

"Come now, Noodles, that won't do. Why you were born twins."

"*Me* a twin!" exclaimed the odd man, indignantly. "I'd like to see the chap who'll dare to say he was a twin brother o' mine."

"There is one, though, and you know it, Noodles," said Lionel. "Why, don't you remember, Charlie, we saw the very image of him in Sutton village once, when we knew that Noodles was a good four miles away, and we all said that he must have over eaten himself into an apoplexy, and what we saw was his ghost."

"Of course, I do," replied Charlie, readily. "The old rascal's up to all sorts of games. I shouldn't wonder if he'd got two or three sets of twin brothers somewhere or other."

"It's no use chaffin' me about twins, as I know better," said the odd man, stolidly. "I'm a lookin' out for a genelman, as you'd better look arter if you valleys your precious skins."

"Oh, dear!" exclaimed Charlie, affecting to shiver violently. "I begin to feel so frightened. Who is it Noodles?"

"Mr. Trixham Trot," replied the odd man—"and a real genelman he is. Just the sort of a schoolmaster. He'd flay a boy easy in two minutes, and think nothink of it."

"Oh, what a nice man!" said Lionel. "What a pity we aren't at his school."

"So I thinks," added Noodles, in a sincere tone of conviction. "He's nigh on seven foot tall, and with a harm as big as my leg. That's the sort of chap as can lay it on, I should think; and you'd better be careful when you gets beyond the gates, for his own boys ain't come yet, and he said he didn't like to be hout o' practice, so he thought he'd wait about a bit on the chance of catching some of you."

"The dickens he did! I believe your yarn's all gammon, Noodles; but if it isn't, let old Trot look out for a stoning. Come on, you fellows."

And away the trio ran along the high road, and then turned into the lane which led by a short cut to the old Manor House.

"Do you believe Noodles' story?" asked Charlie, as soon as the pace admitted of conversation.

"Not all of it," replied our hero; "but Noodles has either seen or heard from Tricksy. Noodles is too slow a chap to be able to invent a whole lie."

"But, I say, if he's a chap seven feet high, and big in proportion, what will poor De Bewty do?"

"That's the part Noodles made up. I never heard of a schoolmaster seven feet high, and I don't believe there is such a thing."

"Cave," said Charlie, suddenly. "I can see the top of old Crocklejack's hat coming down the lane."

"He's coming back in a hurry, then. I wonder if Tricksy set the dogs on him or kicked him out. Don't hide you chaps; he won't stop us."

The next moment Mr. Crocklejack had turned the corner, and came along towards the boys, with a jaunty, self-satisfied air.

"Hallo! you boys," he called out, as soon as he caught sight of them; "where are you going? Don't you know this is out of bounds."

"Only a very little, sir," replied Lionel. "We were only going to take a peep at the new school."

"Ah, I dare say; and what besides was your object in going there? To fight some of Mr. Trot's boys, or insult Mr. Trot himself, or break a few of his windows? You see I know you. It happens that the house is empty—only a couple of servants are there. You may go and look at the new school if you like; but mind you are back to tea."

"Old Tricksy not there? There's a go," said Lionel. "I wonder what it means."

"That he's as big a coward as De Bewty, and he's bolted off to London to get out of the fight."

"I hope he won't, or the game's spoiled," replied our hero. "But that can't be, or Crocklejack wouldn't have looked so happy."

"I know what it is, then," said Charlie. "He's gone to get a second. You must have a second in a duel, and he don't know anybody about here whom he could ask."

"You've hit it, Charlie. That's old Tricksy's game, for a sovereign."

"We needn't go up to the Manor House now. It's no good."

"May as well, now we're so close. It's always a good plan to reconnoitre the enemy's camp."

"Let's run, then, and we shall get back in time for an innings at cricket."

A smart spin of ten minutes, and they were before the high walls which guarded the grounds of the old Manor House from vulgar intrusion.

A glance sufficed to show that it had been once a fine old building; but long neglect had done its work, and it looked as forlorn, desolate, and gloomy as Tennyson's "Moated Grange."

"Well, that is a dismal-looking old crib," was Lionel's criticism on it. "I wouldn't be a pupil there for something."

"Afraid of ghosts, eh, Li?"

"Not I. The very look of the place is enough to give anyone the 'blues' for a month; and I'll bet it's alive with rats, mice, and spiders."

"Ugh, don't," said Charlie, with a shudder. "You make one feel creepy all over. Hallo! there's somebody coming out of that little side door."

"By George, it's that chap we sold the other day," said Lionel, in a low tone. "Look out, he may be rusty."

But Mr. Jubilee, far from evincing any rancour, grinned and nodded in the most amiable way.

"He's all right, I think; but be on your guard. We three are good enough for him."

"Good arternoon, young gentlemen," said Mr. Jubilee, cheerfully, as he came towards the boys. "Nice weather for that gent o' yours as sits on the chimbly pots."

"Beautiful," replied Lionel, with a smile.

"He's up there now, may be," continued Mr. Jubilee, in the same cheerful voice; "a shootin' of the cats with that blunderbuss of his'n."

"I shouldn't wonder," said our hero, keeping a wary eye upon the good-humoured face of John.

"Ah! you reg'lar took me in that day. 'Pon my word, I half believed all you was sayin', you did it so well. But there, I don't bear no malice; I was a boy myself once."

"You do tell the truth sometimes," said Charlie.

"Ah! you're a sharp lad. You ought to be at our school. We'd do credit to you. By-the-way, I 'spose you came up to have a look at it?"

"Well, yes, we did," replied our hero, his first suspicions disarmed by Mr. John Jubilee's frank, good nature.

"Well, you can have a peep round if you like. It's the queerest old place I ever saw. There's the grounds, now—full of fountains, and statues, and secret walks—it must have been a beautiful place at one time; and as for the house itself, all I can say is that if our guv'nor gets pupils enough to fill it,, he'll have the biggest school in England."

"Well, if a fellow's governor or his mother was to come down here first, blow me if I think they'd ever let him come home, unless they wanted to drive him jolly well melancholy mad."

But Mr. Jubilee only grinned amiably as he led the way towards the little door in the wall.

Our hero and his chums passed through, and found themselves instantly in an obscurity almost as deep as night, and in the midst of so tangled and dense a growth of trees, and wild struggling plants and shrubs, that it might well have compared with some primeval forest.

"My stars, what a place for rabbiting!" said Lionel. "I suppose there's lots here, eh?"

"Plenty, as cats in a London square," replied Mr. John Jubilee. "The guv'nor's noticed it, too, and I reckon his young gen'lemen will get pretty sick of rabbit-pie afore the first half is over."

"There! I saw a beauty, then, as fat as butter," exclaimed Charlie, his eyes lighting up. "Lor'! I'd give five shillings for a half holiday here, with the little double-barrel my uncle gave me."

"Can't it be managed somehow?" said Lionel, suggestively, rattling some loose silver in his pocket.

"Not no how," replied Mr. Jubilee, pitching in a formidable negative as a final settler to the question. "The guv'nor comes back to-morrow—p'r'aps to-night; and if the servant gals in the house hears guns, they're sure to blow on me."

"Well, it's a pity, but it can't be helped," said Charlie; "and after all it don't much matter, for it's so precious dark here, that you couldn't see the beggars unless they got up under your very nose. Drive on, old cock."

This latter polite phrase was addressed to Mr. Jubilee, who immediately did as he was requested, and pushed along paths which were quite invisible to the boys, turning now to the right, now to the left, then going straight on for a little while, and then seemingly doubling upon his track, until at length he halted on the edge of what had once been a large clearing, and, stretching out his hand, said—

"What do you think o' that, young gen'lemen?"

In the centre of the clearing were the remains of what had once been a large and beautiful fountain, representing the fable of Diana and Actæon. The water no longer flowed, the lovely figures of the chaste goddess and her nymphs and of the unfortunate hunter were discoloured, but the dim light green-filtered through the dense canopy of leaves, played with a ceaseless motion on the sculptured forms, and gave them a weird semblance of life.

"I say," said Tommy Codlings, down whose back a chill of awe was coldly creeping, "let's go; I don't like the place."

"Here's Tommy funky again," said Charlie, who was nearly as uncomfortable as his chum, but would have died rather than own it.

"No, I ain't," retorted Tommy.

"Then what do you keep getting behind Li for? I say, though," continued Charlie, keeping down his own fears by the clever contrivance of chaffing Tommy, "I shouldn't wonder if at the solemn midnight hour these figures got off and walked about. Should you, Li?"

"*Don't*," almost shrieked Tommy, who became paler every minute."

"Can't say," replied our hero, who had been gazing at Diana, and wondering how she would look in a modern "pull back" costume, with her hair plaited into a pig-tail, and high heels to her boots. "Ask Grinaway."

This was an allusion to their good-humoured conductor, which Charlie instantly recognised; but turning round in search of that gentleman, he discovered that he had quietly vanished.

CHAPTER LXIX.

SOLD AGAIN—IN THE TRACKLESS WILDERNESS—THE VOICE OF THE SCORNER—TOMMY FOLLOWS ITS LEAD, AND MAKES THE ACQUAINTANCE OF SUNDRY INTERESTING SPECIMENS OF INSECT LIFE, TO BE MET WITH ONLY IN VERY STALE DITCHES—THE SEARCH FOR THE PATH RENEWED—EUREKA!—THE VOYAGE HOME—TOMMY IN LUCK AGAIN—IS TREATED TO A WARM BATH OVER NIGHT, AND PROMISED "HOT WATER" IN THE MORNING—LIONEL'S "DODGE," AND HOW IT SUCCEEDED.

"HALLO, Li!" Charlie called out. "The fellow's gone!"

"Gone! Who's gone?"

"Why the chap who brought us here."

"The dickens he has!" exclaimed Lionel, forgetting in an instant all about Diana and Actæon. "Which way has he gone? Why didn't you fellows look better after him."

"I suppose a fellow can look at a statue as well as you," growled Charlie. "Get out of the way, Tommy. What are you catching hold of me for?"

"Do—o—o—n't," shivered poor Tommy. "I—I—sa—sa—saw it move."

"Don't be an ass. Let go, I tell you," said Charlie, wresting himself away from the fear-frenzied grip of Tommy.

"Let's holloa for him first."

"That won't be of any use," said Lionel, savagely. "I see it now. He's given us the slip, to serve us out for the chaff we gave him."

"Dash the beggar!" growled Charlie. "Which way did we come in, Li?"

"I don't know," replied our hero. "I've been walking round looking at these confounded statues."

"Can't you see anything like a path anywhere?"

"Not yet; but if we walk round, and examine the bushes closely, we're sure to find one."

But they didn't; so thick was the undergrowth, so closely did the bushes intertwine their stems, that not a trace of their recent passage was visible to them. Had any of them indeed been one of those miraculous Indians, whose conversation consists of grunts, interlarded with poetry, and who possess eyes which are a combination of the microscope and telescope, they might have found the way out. Being only ordinary mortals, they failed.

"If ever I get hold of that grinning beast, I'll stone him," said Charlie.

"We'll owe him one for this," added Lionel; "but as we can't stay here all night we must find a path for ourselves."

"It wouldn't be such a bad plan to stay all night," said Charlie, with a side wink at Lionel. "I really should like to know for certain whether these statues get down and walk at midnight."

"Oh—oh—oh—oh, don't!" yelled Tommy, upon whose pallid face big beads of perspiration were standing out.

"No nonsense, Charlie—come on," said Lionel, sharply; for to tell the truth, he had lost his temper at the idea of being sold by the good-humoured Mr. Jubilee.

"Which way, then?"

"Oh! any way. All ways are alike when we don't know one of 'em."

"Then let's tie a handkerchief over Tommy's eyes, and turn him round three times, as they do at blind man's buff."

With a faint show of resistance from Tommy, he was blindfolded and turned round with such rapidity, that at the third twirl he lost his balance, and plunged head-first into a dense thicket.

"What did you shove a fellow like that for?" growled Tommy, when he was extricated and unbound. "My face and hands are scratched all to bits."

"If you say another word, Li and I will leave you alone with the statues. So behave yourself, Tommy."

Lionel took the lead, and, first cutting himself a stout hickory stick, beat down the bushes in front with a viciousness that well indicated the excessively bad temper he was in.

"Keep at it, Li," Charlie called out from time to time; "we're sure to land somewhere."

"I wish I could land this stick on that beggar's head," said Lionel.

Just then, and as if in reply to Lionel's threat, there rang through the plantation a loud mocking laugh, followed by the words—

"Don't you wish you may get him?"

"Confound him," said Lionel, coming to a full stop, and getting very red in the face; "it's that rascally grinning chap laughing at us."

"Come on, Li. The sound was just over there; he can't be far."

And turning sharply to the right, they dashed through the bushes—not to catch the adroit Mr. Jubilee—but in the hope of getting near enough to follow him.

Suddenly Lionel uttered a cry of warning, and, catching hold of a branch, brought himself up with a jerk; Charlie, who was just behind, stopped, too; but Tommy, the ever-unlucky, was too late, and, with a howl, he plunged into a very foul and evil-smelling ditch, half full of stagnant, green water, alive with creeping things, enough to make one shudder to look at.

Poor Tommy rolled in head over heels, but the next moment he came up gasping, and with a bright pea-green complexion.

Lionel and Charlie had him out in a moment, and just then the mocking laugh of Mr. Jubilee was heard again on the other side of the ditch.

"Laugh away, you beggar," said Lionel; "I'll bet you don't laugh last. It's a wonder that we weren't all in; I only caught sight of it just in time."

"Let's leave Tommy here, jump the ditch, and run him down," said Charlie.

"Not for me. Don't you see this is only another trap he's laid for us? If we follow him further we shall get into a worst mess. Poor old Tommy! help me scrape him down, Charlie."

Tommy was lying face downwards, and evidently suffering from violent internal derangement; about every minute he would heave and shudder like an earthquake, and then, if anybody had wanted to know what he had had for dinner, they could have satisfied themselves.

"Better leave him alone a little while," suggested Lionel; "it can't last long at that rate."

"He must have swallowed something precious nasty," said Charlie.

"I think he did," replied Lionel, looking at the the ditch. "Poor old chap, he must be pumped empty by this time."

"I don't know, he holds a lot," said Charlie. "Yes, there he goes again."

Another attack of shuddering, a fresh succession of spasms, and then Tommy, with a groan, rolled over on his back.

"How are you now, old fellow; better?" said Charlie, drawing cautiously near his invalid chum.

"Oh, lor!" moaned Tommy; "let me alone—let me die."

"Not a bit of it," said Lionel. "Get up and run a bit, Tommy, or you'll catch your death of cold, or ague, or something of that sort."

"My eye," muttered Charlie, "how that green stuff on him does stink; it makes me heave to go near him. Poor Tommy, and he swallowed at least a quart of it. Ugh!"

"Catch hold of him on that side, Charlie," said Lionel. "We shall have to get him along somehow."

"Can't we leave him here while we find the path?"

"We shall have trouble enough to do that, without taking the extra pains to lose it again," said Lionel, impatiently. "Come on, up with him; never mind the smell."

"Oh, ah! it's all precious fine to say 'Never mind the smell,' when my heart's in my mouth now," growled Charlie; but nevertheless he did as he was told, and hauled away on his side till Tommy was on his legs.

"Now, run him along; never mind getting your clothes torn a bit. It strikes me that we shall be lucky if we get home by bed-time."

They found their way back easily enough to the spot from which they had turned off to follow the beguiling sound of Mr. Jubilee's voice.

It was no easy task to make way through the bushes three abreast, and with only one hand apiece at liberty to push aside the thorny branches. Lionel and Charlie soon presented an appearance that would have procured them instant admission into the casual ward of any workhouse.

But their wanderings in the labyrinth were soon to be ended, for just as Charlie had declared that he could not go a step further, Lionel, in thrusting aside some branches, scraped his knuckles against a brick wall.

"Hurrah! Charlie," he said. "Found at last. Here's the wall."

Charlie dropped his share of Tommy, and hurried to the front to verify the glad tidings.

It was true enough; there was the wall, not more than twelve feet high—a mere nothing to two active school boys, aided by the trees and bushes that grew close to it. But how about the limp and helpless Tommy?

"Dash it!" growled Charlie. "I never saw such a chap. I declare, I'll never come out for a spree again. He always spoils the fun."

"Don't blame him. He can't help it—it's his luck."

"Well, let him keep his luck to himself for the future," said Charlie. "How the deuce are we to get him up that wall?"

"He's better now. Give him a shake, and ask him if he can stand."

Poor Tommy was now shivering with cold, but managed to get upon his feet.

"How are you now, old chap?"

"Awful!" moaned Tommy. "I feel like a gas-pipe. Hasn't anybody got a biscuit, or anything, in his pocket."

But neither Lionel or Charlie had anything more eatable than some beeswax and india-rubber.

"Give me a bit of india-rubber then. It's something to chew, and I'll make it last till we get home."

"We've got to get up this wall first," said Lionel. "Do you feel strong enough to climb, Tommy?"

"I'll climb anything to get out of this dashed place," was the reply.

"All right, then. I'll go first, Charlie. You give Tommy a leg up, and I'll pull him up to the top of the wall."

Lionel climbed up like a cat, and a low whistle announced that he had completed the journey.

"Now then, up with you, Tommy," said Charlie, encouragingly. "Catch hold tight."

The unlucky one commenced the ascent with far more agility then his chums had given him credit for, and he was almost within reach of Lionel's outstretched hand, when suddenly he uttered a strange gurgling noise, and fell through the tree with a crash—upsetting Charlie in his fall.

"What's the matter?" called Lionel from the top of the wall.

"That deuced ass, Tommy, swallowed the india-rubber, blow him!" mumbled Charlie; "and he's loosened all my front teeth with the heel of his boot."

And here followed a dull sound, as if the toe of Charlie's boot was making acquaintance with poor Codlings' ribs.

"Never mind; up with him again, and let's get this over. It must be seven o'clock; the sun's setting."

Another effort was made, poor Tommy being "shoved up" in the most painful and reckless manner.

"I've got him," said Lionel, as he grabbed Tommy by the collar. "Up you come."

"What did you want to keep sticking pins into me for?" demanded Hot Codlings, as Charlie scrambled up and joined his chums on the wall.

"To keep you awake, stupid-head," panted Charlie. "Do you think I wanted you to go to sleep and fall down on me again."

"No quarrelling," said Lionel. "You ought to be thankful that we haven't had to spend a night in that confounded place. Here goes for a drop."

And the next moment our hero was safe in the lane below. Charlie followed, landing lightly on his toes; and then came Tommy, landing heavily on his nose.

"He never can do anything like anybody else," said Lionel, picking him up. "Run now, Tommy, or we shall be locked out for the night."

This awful prospect made Hot Codlings put his shivering limbs to such good use, that he managed to keep up with his chums until the school gates were reached.

"There's nobody about," whispered Charlie, peering through the darkness; "and I think the gate's open."

Creeping stealthily up, crouched almost to the ground, Lionel slipped through the partly open gate, and, keeping in the shadow, slipped by two figures which were outlooking patiently for the culprits.

Charlie was equally successful, but Tommy, as a matter of course, fell into the trap.

He sneezed just as he got within the gates, and, like tigers, De Bewty and Crocklejack pounced on their prey.

"Here's one!" ejaculated tne first.

"I've got him!" cried the second.

Then, as their noses got close to Tommy, they turned their heads away with a jerk.

Phew! Powers above! what's the matter with him?" said Crocklejack.

"It's Codlings," said De Bewty, holding his nose with the fingers of his left hand, while with the right he laid hold of Tommy's ear—"put him under the pump. Where's Noodles?"

AS MR. DE BEWTY TURNED TO RUN, AMID THE SHOUTS OF THE SPECTATORS, MR. TROT PURSUED HIM WITH PISTOL AND STICK.

"Oh, don't, sir. I'm wet through already—I am indeed!"

It was true, for they could feel the unlucky youth shaking like a jelly on a dinner table when one of Pickford's vans is rushing by in the street below.

"He must have a bath," said Crocklejack. "I'll go and have one got ready."

"Take Codlings with you, then," replied De Bewty, by no means anxious to have Tommy nearer to him longer than he could help; "I must watch for the others."

The unlucky one, who, by this time, was almost fainting with cold, exhaustion, and hunger, was tumbled, sans ceremonie, into a tub of hot water, and scrubbed vigorously by Noodles; then he had an interview with Mr. Styngy and the doctor, the latter of whom gave him a dose of the nastiest medicine Tommy had ever tasted, while the schoolmaster held out cheering prospects of a vigorous thrashing on the morrow, to counteract the evil effects of Tommy's dip in the ditch.

"And the other two—Wilful and Drummond—have not returned?" asked Mr. Styngy, of Crocklejack.

"Not yet, sir."

"Very good. It is supper time now, so you and De Bewty had better take your usual places at the table, and send Noodles out to the gate."

Mr. Crocklejack retired to obey.

Meantime, the bell rang, the boys trooped in to supper, and there, to the unspeakable astonishment of Mr. Styngy and his ushers, were both Lionel and Charlie, looking as unconscious and innocent as sucking pigs.

"Wilful and Drummond, where have you been?"

"We went for a walk, sir, this afternoon."

"And how long is it since you returned?"

"A long time, sir. It was after tea, I know, because we were too late for it."

"And where have you been since? You have been missed, and no one in the school has seen you since dinner."

"We went up to the dormitory to study, sir," said Charlie, who was less scrupulous about telling a downright fib than his chum.

"Hum—some mistake," said Mr. Styngy, puzzled. He would have been more particular in his examination, perhaps, but he had caught one culprit, flagranti delicto, and he could visit the sins of the others on him.

After supper there came the usual hour's preparation of the following day's lessons, but Lionel and Charlie used the time for a very different purpose.

They exchanged a look first, as they seated themselves in a quiet corner, and that look was enough to tell them that the same subject occupied their minds.

"Poor old Tommy—in for it again!"

"Yes; and, worse luck, he always gets in for it in such a way that we can't help him."

"I mean to make De Bewty remember it when he flogs him this time, though."

"How? What's the lark?"

Lionel carefully unfolded a small packet he had in his breast pocket, and exhibited the contents to Charlie.

"Why, what on earth are you going to do with that?"

"I'll show you, but I must have a needle and thread."

"I've got plenty in my box, and buttons too, if you want 'em," said Charlie. "My old aunt would make me bring a regular work-box, like a girl's, you know. I wouldn't tell any other chap but you, only I know you won't laugh at me."

"That's prime," said Lionel. "Whoever flogs Tommy to-morrow will recollect it for a day or two, I'll warrant."

* * * *

Three hours passed away, and the pupils of Cheetham Hall were tucked up in their cosy little beds, asleep—with two exceptions.

They were, as our readers have already guessed, none other than Lionel and Charlie, and these two young gentlemen were squatted cross-legged on the ground between two of the beds, and just beneath one of the windows.

"Don't you see, Charlie?" whispered Lionel. "Neither Tommy nor anyone else can be blamed. Tommy's best suit is spoiled, and his new one hasn't come yet, consequently he has to go to the cast-off bag to pick one out. Perhaps I go for him, and I happen to hit upon this particular jacket, the lining of which we have just dosed so beautifully with pepper."

"Yes—it's a jolly dodge, Li. I wonder how you manage to think of 'em?"

"Comes natural, Charlie. Now I'll put this back in the bag, and then we'll get to sleep, for I feel tired."

"Ditto, Li. Here goes."

And in a very few minutes the two chums added their snores to the general chorus.

They only seemed to have been asleep about five minutes, when "Ding, dong, bang! Cling, clash, clang!" came the bellowing of the getting up gong along the corridor, putting Somnus to rout at once, for the noise Noodles made when he performed on that gong was fearful.

Lionel and Charlie were the first to leap out of bed, and playfully strip the sheets and blankets from off Tommy, who lay huddled up in a ball, groaning in his sleep.

"Now then, wake up, Tommy," bawled our hero, giving the fat youth a vigorous punch.

Tommy sleepily opened his eyes, and stared vacantly about him.

"Now, old fellow, up with you, or you won't get any breakfast."

"I can't," replied Tommy, dismally. "I haven't got any togs. I've been thinking of it all night."

"We'll make that all right. You can rig yourself out from the cast-off bag. They'll do till your own things come."

And in less time than it takes to tell it, Tommy was invested in a dilapidated pair of trousers, a waistcoat with only one button, and *the* jacket.

The thought of breakfast put all idea of his coming torture out of Tommy's head, and it was not till he had drained the last drop from his mug, and swallowed the last crumb off his plate, that he began to eye Mr. Styngy with a look suggestive of a wish to assassinate him on the spot.

Mr. Styngy was hungry for vengeance that morning. Everything had gone wrong with him lately, and he eased his mind by "doing his duty" by his pupils, till there was hardly one who did not shiver in his shoes at the master's approach.

"Codlings," he said, in a terrible voice, "come here."

He had his cane in his hand, and Tommy knew what "Come here" meant.

"I'm punishing you, Codlings," he said, "not for going out of bounds, but for returning to this school in a disgraceful condition—impossible to describe—so foul indeed that both Mr. de Bewty and Mr. Crocklejack were taken ill."

"And I was ill too, sir. Dreadfully ill," said Tommy, with a shudder as the flavour of that awful slime seemed to invade his mouth again.

"That was a part of your just punishment, Codlings, and this is the rest. Turn round."

Tommy obeyed, Mr. Styngy's cane descended with a dull thud, and a cloud of reddish dust flew out of the jacket.

Mr. Styngy paused, and a puzzled expression stole over his features; then he opened his mouth as if he wanted to say something; then he shut his eyes as if he wanted to think; then all his features contracted themselves into one hideous grin, and he sneezed with such violence that the window panes rattled.

"It's—it's—the dust," he faltered, trying hard to conquer a second sternutation. "Why don't you brush your jacket, Codlings?"

"It isn't mine, sir. Mine's spoilt. This is an old one out of the cast-off bag. Besides, sir," added Tommy, delivering himself of a rare and brilliant joke, "*you* promised to dust my jacket for me this morning."

Mr Styngy nearly exploded with rage and a fourth sneeze.

"Crocklejack," he said, "come and cane this young reprobate."

The tutor obeyed, and delivered one mighty cut. The dust flew out again, and he did exactly as his reverend principal had done, only with more violence.

Then Mr. de Bewty tried, and then Tomkini; even Noodles was pressed into the service, but by that time the whole of the school was in an uproar, for every body in it, from the head master to the youngest pupil, were sneezing, coughing, or crying, and in some extreme cases all three.

Well indeed had Lionel kept his word, that whoever caned Tommy that morning would dearly remember it.

CHAPTER LXX.

LIONEL MAKES THE PERSONAL ACQUAINTANCE OF MR. TRIXHAM TROT—THE VISIT OF THAT GENTLEMAN TO CHEETHAM HALL—THE INTERVIEW WITH MR. CROCKLEJACK—THE USHERS IN A "FIX," OUT OF WHICH IT IS TO BE HOPED THEY WILL GET IN THE NEXT CHAPTER.

TOMMY CODLINGS, by a wonderful break in his usual luck, little short of miraculous, came out of the "jacket-peppering" business with flying colours.

All work in the class-rooms was, of course, at an end for that morning—indeed, we might say for the whole of the day—so dire was the effect, real in some cases, fancied in others, of red pepper upon the eyes, throats, and noses of the sufferers.

Mr. Styngy had it particularly "warm," to use an appropriate slang epithet, and, retiring to the privacy of his own room, he drank cold water by the jugful, in the vain endeavour to quench the inward fires that tortured him.

De Bewty and Crocklejack were very little better. Noodles declared he was worse than anybody, and sent over to the public-house for two gallons of mild ale, with which, and a long pipe, he managed to make himself pretty comfortable.

I regret to record that the sufferings of the ushers at the dinner table afforded Lionel and his chums intense amusement.

These unhappy gentlemen, who each wore a green shade over his eyes, could not touch a mouthful of solid food, but disposed of the table beer with wonderful avidity; and, when that was gone, emptied several of the water-bottles.

"Prime, isn't it?" chuckled Tommy, with intense delight. "Just look at old De Bewty!"

"You'd better keep a little quiet," said Lionel, in a low tone. "They're like a couple of tigers, and there's no pepper in the jacket you've got on now."

"I don't care," replied Tommy, recklessly. "I'd stand the hottest whacking any of 'em could give me for this slice of fun. Ha, ha! There goes old De Bewty at the cold water again!"

It was fortunate for Tommy that the sufferings of the ushers required their whole attention, or he would certainly have been caught; but the dinner came safely to an end, and De Bewty and Crocklejack led the way, each tightly grasping a full water-bottle and a tumbler.

The afternoon lessons were a farce, of course. Very few of the boys had even smelt the pepper, except Flashaway Junior, whose curiosity had led to its just reward; but so excellent an excuse for neglecting work was not to be lost, and artificial sneezing, coughing, and choking sounded from every part of the schoolroom.

An hour of that was quite enough. The facts of the case were reported to Mr. Styngy, who "confounded" the boys and the ushers too, and ordered the classes to be dismissed.

It was marvellous how soon the fresh air revived the youthful sufferers. In the playground, there was no longer any signs of coughing, choking, or sneezing, and as for the cricketers in the home field, all the "pepper" they had in their possession was given to the ball, by means of a stout cane-handled bat.

Lionel and his chums had joined the cricketers, for, as our hero said, both De Bewty and Crocklejack were in too much torture to say or do anything in the matter of the duel.

Lionel had not had much practice at what is justly entitled "our national game," but he had a quick eye, steady nerves, sound wind, and a strong arm, and if out of such materials a good cricketer cannot be made, it is not the fault of the materials.

He was fielding, and Charlie was in, giving the fielders plenty of work, for he was a capital batter, and sent the ball skimming like a swallow over the ground into all sorts of unexpected places.

Lionel then was anxiously waiting for the ball to be driven in his direction, when he heard a harsh, disagreeable voice calling to him from the gate close by.

"Here, I say, you boy! Hi!"

Lionel looked sharply round, ready to give an angry reply to such an uncivil address; but some undefinable impulse prompted him to advance towards the short, broad-shouldered, big-headed man who had called him.

"Now, what's the matter with you?" he said, shortly.

"Don't you know how to speak to your betters, boy?" said the little man—his big face growing scarlet with passion.

"Yes, when I see 'em," retorted Lionel. "You're not one, though, old turkey cock."

Now this was very disgraceful language for a boy to address to one so many years older, and there is little wonder that the large-headed gentleman got furious, and began to climb over the stile.

"Don't you do that," said Lionel, coolly. "I give you fair warning—there are more than twenty of us in the field, and we'll bait you like a bull."

The big-headed gentleman paused, and kept on his own side of the stile. It was evident that he had had some experience of boys. But he fixed a tremendous scowl on Lionel, and shook his fist at him as he said—

"It's lucky for you, you young rascal, that I've got an appointment close by, or I'd flay you. I shall catch you, though, one of these days, as sure as my name 's Trixham Trot."

"Whew!" whistled our hero; "here's a game. That's old Tricksy, is it? and he's off to the school, I'll wager a sovereign."

Totally disregarding a splendid "catch" that just whistled by him, Lionel ran up to the wickets and whispered his discovery to Charlie.

"Get on your jacket—quick!" he added. "We must be in the school before Tricksy. Crocklejack's sure to see him to avoid a row, for the chap's got a temper like the very deuce."

And in less than three minutes the chums were trotting swiftly away by a short cut to Cheetham Hall, through the gates of which they rushed while yet the large head of Mr. Trot was five hundred yards away.

"You stay here at the gates, Charlie," said

Lionel, in a hurried whisper. "Be very polite; 'sir' him, and take off your cap, and all that sort of thing, then you can offer to take his message to old Crocklejack, and so we shall find out what room they're going to talk in."

"D'ye you think he'll see Tricksy."

"Sure to, especially if you say that he seems in a dreadful temper. I'll hide in the corridor close to Crocklejack's room."

Mr. Trixham Trot arrived at the gate just as our hero's jacket tails disappeared into the house, and the peppery gentleman scowled dreadfully when he saw another boy apparently of the same audacious breed as Lionel.

But Charlie took off his hat so politely, and put on such an innocent expression, that Mr. Trot relaxed his scowl, and opened his mouth.

"Boy," said he.

"Yes, sir," said Charlie.

"Is this Cheetham Hall School?"

"It is, sir."

"And you are one of the pupils, I suppose?"

"Yes, sir."

"Hum. Then you're a better-behaved boy than I expected to find at a school where blackguards are employed as ushers. There's two here, ain't there, called De Bewty and Bottlejack?"

"Crocklejack, if you please, sir," Charlie ventured to hint in a polite way.

"It's all the same. Now I want to see Bottlejack at once. It's no good telling me he's not in, because I know better."

"He is in, sir—in his bedroom, I believe, for he met with an accident."

"Go to him, and tell him from me, Mr. Trixham Trot, that if he don't see me in five minutes he'll meet with another accident."

"With pleasure, sir," and Charlie darted off like an arrow.

In less than the stipulated five minutes he returned out of breath, and with a message that Mr. Crocklejack would be glad to see him in his study.

"Ha, ha! here's a game," chuckled Charlie to himself. "They're going to talk about the duel, but they little think that I gave Li the tip, and that he's hidden under the table."

"This is the door, sir, and there is Mr. Crocklejack," said Charlie, indicating that gentleman, as with the green shade still over his eyes, he approached the door of the species of cupboard which he dignified by the name of study.

"That'll do, boy. Now you can go. Be off, and mind you don't skulk about the passage. Whenever *I* catch a boy listening to what doesn't concern him, I wring his ears off. D'ye hear that?"

"I'd scorn to do such a thing, sir," replied Charlie, as he walked away with an air of virtuous indignation.

Nevertheless Mr. Trot watched him till he had reached the end of the corridor, and then following Mr. Crocklejack into the study, he closed the door with a bang, placed his hat and stick on the table with a bang, and sat down in his chair like an earthquake.

"Now, sir," he said, fixing Crocklejack with a stern glance. "I am a man of few words."

"I—I am very glad to hear it," said the usher.

"Don't interrupt me, sir. An interruption I regard as an insult, and treat as such. Now with regard to this Bewty fellow. Is he ready to be kicked?"

"Qu—qu—quite ready, I believe," stammered Mr. Crocklejack.

"And to have his nose pulled?"

"Certainly,"

"And then to be thrashed within an inch of his life?"

"No—no doubt of it, sir."

"And then to have that last inch shot out of his rascally carcass?"

"Wi—with pleasure, I'm sure," said Mr. Crocklejack, who was himself becoming more than half bewildered with fright at the blood-thirsty aspect of Mr. Trot, as he produced two huge pistols and a horsewhip, and banged them on the table.

"Then," said Mr. Trixham Trot, "bring him here."

"Here, my dear sir!" faltered the tutor, who would have given a whole year's salary to have been a mile away.

"Yes, here—or if he prefers it, as being more convenient, in his own bedroom. They can lay him out there, you know, when I've done with him."

Mr. Crocklejack nearly fainted—the chairs seemed to be heaving beneath him, and the walls to be spinning rapidly round—as he comprehended the awful hint conveyed in Mr. Trot's last words.

"B—b—but," he managed to say, mastering himself by a desperate effort, "it can't be done now. In a room! The whole house will be alarmed—think of that, sir—before you had got well through the kicking."

Mr. Trot fixed his severest stare upon the tutor, until that gentleman writhed like a cockchafer impaled with a pin.

"There would be some reason in what you say," he said, sternly, "if I had not every reason to believe that there is a dodge—a mean-spirited, cowardly dodge—to enable this Bewty fellow to keep out of my way."

"I assure you," began Mr. Crocklejack, earnestly——

"Don't assure *me*," growled Mr. Trot. "I'm going to assure *you* and that Bewty of this. Now listen. I give you and him one more chance to name your own time and place; but, by all that's blue, if you're not there punctual to the minute I march straight here, and shoot you both."

"Cer—certainly. Very proper, and—and—gentlemanlike," stammered Mr. Crocklejack.

"Never mind that. Will you name the time and place, or will you not?" said Mr. Trot, who grew more furious with every moment.

"Say—say—Hampstead Heath," muttered Mr. Crocklejack, who was fast drifting into idiocy from terror, "in—in—a month or two."

"Sir—r—r—r," growled Mr. Trot, rolling the "r's" till they sounded like the rattle of a drum, "you dare to jest, and with *me!*"

"Not at all," murmured Mr. Crocklejack, becoming reckless. "Anywhere'll do for my friend—any time. Say the top of the Monument, in six months."

"You are intoxicated, sir," said Mr. Trot, almost foaming at the mouth. "You dare to confer with a gentleman of my standing in such a beastly state—but that shall not prevent your knowing my meaning. I will write it down here, and, when you are sober, I warn you to attend to what I have written."

And, stabbing the inkstand with a pen, Mr. Trot scribbled a few lines on a sheet of paper, and then held it beneath the usher's nose, as if he wanted him to smell it.

"There," he said, "is the place—the lonely field at the back of my house; and there is the time—four o'clock to-morrow afternoon. Beware!"

Then, laying the paper on the table, while Mr. Crocklejack regarded him with a helpless stare, Mr. Trot gathered up his pistols, whip, hat, and stick, and, with a final withering glare, departed.

Mr. Crocklejack remained in a state of utter prostration for fully a quarter of an hour. Then he arose, and, giving utterance to a sound between a gasp and a groan, he tottered to a little cupboard, and, drawing out a bottle, took a longish sip, and instantly the apartment became aromatic with the fragrance of "Old Tom."

"Getting his courage up," thought Lionel, as he lay curled up under the little table. "Dash him, I hope he'll get it up soon, and go; I've got the pins and needles in both my legs."

Mr. Crocklejack took another sip. Lionel heard the Old Tom gurgling as it flowed down the usher's throat. Then he replaced the bottle, and began to commune with himself.

"What an escape I've had," Lionel heard him murmur. "What a blood-thirsty villain! I really believe, if I had offered the slightest opposition to his wishes, he would have shot me on the spot. But he's gone, thank goodness! Let me see, he said something as he was going. What was it? I can't remember; my brain's in a whirl now. Hallo! what's this paper?"

Mr. Crocklejack took it up, read Mr. Trot's blood-thirsty message, and sat down flat in the arm-chair.

"To-morrow afternoon!" he gasped. "Four o'clock—oh, Lord! I daren't. It'll be like murder, to take De Bewty there; and yet, if I don't, the miscreant will come here, and shoot us both!"

"I wish he'd settled you at once," thought Lionel, savagely. "I can't put up with much more of this—it's positive torture."

"But," he heard the usher murmur, after a while, "De Bewty has brought this on himself, and he must take the penalty. I'd rather, a good deal, that he should be shot than me. Here goes."

And, after one more application to the bottle, the usher hastily left the room, and Lionel, with a deep sigh of relief, crawled out from beneath the table, and, after listening at the door for a moment or two, stepped out, and ran off, to communicate the news to Charlie.

Crocklejack, putting on as good an imitation of a calm and confident expression as he could, at so short a notice, went straight to De Bewty, whom he clapped on the back in a lively and cheerful manner.

"Oh, don't! You'll shake all the pepper up, just as it's beginning to settle down. What's the matter?"

"Good news, De Bewty; I've seen him."

"Seen him—whom do you mean?"

"Trixham Trot."

At the mention of that dread name, De Bewty turned pale, and retreated into the farthest corner of the bed-room.

"Don't be alarmed. I've made it all right for you."

"But is he gone?"

"Yes."

"And didn't want to see me?"

"Yes, he did. But I told him you were unwell, and in the most gentlemanly manner he declared he wouldn't intrude."

Mr. de Bewty started forward, and shook Crocklejack's hands warmly.

"You are indeed a friend. Then it's all settled, eh?"

"No thanks, no thanks; you'd have done as much for me, I know. Yes, it's all settled. There's only that trifle about the letter to be explained."

"What letter?"

"The letter you wrote. The challenge, you know."

"But I *didn't* write it," said De Bewty, turning pale again. "I never wrote a line to him in my life. Why didn't you tell him so?"

"So I did," replied the perfidious Crocklejack, "and he said he didn't disbelieve me for a moment; but you see, De Bewty, he's a very particular man about his honour, and a personal explanation is necessary—only as a matter of form, you know."

"Oh, only as a matter of form!" Mr. de Bewty echoed, faintly.

"That's all," said the deceiver. "It's a—a sort of arbitration, you know, and, as I thought the sooner it was over the better, I appointed four o'clock to-morrow afternoon, at Mr. Trot's house."

"You'll go with me, Crocklejack?"

"Of course I will," replied the perfidious usher, readily. "I'll see it through you."

"See what through me?"

"See you through it, I should have said. Keep your spirits up—it'll soon be over."

"I suppose there's no other way?"

"None at all. Mr. Trot's really a most gentlemanly man, willing to make every allowance, but you see, De Bewty, his honour demands this personal explanation."

"Bother his honour!" replied the victim; "I never make such a fuss about mine."

"I see," said Mr. Crocklejack, "you agree with Shakespeare's idea of honour, when he makes Falstaff say, 'Honour pricks me on. Yea, but how if honour picks me off when I come on? How then? Can honour mend a leg? No. Or an arm? No. Or take away the pain of a wound? No. Honour hath no skill in surgery, then? No. What is honour? A word. What is that word? Air. A true reckoning! Who hath it? He that died o' Wednesday. Doth he feel it? No. Doth he hear it? No. Is it insensible, then? Yea—to the dead. But will it not live with the living? No. Why? Envy will not suffer it; therefore I'll none of it. Honour is a mere scutcheon—and so ends my catechism.'"

"My sentiments exactly," said De Bewty. "Is that really out of Shakespeare?"

"Yes. You'll find it in King Henry IV., part 1, scene 5, act 1."

"Wonderful man, that Shakespeare. That's my idea about honour, to a T."

"Pity it isn't Mr. Trot's," said Crocklejack. with a peculiar smile, "and then you wouldn't have to go to meet him to-morrow."

"If I must go, I must. I only hope I shall get the pepper out of my eyes first. It won't look very dignified to appear with a green shade on."

CHAPTER LXXI.

MR. DE BEWTY'S DOUBTS AND FEARS—PREPARATIONS FOR THE DUEL—THE MEETING—EXULTATION OF LIONEL AND HIS FRIENDS—IGNOMINIOUS RETREAT OF MR. DE BEWTY FROM THE "FIELD OF HONOUR."

HORRIBLE dreams that night haunted both Crocklejack and De Bewty—dreams in which Mr. Trixham Trot played a conspicuous part—now being a lion, with a mouth like the great gate of Westminster Abbey—now a bloated spider, whose body emulated in size the dome of St. Paul's—then changing into the likeness of some other hideous monster, but always in pursuit of the unlucky ushers.

When they awoke at the early hour which habit had made customary to them, each found himself bathed in a cold perspiration, and about as much refreshed as if he had passed the night on the top of a five-barred gate in the pelting rain.

"Oh, dear me!" groaned Mr. de Bewty; "I have had such an awful night."

Mr. Crocklejack was going to say that he had been equally unlucky, when the thought struck him that he might dispirit the victim; so he said cheerfully—

"Dreams always go by contraries, old fellow."

"Oh, it's all very well; but I can't get 'em out of my head. They were all about that confounded Trot."

"Don't talk about him," rejoined Crocklejack; "after four o'clock to-day, you know, you'll never see him any more."

"I hope I shan't. I don't want to see him to-day if he's anything like my dream."

"What was he like, then?"

"Oh, awful; I couldn't describe it," said De Bewty, with a shudder. "What's he like, in reality? Not seven feet high, is he?"

"Why, he isn't nearly so tall as you are," replied Crocklejack. "He's not a handsome man, certainly; some people might say that his head was too big

FOLLOW MY LEADER.

MR. GRUBB DID NOT SEE THE TRAP THAT WAS LAID, TILL HE FOUND HIMSELF IN THE TUB, GRASPING AT THE FLOWER POTS.

No. 16.

for his body, and that he was bandy-legged; but that's nothing to do with us. Hallo! De Bewty, there's the bell for prayers, and you haven't began dressing yet."

Those pupils who had the misfortune to be in the classes of the two ushers, certainly thought, and had good reason for thinking, that their instructors had gone a little mad that day.

One examined the geography class in vulgar fractions, the other insisted that the Euclid handed to him was a delectus, and caned the boys all round when they ventured to remonstrate. Some youngsters were handsomely flogged when they had carefully prepared their lessons; others who had come up shivering in the dread consciousness of not knowing a word, found themselves rewarded with good marks.

It was Wednesday, and should properly have been a half-holiday, but as an instalment had already been given in consequence of the "peppering," on Tuesday, the classes were ordered to work until three o'clock, by order of Mr. Styngy.

"There's a confounded nuisance," thought Mr. Cracklejack. "I shan't have time to dodge De Bewty and get the pistols. Never mind, though, old Trot is sure to bring his."

The agitation of the ushers had not escaped our hero's observation, and to him as well as to Charlie and Codlings, their evident state of "funk" afforded the greatest amusement.

"This is out-and-out—the biggest spree I've had for a twelvemonth. Do just look at Bewty trying to rule that copy-book. Ha! ha! Now he's giving poor Smalls one over the head for grinning at him. Oh! my; I shall burst!"

"Save yourself up for four o'clock, Charlie," said Lionel; "there'll be something worth bursting about, then."

"It can't be far off three, now. How Crocklejack keeps looking at that old silver turnip of his! Hallo! there's the signal. Time's up."

And, amidst a deafening clashing, clattering, and banging of slates, books, and desks, the classes broke up to enjoy the remnant of their half-holiday.

"Now, Li," said Charlie, "what's the first move?"

"Upstairs, my boy, to get a few little pills that I've got ready for that grinning chap, if he puts in an appearance."

"What, the chap who led us that dance at the old Manor House?"

"That's him, Charlie; and I mean to make him dance to-day if he comes within twenty yards of me."

"But how about Crocklejack and De Bewty?"

"We shan't miss them. It's only twenty minutes' easy walk to Trot's crib, and they won't start before half-past; they are in no hurry to go, you can bet."

This was true enough, for when the perfidious Crocklejack and De Bewty were alone in their sanctum, it seemed to the former as if the appointment would not be kept at all, for the victim's fears had returned with doubled force.

"Cheer up, old fellow," said Crocklejack, soothingly. "Keep your pecker up—as the boys say—it'll soon be over."

"Yes," responded De Bewty, in a tone as melancholy as that of a voice from the grave, "it'll soon be over with me; I can't go, Crocklejack."

"Nonsense, nonsense!" said the other. "What has got into your head, now? Didn't I tell you it was all right; that I'd settle everything with Mr. Trot, and that you have only to say half a dozen words to him yourself?"

"Yes, I know, I feel that you have acted like a true friend; but I have a presentiment that Trot only wants to lure me to that solitary place to have my blood."

"Stuff and nonsense!" said Crocklejack, impatiently. He began to get quite angry at his friend's reluctance to go out and be comfortably shot like a gentleman. "Slip your things on at once, De Bewty, or I declare solemnly I'll go to Mr. Trot, and tell him that you decline to satisfy the trifling concession to his honour which he demands. You know what will happen then, I suppose?"

This was spoken in such a grim and meaning tone, that Mr. de Bewty's hair stood on end.

"Wh—what will happen?" he stammered.

"He'll come here after you!"

"Oh, my good gracious! Do you think he will?"

"I'm sure of it—he said so. Unless we're there punctually at four o'clock, he'll consider that you've refused satisfaction to his honour, and he'll come after it with a couple of loaded pistols."

Mr. de Bewty didn't want to hear any more. He made a grab at his hat, and put that on first. Then he kicked off his slippers, with such haste, that they broke a pane of glass, and altogether proceeded to dress himself in such an extraordinary way, that unless Mr. Crocklejack had taken him in hand, he would not have completed his toilette by midnight.

"Now take a sip out of this. It'll put your nerves to rights."

Mr. de Bewty held the neck of the pocket flask against his chattering teeth, and swallowed an amount of neat brandy, which at any other time would have made him helplessly drunk in ten minutes.

"Feel better?"

"Ever so much!" gasped De Bewty, whose courage began almost instantly to rise into his head with the brandy, and, linking his arm with Crocklejack's, he stalked away with a defiant air.

Lionel, Charlie, and Tommy were waiting for them at the corner of the lane which led to the Manor House, and no sooner did they see that the ushers were really bent upon keeping the appointment, than they scudded away like hares, to secure their places.

"I think that Crocklejack's been giving De Bewty a dose of Dutch courage," said Lionel. "Did you notice how red his face was?"

"He'll want a lot of it to get him up to the scratch," replied Drummond. "What a frightened beggar he is, though, Li? Why don't he fight old Trot like a man, for the honour of the school?"

"'Praps he will when he finds himself in for it."

"But I say," cried Tommy, "the pistols won't be loaded with real bullets, will they?"

"Of course, they will," replied Lionel. "What do you think they'd load 'em with—young potatoes or gooseberries?"

"But I say——" began Tommy again, when Lionel peremptorily ordered him to be silent, for they were just upon the house.

"Keep close up under the walls," whispered Lionel, "and tread carefully."

In this way the house was safely passed, and they found themselves under the hedge bordering the field where the duel was to take place.

"It's small enough," said our hero, taking a survey of it through a gap in the hedge. "Why Tommy here could pitch a stone clean over it. But come on round the corner—they'll be here directly."

The young reprobates who had set all this mischief afloat had scarcely esconced themselves in a snug position "round the corner," where they could see and hear everything—for the field might almost have been crossed in any direction with a hop, skip, and a jump—when they saw entering the field, from the side opposite to the lane, Mr. Trot, a tall solemn looking gentleman, dressed in black, Mr. Jubilee, carrying an oblong mahogany box, bound with brass, and a short, stout gentleman with a red face, a stiff back, and a military swagger.

With Mr. Trot at the head, this little party marched slowly into the very centre of the field, or paddock, and then halted.

Mr. Trot looked very carefully all round the field, and up and down the lane, and then, taking out his watch, said—

"Five minutes to four, gentlemen. Do your watches agree with mine?"

They all did with the exception of the long gentleman, who said that Mr. Trot was five seconds and a fraction too slow.

"Never mind," said Mr. Trot. "We will give them the benefit of the doubt, sir. John."

Mr. Jubilee advanced with his usual good-humoured grin widening his mouth.

"What do you mean, sir?" demanded Mr. Trot, looking sternly at him. "How dare you grin like a bumpkin through a horse collar, on such an occasion as this?"

Mr. Jubilee tried his hardest to look like a mute on duty, but the attempt was a failure—grinning was constitutional with him.

Luckily Mr. Trot's anger was averted by the appearance of two hats just coming into view above the hedge.

"Here they come," said the military gentleman, in a husky whisper. "No apologies, Trot."

The next moment the two ushers pushed open the little gate, and entered the field of combat.

"There they are," whispered Crocklejack. "Now, old fellow, throw your chest out, and march up to 'em like a man who doesn't care for anybody."

"Just give me another little drop," said De Bewty, huskily.

"You can't drink with these fellows looking at you. Go in and get it over, and then yon can drink as much as you like."

Thus urged, De Bewty, with a pallid face, and very shaky legs, moved on. He had been brave enough coming up the lane, but at the sight of the blood-thirsty Mr. Trot all his Dutch courage oozed out at his finger ends, like unto that of the immortal Bob Acres; but if he had only known how the faithless Crocklejack had deceived him, what would have been his feelings then?"

"Good afternoon, sir," he managed to say in his politest tones. "I hope you're quite well. You wished to see me, I believe, about—er—about a letter."

"I certainly did," returned Mr. Trot, with a horrible frown, "if your name's Bewty."

"It is, sir."

"Ha!" said Mr. Trot, producing Lionel's letter, and holding it so close to the usher's nose that he recoiled a step or two. "That filthy and disgusting scrawl was written by you, I believe?"

"Certainly not," replied De Bewty. "I am here to deny all knowledge of it."

"That evasion will not avail you," said Mr. Trot, twisting the letter into a species of pipe light. "Now, sir, eat that letter instantly."

"Wh—wh—a—a—t?"

"Eat it!" roared Mr. Trot, seizing the unfortunate De Bewty by the nape of the neck with one hand, and cramming the letter into his mouth with the other. "Swallow it—every morsel, you rascal, or I'll blow your brains out."

The terrified usher closed his eyes in the fear of instant death, chewed the paper for a few minutes, and then, with a desperate gulp, swallowed it.

"Good," said Mr. Trot, as he peered down the usher's throat to satisfy himself that it was all gone. "Now, my friend, according to the programme I arranged with your friend, Bottlejack, yonder, I'm going to pull your nose, then kick you round the paddock half a dozen times, then horsewhip you, and finally, if there's any life left in you, I'll have that with a pistol bullet."

Here was a startling revelation for the unhappy De Bewty, as the awful truth flashed upon him that he had been deceived by his false friend into a mortal combat with the ferocious Trixham Trot! He broke out into a perspiration all over him, and every hair on his head stood on end!

"Murder!" he yelled. "It's a mistake. I never ——oh, oh, oh!"

These later ejaculations were caused by Mr. Trot seizing the opportunity and Mr. de Bewty's nose at the same time. Mr. Trot's fingers were strong, and the usher's nose a beauty for the purpose, being long and flexible.

For fully five minutes did Mr. de Bewty suffer this humiliating torture; then Mr. Trot let go the nose, and, taking him by the collar, lifted his right foot, and kicked a hideous yell out of the unlucky usher.

In vain did he writhe, roar, and alternately beg for mercy, or curse his assailant. Mr. Trot was a strong man, and never relaxed his hold, while his right foot kicked away with the regularity of a machine.

"My eye," said Charlie to Lionel, "old Tricksy is giving it to him. I hope he won't go too far; but those kicks are tremendous."

"Serves him right for being a coward. Trot's only a bully, I know, by his way, and if De Bewty had stood up to him like a man, he might have been doing the kicking himself. But it's time we joined in the fun; give me a little room for my elbow, I'm going to pepper that grinning chap."

Lionel took a large and very powerful catapult from his pocket, and then a supply of ammunition in the form of sundry bullets, so notched with a knife, that the jagged pieces of lead stood up like spikes upon the surface.

"I say, Li, you're not going to use these in that catapult? They're dangerous."

"They'd kill a man," replied Lionel, coolly; "if he was hit in the head; but I'm going to let fly at Grinaway's tail."

There was a convenient little gap in the hedge just large enough for Lionel to aim through. He waited patiently till Mr. Jubilee suddenly stooped to pick up something, and then fired.

The aim was excellent, and Mr. Jubilee, with a tremendous oath, bounced up into the air like an india-rubber ball, and then began dancing a species of frantic hornpipe to the music of his own sweet voice.

And this was the song that he sang—

"Oh, my! where the devil did that come from? Oh, lor! don't it hurt. Oh, dear! I believe I'm bleeding to death, I do; I can feel it running down my legs." (Chorus.)

But we are compelled to omit the chorus on account of its extreme profanity.

Just then, too, Mr. Trot had completed the kicking portion of the programme, and, halting just opposite the gate, beckoned to John to come and hold his captive, while he recovered breath and prepared for the horse-whipping.

Mr. Jubilee advanced, not walking like an ordinary Christian, but dancing a curious kind of waltz-step, with one hand pressed to his coat tails.

"What the devil's the matter with you?" growled Mr. Trot. "Here, catch hold of this fellow, will you, and hold him tight; d'ye hear?"

Mr. John Jubilee grasped the unfortunate De Bewty by the collar of his coat with his left hand, but he still kept his right behind him, and danced the waltz-step.

"Now, here's a chance," whispered Lionel; "I think De Bewty's had enough. Here goes."

Lionel took steady aim, and sent bullet number two whizzing on its errand. It was just as well aimed as the first; but, unfortunately for Mr. Jubilee his fingers got in the way.

The doleful howl he uttered could have been heard for half a mile. He forgot all about De Bewty, and, releasing him, spun about the field like a gigantic teetotum attacked with a brain fever.

"Run!" shouted Lionel; "now is your time—run!"

The tutor needed no second hint; he turned, took

the gate at a leap, and scudded away down the lane like a fox with a pack of hounds at his brush.

But quick as he was, Mr. Trot was very little behind in the pursuit, and only pausing to pick up a pistol in one hand and snatch the tall gentleman's stick with the other, he shot away, getting a good ten miles an hour out of his bandy-legs.

Lionel and Charlie were both good runners, and kept the chase well in view, though more than once they were compelled to stop and have their laugh out, giving Tommy Codlings an opportunity to catch up to them.

"Oh, my eye!" panted Charlie, "this will be the death of me, Li. Look at De Bewty just turning the corner, and old Tricksy with the pistol, roaring to him to stop. Come on, old fellow; off we go again, or we shall miss all the fun."

And away they sped, at a rate which soon brought them up with the chase.

The end of the lane was now reached, and De Bewty, who was only three or four yards in advance of his terrible opponent, made straight for Cheetham Hall, with the instinct of the hunted fox, which always makes for its own cover.

It so happened that the Rev. Mr. Styngy, feeling a little better, had come down to the gates, with Professor Tomkini, for the benefit of a little fresh air, and as it was a particularly warm and genial day, Noodles had just been ordered to bring out a certain little table and a couple of chairs, whereon his employer and the professor might rest while they chatted.

It was just then that the sound of many voices, uplifted as in strife, made itself heard, advancing towards the school at a rapid pace.

"Dear me," said Mr. Styngy, "what can that be. Is it a riot? Noodles, step into the road and ascertain."

Noodles obeyed, and reported—"Mr. de Bewty coming down the road like one o'clock, with a mob o' people arter him."

"Stand ready, Noodles," said Mr. Styngy, hastily. "Let Mr. de Bewty in, and close the gates—an'——"

Before he could complete the sentence the usher rushed in full tilt against Tomkini, and, clasping him tightly in his arms, they plunged with a crash amongst the chairs.

Mr. Trot and the mob, which was now a pretty large one, were so close upon his heels, that there was no time to close the gates; they were dashed back, and Mr. Trixham Trot, in his turn, ran head first against Mr. Styngy, and rolled him over like a nine-pin.

There was a dull thud as they struck the ground, then a bright flash, a loud report, and a cloud of dense white smoke, as Mr. Trot's pistol, dashed from his grasp, exploded, without doing further damage than taking off the tip of Noodles' ear.

For a few minutes there was a dead silence amongst the spectators, but when the rival schoolmasters scrambled to their feet unhurt, but wrathful—

"Where is he?" roared Mr. Trot, looking viciousfully about him.

"Whom do you mean, sir?" said Styngy, now blazing with wrath as hot as that which burned within the bosom of his rival. "How dare you intrude upon my premises with this blackguard mob, and discharge pistols at unoffending people."

"Because I choose," retorted Trot. "A low contemptible cur of an usher, who calls himself Bewty, insulted me grossly, and when I invited him to meet me, and give the satisfaction due to a gentleman, the cowardly whelp runs away, and I ran after him—and I'll have him, too, as sure as my name's Trixham Trot."

"What!" ejaculated Mr. Styngy, in a voice that made those nearest to him jump nervously into the air; "are *you* Trixham Trot? The mean scoundrel who has been trying for weeks past to injure my school and my reputation? The rascal who bribed the upholsterer to damage my furniture?"

"Dare you apply those epithets to me, sir?" said Mr. Trot, advancing to Mr. Styngy, and putting his head temptingly close to that gentleman.

"I do," retorted Mr. Styngy, emphatically.

"Then if it were not for your profession as a clergyman, which you disgrace," said Mr. Trot, "hang me if I wouldn't knock your ugly head off!"

This was too much. Mr. Styngy forgot that he was a clergyman, and remembering only that he was a man with a pair of good long arms and fists at the end of them, he bestowed upon the nose of his foe such a "punch," that it seemed to spread that feature all over his face.

"Brayvo!" shouted Tommy Codlings; and "Brayvo," uttered the mob, who had got inside the gates, and now formed a ring for the combatants.

But the cries and the disgraceful exhibition they were making of themselves had no influence now with either.

Trot, enraged by the pain of the blow and the taste of his own blood, which was trickling into his mouth at the rate of a quarter of a pint a minute, sprang up, and rushed at Mr. Styngy with a roar like that of a mad bull.

But the reverend schoolmaster had not forgotten the fistic lessons of his youth. In his young days boxing had the patronage of the aristocracy, and many a time at Oxford had Philo Styngy doubled up, by force of science, a rough or bargee twice his own weight and size.

In the language of the "noble science," Trot was nowhere. In three rounds Mr. Styngy had peppered his smeller out of all human shape, put up both his shutters, spilt all his ivories, and made him so groggy that he could not come up to time.

"There," panted the schoolmaster, flushed, but triumphant, "I hope I have taught you a lesson that you will not readily forget. Noodles, turn him out."

The odd man had just returned from the house, where he had persuaded one of the servants to plaister the tip of his ear. It was with a ferocious joy, then, that he pounced upon the beaten Mr. Trot, and bumped him out of the gates into the road, whither the crowd followed, ready for more fun.

"Oh!" growled Noodles, giving his half unconscious captive a violent shake, "you'll come here, will you, shootin' people's ears orf. You only show your 'ed here again, and I'll give it a dose similar to wot the gov'nor purwided—and there's a kick on account. Hooray, boys! Chevey him!"

It is doubtful whether Mr. Trot would ever have reached home alive if Mr. John Jubilee had not met him half way, still followed by the mob, who were pelting him with anything they could pick up, but judiciously fled upon the arrival of assistance.

Let it suffice to record here that he lay in bed for a week, and at the expiration of that time started for London, where he resolved to remain, cursing heartily Cheetham Hall and every one connected with it.

CHAPTER LXXII.

AN EVIL SHADOW CROSSES LIONEL'S PATH—MR. GRUBBE MAKES HIS RE-APPEARANCE—LIONEL'S LAST PRACTICAL JOKE AT CHEETHAM HALL—THE LETTER—FAREWELL.

AND now a dark page has to be turned in this veracious history of our hero's career, a page which chronicles sorrow and evil fortunes, a page which is turned by the fat fingers of his old enemy—the sanctimonious Mr. Grubbe.

The events detailed in our last chapter had

scarcely yet been consigned to that limbo—the receptacle of all things which have had their day—when the evil shadow of Mr. Grubbe crossed Lionel's path, and chilled him with an involuntary shudder—not of fear, but of aversion.

It was in the evening when they met, during the interval allotted for the preparation of the morrow's lessons. Lionel had completed his task more rapidly than usual, and had sauntered into the playground, when he felt a hand touch his shoulder, and, looking round suddenly, he found himself face to face with Mr. Grubbe.

"Ah, Lionel, my dear boy," he said, in his smooth measured tones; "I see that you remember me."

"I do sir," replied our hero, in a tone that very plainly expressed that he felt no very great amount of joy at seeing him again.

"A—h—h—h!" continued Mr. Grubbe, with a long sigh. "It is not very long since we met, and yet in that comparatively short space of time how many important events, affecting not only ourselves, but the future of those near and dear to us, may have occurred; but there is a Providence that ordereth all things."

"Have you anything to say to me, sir?" said Lionel, who hated, above all things, cant and hypocrisy.

"Not at present," returned Mr. Grubbe, in an uneasy, hesitating way; "there is no opportunity now. But to-morrow I may have some intelligence to communicate. You rise at six, I believes?"

Lionel replied that such was the hour at which Noodles performed his solo on the gong.

"I rise early, too," said Mr. Grubbe, with a flourish of his hand towards the sky, "to commune with nature whilst the morn is yet fresh and lovely. You know the entrance to Mr. Styngy's private garden?"

"Yes, sir."

"Then I shall be walking there at six to-morrow morning," said Mr. Grubbe; "meet me, and we will have a little pleasant and instructive conversation."

Lionel promised, and then darted off, without taking any heed of Mr. Grubbe's fat fingers outstretched for him to shake. He would have promised anything to have got out of sight of the unwieldly figure and pale, fat, flabby face of Grubbe.

"Who do you think's come back?" said our hero, as soon as he had sought and found his chums.

"Give it up. Who is it?"

"Why that fat, sneaking chap, Grubbe, that came here with me."

"Oh, I remember; he was usher here, years ago, long before my time, but even then there used to be all sorts of tales about him. One was, I remember, that he had sold himself to the devil."

"I can't bear him," said Lionel; "and ever since he had the confounded cheek to hint at marrying my mother, I feel as if I could poison him."

"I should like to catch him trying it on with mine," added Charlie.

"He hasn't got the sense to see that I'd rather have his room than his company," Lionel continued; "and he has just been bothering me to go for a walk with him at six to-morrow morning, in Styngy's garden."

"What, the private part?"

"Yes."

"He'd better look where he goes to, then," continued Charlie, "for the gardener's been digging a deep hole just in front of the door, to get gravel, I believe."

"I wonder if old Grubbe knows it."

"Most likely; but why?"

"What a game it would be if we filled the hole with water, and Grubbe walked into it."

"He's too wide awake, Li. It's rather dark at six; but he'd be sure to see a big hole like that."

"Not if we covered it up a little, as the elephant hunters in Africa do to their pits," replied Lionel. "You remember that book of travels we read?"

"Yes; it's a good plan. But when is it to be done?"

"To-night; you and I can slip down after the other fellows are asleep."

"And me," said Tommy.

"No, no, old chap, you won't do for night work; you'd be tumbling into the hole."

"Besides, he's too nervous," added Charlie; "he'd see ghosts all the time."

"No, I won't, I promise faithfully," pleaded Tommy. "Do let me come, Li."

"No, my boy. What we've got to do will have to be done in a hurry. You go to bed, and be satisfied with seeing the fun in the morning."

* * * *

Everything gave promise of a beautiful morning, when, at his accustomed early hour, Mr. Grubbe detached himself from his bed, and looked out of window.

The sun was not yet up, but the sky was clear, a balmy south wind was stirring the branches of the trees, just lazily awakening—answering in rustling whispers—the morning music of the birds.

There was a peculiar evil-looking smile hovering about the corners of Mr. Grubbe's mouth as he dressed himself in his semi-clerical costume, and from time to time he muttered a name which sounded very much like that of our hero.

When he had finished, he looked at his watch.

"Ten minutes past six," he muttered half aloud. "I had better go, or the young whelp will be offended, and go. How will he bear the news, I wonder?"

He paused, and as he turned the handle of the door which led into the garden, that evil smile flitted across his face again.

"I would give fifty pounds," he went on, as he closed the door behind him, "to see the young cur on his knees, begging for ——. Oh, murder! Help!"

Mr. Grubbe had stepped neatly into Lionel's pitfall, and was up to his neck in foul, muddy water, smelling of all sorts of abominations.

"Here—hi! (Splutter.) Ugh! Help! help!"

Some boards had been fitted to the sides of the hole, giving it much the appearance of a large water-butt, but Mr. Grubbe found appearances deceptive, for as fast as he caught hold of them to drag himself up thereby, they gave way, and he fell in again.

"Help! murder!" roared Mr. Grubbe again.

At a certain little window overlooking that portion of Mr. Styngy's private garden, which window has already figured in this story, three youthful heads were clustered together, beaming down with silent delight upon the struggles of the unfortunate Mr. Grubbe.

"Ha—ha—ha!" laughed Lionel. "It's as good as a pantomime. Come away from the window, I must have my laugh out, and he'll hear me."

"Not he," replied Charlie, with a grin; "he's got too much of that muddy water in his ears. Hallo, here comes the gardener, pelting up."

"Holloa! hi—help!" roared Mr. Grubbe.

"Hillo," responded the man, who at first could not see anyone in need of assistance, "who be kickin' up a' this 'ere rumpus?"

"Me—it's me; here in this hole. Confound you, help me out."

The gardener saw him this time, and in a twinkling had Mr. Grubbe out on dry land—very cold and wet without, but burning inwardly with rage.

"Now, who'd ha' thought," said the old gardener, as he stood at the hole and scratched his head reflectively, "o' anyone tumblin' into that there."

"What!" ejaculated Mr. Grubbe, "did *you* dig it?"

"I did, and main hard it were to get down so fur," replied the gardener, wiping his mouth with the back of his hand, as if he expected a trifle for beer.

"Then go down again, you confounded old fool," said Mr. Grubbe, savagely, as he gave the unfortunate gardener a push, which sent him reeling into the hole, "and learn for the future not to dig holes where gentlemen are likely to fall into them."

This little occurrence did not help to smooth Mr. Grubbe's temper, especially as it involved the necessity of washing and dressing again from top to toe, operations which consumed the better portion of an hour, and then—a thing which he particularly disliked in general—he was obliged to hurry over his breakfast in order to reach the schoolroom just as the pupils took up their places at the desks.

Mr. Grubbe, with that same evil smile still hovering about the corners of his mouth, took up his place by the side of Mr. Styngy, who, for some reason, looked pale and excessively uncomfortable, and then, with a preliminary cough, pronounced Lionel's name.

Lionel rose from his seat and walked up to the desk, fully believing that the practical joke of that morning would be placed to his account. He little thought then of the real nature of the blow Mr. Grubbe was going to deal.

"Master Wilful," he said, twirling a folded piece of paper in his fat fingers, "a letter arrived yesterday for you from your mother. In accordance with the rules of this school, Mr. Styngy exercised his prerogative of opening it and reading it. It contains some information that will interest you, and some scandalous insinuations against myself, which, as an erring though sincere Christian, I trust I know how to forgive."

Lionel had snatched the letter before Mr. Grubbe finished his hypocritical speech. His sight seemed strangely blurred, there was a singing in his ears, and the floor seemed to heave and sway like the deck of a ship at sea as he read these few lines :—

"My own dear Lionel—

"Almost as soon as you receive this, I shall have landed in England. I hardly know how to write the words, for I am distracted, and sometimes, I think, not in my right mind ; but we are ruined, Lionel, my darling—utterly ruined. Beyond the little money in my purse, I have not a shilling in the world, and I believe your aunt's friend—Mr. Grubbe—to be alone responsible for our misfortunes. May God pardon him, for I cannot. You must leave school at once, dear Lionel, for I am quite unable to pay what is already due to Mr. Styngy ; but I do not think he is a hard man, he will give us time. I shall reach London on Thursday, the 17th, and will stay at the Great Southern Terminus Hotel till I see or hear from you."

And with many tender epithets and loving wishes, each one of which had cost the poor lady many tears, the letter ended.

Lionel, if he had been alone, would, there is little doubt, have had a hearty cry over his mother's letter ; but he would sooner have died upon the spot then have shown a sign of weakness before his enemy.

"You will, doubtless, Wilful," continued Mr. Grubbe, knitting his thick eyebrows heavily together, "see the propriety of following your mother's wishes. She is ruined and a beggar, you are in the same position, and you cannot reasonably expect Mr. Styngy to provide education, board, and lodging for paupers."

Lionel glanced once at the sanctimonious Mr. Grubbe, and such concentration of scorn and loathing was in that look, that the hypocrite shrank beneath it.

"I will go at once, if you please, sir," said Lionel to Mr. Styngy, in a voice that trembled a little in spite of his efforts to steady it. "I will not stop a minute longer than I can help beneath the same roof with the man who has robbed my mother."

Then turning on his heel, Lionel walked away, only stopping to exchange a hasty "good-bye" with his most particular friends. Tommy Codlings was fairly blubbering, and Charlie Drummond's eyes were full, and an obstinate lump was in his throat as he said farewell.

And so, with this dark cloud of misfortune that has closed so suddenly and heavily about our hero, we write—

THE END OF PART I.

www.ingramcontent.com/pod-product-compliance
Lightning Source LLC
Chambersburg PA
CBHW080840250626
47161CB00009B/3139